THE BRIDE OF LAMMERMOOR

WALTER SCOTT was born in Edinburgh in 1771, educated at the High School and University there and admitted to the Scottish Bar in 1792. From 1799 until his death he was Sheriff-Depute of Selkirkshire, and from 1806 to 1830 he held a well-paid office as a principal clerk to the Court of Session in Edinburgh, the supreme Scottish civil court. From 1805, too, Scott was secretly an investor in, and increasingly controller of, the printing and publishing businesses of his associates, the Ballan-tyne brothers.

Despite suffering crippling polio in infancy, conflict with his Calvinist lawyer father in adolescence, rejection by the woman he loved in his twenties, and financial ruin in his fifties, Scott displayed an amazingly productive energy, and his personal warmth was attested by almost everybody who met him. His first literary efforts, in the late 1790s, were translations of romantic and historical German poems and plays. In 1805 Scott's first considerable original work, *The Lay of the Last Minstrel*, began a series of narrative poems that popularized key incidents and settings of early Scottish history, and brought him fame and fortune.

In 1813 Scott, having declined the poet-laureateship and recom-mended Southey instead, moved towards fiction and devised a new form that was to dominate the early-nineteenth-century novel. *Waverley* (1814) and its successors draw on the social and cultural contrasts and the religious and political conflicts of recent Scottish history to illustrate the nature and cost of political and cultural change and the relationship between the historical process and the individual. *Waverley* was pub-lished anonymously and, although many people guessed, Scott did not acknowledge authorship of the Waverley Novels until 1827. Many of the novels from *Ivanhoe* (1819) on extended their range to the England and Europe of the Middle Ages and Renaissance. Across the English-speaking world, and by means of innumerable translations throughout Europe, the Waverley Novels changed forever the way people con-structed their personal and national identities.

Scott was created a baronet in 1820. During the financial crisis of 1825-6 Scott, his printer Ballantyne, and his publishers Constable and their London partner became insolvent. Scott chose not to be declared bankrupt, determining instead to work to generate funds to pay his creditors. Despite his failing health he continued to write new novels, to revise and annotate the earlier ones for a new edition, and to write a nine-volume *Life of Napoleon* and a history of Scotland under the title *Tales of a Grandfather*. His private thoughts during and after his financial crash are set down in a revealing and moving *Journal*. Scott died in September 1832; his creditors were finally paid in full in 1833 from the proceeds of his writing.

J. H. ALEXANDER is a graduate of Oxford University and is currently Reader in English at the University of Aberdeen. He has published critical studies of Walter Scott's poetry and of Wordsworth, and has edited a selection from the *Noctes Ambrosianae* and (with William Baker) the second series of Scott's *History of France*. For the Edinburgh Edition of the Waverley Novels he has edited *The Bride of Lammermoor*, *A Legend of the Wars of Montrose*, *Kenilworth* and *Anne of Geierstein*, and is currently editing *Quentin Durward* (with G. A. M. Wood).

KATHRYN SUTHERLAND is Professorial Fellow in English Literature at St Anne's College, Oxford. She has published widely on fictional and non-fictional writings of the Scottish Enlightenment and Romantic periods. Her editions include Adam Smith's *An Inquiry into the Nature and Causes of the Wealth of Nations*, Jane Austen's *Mansfield Park* (for Penguin Classics) and Walter Scott's *Redgauntlet*.

DAVID HEWITT, born in 1942, was brought up in the Borders, and studied English at the University of Edinburgh. Since 1994 he has been Professor in Scottish Literature at the University of Aberdeen. He has published widely on Scottish and Romantic literature, and is editor-in-chief of the Edinburgh Edition of the Waverley Novels. He is editor of Scott's *The Antiquary* for Penguin Classics.

CLAIRE LAMONT is a graduate of the universities of Edinburgh and Oxford and is currently a Senior Lecturer in English at the University of Newcastle. She specialises in late-eighteenth- and early-nineteenth-century English and Scottish literature. She has published editions of Scott's *Waverley* (1981) and *The Heart of Midlothian* (1982), and is editing *Chronicles of the Canongate* for the Edinburgh Edition of the Waverley Novels. She is Advisory Editor for the Waverley Novels in Penguin and the Textual Adviser for the new Penguin edition of the novels of Jane Austen.

WALTER SCOTT

THE BRIDE
OF LAMMERMOOR

Edited by
J. H. ALEXANDER
with an introduction by
KATHRYN SUTHERLAND

PENGUIN BOOKS

PENGUIN BOOKS

Published by the Penguin Group
Penguin Books Ltd, 27 Wrights Lane, London w8 5tz, England
Penguin Putnam Inc., 375 Hudson Street, New York, New York 10014, USA
Penguin Books Australia Ltd, Ringwood, Victoria, Australia
Penguin Books Canada Ltd, 10 Alcorn Avenue, Toronto, Ontario, Canada m4v 3b2
Penguin Books India (P) Ltd, 11, Community Centre, Panchsheel Park, New Delhi – 110 017, India
Penguin Books (NZ) Ltd, Private Bag 102902, NSMC Auckland, New Zealand
Penguin Books (South Africa) (Pty) Ltd, 5 Watkins Street, Denver Ext 4, Johannesburg 2094, South Africa

Penguin Books Ltd, Registered Offices: Harmondsworth, Middlesex, England

First published 1819
Published in the Edinburgh Edition of the Waverley Novels by the Edinburgh University Press 1995

Published with revised critical apparatus in Penguin Classics 2000
1

Text, historical note, explanatory notes and glossary copyright © The University Court
of the University of Edinburgh, 1995
Editor-in-chief's Preface and Chronology copyright © David Hewitt, 1998
Introduction copyright © Kathryn Sutherland, 2000
Note on the Text copyright © J. H. Alexander, 2000
All rights reserved

The moral right of the editors has been asserted

Typeset in Linotype Ehrhardt
Printed in England by Clays Ltd, St Ives plc

CONTENTS

ACKNOWLEDGEMENTS

The editors of a critical edition incur many debts, but the indebtedness of the editors of the Edinburgh Edition of the Waverley Novels and of its paperback progeny in the Penguin Scott is particularly heavy. The universities which employ the editors (in this case Aberdeen) have, in practice, provided the most substantial assistance, but in addition the Universities of Edinburgh and of Aberdeen have been particularly generous with their grants towards the costs of editorial preparation, and the support of the Humanities Research Board of the British Academy has allowed the Edition to employ a research fellow.

The Edinburgh Edition of the Waverley Novels has been most fortunate in having as its principal financial sponsor the Bank of Scotland, which has continued its long and fruitful involvement with the affairs of Walter Scott. In addition, the P.F. Charitable Trust and the Robertson Trust have given generous grants, and the Carnegie Trust for the Universities of Scotland has been most helpful.

Scott's manuscripts are widely distributed, but the greatest concentrations are in the National Library of Scotland in Edinburgh, and the Pierpont Morgan Library in New York. Without their preparedness to make manuscripts readily accessible, and to provide support beyond the ordinary, this edition would not have been feasible.

The editors have had, perforce, to seek specialist advice on many matters, and they are most grateful to their consultants Dr John Cairns, Professor Thomas Craik, Caroline Jackson-Houlston, Professor David Nordloh, Roy Pinkerton, and Professor David Stevenson. They owe much to their research fellows, Mairi Robinson, Dr Alison Lumsden, and Gerard Carruthers. They have continuously sought advice from the members of the Scott Advisory Board, and are particularly grateful for the support of Sir Kenneth Alexander, Professor David Daiches, Professor Douglas S. Mack, Professor Jane Millgate, and Dr Archie Turnbull.

The editor of *The Bride of Lammermoor* is specifically indebted to the late Dr J. C. Corson for the identification of several quotations, and is grateful to Dr W. E. K. Anderson, Dr Corson's literary executor, for making Dr Corson's material available. The manuscript of *The Bride* is in the Signet Library, Edinburgh, and special thanks are due to the Library and its Librarian, G. H. Ballantyne, for their generous help in making the manuscript available. The editor's thanks are due

viii ACKNOWLEDGEMENTS

also to: Flora Alexander, Mark Alexander, many members of the academic, library, and secretarial staff of the University of Aberdeen, Dr Brian Allen, Dr Penny Fielding, Dr P. D. Garside, Professor Douglas Gifford, the late A. P. Gorringe, P. E. Hewison, Professor David Irwin, Claire Lamont, Professor Douglas S. Mack, Professor John MacQueen, Patricia Marshall, Dame Jean and the late Mrs Patricia Maxwell-Scott, Professor Donald Meek, Professor Jane Millgate, Professor W. F. H. Nicolaisen, Professor Colm J. M. Ó Baoill, Professor M. G. H. Pittock, Dr David Reid, Dr Michael J. Robson, the late Margaret Tait, Professor D. E. R. Watt, and G. A. M. Wood.

In connection with *The Bride of Lammermoor* thanks are due also to the numerous libraries that have responded to requests for details of their Scott holdings, in particular Aberystwyth University Library; the Bodleian Library, Oxford; Bristol University Library; the British Library, London; Cambridge University Library; Houghton Library, Harvard University; Hull University Library; St Andrews University Library; Selwyn College, Cambridge; Sheffield University Library; Stirling University Library; and the Victoria and Albert Museum, London.

To all of these the editors express their thanks, and acknowledge that the production of the Edinburgh Edition of the Waverley Novels and the Penguin Scott has involved a collective effort to which all those mentioned by name, and very many others, have contributed generously and with enthusiasm.

Notes from Fiona Robertson's edition of *The Bride of Lammermoor* in the World's Classics series (1991) are quoted by permission of Oxford University Press.

David Hewitt
Editor-in-chief and General Editor for this title

Claire Lamont
Advisory Editor, the Penguin Scott

J. H. Alexander,
P. D. Garside,
G. A. M. Wood
General Editors

THE WAVERLEY NOVELS IN PENGUIN

The novels of Walter Scott published in Penguin are based on the volumes of the Edinburgh Edition of the Waverley Novels (EEWN). This series, which started publication in 1993 and which when complete will run to thirty volumes, is published in hardback by Edinburgh University Press. The Penguin edition of *The Bride of Lammermoor* reproduces the text of the novel, Historical Note, Explanatory Notes and Glossary unaltered from the EEWN volume. It does not reproduce the substantial amount of textual information in the Edinburgh Edition but instead provides, in the following paragraphs, a summary of general issues common to all Scott's novels and, in the Note on the Text, a succinct statement of the textual history of *The Bride of Lammermoor*. A new critical Introduction has been written specifically for the paperback, as well as a Chronology of Scott's life and a list of recommended Further Reading.

The most important aspect of the EEWN is that the text of the novels is based on the first editions, corrected so as to present what may be termed an 'ideal first edition'. Normally Scott's novels gestated over a long period: for instance, the historical works on which he drew for *The Tale of Old Mortality* (1816) had all been read by 1800. By contrast the process of committing a novel to paper, and of converting the manuscript into print, was in most cases extremely rapid. Scott wrote on only one side of his paper, and he used the blank back of the preceding leaf for additions and corrections, made both as he wrote and as he read over what he had written the previous day. Scott's novels were published anonymously – hence the title 'The Waverley Novels', named after the first of them – which meant that only a few people could be allowed to see his handwritten manuscript. Before delivery to the printing-house, therefore, the manuscript was copied and it was the copy that went to the compositor. The person who oversaw the printing of Scott's novels was his friend and business partner James Ballantyne, with whom he jointly owned the printing firm of James Ballantyne & Co. from 1805 (except for the period 1816–22 when Scott was sole partner) until they both became insolvent in 1826.

The compositors in the printing-house set the novels as copy arrived, and while doing so they inserted the great majority of the punctuation marks, normalised and regularised the spelling without standardising it, and corrected many small errors. It was in the printing-house that the presentation of the texts of the novels was changed from the conventions appropriate to manuscript to those of a printed novel of the early nineteenth century. Proofs were corrected in-house, and then a new set of proofs was given to Ballantyne who annotated them prior to sending them to the author. Scott did not read his proofs against his manuscript or against the printer's copy; he read for sense and, making full use of the prerogatives of ownership, he took the opportunity of revising, amplifying, and even introducing new ideas. Thus for Scott reading proofs was a creative rather than just a corrective engagement with his texts. The proofs went back to Ballantyne who oversaw the copying of Scott's new material on to a clean set of proofs and its incorporation into the printed text. Only occasionally did Scott see revised proofs. Two points in particular might be noted about the above procedures. First, Scott delivered his manuscript in batches as he wrote it, and the result was that the first part of a novel was set in type, and proofs corrected, before the end was written. And second, in the business of turning a rapidly written text from manuscript to print Scott was indebted to a series of people, copyist, printer, proof-reader, whom Scott editors have come to refer to as 'the intermediaries'.

The business of producing a Waverley novel was so pressurised that mistakes were inevitable. The manuscript was sometimes misread or misunderstood (Scott's handwriting is neat but his letters poorly differentiated); punctuation was often inserted in a mechanical way and the implication of Scott's light manuscript punctuation lost; period words were sometimes not recognised and more obvious, modern terms were substituted for them. The EEWN has examined every aspect of the first-edition texts in the light of the manuscript and the full textual history of the novel. This has enabled the editors to correct the text where Scott's intentions were clearly not fulfilled in the first edition. The EEWN corrects errors, but it does so conservatively bearing in mind that the production of the printed text was a collective effort to which Scott had given his sanction.

Most of the Waverley Novels went through many editions in Scott's lifetime; Scott was not normally involved in the later editions although very occasionally he did see proofs. But in 1827, after his insolvency the previous year, it was decided to issue the first full collected edition of the Waverley Novels, and much of Scott's time in the last years of his life was committed to writing introductions and notes, and to reviewing his text for what he called his 'Magnum Opus' ('Great Work'), or Magnum for short. Scott had acknowledged his authorship of the novels in 1827, and this enabled him to describe the origins of his novels in the introductions to the Magnum edition in a way which was impossible to an author seeking anonymity. The Magnum has formed the basis of every edition of the Waverley Novels published from Scott's death in 1832 until the EEWN chose the first editions as its base-text. In the EEWN the additions made for the Magnum will be published in two volumes at the end of the series. In the volumes published in Penguin passages from the Magnum Introduction relating to the genesis of the novel are included in the new original material produced for the paperback edition.

This edition of Scott in Penguin offers the reader a text which is not only closer to what the author actually wrote and intended but is also new in that it uses for the first time material recovered from manuscripts and proof-sheets, revealing to fuller view the flair and precision of Scott's writing. In addition it supplies the editorial assistance necessary for a modern reader to interpret and enjoy the novel.

David Hewitt
Editor-in-chief
The Edinburgh Edition of the Waverley Novels

INTRODUCTION

(New readers are advised that this Introduction makes details of the plot explicit)

STORIES WITHIN STORIES

Among Scott's novels, *The Bride of Lammermoor* appears to be the exception. It is that un-Scott-like thing, 'a perfect specimen of form', as Thomas Hardy described it.[1] It lacks the general expansiveness of style, with contrasted regional settings and leisurely textual digressions, which we have come to recognize as constituting the typical Scott narrative. In *The Bride of Lammermoor*, on the contrary, the hero's destiny is not played out geographically in the symbolic distances between regions of adventure and reality, between the dangerous excitement represented by Highland clansmen, smugglers, social outcasts, or religious extremists, and the domestic safety of compromised lives in modern cities and on well-managed estates – those ingredients which we know as the familiar 'north' and 'south' of a Scott story. Even E. M. Forster, no advocate for the lumbering style ('think how all Scott's laborious mountains and scooped-out glens and carefully ruined abbeys call out for passion, passion, and how it is never there!'), found in *The Bride* an economy of expression and a liberated passion which provided him with an effective shorthand for the submerged emotions of his own constrained characters.[2] Forster, like Flaubert in *Madame Bovary* (1856), came to Scott's romantic tragedy by way of Donizetti's opera, *Lucia di Lammermoor* (1835); and for Donizetti the love-story is the novel's emotional core. Partly because of these influential reinterpretations, this is a novel we open with certain expectations: it is a tale we feel we already know.

Defending the general construction of his novels, Scott wrote in the Introductory Epistle to *The Fortunes of Nigel* (1822) that his typical style resembled the rambling, picaresque method of his eighteenth-century predecessors Smollett and Le Sage, who 'have been satisfied if they amused the reader upon the road, though the conclusion only arrived because the tale must have an end, just as the traveller alights at the inn because it is evening'. This is the style of his best known novels, *Waverley*, *The Heart of Mid-Lothian*, *Ivanhoe*, and *Redgauntlet*. In the Epistle he compared their episodic, loosely strung story lines, his preferred mode, with something different, 'the plot of a regular and connected epopeia, where every step brings us a point nearer to the final catastrophe'.[3] It is this different thing that he offers in *The Bride of Lammermoor*, his eighth novel, which displays from its opening scenes the signs of an inevitable conclusion, with little to distract the reader from its anticipation. It exhibits a strict formal and thematic unity, or, in Forster's equivocal words, it is a novel 'that professes to be lean and tragic'.[4]

As if to confirm its anomalous position among his fictions, a belief soon gained credence that in this novel Scott was tapping a deeper and less conscious area of his imagination. During the early months of 1819, when much of *The Bride* was written, an agonizing (and undiagnosed) attack of gallstones meant that he worked in excruciating pain, relieved only by high doses of opiates. It was feared he was dying. Almost twenty years later, when Scott was dead, his son-in-law and early biographer, John Gibson Lockhart, wove together a remarkable set of eye-witness accounts of the novel's composition. These describe how, unable to lift a pen, Scott dictated a large part of the work to his friends, William Laidlaw and John Ballantyne; how Scott's groans of pain interrupted but never stopped the flow of composition; how incapacitated by suffering Scott nevertheless, under the influence of the narrative, rose up from time to time to walk about and act out parts of the dialogue; how Ballantyne equipped himself with a dozen pens for each session at the strangely productive sick-bed. As further confirmation, Lockhart recorded, too, the deathbed statement of the printer James Ballantyne, Scott's business partner, that the novel 'was not only written, but published, before Mr Scott was able to rise from his bed; and he assured me, that when it was first put into his hands in a complete shape, he did not recollect one single incident, character, or conversation it contained!'[5]. Edgar Johnson, Scott's most industrious twentieth-century biographer, has further embellished Ballantyne's dying account with his own flight of fancy, claiming,

> *The Bride of Lammermoor* is the most perfectly constructed of all Scott's novels ... Though Scott had written it in drugged near-somnambulism, and though he himself, on rereading, felt it to be monstrous and grotesque, the truth is that its brooding fatality is fused with the reality it envelopes; its Gothic warnings are dark mists swirling through a solid world. Released by Scott's illness, his imagination dredged up primitive tremors from primordial deeps.[6]

Pain, narcotic trance, and the unacknowledged workings of the unconscious mind provide suitable origins for what might have been Scott's last novel, a tale of family ruin, madness and death, which John

Sutherland, in a recent biography, has called 'an appropriately terminal work'.[7] Only a few years earlier, in 1816, Coleridge had published his opium experiments in poetry, notable among them 'Kubla Khan', with its preface outlining the poem's hallucinogenic origins in incomplete consciousness. Coleridge's explanatory preface and the anecdotes surrounding Scott's composition of *The Bride of Lammermoor* share an anxiety about creation and a concern with the mechanism of the imagination. In both cases, some trouble is taken to explain the anterior life of the literary work as in some sense written upon and written out of the distressed body of the author. In Scott's case, only the invasive action of drugs and extreme personal anguish can explain to his critics the violence which shapes the novel and which releases a hitherto unsuspected fictional capacity for psychological intensity. There is further corroboration in the complex of personal emotions which, biographers have argued, welled up at this crisis (as at other, later, crises) from the memory of Scott's failed love-affair with Williamina Belsches some twenty years earlier. In this reading of the novel, the conditions of near-mortal illness and the unusual recourse to opiates may have exposed the ultimate psychic source (in lost love and betrayal) of all Scott's fictions.[8]

But some of these details of involuntary composition are not borne out by the facts. In contrast to Lockhart's romantic description of prolific dictation interrupted only by groans of pain, J. H. Alexander's investigation of the manuscript of the novel for the present edition confirms that the four fifths that survive are in Scott's own usual hand, with an amanuensis (probably Laidlaw) employed only for the last part (no more than the missing fifth). Against Johnson's Ballantyne-derived account of Scott himself penning the novel, but 'in a blurred trance', unaware of his actions from composition to publication, surviving proof sheets show that, gravely ill though he undoubtedly was, he was sufficiently conscious to insert pre-publication corrections.[9] What the discrepancy should alert us to is the shifting ground on which all stories are built. Not only is such instability a condition of the stories which surround the writing of *The Bride of Lammermoor*, but it is driven deep into the novel itself, where the nature and 'truth'-status of story becomes a chief concern, for the reader and for the central characters. In this instance, the discrepancy over the facts of composition expresses a need to derive Scott's least Scott-like novel from a set of ultimate biographical circumstances, whose very resistance to proof provides a peculiarly modern, because neurotic, pedigree. This derivation becomes even more problematic when we discover that *The Bride of Lammermoor* is a tale which came to Scott ready-made, with at least as many outward, historical determinants as inward and psychic ones, and that it is therefore apparently indisposed to convey a personal voice or intention.

The original of *The Bride of Lammermoor* was communicated to Scott orally by at least two routes: he heard it from his maternal great-aunt Margaret Swinton, who died in 1780 when he was nine; and his mother used to tell it regularly in the family circle. Writing to his friend Lady Louisa Stuart in January 1820, a month after his mother's death, Scott acknowledged her oral tales as the originals of many of his printed fictions:

> She had a mind peculiarly well stored with much acquired infor-
> mation and natural talent, and as she was very old, and had an
> excellent memory, she could draw without the least exaggeration
> or affectation the most striking pictures of the past age. If I have
> been able to do anything in the way of painting the past times, it
> is very much from the studies with which she presented me. She
> connected a long period of time with the present generation, for
> she remembered, and had often spoken with, a person who
> perfectly recollected the battle of Dunbar, and Oliver Cromwell's
> subsequent entry into Edinburgh. She preserved her faculties to
> the very day before her final illness; for our friends Mr and Mrs
> Scott of Harden visited her on the Sunday; and, coming to our
> house after, were expressing their surprise at the alertness of her
> mind, and the pleasure which she had in talking about ancient
> and modern events. She had told them with great accuracy the
> real story of the Bride of Lammermuir, and pointed out wherein
> it differed from the novel. She had all the names of the parties,
> and detailed (for she was a very great genealogist) their connexion
> with existing families.[10]

Margaret Swinton, Scott's other authority for the story, was the 'Aunt Margaret' of 'My Aunt Margaret's Mirror', a late supernatural tale published in *The Keepsake* in 1828 and bearing some slight similarities to *The Bride*, and she was 'a near connexion of the family in which the event happened'. When young she had known the brother of Janet Dalrymple, the original of Lucy Ashton, and so got some of the details of the 'melancholy tale' at first hand:

> The female relative, by whom the melancholy tale was communi-
> cated to me many years since, was a near connexion of the
> family in which the event happened, and always told it with an
> appearance of melancholy mystery, which enhanced the interest.
> She had known, in her youth, the brother who rode before the
> unhappy victim to the fatal altar, who, though then a mere
> boy, and occupied almost entirely with the gallantry of his own

appearance in the bridal procession, could not but remark that the hand of his sister was moist, and cold as that of a statue.[11]

There were several versions of the Dalrymple story, but the version Scott heard in his own family is the one he records in the 1830 Introduction to the Magnum edition of the novel as 'the real source' for his narrative. Its kernel is that on 24 August 1669 Janet Dalrymple, daughter of James Dalrymple, the first Viscount Stair, and of his wife Margaret, publicly celebrated her marriage to David Dunbar of Baldoon. Previously, she had secretly become engaged to a man of her own choice, Lord Rutherford, but renounced him under family pressure and accepted Baldoon, who was her parents' choice. On the wedding night the bridal chamber was opened, the bridegroom discovered severely wounded, and the bride insane. Though he recovered, she died in a matter of weeks, on 12 September. Baldoon never afterwards spoke of how he received his injury.[12]

In a letter to James Ballantyne in September 1818, Scott, then at work on the novel, expressed some doubts about translating the oral account into print:

> The story is a dismal one, and I doubt sometimes whether it will bear working out to much length after all. Query, if I shall make it so effective in two volumes as my mother does in her quarter of an hour's crack by the fireside? But nil desperandum. You shall have a bunch to-morrow or next day – and when the proofs come in, my pen must and shall step out.[13]

This alternative origin for the novel, in local legend and family history as distinct from psycho-biography, relocates its imagined source in a second area of personally unwilled association. What he sees as the special conditions of existence of traditional stories also sets Scott on pondering the possible meanings that inhere in different methods of recording history: how far, for example, a tale is identifiable with the way it is told, and what it therefore means to represent it in a different form. Between the 'quarter of an hour's crack by the fireside' and the 'pen [which] must and shall step out' lies the huge transformation that print technology works on the impermanence, provisionality, and stark power of the spoken tale. Scott's mother registered the fact of change when she told her visitors 'the real story of the Bride of Lammermuir, and pointed out wherein it differed from the novel'. In recording his debt to his great-aunt Margaret Swinton, Scott chose words that reveal something of the nature of the difference: she was, he wrote, closely related to the family 'in which the event happened'. Through the renewed activity of telling and retelling which constitutes the life of the oral story, its existence is shown to be of the moment, bound by the occasion. In reconstituting one moment in another (the moment of happening in the moment of telling), oral storytelling is itself an event rather than an account, and as an event it is not accountable in the way that a written or printed narrative is. This is why Scott's mother can test the authenticity of the novel against 'the real story', though that real story leaves no obvious mark.

This is a distinction which we as modern readers understand only ironically: that is, less from our experience of an oral culture than from reading of its loss. In his classic study *Orality and Literacy*, Walter Ong describes the difference between oral and written sources as a difference between sound and vision: being only sound, spoken words 'have no focus and no trace'.[14] Walter Benjamin, in his influential essay 'The Storyteller: Reflections on the Works of Nikolai Leskov', makes the same point when he writes of the art of the oral teller as non-referential. According to Benjamin, the tale told and the tale written or printed occupy distinct cultural spaces; the one will irresistibly drive out the other. Benjamin expands this distinction by opposing the reciprocal, sociable activity of the tale told and heard to the insulated and private representation of human complexity that is found in the novel. The novel, unlike the oral tale, is characterised by its weight of information. This information is the price we pay for a book-bound culture which, by its very reliance on verification, or looking things up, is unable to accommodate what is occasional and explanation-free in the oral performance, the story's re-event.[15] More recently, experimental narrators like Jorge Luis Borges and Italo Calvino have attempted to recover for print, through the disruption of print's own conventional certainties, something of the unaccountability and provisional status of the oral performance. Within the novel this is often described as the challenge of romance to realism. If the apparent aim of realism is to construct a narrative which is intelligible, graspable, and knowable, then the function of romance is to create doubt about what it is we know and how we come to know it. This distinction – between the unfixed (eventful) and the contextual (informational) lives of oral and print narration, and between the tasks of romance and realism – goes to the heart of Scott's concern in *The Bride of Lammermoor*. Driven deep into the novel's structure is a tension between different ways of accounting for experience, where the discrepancies between the local and the extended meanings of the stories which people tell one another are shown to impact decisively and tragically on behaviour.

All Scott's novels were written in disguise, as if by someone else. They follow two general lines of fictional descent: one group form the Waverley Novels, issued as by 'the Author of *Waverley*', while the other group belong to the four series of *Tales of My Landlord*. The tendentious prefaces, mock-scholarship, and pseudonymous identities which accompany most of the novels in both groups can test the stamina of the modern reader, who is frustrated by their digressions and impatient to arrive at the action. But these frame-stories are never merely wanton evasion or tedious playfulness: in some way the textual excesses which characterise them were a vital stimulant for Scott to the writing of fiction; and they always contain important clues to the narratives which follow. The novels that make up *Tales of My Landlord* are all presented as the work of Peter Pattieson, in whom Scott refashions himself as a sickly and sensitive young writer with a romantic fascination for morbid tales. Assistant schoolmaster in the imaginary village of Gandercleugh, Pattieson compiles his novels from the communications of travellers who find their way to the village pub. After Pattieson's death, the tales are edited by his executor, the pedantic Jedidiah Cleishbotham, parish-clerk and schoolmaster, before being committed 'to the Ballantynian ordeal' of print. The original plan was for Scott to write as Pattieson 'four tales illustrative of the manners of Scotland in her different provinces', but the scheme was more or less abandoned at once. After a false start with *The Black Dwarf*, from which Scott managed to spin only one of the two volumes it was designed to fill, the next, *The Tale of Old Mortality*, grew into a three-volume novel, and these four volumes were issued as the first series of *Tales* in 1816. Until almost the last moment, *The Heart of Mid-Lothian* was to have been published with *The Bride of Lammermoor* as the second series of *Tales* in 1818, but the excessive length of the former novel (alone, it filled four volumes) pushed *The Bride* into a third series, with *A Legend of Montrose* added to bulk out its two-and-a-half volumes to the requisite four.[16] What the three series of *Tales of My Landlord* have in common is the statement in their frame-stories that they all derive at some stage from oral sources and (which seems to follow from their oral origins) an unruly resistance to the novelistic shaping so profusely written into their opening pages.

In its fictional frame, *The Bride of Lammermoor* is offered as a piece of local East Lothian history, 'by tradition, affirmed to be truth', told to Dick Tinto, a travelling painter, by an 'aged goodwife' living in the Lammermoor hills (12,14). Through the device of Tinto, the narrative's real and fictitious oral beginnings are represented by means of an extended equivalence in painting. From the evidence of the manuscript, the opening chapter in which Peter Pattieson tells the story of his friend Tinto appears to have been an afterthought. But in its anecdotal comparison of the methods of the painter and the novelist in presenting a tale, it offers a more carefully judged interpretative statement about what follows than critics have allowed. For Tinto, the painter has the advantage in suggesting, through look or gesture, rather than protracting through accumulated detail and conversation, the life of his characters, while Pattieson's starting point as a writer is his distrust of the whole idea of the momentary insight. Tinto believes that pictures are more communicative than written words because the economy of expression that a narrative on canvas demands produces a more intense imaginative engagement in the spectator.[17] In contrast, he claims that Pattieson's characters dissipate effects by making 'too much use of the *gob-box*' (10). Challenging his friend to revise his style, Tinto illustrates his criticisms by means of a sketch for a painting inspired by the legend he heard in the Lammermoor hills. But deprived of words, Pattieson fails to deduce its story, and this is sure proof for Tinto.

> "That is the very thing I complain of . . . you have accustomed yourself so much to these creeping twilight details of yours, that you are become incapable of receiving that instant and vivid flash of conviction, which darts on the mind from seeing the happy and expressive combinations of a single scene, and which gathers from the position, attitude, and countenance of the moment, not only the history of the past lives of the personages represented, and the nature of the business on which they are immediately engaged, but lifts even the veil of futurity, and affords a shrewd guess at their future fortunes." (13)

Pattieson is accordingly referred, for the fuller explanation he craves, to Tinto's manuscript notes of the tale, and these he transforms into his novel *The Bride of Lammermoor*.

The inset 'life' of Dick Tinto is elaborated until it threatens to bury the real significance of the frame. But not quite, for this whimsical morality tale, of Tinto's failure and Pattieson's caution, contains a shrewd critical comment from the celebrated novelist on the fickleness of popularity and the relationship of art to consumer demands. An obscure provincial painter of inn-signs, Tinto takes his large dreams and small talent to Edinburgh and London, where his ambitions as a portraitist and painter of historical scenes soon end in bankruptcy and death. If his own history hints at the general arbitrariness and waste in the individual life, the inability to control circumstances and outcomes, the sketch that Pattieson fails to 'read' contains a direct visual clue to what follows. The scene it depicts – of a beautiful young woman, her impatient mother, and a proud, angry young man – occurs towards the end of the novel (at Volume 3, Chapter 6) and represents a detail from Scott's 'real source', only revealed in the 1830 Introduc-

tion. The thread connecting the painter's art and the tale's real source
is both slight and strong. When Pattieson fails to interpret the sketch,
it is set aside in favour of a manuscript, but one in which 'outlines of
caricatures, sketches of turrets, mills, old gables, and dove-cotes,
disputed the ground with [the] written memoranda' (14). *The Bride*'s
uncharacteristic reliance, among Scott's novels, on pictorial compression, whereby landscape, architecture, and character are persistently combined for interpretative effect, transfers to print the
expressive art of the painter. In apparent compliance with Tinto's
advice, the narrative is loaded with portraiture, whose function it is to
contest the slower unfolding of events in the temporal dimension.
Within the frame of the canvas, visual detail transforms social and
psychological symptoms into spatial features, capturing the life lived
through time all at once, as a picture. The effect of such pictorial clues
is not only to anticipate subsequent explanation by narrative enlarge-
ment but more poignantly, and through their very economy, to suggest
the constriction of opportunity and of individual human identity.

This compressed pictorial method dominates the scene, in Volume
2, Chapter 4, which returns Edgar Ravenswood to Ravenswood Castle
as the guest of his enemy Sir William Ashton. Ravenswood's inheritance of mouldering tapestries, rusted weapons, and old family portraits
has been swept aside for the comforts favoured by new money –
oak-panelled walls, rich carpets, and a selection of carefully chosen
paintings, which attest to Sir William's modern loyalties and social
pretensions. By a nicely judged touch, there is a picture of Lord Stair,
the great Scottish lawyer and political opportunist, whose daughter's
tragedy originates the novel. But it is the portrait of his parents and
the more splendid full-length study of Lady Ashton and himself, in
the ceremonial robes of his state office of Lord Keeper, which suggest
details that unsettle any straightforward reading of their owner's progress. Sir William's parents gaze out from the canvas 'sour . . . peevish,
puritanical . . . hungry', while the Lord Keeper himself it 'was obvious,
at the first glance . . . was somewhat hen-pecked' (144). Not only
Sir William, but Edgar Ravenswood, too, is shown to be a careless
interpreter of the painter's condensed art when he fails to trace in
Lucy Ashton's features any grounds for comparison with the portraits
of her parents and grandparents. In contrast, during the same scene
young Henry Ashton sees in Edgar Ravenswood a living replica of the
portrait of his bloody ancestor Sir Malise, now consigned to the laundry
but threatening, in Edgar's shape, to break out of its frame (as in a
sense it does in a crudely Gothic moment at the novel's close) and
avenge his family's wrongs. The attempt to fix the moment (fictionally,
the painter's, and, historically, the oral teller's province) appears in

context to serve a merely supplementary rather than a definitive purpose. But it leaves ominous local deposits.

Caleb Balderstone, devoted retainer to the fallen family of Ravenswood, derives his resilience from understanding the correct way to live in the moment, a capacity that he tries unsuccessfully to communicate to his young master. In Caleb's world, storytelling is a way to remake the tragic wastes of history as a comedy of manners. His efforts at domestic economy, the only subject for his narrative skills, weave a contrasting thread of humour through Edgar Ravenswood's inherited gloom and fatalism. In this respect, Caleb is as locked inside his role as Ravenswood in his. Where early reviewers judged him a caricature, modern critics have tended to see him as tiresomely facetious but vital to placing the novel against its socio-political background, a world in which feudal loyalties are being driven out by the less stable relationships of commerce.[18] All Caleb's actions are motivated by his desire to uphold the 'honour of the family' and the 'credit of the house', but the discreditable extremes that his notions of honour lead him into provide a knockabout comedy which is by turns zany and poignant in its lavish excess: 'if it's my pleasure to hazard my soul in telling lies for the honour of the family, it's nae business of yours', he threatens Ravenswood, 'and if ye let me gang on quietly, I'se be moderate in my banquet; but if ye contradict me, de'il but I dress ye a dinner for a duke' (96). Despite a fanatical adherence to old values, Caleb's capacity for improvisation is his survivor's response to the mutability of life in history.

By contrast, Lucy Ashton and Edgar Ravenswood seem temperamentally incapable of resilience or change – 'unless the Master learns mair the ways of this warld . . .', Caleb prophetically warns after one of his own successful forays into the village of Wolfshope (210). The sentence hangs in the air. In a comic scene that grotesquely anticipates the tragic end of the Ravenswoods, Caleb stages a mock-fire in which he pretends to destroy Wolfscrag, the family's remaining dwelling. It is his most extreme piece of housekeeping, designed to maintain the Ravenswood reputation for wealth. As he explains it to Edgar, the fiction was necessary: besides, 'in some sort, a gude excuse is better than the things themselves' (215). In Caleb, Scott offers the reader a storyteller whose stories exceed their occasions and in so doing bring with them their own comforts. Caleb's stories are not records of events but free-wheeling, fertile banquets – feasts of words untrammelled by subordination to external circumstances. It is this that provides their most valuable social function, not their openness to proof of having really happened but their capacity for relevance to the moment of narration. It is a capacity to release meaning at the appropriate time, and then to set it aside when it no longer applies.

According to Caleb, 'young folk are no judicious – they cannot make the maist of a bit figment' (215). Lucy and Edgar, the doomed lovers, are both romantics, given to living in fictions; but they seem perversely set on choosing the least promising fictions to act out. Lucy, dreamy, secretive, and vulnerable, is introduced to the reader in a song, overheard by her father: 'Look not thou on Beauty's charming'. 'The words she had chosen seemed peculiarly adapted to her character', comments the narrator about this emphatically negative little song (25). In his novel *A Room with a View* (1908), in a scene which contains a direct critical assessment of Scott's Lucy, E. M. Forster gives his heroine, Lucy Honeychurch, the same song to sing. But what, in Forster's social comedy, provides the occasion for the healthy release of natural desire, contains for Scott's heroine only a terrible warning of the danger of following one's passions. Where 'Lucy's song' gives Lucy Honeychurch the late opportunity to consider the emotional bankruptcy which will attend a life lived according to social form, the earlier narrator wastes no time in presenting a picture of Lucy Ashton in which a narrowness of reference is ominously adequate to the limited part she must play. We have it all in a few sentences: outwardly, she is easily ruled by the opinions of others, passive and silent in society, and anxious to please; inwardly, she is equally vulnerable to the rigid moral codes of the literary romances which have formed her education, 'old legendary tales of ardent devotion and unalterable affection, chequered as they so often are with strange adventures and supernatural horrors'. Lucy is a study in compliance, 'in the last degree gentle, soft, timid, and feminine' (25). She is malleable – to the will of others and to the invasive shapes which impress her vivid sensibility. What might seem her refuge, the life of the imagination, is no such thing but uncannily identifiable with her social dealings among her family. In her the pliancy that seemed to ensure her father's political success and the hunger to be read in the faces of her puritanical grandparents have resolved into a terrible emptiness of personality, a vacancy filled instead with the tyrannical forms of outer and inner forces which she is powerless to control. By the end of her story, and through the contrivances of an unscrupulous mother, Lucy's secret and social selves have collapsed into a frightening singularity. As the narrator records, 'The fairy wand, with which in her solitude she had delighted to raise visions of enchantment, became now the rod of a magician, the bond slave of evil genii . . .' (237).

'The first sight of Lucy Ashton had been less impressive than her image proved to be upon reflection', observes the narrator of Edgar Ravenswood's incipient passion (69). Edgar is held captive by an imagined future that promises to change the course of his life, offering love in the shape of his enemy's daughter as the antidote to his inherited purpose of revenge. In this way he, too, appears to set an inner, spiritual preserve against the exigencies of external reality. But in his case, as in Lucy's, romantic love is a second-hand emotion: less the victim of his reading, he is nonetheless impressed by her impression-ability. The narrator comments, in terms which are not designed to reassure the reader, that 'the softness of a mind, amounting almost to feebleness, rendered her even dearer to him' (164). But the sheer impossibility of turning their situation to domestic romance is never absent; their every encounter is against an unambiguous, ritualised backdrop, which appears to announce the story's fatal outcome as already determined. As the emblematic use of family portraits suggests, in *The Bride of Lammermoor* the real, physical space that characters seek to inhabit has already been occupied before them. Sir William Ashton's crass attempts in the novel's opening scenes to play the part of the traditional laird reveal only the social discomfort of the newly rich as he misjudges his relationship first with his forester Norman and then with blind Alice Gray. Like Sir William, the central characters are all intruders upon a previous scene which they misread or ignore at their peril. In retracing old ground they deviate, occasionally, as does Sir William, into comedy, but more often into tragedy.

Saved early in the novel from a wild bull which threatens her forest walk, Lucy awakes from 'her long and almost deadly swoon' to the first sight of her rescuer, Edgar Ravenswood (40). He has carried her to the safety of a ruined Gothic fountain, known locally as the Mermaiden's Well, from a legend which we are told makes the spot fatal to the Ravenswood family. The narrator breaks off the account of Lucy's rescue to tell the 200-year-old tale of Raymond of Ravenswood and the nymph of the fountain. The violent sexual symbolism of the old tale is reinvoked when the Well later becomes the setting for Edgar and Lucy's secret engagement. If that were not sufficient, just as the couple exchange their vows a raven falls dead at Lucy's feet, spattering her white dress with its blood. The raven, it need hardly be said, is a bird ominous to the Ravenswoods. What the heavy irony of the Well legend implies for the novel's characters, of course, is the impossibility of acting for or as oneself, of taking control of one's actions. This is represented by a plot whose unfolding in the fictional present is regularly interrupted by tales of the past. At some simple level, Edgar Ravenswood and Lucy Ashton appeal to the reader as archetypal romance hero and heroine: he is the dark avenger, the man of action; she is blonde and delicate, a study in feminine sensibility. But just as her interiority proves a false construction, so Edgar's activity is effectively undermined. Either fate or hereditary law or the workings of his own superstitious imagination – it is any and all of these – consign him to the impotent repetition of past deeds and surrender him finally to a gruesome personal destiny, fulfilling the prophecy of Thomas the Rhymer, told by Caleb Balderstone, and the predictions made at his birth and repeated by the old hag Ailsie Gourlay.

The oppressive sense that the tale has already been told is driven deep into *The Bride of Lammermoor*, not only in the shape of old Border ballad and superstition but by the sheer weight of literary allusions. Chapter mottoes, narrative references, and the words of the characters themselves conspire to cast a spell over the present action and to absorb it into the supercharged imaginative categories of Gothic fiction and Shakespearean tragedy. Lucy Ashton is by turns traumatised Gothic heroine, the victim of oppressive and distorted family relations, like those described in the hugely popular 1790s novels of Ann Radcliffe, and she is also Ophelia or Desdemona, driven mad by love; her mother, who in the words of the favoured suitor Bucklaw 'understands every machine for breaking in the human mind' (227), combines the cruelty and ambition of Lady Macbeth (to whom the narrator compares her the first time she is mentioned) with the surveillance of Radcliffe's Marchesa Vivaldi in *The Italian* (1797); the village hags are the three witches, and the sexton Mortsheugh plays the philosophical grave-digger to Ravenswood's melancholy Hamlet. References to *Romeo and Juliet* (for example, in chapter mottoes at Volume 1, Chapter 5, and Volume 3, Chapter 6) serve to render this improbable love-story more, not less, convincing to the reader: the sense that the central characters are playing roles simultaneously raises the emotional temperature and emphasises their powerlessness to control their destinies. In particular, the extent to which the lovers fail to resist literary stereotyping is an index of their inability to engage purposefully with their immediate environment.

As its fictional and historical frames work hard to imply, *The Bride of Lammermoor* is structured out of the linked psychic and temporal processes of remembering and forgetting indispensable to storytelling: all stories take shape through selection. Where Caleb contrives this as comic improvisation, Ravenswood's untimely capacity for suppressing relevant narrative details condemns him to an unnuanced tragic fate. Not only is he the living image of his ancestor Sir Malise, but he is well rehearsed in those family legends, including that of the Mermai-den's Well, which he persistently chooses to ignore. To place the wilfulness of his forgetting in no doubt, he is provided with an old nurse, blind Alice Gray, one of the last surviving retainers of the Ravenswood family and the living repository of its lore. Alice represents folk memory; her function is to link long tradition to the psychic time of Ravenswood's personal actions, as is made clear in the scene in which her ghost appears to him. Pattieson, the tale's modern narrator, is concerned to equivocate over the 'real' nature of her apparition, whether a true manifestation or the consequence of Ravenswood's overwrought imagination. But this distinction is beside the point. From the moment of her ghostly appearance, the fragile barrier by which Ravenswood sought to separate the dead weight of precedent from the independent assertions of the individual life collapses. From that moment, he is wholly the prey of the inheritance he seemed always to court in the unpromising materials from which he tried to fashion an alternative reality and a different story.

THE DEBATE OVER HISTORY

Readers and critics of *The Bride of Lammermoor* have found it difficult to reconcile the intensity and insulation of a tale of family and sexual passions with other indications that the action is also historical and political. By convention, the concentration on a central personal tragedy requires different fictional practices and implies a different understanding of the significance of character from that developed within a wider and more diffused historical vision. What, then, is the nature of the relationship between individual and social realities in *The Bride of Lammermoor*? Above all, is this a novel in Scott's usual manner, wherein historical process wins out over the individual life? Two recent contrasted studies find in the novel's special blend of politics and passion a reason to revisit the old, related debate over whether Scott is a realist or a romantic – that is, whether his novels come down on the side of external circumstance or private experience as more determining of identity. In *The Forms of Historical Fiction*, Harry Shaw identifies *The Bride* as the exception to Scott's rule that 'heroes are not ends but means, existing to mediate between historical forces, or to see historical sights ... but not to have deep souls or interesting minds'. He concludes that '*The Bride* has a unique power to fascinate and disturb us because it expresses a complex of personal emotions with less historical mediation than any other of Scott's works'.[19] Against this view, Ian Duncan's premises in *Modern Romance and Transformation, of the Novel*, that Scott's novelistic project is to recover romance for serious historical use, finds him transforming romance in the opposite direction, into the energy that reconciles private with national interests. But what is most interesting about Duncan's interpretation is that, like Shaw, he reads *The Bride* as contradicting his general conclusion about how Scott's fiction works. He writes: 'Public politics, with their private effects of ambition, avarice and betrayal, wreck the domestic romance between Edgar Ravenswood and Lucy Ashton ...

it fails to transcend the political pressures which have set it in motion and end up defining it.'[20] Where Shaw concludes that *The Bride* represents among Scott's fictions the unique transcendence of the private and psychological over the outward and historical, in Duncan's opposed interpretation it displays the 'vulnerability of character and action to circumstance'.[21] What both readings identify as problematic – as against the grain of the thesis they each propose – is the extent to which in *The Bride* the private self is grounded in political setting. For Shaw, the historically attuned reader, the political environment against which actions occur is vivid but finally irrelevant; for Duncan, the romance reader, the same environment functions as a constant against which individual identity is pitted and shown to be powerless.

In what senses, then, is this a historical novel? We know that the immediate political context of the action is some time shortly before the Union of Scotland and England in 1707, itself a historically momentous time, and that this setting required Scott to transfer the events of his oral source, the Dalrymple tragedy, from their actual date of 1669. The upturn in Edgar Ravenswood's fortunes, occurring between Volumes 2 and 3, which finds him in Edinburgh and subsequently sent on a foreign mission, points more precisely to the period of the brief Tory ascendancy, beginning in May 1704 and lasting about a year. We also know that Scott inserted several additional passages into the 1830 text when he revised the novel for publication in the collected edition of his works, and that these establish a new, post-Union (post-1707) setting.[22] Though as a matter of detail this does not bear upon the present edition, based as it is on the 1819 first-edition text, as a matter of general fact these later changes are worth a moment's consideration if only because they show Scott resituating the novel's private emotional waste and the fall of the house of Ravenswood to a time, post-1707, when Scotland, too, has lost a distinct identity, by absorption into the new kingdom of Great Britain. More important to the present reading, though, is the setting of the novel in a period of vacillation and transition, when political reputations are in flux and no clear leadership (or historical shape) has emerged.

Introducing Sir William Ashton, the narrator explains the personal opportunism that dictates his actions as the consequence of a deeper political failure. At the Union of the Crowns in 1603, James VI of Scotland and I of England moved his court from Edinburgh to London, and for the ensuing century there was in Scotland 'no supereminent power, claiming and possessing a general interest with the community at large' (16). The biblical half-quotation, from Judges 17.6 ('In those days there was no king in Israel'), is offered to suggest that the king's withdrawal from Scotland left behind a moral vacuum, and the reader is expected to complete the verse: 'In those days there was no king in Israel, but every man did that which was right in his own eyes.' Sir William's family are Puritans, and as such they consider themselves as justified by faith to be the monitors of their own private morality. They date their wealth and growing influence from the unstable times of the 'great civil wars' (15; 1642–51). In other words, the novel defines the present time of history as shaped by and for the individual acting self-interestedly. The narrator continues with an analogy: 'The evils attending upon this system of government, resembled those which afflict the tenants of an Irish estate owned by an absentee' (16). It is a comment which shifts the present of history, suddenly and unexpectedly, to the present of writing – from the opening years of the eighteenth century to 1818. In 1800, within the recent memory of Scott's contemporary readers, Ireland had followed the 1707 example of Scotland and entered into political union with England. Several novels of the early nineteenth century take as their subject the contrast between an ancient family dispossessed of their estates and an incoming Anglo-Irish owner, often an absentee landlord, who governs their usurped lands for profit.[23] Lady Morgan's *The Wild Irish Girl* (1806) and Charles Maturin's *The Milesian Chief* (1812) are both likely models, directly or indirectly, for a national romance, a tale of personal *and* political union, that Scott transplants to the different but related situation of Scotland, adapting it first of all comically in *Guy Mannering* (1815) and then tragically in *The Bride of Lammermoor*.

The profound sense of a broken allegiance between the old aristocracy and the folk provides the immediate context in which to understand the social displacement governing the actions of both Ravenswood, as proud representative of an ancient but ruined family, and Sir William, as the anxious, ill-at-ease incomer. This is a society viewed through the lens of Scott's Enlightenment training in sociological history – history, that is, which is dedicated to identifying the links between economic modes, social formations, and cultural mentalities at any given period.[24] In *The Bride of Lammermoor* we witness feudalism, as a stage in the progressive social march, giving place to commerce, and, in consequence, we see a community adjusting its material conditions and its 'class' relations. The local setting of the novel is the eastern Scottish Borders, possibly a fictional Berwickshire. A geographic and socio-economic space, the imagined boundaries of Lammermoor are mapped in terms of the symbolic locations of ruined ancestral fortress (Wolfscrag), usurped castle (Ravenswood Castle), and flourishing fishing community (Wolfshope). These are places which also represent the temporal range of identities (feudal aristocracy, newly ennobled wealth, and emergent bourgeoisie) possible in this community in crisis. The confined spaces of these physical locations act upon style, heightening it to the point of allegorical intensity.[25] For example, the improvised feast that Caleb musters for an astonished Ravenswood and his guests in the crumbling austerity of Wolfscrag is to be set against the formal banquet prepared with such ceremony by Sir William Ashton for the Marquis of A— at Ravenswood Castle, on which event the narrator comments that it was attended by 'a pomp and display of luxury very uncommon in Scotland at that remote period' (162). In turn, both are to be compared with the reception of Ravenswood, the Marquis, and his attendants by the Wolfshope community. John Girder, a prosperous cooper and local leader, cannily balances 'the distinction which he had attained [from housing and feeding a Marquis] with the expences of the entertainment' (219). Set pieces, and all in their different ways opportunities for critical observation and comedy, they are each the occasion for that strategic description of the manners and customs of former times which we recognise as a vital ingredient of Scott's anthropological vision of history. But they are more than this. For the Scottish Enlightenment thinkers, the real motor of historical change, the force moving us from one social stage to the next, is desire or appetite. The supply of food and drink, not as necessity but as acts of conspicuous consumption, provides Scott with a measure by which we discover what is literally sustainable as a way of life among this community. Significantly, Girder's household economy, self-consciously modelled, as the narrator is at some pains to insist, on that of his 'betters', is also the most comfortable and socially secure. Girder and the villagers he represents are the future, and in that sense they figure a present reality for the reader, distinct from the past-historical world which closes over Ravenswood and even the time-serving Sir William. In Girder and the other inhabitants of Wolfshope, the mystified and arbitrary obligations of feudal duty are gradually being replaced, not by a freedom from distinction and hierarchy, but by a new consciousness of class and its opportunities.[26]

The margins of the central story contain examples of the deforming effects of centuries of feudalism, from the early, vivid description of the village of Wolfshope itself as 'a man . . . long fettered, who, even at liberty, feels, in imagination, the grasp of the hand-cuffs' (101), to the sexton Mortsheugh's denunciation of battle as bloody conscription, and the explanation, in poverty, petty crime, and social powerlessness, of witchcraft. In contrast to history's official, public definition as the record of famous men and famous deeds, this is 'history from below',[27] and its humble commentators exert a palpable force over the interpretation of events, notably the tragic denouement. At first meeting, Edgar, Master of Ravenswood, and Sir William Ashton appear to represent respectively the old and the new political orders. But this simple construction is thrown into doubt by a number of qualifications: by Sir William's obvious failure at social and domestic governance; by the reversal in national affairs placing his political enemy, the Tory and natural supporter of the exiled Stewart monarchy, the Marquis of A—, in a position of power in Queen Anne's court; and by repeated indications that, regardless of party fortunes, his own hand has been overplayed. As a Tory and adherent of the Stewart inheritance, Ravens-wood's father had supported the losing side in the 1688–89 Revolution which brought the Protestant William and Mary of Orange to the English throne, consolidated Sir William Ashton's success, and sent the last Stewart king, the Roman Catholic James II of England (VII of Scotland), into exile in France. The revival of the fortunes of the Marquis, his kinsman, promises to restore Ravenswood's family, but it appears that Ravenswood himself is no unthinking adherent of the old ways. Intellectually, at least, he is a progressive and a political realist. He tells the spendthrift Tory squire, Bucklaw, 'when I recollect the times of the first and second Charles, and of the last James, truly, I see little reason, that, as a man or patriot, I should draw my sword for their descendants' (73). As for the factious terms of 'Whig' and 'Tory', rather than deriving from them personal honour or principles, he anticipates a thoroughly modern compromise, whereby, 'as social life is better protected, its comforts will become too dear to be hazarded without some better reason than speculative politics' (74). In some senses, then, it would appear that Ravenswood is the coming man and Sir William the supplanted, and that this is so regardless of the larger frame in which all historical fiction operates – the real time of history itself – which tells us that the Tory revival, context for the novel's imagined events, barely outlived them.

It is a critical commonplace that Scott's novels enact the myth of history as the confrontation of old and new, in which extremes are moderated, differences synthesised, and a recognisably modern world is secured. The notoriously wavering hero – Scott's contribution to an understanding of how history mediates personal identity – is instrumental in brokering this agreement. It is his sympathetic leaning towards the old ways – those elements which as record and event are designated dangerous and obsolete – which is vital to deliver the past to the reader as matter for safe aesthetic contemplation; as it is also his return to domestic and political orthodoxy at the novel's close which enacts the successful progress of the modern state, through and out of history. Edward Waverley, the protagonist of Scott's first novel, is cast in this mould, as a romantic but ultimately commonsensical and resilient survivor. Ravenswood, too, his early comments suggest, would fill such an instrumental role. But another way of dealing with events overtakes him; in place of moderation and compromise between old and new, is set the obsessive unforgiveness of revenge.

As a way of describing the workings of history, the replacement of compromise by revenge is the replacement of progress by primitivism, and of reason by fate. This is history as the repetition of the past rather than the bringing to birth of the future. Scott's novels conventionally depict a confrontation between these two modes of historical explanation, which is often figured in the hero's apprenticeship to the teachings of a prophetic outcast, a madwoman who is also a folk representative, but who, in the course of the action's resolution, dies or is otherwise outgrown and reconsigned to the margins of events. In Scott's Enlightenment reading of history, this development is associated with a gendered interpretation of events, whereby fate and revenge, history's 'older' forms, are defined as feminine, while reason and negotiation, its modern arbiters, are masculine. In Lucy Ashton's impressionable psychology (easily invaded by terror and superstition), in Alice Gray's guardianship of Ravenswood family lore, in the ghoulish torments and spells of Ailsie Gourlay, and above all in Lady Ashton's fanatical preoccupation with genealogy and genetic determinism, can be found the ingredients for a violent parochial history which disregards the compromises of any grander, universalising scheme and disruptively returns the primitive from the margins of the story to its centre. It is as if history in its rawest form – superstition and vengeance – expunged from the official record in modern times, is here not only given voice but legitimacy, while the language of appeasement (in Scott's version, a masculine language) is decisively suppressed.

In several senses, *The Bride of Lammermoor* embodies Scott's vision of history as it came to him in its sensational feminine form – from oral tales preserved by the women in his family, but also from the Gothic novels of his precursor Ann Radcliffe – rather than in its rational, masculine form – from the printed authorities of his Enlightenment teachers, David Hume, Adam Smith, and Dugald Stewart. This is a tale that could be told in no other way: its every connection was for Scott feminine and steeped in violence. Great-aunt Margaret Swinton, its most authoritative source, was hacked to death by a crazed woman servant, and her murder, he later recalled, was associated with 'the first images of horror that the scenes of real life stamped on my mind'.[28] History's definition in the novel as the record of a destruction beyond recovery finds its explanation here, and in the shocking realization that this is Lucy Ashton's tale – only its consequences are Ravenswood's. Pliant and sentimental, as befits her bourgeois inheritance on the father's side, Lucy is also and more insidiously her mother's daughter. In Lucy, Lady Ashton's patrician tyranny, the legacy of her Douglas blood, finally resolves into a desperate negative energy. Something of this is implied in the lyric by which the narrative first introduces Lucy:

> "Look not thou on Beauty's charming, –
> Sit thou still when Kings are arming, –
>
> . . .
>
> Vacant heart, and hand, and eye, –
> Easy live and quiet die".(25)

The song's message, whether interpreted as a series of commands or cast in the conditional tense (its syntax remains unclear), carries a double irony: where an easy life depends upon retreat, peace may be bought at too high a price; but where ease is lost in the pursuit of fulfilment, the price paid may be even higher. Lucy's withdrawal is not a determined commitment to ease – neither the choice of the wise philosopher nor the dutiful daughter – but the deceptive, seeming vacancy of one who is prepossessed by attachments whose outcome, as the song implies, can be neither quiet nor happy.[29] In a final decisive action, she wreaks havoc upon the domestic restraint within which she only ever appeared to exist.

The Bride of Lammermoor offers history on a small scale whose intensity perverts and recombines in terrible ways our usual gender expectations: Lucy Ashton is passive victim *and* would-be murderer; Lady Ashton is mother *and* demonic persecutor; Ailsie Gourlay is nurse *and* tormentor. The anarchic forces which these domestic distortions unleash are not spent until there is nothing left of the Ashtons or Ravenswoods. Where history written along the masculine, Enlightenment line resolves, for Scott, into an amalgam of disparate viewpoints, ushered in by the hero's sympathetic recognition of other ways of living, feminine history permits no such compromise. Exclusively concerned with its own utterances, feminine history denies the validity of other points of view. Throughout the novel, two opposed voices – the one temporizing and contextual, the other disruptive and local – have competed for narrative possession. Ultimately, the local and disruptive voice makes the more urgent claim to attention. Unlike other Scott novels, *The Bride of Lammermoor* does not offer history according to general rules but according to the primitive law of exception, the feminine law.

The penultimate chapter, already withdrawn and abrupt in its haste to have done with the characters, records Lucy's insane attack upon her new husband and her eventual discovery by his rescuers, 'couched, like a hare upon its form . . . her night-clothes torn and dabbled with blood' (260). The blood-spotted night-gown provides its own grim comment on the unexpected transformation of the wedding night. But it also carries echoes of an earlier occasion, when the blood of the dead raven spattered Lucy's dress on her engagement to Edgar. In turn, this earlier scene finds its full significance in the symbolism of the bloodied waters of the Mermaiden's Well. Lucy's final words, too, – 'So, you have ta'en up your bonnie bridegroom.' (260) – appropriately release her from a sense of personal responsibility for what she does, returning her actions and her person to legend and superstition. She speaks in dialect, for the first and only time, in language which resonates with the rhythms and prophetic tones of Border ballad and folk curse. In word and deed Lucy has become the instrument of an older tale whose ingredients she was always powerless to refashion. The chapter concludes with the emphatic epilogue:

> By many readers this may be deemed overstrained, romantic, and composed by the wild imagination of an author, desirous of gratifying the popular appetite for the horrible; but those who are read in the private family history of Scotland during the period in which the scene is laid, will readily discover, through the disguise of borrowed names and added incidents, the leading particulars of AN OWER TRUE TALE. (262)

There is still a chapter to go, and Ravenswood's end to be told, but the tale, as Scott's sources require it to be shaped, is over. Ravenswood may ride out to a duel with Lucy's brother, but one last irony confirms the redundancy of his heroism, and with it the hopelessness, too, of any reconciliation with the past: it is not the duel which puts an end to the recent violent events but an old prophecy. Like the public affairs of state, which only punctuate the narrative occasionally, Ravenswood's final act of masculine honour is thwarted and proves as irrelevant as his potential for moderation to the purpose of a darker, private history.

NOTES

1 Thomas Hardy, 'The Profitable Reading of Fiction', *Life and Art* (London, 1925), 69. The essay first appeared in *The Forum* (1888).

2 E. M. Forster, *Aspects of the Novel* (1927; Harmondsworth, 1962), 38. Forster draws on expressive emotional features of Scott's tale and Donizetti's subsequent operatic redaction in *Where Angels Fear to Tread* (1905) and *A Room with a View* (1908).

3 Walter Scott, *The Fortunes of Nigel*, 3 vols (Edinburgh, 1822), 1.xv. ('epopeia', 'the making of epics', from the Greek; Scott is using the term to mean something like 'a narrative made in the epic mode').

4 Forster, *Aspects of the Novel*, 41.

5 John Gibson Lockhart, *Memoirs of the Life of Sir Walter Scott, Bart.*, 2nd edn, 10 vols (Edinburgh, 1839), 6.66–68 and 89.

6 Edgar Johnson, *Sir Walter Scott: The Great Unknown*, 2 vols (London, 1970), 1.670.

7 John Sutherland, *The Life of Sir Walter Scott: A Critical Biography* (Oxford, 1995), 220.

8 For interpretations of *The Bride of Lammermoor* which develop from readings of Scott's unconscious imagination, see John Buchan, *Sir Walter Scott* (London, 1932), 193; Alethea Hayter, *Opium and the Romantic Imagination* (London, 1968), 292–94; and Harry E. Shaw, *The Forms of Historical Fiction: Sir Walter Scott and His Successors* (Ithaca, NY, 1983), 215–16.

9 See the Essay on the Text, *The Bride of Lammermoor*, EEWN 7a, ed. J. H. Alexander (Edinburgh, 1995), 271–79.

10 *The Letters of Sir Walter Scott*, ed. H. J. C. Grierson and others, 12 vols (London, 1932–37), 6.118–19.

11 Walter Scott, *Chronicles of the Canongate*, 2 vols (Edinburgh, 1827), 1.x–xi.

12 Scott first published an account of the historical original in his revised, 1830, edition of the novel. See *Waverley Novels*, 48 vols (Edinburgh, 1829–33), 13.237–55. For a modern explanation of his source in the Dalrymple legend, see John W. Cairns, 'A Note on *The Bride of Lammermoor*: Why Scott did not mention the Dalrymple Legend until 1830', *Scottish Literary Journal*, 20:1 (May 1993), 19–36. For Scott's use of his source-tale, see Claire Lamont, 'Scott as Story-teller: *The Bride of Lammermoor*', *Scottish Literary Journal*, 7:1 (May 1980), 113–26. Coleman O. Parsons, 'The Dalrymple Legend in *The Bride of Lammermoor*', *Review of English Studies*, 19 (1943), 51–58, provides a survey of the four versions of the legend known to Scott. Much of this material is incorporated into Parsons's later study, *Witchcraft and Demonology in Scott's Fiction* (Edinburgh and London, 1964). In a recent article, J. H. Alexander suggests that Scott may have combined the traditional Dalrymple story with features from a German supernatural tale published in 1818. See ' "Das Goldene Schloss"; A Likely Source for *The Bride of Lammermoor*', *Scott Newsletter*, 34 (Summer 1999), 2–6.

13 *The Letters of Sir Walter Scott*, 5.186.

14 Walter J. Ong, *Orality and Literacy: The Technologizing of the Word* (London, 1982), 31.

15 Walter Benjamin, 'The Storyteller', in *Illuminations*, ed. Hannah Arendt (English translation, 1968; London, 1973), 87–89.

16 Jedidiah Cleishbotham (pseudonym), Introductory Address to *Count Robert of Paris* (1831), *Waverley Novels*, 46.xxv; *The Letters of Sir Walter Scott*, 4.292 and 5.135 and note 2; and Lockhart, *Memoirs*, 5.179–80 and 363.

17 Tinto's understanding of how paintings function is comparable in this respect to Benjamin's description of the method of the oral tale, whose compression exhibits the 'amplitude that information lacks' ('The Storyteller', 89).

18 See Lockhart, *Memoirs*, 6.88. Among modern commentators, David Brown, *Walter Scott and the Historical Imagination* (London, 1979), 145, relegates Caleb to 'the almost self-contained, and predominantly comic sub-plot', where he 'shows the inevitable degradation of the feudal ideal in the modern age'.

19 Shaw, *The Forms of Historical Fiction*, 214–15.

20 Ian Duncan, *Modern Romance and Transformations of the Novel: The Gothic, Scott, Dickens* (Cambridge, 1992), 136.

21 Shaw, *The Forms of Historical Fiction*, 222; Duncan, *Modern Romance*, 137.

22 For the dating of the novel's action, see Jane Millgate, 'Text and Context: Dating the Events of *The Bride of Lammermoor*', *Bibliotheck*, 9 (1979), 200–13; and Peter Dignus Garside, 'Union and *The Bride of Lammermoor*', *Studies in Scottish Literature*, 19 (1984), 72–93.

23 I owe the comment to Katie Trumpener, *Bardic Nationalism: The Romantic Novel and the British Empire* (Princeton, NJ, 1997), 45. Aesthetic and political connections between *The Bride* and Maturin's *The Milesian Chief* have long been assumed. For this, see Fiona Robertson, *Legitimate Histories: Scott, Gothic, and the Authorities of Fiction* (Oxford, 1994), 216–24.

24 For Scott's debt to the Scottish Enlightenment historians, see Duncan Forbes, 'The Rationalism of Sir Walter Scott', *Cambridge Journal*, 7 (1953), 20–35; and P. D. Garside, 'Scott and the "Philosophical" Historians', *Journal of the History of Ideas*, 36 (1975), 497–512.

25 See Franco Moretti, *Atlas of the European Novel 1800–1900* (Oxford, 1998), 38–45, which attempts to explore the nineteenth-century novel in terms of the inter-relationships and symbolic topographies of its real and fictional geographic spaces.

26 Critics have not always viewed the Wolfshope community as a locus of healthy enterprise. R. C. Gordon's influential reading of the novel through the lens of Scott's Tory pessimism regards the villagers as evidence of society's moral decay, see '*Under Which King?' A Study of the Scottish Waverley Novels* (Edinburgh, 1969), 103.

27 The phrase derives from the socialist historian E. P. Thompson but is here taken from the feminist historian Joan Wallach Scott's interpretation of Thompson's work, in *Gender and the Politics of History* (New York, 1988), 69.

28 Walter Scott, Introduction to 'My Aunt Margaret's Mirror' (1831), *Waverley Novels*, 41,293.

29 See Claire Lamont, 'The Poetry of the Early Waverley Novels', *Proceedings of the British Academy*, 61 (1975), for a closer examination of Lucy Ashton's character as illuminated by her song, and in particular for a persuasive account of the negative strength of her character. For a politicised reading of Lucy's madness, that implicates her distress in 'the narration of a wider social distress' which is 'the unofficial public history of Scotland', see Helen Small, *Love's Madness: Medicine, the Novel, and Female Insanity, 1800–1865* (Oxford, 1996), 123–38 (138).

1771	*15 August.* Born in College Wynd, Edinburgh. His father, Walter (1729–99), son of a sheep-farmer at Sandyknowe, near Smailholm Tower, Roxburghshire, was a lawyer. His mother, Anne Rutherford (1732–1819), was daughter of Dr John Rutherford, Professor of Medicine at the University of Edinburgh. His parents married in April 1758; Walter was their ninth child. The siblings who survived were Robert (1767–87), John (1769–1816), Anne (1772–1801), Thomas (1774–1823), and Daniel (?1776–1806).
1772–73	*Winter.* Contracted what is now termed poliomyelitis, and became permanently lame in his right leg. His grandfather Rutherford advised that he be sent to Sandyknowe to benefit from country air, and, apart from a period of 'about a year' in 1775 spent in Bath, a spell in 1776 with his family in their new home on the west side of George Square, Edinburgh, and a time in 1777 at Prestonpans, near Edinburgh, he lived there until 1778. From his grandmother and his aunt Janet he heard many ballads and stories of the Border past, and these narratives were crucial to his intellectual and imaginative development.
1779–83	Attended the High School of Edinburgh; he was particularly influenced by the Rector, Dr Alexander Adam, and his teaching of literature in Latin. After the High School, he spent 'half a year' with his aunt Janet in Kelso, where he attended the grammar school, and read for the first time Thomas Percy's *Reliques of Ancient English Poetry*.
1783–86	Attended classes at Edinburgh University, including Humanity (Latin), Greek, Logic and Metaphysics, and Moral Philosophy.
1786	Studies terminated by serious illness; convalescence in Kelso. Apprenticed as a lawyer to his father.
1787	Met Robert Burns at the house of the historian and philosopher, Adam Ferguson.
1789	Decided to prepare for the Bar.
1789–92	Attended classes at Edinburgh University, including History, Moral Philosophy, Scots Law, and Civil Law.
1792	*11 July.* Admitted to the Faculty of Advocates.

Autumn. First visit to Liddesdale, in the extreme south of Scotland, with Robert Shortreed, in search of ballads and ballad-singers. Seven such 'raids' followed over seven years. Shortreed later commented: 'He was makin' himsell a' the time'. His tours took him into many parts of Scotland and the north of England: e.g. in 1793 to Perthshire and the Trossachs; in 1796 to the north-east of Scotland; and in 1797 to Cumberland and the Lake District.

1794 In April involved in a brawl with some political radicals and bound to keep the peace. In September attended the trials of the radicals Watt and Downie, and in November Watt's execution.

*c.*1794–96 In love with Williamina Belsches, culminating in April 1796 with an invitation to her home, Fettercairn House, Kincardineshire.

1796 Anonymous publication of *The Chase and William and Helen*, Scott's translations of two of Bürger's poems.
October. Announcement of the engagement of Williamina Belsches to William Forbes.

1797 Volunteered for the new volunteer cavalry regiment, the Royal Edinburgh Light Dragoons, and appointed quartermaster.
September. Met Charlotte Carpenter (1770–1826), at Gilsland, Cumberland, and within three weeks proposed marriage. Charlotte's parents were Jean François Charpentier and Margaret Charlotte Volère (d. 1788), of Lyons. Sometime after the break-up of the marriage around 1780, her mother brought Charlotte and her brother Charles (1772–1818) to England; Charlotte and Charles later became the wards of the 2nd Marquess of Downshire, and changed their name to Carpenter.
24 December. Married Charlotte in Carlisle and set up house at 50 George Street, Edinburgh.

1798 Met Matthew Gregory ('Monk') Lewis and agreed to contribute to *Tales of Wonder* (published 1801).
Rented cottage in Lasswade near Edinburgh for the summer, and made many political and literary contacts, including Lady Louisa Stuart, who proved to be one of the most acute and trusted of his friends and critics.
Moved to 19 Castle Street, Edinburgh.
October. Birth and death of first son.

1799 Publication of *Goetz of Berlichingen*, Scott's translation of Goethe's tragedy.

April. Death of Scott's father.

Met John Leyden and the publisher Archibald Constable, and had his first discussion with the printer James Ballantyne about undertaking book-printing: Ballantyne brought out Scott's anthology *An Apology for Tales of Terror* in 1800.

October. Birth of daughter, Charlotte Sophia Scott.

December. Appointed Sheriff-Deputy of Selkirkshire.

1801   *October*. Birth of son, Walter Scott.

Moved to 39 Castle Street, Edinburgh.

1802   Publication of *Minstrelsy of the Scottish Border*, Vols 1 and 2. The *Minstrelsy* was the first publication in a lifetime of scholarly editing, and it shows both the strengths and weaknesses of Scott as editor. He found new texts (of the 72 ballads he published, 38 had not appeared in print before), and his literary, historical, and anthropological essays and notes are always illuminating; but, following the editorial practice of the time, he had no settled methods or principles for choosing or establishing a text.

Met James Hogg.

1803   *February*. Birth of daughter, Anne Scott.

Second edition of *Minstrelsy of the Scottish Border*, Vols 1 and 2, and first edition of Vol. 3.

Began to contribute reviews to the *Edinburgh Review*. Scott was an acute reviewer, in the expansive manner characteristic of heavyweight reviews in the early nineteenth century, and was particularly perceptive about such contemporaries as Jane Austen, Byron, and Mary Shelley.

September. Visit from William and Dorothy Wordsworth.

1804   Took the lease of Ashestiel near Selkirk as his country house in place of the cottage in Lasswade.

Publication of Scott's edition of the medieval metrical romance, *Sir Tristram*.

1805   Publication of *The Lay of the Last Minstrel*, the first of a series of verse romances which established his fame as a poet.

Entered into partnership with James Ballantyne in the printing business of James Ballantyne & Co. Until the financial crash in 1826, the partnership was not just a financial arrangement, but a unique collaboration: Ballantyne managed the business, but also acted as Scott's editor; Scott seems to have been responsible for much of the financial planning, and it was a standard part of his contracts with publishers that his works should be printed by James Ballantyne & Co.

December. Birth of son, Charles Scott.

1806   Hurried to London to secure his appointment as one of the Principal Clerks to the Court of Sessions, a position which had been under negotiation for much of the previous year but which was imperilled by the advent of a new government after the death of William Pitt on 23 January. The appointment was announced on 8 March. Scott took the place of an elderly Clerk, but, as there was no retirement and pension scheme, allowed his predecessor to keep the salary of £800 per annum for life. While in London Scott was 'taken up' by high society.

1807   Brother Tom bankrupt. It also emerged that Tom, a lawyer who had inherited his father's practice, and who had been retained as agent for the Duddingston estate of the Marquess of Abercorn, had misappropriated some of his client's money. Scott felt financially and morally endangered by his brother's breach of trust, and extended efforts were required over several years to protect his own financial credit and provide for his brother and his family.

1808   Publication of poem *Marmion* (the rights of which the publisher Archibald Constable had bought for £1050 in 1807).

Appointed secretary to the Parliamentary Commission to Inquire into the Administration of Justice in Scotland. The Commission ended its work in 1810.

Publication of *The Works of John Dryden . . . with Notes . . . and a Life of the Author*, 18 vols.

Cancelled his subscription to the *Edinburgh Review* because of its 'defeatist' view of the war in Spain, and began (with others) planning the *Quarterly Review* and the *Edinburgh Annual Register*, both launched in 1810. The political disagreement developed into a quarrel with Archibald Constable & Co., and Scott and the Ballantyne brothers, James and John, set up and became the partners in a rival publishing business, John Ballantyne & Co. Scott entrusted his own works to the new business and whenever possible directed other writers and new ventures to it, but Constable withdrew printing work from James Ballantyne & Co., and the printing firm stopped making significant profits.

1809   Publication of *A Collection of Scarce and Valuable Tracts*

(Somers' Tracts), Vols 1–3; completed in 13 vols 1812.

1810   Publication of *The Lady of the Lake*, his most commercially successful poem.   ·

1811   Scott's predecessor as Clerk of Session agreed to apply for a pension, and from 1812 Scott was paid a salary of £1300 per annum.

Publication of poem *The Vision of Don Roderick*.

Purchase of Cartley Hole, the nucleus of the Abbotsford Estate, between Galashiels and Melrose.

1812   Byron began correspondence with Scott.

Removal from Ashestiel to Abbotsford, and plans for rebuilding the small farmhouse there.

1813   Publication of poems *Rokeby* and *The Bridal of Triermain*. First financial crisis. It became apparent in 1812 that the publishing firm of John Ballantyne & Co. was making losses on every publication except Scott's poetry, and that the *Edinburgh Annual Register* was losing £1000 per issue. The firm was undercapitalized, and depended overmuch on bank credit. The national financial crisis of 1812–14 led to reduced orders for books from retailers, late payments, and to the bankruptcy of many companies whose debts to John Ballantyne & Co. were either not paid or paid in part. John Ballantyne & Co. found itself unable to pay its own bills and repay the banks on time, and *Rokeby*, greatly profitable though it was, failed to generate enough ready money to meet obligations. Protracted negotiations with Constable over much of 1813 led to the purchase of Ballantyne stock, on the condition that John Ballantyne & Co. ceased to be an active publisher, to the sale of a share in *Rokeby*, and later to the advance sale to Constable of rights for the publication of the long poem *The Lord of the Isles*. Scott had to ask the Duke of Buccleuch to guarantee a bank loan of £4000, and many friends gave small loans. All the personal loans were repaid in 1814, and the publishing business was eventually wound up profitably in 1817, largely through Scott's efforts. As part of the reconciliation Constable commissioned essays on Chivalry and the Drama for the Supplement to the *Encyclopaedia Britannica* (published 1818 and 1819 respectively).

Offered and declined the poet laureateship.

1814   Publication of his first novel, *Waverley*. The novel was probably begun in 1808 (the date '1st November, 1805' in the first chapter is part of the fiction), continued in 1810, and completed 1813–14; it was first advertised in 1810, and again in January 1814. The early parts (up to the beginning of Chapter 5, and Chapters 5–7) were probably written in parallel with Scott's autobiography (first published at the beginning of Lockhart's *Life of Scott* in 1837). Publication of *The Works of Jonathan Swift . . . with Notes and a Life of the Author*, 19 vols.

Toured the northern and western isles of Scotland with the Lighthouse Commissioners. His diary of the voyage is published in Lockhart's *Life of Scott* (1837).

1815 Publication of poem *The Lord of the Isles* and *Guy Mannering*, his second novel.

First visit to the Continent, including Waterloo and Paris, where he was lionized.

1816 Publication of *Paul's Letters to His Kinsfolk*, *The Antiquary*, and *Tales of my Landlord* (*The Black Dwarf* and *The Tale of Old Mortality*).

1817 Publication of *Harold the Dauntless* (Scott's last long poem), and *Rob Roy* (1818 on title page).

1817–19 First phase of the building of Abbotsford.

1818 Publication of *Tales of My Landlord*, second series (*The Heart of Midlothian*).

Offered and accepted a baronetcy (announced March 1820).

1819 Seriously ill, probably from gallstones. From 1817 Scott had been suffering stomach cramps, but in the spring and early summer of 1819 he was thought to be dying. Nonetheless he continued to work, dictating to an amanuensis when he was too ill to write. He completed *The Bride of Lammermoor* in April (the greater part of the manuscript is in his own hand) but the latter part of the novel and most of *A Legend of the Wars of Montrose* must have been dictated. The two tales constitute *Tales of My Landlord*, third series, and were published in June 1819.

Purchase by Constable of the copyrights of the 'Scotch novels' and publication of the first collection of Scott's fiction as *Novels and Tales of the Author of Waverley*, 16 vols. All the novels eventually appeared in collected editions in three formats: 8vo, 12mo, and 18mo. Publication of three articles in the *Edinburgh Weekly Journal*, later issued as a pamphlet entitled *The Visionary*, which was in essence political propaganda for the constitutional status

quo in the period after Peterloo, when there was a real possibility of a radical rising in the west of Scotland.
December. Death of Scott's mother.
Publication of *Ivanhoe* (1820 on title-page).

1820   Publication of *The Monastery* and *The Abbot.*
Marriage of daughter Sophia to John Gibson Lockhart.
Elected President of the Royal Society of Edinburgh.

1821   Publication of *Kenilworth* and *The Pirate* (1822 on title-page).

1821–24   Publication of *Ballantyne's Novelist's Library*, for which Scott wrote the lives of the novelists.

1822   Publication of *The Fortunes of Nigel* and *Peveril of the Peak* (1823 on title-page).
Visit of King George IV to Edinburgh.

1822–25   Demolition of the original house and second phase of the building of Abbotsford.

1823   Bannatyne Club founded and Scott made first president.
Publication of *Quentin Durward* and *St Ronan's Well* (1824 on title-page).

1824   Publication of *Redgauntlet.*

1825   Marriage of son Walter to Jane Jobson.
Publication of *Tales of the Crusaders* (*The Betrothed* and *The Talisman*).
Began his Journal.

1826   *January.* Scott insolvent. There was a severe economic recession in the winter of 1825–26 and many companies and individuals became bankrupt. Scott's principal publishers, Archibald Constable & Co., and the printers James Ballantyne & Co. in which he was co-partner, had always been undercapitalized, and relied on bank borrowings for working capital. In paying for goods and services, including such things as paper, printing, and publication rights, all parties used promissory bills, a system in which the drawer promised to pay stated sums on stated dates, and which the acceptor 'discounted' at the banks, i.e. got the money in advance of the date less the amount the banks charged in interest for what was in fact a loan. Both Constable's and Ballantyne's hoped that the money coming in from the sale of books when they were published would be sufficient to pay off the money due to the banks, but in practice both firms too often borrowed more money to pay off debts when they were due, and acted as guarantors for each other's loans. In December 1825 it was realized that they were unable to get further credit from the banks; and in January the bankruptcy of the London publishers of Scott's works, Hurst, Robinson & Co., precipitated the collapse of Constable's, then Ballantyne's, and the ruin of all the partners. Scott, the only one of those involved with a capacity to generate a large income, signed a trust deed undertaking to repay his own private debts (£35,000), all the debts of the printing business for which he and James Ballantyne were jointly liable (£41,000), the debts of Archibald Constable & Co. for which he was legally liable (£40,000), and a mortgage on Abbotsford (£10,000), amounting in all to over £126,000. Such were the profits from works like *Woodstock*, *The Life of Napoleon Buonaparte*, and above all the Magnum Opus, the collected edition of the Waverley Novels with introductions and notes specially written by Scott, and issued in monthly parts from 1829–33, that by Scott's death in 1832 more than £53,000 had been repaid, and the remaining debts were paid in 1833.

Publication of three letters in the *Edinburgh Weekly Journal*, later issued as *The Letters of Malachi Malagrowther*, in which Scott attacked a government proposal to restrict the rights of the Scottish banks to issue their own banknotes; Scott was so effective that the government withdrew its proposal.

Sale of 39 Castle Street, Edinburgh, on behalf of creditors.

15 May. Death of wife, Charlotte Scott.

Publication of *Woodstock*.

Autumn. Visit to Paris.

1827   Public acknowledgement of the authorship of the Waverley Novels.

Publication of *The Life of Napoleon Buonaparte*, 9 vols, *Chronicles of the Canongate* (Chrystal Croftangry's Narrative, 'The Highland Widow', 'The Two Drovers', and 'The Surgeon's Daughter'), and *Tales of a Grandfather* (Scotland to 1603).

1828   Publication of *Chronicles of the Canongate*, second series (*The Fair Maid of Perth*), and *Tales of a Grandfather*, second series (Scotland 1603–1707).

1829   Publication of *Anne of Geierstein*, *History of Scotland*, Vol. 1, and *Tales of a Grandfather*, third series (Scotland 1707–45). The first volume of the Magnum Opus, completed in 48 vols in 1833, appeared on 1 June.

1830   *February*. First stroke.

November. Retired as Clerk to the Court of Session with pension of £864 per annum. Second stroke.

Publication of *Letters on Demonology and Witchcraft*, *Tales of a Grandfather* (France), and *History of Scotland*, Vol. 2.

1831   *April*. Third stroke.

Publication of *Tales of my Landlord*, fourth series (*Count Robert of Paris* and *Castle Dangerous*).

October. Departure on HMS *Barham* to the Mediterranean, Malta and Naples.

1832   Overland journey home, via Rome, Florence, Venice, Verona, the Brenner Pass, Augsburg, Mainz, and down the Rhine, but had his fourth stroke at Nijmegen. Travelling by sea to London and then Edinburgh, he reached Abbotsford on 11 July.

21 September. Death at Abbotsford.

FURTHER READING

THE WORKS OF SCOTT

The Journal of Sir Walter Scott, ed. W. E. K. Anderson (Oxford, 1972).

The Letters of Sir Walter Scott, ed. H. J. C. Grierson and others, 12 vols (London, 1932–37). The index to this edition is by James C. Corson, *Notes and Index to Sir Herbert Grierson's Edition of the Letters of Sir Walter Scott* (Oxford, 1979).

'Memoirs', in *Scott on Himself: A Selection of the Autobiographical Writings of Sir Walter Scott*, ed. David Hewitt (Edinburgh, 1981).

The Poetical Works of Sir Walter Scott, ed. J. Logie Robertson (Oxford, 1904; frequently reprinted).

The Poetical Works of Sir Walter Scott, Bart. [ed. J. G. Lockhart], 12 vols (Edinburgh, 1833–34).

The Prose of Sir Walter Scott, Bart., 28 vols (Edinburgh, 1834–36).

Waverley Novels, 48 vols (Edinburgh, 1829–33), known as the 'Magnum Opus'.

The Waverley Novels were among the most frequently reprinted works of the nineteenth century, and all editions after Scott's death were based upon the edition of 1829–33. Of these, the best are the Centenary Edition, 25 vols (London, 1871), the Dryburgh Edition, 25 vols (London, 1892–94), and the Border Edition, ed. Andrew Lang, 48 vols (London, 1892–94). The first critical edition is the Edinburgh Edition of the Waverley Novels (1993–) on which the volumes of the new Penguin Scott are based.

The complete listing of the works of Scott is in

William B. Todd and Ann Bowden, *Sir Walter Scott: A Bibliographical History 1796–1832* (Newcastle, DE, 1998).

There are two simpler listings:

J. G. Lockhart, 'Chronological List of the Publications of Sir Walter Scott', in *Memoirs of the Life of Sir Walter Scott, Bart.*, 7 vols (Edinburgh, 1837–38; many times republished), 7.433–39.

J. H. Alexander, 'Sir Walter Scott', in *The Cambridge Bibliography of English Literature, Volume 4: 1800–1900*, 3rd edn, ed. Joanne Shattock (Cambridge, 2000) 992–1963.

BIOGRAPHY

There are very many biographies of Scott. The most important is still by J. G. Lockhart for although it is unreliable in much of its detail it is the work of a writer and an intimate who knew Scott well. The most comprehensive of the modern works is by Edgar Johnson; it is generally reliable. John Buchan's one-volume life is the most sympathetic of all the studies of Scott, while John Sutherland takes a harsher view of the way in which Scott used those in his circle for his own advantage.

James Hogg, *Anecdotes of Scott*, ed. Jill Rubenstein (Edinburgh, 1999).

J. G. Lockhart, *Memoirs of the Life of Sir Walter Scott, Bart.*, 7 vols (Edinburgh, 1837–38; many times republished).

John Buchan, *Sir Walter Scott* (London, 1932).

Sir Herbert Grierson, *Sir Walter Scott, Bart.: A New Life supplementary to, and corrective of, Lockhart's Biography* (London, 1938).

Arthur Melville Clark, *Sir Walter Scott: The Formative Years* (Edinburgh, 1969).

Edgar Johnson, *Sir Walter Scott: The Great Unknown*, 2 vols (London, 1970).

John Sutherland, *The Life of Walter Scott* (Oxford, 1995).

CRITICISM

Complete listings of critical works on Scott are to be found in:

James C. Corson, *A Bibliography of Sir Walter Scott: A Classified and Annotated List of Books and Articles relating to his Life and Works 1797–1940* (Edinburgh, 1943).

Jill Rubenstein, *Sir Walter Scott: A Reference Guide* (Boston, MA, 1978) [covers the period 1932–77].

Jill Rubenstein, *Sir Walter Scott: An Annotated Bibliography of Scholarship and Criticism 1975–1990* (Aberdeen, 1994).

THE FOLLOWING ARE USEFUL FOR THE STUDY OF *THE BRIDE OF LAMMERMOOR*:

Robert C. Gordon, '*The Bride of Lammermoor*: A Novel of Tory Pessimism', *Nineteenth Century Fiction*, 12 (1957), 110–24.

Alexander Welsh, *The Hero of the Waverley Novels* (New Haven, CT, 1963).

Francis R. Hart, *Scott's Novels: The Plotting of Historic Survival* (Charlottesville, VA, 1966).

Andrew D. Hook, '*The Bride of Lammermoor:* A Reexamination', *Nineteenth Century Fiction*, 22 (1967), 111–26.

Donald Cameron, 'The Web of Destiny: The Structure of *The Bride of Lammermoor*', in *Scott's Mind and Art*, ed. A. Norman Jeffares (Edinburgh, 1969), 185–205.

A. O. J. Cockshut, *The Achievement of Walter Scott* (London, 1969).

Robert C. Gordon, *Under Which King? A Study of the Scottish Waverley Novels* (Edinburgh, 1969).

Robert C. Gordon and Andrew D. Hook, '*The Bride of Lammermoor* Again: An Exchange', *Nineteenth Century Fiction*, 23 (1969), 493–99.

Douglas Brooks, 'Feast and Structure in *The Bride of Lammermoor*', *Ariel*, 2:3 (1971), 66–76.

D. D. Devlin, *The Author of Waverley: A Critical Study of Walter Scott* (London, 1971).

Robin Mayhead, *Walter Scott* (Cambridge, 1973).

Claire Lamont, 'The Poetry of the Early Waverley Novels', *Proceedings of the British Academy*, 61 (1975), 315–36.

Frank McCombie, 'Scott, Hamlet, and *The Bride of Lammermoor*', *Essays in Criticism*, 25 (1975), 419–36.

Jane Millgate, 'Two Versions of Regional Romance: Scott's *The Bride of Lammermoor* and Hardy's *Tess of the D'Urbervilles*', *Studies in English Literature 1500–1900*, 17 (1977), 729–38.

Jane Millgate, 'Text and Context: Dating the Events of *The Bride of Lammermoor*', *Bibliotheck*, 9 (1979), 200–13.

John P. Farrell, *Revolution as Tragedy: The Dilemma of the Moderate, from Scott to Arnold* (Ithaca, NY, 1980).

Claire Lamont, 'Scott as Story-teller: *The Bride of Lammermoor*', *Scottish Literary Journal*, 7:1 (May 1980), 113–26.

David Punter, *The Literature of Terror: A History of Gothic Fictions from 1765 to the Present Day* (London, 1980).

George Levine, *The Realistic Imagination: English Fiction from Frankenstein to Lady Chatterley* (Chicago, 1981).

Graham McMaster, *Scott and Society* (Cambridge, 1981).

Thomas Crawford, *Scott* (Edinburgh, 1982: original version published 1965).

Harry E. Shaw, *The Forms of Historical Fiction: Sir Walter Scott and His Successors* (Ithaca, NY, 1983).

Peter Dignus Garside, 'Union and *The Bride of Lammermoor*', *Studies in Scottish Literature*, 19 (1984), 72–93.

Jane Millgate, *Walter Scott: The Making of the Novelist* (Edinburgh, 1984).

Robert C. Gordon, 'The Marksman of Ravenswood: Power and Legitimacy in *The Bride of Lammermoor*', *Nineteenth Century Literature*, 41 (1986), 49–71.

Caroline Franklin, 'Feud and Faction in *The Bride of Lammermoor*', *Scottish Literary Journal*, 14:2 (November 1987), 18–31.

Philip W. Martin, *Mad Women in Romantic Writing* (Brighton, 1987).

Jina Politi, 'Narrative and Historical Transformation in *The Bride of Lammermoor*', *Scottish Literary Journal*, 15:1 (May 1988), 70–81.

James Kerr, *Fiction Against History: Scott as Storyteller* (Cambridge, 1989).

Robert M. Polhemus, *Erotic Faith: Being in Love from Jane Austen to D. H. Lawrence* (Chicago, 1990).

Daniel S. Butterworth, 'Tinto, Pattieson and the Theories of Pictorial and Dramatic Representation in Scott's *The Bride of Lammermoor*', *South Atlantic Review*, 56 (1991), 1–15.

Ina Ferris, *The Achievement of Literary Authority: Gender, History, and the Waverley Novels* (Ithaca, NY, 1991).

Sir Walter Scott, *The Bride of Lammermoor*, ed. Fiona Robertson (Oxford, 1991).

Ian Duncan, *Modern Romance and Transformations of the Novel: The Gothic, Scott, Dickens* (Cambridge, 1992).

Bruce Beiderwell, 'Death and Disappearance in *The Bride of Lammermoor*', in *Scott in Carnival*, ed. J. H. Alexander and David Hewitt (Aberdeen, 1993), 245–53.

John W. Cairns, 'A Note on *The Bride of Lammermoor*: Why Scott did not Mention the Dalrymple Legend until 1830', *Scottish Literary Journal*, 20:1 (May 1993), 19–36.

Simon Edwards, '*The Bride of Lammermoor* and the Borders of Character', in *Scott in Carnival*, ed. J. H. Alexander and David Hewitt (Aberdeen, 1993), 254–63.

James Chandler, 'Scott and the Scene of Explanation: Framing Contextuality in *The Bride of Lammermoor*', *Studies in the Novel* (University of North Texas), 26 (1994), 69–98.

Fiona Robertson, *Legitimate Histories: Scott, Gothic, and the Authorities of Fiction* (Oxford, 1994).

Penny Fielding, *Writing and Orality: Nationality, Culture, and Nineteenth-Century Scottish Fiction* (Oxford, 1996).

Helen Small, *Love's Madness: Medicine, the Novel, and Female Insanity 1800–1865* (Oxford, 1996).

Janet Sorenson, 'Writing Historically, Speaking Nostalgically: The Competing Languages of Nation in Scott's *The Bride of Lammer-*

moor', in *Narratives of Nostalgia, Gender and Nationalism*, ed. Jean Pickering and Suzanne Kehde (Basingstoke, 1997), 30–51.

J. H. Alexander, 'A Key, a Bonnie Bridegroom, and an Ower True Tale', *The Edinburgh Sir Walter Scott Club Bulletin* (1997–98), 31–39.

J. H. Alexander, ' "Das Goldene Schloss": A Likely Source for *The Bride of Lammermoor*', *Scott Newsletter*, 34 (Summer 1999), 2–6.

A NOTE ON THE TEXT

The Bride of Lammermoor was published along with *A Legend of Montrose* as *Tales of my Landlord (Third Series)* in four volumes on 21 June 1819. *The Bride* occupies the first two volumes of the set and rather more than one third of the third. The present text, which is taken from Volume 7a in the Edinburgh Edition of the Waverley Novels series,[1] is based on the first edition, for the reasons and on the general principles explained above in the Waverley Novels in Penguin. In Scott's time it was not expected that spelling or punctuation would be rigorously standardized throughout a novel: each compositor had a good deal of freedom to follow his own preferences. The EEWN text standardizes on Scott's preferred forms only where variation (in the name of a character, for example) might cause confusion. Variations between spellings of common words such as 'sho/ew' or 'e/inquire' are preserved, since they are as much part of the characteristic texture of the 1819 text as the physical division into volumes with chapter numbers beginning afresh in each volume.

The manuscript, preserved in the Signet Library, Edinburgh, is complete for the first volume, and (except for three leaves) for most of the second (to 213.1: 'and let me know the' in the present edition). On the otherwise blank verso, or back, of the final surviving leaf there are short passages designed for insertion in a now missing following leaf, and Scott may have written more in his own hand before he was forced by an excruciating attack of gallstones to dictate the final chapters. The National Library of Scotland preserves proofs corrected by Scott for the closing pages of the novel (240.28: '[attri]butes. The story' to the end).

After the first edition, *The Bride of Lammermoor* appeared in five different versions of the collected *Novels and Tales* between 1819 and 1825, and again in the 'Magnum Opus' edition in 1830. (A 'second' and 'third' edition published shortly after the first were simply copies of the first edition with new title-pages designed to shift stock.)

The present text aims to correct the first-edition base-text primarily by reference to the manuscript and to the proofs where extant. More than 30,000 changes in punctuation and capitalization were made between manuscript and first edition, along with more than 2000 verbal alterations. Although the conversion of Scott's manuscript punctuation and capitalization in conformity with the print conventions of his time

1

is accepted in the present edition, in some 250 cases the force or
movement of the manuscript has been lost and emendation is called
for. So, Lucy cautions against 'Beauty's' [not 'beauty's'] charming',
where the manuscript capital denotes a personification (25.5); but 'old
Alice' is simply that, not 'Old Alice' (29.39) as in the first edition.
Occasionally, the intermediaries lost the movement which Scott must
have heard in a particular speech. Thus, three of the five manuscript
dashes in the Lord Keeper's meditating speech 'as if half speaking
with himself' were changed to commas or full, stops; the dashes are
restored in the present text (134.34–37).

In addition to supplying punctuation, the intermediaries had 'standing orders' authorizing them to, for example, change words repeated
in close proximity to each other, introduce additional Scots forms in
the speech of Scots speakers, correct clear grammatical errors, insert
speech indicators, and add appropriate (usually single) words to fill
obvious lacunae left by Scott in his haste. Except where standing
orders were applied in an insensitive and mechanical way, such changes
are accepted in the present edition. However, over a thousand verbal
emendations have been made to the first-edition base-text.[2]

The commonest reason for verbal emendation is that the manuscript
was misread. Going back to the manuscript has made it possible to
restore, for example, the important singular forms 'eye' (18.6) and
'step' (31.29). Also: Lucy's sentiments seemed 'dull', not 'chill' (27.17);
Bucklaw had 'cut', not 'eat', a portion of ham (65.16), and he is
'frack' rather than 'frank' (77.15); and 'town, and' is a misreading of
'town-end' (105.17). Sometimes, being less inward with the linguistic
usages of the period of the novel than the author, the intermediaries
failed to recognize an idiom, inserting for example a word (here
indicated by arrows) in 'something of ↑ a ↓ nourice-ship' (30.18) and
deleting one (indicated by angle brackets) in 'play <you> your own
part' (51.7). On occasion, phrases or even complete sentences were
omitted. Three important nuances in the presentation of Lucy were
missed by the intermediaries. First, in the manuscript her voice as she
sings her celebrated song mingles with the accompaniment '<of an>
in ancient and solemn air' (25.3): for the first edition either Scott or
the intermediaries have correctly inserted 'an' before 'ancient', but the
words 'and solemn' have probably dropped out rather than been
deliberately removed. Second, a straightforward slip of the eye from
one 'Alice' to the next accounts for the unfortunate loss to the first
edition of the last part of Lucy's speech at the end of Chapter 3: 'her
cottage is so bad besides and I am sure you<r> will cause Former the
carpenter to put it somewhat to rights if you see how decayd it is—
Do come to see old Alice—'(30.34–36). And third, though it involves

only three words, the restoration in the present text of the confidently written manuscript 'and she sang' at 117.8 alters a little our view both of Lucy and of Edgar's response to her: if the words were deliberately removed, rather than accidentally omitted, it would probably have been a result of James Ballantyne's often prissy sense of what constituted ladylike behaviour. At 70.12–22 it has been possible to recover two phrases inserted by Scott on the otherwise blank versos, and these also fill in details of Edgar's feelings: 'and these were powerfully connected with the image of Lucy Ashton'; and death 'was now opening his bosom to a passion for the daughter of that very person'. The first edition had to change the main text of the manuscript a little to accommodate the inadvertent omissions: in the present text the full manuscript reading is restored. Caleb's rhetoric is enhanced by two other recoveries of verso readings: 'before we are blessd wi' better provision', and 'and I'll no say but some o' them may make themselves heard in the field yet unless times be a' the quieter' (213.15–16, 214.29–30).

All Scott's extant proof changes have been accepted in the present text, including a handful missed or ignored by the intermediaries. The same is true of most of James Ballantyne's, but not quite all. His changing of 'death chamber' to 'cottage' at 240.35 is diminishing: he probably fancied that the echo of 'dead bride' four lines earlier ought to be removed. More importantly, at 268.41–42 Ballantyne seems to have marked for deletion the phrase 'in a great degree' (and he wrote, 'Old jade! They were *altogether* owing to her implacability'), but Scott did not actually delete the phrase, so it is here restored.

The readings incorporated for the first time in the present edition – 1,250 of them – will, it is hoped, have produced a text with something of the same impression as a freshly restored painting. Like the innumerable swabbings and applications of adhesive by the conservator, the individual emendations are mostly tiny, but the cumulative effect is revelatory of Scott's skill and judgement as a master craftsman.

NOTES

1 *The Bride of Lammermoor*, ed. J. H. Alexander, EEWN 7a (Edinburgh: Edinburgh University Press, and New York: Columbia University Press, 1995).

2 An analysis of the transmission from manuscript to first edition and a full list of emendations to the first-edition text will be found in the EEWN volume on 279–83 and 305–31.

TALES OF MY LANDLORD,

Third Series,

COLLECTED AND REPORTED

BY

JEDIDIAH CLEISHBOTHAM,

PARISH-CLERK AND SCHOOLMASTER OF GANDERCLEUGH.

> Hear, Land o' Cakes and brither Scots,
> Frae Maidenkirk to Jonny Groats',
> If there's a hole in a' your coats,
>   I rede ye tent it,
> A chiel's amang you takin' notes,
>   An' faith he'll prent it.
>
> BURNS.

IN FOUR VOLUMES.

VOLS. I, II & III (PART).

EDINBURGH:

PRINTED FOR ARCHIBALD CONSTABLE AND CO. EDINBURGH;

LONGMAN, HURST, REES, ORME, AND BROWN, PATERNOSTER-ROW;
AND HURST, ROBINSON, AND CO. 90, CHEAPSIDE, LONDON.

1819.

Ahora bien, dixo el Cura, traedme, senor huésped, aquesos libros, que los quiero ver. Que me place, respondió el, y entrando, en su aposento, sacó dél una maletilla vieja cerrada con una cadenilla, y abriéndola, halló en ella tres libros grandes y unos papeles de muy buena letra escritos de mano.—DON QUIXOTE, Parte I. Capitulo 32.

It is mighty well, said the priest; pray, landlord, bring me those books, for I have a mind to see them. With all my heart, answered the host; and, going to his chamber, he brought out a little old cloke-bag, with a padlock and chain to it, and opening it, he took out three large volumes, and some manuscript papers written in a fine character.— JARVIS's *Translation*.

THE
BRIDE OF LAMMERMOOR

Chapter One

By cauk and keel to win your bread,
Wi' whigmaleeries for them wha need,
Whilk is a gentle trade indeed
To carry the gaberlunzie on.
Old Song

FEW HAVE been in my secret while I was engaged in compiling these narratives, nor is it probable that they will ever become public during the life of their author. Even were that event to happen, I am not ambitious of the honoured distinction, *monstrari digito*. I confess, that, were it safe to cherish such dreams at all, I should more enjoy the thought of remaining behind the curtain unseen, like the ingenious manager of Punch and his wife Joan, and enjoying the astonishment and conjectures of my audience. Then might I, perchance, hear the productions of the obscure Peter Pattieson praised by the judicious, and admired by the feeling, engrossing the young, and attracting even the old; while the critic traced their style and sentiments up to some name of literary celebrity, and the question when, and by whom, these tales were written, filled up the pause of conversation in a hundred circles and coteries. This I may never enjoy during my lifetime; but farther than this, I am certain, my vanity should never induce me to aspire.

I am too stubborn in habits, and too little flexible in manners, to envy or aspire to the honours assigned to my literary contemporaries. I could not think a whit more highly of myself, were I even found worthy to "come in place as a lion" for a winter in the great metropolis. I cannot rise, turn round, and shew all my honours, from the shaggy mane to the tufted tail, roar ye as it were any nightingale, and so lie down again like a well-behaved beast of show, and all at the cheap and

3

easy rate of a cup of coffee, and a slice of bread and butter as thin as a wafer. And I could ill stomach the fulsome flattery with which the lady of the evening indulges her show-monsters on such occasions, as she crams her parrots with sugar-plumbs, in order to make them talk before company. I care not for these marks of distinction, and, like imprisoned Sampson, I would rather remain—if such must be the alternative—all my life in the mill-house, grinding for my very bread, than be brought forth to make sport for the Philistian lords and ladies. This proceeds from no dislike, real or affected, to the aristocracy of these realms. But they have their place, and I have mine; and, like the iron and earthen vessels in the old fable, we can scarce come into collision without my being the sufferer in every sense. It may be otherwise with the sheets which I am now writing. These may be opened and laid aside at pleasure; by amusing themselves with the perusal, the great will excite no false hopes; by neglecting or condemning them, they will inflict no pain; and how seldom can they converse with those whose minds have toiled for their delight, without doing either the one or the other.

In the better and wiser tone of feeling, which Ovid only expresses in one line to retract in that which follows, I can address these quires—

Parve, nec invideo, sine me, liber, ibis in urbem.

Nor do I join the regret of the illustrious exile, that he himself could not in person accompany the volume, which he sent forth to the mart of literature, pleasure, and luxury. Were there not a hundred similar instances on record, the fate of my poor friend and school-fellow, Dick Tinto, would be sufficient to warn me against seeking happiness, in the celebrity which attaches itself to the successful cultivator of the fine arts.

Dick Tinto, when he wrote himself Artist, was wont to derive his origin from the ancient family of Tinto, of that ilk, in Lanarkshire, and occasionally hinted that he had somewhat derogated from his gentle blood, in using his pencil for his principal means of support. But if Dick's pedigree was correct, some of his ancestors must have suffered a more heavy declension, since the goodman his father executed the necessary, and, I trust, the honest, but certainly not very distinguished employment, of tailor in ordinary to the village of Langdirdum in the west. Under his humble roof was Richard born, and to his father's humble trade was Richard, greatly contrary to his inclination, early indentured. Old Mr Tinto had, however, no reason to congratulate himself upon having compelled the youthful genius of his son to forsake its natural bent. He fared like the school-boy, who attempts to stop with his finger the spout of a water cistern, while the stream, exasperated at this compression, escapes by a thousand uncalculated spirts, and wets him all over for his pains. Even so fared the senior Tinto, when his hopeful apprentice not only exhausted all the chalk in making sketches upon the shopboard, but even executed several caricatures of his father's best customers, who began loudly to murmur, that it was too hard to have their persons deformed by the vestments of the father, and to be at the same time turned into ridicule by the pencil of the son. This led to discredit and loss of practice, until the old tailor, yielding to destiny, and to the entreaties of his son, permitted him to attempt his fortune in a line for which he was better qualified.

There was about this time, in the village of Langdirdum, a peripatetic brother of the brush, who exercised his vocation *sub Jove frigido*, the object of admiration to all the boys of the village, but especially to Dick Tinto. The age had not yet adopted, amongst other unworthy retrenchments, that illiberal measure of economy, which, supplying by written characters the lack of symbolical representation, closes one open and easily accessible avenue of instruction and emolument against the students of the fine arts. It was not yet permitted to write upon the plaistered door-way of an ale-house, or the suspended sign of an inn, "The Old Magpie," or "The Saracen's Head," substituting this cold description for the lively effigies of the plumed chatterer, or the turban'd frown of the terrific soldan. That early and more simple age considered alike the necessities of all ranks, and so depicted the symbols of good cheer as to be obvious to all capacities; well judging, that a man, who could not read a syllable, might nevertheless love a pot of good ale as well as his better educated neighbours, or even the parson himself. Acting upon this liberal principle, publicans as yet hung forth the painted emblems of their calling, and sign-painters, if they seldom feasted, did not at least absolutely starve.

To the worthy of this decadent profession whom we have already indicated, Dick Tinto became an assistant; and thus, as is not unusual among heaven-born geniuses in this department of the fine arts, began to paint before he had any notion of drawing.

His natural talent for observing nature soon induced him to rectify the errors, and soar above the instructions, of his teacher. He particularly shone in painting horses, that have been a favourite sign in the Scottish villages; and, in tracing his progress, it is beautiful to observe, how by degrees he learned to shorten the backs, and prolong the legs, of these noble animals, until they came to look less like crocodiles, and more like nags. Detraction, which always pursues merit with strides proportioned to its advancement, has indeed alleged, that Dick once upon a time painted a horse with five legs, instead of four. I might have rested his defence upon the licence allowed to this branch of his profession, which, as it permits all sort of singular and irregular combinations, may be allowed to extend itself so far as to bestow a limb supernumerary on a favourite subject. But the cause of a deceased friend is sacred; and I disdain to bottom it so superficially. I have visited the sign in question, which yet swings exalted in the village of Langdirdum, and I am ready to depone upon oath, that what has been idly mistaken or misrepresented as being the fifth leg of the horse, is, in fact, the tail of that quadruped, and, considered with reference to the posture in which he is represented, forms a circumstance, introduced and managed with great and successful, though daring art. The nag being represented in a rampant or rearing posture, the tail, which is prolonged till it touches the ground, appears to form a *point d'appui*, and gives the firmness of a tripod to the figure, without which it would be difficult to conceive, placed as the feet are, how the courser could maintain his ground without tumbling backwards. This bold conception has fortunately fallen into the custody of one by whom it is duly valued; for, when Dick, in his more advanced state of proficiency, became dubious of the propriety of so daring a deviation from the established rules of art, and was desirous to execute a picture of the publican himself in exchange for this juvenile production, the courteous offer was declined by his judicious employer, who had observed, it seems, that when his ale had failed to do its duty in conciliating his guests, one glance at his sign was sure to put them into good-humour.

It would be foreign to my present purpose to trace the steps by which Dick Tinto improved his touch, and corrected, by the rules of art, the luxuriance of a fervid imagination. The scales fell from his eyes on viewing the sketches of a contemporary, the Scottish Teniers, as Wilkie has been deservedly styled. He threw down the brush, took up the crayons, and, amid hunger and toil, and suspense and uncertainty, pursued the path of his profession under better auspices than those of his original master. Still the first rude emanations of his genius (like the nursery rhymes of Pope, could these be recovered,) will be dear to the companions of Dick Tinto's youth. There is a tankard and gridiron painted over the door of an obscure changehouse in the back-wynd of Gandercleugh—But I feel I must tear myself from the subject, or dwell on it too long.

Amid his wants and struggles, Dick Tinto had recourse, like his brethren, to levying that tax upon the vanity of mankind which he could not extract from their taste and liberality—in a word, he painted portraits. It was in this more advanced stage of proficiency, when Dick had soared above his original line of business, and highly disdained all allusions to it, that, after having been estranged for several years, we again met in the village of Gandercleugh, I holding my present situation, and Dick painting copies of the human face divine at a guinea per head. This was a small premium, yet, in the first burst of business, it more than sufficed for all Dick's moderate wants; so that he occupied an apartment at the Wallace Inn, cracked his jest with impunity even upon mine host himself, and lived in respect and observance with the chambermaid, hostler, and waiter.

These halcyon days were too serene to last long. When his honour the Laird of Gandercleugh, with his wife and three daughters, the minister, the gauger, mine esteemed patron Mr Jedidiah Cleishbotham, and some round dozen of the neighbouring feuars and farmers, had been consigned to immortality by Tinto's brush, custom began to slacken, and it was impossible to wring more than crowns and half-crowns from the hard hands of the peasants, whose ambition led them to Dick's painting-room.

Still, though the horizon was overclouded, no storm for some time ensued. Mine host had Christian faith with a lodger, who had been a good paymaster as long as he had the means. And from a portrait of our landlord himself, grouped with his wife and daughters, in the style of Rubens, which suddenly appeared in the best parlour, it was evident that Dick had found some mode of bartering art for the necessaries of life.

Nothing, however, is more precarious than resources of this nature. It was observed, that Dick became in his turn the whetstone of mine host's wit, without venturing either at defence or retaliation; that his easel was transferred to a garret-room, in which there was scarce space for it to stand upright; and that he no longer ventured to join the weekly club, of which he had been once the life and soul. In short, Dick Tinto's friends feared that he had acted like the animal called the sloth, which, having eaten up the very last green leaf upon the tree where it has established itself, ends by tumbling down from the top, and dying of inanition. I ventured to hint this to Dick, recommended his transferring the exercise of his inestimable talent to some wider sphere, and forsaking the common which he might be said to have eaten bare.

"There is an obstacle to my change of residence," said my friend, grasping my hand with a look of solemnity.

"A bill due to my landlord, I am afraid," replied I, with heartfelt sympathy; "if any part of my slender means can assist in this emergence"——

"No, by the soul of Sir Joshua," answered the generous youth, "I will never involve a friend in the consequences of my own misfortunes. There is a mode by which I can regain my liberty; and to creep even through a common sewer, is better than to remain in prison."

I did not perfectly understand what my friend meant. The muse of painting appeared to have failed him, and what other goddess he could invoke in his distress, was a mystery to me. We parted, however, without further explanation, and I did not again see him until three days after, when he summoned me to partake of the *foy* with which his landlord proposed to regale him ere his departure for Edinburgh.

I found Dick in high spirits, whistling while he buckled the small knapsack, which contained his colours, brushes, pallets, and clean shirt. That he parted on the best terms with mine host, was obvious from the cold beef set forth in the low parlour, flanked by two mugs of admirable brown stout; and I own my curiosity was excited concerning the means through which the face of my friend's affairs had been so suddenly improved. I did not suspect Dick of dealing with the devil, and by what earthly means he had extricated himself thus happily, I was at a total loss to conjecture.

He perceived my curiosity, and took me by the hand. "My friend," he said, "fain would I conceal, even from you, the degradation to which it has been necessary to submit, in order to accomplish an honourable retreat from Gandercleugh. But what avails attempting to conceal that, which must needs betray itself even by its superior excellence? All the village—all the parish—all the world—will soon discover to what poverty has reduced Richard Tinto."

A sudden thought here struck me—I had observed that our landlord wore, on that memorable morning, a pair of bran new velveteens, instead of his ancient thicksets.

"What," said I, drawing my right hand, with the forefinger and thumb pressed together, nimbly from my right haunch to my left shoulder, "you have condescended to resume the paternal arts to which you were first bred—long stitches, ha, Dick?"

He repelled this unlucky conjecture with a frown and a "pshaw," indicative of indignant contempt, and leading me into another room, shewed me, resting against the wall, the majestic head of Sir William Wallace, grim as when severed from the trunk by the orders of the felon Edward.

The painting was executed on boards of a substantial thickness, and the top decorated with irons, for suspending the honoured effigy upon a sign-post.

"There," he said, "my friend, stands the honour of Scotland, and my shame—yet not so—rather the shame of those, who, instead of encouraging art in its proper sphere, reduce it to these unbecoming and unworthy extremities."

I endeavoured to smooth the ruffled feelings of my misused and indignant friend. I reminded him, that he ought not, like the stag in the fable, to despise the quality which had extricated him from difficulties, in which his talents, as a portrait or landscape painter, had been found unavailing. Above all, I praised the execution, as well as the conception, of his painting, and reminded that far from being dishonoured by so superb a specimen of his talents being exposed to the general view of the public, he ought rather to congratulate himself upon the augmentation of his celebrity, to which its public exhibition must necessarily give rise.

"You are right, my friend—you are right," replied poor Dick, his eye kindling with enthusiasm; "why should I shun the name of an—an —(he hesitated for a phrase)—an out-of-doors artist? Hogarth has introduced himself in that character in one of his best engravings— Domenichino, or some body else, in ancient times—Moreland in our own, have exercised their talents in this manner. And wherefore limit to the rich and better classes alone the delight which the exhibition of works of art is calculated to inspire into all classes? Statues are placed in the open air, why should Painting be more niggardly in displaying her master-pieces than her sister Sculpture? And yet, my friend, we must part suddenly; the men are coming in an hour to put up the—the emblem;—and truly, with all my philosophy, and your consolatory encouragement to boot, I would rather wish to leave Gandercleugh before that operation commences."

We partook of our genial host's parting banquet, and I escorted Dick on his walk to Edinburgh. We parted about a mile from the village, just as we heard the distant cheer of the boys which accompanied the mounting of the new symbol of the Wallace-Head. Dick Tinto mended his pace to get out of hearing, so little had either early practice or recent philosophy reconciled him to the character of a sign-painter.

In Edinburgh, Dick's talents were discovered and appreciated, and he received dinners and hints from several distinguished judges of the fine arts. But these gentlemen dispensed their criticism more willingly than their cash, and Dick thought he needed cash more than criticism. He therefore sought London, the universal mart of talent, and where, as is usual in general marts of most descriptions, much more of the commodity is exposed to sale than can ever find purchasers.

Dick, who, in serious earnest, was supposed to have considerable natural talents for his profession, and whose vain and sanguine disposition never permitted him to doubt for a moment of ultimate success, threw himself headlong into the crowd which jostled and struggled for notice and preferment. He elbowed others, and was elbowed himself; and finally, by dint of intrepidity, fought his way into some notice, painted for the prize at the Institution, had pictures at the Exhibition at Somerset-house, and damned the hanging committee.

But poor Dick was doomed to lose the field which he fought so gallantly. In the fine arts, there is scarce an alternative betwixt distinguished success and absolute failure; and as Dick's zeal and industry were unable to ensure the first, he fell into the distresses which, in his condition, were the natural consequences of the latter alternative. He was for a time patronized by one or two of those judicious persons who make a virtue of being singular, and of pitching their own opinions against those of the world in matters of taste and criticism. But they soon tired of poor Tinto, and laid him down as a load, upon the principle on which a spoilt child throws away its plaything. Misery, I fear, took him up, and accompanied him to a premature grave, to which he was carried from an obscure lodging in Swallow-street, where he had been dunned by his landlady within doors, and watched by bailiffs without, until death came to his relief. A corner of the Morning Post noticed his death, generously adding, that his manner displayed considerable genius, though his style was rather sketchy; and referred to an advertisement, which announced that Mr Varnish, the well-known print-seller, had still on hand a very few drawings and paintings by Richard Tinto, Esquire, which those of the nobility and gentry, who might wish to complete their collections of modern art, were invited to visit without delay. So ended Dick Tinto, a lamentable proof of the great truth, that in the fine arts mediocrity is not permitted, and that he who cannot ascend to the very top of the ladder will do well not to put his foot upon it at all.

The memory of Tinto is dear to me, from the recollection of the many conversations which we have had together, most of them turning upon my present task. He was delighted with my progress, and talked of an ornamented and illustrated edition, with heads, vignettes, and *culs de lampe*, all to be designed by his own patriotic and friendly pencil. He prevailed upon an old serjeant of invalids to sit to him in the character of Bothwell, the life-guard's-man of Charles the Second, and the bell-man of Gandercleugh in that of David Deans. But while he thus proposed to unite his own powers with mine for the illustration of these narratives, he mixed many a dose of salutary criticism with the panegyrics which my composition was at times so fortunate as to call forth. "Your characters," said he, "my dear Pattieson, make too much use of the *gob-box;* they *patter* too much—(an elegant phraseology, which Dick had learned while painting the scenes of an itinerant company of players)—there is nothing in whole pages but mere chat and dialogue."

"The ancient philosopher," said I in reply, "was wont to say, 'Speak, that I may know thee;' and how is it possible for an author to introduce his *personæ dramatis* to his readers in a more interesting and effectual manner, than by the dialogue in which each is represented as supporting his own appropriate character?"

"It is a false conclusion," said Tinto; "I hate it, Peter, as I hate an unfilled cann. I will grant you, indeed, that speech is a faculty of some value in the intercourse of human affairs, and I will not even insist on the doctrine of that Pythagorean toper, who was of opinion, that over a bottle speaking spoiled conversation. But I will not allow that a professor of the fine arts has occasion to embody the idea of his scene in language, in order to impress upon the reader its reality and its effect. On the contrary, I will be judged by most of your readers, Peter, should these tales ever become public, whether you have not given us a page of talk for every single idea which two words might have communicated, while the posture, manner, and incident, accurately drawn, and brought out by appropriate colouring, would have preserved all that was worthy of preservation, and saved these everlasting said he's and said she's, with which it has been your pleasure to encumber your pages."

I replied, "that he confounded the operations of the pencil and the pen; that the serene and silent art, as painting has been called by one of our first living poets, necessarily appealed to the eye, because it had not the organs for addressing the ear; whereas poetry, or that species of composition which approaches to it, lay under the necessity of doing absolutely the reverse, and addressed itself to the ear, for the purpose of exciting that interest which it could not attain through the medium of the eye."

Dick was not a whit staggered by my argument, which he contended was founded on misrepresentation. Description, he said, was to the author of a romance exactly what drawing and tinting were to a painter; words were his colours, and, if properly employed, they could not fail to place the scene, which he wished to conjure up, as effectually before the mind's eye, as the tablet or canvas presents it to the bodily organ. The same rules, he contended, applied to both, and an exuberance of dialogue, in the former case, was a verbose and laborious mode of composition, which went to confound the proper art of fictitious narrative with that of the drama, a widely different species of composition, of which dialogue was the very essence; because all, excepting the language to be made use of, was presented to the eye by the dresses, and persons, and action of the performers upon the stage. "But as nothing," said Dick, "can be more dull than a long narrative written upon the plan of a drama, so where you have approached most near to that species of composition, by indulging in prolonged scenes of mere conversation, the course of your story has become chill and constrained, and you have lost the power of arresting the attention and exciting the imagination, in which upon other occasions you may be considered as having succeeded tolerably well."

I made my bow in requital of the compliment, which was probably thrown in by way of *placebo*, and expressed myself willing at least to make one trial of a more straight forward style of composition, in which my actors should do more, and say less, than in my former attempts of this kind. Dick gave me a patronizing and approving nod, and observed, that, finding me so docile, he would communicate, for the benefit of my muse, a subject which he studied with a view to his own art. The story, he said, was, by tradition, affirmed to be truth, although, as upwards of a hundred years had passed away since the events took place, some doubt upon all the accuracy of the particulars might be reasonably entertained.

When Dick Tinto had thus spoken, he rummaged his portfolio for the sketch from which he proposed one day to execute a picture on a canvas of fourteen feet by eight. The sketch, which was cleverly executed, to use the appropriated phrase, presented an ancient hall, fitted up and furnished in what we now call the taste of Queen Elizabeth's age. The light, admitted from the upper part of a high casement, fell upon a female figure of exquisite beauty, who, in an attitude of speechless terror, appeared to watch the issue of an animated debate betwixt two other persons. The one was a young man, in the Vandyke dress common to the time of Charles I., who, with an air of indignant pride, testified by the manner in which he raised his head and extended his arm, seemed to be urging a claim of right, rather than of favour, to a lady, whose age, and some resemblance in their features, pointed her out as the mother of the younger female, and who appeared to listen with a mixture of displeasure and impatience.

Tinto produced his sketch with an air of mysterious triumph, and gazed on it as a fond parent looks upon a hopeful child, while he anticipates the future figure he is to make in the world, and the height to which he will raise the honour of his family. He held it at arm's length from me,—he held it closer,—he placed it upon the top of a chest of drawers, closed the lower shutters of the casement, to adjust a downward and favourable light,—fell back to the due distance, dragging me after him,—shaded his face with his hand, as if to exclude all but the favourite object,—and ended by spoiling a child's copy-book, which he rolled up so as to serve for the darkened tube of an amateur. I fancy my expressions of enthusiasm had not been in proportion to his own, for he presently exclaimed with vehemence, "Mr Pattieson, I used to think you had an eye in your head."

I vindicated my claim to the usual allowance of visual organs.

"Yet, on my honour," said Dick, "I would swear you had been born blind, since you have failed at the first glance to discover the subject and meaning of that sketch. I do not mean to praise my own perform-ance—I leave these arts to others—I am sensible of my own deficien-cies, conscious that my drawing and colouring may be improved by the time I intend to dedicate to the art. But the conception—the expres-sion—the positions—these tell the story to every one who looks at the sketch; and if I can finish the picture without diminution of the original conception, the name of Tinto shall no more be smothered by the mists of envy and intrigue."

I replied that I admired the sketch exceedingly; but that to under-stand its full merit, I felt it absolutely necessary to be informed of the subject.

"That is the very thing I complain of," answered Tinto; "you have accustomed yourself so much to these creeping twilight details of yours, that you are become incapable of receiving that instant and vivid flash of conviction, which darts on the mind from seeing the happy and expressive combinations of a single scene, and which gathers from the position, attitude, and countenance of the moment, not only the history of the past lives of the personages represented, and the nature of the business on which they are immediately engaged, but lifts even the veil of futurity, and affords a shrewd guess at their future fortunes."

"In that case," replied I, "Painting excels the Ape of the renowned Gines de Passamonte, which only meddled with the past and the present; nay, she excels that very Nature who affords her subjects; for I protest to you, Dick, that were I permitted to peep into that Eliza-beth-chamber, and see the persons whom you have sketched convers-ing in flesh and blood, I should not be a jot nearer guessing the nature of their business, than I am at this moment while looking at your sketch. Only generally, from the languishing look of the young lady, and the care you have taken to present a very handsome leg on the part of the gentleman, I presume there is some reference to a love affair between them."

"Do you really presume to form such a bold conjecture?" said Tinto. "And the indignant earnestness with which you see the man urge his suit—the unresisting and passive despair of the younger female—the stern air of inflexible determination in the elder woman, whose looks express at once consciousness that she is acting wrong, and a firm determination to persist in the course she has adopted"——

"If her looks express all this, my dear Tinto," replied I, "your pencil rivals the dramatic art of Mr Puff in the Critic, who crammed a whole complicated sentence into the expressive shake of Lord Burleigh's head."

"My good friend Peter," replied Tinto, "I observe you are perfectly incorrigible; however, I have compassion on your dulness, and am unwilling you should be deprived of the pleasure of understanding my picture, and of gaining, at the same time, a subject for your own pen. You must know that last summer, while I was taking sketches on the coast of East Lothian and Berwickshire, I was seduced into the mountains of Lammermoor by the account I received of some remains of antiquity in that district. Those with which I was most struck, were the ruins of the ancient castle in which that Elizabeth-chamber, as you call it, once existed. I resided for two or three days at a farm-house in the neighbourhood, where the aged goodwife was well acquainted with the history of the castle, and the events which had taken place in it. One of these was of a nature so interesting and singular, that my attention was divided between my wish to draw the old ruins in landscape, and to represent in a history-piece the singular events which have taken place in it. Here are my notes of the tale," said poor Dick, handing a parcel of loose scraps, partly scratched over with his pencil, partly with his pen, where outlines of caricatures, sketches of turrets, mills, old gables, and dove-cotes, disputed the ground with his written memoranda.

I proceeded, however, to decypher the substance of the manuscript as well as I could, and weave it into the following Tale, in which, following in part, though not entirely, my friend Tinto's advice, I endeavoured to render my narrative rather descriptive than dramatic. My favourite propensity, however, has at times overcome me, and my persons, like many others in this talking world, speak now and then a great deal more than they act.

Chapter Two

Well, lords, we have not got that which we have;
'Tis not enough our foes are this time fled,
Being opposites of such repairing nature.
                                        Second Part of Henry VI

IN THE gorge of a pass or mountain glen, ascending from the fertile plains of East Lothian into the mountainous and moorish district of Lammermoor, there stood in former times an extensive castle, of which only the ruins are now visible. Its ancient proprietors were a race of powerful and warlike barons, who bore the same name with the castle itself, which was Ravenswood. Their line extended to a remote period of antiquity, and they had intermarried with the Douglasses,

Homes, Swintons, Hays, and other families of power and distinction in the same country. Their history was frequently involved in that of Scotland itself, in whose annals their feats are recorded. The Castle of Ravenswood, occupying, and in some measure commanding, a pass betwixt Berwickshire or the Merse, as the south-eastern province of Scotland is termed, and the Lothians, was of importance both in foreign war and domestic discord. It was frequently besieged with ardour and defended with obstinacy, and of course, its lords and owners played a conspicuous part in story. But their house had its revolutions, like all sublunary things; became greatly declined from its splendour about the middle of the 17th century; and towards the period of the Revolution, the last proprietor of Ravenswood Castle saw himself compelled to part with the ancient family seat, and to remove himself to a lonely and sea-beaten tower, which, situated on the bleak shores between Saint Abb's Head and the village of Eyemouth, looked out on the lonely and boisterous German Ocean. A black domain of wild pasture-land surrounded their new residence, and formed the remains of their property.

Lord Ravenswood, the heir of this ruined family, was far from bending his mind to his new condition of life. In the civil war of 1689, he had espoused the sinking side, and although he had escaped without the forfeiture of life or land, his blood had been attainted, and his title abolished. He was now called Lord Ravenswood only in courtesy.

This forfeited nobleman inherited the pride and turbulence, though not the fortune of his family, and, as he imputed the final declension of his family to a particular individual, he honoured that person with his full portion of hatred. This was the very man who had now become, by purchase, proprietor of Ravenswood, and the domains of which the heir of the house now stood dispossessed. He was descended of a family much less ancient than that of Lord Ravenswood, and which had only risen to wealth and political importance during the great civil wars. He himself had been bred to the bar, and had held high offices in the state, maintaining through life the character of a skilful fisher in the troubled waters of a state divided by factions, and governed by delegated authority; and of one who contrived to amass considerable sums of money in a country where there was but little to be gathered, and who equally knew the value of wealth, and the various means of augmenting it, and using it as an engine of increasing his power and influence.

Thus qualified and gifted, he was a dangerous antagonist to the fierce and imprudent Ravenswood. Whether he had given him good cause for the enmity with which the Baron regarded him, was a point on which men spoke differently. Some said the quarrel arose merely from the vindictive spirit and envy of Lord Ravenswood, who could not patiently behold another, though by just and fair purchase, become the proprietor of the estate and castle of his forefathers. But the greater part of the public, prone to slander the wealthy in their absence, as to flatter them in their presence, held a less charitable opinion. They said, that the Lord Keeper, (for to this height Sir William Ashton had ascended,) had, previous to the final purchase of the estate of Ravenswood, been concerned in extensive pecuniary transactions with the former proprietor; and, rather intimating what was probable, than affirming any thing positively, they asked which party was likely to have the advantage in stating and enforcing the claims arising out of these complicated affairs, and more than hinted the advantages which the cool lawyer and able politician must necessarily possess over the hot, fiery, and imprudent character, whom he had involved in legal toils and pecuniary snares.

The character of the times aggravated these suspicions. "In those days there was no king in Israel." Since the departure of James VI. to assume the richer and more powerful crown of England, there had existed in Scotland contending parties, formed among the aristocracy, by whom, as their intrigues at the court of St James's chanced to prevail, the delegated powers of sovereignty were alternately swayed. The evils attending upon this system of government, resembled those which afflict the tenants of an Irish estate owned by an absentee. There was no supereminent power, claiming and possessing a general interest with the community at large, to whom the oppressed might appeal from subordinate tyranny, either for justice or for mercy. Let a monarch be as indolent, as selfish, as much disposed to arbitrary power as he will, still, in a free country, his own interests are so closely connected with those of the public at large, and the evil consequences to his own authority are so obvious and imminent when a different course is pursued, that common policy, as well as common feeling, point to the equal distribution of justice, and to the establishment of the throne in righteousness. Thus, even sovereigns who were remarkable for usurpation and tyranny, have been found rigorous in the administration of justice among their subjects, in cases where their own power and passions were not compromised.

It is very different when the powers of sovereignty are delegated to the head of an aristocratic faction, rivalled and pressed closely in the race of ambition by an adverse leader. His brief and precarious enjoyment of power must be employed in rewarding his partizans, in extending his influence, in oppressing and crushing his adversaries. Even Abon Hassan, the most disinterested of all viceroys, forgot not, during his caliphate of one day, to send a douçeur of one thousand pieces of gold to his own household; and the Scottish vicegerents, raised to power by the strength of their faction, failed not to embrace the same means of rewarding them.

The administration of justice, in particular, was infected by the most gross partiality. Scarce a case of importance could occur, in which there was not some ground for bias or partiality on the part of the judges, who were so little able to withstand the temptation, that the adage, "Show me the man, and I will show you the law," became as prevalent as it was scandalous. One corruption led the way to others still more gross and profligate. The judge who lent his sacred authority in one case to support a friend, and in another to crush an enemy, and whose decisions were founded on family connections, or political relations, could not be supposed inaccessible to direct personal motives, and the purse of the wealthy was too often believed to be thrown into the scale to weigh down the cause of the poorer litigant. The subordinate officers of the law affected little scruple concerning bribery. Pieces of plate, and bags of money, were sent in presents to the king's counsel, to influence their conduct, and poured forth, says a contemporary writer, like billets of wood upon their floors, without even the decency of concealment.

In such times, it was not over uncharitable to suppose, that the statesman, practised in courts of law, and a powerful member of a triumphant cabal, might find and use means of advantage over his less skilful and less favoured adversary; and if it had been supposed that Sir William Ashton's conscience had been too delicate to profit by these advantages, it was believed that his ambition and desire of extending his wealth and consequence, found as strong a stimulus in the exhortations of his lady, as the daring aim of Macbeth in the days of yore.

Lady Ashton was of a family more distinguished than that of her lord, an advantage which she did not fail to use to the uttermost, in maintaining and extending her husband's influence over others, and, unless she was greatly belied, her own over him. She had been beautiful, and was still stately and majestic in her appearance. Endowed by nature with strong powers and violent passions, experience had taught her to employ the one, and to conceal, if not to moderate, the other. She was a severe and strict observer of the external forms, at least, of devotion; her hospitality was splendid, even to ostentation; her address and manners, agreeable to the pattern most valued in Scotland at the period, were grave, dignified, and severely regulated by the rules of etiquette. Her character had always been beyond the breath of slander, and yet, with all these qualities to excite respect, Lady Ashton was seldom mentioned in the terms of love or affection.

Interest,—the interest of her family, if not her own,—seemed too obviously the motive of her actions; and where this is the case, the sharp-judging and malignant public are not easily imposed upon by outward show. It was seen and ascertained, that, in her most graceful courtesies and compliments, Lady Ashton no more lost sight of her object than the falcon in his airy wheel turns his quick eye from his destined quarry; and hence, something of doubt and suspicion qualified the feelings with which her equals received her attentions. With her inferiors these feelings were mingled with fear, an impression useful to her purposes, so far as it enforced ready compliance with her requests, and implicit obedience to her commands, but detrimental, because it cannot exist with affection or regard.

Even her husband, it is said, upon whose fortunes her talents and address had produced such emphatic influence, regarded her with respectful awe rather than confiding attachment; and report said, there were times when he considered his grandeur as dearly purchased at the expence of domestic thraldom. Of this, however, much might be suspected, but little could be accurately known. Lady Ashton regarded the honour of her husband as her own, and was well aware how much it would suffer in the public eye should he appear a vassal to his wife. In all her arguments, his opinion was quoted as infallible, his taste appealed to and his sentiments received with the air of deference, which a dutiful wife might seem to owe to a husband of Sir William Ashton's rank and character. But there was something under all this which rung false and hollow; and to those who watched this couple with close, and perhaps malicious scrutiny, it seemed evident, that, in the haughtiness of a firmer character, higher birth, and more decided views of aggrandizement, the lady looked with some contempt on her husband, and that he regarded her with jealous fear rather than with love or admiration.

Still, however, the leading and favourite interests of Sir William Ashton and his lady were the same, and they failed not to work in concert, although without cordiality, and to testify, in all exterior circumstances, that respect for each other which they were aware was necessary to secure that of the public.

Their union was crowned with several children, of whom three survived. One, the eldest son, was absent on his travels; the second, a girl of seventeen, and the third, a boy about three years younger, resided with their parents in Edinburgh, during the sessions of the Scottish Parliament and Privy-council, at other times in the old Gothic castle of Ravenswood, to which the Lord Keeper had made large additions in the style of the seventeenth century.

Allan Lord Ravenswood, the late proprietor of that ancient mansion and the large estate annexed to it, continued for some time to wage ineffectual war with his successor concerning various points to which their former transactions had given rise, and which were successively determined in favour of the wealthy and powerful competitor, until death closed the litigation, by summoning Ravenswood to a higher bar. The thread of life, which had been long wasting, gave way during a fit of violent and impotent fury, with which he was assailed on receiving the news of the loss of a cause, founded, perhaps, rather in equity than in law, the last which he had maintained against his powerful antagonist. His son witnessed his dying agonies, and heard the curses which he breathed against his adversary, as if they had conveyed to him a legacy of vengeance. Other circumstances happened to exasperate a passion, which was, and had long been, a prevalent vice in the Scottish disposition.

It was a November morning, and the cliffs which overlooked the ocean were hung with thick and heavy mist, when the portals of the ancient and half-ruinous tower, in which Lord Ravenswood had spent the last and troubled years of his life, opened, that his mortal remains might pass forward to an abode yet more dreary and lonely. The pomp of attendance, to which the deceased had, in his latter years, been a stranger, was revived as he was about to be consigned to the realms of forgetfulness.

Banner after banner, with the various devices and coats of this ancient family and its connections, followed each other in mournful procession from under the low-browed archway of the court-yard. The principal gentry of the country attended in the deepest mourning, and tempered the pace of their long train of horses to the solemn march befitting the occasion. Trumpets, with banners of crape attached to them, sent forth their long and lugubrious notes to regulate the movements of the procession. An immense train of inferior mourners and menials closed the rear, which had not yet issued from the castle-gate, when the van had reached the chapel where the body was to be deposited.

Contrary to the custom, and even to the law of the time, the body was met by a priest of the English communion, arrayed in his surplice, and prepared to read over the coffin of the deceased the funeral service of the church. Such had been the desire of Lord Ravenswood in his last illness, and it was readily complied with by the tory gentlemen, or cavaliers, as they affected to style themselves, in which faction most of his kinsmen were enrolled. The presbyterian church-judicatory of the bounds, considering the ceremony as a bravading insult upon their authority, had applied to the Lord Keeper, as the nearest privy counsellor, for a warrant to prevent its being carried into effect;

so that, when the clergyman had opened his prayer-book, an officer of the law, supported by some armed men, commanded him to be silent. An insult, which fired the whole assembly with indignation, was particularly and instantly resented by the only son of the deceased, Edgar, popularly called the Master of Ravenswood, a youth of about twenty years of age. He clapped his hand on his sword, and, bidding the official person to desist at his peril from further interruption, commanded the clergyman to proceed. The man attempted to enforce his commission, but as an hundred swords at once glittered in the air, he contented himself with protesting against the violence which had been offered to him in the execution of his duty, and stood aloof, a sullen and moody spectator of the ceremonial, humming as who should say, "You'll rue the day that clogs me with this answer."

The scene was worthy of an artist's pencil. In the very arch of the house of death, the clergyman, affrighted at the scene, and trembling for his own safety, hastily and unwillingly rehearsed the solemn service of the church, and spoke dust to dust, and ashes to ashes, over ruined pride and decayed posterity. Around stood the relations of the deceased, their countenances more in anger than in sorrow, and the drawn swords which they brandished forming a violent contrast with their deep mourning habits. In the countenance of the young man alone, resentment seemed for the moment overpowered by the deep agony with which he beheld his nearest, and almost his only friend, consigned to the tomb of his ancestry. A relative observed him turn deadly pale, when, all rites being now duly observed, it became the duty of the chief mourner to lower down into the charnel vault, where mouldering coffins shewed their tattered velvet and decayed plating, the head of the corpse which was to be their partner in corruption. He stept to the youth and offered his assistance, which, by a mute motion, Edgar Ravenswood rejected. Firmly, and without a tear, he performed that last duty. The stone was laid on the sepulchre, the door of the aisle was locked, and the youth took possession of its massive key.

As the crowd left the chapel, he paused on the steps which led to its Gothic chancel. "Gentlemen and friends," he said, "you have this day done no common duty to the body of your deceased kinsman. The rites of due observance, which, in other countries, are allowed as the due of the meanest Christian, would this day have been denied to the body of your relative—not certainly sprung of the meanest house in Scotland—had it not been assured to him by your courage. Others bury their dead in sorrow and tears, in silence and in reverence; our funeral rites are marred by the intrusion of bailiffs and ruffians, and our grief—the grief due to our departed friend—is chased from our cheeks by the glow of just indignation. But it is well that I know from what quiver this arrow hath come forth. It was only he that dug the grave who could have the mean cruelty to disturb the obsequies; and Heaven do as much to me and more, if I requite not to this man and his house the ruin and disgrace he has brought on me and mine."

The more numerous part of the assembly applauded this speech, as the spirited expression of just resentment; but the more cool and judicious regretted that it had been uttered. The fortunes of the heir of Ravenswood were too low to brave the further hostility which they imagined these open expressions of resentment must necessarily provoke. Their apprehensions, however, proved groundless, at least in the immediate consequences of this affair.

The mourners returned to the tower, there, according to a custom but recently abolished in Scotland, to carouse deep healths to the memory of the deceased, to make the house of sorrow ring with sounds of joviality and debauch, and to diminish, by the expense of a large and profuse entertainment, the limited revenues of the heir of him whose funeral they thus strangely honoured. It was the custom, however, and on the present occasion it was fully observed. The tables swam in wine, the populace feasted in the court-yard, the yeomen in the kitchen and buttery, and two years' rent of Ravenswood's remaining property hardly defrayed the charge of the funereal revel. The wine did its office on all but the Master of Ravenswood, a title which he still retained, though forfeiture had attached to that of his father. He, while passing around the cup which he himself did not taste, soon listened to a thousand exclamations against the Lord Keeper, and passionate protestations of attachment to himself, and to the honour of his house. He listened with dark and sullen brow to ebullitions which he considered justly as equally evanescent with the crimson bubbles on the brink of the goblet, or at least with the vapours which the draughts excited in the brains of the revellers around him.

When the last flask was emptied, they took their leave, with deep protestations—to be forgotten on the morrow, if, indeed, those who made them should not think it necessary for their safety to make a more solemn retractation.

Accepting their adieus with an air of contempt which he could scarce conceal, Ravenswood at length beheld his ruinous habitation cleared of this confluence of riotous guests, and returned to the deserted hall, which now appeared doubly lonely from the cessation of that clamour to which it had so lately echoed. But its space was peopled by phantoms, which the imagination of the young heir conjured up before him—the tarnished honour and degraded fortunes of his family, the destruction of his own hopes, and the triumph of that family by whom they had been ruined. To a mind naturally of a gloomy cast, here was ample room for meditation, and the musings of young Ravenswood were deep and unwitnessed.

The peasant, who shows the ruins of the tower, which still crown the beetling cliff and behold the war of the waves, though no more tenanted save by the sea-mew and cormorant, even yet affirms, that on this fatal night the Master of Ravenswood, by the bitter exclamations of his despair, evoked some evil fiend, under whose malignant influence the future tissue of incidents was woven. Alas! what fiend can suggest more desperate counsels, than those adopted under the guidance of our own violent and unresisted passions?

Chapter Three

Over Gods forebode, then, said the King,
That thou shouldst shoot at me.
        Adam Bell, Clym of the Clough, and
                William of Cloudesly

ON THE morning after the funeral, the legal officer, whose authority had been found insufficient to effect an interruption of the funeral solemnities of the late Lord Ravenswood, hastened to state before the Keeper the interruption which he had received in the execution of his office.

The statesman was seated in a spacious library, once a banquetting-room in the old Castle of Ravenswood, as was evident from the armorial insignia still displayed on the carved roof, which was vaulted with Spanish chesnut, and on the stained glass of the casement, through which gleamed a dim yet rich light, on the long rows of shelves, bending under the weight of legal commentators and monkish historians, whose ponderous volumes formed the chief and most valued contents of a Scottish library of the period. On the massive oaken table and reading-desk, lay a confused mass of letters, petitions, and parchments; to toil amongst which was the pleasure at once and plague of Sir William Ashton's life. His appearance was grave and even noble, well becoming one who held an high office in the state; and it was not, save after long and intimate conversation with him upon topics of pressing and personal interest, that a stranger could have discovered something vacillating and uncertain in his resolution; an infirmity of purpose, arising from a cautious and somewhat timid disposition, which, as he was conscious of its internal influence on his mind, he was, from pride as well as policy, most anxious to conceal from others.

He listened with great apparent composure to an exaggerated account of the tumult which had taken place at the funeral, of the contempt thrown on his own authority, and that of the church and state; nor did he seem moved even by the faithful report of the insulting and threatening language which had been uttered by young Ravenswood and others, and obviously directed against himself. He heard, also, what the man had been able to collect, in a very distorted and aggravated shape, of the toasts which had been drunk, and the menaces uttered at the subsequent entertainment. In fine, he made careful notes of all these particulars, and of the names of the persons by whom, in case of need, an accusation, founded upon these violent proceedings, could be witnessed and made good, and dismissed his informer, secure that he was now master of the remaining fortune, and even the personal liberty, of young Ravenswood.

When the door had closed upon the officer of the law, the Lord Keeper remained for a moment in deep meditation; then, starting from his seat, paced the apartment as one about to take a sudden and energetic resolution. "Young Ravenswood," he muttered, "is now mine—he is my own—he has placed himself in my hand, and he shall bend or break. I have not forgot the determined and dogged obstinacy with which his father fought every point to the last, resisted every offer at compromise, embroiled me in law-suits, and attempted to assail my character when he could not otherwise impugn my rights. This boy he has left behind him—this Edgar—this hot-headed, hare-brained fool, has wrecked his vessel before she has cleared the harbour. I must see he gains no advantage of some turning tide which may again float him off. These memoranda, properly stated to the Privy-council, cannot but be construed into an aggravated riot, in which the dignity both of the civil and ecclesiastical authorities stand committed. A heavy fine might be imposed—an order for committing him to Edinburgh or Blackness Castle seems not improper—even a charge of treason might be laid on many of these words and expressions—though God forbid I should prosecute the matter to that extent—No —I will not—I will not touch his life, even if it should be in my power —and yet, if he lives till a change of times, what follows? Restitution— perhaps revenge—I know Athole promised his interest to old Ravenswood, and here is his son already bandying and making a faction by his own contemptible influence—What a ready tool he would be for the use of those who are watching the downfall of our administration!"

While these thoughts were agitating the mind of the wily statesman, and while he was persuading himself that his own interest and safety, as well as those of his friends and party, depended on using the present advantage to the uttermost against young Ravenswood, the Lord Keeper sate down to his desk, and proceeded to draw up, for the information of the Privy-council, an account of the disorderly proceedings which, in contempt of his warrant, had taken place at the

funeral of Lord Ravenswood. The names of most of the parties concerned, as well as the fact itself, would, he was well aware, sound odi-
ously in the ears of his colleagues in administration, and most likely
instigate them to make an example of young Ravenswood at least, *in
terrorem*.

It was a point of delicacy, however, to select such expressions as
might infer his culpability, without seeming directly to urge it, which,
on the part of Sir William Ashton, his father's ancient antagonist,
could not but appear odious and invidious. While he was in the act of
composition, labouring to find words which might indicate Edgar
Ravenswood to be the cause of the uproar, without directly urging the
charge, Sir William, in a pause of his task, chanced, in looking
upward, to see the crest of the family for whose heir he was whetting
the arrows and disposing the toils of the law, carved upon one of the
corbeilles from which the vaulted roof of the apartment sprung. It was
a black bull's head, with the legend, "I bide my time;" and the
occasion upon which it was adopted mingled itself singularly and
impressively with the subject of his present reflections.

It was said by a constant tradition, that a Malisius de Ravenswood
had, in the thirteenth century, been deprived of his castle and lands by
a powerful usurper, who had for a while enjoyed his spoils in quiet. At
length, on the eve of a costly banquet, Ravenswood, who had watched
his opportunity, introduced himself into the castle with a small band of
faithful retainers. The serving of the expected feast was impatiently
looked for by the guests, and clamorously demanded by the temporary
master of the castle. Ravenswood, who had assumed the disguise of a
sewer upon the occasion, answered, in a stern voice, "I bide my time;"
and at the same moment a bull's head, the ancient symbol of death,
was placed upon the table. The explosion of the conspiracy took place
upon the signal, and the usurper and his followers were put to death.
Perhaps there was something in this still known and often repeated
story, which came immediately home to the breast and conscience of
the Lord Keeper; for, putting from him the paper on which he had
begun his report, and carefully locking the memoranda which he had
prepared, into a cabinet which stood beside him, he proceeded to walk
abroad, as if for the purpose of collecting his ideas, and reflecting
farther on the consequences of the step which he was about to take,
ere yet they became unavoidable.

In passing through a large Gothic anti-room, Sir William Ashton
heard the sound of his daughter's lute. Music, when the performers
are concealed, affects us with a pleasure mingled with surprise, and
reminds us of the natural concert of birds among the leafy bowers.
The statesman, though little accustomed to give way to emotions of

this natural and simple class, was still a man and a father. He stopped, therefore, and listened, while the silver tones of Lucy Ashton's voice mingled with the accompaniment in an ancient and solemn air, to which some one had adapted the following words:—

> "Look not thou on Beauty's charming,—
> Sit thou still when Kings are arming,—
> Taste not when the wine-cup glistens,—
> Speak not when the people listens,—
> Stop thine ear against the singer,—
> From the red gold keep thy finger,—
> Vacant heart, and hand, and eye,—
> Easy live and quiet die."

The sounds ceased, and the Keeper entered his daughter's apartment.

The words she had chosen seemed peculiarly adapted to her character; for Lucy Ashton's exquisitely beautiful, yet somewhat girlish features, were formed to express peace of mind, serenity, and indifference to the tinsel of worldly pleasure. Her locks, which were of shadowy gold, divided on a brow of exquisite whiteness, like a gleam of broken and pallid sunshine upon a hill of snow. The expression of the countenance was in the last degree gentle, soft, timid, and feminine, and seemed rather to shrink from the most casual look of a stranger, than to court his admiration. Something there was of a Madonna cast, perhaps the result of delicate health, and of residence in a family, where the dispositions of the inmates were fiercer, more active, and more energetic than her own.

Yet her passiveness of disposition was by no means owing to an indifferent or unfeeling mind. Left to the impulse of her own taste and feelings, Lucy Ashton was peculiarly accessible to those of a romantic cast. Her secret delight was in the old legendary tales of ardent devotion and unalterable affection, chequered as they so often are with strange adventures and supernatural horrors. This was her favoured fairy realm, and here she erected her aërial palaces. But it was only in secret that she laboured at this delusive, but delightful architecture. In her retired chamber, or in the woodland bower which she had chosen for her own, and called after her name, she was in fancy distributing the prizes at the tournament, or raining down influence from her eyes on the valiant combatants, or she was wandering in the wilderness with Una, or she was identifying herself with the simple, yet noble-minded Miranda, in the isle of wonder and enchantment.

But in her exterior relations to things of this world, Lucy willingly received the ruling impulse from those around her. The alternative was, in general, too indifferent to her to render resistance desirable, and she willingly found a motive for decision in the opinion of her friends, which perhaps she might have sought for in vain in her own choice. Every reader must have observed in some family of his acquaintance, some individual of a temper so soft and yielding, who, mixed with stronger and more ardent minds, is borne along by the will of others, with as little power of opposition as the flower which is flung into a running stream. It usually happens that such a compliant and easy disposition, which resigns itself without murmur to the guidance of others, becomes the darling of those to whose inclinations its own seem to be offered, in ungrudging and ready sacrifice.

This was eminently the case with Lucy Ashton. Her politic, wary, and worldly father, felt for her an affection, the strength of which sometimes surprised him into unusual emotion. Her elder brother, who trode the path of ambition with a haughtier step than his father, had also more of human and domestic affection. A soldier, and in a dissolute age, he preferred his sister Lucy even to pleasure, and to military preferment and distinction. Her younger brother, at an age when trifles chiefly occupied his mind, made her the confidante of all his pleasures and anxieties,—his success in field-sports, and his quarrels with his tutor and instructors. To these details, however trivial, Lucy lent patient and not indifferent attention. They moved and interested Henry, and that was enough to secure her ear.

Her mother alone did not feel that distinguished and predominating affection, with which the rest of the family cherished Lucy. She regarded what she termed her want of spirit, as a decided mark, that the more plebeian blood of her father predominated in Lucy's veins, and used to call her in derision her Lammermoor Shepherdess. To dislike so gentle and inoffensive a being was impossible; but Lady Ashton preferred her eldest son, on whom had descended a large portion of her own ambitious and undaunted disposition, to a daughter whose softness of temper seemed allied to feebleness of mind. Her eldest son was the more partially beloved by his mother, because, contrary to the usual custom in Scottish families of distinction, he had been named after the head of her house.

"My Sholto," she said, "will support the untarnished honour of his maternal house, and elevate and support that of his father. Poor Lucy is unfit for courts, or crowded halls. Some country laird must be her husband, rich enough to supply her with every comfort, without an effort on her own part, so that she may have nothing to shed a tear for but the tender apprehension lest he may break his neck in a fox-chase. It was not so, however, that our house was raised, nor is it so that it can be fortified and augmented. The Lord Keeper's dignity is yet new; it must be borne as if we were used to its weight, worthy of it, and prompt to assert and maintain it. Before ancient authorities, men bend, from customary and hereditary deference; in our presence, they will stand erect, unless they are compelled to prostrate themselves. A daughter fit for the sheep-fold, or the cloister, is ill qualified to exact respect where it is yielded with reluctance; and since Heaven refused us a third boy, Lucy should have held a character fit to supply his place. The hour will be a happy one which disposes her hand in marriage to some one whose energy is greater than her own, or whose ambition is of as low an order."

So meditated a mother, to whom the qualities of her children's hearts, as well as the prospect of their domestic happiness, seemed light in comparison to their rank and temporal greatness. But, like many a parent of hot and impatient character, she was mistaken in estimating the feelings of her daughter, who, under a semblance of extreme indifference, nourished the germ of those passions which sometimes spring up in one night, like the gourd of the prophet, and astonish the observer by their unexpected ardour and intensity. In fact, Lucy's feelings seemed dull, because nothing had occurred to interest or awaken them: her life had hitherto flowed on in an uniform and gentle tenor, and happy for her had not its present smoothness of current resembled that of the stream as it glides downwards to the waterfall!

"So Lucy," said her father, entering as her song was ended, "does your musical philosopher teach you to contemn the world before you know it?—that is surely something premature—or did you but speak according to the fashion of fair maidens, who are always to hold the pleasures of life in contempt till they are pressed upon them by the address of some gentle knight?"

Lucy blushed, disclaimed any inference respecting her own choice being inferred from her selection of a song, and readily laid aside her instrument at her father's request that she would attend him in his walk.

A large and well wooded park, or rather chase, stretched along the hill behind the castle, which occupying, as we have noticed, a pass ascending from the plain, seemed built in its very gorge to defend the forest ground which arose behind it in shaggy majesty. Into this romantic region the father and daughter proceeded, arm in arm, by a noble avenue overarched by embowering elms, beneath which groups of the fallow-deer were seen to stray in distant perspective. As they paced slowly on, admiring the different points of view, for which Sir William Ashton, notwithstanding the nature of his usual avocations, had considerable taste and feeling, they were overtaken by the forester, or park-keeper, who, intent on sylvan sport, was proceeding with his cross-bow over his arm, and a hound led in leash by his boy, into the interior of the wood.

"Going to shoot us a piece of venison, Norman?" said his master, as he returned the woodsman's salutation.

"Saul, your honour, and that I am—wull it please you to see the sport?"

"O no," said his lordship, after looking at his daughter, whose colour fled at the idea of seeing the deer shot, although, had he expressed his wish that they should accompany Norman, it was probable she would not even have hinted her reluctance.

The forester shrugged his shoulders. "It was a disheartening thing," he said, "when none of the gentles came doun to see the sport. He hoped Mr Sholto would be soon hame, or he might shut up his shop entirely; for Mr Harry was kept sae close wi' his Latin nonsense, that, though his will was very gude to be in the wood from morning till night, there would be a hopeful lad lost, and no making a man of him. It was not so, he had heard, in Lord Ravenswood's time—when a buck was to be killed, man and mother's son ran to see; and when the deer fell, the knife was always presented to the knight, and he never gave less than a dollar for the compliment. And there was Edgar Ravenswood—Master of Ravenswood that is now—when he goes up to the wood there hasna been a better hunter since Tristrem's time—When Sir Edgar hauds out, down goes the deer, faith—But we hae lost a' sense of wood-craft on this side of the hill."

There was much in this harangue highly displeasing to the Lord Keeper's feelings; he could not help observing that his menial despised him almost avowedly for not possessing the taste for sport, which in these times was deemed the natural and indispensible attribute of a real gentleman. But the master of the game is, in all country houses, a man of great importance, and entitled to use considerable freedom of speech. Sir William, therefore, only smiled and replied, he had something else to think upon to-day than killing deer; meantime, taking out his purse, he gave the ranger a dollar for his encouragement. The fellow received it as the waiter of a fashionable hotel receives double his proper fee from the hand of a country gentleman, —that is, with a smile, in which pleasure at the gift is mingled with contempt for the ignorance of the donor. "Your honour is the bad paymaster," he said, "who pays before it is due. What would you do were I to miss the buck after you have paid me my wood-fee?"

"I suppose," said the Keeper, smiling, "you would hardly guess what I mean were I to tell you of a *condictio indebiti.*"

"Not I, on my saul—I guess it is some law phrase—but sue a beggar, and your honour knows what follows.—Well, but I will be just with you, and if bow and brach fail not, you shall have a piece of game two fingers fat on the brisket."

As he was about to go off, his master again called him, and asked, as if by accident, whether the Master of Ravenswood was actually so brave a man and so good a shooter as the world spoke him.

"Brave?—brave enough, I warrant ye," answered Norman; "I was in the wood at Tyninghame, when there was a sort of gallants hunting with my lord; on my saul, there was a buck turned to bay made us all stand back; a stout old Trojan of the first-head, ten-tyned branches, and a brow as broad as e'er a bullock's. Egad, he dashed at the old lord, and there would have been inlake among the peerage, if the Master had not whipt roundly in, and hamstrung him with his cutlace. He was but sixteen then, bless his heart!"

"And he is as ready with the gun as with the couteau?" said Sir William.

"He'll strike this silver dollar out from between my finger and thumb at fourscore yards, and I'll hold it out for a gold merk; what more would ye have of eye, hand, lead, and gunpowder?"

"O no more to be had, certainly," said the Lord Keeper; "but we keep you from your sport, Norman—good morrow, good Norman."

And humming his rustic roundelay, the yeoman went on his road, the sound of his rough voice gradually dying away as the distance betwixt them increased.

> "The monk must arise when the matins ring,
>   The abbot may sleep to their chime;
> But the yeoman must start when the bugles sing,
>   'Tis time, my hearts, 'tis time.
>
> "There's bucks and raes in Bilhope braes,
>   There's a herd in Shortwood Shaw;
> But a lily white doe in the garden gaes,
>   She's fairly worth them a'."

"Has this fellow," said the Lord Keeper, when the yeoman's song had died on the wind, "ever served the Ravenswood people, that he seems so much interested in them? I suppose you know, Lucy, for you make it a point of conscience to record the special history of every boor about the castle."

"I am not quite so faithful a chronicler, my dear father; but I believe that Norman once served here while a boy, and before he went to Ledington, whence you hired him. But if you want to know any thing about the former family, old Alice is the best authority."

"And what should I have to do with them, pray, Lucy," said her father, "or with their history or accomplishments?"

"Nay, I do not know, sir; only that you were asking questions at Norman about young Ravenswood."

"Pshaw, child!"—replied her father, yet immediately added, "And who is old Alice? I think you know all the old women in the country."

"To be sure I do, or how could I help the old creatures when they are in hard times? And as to old Alice, she is the very empress of old women, and queen of gossips, so far as legendary lore is concerned. She is blind, poor old soul, but when she speaks to you, you would think she has some way of looking into your very heart. I am sure I often cover my face, or turn it away, for it seems as if she saw one change colour, though she has been blind these twenty years. She is worth visiting, were it but to say you had seen a blind and paralytic old woman have so much acuteness of perception, and dignity of manner. I assure you, she might be a countess from her language and behaviour.—Come, you must go to see Alice; we are not a quarter of a mile from her cottage."

"All this, my dear," said the Lord Keeper, "is no answer to my question, who this woman is, and what is her connection with the former proprietor's family?"

"O, it was something of nourice-ship, I believe; and she remained here, because her two grandsons were engaged in your service. But it was against her will, I fancy; for the poor old creature is always regretting the change of times and of property."

"I am much obliged to her," answered the Lord Keeper. "She and her folks eat my bread and drink of my cup, and are lamenting all the while that they are not still under a family which never could do good, either to themselves or any one else."

"Indeed," replied Lucy, "I am certain you do old Alice injustice. She has nothing mercenary about her, and would not accept a penny in charity, if it were to save her from being starved. She is only talkative, like all old folks, when you put them upon stories of their youth; and she speaks about the Ravenswoods because she lived under them so many years. But I am sure she is grateful to you, sir, for your protection, and that she would rather speak to you, than to any other person in the whole world beside. Do, sir, come and see old Alice—her cottage is so bad besides, and I am sure you will cause Former the carpenter put it somewhat to rights if you see how decayed it is—Do come to see old Alice."

And with the freedom of an indulged daughter, she dragged on the Lord Keeper in the direction she desired.

Chapter Four

Through tops of the high trees she did descry
A little smoke, whose vapour, thin and light,
Reeking aloft, uprolled to the sky,
Which cheerful sign did send unto her sight,
That in the same did wonne some living wight.
                                                SPENSER

LUCY acted as her father's guide, for he was too much engrossed with his political labours, or with society, to be perfectly acquainted with his own extensive domains, and, moreover, was generally an inhabitant of the city of Edinburgh; and she, on the other hand, had, with her mother, resided the whole summer in Ravenswood, and, partly from taste, partly from want of any other amusement, had, by her frequent rambles, learned to know each lane, alley, dingle, or bushy dell,

And every bosky bourne from side to side.

We have said, that the Lord Keeper was not indifferent to the beauties of nature, and we must add, in justice to him, that he felt them doubly, when pointed out by the beautiful, simple, and interesting girl, who, hanging on his arm with filial fondness, now called him to admire the size of some ancient oak, and now the unexpected turn, where the path developing its maze from glen or dingle, suddenly reached an eminence commanding an extensive view of the plains beneath them, and then gradually glided away from the prospect to lose itself among rocks and thickets, and guide to scenes of deeper seclusion.

It was when pausing on one of those points of extensive and commanding view, that Lucy told her father they were close by the cottage of her blind protegée; and on turning from the little hill, a path which led around it, worn by the daily step of the infirm inmate, brought them in sight of the hut, which, embosomed in a deep and obscure dell, seemed to have been situated purposely to bear a correspondence with the darkened state of its inhabitant.

The cottage was situated immediately under a tall rock, which in some measure beetled over it, as if threatening to drop some detached fragment from its brow on the frail tenement beneath. The hut itself was constructed of turf and stones, and rudely roofed over with thatch, much of which was in a dilapidated condition. The thin blue smoke rose from it in a light column, and curled upward along the white face of the incumbent rock, giving to the scene a tint of exquisite softness. In a small and rude garden, surrounded by straggling elder bushes, which formed a sort of imperfect hedge, sat near to the bee-hives, by the produce of which she lived, that "woman old," whom Lucy had brought her father hither to visit.

Whatever there had been which was disastrous in her fortune— whatever there was miserable in her dwelling, it was easy to judge, by the first glance, that neither years, poverty, misfortune, nor infirmity, had broken the spirit of this remarkable woman.

She occupied a turf-seat, placed under a weeping birch of unusual magnitude and age, as Judah is represented in coins sitting under her palm-tree, with an air at once of majesty and of dejection. Her figure was tall, commanding, and but little bent by the infirmities of old age. Her dress, though that of a peasant, was remarkably clean, forming in that particular a strong contrast to those of her rank, and was disposed with an attention to neatness, and even to taste, equally unusual. But it was her expression of countenance which chiefly struck the spectator, and induced most persons to address her with a degree of deference and civility very inconsistent with the miserable state of her dwelling; and which, nevertheless, she received with that easy composure which showed she felt it to be her due. She had once been beautiful, but her beauty had been of a bold and masculine cast, such as does not survive the bloom of youth; yet her features continued to express strong sense, deep reflection, and a character of sober pride, which, as we have already said of her dress, appeared to argue a conscious superiority to those of her own rank. It scarce seemed possible that a face, deprived of the advantage of sight, could have expressed character so strongly; but her eyes, which were almost totally closed, did not, by the display of their sightless orbs, mar the countenance to which they could add nothing. She seemed in a ruminating posture, soothed, perhaps, by the murmurs of the busy tribe around her, to abstraction, though not to slumber.

Lucy undid the latch of the little garden gate, and solicited the old woman's attention. "My father, Alice, is come to see you."

"He is welcome, Miss Ashton, and so are you," said the old woman, turning and inclining her head towards her visitors.

"This is a fine morning for your bee-hives, mother," said the Lord Keeper, who, struck with the outward appearance of Alice, was somewhat curious to know if her conversation would correspond with it.

"I believe so, my lord," she replied; "I feel the air breathe milder than of late."

"You do not," resumed the statesman, "take charge of these bees yourself, mother—how do you manage them?"

"By delegates, as kings do their subjects," returned Alice, "and I am fortunate in a prime minister—Here, Babie."

She whistled on a small silver call which hung around her neck, and which at that time was sometimes used to summon domestics, and Babie, a girl of fifteen, made her appearance from the hut, not altogether so cleanly arrayed as she would probably have been had Alice had the use of her eyes, but with a greater air of neatness than was upon the whole to have been expected.

"Babie," said her mistress, "offer some bread and honey to the Lord Keeper and Miss Ashton; they will excuse your awkwardness, if you use cleanliness and despatch."

Babie performed her mistress's command with the grace which was naturally to be expected, moving to and again in a lobster-like gesture, her feet and legs tending one way, while her head, turned in a different direction, was fixed in wonder upon the laird, who was more frequently heard of than seen by his tenants and dependents. The bread and honey, however, deposited on a plantain leaf, was offered and accepted in all due courtesy. The Lord Keeper, still keeping the place which he had occupied on the decayed trunk of a felled tree, looked as if he wished to prolong the interview, but was at a loss how to introduce a suitable subject.

"You have been long a resident on this property," he said, after a pause.

"It is now nearly sixty years since I first knew Ravenswood," answered the old dame, whose conversation, though perfectly civil and respectful, seemed cautiously limited to the unavoidable and necessary task of replying to Sir William.

"You are not, I should judge by your accent, of this country originally," said Sir William in continuation.

"No; I am by birth an Englishwoman."

"Yet you seem attached to this country as if it were your own."

"It is here," replied the blind woman, "that I have drank the cup of joy and of sorrow which Heaven destined for me—I was here the wife of an upright and affectionate husband for more than twenty years—I was here the mother of six promising children—it was here that God deprived me of all these blessings—it was here they died, and yonder, by yon ruined chapel, they lie all buried—I had no country but theirs while they lived—I have none but theirs now they are no more."

"But your house," said the Lord Keeper, looking at it, "is miserably ruinous."

"Do, my dear father," said Lucy, eagerly, yet bashfully, catching at the hint, "give orders to make it better,—that is, if you think it proper."

"It will last my time, my dear Miss Lucy," said the blind woman; "I would not have my lord give himself the least trouble about it."

"But," said Lucy, "you once had a much better house, and were rich, and now in your old age to live in this hovel!"

"It is as good as I deserve, Miss Lucy; if my heart has not broken with what I have suffered, and seen others suffer, it must have been strong enough, and the rest of this old frame has no right to call itself weaker."

"You must have witnessed many changes," said the Lord Keeper; "but your experience must have taught you to expect them."

"It has taught me to endure them, my lord," was the reply.

"Yet you knew that they must needs arrive in the course of years?" said the statesman.

"Ay; as I know that the stump, on or beside which you sit, once a tall and lofty tree, must needs one day fall by decay, or by the axe; yet I hoped my eyes might not witness the downfall of the tree which over-shadowed my dwelling."

"Do not suppose," said the Lord Keeper, "that you will lose any interest with me, for looking back with regret to the days when another family possessed my estates—you had reason, doubtless, to love them, and I respect your gratitude. I will order some repairs on your cottage, and I hope we shall live to be friends when we know each other better."

"Those of my age," returned the dame, "make no new friends. I thank you for your bounty—it is well intended undoubtedly; but I have all I want, and I cannot accept more at your lordship's hands."

"Well then," continued the Lord Keeper, "at least allow me to say, that I look upon you as a woman of sense and education beyond your appearance, and that I hope you will continue to reside on this prop-erty of mine rent-free for your life."

"I hope I shall," said the old dame, composedly; "I believe that was made an article in the sale of Ravenswood to your lordship, though such a trifling circumstance may have escaped your recollection."

"I remember—I recollect," said his lordship, somewhat confused. "I perceive you are too much attached to your old friends to accept any benefit from their successor."

"Far from it, my lord; I am grateful for the benefits which I decline, and I wish I could pay you for offering them better than by what I am now about to say." The Lord Keeper looked at her in some surprise, but said not a word. "My lord," she continued, in an impressive and solemn tone, "take care what you do—you are on the brink of a precipice."

"Indeed?" said the Lord Keeper, his mind reverting to the political circumstances of the country; "has any thing come to your knowledge —any plot or conspiracy?"

"No, my lord; those who traffic in such commodities do not call into their councils the old, blind, and infirm. My warning is of another kind. You have driven matters hard on with the house of Ravenswood. Believe a true tale—they are a fierce house, and there is danger in dealing with men when they become desperate."

"Tush," answered the Keeper; "what has been between us has been the work of the law, not my doing; and to the law they must look, if they would impugn my proceedings."

"Ay, but they may think otherwise, and take the law into their own hand, when they fail of other means of redress."

"What mean you?" said the Lord Keeper. "Young Ravenswood would not have recourse to personal violence?"

"God forbid I should say so; I know nothing of the youth but what is honourable and open—honourable and open, said I?—I should have added, free, generous, noble—but he is still a Ravenswood, and may bide his time—remember the fate of Sir George Lockhart."*

The Lord Keeper started as she called to his recollection a tragedy so deep and so recent. The old woman proceeded, "Chiesley, who did the deed, was a relative of Lord Ravenswood. In the hall at Ravenswood, in my presence, and in that of others, he avowed publicly his determination to do the cruelty which he afterwards committed. I could not keep silence, though to speak ill became my station. 'You are devising a dreadful crime,' I said, 'for which you must reckon before the judgment-seat.' Never shall I forget his look, as he replied, 'I must reckon then for many things, and will reckon for this also.' Therefore I may well say beware of pressing a desperate man with the hand of authority. There is blood of Chiesley in the veins of Ravenswood, and one drop of it were enough to fire him in the circumstances in which he is placed—I say beware of him."

The old dame had, either intentionally or by accident, harped

* President of the Court of Session. He was pistolled in the High Street of Edinburgh, by John Chiesley, of Dalry, in the year 1689. The revenge of this desperate man was stimulated by an opinion that he had sustained injustice in a decreet-arbitral pronounced by the President, assigning an alimentary provision of about 93l. in favour of his wife and children. He is said at first to have designed to shoot the judge while attending upon divine worship, but was diverted by some feeling concerning the sanctity of the place. After the congregation was dismissed, he dogged his victim as far as the head of the small close on the south side of the Lawnmarket, in which the President's house was situated, and shot him dead as he was about to enter it. This act was done in the presence of numerous spectators. The assassin made no attempt to fly, but boasted of the deed, saying, "I have taught the President how to do justice." He had at least given him fair warning, as Jack Cade says on a similar occasion. The murderer, after undergoing the torture, by a special Act of the Estates of Parliament, was tried before the Lord Provost of Edinburgh, as High Sheriff, and condemned to be dragged on a hurdle to the place of execution, to have his right hand struck off while he yet lived, and finally, to be hung on the gallows with the pistol wherewith he shot the President tied round his neck. This execution took place on the 3d April, 1689; and the incident was long remembered as a dreadful instance of what the law books call the *perfervidum ingenium Scotorum.*

aright the fear of the Lord Keeper. The desperate and dark resource of private assassination, so familiar to a Scottish baron in former times, had even in the present age been too frequently resorted to under the pressure of unusual temptation, or where the mind of the actor was prepared for such a crime. Sir William Ashton was aware of this; as also that young Ravenswood had received injuries sufficient to prompt him to that sort of revenge, which becomes a frequent though fearful consequence of the partial administration of justice. He endeavoured to disguise from Alice the nature of the apprehensions which he entertained, but so ineffectually, that a person even of less penetration than nature had endowed her with must necessarily have been aware that the subject lay near his bosom. His voice was changed in its accent as he replied to her, that the Master of Ravenswood was a man of honour; and, were it otherwise, that the fate of Chiesley of Dalry was a sufficient warning to any one who should dare to assume the office of avenger of his own imaginary wrongs. And having hastily uttered these expressions, he rose and left the place without waiting for a reply.

Chapter Five

————Is she a Capulet?
O dear account! my life is my foe's debt.
SHAKESPEARE

THE LORD Keeper walked for nearly a quarter of a mile in profound silence. His daughter, naturally timid and bred up in those ideas of filial awe and implicit obedience which were inculcated upon the youth of that period, did not venture to interrupt his meditations.

"Why do you look so pale, Lucy?" said her father, turning suddenly around and breaking silence.

According to the ideas of the time, which did not permit a young woman to offer her sentiments on any subject of importance unless especially required to do so, Lucy was bound to appear ignorant of the meaning of all that had passed betwixt Alice and her father, and imputed the emotion he had observed to the fear of the wild cattle which grazed in that part of the extensive chase through which they were now walking.

Of these animals, the descendants of the savage herds which anciently roamed free in the Caledonian forests, it was formerly a point of state to preserve a few in the parks of the Scottish nobility. Specimens continued within the memory of man to be kept at least at three houses of distinction, Hamilton namely, Drumlanrick, and Cumbernauld. They were degenerated from the ancient race in size and strength, if we are to judge from the accounts of old chronicles, and from the formidable remains frequently discovered in bogs and morasses when drained and laid open. The bull had lost the shaggy honours of his mane, and the race was small and light-made, in colour a dingy white, or rather a pale yellow, with black horns and hoofs. They retained, however, in some measure, the ferocity of their ancestry, could not be domesticated on account of their antipathy to the human race, and were often dangerous if approached unguardedly, or wantonly disturbed. It was this last reason which has occasioned their being extirpated at the places we have mentioned, where probably they would otherwise have been retained as appropriate inhabitants of the Scottish woodland, and fit tenants for a baronial forest. A few, if I mistake not, are yet preserved at Chillingham Castle, in Northumberland, the seat of the Earl of Tankerville.

It was to her finding herself in the vicinity of a group of three or four of these animals, that Lucy thought proper to impute those signs of fear, which had arisen in her countenance for a different reason. For she had been familiarized with the appearance of the wild cattle, during her walks in the chace; and it was not then, as now, a necessary part of a young lady's education, to indulge in causeless tremors of the nerves. On the present occasion, however, she speedily found cause for real terror.

Lucy had scarcely replied to her father in the words we have mentioned, and he was just about to rebuke her supposed timidity, when a bull, stimulated either by the scarlet colour of Miss Ashton's screen or mantle, or by one of those fits of capricious ferocity to which their dispositions are liable, detached himself suddenly from the group which were feeding at the upper extremity of a grassy glade, that seemed to lose itself among the crossing and entangled boughs of the forest. The animal approached the intruders on his pasture ground, at first slowly, pawing the ground with his hoof, bellowing from time to time, and tearing up the sand with his horns, as if to lash himself up into rage and violence.

The Lord Keeper, who observed the animal's demeanour, was aware that he was about to become mischievous, and, drawing his daughter's arm under his own, began to walk fast along the avenue, in hopes to get out of his sight and his reach. This was the most injudicious course he could have adopted, for, encouraged by the appearance of flight, the bull began to pursue them at full speed. Assailed by a danger so imminent, firmer courage than that of the Lord Keeper might have given way. But paternal tenderness, "love strong as death," supported him. He continued to support and drag onward his daughter, until, her fears altogether depriving her of the power of flight, she sunk down by his side; and when he could no longer assist her to escape, he turned round and placed himself betwixt her and the raging animal, which advancing in full career, its brutal fury enhanced by the rapidity of the pursuit, was now within a few yards of them. The Lord Keeper had no weapons: his age and gravity dispensed even with the usual appendage of a walking sword,—could such appendage have availed him any thing.

It seemed inevitable that the father or daughter, or both, should have fallen victims to the impending danger, when a shot from the neighbouring thicket arrested the progress of the animal. He was so truly struck between the junction of the spine with the skull, that the wound, which in any other part of his body might scarce have impeded his career, proved instantly fatal. Stumbling forward with a hideous bellow, the progressive force of his previous motion, rather than any operation of his limbs, carried him up to within three yards of the astonished Lord Keeper, where he rolled on the ground, his limbs darkened with the black death-sweat, and quivering with the last convulsions of muscular motion.

Lucy lay senseless on the ground, insensible of the wonderful deliverance which she had experienced. Her father was almost equally stupified, so rapid and so unexpected had been the transition from the horrid death which seemed inevitable, to perfect security. He gazed on the animal, terrible even in death, with a species of mute and confused astonishment, which did not permit him distinctly to understand what had taken place; and so inaccurate was his consciousness of what had passed, that he might have supposed the bull had been arrested in its career by a thunderbolt, had he not observed among the branches of the thicket the figure of a man, with a short gun or musquetoon in his hand.

This instantly recalled him to a sense of their situation—a glance at his daughter reminded him of the necessity of procuring her assistance. He called to the man, whom he concluded to be one of his foresters, to give immediate attention to Miss Ashton, while he himself hastened to call assistance. The huntsman approached them accordingly, and the Lord Keeper saw he was a stranger, but was too much agitated to make any farther remarks. In a few hurried words, he directed the shooter, as stronger and more active than himself, to carry the young lady to a neighbouring fountain, while he went back to Alice's hut to procure more aid.

The man to whose timely interference they had been so much indebted, did not seem inclined to leave his good work half finished. He raised Lucy from the ground in his arms, and conveying her through the glades of the forest by paths with which he seemed well acquainted, stopped not until he laid her in safety by the side of a plentiful and pellucid fountain, which had been once covered in, screened and decorated with architectural ornament of a Gothic character. But now the vault which had covered it being broken down and riven, and the Gothic front ruined and demolished, the stream burst forth from the recess of the earth in open day, and winded its way among the broken sculpture and moss-grown stones which lay in confusion around its source.

Tradition, always busy, at least in Scotland, to grace with a legendary tale a spot in itself interesting, had ascribed a cause of peculiar veneration to this fountain. A beautiful young lady met one of the Lords of Ravenswood while hunting near this spot, and, like a second Egeria, had captivated the affections of the feudal Numa. They met frequently afterwards, and always at sunset, the charms of the nymph's mind completing the conquest which her beauty had begun, and the mystery of the intrigue adding zest to both. She always appeared and disappeared close by the fountain, with which, therefore, her lover judged she had some inexplicable connection. She placed certain restrictions on their intercourse, which also savoured of mystery. They met only once a week; Friday was the appointed day, and she explained to the Lord of Ravenswood, that they were under the necessity of separating so soon as the bell of a chapel, belonging to a hermitage in the adjoining wood, now long ruinous, tolled the hour of vespers. In the course of his confession, the Baron of Ravenswood entrusted the hermit with the secret of this singular amour, and Father Zachary drew the necessary and obvious consequence, that his patron was enveloped in the toils of Satan, and in danger of destruction both to body and soul. He urged these perils to the Baron with all the force of monkish rhetoric, and described, in the most frightful colours, the real character and person of the apparently lovely Naiad, whom he hesitated not to denounce as a limb of the kingdom of darkness. The lover listened with obstinate incredulity; and it was not until worn out by the obstinacy of the anchoret, that he consented to put the state and condition of his mistress to a certain trial, and for that purpose acquiesced in Zachary's proposal, that on their next interview the vespers bell should be rung at half an hour later than usual. The hermit maintained and bucklered his opinion, by quotations from the *Malleus Maleficarum*, *Sprengerus*, *Remigius*, and other learned dæmonologists, that the Evil One, thus seduced to remain behind the appointed hour, would assume her true shape, and having appeared to her terrified lover as a fiend of hell, would vanish from him in a flash of sulphureous lightning. Raymond of Ravenswood acquiesced in the experiment, not incurious concerning the issue, though confident it would disappoint the expectations of the hermit.

On the appointed hour the lovers met, and their interview was protracted beyond that at which they usually parted, by the delay of the priest to ring his usual curfew. No change took place upon the nymph's outward form; but as soon as the lengthening shadows made her aware that the usual hour of the vesper chime was passed, she tore herself from her lover's arms with a shriek of despair, bid him adieu for ever, and plunging into the fountain, disappeared from his eyes. The bubbles occasioned by her descent were crimsoned with blood as they arose, leading the distracted Baron to infer, that his ill-judged curiosity had occasioned the death of this interesting and mysterious being. The remorse which he felt, as well as the recollection of her charms, proved the penance of his future life, which he lost in the battle of Flodden not many months after. But, in memory of his Naiad, he had previously ornamented the fountain in which she appeared to reside, and secured its waters from profanation or pollution, by the small vaulted building of which the fragments still remained scattered around it. From this period the house of Ravenswood was supposed to have dated its decay.

Such was the generally received legend, which some, who would seem wiser than the vulgar, explained, as obscurely intimating the fate of a beautiful maid of plebeian rank, the mistress of this Raymond, whom he slew in a fit of jealousy, and whose blood was mingled with the waters of the locked fountain, as it was commonly called. Others imagined that the tale had a more remote origin in the ancient heathen mythology. All however agreed, that the spot was fatal to the Ravenswood family; and that to drink of the waters of the well, or even approach its brink, was as ominous to the descendant of that house, as for a Grahame to wear green, a Bruce to kill a spider, or a St Clair to cross the Ord on a Monday.

It was in this ominous spot that Lucy Ashton first drew breath after her long and almost deadly swoon. Beautiful and pale as the fabulous Naiad in the last agony of separation from her lover, she was seated so as to rest with her back against a part of the ruined wall, while her mantle, dripping with the water that her protector had used profusely to recal her senses, clung to her slender and beautifully proportioned form.

The first moment of recollection brought to her mind the danger which had overpowered her senses—the next remembered that of her father. She looked around—he was no where to be seen—"My father—my father!" was all that she could ejaculate.

"Sir William is safe," answered the voice of a stranger—"perfectly safe, and will be with you instantly."

"Are you sure of that?" exclaimed Lucy—"the bull was close by us —do not stop me—I must go to seek my father."

And she arose with that purpose; but her strength was so much exhausted, that, far from possessing the power to execute her purpose, she must have fallen against the stone on which she had leant, probably not without sustaining serious injury.

The stranger was so near to her, that, without actually suffering her to fall, he could not avoid catching her in his arms, which, however, he did with a momentary reluctance, very unusual when youth interposes to prevent beauty from danger. It seemed as if her weight, slight as it was, proved too heavy for her young and athletic assistant, for, without feeling the temptation of detaining her in his arms even for a single instant, he again placed her on the stone from which she had risen, and retreating a few steps, repeated hastily, "Sir William Ashton is perfectly safe, and will be here instantly. Do not make yourself anxious on his account—Fate has singularly preserved him—You, madam, are exhausted, and must not think of rising until you have some assistance more suitable than mine."

Lucy, whose senses were by this time more effectually collected, was naturally led to look at the stranger with attention. There was nothing in his appearance which should have rendered him unwilling to offer his arm to a young lady who required support, or which could have induced her to refuse his assistance; and she could not help wonder, even in that moment, that he seemed cold and reluctant to offer it. A shooting-dress of dark green, richly laced with gold, intimated the rank of the wearer, though concealed in part by a large and loose cloak of a dark brown colour. A Montero cap and a black feather drooped over the wearer's brow, and partly concealed his features, which, so far as seen, were dark, regular, and full of majestic, though somewhat sullen, expression. Some secret sorrow, or the brooding spirit of some moody passion, had quenched the light and the ingenuous vivacity of youth in a countenance singularly fitted to display both, and it was not easy to gaze on the stranger without a secret impression either of pity or fear, or at least of doubt and curiosity allied to both.

The impression which we have necessarily been long in describing, Lucy felt in the glance of a moment, and had no sooner encountered the keen black eyes of the stranger, than her own were bent on the ground with a mixture of bashful embarrassment and fear. Yet there was a necessity to speak, or at least she thought so, and in a fluttered accent began to mention her wonderful escape, in which she was sure that the stranger must, under Heaven, have been her father's protector, and her own.

He seemed to shrink from her expressions of gratitude, while he replied abruptly, "I leave you, madam;" the deep melody of his voice rendered powerful, but not harsh, by something like a severity of tone —"I leave you to the protection of those to whom you have been this day a guardian angel."

Lucy was surprised at the ambiguity of his language, and, with a feeling of artless and unaffected gratitude, began to deprecate the idea of having intended to give any offence, as if such a thing had been possible. "I have been unfortunate," she said, "in endeavouring to express my thanks—I am sure it must be so, though I cannot recollect what I said—but would you but stay till my father—till the Lord Keeper comes—would you only permit him to pay you his thanks, and to enquire your name——"

"My name is unnecessary," answered the stranger; "your father—I would rather say Sir William Ashton—will learn it soon enough, for all the pleasure it will afford him."

"You mistake him," said Lucy earnestly; "he will be grateful for my sake and for his own—you do not know my father, or you are deceiving me with a story of his safety, when he has already fallen a victim to the fury of that animal."

When she had caught this idea, she started from the ground, and endeavoured to press towards the avenue in which the accident had taken place, while the stranger, though he seemed to hesitate between the desire to assist and the wish to leave her, was obliged, in common humanity, to oppose her both by entreaty and action.

"On the word of a gentleman, madam, I tell you the truth; your father is in perfect safety; you will expose yourself to injury if you venture back where the herd of wild cattle graze—If you will go"—for, having once adopted the idea that her father was still in danger, she pressed forwards in spite of him—"if you will go, accept my arm, though I am not the person who can with most propriety offer you support."

But, without heeding this intimation, Lucy took him at his word. "O if you be a man," she said,—"if you be a gentleman, assist me to find my father—You shall not leave me—you must go with me—he is dying perhaps while we are talking here."

Then, without listening to excuse or apology, and holding fast by the stranger's arm, though unconscious of any thing save the support which it gave, and without which she could not have moved, mixed with a vague feeling of preventing his escape from her, she was urging, and almost dragging him forward, when Sir William Ashton came up, followed by the female attendant of blind Alice, and by two wood-cutters, whom he had summoned from their occupation to his assistance. His joy at seeing his daughter safe, overcame the surprise with which he would at another time have beheld her hanging as familiarly on the arm of a stranger, as she might have done upon his own.

"Lucy, my dear Lucy, are you safe?—are you well?" were the only words that broke from him as he embraced her in ecstasy.

"I am well, sir—thank God—and still more that I see you so;—but this gentleman," she said, quitting his arm, and shrinking from him, "what must he think of me?" and her eloquent blood, flushing over neck and brow, spoke how much she was ashamed of the freedom with which she had craved, and even compelled his assistance.

"This gentleman," said Sir William Ashton, "will, I trust, not regret the trouble we have given him, when I assure him of the gratitude of the Lord Keeper for the greatest service which one man ever rendered to another—for the life of my child—for my own life, which he has saved by his bravery and presence of mind. He will, I am sure, permit us to request"——

"Request nothing of ME, my lord," said the stranger, in a stern and peremptory tone; "I am the Master of Ravenswood."

There was a dead pause of surprise, not unmixed with less pleasing feelings. The Master wrapt himself in his cloak, made a haughty inclination towards Lucy, muttering a few words of courtesy, as indistinctly heard as they seemed to be reluctantly uttered, and turning from them was immediately lost in the thicket.

"The Master of Ravenswood!" said the Lord Keeper, when he had recovered his momentary astonishment. "Hasten after him—stop him —beg him to speak to me for a single moment."

The two foresters accordingly set off in pursuit of the stranger. They speedily returned, and, in an embarrassed and awkward manner, said the gentleman would not return. The Lord Keeper took one of the fellows aside, and questioned him more closely what the Master of Ravenswood said.

"He just said he wadna come back," said the man, with the caution of a prudent Scotchman, who cared not to be the bearer of an unpleasant errand.

"He said something more, sir," said the Lord Keeper, "and I insist on knowing what it was."

"Why, then, my lord," said the man, looking down, "he said—but it wad be nae pleasure to your lordship to hear it, for I dare say the Master meant nae ill."

"That's none of your concern, sir; I desire to hear the very words."

"Weel then," replied the man, "he said, tell Sir William Ashton, that the next time he and I forgather, he will not be half sae blythe of our meeting as of our parting."

"Very well, sir," said the Lord Keeper, "I believe he alludes to a wager we have on our hawks—it is a matter of no consequence."

He turned to his daughter, who was by this time so much recovered as to be able to walk home. But the effect which the various recollections, connected with a scene so terrific, made upon a mind which was susceptible in an extreme degree, was more permanent than the injury which her nerves had sustained. Visions of terror, both in sleep and in waking reveries, recalled to her the form of the furious animal, and the dreadful bellow with which he accompanied his career; and it was always the image of the Master of Ravenswood, with his native nobleness of countenance and form, that seemed to interpose betwixt her and assured death. It is, perhaps, at all times dangerous for a young person to suffer their recollection to dwell repeatedly, and with too much complacence, on the same individual; but in Lucy's situation it was almost unavoidable. She had never happened to see a young man of mien and features so romantic and so striking as young Ravenswood; but had she seen an hundred his equals or his superiors in those particulars, no one else could have been linked to her heart by the strong associations of remembered danger and escape, of gratitude, wonder, and curiosity. I say curiosity, for it is likely that the singularly restrained and unaccommodating manners of the Master of Ravenswood, so much at variance with the natural expression of his features and grace of his deportment, as they excited wonder by the contrast, had their effect in rivetting her attention to the recollection. She knew little of Ravenswood, or the disputes which had existed betwixt her father and his, and perhaps could in her gentleness of mind hardly have comprehended the angry and bitter passions which they had engendered. But she knew that he was come of noble stem; was poor, though descended from the noble and the wealthy; and she felt that she could sympathize with the feelings of a proud mind, which urged him to recoil from the proffered gratitude of the new proprietors of his father's house and domains. Would he have equally shunned their acknowledgments and avoided their intimacy, had her father's request been urged more mildly, less abruptly, and softened with the grace which women so well know how to throw into their manner, when they mean to mediate betwixt the headlong passions of the ruder sex? This was a perilous question to ask her own mind— perilous both in the idea and in its consequences.

Lucy Ashton, in short, was involved in those mazes of the imagination which are most dangerous to the young and the sensitive. Time, it is true, absence, change of place and of face, might probably have destroyed the illusion in her instance as it has done in many others; but her residence remained solitary, and her mind without those means of dissipating her pleasing visions. This solitude was chiefly owing to the absence of Lady Ashton, who was at this time in Edinburgh, watching the progress of some state-intrigue; the Lord Keeper only received society out of policy or ostentation, and was by nature rather reserved and unsociable; and thus no cavalier appeared to rival or to obscure the ideal picture of chivalrous excellence which Lucy had pictured to herself in the Master of Ravenswood.

While Lucy indulged in these dreams, she made frequent visits to old blind Alice, hoping it would be easy to lead her to talk on the subject, which at present she had imprudently admitted to occupy so large a portion of her thoughts. But Alice did not in this particular altogether gratify her wishes and expectations. She spoke readily, and with pathetic feeling, concerning the family in general, but seemed to observe an especial and cautious silence on the subject of the present representative. The little she said of him was not altogether so favourable as Lucy had anticipated. She hinted that he was of a stern and unforgiving character, more ready to resent than to pardon injuries; and Lucy combined with great alarm the hints which she now dropped of these dangerous qualities, with Alice's advice to her father, so emphatically given, "to beware of Ravenswood."

But that very Ravenswood, of whom such unjust suspicions had been entertained, had, almost immediately after they had been uttered, confuted them by saving at once her father's life and her own. Had he nourished such black revenge as Alice's dark hints seemed to indicate, no deed of active guilt was necessary for the full gratification of that evil passion. He needed but to have withheld for an instant his indispensable and effective assistance, and the object of his resentment must have perished, without any direct aggression on his part, by a death equally fearful and certain. She conceived, therefore, that some secret prejudice, or the suspicions incident to age and to misfortune, had led Alice to form conclusions injurious to the character, and irreconcileable both with the generous conduct and noble features of the Master of Ravenswood. And in this belief Lucy reposed her hope, and went on weaving her enchanted web of fairy tissue, as beautiful and transient as the film of the gossamer, when it is pearled with the morning dew, and glimmering to the morning sun.

Her father, in the meanwhile, as well as the Master of Ravenswood, were making reflections, as frequent, though more solid than those of Lucy, upon the singular event which had taken place. His first task, when he returned home, was to ascertain by medical assistance that his daughter had sustained no injury from the dangerous and alarming situation in which she had been placed. Satisfied on this topic, he proceeded to revise the memoranda which he had taken down from the mouth of the person employed to interrupt the funeral service of the late Lord Ravenswood. Bred to casuistry, and well accustomed to practise the ambi-dexter ingenuity of the bar, it cost him little trouble to soften the features of the tumult which he had been at first so anxious to exaggerate. He preached to his colleagues of the privy council the necessity of using conciliating measures with young men whose blood and temper were hot, and their experience of life limited. He did not hesitate to attribute some censure to the conduct of the officer, as having been unnecessarily irritating.

These were the contents of his public dispatches. The letters which he wrote to those private friends into whose management the matter was like to fall, were of a yet more favourable tenor. He represented that lenity in this case would be equally politic and popular, whereas, considering the high respect with which the rites of interment are regarded in Scotland, any severity exercised against the Master of Ravenswood for protecting those of his father from interruption, would be on all sides most unfavourably construed. And, finally, assuming the language of a generous and high-spirited man, he made it his particular request that this affair should be passed over without severe notice. He alluded with delicacy to the predicament in which he himself stood with young Ravenswood, as having succeeded in the long train of litigation by which the fortunes of that noble house had been so much reduced, and confessed it would be most peculiarly acceptable to his own feelings, could he find means in some sort to counterbalance the disadvantages which he had occasioned the family, though only in the prosecution of his just and lawful rights. He therefore made it his particular and personal request that the matter should have no further consequences, and insinuated a desire that he himself should have the merit of having put a stop to it by his favourable report and intercession. It was particularly remarkable, that, contrary to his uniform practice, he made no special communication to Lady Ashton upon the subject of the tumult; and although he mentioned the alarm which Lucy had received from one of the wild cattle, yet he gave no detailed account of an incident so interesting and terrible.

There was much surprise among Sir William Ashton's political friends and colleagues on receiving letters of a tenor so unexpected. On comparing notes together, one smiled, one put up his eye-brows, a third nodded acquiescence in the general wonder, and a fourth asked, if they were sure these were *all* the letters the Lord Keeper had written on the subject. "It runs strangely in my mind, my lords, that none of these advices contain the root of the matter."

But no secret letters of a contrary nature had been received, although the question seemed to imply the possibility of their exist-ence.

"Weel," said an old grey-headed statesman, who had contrived, by shifting and trimming, to maintain his post at the steerage through all the changes of course which the vessel had held for thirty years, "I thought Sir William would hae verified the auld Scottish saying, 'as soon comes the lamb's skin to market as the auld tup's.'"

"We must please him after his own fashion," said another, "though it be an unlooked-for one."

"A wilful man maun hae his way," answered the old counsellor.

"The Keeper will rue this before year and day are out," said a third; "the Master of Ravenswood is the lad to wind him a pirn."

"Why, what would you do, my lords, with the poor young fellow?" said a noble Marquis present; "the Lord Keeper has got all his estate —he has not a cross to bless himself with."

To which the ancient Lord Turntippet replied,

"If he hasna gear to fine,
He has shins to pine—

And that was our way before the Revolution—*Luitur cum persona, qui luere non potest cum crumena*—Hegh, my lords, that's gude law Latin."

"I can see no motive," replied the Marquis, "that any noble lord can have for urging this matter farther; let the Lord Keeper have the power to deal in it as he pleases."

"Agree, agree—remit to the Lord Keeper, with any other person for fashion's sake—Lord Hirplehooly, who is bed-ridden—one to be a quorum—Make your entry in the minutes, Mr Clerk.—And now, my lords, there is that young scattergood, the Laird of Bucklaw's fine to be disponed upon—I suppose it goes to my Lord Treasurer."

"Shame be in my meal-poke then," exclaimed Lord Turntippet, "and your hand aye in the nook of it. I had set that down for a bye bit between meals for mysel."

"To use one of your favourite saws, my lord," replied the Marquis, "you are like the miller's dog, that licks his lips before the bag is untied —the man is not fined yet."

"But that costs but twa skarts of a pen," said Lord Turntippet; "and surely there is nae noble lord that will presume to say, that I, wha hae complied wi' a' compliances, tane all manner of tests, abjured all that was to be abjured, and sworn a' that was to be sworn, for these thirty years by-past, sticking fast by my duty to the state through good report and bad report, shouldna hae something now and than to synde my mouth wi' after sic drouthy wark."

"It would be very unreasonable indeed, my lord," replied the Marquis, "had we either thought that your lordship's drought was quenchable, or observed any thing stick in your throat that required washing down."

And so we close the scene on the Privy-council of that period.

Chapter Six

> For this are all these warriors come,
>   To hear an idle tale;
> And o'er our death-accustomed arms
>   Shall silly tears prevail?

ON THE evening of the day when the Lord Keeper and his daughter were saved from such eminent peril, two strangers were seated in the most private apartment of a small obscure inn, or rather alehouse, called the Tod's-hole, about five or six miles from the Castle of Ravenswood, and as far from the ruinous tower of Wolfscrag, betwixt which two places it was situated.

One of these strangers was about forty years of age, tall, and thin in the flanks, with an aquiline nose, dark penetrating eyes, and a shrewd but sinister cast of countenance. The other was about fifteen years younger, short, stout, ruddy-faced, and red-haired, with an open, resolute, and cheerful eye, to which careless and fearless freedom, and inward daring, gave fire and expression, notwithstanding its light grey colour. A stoup of wine, for in those days it was served out from the cask in pewter flaggons, was placed on the table, and each had his quaigh or bicker* before him. But there was little appearance of conviviality. With folded arms, and looks of anxious expectation, they eyed each other in silence, each wrapt in his own thoughts, and holding no communication with his neighbour.

At length the younger broke silence by exclaiming, "What the foul fiend can detain the Master so long? he must have miscarried in his enterprize.—Why did you dissuade me from going with him?"

"One man is enough to right his own wrong," said the taller and older personage; "we venture our lives for him in coming thus far on such an errand."

"You are but a craven after all, Craigengelt," answered the younger, "and that's what many folks have thought you before now."

"But what none has dared to tell me," said Craigengelt, laying his hand on the hilt of his sword; "and, but that I hold a hasty man no better than a fool, I would——" he paused for his companion's answer.

---

*Drinking cups, of different sizes, made out of staves hooped together. The *quaigh* was used chiefly for drinking wine or brandy: it might hold about a gill, and was often composed of rare wood, and curiously ornamented with silver.

"*Would* you?" said the other coolly; "and why do you not then?"

Craigengelt drew his cutlass an inch or two, and then returned it with violence into the scabbard—"Because there is a deeper stake than the lives of twenty hair-brained gowks like you."

"You are right there," said his companion, "for if it were not that these forfeitures, and that last fine that the old driveller Turntippit is gaping for, and which, I dare say, is laid on by this time, have fairly driven me out of house, I were a coxcomb and a cuckoo to boot, to trust your fair promises of getting me a commission in the Irish brigade. What have I to do with the Irish brigade? I am a plain Scotchman, as my father was before me; and my grand aunt, Lady Girnington, cannot live for ever."

"Ay, Bucklaw," observed Craigengelt, "but she may live many a long day; and for your father, he had land and living, kept himself close from wadsetters and money-lenders, paid each man his due, and lived on his own."

"And whose fault is it that I have not done so too?" said Bucklaw— "whose but the devil's and your's, and such like as you, that have led me to the far end of a fair estate; and now I shall be obliged, I suppose, to skelder and shift about like yourself—live one week upon a line of secret intelligence from Saint Germains—another upon a report of a rising in the Highlands—get my breakfast and morning draught of sack from old Jacobite ladies, and give them locks of my old wig for the Chevalier's hair—second my friend in his quarrel till he comes to the field, and then flinch from him lest so important a political agent should perish from the way. All this I must do for bread, besides calling myself a captain!"

"You think you are making a fine speech now," said Craigengelt, "and shewing much wit at my expence. Is starving or hanging better than the life I am obliged to lead, because the present fortunes of the king cannot sufficiently support his envoys?"

"Starving is honester, Craigengelt, and hanging is like to be the end on't—But what you mean to make of this poor fellow Ravenswood, I know not—he has no money left, any more than I—his lands are all pawned and pledged, and the annual rent eats up the rents, and is not satisfied, and what do you hope to make by meddling in his affairs?"

"Content yourself, Bucklaw; I know my business," replied Craigengelt. "Besides that his name, and his father's services in 1689, will make such an acquisition sound well both at Versailles and Saint Germains, you will also please be informed, that the Master of Ravenswood is a very different kind of a young fellow from you. He has parts and address, as well as courage and talents, and will present himself abroad like a young man of head as well as heart, who knows something more than the speed of a horse or the flight of a hawk. I have lost credit of late, by bringing over no one that had sense to know more than how to unharbour a stag, or take and reclaim an eyess—the Master has education, sense, and penetration."

"And yet not wise enough to escape the tricks of a kidnapper, Craigengelt—but don't be angry; you know you will not fight, and so it is as well to leave your hilt in peace and quiet, and tell me in sober guise how you drew the Master into your confidence."

"By flattering his love of vengeance, Bucklaw—he has always distrusted me—but I watched my time, and struck while his temper was red-hot with the sense of insult and of wrong. He goes now to expostulate, as he says—and perhaps thinks—with Sir William Ashton.—I say, that if they meet, and the lawyer puts him to his defence, the Master will kill him; for he had that sparkle in his eye which never deceives you when you would read a man's purpose. At any rate, he will give him such a tight bullying as will be construed into an assault on a privy-counsellor. So there will be a total breach betwixt him and government; Scotland will be too hot for him, France will gain him, and we will all set sail together in the French brig L'Espoir, which is hovering for us off Eyemouth."

"Content am I," said Bucklaw; "Scotland has little left that I care about; and if carrying the Master with us will get us a better reception in France, why, so be it, a God's name. I doubt our own merits will procure us but slender preferment. And I trust he will send a ball through the Keeper's head before he joins us. One or two of these scoundrel statesmen should be shot once a-year, just to keep the others on their good behaviour."

"That is very true," replied Craigengelt; "and it reminds me that I must go and see that our horses have been fed, and are in readiness; for, should such deed be done, it will be no time for grass to grow beneath their heels." He proceeded as far as the door, then turned back with a look of earnestness, and said to Bucklaw, "Whatever should come of this business, I am sure you will do me the justice to remember, that I said nothing to the Master which could imply my accession to any act of violence which he may take it into his head to commit."

"No, no, not a single word like accession," replied Bucklaw; "you know too well the risk belonging to those two terrible words, art and part." Then, as if to himself, he recited the following lines:

> "The dial spoke not, but it made shrewd signs,
> And pointed full upon the stroke of murder."

"What is that you are talking to yourself?" said Craigengelt, turning back with some anxiety.

"Nothing—only two lines I have heard upon the stage," replied his companion.

"Bucklaw," said Craigengelt, "I sometimes think you should have been a stage-player yourself; all is fancy and frolic with you."

"I have often thought so myself," said Bucklaw. "I believe it would be safer than acting with you in the Fatal Conspiracy.—But away, play you your own part, and look after the horses like a groom as you are.—A play-actor! a stage-player! that would have deserved a stab, but that Craigengelt's a coward—And yet I should like the profession well enough. Stay—let me see—ay—I would come out in Alexander—

> Thus from the grave I rise to save my love,
> Draw all your swords, and quick as lightning move;
> When I rush on, sure none will dare to stay,
> 'Tis love commands, and glory leads the way."

As with a voice of thunder, and his hand upon his sword, Bucklaw repeated the ranting couplets of poor Lee, Craigengelt re-entered with a face of alarm.

"We are undone, Bucklaw! the Master's led horse has cast himself over his halter in the stable, and is dead lame—his hackney will be set up with the day's work, and now he has no fresh horse; he will never get off."

"Egad there will be no moving with the speed of lightning this bout," said Bucklaw, drily. "But stay, you can give him yours."

"What, and be taken myself? I thank you for the proposal," said Craigengelt.

"Why, if the Lord Keeper should have met with a mischance, which for my part I cannot suppose, for the Master is not the lad to shoot an old and unarmed man—But *if* there should have been a fray at the Castle, you are neither art nor part in it you know, so have nothing to fear."

"True, true," answered the other, with embarrassment; "but consider my commission from Saint Germains."

"Which many men think is a commission of your own making, noble captain. Well, if you will not give him your horse, why, d—n it, he must have mine."

"Yours?" said Craigengelt.

"Ay, mine," repeated Bucklaw; "it shall never be said that I agreed to back a gentleman in a little affair of honour, and neither helped him on with it or off from it."

"You will give him your horse? and have you considered the loss?"

"Loss! why Grey Gilbert cost me twenty Jacobuses, that's true; but then his hackney is worth something, and his Black Moor is worth twice as much were he sound, and I know how to handle him.—Take a fat sucking mastiff whelp, flay and bowel him, stuff the body full of black and grey snails, roast a reasonable time, and baste with oil of spikenard, saffron, cinnamon and honey, anoint with the dripping, working it in"——

"Yes, Bucklaw, but in the meanwhile, before the sprain is cured, nay before the whelp is roasted, you will be caught and hung. Depend on it, the chase will be hard after Ravenswood. I wish we had made our place of rendezvous nearer to the coast."

"On my faith then," said Bucklaw, "I had best off just now, and leave my horse for him—Stay, stay, he comes, I hear a horse's feet."

"Are you sure there is only one?" said Craigengelt; "I fear there is a chase; I think I hear three or four galloping together; I am sure I hear more horses than one."

"Pooh, pooh, it is the wench of the house that is clattering to the well in her pattens: by my faith, captain, you should give up both your captainship and your secret service, for you are as easily scared as a wild goose. But here comes the Master alone, and looking as gloomy as a night in November."

The Master of Ravenswood entered the room accordingly, his cloak muffled around him, his arms folded, his looks stern, and at the same time dejected. He flung his cloak from him as he entered, threw himself upon a chair, and appeared sunk in a profound reverie.

"What has happened? What have you done?" was hastily demanded by Craigengelt and Bucklaw in the same moment.

"Nothing," was the short and sullen answer.

"Nothing? and left us, so determined to call the old villain to account for all the injuries that you, we, and the country have received at his hand? Have you seen him?"

"I have," replied the Master of Ravenswood.

"Seen him and come away without settling scores which have been so long due?" asked Bucklaw; "I would not have expected that at the hand of the Master of Ravenswood."

"No matter what you expected," replied Ravenswood; "it is not to you, sir, that I shall be disposed to render any reason for my conduct."

"Patience, Bucklaw," said Craigengelt, interrupting his companion, who seemed about to make an angry reply. "The Master has been interrupted in his purpose by some accident, but he must excuse the anxious curiosity of friends, who are devoted to his cause like you and me."

"Friends, Captain Craigengelt!" retorted Ravenswood haughtily, "I am ignorant what familiarity has passed betwixt us to entitle you to use that expression. I think our friendship amounts to this, that we agreed to leave Scotland together so soon as I should have visited the alienated mansion of my fathers, and had an interview with its present possessor, I will not call him proprietor."

"Very true, Master," answered Bucklaw; "and as we thought you had a mind to do something to put your neck in jeopardy, Craigie and I very courteously agreed to tarry for you, although ours might run some risk in consequence. As to Craigie, indeed, it does not very much signify, he had gallows written on his brow in the hour of his birth; but I should not like to discredit my parentage by coming to such an end in another man's cause."

"Gentlemen," said the Master of Ravenswood, "I am sorry if I have occasioned you any inconvenience, but I must claim the right of judging what is best for my own affairs, without rendering any explanations to any one. I have altered my mind, and do not design to leave the country this season."

"Not to leave the country, Master!" exclaimed Craigengelt. "Not to go over, after all the trouble and expence I have incurred—after all the risk of discovery, and the expence of freight and demurrage!"

"Sir," replied the Master of Ravenswood, "when I designed to leave this country in haste, I made use of your obliging offer to procure me means of conveyance; but I do not recollect that I pledged myself to go off, if I found occasion to alter my mind. For your trouble on my account, I am sorry, and I thank you; your expence," he added, putting his hand in his pocket, "admits a more solid compensation— freight and demurrage are matters with which I am unacquainted, Captain Craigengelt, but take my purse and pay yourself according to your own conscience." And accordingly he tendered a purse with some gold in it to the soi-disant captain.

But here Bucklaw interposed in his turn. "Your fingers, Craigie, seem to itch for that same piece of green net-work," said he; "but I make my vow to God, that if they offer to close upon it, I will chop them off with my whinger. Since the Master has changed his mind, I suppose we need stay here no longer; but in the first place I beg leave to tell him"——

"Tell him any thing you will," said Craigengelt, "if you will first allow me to state to him the inconveniencies to which he will expose himself by quitting our society, to remind him of the obstacles to his remaining here, and of the difficulties attending his proper introduction at Versailles and Saint Germains, without the countenance of those who have established useful connections."

"Besides forfeiting the friendship," said Bucklaw, "of at least one man of spirit and honour."

"Gentlemen," said Ravenswood, "permit me once more to assure you, that you have been pleased to attach to our temporary connection more importance than I ever meant that it should have. When I repair to foreign courts, I shall not need the introduction of an intriguing adventurer, nor is it necessary for me to set value on the friendship of an hot-headed bully." With these words, and without waiting for an answer, he left the apartment, remounted his horse, and was heard to ride off.

"Mortbleu!" said Captain Craigengelt, "my recruit is lost."

"Ay, captain," said Bucklaw, "the salmon is off with hook and all. But I will after him, for I have had more of his insolence than I can well digest."

Craigengelt offered to accompany him, but Bucklaw replied, "No, no, captain, keep you the cheek of the chimney-nook till I come back. Its good sleeping in a hale skin.

> Little kens the auld wife that sits by the fire,
> How cauld the wind blaws in hurle-burle-swire."

And singing as he went, he left the apartment.

Chapter Seven

> Now, Billy Bewick, keep good heart,
>   And of thy talking let me be;
> But if thou art a man, as I'm sure thou art,
>   Come ower the dike and fight with me.
>   *Old Ballad*

THE MASTER of Ravenswood had mounted the ambling hackney which he before rode, on finding the accident which had happened to his led horse, and, for the animal's ease, was proceeding at a slow pace from the Tod's-hole towards his old tower of Wolfscrag, when he heard the gallopping of a horse behind him, and, looking back, perceived that he was pursued by young Bucklaw, who had been delayed a few minutes in the pursuit by the irresistible temptation of giving the hostler at the Tod's-hole some receipt for treating the lame horse. This brief delay he had made up by hard gallopping, and now overtook the Master where the road traversed a waste moor. "Halt, sir," cried Bucklaw; "I am no political agent—no Captain Craigengelt, whose life is too important to be hazarded in defence of his honour. I am Frank Hayston of Bucklaw, and no man injures me by word, deed, sign, or look, but he must render me an account of it."

"This is all very well, Mr Hayston of Bucklaw," replied the Master of Ravenswood, in a tone the most calm and indifferent; "but I have no quarrel with you, and desire to have none. Our roads homeward, and our roads through life, lie in different directions; there is no occasion for our crossing each other."

"Is there not?" said Bucklaw, impetuously. "By Heaven! but I say that there is though—you called us intriguing adventurers."

"Be correct in your recollection, Mr Hayston; it was to your companion only I applied that epithet, and you know him to be no better."

"And what then? he was my companion for the time, and no man shall insult my companion, right or wrong, while he is in my company."

"Then, Mr Hayston," replied Ravenswood, with the same composure, "you should chuse your society better, or you are like to have much work in your capacity of their champion. Go home, sir, sleep, and have more reason in your wrath to-morrow."

"Not so, Master, you have mistaken your man; high airs and wise saws shall not carry it off thus. Besides, you termed me bully, and you shall retract the word before we part."

"Faith, scarcely," said Ravenswood, "unless you shew me better reason for thinking myself mistaken than you are now producing."

"Then, Master," said Bucklaw, "though I should be sorry to offer it to a man of your quality, if you will not justify your uncivility, or retract it, or name a place of meeting, you must here undergo the hard word and the hard blow."

"Neither will be necessary," said Ravenswood; "I am satisfied with what I have done to avoid an affair with you—if you are serious, this place will serve as well as another."

"Dismount then, and draw," said Bucklaw, setting him the example. "I always thought and said you were a pretty man; I should be sorry to report you otherwise."

"You shall have no reason, sir," said Ravenswood, alighting, and putting himself into a posture of defence.

Their swords crossed, and the combat commenced with great spirit on the part of Bucklaw, who was well accustomed to affairs of the kind, and distinguished by address and dexterity at his weapon. In the present case, however, he did not use his skill to the best advantage; for having lost temper at the cool and contemptuous manner in which the Master of Ravenswood had long refused, and at length granted him satisfaction, and urged by his impatience, he adopted the part of an assailant with inconsiderate eagerness. The Master, with equal skill, and much greater composure, remained chiefly on the defensive, and even declined to avail himself of one or two advantages afforded him by the eagerness of his adversary. At length, in a desperate lounge, which he followed up with an attempt to close, Bucklaw's foot slipped, and he fell on the short grassy turf on which they were fighting. "Take your life, sir," said the Master of Ravenswood, "and mend it, if you can."

"It would be but a cobbled piece of work, I fear," said Bucklaw, rising slowly and gathering up his sword, much less disconcerted with the issue of the combat than could have been expected from the impetuosity of his temper. "I thank you for my life, Master," he pursued. "There is my hand, I bear no ill will to you either for my bad luck, or your better swordmanship."

The Master looked steadily at him for an instant, then extended his hand to him.—"Bucklaw," he said, "you are a generous fellow, and I have done you wrong. I heartily ask your pardon for the expression which offended you; it was hastily and incautiously uttered, and I am convinced it is totally misapplied."

"Are you indeed, Master?" said Bucklaw, his face resuming at once its natural expression of light-hearted carelessness and audacity; "that is more than I expected of you, for, Master, men say you are not too ready to retract your opinions and your language."

"Not when I have well considered them," said the Master.

"Then you are little wiser than I am; for I always give my friend satisfaction first, and explanation afterwards—if one of us falls, all accounts are settled—if not, men are never so ready for peace as after war. But what does that bawling beast of a boy want?" said Bucklaw. "I wish to Heaven he had come a few minutes sooner, and yet it must have been ended some time, and perhaps this way is as well as any other."

As he spoke, the boy he mentioned came up, cudgelling an ass, on which he was mounted, to the top of its speed, and sending, like one of Ossian's heroes, his voice before him,—"Gentlemen,—gentlemen, save yoursells, for the gudewife bade us tell ye that there were folk in her house had ta'en Captain Craigengelt, and were seeking for Bucklaw, and that ye behoved to ride for it."

"By my faith, and that's very true, my man," said Bucklaw; "and there is a silver sixpence for your news, and I would give any man twice as much would tell me which way I should ride."

"That will I, Bucklaw," said Ravenswood; "ride home to Wolfscrag with me; there are places in the old tower you might lie hid, were a thousand men to seek you."

"But that will bring you into trouble yourself, Master; and unless you be in the Jacobite scrape already, it is needless for me to drag you in."

"Not a whit; I have nothing to fear."

"Then I will ride with you blithely, for, to say the truth, I do not know the rendezvous that Craigie was to guide us to this night; and I am sure that, if he is taken, he will tell all the truth on me, and twenty lies on you, in order to save himself from the withie."

They mounted, and rode off in company accordingly, striking off the ordinary road, and holding their way by wild moorish unfrequented paths, with which the gentlemen were well acquainted from the exercise of the chace, but through which others would have had much difficulty in tracing their course. They rode for some time in silence, making such haste as the condition of Ravenswood's horse permitted, until night having gradually closed around them, they discontinued their speed, both from the difficulty of discovering their path, and from the hope that they were beyond the reach of pursuit or observation.

"And now that we have drawn bridle a bit," said Bucklaw, "I would fain ask you a question, Master."

"Ask, and welcome," said Ravenswood, "but forgive my not answering it, unless I think proper."

"Well, it is simply this," answered his late antagonist, "What, in the name of old Sathan, could make you, who stand so high on your reputation, think for a moment of drawing up with such a rogue as Craigengelt, and such a scape-grace as folks call Bucklaw?"

"Simply, because I was desperate, and sought desperate associates."

"And what made you break off from us at the nearest?" again demanded Bucklaw.

"Because I had changed my mind," said the Master, "and renounced my enterprize, at least for the present. And now that I have answered your questions fairly and frankly, tell me what makes you associate with Craigengelt, so much beneath you both in birth and in spirit?"

"In plain terms," answered Bucklaw, "because I am a fool, who have gambled away my land in these times. My grand-aunt, Lady Girnington, has ta'en a new tack of life, I think, and I could only hope to get something by a change of government. Craigie was a sort of gambling acquaintance. He saw my condition, and, as the devil is always at one's elbow, told me fifty lies about his credentials from Versailles, and his interest at Saint Germains, promised me a captain's commission at Paris, and I have been ass enough to put my thumb under his belt. I dare say, by this time, he has told a dozen pretty stories of me to the government. And this is what I have got by wine, women, and dice, cocks, dogs, and horses."

"Yes, Bucklaw," said the Master, "you have indeed nourished in your bosom the snakes that are now stinging you."

"That's home as well as true, Master," replied his companion;

"but, by your leave, you have nursed in your bosom one great goodly snake that has swallowed all the rest, and is as sure to devour you as my half dozen are to make a meal on all that's left of Bucklaw, which is but what lies between bonnet and boot-heel."

"I must not," answered the Master of Ravenswood, "challenge the freedom of speech in which I have set example. What, to speak without a metaphor, do you call this monstrous passion which you charge me with fostering?"

"Revenge, my good sir, revenge, which, if it be as gentleman-like a sin as wine and wassail, with all their *et cæteras*, is equally unchristian, and not quite so bloodless. It is better breaking a park-pale to watch a doe or damsel, than to shoot at an old man."

"I deny the purpose," said the Master of Ravenswood. "On my soul, I had no such intention; I meant but to confront the oppressor ere I left my native land, and upbraid him with his tyranny and its consequences. I would have stated my wrongs so that they would have shaken his soul within him."

"Yes," answered Bucklaw, "and he would have collared you, and cried help, and then you would have shaken the soul out of him, I suppose. Your very look and manner would have frightened the old man to death."

"Consider the provocation," answered Ravenswood,—"consider the ruin and death procured and caused by his hard-hearted cruelty— an ancient house destroyed, an affectionate father murdered. Why, in our old Scottish days, he that sat quiet under such wrongs, would have been held neither fit to back a friend or face a foe."

"Well, Master, I am glad to see that the devil deals as cunningly with other folks as he does with me; for whenever I am about to commit any folly, he persuades me it is the most necessary, gallant, gentlemanlike thing on earth, and I am up to saddlegirths in the bog before I see that the ground is soft. And you, Master, might have turned out a murd ——a homicide, just out of pure respect for your father's memory."

"There is more sense in your language, Bucklaw," replied the Master, "than might have been expected from your conduct—it is too true, our vices steal upon us in forms outwardly as fair as those of the demons whom the superstitious represent as intriguing with the human race, and are not discovered in their native hideousness until we have clasped them in our arms."

"But we may throw them from us though," said Bucklaw, "and that is what I shall think of doing one of these days, that is when old Lady Girnington dies."

"Did you ever hear the expression of the English divine?" said Ravenswood—" 'Hell is paved with good intentions'—As much as to say, they are more often formed than executed."

"Well," replied Bucklaw, "but I will begin this blessed night, and not drink above one quart of wine—unless your claret be of extraordinary quality."

"You will find little to tempt you at Wolfscrag," said the Master. "I know not that I can promise you more than the shelter of my roof; all, and more than all our stock of wine and provisions were exhausted on the late occasion."

"Long may it be ere provision is needed for the like purpose," answered Bucklaw; "but you should not drink up the last flask at a dirgie; there is ill luck in that."

"There is ill luck, I think, in whatever belongs to me," said Ravenswood. "But yonder is Wolfscrag, and whatever it still contains is at your service."

The roar of the sea had long announced their approach to the cliffs, on the summit of which, like the nest of some sea-eagle, the founder of the fortalice had perched his eyry. The pale moon, which had hitherto been contending with flitting clouds, now shone out, and gave them a view of the solitary and naked tower, situated on a projecting cliff that beetled over the German ocean. On three sides the rock was precipitous; on the fourth, which was that towards the land, it had been originally fenced by an artificial ditch and draw-bridge, but the latter was broken down and ruinous, and the former had been in part filled up, so as to allow passage for a horseman into the narrow court-yard, encircled on two sides with low offices and stables, partly ruinous, and closed on the landward front by a low embattled wall, while the remaining side of the quadrangle was occupied by the tower itself, which, tall and narrow, and built of a greyish stone, stood glimmering in the moonlight, like the sheeted spectre of some huge giant. A wilder, or a more disconsolate dwelling, it was perhaps difficult to conceive. The sombrous and heavy sound of the billows, successively dashing against the rocky beach at a profound distance beneath, was to the ear what the landscape was to the eye— a symbol of unvaried and monotonous melancholy, not unmingled with horror.

Although the night was not far advanced, there was no sign of living inhabitant about this forlorn abode, excepting that one, and only one, of the narrow and staunchelled windows which appeared at irregular heights and distances in the walls of the building, showed a small glimmer of light.

"There," said Ravenswood, "sits the only male domestic that remains to the house of Ravenswood; and it is well that he does remain there, since otherwise, we had little hope to find either light or fire. But follow me cautiously; the road is narrow, and admits only one horse in front."

In effect, the path led along a kind of an isthmus, at the peninsular extremity of which the tower was situated, with that exclusive attention to strength and security, in preference to every circumstance of convenience, which dictated to the Scottish barons the choice of their situations, as well as their style of building.

By adopting the cautious mode of approach recommended by the proprietor of this wild hold, they entered the court-yard in safety. But it was long ere the efforts of Ravenswood, though loudly exerted by knocking at the low-browed entrance, and repeated shouts to Caleb to open the gate and admit them, received any answer. "The old man must be departed," he began to say, "or he has fallen into some fit; for the noise I have made would have waked the seven sleepers."

At length a timid and hesitating voice replied,—"Master—Master of Ravenswood—is it you?"

"Yes, it is I, Caleb; open the door quickly."

"But is it you in very blood and body?—for I would sooner face fifty devils as my master's ghaist, or even his wraith,—wherefore aroint ye, if ye were ten times my master, unless ye come in bodily shape, lith and limb."

"It is I, you old fool," answered Ravenswood, "in bodily shape, and alive, save that I am half dead with cold."

The light at the upper window disappeared, and glancing from loop-hole to loop-hole in slow succession, gave intimation that the bearer was in the act of descending, with great deliberation, a winding stair-case occupying one of the turrets which graced the angles of the old tower. The tardiness of its descent extracted some exclamations of impatience from Ravenswood, and several oaths from his less patient and more mercurial companion. Caleb again paused ere he unbolted the door, and once more asked, if they were men of mould that demanded entrance at this time of night?

"Were I near you, you old fool," said Bucklaw, "I would give you sufficient proofs of my bodily condition."

"Open the gate, Caleb," said his master, in a more soothing tone, partly from his regard to the ancient and faithful seneschal, partly perhaps because he thought that angry words would be thrown away, so long as Caleb had a stout iron-clenched oaken door betwixt his person and the speakers.

At length Caleb, with a trembling hand, undid the bars, opened the heavy door, and stood before them, exhibiting his thin grey hairs, bald forehead, and sharp high features, illuminated by a quivering lamp which he held in one hand, while he shaded and protected its flame with the other. The timorous cautious glance which he threw around him—the effect of the partial light upon his white hair and illumined features, might have made a good painting; but our travellers were too impatient for security against the rising storm, to permit them to indulge themselves in studying the picturesque. "Is it you, my dear master? is it yoursell indeed?" exclaimed the old domestic. "I am wae ye suld hae stude waiting at your ain yate, but wha wad hae thought o' seeing ye sae sune, and a strange gentleman with a'—(here he exclaimed apart as it were, and to some inmate of the tower, in a voice not meant to be heard by those in the court)—Mysie—Mysie, woman —stir for dear life and get the fire mended—take the auld three-legged stool, or ony thing that's readiest that will mak a lowe.—I doubt we are but puirly provided, no expecting ye this some months, when doubtless ye wad hae been received conform till your rank, as gude right is; but natheless"——

"Natheless, Caleb," said the Master, "we must have our horses put up, and ourselves too, the best way we can. I hope ye are not sorry to see me sooner than you expected?"

"Sorry, my lord!—I am sure ye sall aye be my lord wi' honest folk, as your noble ancestors hae been these three hundred years, and never asked a whig's leave—sorry to see the Lord of Ravenswood at ane o' his ain castles!—(Then again apart to his unseen associate behind the screen)—Mysie, kill the brood-hen without thinking twice on it; let them care that come ahint.—No to say its our best dwelling," he added, turning to Bucklaw, "but just a strength, Sir, for the Lord of Ravenswood to flee until,—that is, no to *flee*, but to retreat until in troublous times, like the present, when it was ill convenient for him to live farther in the country in ony of his better and mair principal manors; but, for its antiquity, maist folks think that the outside of Wolfscrag is worthy of a large perusal."

"And you are determined we shall have time to make it," said Ravenswood, somewhat amused with the shifts the old man used to detain them without doors, until his confederate Mysie had made her preparations within.

"O, never mind the outside of the house, my good friend," said Bucklaw; "let us see the inside, and let our horses see the stable, that's all."

"O yes, sir—ay, sir—unquestionably, sir,—my lord and ony of his honourable companions"——

"But our horses, my old friend—our horses; they will be dead-foundered by standing here in the cold after riding hard, and mine is too good to be spoiled—therefore, once more, our horses," exclaimed Bucklaw.

"True—ay—your horses—yes—I will call the grooms;" and sturdily did Caleb roar till the old tower rung again,—"John—William—Saunders!—The lads are gane out, or sleeping," he observed, after pausing for an answer, which he knew that he had no human chance of receiving. "A' gaes wrang when the Master's out bye; but I'll take care o' your cattle mysell."

"I think you had better," said Ravenswood, "otherwise I see little chance of their being attended to at all."

"Whisht, my lord,—whisht, for God's sake," said Caleb, in an imploring tone, and apart to his master; "if ye dinna regard your ain credit, think on mine; we'll hae hard eneugh wark to make a decent night o't, wi' a' the lies I can tell."

"Well, well, never mind," said his master; "go to the stable—there is hay and corn, I trust?"

"Ow ay, plenty of hay and corn;" this was uttered boldly and aloud, and, in a lower voice, "there was some half fous o' aits, and some taits o' meadow-hay, left after the burial."

"Very well," said Ravenswood, taking the lamp from his domestic's unwilling hand, "I will shew the stranger up stairs myself."

"I canna think o' that, my lord;—if ye wad but have five minutes, or ten minutes, or, at maist, a quarter of an hour's patience, and look at the fine moonlight prospect of the Bass and North-Berwick Law till I sort the horses, I would marshal ye up, as reason is ye suld be marshalled, your lordship and your honourable visitor. And I hae lockit up the siller candlesticks, and the lamp is not fit"——

"It will do very well in the meantime," said Ravenswood, "and you will have no difficulty for want of light in the stable, for, if I recollect right, half the roof is off."

"Vera true, my lord," replied the trusty adherent, and with ready wit instantly added, "and the lazy sclater loons have never come to put it on a' this while, your lordship."

"If I were disposed to jest at the calamities of my house," said Ravenswood, as he led the way up stairs, "poor old Caleb would furnish me with ample means. His passion consists in representing things about our miserable *menage*, not as they are, but as, in his opinion, they ought to be; and, to say truth, I have been often diverted with the poor wretch's expedients to supply what he thought was essential for the credit of the family, and his still more ingenious apologies for the want of those articles for which his ingenuity could discover no substitute. But though the tower is none of the largest, I shall have some trouble without him to find the apartment in which there is a fire."

As he spoke thus, he opened the door of the hall. "Here, at least," he said, "there is neither hearth nor harbour."

It was indeed a scene of desolation. A large vaulted room, the beams of which, combined like those of Westminster-Hall, were rudely carved at the extremities, remained nearly in the situation in which it had been left after the entertainment at Allan Lord Ravenswood's funeral. Overturned pitchers, and black jacks, and pewter stoups, and flagons, still cumbered the large oaken table; glasses, those more perishable implements of conviviality, many of which had been voluntarily sacrificed by the guests in their enthusiastic pledges to favourite toasts, strewed the stone floor with their fragments. As for the articles of plate, lent for the purpose by friends and kinsfolks, these had been carefully withdrawn so soon as the ostentatious display of festivity, equally unnecessary and strangely timed, had been made and ended. Nothing, in short, remained that indicated wealth: all the signs were those of recent wastefulness, and present desolation. The black cloth hangings, which, on the late mournful occasion, had replaced the tattered and moth-eaten tapestries, had been partly pulled down, and, dangling from the wall in irregular festoons, disclosed the rough stone-work of the building, unsmoothed either by plaster or hewn stone. The seats thrown down, or left in disorder, intimated the careless confusion which had concluded the mournful revel. "This room," said Ravenswood, holding up the lamp—"this room, Mr Hayston, was riotous when it should have been sad; it is a just retribution that it should now be sad when it ought to be cheerful."

They left this disconsolate apartment, and went up stairs, where, after opening one or two doors in vain, Ravenswood led the way into a little matted anti-room, in which, to their great joy, they found a tolerably good fire, which Mysie, by some such expedient as Caleb had suggested, had supplied with a reasonable quantity of fuel. Glad at the heart to see more of comfort than the castle had yet seemed to offer, Bucklaw rubbed his hands heartily over the fire, and now listened with more complacence to the apologies which the Master of Ravenswood offered. "Comfort," he says, "I cannot provide for you, for I have it not for myself; it is long since these walls have known it, if, indeed, they were ever acquainted with it. Shelter and safety, I think, I can promise you."

"Excellent matters, Master," replied Bucklaw, "and, with a mouthful of food and wine, positively all that I can require to-night."

"I fear," said the Master, "your supper will be a poor one—I hear the matter in discussion betwixt Caleb and Mysie—poor Balderstone is something deaf, amongst his other accomplishments, so that much of what he means should be spoken aside is overheard by the whole audience, and especially by those from whom he is most anxious to conceal his private manœuvres—Hark!"

They listened, and heard the old domestic's voice in conversation with Mysie to the following effect. "Just mak the best o't, mak the best o't, woman; it is easy to put a fair face on ony thing."

"But the auld brood-hen?—she'll be as teugh as bow-strings and bend-leather."

"Say ye made a mistak—say ye made a mistak, Mysie," replied the faithful seneschal, in a soothing and undertoned voice; "tak it a' on yoursel; never let the credit o' the house suffer."

"But the brood-hen," remonstrated Mysie,—"ou, she's sitting some gate aneath the dais in the hall—and I am feared to gae in in the dark for the bogle—and if I didna see the bogle, I could as ill see the hen, for it's pit-mirk, and there's no another light in the house, save that very blessed lamp whilk the Master has in his ain hand—and if I had the hen, she's to pu', and to draw, and to dress—and how can I do that, and them sitting by the only fire we hae?"

"Weel, weel, Mysie," said the butler, "bide ye there a wee, and I'll try to get the lamp wiled away frae them."

Accordingly, Caleb Balderstone entered the apartment, little aware that so much of his bye-play had been audible there. "Well, Caleb, my old friend, is there any chance of supper?" said the Master of Ravens-wood.

"*Chance* of supper, your lordship?" said Caleb, with an emphasis of strong scorn at the implied doubt,—"How should there be ony question o' that, and we in your lordship's house?—Chance of supper, indeed?—but ye'll no be for butcher-meat—there's walth o' fat poultry, ready either for spit or brander—The fat capon, Mysie," he added, calling out as boldly as if such a thing had been in existence.

"Quite unnecessary," said Bucklaw, who deemed himself bound in courtesy to relieve some part of the anxious Butler's perplexity, "if you have any thing cold, or a morsel of bread."

"The best of bannocks!" exclaimed Caleb, much relieved; "and, for cauld meat, aw that we hae is cauld aneugh,—howbeit maist of the cauld meat and pastry was gi'en to the poor folk after the ceremony of interment, as gude reason was; nevertheless"——

"Come, Caleb," said the Master of Ravenswood, "I must cut this matter short—this is the young laird of Bucklaw—he is under hiding, and therefore you know"——

"He'll be nae nicer than your lordship's honour, I'se warrant," answered Caleb, chearfully, with a nod of intelligence; "I am sorry that the gentleman is under distress, but I am blyth that he canna say mickle again our house-keeping, for I believe his ain pinches may match ours;—no that we are pinched, thank God," he added, retracting the admission which he had made in his first burst of joy, "but nae doubt we are waur aff than we hae been, or suld be. And for eating,— what signifies telling a lee? there's just the hinder end of the mutton-ham that has been but three times on the table, and the nearer the bane the sweeter, as your honours weel ken—and there's the heel of the ewe-milk kebbuck, wi' a bit of nice butter, and—and—and that's a' that's to trust to." And with great alacrity he produced his slender stock of provisions, and placed them with great formality upon a small round table betwixt the two gentlemen, who were not deterred either by the homely quality or limited quantity of the repast from doing it full justice. Caleb in the mean-while waited on them with grave officiousness, as if anxious to make up, by his own respectful assiduity, for the want of all other attendance.

But alas! how little on such occasions can form, however anxiously and scrupulously observed, supply the lack of substantial fare! Bucklaw, who had eagerly cut a considerable portion of the thrice sacked mutton-ham, now began to demand ale.

"I wadna just presume to recommend our ale," said Caleb; "the maut was ill made, and there was awfu' thunner last week; but siccan water as the Tower well has, ye'll seldom see, Bucklaw, and that I'se engage fur."

"But if your ale is bad you can let us have some wine," said Bucklaw, making a grimace at the mention of the pure element which Caleb so earnestly recommended.

"Wine," answered Caleb undauntedly, "eneugh of wine; it was but twa days syne—waes me for the cause—there was as much wine drunk in this house as would hae floated a pinnace. There never was lack of wine at Wolfscrag."

"Do fetch us some then," said his master, "instead of talking about it." And Caleb boldly departed.

Every expended butt in the old cellar did he set atilt and shake with the desperate expectation of collecting enough of the grounds of claret to fill the large pewter measure which he carried in his hand. Alas! each had been too devoutly drained; and, with all the squeezing and manœuvring which his craft as a butler suggested, he could only collect about half a quart that seemed presentable. Still, however, Caleb was too good a general to renounce the field without a stratagem to cover his retreat. He undauntedly threw down an empty flagon, as if he had stumbled at the entrance of the apartment; called upon Mysie to wipe up the wine that had never been spilt, and placing the other vessel on the table, hoped there was still enough left for their honours. There was indeed; for even Bucklaw, sworn friend to the grape as he was, found no encouragement to renew his first attack

upon the vintage of Wolfscrag, but contented himself, however reluctantly, with a draught of fair water. Arrangements were now made for
his repose; and as the secret chamber was assigned for this purpose, it
furnished Caleb with a first-rate and most plausible apology for all
deficiencies of furniture, bedding, &c.

"For wha," said he, "would have thought of the secret chaumer
being needed? it has not been used since the time of the Gowrie
Conspiracy, and I durst never let a woman ken of the entrance to it, or
your honour will allow that it wad not hae been a secret chaumer
lang."

Chapter Eight

> The hearth in hall was black and dead,
>   No board was dight in bower within,
> Nor merry bowl nor welcome bed;
>   "Here's sorry cheer," quoth the Heir of Linne.
> *Old Ballad*

THE FEELINGS of the prodigal Heir of Linne, as expressed in that
excellent old song, when, after dissipating his whole fortune, he found
himself the deserted inhabitant of "the lonely lodge," might perhaps
have some resemblance to those of the Master of Ravenswood
in his deserted mansion of Wolfscrag. The Master, however, had this
advantage over the spendthrift in the legend, that if he was in similar
distress, he could not impute it to his own imprudence. His misery
had been bequeathed to him by his father, and, joined to his high
blood, and to a title which the courteous might give, or the churlish
withhold at their pleasure, it was the whole inheritance he had derived
from his ancestry.

Perhaps this melancholy, yet consolatory reflection, crossed the
mind of this unfortunate young nobleman with a breathing of comfort.
Favourable to calm reflection, as well as to the Muses, the morning,
while it dispelled the shades of night, had a composing and sedative
effect upon the stormy passions by which the Master of Ravenswood
had been agitated on the preceding day. He now felt himself able to
analyze the different feelings by which he was agitated, and much
resolved to combat and to subdue them. The morning, which had
arisen calm and bright, gave a pleasant effect even to the waste moorland view which was seen from the castle on looking to the landward;
and the glorious ocean, crisped with a thousand rippling waves of
silver, extended on the other side in awful yet complacent majesty to
the verge of the horizon. With such scenes of calm sublimity the

human heart sympathizes even in its most disturbed moods, and deeds of honour and virtue are inspired by their majestic influence.

To seek out Bucklaw in the retreat which he had afforded him was the first occupation of the Master, after he had performed, with a scrutiny unusually severe, the important task of self-examination. "How now, Bucklaw?" was his morning salutation—"how like you the couch in which the exiled Earl of Angus once slept in security, when he was pursued by the full energy of a king's resentment?"

"Umph!" returned the sleeper awakened; "I have little to complain of where so great a man was quartered before me, only the mattress is of the hardest, the vault somewhat damp, the rats more mutinous than I would have expected from the state of Caleb's larder; and if there were shutters to that grated window, or a curtain to the bed, I should think it, upon the whole, an improvement in your accommodation."

"It is, to be sure, forlorn enough," said the Master, looking around the small vault; "but if you will rise and leave it, Caleb will endeavour to find you a better breakfast than your supper of last night."

"Pray, let it be no better," said Bucklaw, getting up and endeavouring to dress himself as well as the obscurity of the place would permit, —"let it, I say, be no better, if you mean me to persevere in my proposed reformation. The very recollection of Caleb's beverage has done more to suppress my longing to open the day with a morning-draught than twenty sermons would have done. And you, Master?— have you been able to give battle valiantly to your bosom-snake? you see I am in the way of smothering my vipers one by one."

"I have commenced the battle, at least, Bucklaw, and I have had a fair vision of an angel who descended to my assistance," replied the Master.

"Woes me!" said his guest, "no vision can I expect, unless my aunt, Lady Girnington, should betake herself to the tomb; and then it would be the substance of her heritage rather than the appearance of her phantom that I should consider as the support of my good resolutions.—But this same breakfast, Master,—does the deer that is to make the pasty run yet on foot, as the ballad has it?"

"I will enquire into that matter," said his entertainer; and, leaving the apartment, he went in search of Caleb, whom, after some difficulty, he found in an obscure sort of dungeon, which had been in former times the buttery of the castle. Here the old man was employed busily in the doubtful task of burnishing a pewter flagon until it should take the hue and semblance of silver-plate. "I think it may do—I think it might pass, if they winna bring it ower mickle in the light o' the window;" were ejaculations which he muttered from time to time as if to encourage himself in his undertaking, when he was interrupted by the voice of his master. "Take this," said the Master of Ravenswood, "and get what is necessary for the family." And with these words he gave to the old butler the purse which had on the preceding evening so narrowly escaped the fangs of Craigengelt. The old man shook his silvery and thin locks, and looked with an expression of the most heartfelt anguish at his master as he weighed in his hand the slender treasure, and said in a sorrowful voice, "And is this a' that's left?"

"All that is left at present," said the Master, affecting more cheer-fulness than perhaps he really felt, "is just the green purse and the wee pickle gowd, as the old song says; but we shall do better one day, Caleb."

"Before that day comes," said Caleb, "I doubt there will be an end of an auld sang, and an auld serving-man to boot. But it disna become me to speak that gate to your honour, and you looking sae pale. Tak back the purse, and keep it to be making a shew before company; for if your honour would just tak a bidding, and be whiles taking it out afore folk and putting it up again, there's naebody would refuse us trust, for a' that's come and gane yet."

"But, Caleb," said the Master, "I still intend to leave this country very soon, and desire to do so with the reputation of an honest man, leaving no debt behind me, at least of my own contracting."

"And gude right ye suld gang away as a true man, and so ye shall; for auld Caleb can tak the wyte of whatever is ta'en on for the house, and then it will be a' just ae man's burden; and I will live just as weel in the tolbooth as out of it, and the credit of the family will be a' safe and sound."

His master endeavoured, in vain, to make Caleb comprehend, that the butler's incurring the responsibility of debts in his own person would rather add to than remove the objections which he had to their being contracted. He spoke to a premier, too busy in devising ways and means to puzzle himself with refuting the arguments offered against their justice or expediency.

"There's Eppie Sma'trash will trust us for ale," said Caleb to him-self; "she has lived a' her life under the family—and maybe wi' a sowp brandy—I canna say for wine—she is but a lone woman, and gets her claret by a runlet at a time—but I'll work a wee drap out o' her by fair means or foul. For doos, there's the doo-cot—There will be poultry amang the tenants, though Luckie Chirnside says she has paid the kain twice ower—We'll mak shift, an it like your honour—we'll mak shift—Keep your heart aboon, for the house sall keep its credit, as lang as auld Caleb is to the fore."

The entertainment which Caleb's exertions of various kinds enabled him to present to the young gentlemen for three or four days was certainly of no splendid description, but it may readily be believed it was set before no critical guests; and even the distresses, excuses, evasions, and shifts of Caleb, afforded amusement to the young men, and added a sort of interest to the scrambling and irregular style of their table. They had indeed occasion to seize on every circumstance that might serve to diversify or enliven time, which otherwise past away so heavily.

Bucklaw, shut out from his usual field-sports and joyous carouses by the necessity of remaining concealed within the walls of the castle, became a joyless and uninteresting companion. When the Master of Ravenswood would no longer fence or play at shovel-board—when he himself had polished to the extremity the coat of his palfrey with brush, curry-comb, and hair-cloth—when he had seen him eat his provender, and quietly lie down in his stall, he could hardly help envying the animal's apparent acquiescence in a life so monotonous. "The stupid brute," he said, "thinks neither of the race-ground or the hunting-field, or his green paddock at Bucklaw, and enjoys himself as comfortably when haltered to the rack in this ruinous vault, as if he had been foaled in it; and I, who have the freedom of a prisoner at large, to range through the dungeons of this wretched old tower, can hardly, betwixt whistling and sleeping, contrive to pass away the hour to dinner-time."

And with this disconsolate reflection he wended his way to the bartizan or battlements of the tower, to watch what objects might appear upon the distant moor, or to pelt, with pebbles and pieces of lime, the sea-mews and cormorants which established themselves incautiously within the reach of an idle young man.

Ravenswood, with a mind incalculably deeper and more powerful than that of his companion, had his own anxious subjects of reflection, which wrought for him the same unhappiness that sheer ennui and want of occupation inflicted on his companion. The first sight of Lucy Ashton had been less impressive than her image proved to be upon reflection. As the depth and violence of that revengeful passion, by which he had been actuated in seeking an interview with the father, began to abate by degrees, he looked back on his conduct towards the daughter as harsh and unworthy towards a female of rank and beauty. Her looks of grateful acknowledgment—her words of affectionate courtesy, had been repelled with something which approached to disdain; and if the Master of Ravenswood had sustained wrongs at the hand of Sir William Ashton, his conscience told him they had been unhandsomely resented towards his daughter. When his thoughts took this turn of self-reproach, the recollection of Lucy Ashton's beautiful features, rendered yet more interesting by the circumstances in which their meeting had taken place, made an impression upon his mind at once soothing and painful. The sweetness of her voice, the delicacy of her expressions, the vivid glow of her filial affection, embittered his regret at having repulsed her gratitude with rudeness, while, at the same time, they placed before his imagination a picture of the most seducing sweetness.

Even young Ravenswood's strength of moral feeling and rectitude of purpose at once increased the danger of cherishing these recollections, and the propensity to entertain them. Firmly resolved as he was to subdue, if possible, the predominating vice in his character, he admitted with willingness—nay, he summoned up in his imagination, the ideas by which it could be most powerfully counteracted, and these were powerfully connected with the image of Lucy Ashton; and, on the other hand, a sense of his own harsh conduct towards her naturally induced him, as if by way of recompense, to invest her with more of grace and beauty than perhaps she could actually claim.

Had any one at this period told the Master of Ravenswood that he who had so lately vowed vengeance against the whole lineage of him whom he considered, not unjustly, as author of his father's ruin and death, was now opening his bosom to a passion for the daughter of that very person, he might at first have repelled the charge as a foul calumny; yet, upon serious self-examination, he would have been compelled to admit, that, if it were not already founded in truth it might, according to the present tone of his sentiments, very soon be so.

There already existed in his bosom two contradictory passions,—a desire to revenge the death of his father, strangely qualified by admiration of his enemy's daughter. Against the former feeling he had struggled, until it seemed to him upon the wane; against the latter he used no means of resistance, for he did not suspect its existence. That this was actually the case, was chiefly evinced by his resuming his resolution to leave Scotland. Yet, though he told Bucklaw, and though probably he himself believed that such was his purpose, he remained day after day at Wolfscrag, without taking measures for carrying it into execution. It is true, that he had written to one or two kinsmen, who resided in a distant quarter of Scotland, and particularly to the Marquis of A——, intimating his purpose; and when pressed upon the subject by Bucklaw, he was wont to allege the necessity of waiting for their reply, especially that of the Marquis, before taking so decisive a measure.

The Marquis was rich and powerful; and although he was suspected to entertain sentiments unfavourable to the government established at the Revolution, he had nevertheless address enough to head a party in the Scottish Privy Council, connected with the high church faction of England, and powerful enough to menace those to whom the Lord Keeper adhered, with a probable subversion of their power. The consulting with a personage of such importance was a plausible excuse, which Ravenswood used to Bucklaw, and probably to himself, for continuing his residence at Wolfscrag; and it was rendered yet more so by a general report which began to be current, of a probable change of ministers and measures in the Scottish administration. These rumours, strongly asserted by some, and as resolutely denied by others, as their wishes or interest dictated, found their way even into the ruinous tower of Wolfscrag, chiefly through the medium of Caleb the butler, who, among his other excellencies, was an ardent politician, and seldom made an excursion from the old fortress to the neighbouring village of Wolfshope, without bringing back what tidings were current in the vicinity.

But if Bucklaw could not offer any satisfactory objections to the delay of the Master in leaving Scotland, he did not the less suffer with impatience the state of inaction to which it confined him, and it was only the ascendance which his new companion had acquired over him, that induced him to submit to a course of life so alien to his habits and inclinations.

"You were wont to be thought a stirring active young fellow, Master," was his frequent remonstrance; "and yet here you seem determined to live on and on like a rat in a hole, with this trifling difference, that the wiser vermin chuses a hermitage where he can find food at least; but as for us, Caleb's excuses become longer as his diet turns more spare, and I fear we shall realize the stories they tell of the sloth,—we have almost eat up the last green leaf on the plant, and have nothing left for it but to drop from the tree and break our necks."

"Do not fear it," said Ravenswood; "there is a fate watches for us, and we too have a stake in the revolution which is now impending, and which already has alarmed many a bosom."

"What fate—what revolution?" answered his companion. "We have had one revolution too much already, I think."

Ravenswood interrupted him by putting into his hands a letter.

"O," answered Bucklaw, "my dream's out—I thought I heard Caleb this morning pressing some unfortunate fellow to a drink of cold water, and assuring him it was better for his stomach in the morning than ale or brandy."

"It was my Lord of A——'s footpost," said Ravenswood, "who was doomed to experience his ostentatious hospitality, which I believe ended in sour beer and herrings—Read, and you will see the news he has brought us."

"I will as fast as I can," said Bucklaw; "but I am no great clerk, nor does his lordship seem to be the first of scribes."

The reader will peruse, in a few seconds, by the aid of our friend Ballantyne's types, what took Bucklaw a good half hour in perusal, though assisted by the Master of Ravenswood. The tenor was as follows:—

"RIGHT HONOURABLE OUR COUSIN,

"Our hearty commendations premised, these come to assure you of the interest which we take in your welfare, and in your purposes towards its augmentation. If we have been less active in shewing forth our effective good will towards you than, as a loving kinsman and blood-relative, we would willingly have desired, we request that you will impute it to lack of opportunity to shew our good liking, not to any coldness of our will. Touching your resolution to travel in foreign parts, as at this time we hold the same little advisable, in respect that your ill-willers may, according to the custom of such persons, impute motives for your journey, whereof, although we know and believe you to be as clear as we ourselves, yet natheless their words may find credence in places where the belief in them may much prejudice you, and which we should see with more unwillingness and displeasure than with means of remeid.

"Having thus, as becometh our kindred, given you our poor mind on the subject of your journeying forth of Scotland, we would willingly add reasons of weight, which may materially advantage you and your father's house, thereby to determine you to abide at Wolfscrag, until this harvest season ensuing shall be passed over. But what sayeth the proverb, *verbum sapienti*,—a word is more to him that hath wisdom than a sermon to a fool. And albeit we have written this poor scroll with our own hand, and are well assured of the fidelity of our messenger, as him that is many ways bounden to us, yet so it is, that sliddery ways crave wary walking, and that we may not peril upon paper matters which we would gladly impart to you by word of mouth. Wherefore, it was our purpose to have prayed you heartily to come to this our barren Highland country to kill a stag, and to treat of the matters which we are now more painfully inditing to you anent. But commodity does not serve at present for such our meeting, which, therefore, shall be deferred until sic time as we may in all mirth rehearse those things whereof we now keep silence. Meantime, we pray you to think that we are, and will still be your good kinsman and well-wisher, waiting but for times of whilk we do, as it were, entertain a twilight prospect, and appear and hope to be also your effectual well-doer. And in which hope we heartily write ourself,

> "Right honourable,
> Your loving cousin,
> A——."

"Given from our poor
house of B——, &c."

Superscribed—"For the right honourable, and our honoured kinsman, the Master of Ravenswood—These—With haste, haste, posthaste—ride and run until these be delivered."

"What think you of this epistle, Bucklaw?" said the Master, when his companion had hammered out all the sense, and almost all the words of which it consisted.

"Truly that the Marquis's meaning is as great a riddle as his manuscript. He is really in much need of Wit's Interpreter, or the Complete Letter-Writer, and were I you, I would send him a copy by the bearer. He writes you very kindly to remain wasting your time and your money in this vile, stupid, oppressed country, without so much as offering you the countenance and shelter of his house. In my opinion, he has some scheme in view in which he supposes you can be useful, and he wishes to keep you at hand, to make use of you when it ripens, reserving the power of turning you adrift, should his plot fail in the concoction."

"His plot?—then you suppose it is a treasonable business," answered Ravenswood.

"What else can it be?" replied Bucklaw; "the Marquis has been long suspected to have an eye to Saint Germains."

"He should not engage me rashly in such an adventure," said Ravenswood; "when I recollect the times of the first and second Charles, and of the last James, truly, I see little reason, that, as a man or patriot, I should draw my sword for their descendants."

"Humph!" replied Bucklaw; "so you are set yourself down to mourn over the crop-eared dogs, whom honest Claverse treated as they deserved."

"They gave the dog an ill name, and then they hanged him," replied Ravenswood. "I hope to see the day when justice shall be open to Whig and Tory, and when these nick-names shall only be used among coffee-house politicians, as slut and jade are among applewomen, as cant terms of idle spite and rancour."

"That will not be in our days, Master—the iron has entered too deeply into our sides and our souls."

"It will be, however, one day," replied the Master; "men will not always start at these nick-names as at a trumpet-sound—as social life is better protected, its comforts will become too dear to be hazarded without some better reason than speculative politics."

"It is fine talking," answered Bucklaw; "but my heart is with the old song,—

> To see good corn upon the rigs,
> And a gallows built to hang the Whigs,
> And the right restored where the right should be,
> O that is the thing that would wanton me."

"You may sing as loudly as you will, *cantabit vacuus*,"—answered the Master; "but I believe the Marquis is too wise—at least too wary, to join you in such a burthen. I suspect he alludes to a revolution in the Scottish Privy-council, rather than in the British kingdoms."

"O, confusion to your state-tricks," exclaimed Bucklaw, "your cold calculating manœuvres, which old gentlemen in wrought night-caps and furred gowns execute like so many games at chess, and displace a treasurer or lord commissioner as they would take a rook or a pawn. Tennis for my sport, and battle for my earnest—my racket and my sword for my play-thing and my bread-winner. And you, Master, so deep and considerate as you would seem, you have that within you makes the blood boil faster than suits your present humour of moralizing on political truths. You are one of those wise men who see every thing with great composure till their blood is up, and then—woe to any one should put them in mind of their own prudential maxims."

"Perhaps," said Ravenswood, "you read me more rightly than I can myself. But to think justly will certainly go some length in helping me to act so. But hark! I hear Caleb tolling the dinner-bell."

"Which he always does with the more sonorous grace, in proportion to the meagreness of the cheer which he has provided," said Bucklaw, "as if that infernal clang and jangle, which will one day bring the old belfry down the cliff, could convert a starved hen into a fat capon, and a blade-bone of mutton into a haunch of venison."

"I wish we may be so well off as your worst conjectures surmize, Bucklaw, for from the extreme solemnity and ceremony with which Caleb seems to place on the table that solitary covered dish"——

"Uncover, Caleb! uncover, for Heaven's sake!" said Bucklaw; "let us have what you can give us without preface—why it stands well enough, man," he continued, addressing impatiently the ancient butler, who, without reply, kept shifting the dish, until he had at length placed it with mathematical precision in the very midst of the table.

"What have we got here, Caleb?" enquired the Master in his turn.

"Ahem! sir, ye suld have known before; but his honour the Laird of Bucklaw is so impatient," answered Caleb, still holding the dish with one hand, and the cover with the other, with evident reluctance to disclose the contents.

"But what is it, a God's name—not a pair of clean spurs, I hope, in the Border fashion of old times?"

"Ahem! ahem!" reiterated Caleb, "your honour is pleased to be facetious—natheless I might presume to say it was a convenient fashion, and used, as I have heard, in an honourable and thriving family. But touching your present dinner, I judged that this being Saint Magdalen's Eve, who was a worthy queen of Scotland in her day, your honours might judge it decorous, if not altogether to fast, yet only to sustain nature with some slight reflection, as ane saulted herring or the like." And uncovering the dish, he displayed four of the savoury fishes which he mentioned, adding, in a subdued tone, "that they were no just common herrings neither, being every ane melters, and sauted with uncommon care by the housekeeper (poor Mysie) for his honour's especial use."

"Out upon all apologies," said the Master, "let us eat the herrings since there is nothing better to be had—but I begin to think with you, Bucklaw, that we are consuming the last green leaf, and that, in spite of the Marquis's political machinations, we must positively shift camp for want of forage, without waiting the issue of them."

Chapter Nine

> Aye, and when huntsmen wind the merry horn,
> And from its covert starts the fearful prey,
> Who, warm'd with youth's blood in his swelling veins,
> Would like a lifeless clod outstretched lie,
> Shut out from all the fair creation offers?
> *Ethwald, Act I. Scene I*

LIGHT meals procure light slumbers; and therefore it is not surprising, that, considering the fare which Caleb's conscience, or his necessity, assuming, as will sometimes happen, that disguise, had assigned to the guests of Wolfscrag, their slumbers should have been short.

In the morning Bucklaw rushed into his host's apartment with a view hollo, which might have waked the dead.

"Up! up! in the name of Heaven—the hunters are out, the only piece of sport I have seen this month; and you lie here, Master, on a bed that has little to recommend it, except that it may be something softer than the stone floor of your ancestors' vault."

"I wish," said Ravenswood, raising his head peevishly, "you had forborne so early a jest, Mr Hayston—it is really no pleasure to lose the very short repose which I had just begun to enjoy, after a night spent in thoughts upon fortune far harder than my couch, Bucklaw."

"Pshaw! pshaw!" replied his guest, "get up—get up—the hounds are abroad—I have saddled our horses myself, for old Caleb was calling for grooms and lacqueys, and would never have proceeded without two hours' apology, for the absence of men that were a hundred miles off—get up, Master—I say the hounds are out—get up, I say—the hunt is up." And off ran Bucklaw.

"And I say," said the Master, rising slowly, "that nothing can concern me less—Whose hounds come so near us?"

"The Honourable Lord Bittlebrain's," answered Caleb, who had followed the impatient Laird of Bucklaw into his master's bed-room, "and truly I ken nae title they have to be yowling and howling within the freedoms and immunities of your lordship's right of free-forestry."

"Nor I, Caleb," replied Ravenswood, "excepting that they have bought both the lands and the right of forestry, and may think themselves entitled to exercise the rights they have paid their money for."

"It may be sae, my lord," replied Caleb; "but its no gentleman's deed of them to come here and exercise such a like right, and your lordship living at your ain castle of Wolfscrag. Lord Bittlebrain wad do weel to remember what his folks have been."

"And we what we now are," said the Master, with suppressed bitterness of feeling. "But reach me my cloak, Caleb, and I will indulge Bucklaw with a sight of this chase. It is selfish to sacrifice my guest's pleasure to my own."

"Sacrifeese?" echoed Caleb, in a tone which seemed to imply the total absurdity of his master making the least concession in deference to any one—"Sacrifeese indeed?—but I crave your honour's pardon—and whilk doublet is it your pleasure to wear?"

"Any one you will, Caleb—my wardrobe, I suppose, is not very extensive."

"Not extensive?" echoed his assistant; "when there is the grey and silver that your lordship bestowed on Hew Hildebrand, your out-rider —and the French velvet that went with my lord your father (Be gracious to him)—my lord your father's auld wardrope to the puir friends of the family, and the drap-de-berry"——

"Which I gave to you, Caleb, and which, I suppose, is the only dress we have any chance to come at, except that I wore yesterday—pray, hand me that, and say no more about it."

"If your honour has a fancy," replied Caleb, "and doubtless it's a sad-coloured suit, and you are in mourning—nevertheless I have never say'd on the drap-de-berry—ill wad it become me—and your honour having no change of claiths at this present—and it weel brushed, and as there are leddies doun yonder"——

"Ladies?" said Ravenswood; "and what ladies?"

"What do I ken, your lordship?—looking down at them from the Warden's Tower, I could but see them glent by wi' their bridles ringing, and their feathers fluttering, like the court of Elfland."

"Well, well, Caleb," replied the Master, "help me on with my cloak, and hand me my sword-belt.—What clatter is that in the court-yard?"

"Just Bucklaw bringing out the horses," said Caleb, after a glance through the window, "as if there werena men aneugh in the castle, or as if I couldna serve the turn of ony o' them that are out o' the gate."

"Alas! Caleb, we should want little, if your ability was equal to your will," replied his master.

"And I hope your lordship disna want that mickle," said Caleb; "for considering a' things, I trust we support the credit of the family sae weel as things will permit of. Only Bucklaw is aye sae frack and sae forward, and there he has brought out your lordship's palfrey, without the saddle being decored wi' the broidered sumpter-cloath, and I could have brushed it in a minute."

"It is all very well," said his master, escaping from him, and descending the narrow and steep winding stair-case, which led to the court-yard.

"It may be a' very weel," said Caleb, somewhat peevishly; "but if your lordship wad tarry a bit, I will tell you what will *not* be very weel."

"And what is that?" said Ravenswood impatiently, but stopping at the same time.

"Why, just that ye suld speer ony gentleman hame to denner; for I canna mak anither fast on the feast day, and sae, if your lordship wad but please to cast yoursell in the way of dining wi' Lord Bittlebrain, I'se warrand I wad cast about brawly for the morn; or if, stead o' that, ye wad but dine wi' them at the Change-house, ye might mak some shift for the lawing; ye might say ye had forgot your purse—or that the carline awed ye rent, and that ye wold allow it in the settlement."

"Or any other lie that came uppermost, I suppose," said his master. "Good bye, Caleb; I commend your care for the honour of the family." And, throwing himself on his horse, he followed Bucklaw, who, at the manifest risk of his neck, had begun to gallop down the steep path which led to the tower, as soon as he saw Ravenswood have his foot in the stirrup.

Caleb Balderstone looked anxiously after them, and shook his thin grey locks—"And I trust they will come to no evil—but they have reached the plain, and folks cannot say but that the horse are hearty and in spirits."

Animated by the natural impetuosity and fire of his temper, young Bucklaw rushed on with the careless speed of a whirlwind. Ravenswood was scarce more moderate in his pace, for his was a mind unwillingly roused from contemplative inactivity, but which, when once put into motion, acquired a spirit of forcible and violent progression. Neither was his eagerness proportioned in all cases to the motive of impulse, but might be compared to the speed of a stone, which rushes with like fury down the hill, whether it was first put in motion by the arm of a giant or the hand of a boy. He felt, therefore, in no ordinary degree, the headlong impulse of the chase, a pastime so natural to youth of all ranks, that it seems rather to be an inherent passion in our animal nature, which levels all differences of rank and education, than an acquired habit of rapid exercise.

The repeated blasts of the French horn, which were then always used for the encouragement and direction of the hounds—the deep, though distant baying of the pack—the half-heard cries of the huntsmen—the half-seen forms which were discovered now emerging from glens which crossed the moor, now sweeping over its surface, now picking their way where it was impeded by morasses, and, above all, the feeling of his own rapid motion, animated the Master of Ravenswood, at least for the moment, above the recollections of a more painful nature by which he was surrounded. The first thing which recalled him to those unpleasing circumstances was feeling that his horse, notwithstanding all the advantages which he received from his rider's knowledge of the country, was unable to keep up with the chace. As he drew his bridle up with the bitter feeling that his poverty excluded him from the favourite recreation of his forefathers, and indeed their sole employment when not engaged in military pursuits, he was accosted by a well-mounted stranger, who, unobserved, had kept near him during the earlier part of his career.

"Your horse is blown, sir," said the man, with a complaisance seldom used in a hunting-field; "Might I crave your honour to make use of mine?"

"Sir," said Ravenswood, more surprised than pleased at such a proposal, "I really do not know how I have merited such a favour at a stranger's hands."

"Never ask a question about it, Master," said Bucklaw, who, with great unwillingness, had hitherto reined in his own gallant steed, not to outride his host and entertainer. "Take the goods the gods provide you, as the great John Dryden says—or stay—here, my friend, lend me that horse; I see you have been puzzled to rein him up this half hour. I'll take the devil out of him for you.—Now, Master, do you ride mine, which will carry you like an eagle."

And throwing the rein of his own horse to the Master of Ravenswood, he sprung upon that which the stranger resigned to him, and continued his career at full speed.

"Was ever so thoughtless a being," said the Master; "and you, my friend, how could you trust him with your horse?"

"The horse," said the man, "belongs to a person who will make your honour, or any of your honourable friends, most welcome to him, flesh and fell."

"And the owner's name is ——?" asked Ravenswood.

"Your honour must excuse me, you will learn that from himself—if you please to take your friend's horse, and leave me your galloway, I will meet you after the fall of the stag, for I hear they are blowing him at bay."

"I believe, my friend, it will be the best way to recover your good horse for you," answered Ravenswood; and mounting the horse of his friend Bucklaw, he made all the haste in his power to the spot where the blast of the horn announced that the stag's career was nearly terminated.

These jovial sounds were intermixed with the huntsmen's shouts of "Hyke a Talbot! Hyke a Teviot! now, boys, now!" and similar cheering halloos of the olden hunting field, to which the impatient yelling of the hounds, now close on the object of their pursuit, gave a lively and unremitting chorus. The straggling riders began now to rally towards the scene of action, collecting from different points as to a common centre.

Bucklaw kept the start which he had gotten, and arrived first at the spot, where the stag, incapable of sustaining a more prolonged flight, had turned upon the hounds, and, in the hunter's phrase, was at bay. With his stately head bent down, his sides white with foam, his eyes strained betwixt rage and terror, the hunted animal had now in his turn become an object of intimidation to his pursuers. The hunters came up one by one, and watched an opportunity to assail him with some advantage, which, in such circumstances, can only be done with caution. The dogs stood aloof and bayed loudly, intimating at once eagerness and fear, and each of the sportsmen seemed to expect that his comrade would take upon him the perilous task of assaulting and disabling the animal. The ground, which was a hollow in the common or moor, afforded little advantage for approaching the stag unobserved, and general was the shout of triumph when Bucklaw, with the dexterity proper to an accomplished cavalier of the day, sprang from his horse, and dashing suddenly and swiftly at the stag, brought him to the ground by a cut on the hind leg, with his short hunting sword. The pack rushing in upon their disabled enemy, soon

ended his painful struggles, and solemnized his fall with their clamour
—the hunters with their horns and voices whooping and blowing a
mort, or death-note, which resounded far over the billows of the
adjacent ocean.

The huntsman then withdrew the hounds from the throttled stag,
and on his knee presented his knife to a fair female form, on a white
palfrey, whose terror, or perhaps her compassion, had till then kept
her at some distance. She wore a black silk riding mask, which was
then a common fashion, as well for preserving the complexion from
sun and rain, as from an idea of decorum, which did not permit
a lady to appear bare-faced while engaged in a boisterous sport, and
attended by a promiscuous company. The richness of her dress, however, as well as the mettle and form of her palfrey, together with the
sylvan compliment paid to her by the huntsman, pointed her out to
Bucklaw as the principal person in the field. It was not without a
feeling of pity, approaching even to contempt, that this enthusiastic
hunter observed her refuse the huntsman's knife, presented to her for
the purpose of making the first incision in the stag's breast, and
thereby discovering the quality of the venison. He felt more than half
inclined to pay his compliments to her; but it had been Bucklaw's
misfortune, that his habits of life had not rendered him familiarly
acquainted with the higher and better classes of female society, so
that, with all his natural audacity, he felt sheepishly bashful when it
became necessary to address a lady of distinction.

Taking unto himself heart of grace (to use his own phrase,) he did
at length summon up resolution enough to give the fair huntress good
time of the day, and trust that her sport had answered her expectation.
Her answer was very courteously and modestly expressed, and testified some gratitude to the gallant cavalier, whose exploit had terminated the chase so adroitly, when the hounds and huntsmen seemed
somewhat at a stand.

"Uds daggers and scabbard, madam," said Bucklaw, whom this
observation brought at once upon his own ground, "there is no difficulty or merit in that matter at all, so that a fellow is not too much
afraid of having a pair of antlers in his guts. I have hunted at force five
hundred times, madam; and I never yet saw the stag at bay, by land or
water, but I durst have gone roundly in on him. It is all use and wont,
madam; and I'll tell you, madam, for all that, it must be done with
good heed and caution; and you will do well, madam, to have your
hunting-sword both right sharp and double-edged, that you may
strike either fore-handed or back-handed, as you see reason, for a
hurt with a buck's horn is a perilous and somewhat venomous matter."

"I am afraid, sir," said the young lady, and her smile was scarce

concealed by her vizard, "I shall have little use for such careful preparation."

"But the gentleman says very right for all that, my lady," said an old
huntsman, who had listened to Bucklaw's harangue with no small
edification; "and I have heard my father say, who was a forester at the
Cabrach, that a wild-boar's gaunch is more easily healed than a hurt
from the deer's-horn, for so says the old woodsman rhyme,

> If thou be hurt with horn of hart, it brings thee to thy bier;
> But tusk of boar shall leeches heal—thereof have lesser fear."

"And if I might advise," continued Bucklaw, who was now in his
element, and desirous of assuming the whole management, "as the
hounds are surbated and weary, the head of the stag should be cab-
aged in order to reward them; and if I may presume to speak, the
huntsman, who is to break up the stag, ought to drink to your good
ladyship's health a good lusty bicker of ale, or a tass of brandy; for if he
breaks him up without drinking, the venison will not keep well."

This very agreeable prescription received, as will be readily
believed, all acceptation from the huntsman, who in requital offered
to Bucklaw the compliment of his knife, which the young lady had
declined. This polite proffer was seconded by his mistress.

"I believe, sir," said she, withdrawing herself from the circle, "that
my father, for whose amusement Lord Bittlebrain's hounds have been
out to-day, will readily surrender all care of these matters to a gentleman of your experience."

Then, bending gracefully from her horse, she wished him good
morning; and attended by one or two domestics, who seemed
immediately attached to her service, retired from the scene of action,
to which Bucklaw, too much delighted with an opportunity of displaying his wood-craft to care about man or woman either, paid little
attention; but was soon stript to his doublet, with tucked-up sleeves,
and naked arms up to the elbows in blood and grease, slashing, cutting, hacking, and hewing, with the precision of Sir Tristrem himself,
and wrangling and disputing with all around him concerning nombles,
briskets, flankards, and raven-bones, then usual terms of the art of
hunting, or of butchery, whichever the reader chuses to call it, which
are now probably antiquated.

When Ravenswood, who followed a short space behind his friend,
saw that the stag had fallen, his temporary ardour for the chace gave
way to that feeling of reluctance which he felt, at encountering in his
fallen fortunes the gaze whether of equals or inferiors. He reined up
his horse on the top of a gentle eminence, from which he observed the
busy and gay scene beneath him, and heard the whoops of the huntsmen gaily mingled with the cry of the dogs, and the neighing and

trampling of the horses. But these jovial sounds fell sadly on the ear of the ruined nobleman. The chace, with all its train of excitations, has ever since feudal times been accounted the almost exclusive privilege of the aristocracy, and was anciently their chief employment in times of peace. The sense that he was excluded by his situation from enjoying the sylvan sport, which his rank assigned to him as a special prerogative, and the feeling that new men were now exercising it over the downs, which had been jealously reserved by his ancestors for their own amusement, while he, the heir of the domain, was fain to hold himself at a distance from their party, awaked reflections calculated to press deeply a mind like Ravenswood's, which was naturally contemplative and melancholy. His pride, however, soon shook off this feeling of dejection, and it gave way to impatience upon finding that his volatile friend Bucklaw seemed in no hurry to return with his borrowed steed, which Ravenswood, before leaving the field, wished to see restored to the obliging owner. As he was about to move towards the groupe of assembled huntsmen, he was joined by a horseman, who like himself had kept aloof during the fall of the deer.

This personage seemed stricken in years. He wore a scarlet cloak, buttoning high upon his face, and his hat was unlooped and slouched, probably by way of defence against the weather. His horse, a strong and steady palfrey, was calculated for a rider who proposed to witness the sport of the day, rather than to share it. An attendant waited at some distance, and the whole equipment was that of an elderly gentleman of rank and fashion. He accosted Ravenswood very politely, but not without some embarrassment.

"You seem a gallant young gentleman, sir," he said, "and yet appear as indifferent to this brave sport as if you had my load of years on your shoulders."

"I have followed the sport with more spirit on other occasions," replied the Master; "at present late events in my family must be my apology—and besides," he added, "I was but indifferently mounted at the beginning of the sport."

"I think," said the stranger, "one of my attendants had the sense to accommodate your friend with a horse."

"I was much indebted to his politeness and yours," replied Ravenswood. "My friend is Mr Hayston of Bucklaw, whom I dare say you will be sure to find in the thick of the keenest sportsmen. He will return your servant's horse, and take my poney in exchange —and will add," he concluded, turning his horse's head from the stranger, "his best acknowledgments to mine for the accommodation."

The Master of Ravenswood having thus expressed himself, began to move homewards, with the manner of one who has taken leave of his company. But the stranger was not so to be shaken off. He turned his horse at the same time, and rode in the same direction so near to the Master, that, without out-riding him, which the formal civility of the time, and the respect due to the stranger's age and recent civility, would have rendered improper, he could not easily escape from his company.

The stranger did not long remain silent. "This then," he said, "is the ancient Castle of Wolfscrag, often mentioned in the Scottish records," looking to the old tower then darkening under the influence of a stormy cloud, that formed its background; for at the distance of a short mile, the chace having been circuitous had brought the hunters back nearly to the point which they had attained when Ravenswood and Bucklaw set forth to join them.

Ravenswood answered his observation with a cold and distant assent.

"It was, as I have heard," continued the stranger, unabashed by his coldness, "one of the most early possessions of the honourable family of Ravenswood?"

"Their earliest possession," answered the Master, "and probably their latest."

"I—I—I should hope not, sir," answered the stranger, clearing his voice with more than one cough, and making an effort to overcome a certain degree of hesitation,—"Scotland knows what she owes to this ancient family, and remembers their frequent and honourable achievements. I have little doubt, that, were it properly represented to her majesty that so ancient and noble a family were subjected to dilapidation—I mean to decay—means might be found, *ad re-ædifi- candam antiquam domum*"——

"I will save you the trouble, sir, of discussing this point farther," said the Master haughtily. "I am the heir of that unfortunate House— I am the Master of Ravenswood—and you, sir, who seem a gentleman of fashion and education, must be sensible, that the next mortification after being unhappy, is the being loaded with undesired commisera- tion."

"I beg your pardon, sir," said the elder horseman—"I did not know —I am sensible I ought not to have mentioned—nothing could be farther from my thoughts than to suppose"——

"There are no apologies necessary, sir," answered Ravenswood, "for here, I suppose, our roads separate, and I assure you that we part in perfect equanimity on my side."

As speaking these words, he directed his horse's head towards a narrow causeway, the ancient approach to Wolfscrag, of which it might be truly said, in the words of the Bard of Hope, that

> Frequented by few was the grass-cover'd road,
> Where the hunter of deer and the warrior trode,
>   To his hills that encircle the sea.

But ere he could disengage himself from his companion, the young lady we have already mentioned came up to join the stranger, followed by her servants.

"Daughter," said the stranger to the masked damsel, "this is the Master of Ravenswood."

It would have been natural that the gentleman should have replied to this introduction; but there was something in the graceful form and retiring modesty of the female to whom he was thus presented, which not only prevented him from enquiring to whom, and by whom, the annunciation had been made, but which even for the time struck him absolutely mute. At this moment the cloud which had long lowered above the height on which Wolfscrag is situated, and which now, as it advanced, spread itself in darker and denser folds both over land and sea, hiding the distant objects and obscuring those which were more near, turning the sea to a leaden complexion, and the heath to a darker brown, began now, by one or two distant peals, to announce the thunders with which it was fraught; while two flashes of lightning, following each other very closely, shewed in the distance the grey turrets of Wolfscrag, and, more nearly, the rolling billows of the sea, crested suddenly with red and dazzling light.

The horse of the fair huntress shewed symptoms of impatience and restiveness, and it became impossible for Ravenswood, as a man or a gentleman, to leave her abruptly to the care of an aged father or her menial attendants. He was, or believed himself, obliged in courtesy to take hold of her bridle, and assist her in managing the unruly animal. While he was thus engaged, the old gentleman observed that the storm seemed to increase—that they were far from Lord Bittlebrain's, whose guests they were for the present—and that he would be obliged to the Master of Ravenswood to point him the way to the nearest place of refuge from the storm. At the same time he cast a wistful and embarrassed look towards the Tower of Wolfscrag, which seemed to render it almost impossible for the owner to avoid offering an old man and a lady, in such an emergency, the temporary use of his house. Indeed, the condition of the young huntress rendered this courtesy indispensable; for, in the course of the services which he rendered, he could not but perceive that she trembled much, and was extremely agitated, from her apprehensions, doubtless, of the coming storm.

I know not if the Master of Ravenswood shared her terrors, but he was not entirely free from something like a similar disorder of nerves, as he observed, "The Tower of Wolfscrag has nothing to offer beyond the shelter of its roof, but if that can be acceptable at such a moment" —he paused, as if the rest of the invitation stuck in his throat. But the old gentleman, his self-constituted companion, did not allow him to recede from the invitation, which he had rather suffered to be implied than directly expressed.

"The storm," said the stranger, "must be an apology for waiving ceremony—his daughter's health was weak—she had suffered much from a recent alarm—he trusted their intrusion on the Master of Ravenswood's hospitality would not be altogether unpardonable in the circumstances of the case—his child's safety must be dearer to him than ceremony."

There was no room to retreat. The Master of Ravenswood led the way, continuing to keep hold of the lady's bridle to prevent her horse from starting at some unexpected explosion of thunder. He was not so bewildered in his own hurried reflections, but what he remarked, that the deadly paleness which had occupied her neck and temples, and such of her features as the riding-mask left exposed, gave place to a deep and rosy suffusion; and he felt with embarrassment that a flush was by a tacit sympathy excited in his own cheeks. The stranger, with a watchfulness which he disguised under apprehensions for the safety of his daughter, continued to observe the expression of the Master's countenance as they ascended the hill to Wolfscrag. When they stood in front of that ancient fortress, Ravenswood's emotions were of a very complicated description; and as he led the way into the rude court-yard, and halloo'd to Caleb to give attendance, there was a tone of sternness, almost of fierceness, which seemed somewhat alien from the courtesies of one who is receiving honoured guests.

Caleb came and saw—and not the paleness of the fair stranger at the first approach of the thunder, nor the paleness of any other person, in any other circumstances whatsoever, equalled that which overcame the thin cheeks of the disconsolate seneschal, when he beheld this accession of guests to the castle, and reflected that the dinner hour was fast approaching. "Is he daft?" he muttered to himself,—"is he clean daft a'thegither, to bring lords and leddies, and a host of folk behint them, and twal-o'-clock chappit?" Then approaching the Master, he craved pardon for having permitted the rest of his people to go out to see the hunt, observing, that "they wad never think of his lordship coming back till mirk night, and that he dreaded they might play the truant."

"Silence, Balderstone!" said Ravenswood sternly; "your folly is unseasonable.—Sir and madam," he said, turning to his guests, "this old man, and a yet older and more imbecile female domestic, furnish my whole retinue. Our means of refreshing you are more scanty than even so miserable a retinue, and a dwelling so dilapidated, might seem to promise; but, such as it is, you may command it."

The elder stranger, struck with the ruined and even savage appearance of the tower, rendered still more disconsolate by the lowering and gloomy sky, and perhaps not altogether unmoved by the grave and determined voice in which their host addressed them, looked round him anxiously, as if he half repented the readiness with which he had accepted the offered hospitality. But there was now no opportunity of receding from the situation in which he had placed himself.

As for Caleb, he was so utterly stunned by his master's public and unqualified acknowledgment of the nakedness of the land, that for two minutes he could only mutter within his hebdomadal beard, which had not felt the razor for six days, "He's daft—clean daft—red wud, and awa' wi't! But de'il hae Caleb Balderstone," said he, collecting his powers of invention and resource, "if the family shall lose credit, if he were as mad as the seven wise masters." He then boldly advanced, and in spite of his master's frowns and impatience, gravely asked, "if he should not serve up some slight refection for the young leddy, and a glass of tokay, or old sack—or"——

"Truce to this ill-timed foolery," said the Master, sternly—"put the horses into the stable, and interrupt us no more with your absurdities."

"Your honour's pleasure is to be obeyed aboon a' thing," said Caleb; "nevertheless, as for the sack and tokay which it is not your noble guests' pleasure to accept"——

But here the voice of Bucklaw, heard even above the clattering of hoofs and braying of horns with which it intermingled, announced that he was scaling the path-way to the tower at the head of the greater part of the gallant hunting train.

"The de'il be in me," said Caleb, taking heart in spite of this new invasion of Philistines, "if they shall beat me yet. The hellicat ne'er-do-weel!—to bring such a crew here, that will expect to find brandy as plenty as ditch-water, and he kenning sae absolutely the case in whilk we stand for the present. But I trow, could I get rid of these gaping gowks of flunkies that hae won into the court-yard at the back of their betters, as mony a man gets preferment, I could make a' right yet."

The measures which he took to execute this dauntless resolution, the reader shall learn in the next chapter.

Chapter Ten

With throat unslaked, with black lips baked,
    Agape they heard him call;
Gramercy they for joy did grin,
And all at once their breath drew in
    As they had been drinking all.
                COLERIDGE'S "Rime of the
                        Ancient Mariner"

HAYSTON of Bucklaw was one of the thoughtless class who never hesitate between their friend and their jest. When it was announced that the principal persons of the chace had taken their route towards Wolfscrag, the huntsmen, as a point of civility, offered to transfer the venison to that mansion, a proffer which was readily accepted by Bucklaw, who thought much of the astonishment which their arrival in full body would occasion poor old Caleb Balderstone, and very little of the dilemma to which he was about to expose his friend the Master, so ill circumstanced to receive such a party. But in old Caleb he had to do with a crafty and alert antagonist, prompt at supplying, upon all emergencies, evasions and excuses suitable, as he thought, to the dignity of the family.

"Praise be blessed!" said Caleb to himself, "ae leaf of the muckle yate has been swung to wi' yestreen's wind, and I think I can manage to shut the ither."

But he was desirous, like a prudent governor, at the same time to get rid, if possible, of the internal enemy, in which light he considered almost every thing which eat and drank, ere he took measures to exclude those whom their jocund noise now pronounced to be near-hand. He waited, therefore, with impatience until his master had shewn his two principal guests into the tower, and then commenced his operations.

"I think," said he to the stranger menials, "that, as they are bringing the stag's head to the castle in all honour, we, who are in-dwellers, should receive them at the gate."

The unwary grooms had no sooner hurried out, in compliance with this insidious hint, than one leaf of the ancient gate being already closed by the wind, as has been already intimated, honest Caleb lost no time in shutting the other with a clang, which resounded from donjon-vault to battlement. Having thus secured the pass, he forthwith indulged the excluded huntsmen in brief parley, from a small projecting window, or shot-hole, through which, in former days, the warders were wont to reconnoitre those who presented themselves before the gates. He gave them to understand, in a short and pithy speech, that the gate of the Castle was never on any account opened during meal-times—that his honour, the Master of Ravenswood, and some guests of quality, had just set down to dinner—that there was excellent brandy at the hostler-wife's at Wolfshope down below—and he held out some obscure hope that the reckoning would be discharged by the Master; but this was uttered in a very dubious and oracular strain, for, like Louis XIV., Caleb Balderstone hesitated to carry finesse so far as direct falsehood, and was content to deceive, if possible, without directly lying.

This annunciation was received with surprise by some, with laughter by others, and with dismay by the expelled lacqueys, who endeavoured to demonstrate that their right of re-admission, for the purpose of waiting upon their master and mistress, was at least indisputable. But Caleb was not in a humour to understand or admit any distinctions. He stuck to his original proposition with that dogged, but convenient pertinacity, which is armed against all conviction and deaf to all reasoning. Bucklaw now came from the rear of the party, and demanded admittance in a very angry tone. But the resolution of Caleb was immovable.

"If the king on the throne were at the yate," he declared, "that his ten fingers should never open it contrair to the established use and wont of the family of Ravenswood, and his duty as their head-servant."

Bucklaw was now extremely incensed, and with more oaths and curses than we care to repeat, declared himself most unworthily treated, and demanded peremptorily to speak with the Master of Ravenswood himself. But to this Caleb also turned a deaf ear.

"He's as soon a-bleeze as a tap of tow the lad Bucklaw," he said, "but the de'il of ony master's face he shall see till he has sleep'd and waked on't. He'll ken himsel better the morn's morn. It sets the like of him, to be bringing a crew of drunken hunters here, when he kens there is but little preparation to sloken his ain drought." And he disappeared from the window, leaving them all to digest their exclusion as they best might.

But another person, of whose presence, Caleb, in the animation of debate, was not aware, had listened in silence to its progress. This was the principal domestic of the stranger—a man of trust and consequence—the same, who, on the hunting-field, had accommodated Bucklaw with the use of his horse. He was in the stable when Caleb had contrived the expulsion of his fellow-servants, and thus avoided sharing the same fate from which his personal importance would certainly not have otherwise saved him.

This personage perceived the manœuvre of Caleb, easily appreciated the motive of his conduct, and knowing his master's intentions
towards the family of Ravenswood, had no difficulty as to the line of
conduct he ought to adopt. He took the place of Caleb (unperceived
by the latter,) at the post of audience which he had just left, and
announced to the assembled domestics, "that it was his master's
pleasure that Lord Bittlebrain's retinue and his own should go down
to the adjacent change-house, and call for what refreshments they
might have occasion for, and he should take care to discharge the
lawing."

The jolly troop of huntsmen retired from the inhospitable gate of
Wolfscrag, execrating, as they descended the steep path-way, the
niggard and unworthy disposition of the proprietor, and damning,
with more than sylvan licence, both the castle and its inhabitants.
Bucklaw, with many qualities which would have made him a man of
worth and judgment in more favourable circumstances, had been so
utterly neglected in point of education, that he was apt to think and
feel according to the ideas of the companions of his pleasures. The
praises which had recently been heaped upon himself he contrasted
with the general abuse now levelled against Ravenswood—he recalled
to his mind the dull and monotonous days he had spent in the tower of
Wolfscrag, compared with the joviality of his usual life—he felt, with
great indignation, his exclusion from the castle, which he considered
as a gross affront, and every mingled feeling led him to break off the
union which he had formed with the Master of Ravenswood.

On arriving at the Change-house of the village of Wolfshope, he
unexpectedly met with an old acquaintance just alighting from his
horse. This was no other than the very respectable Captain Craigengelt, who immediately came up to him, and, without appearing to
retain any recollection of the indifferent terms on which they had
parted, shook him by the hand in the warmest manner possible. A
warm grasp of the hand was what Bucklaw could never help returning
with cordiality, and no sooner had Craigengelt felt the pressure of his
fingers than he knew the terms on which he stood with him.

"Long life to you, Bucklaw," he exclaimed; "there's life for *honest*
folks in this bad world yet!"

The jacobites at this period, with what propriety I know not, used, it
must be noticed, the term of *honest men* as peculiarly descriptive of
their own party.

"Ay, and for others besides, it seems," answered Bucklaw;
"otherways how came you to venture hither, noble Captain?"

"Who—I?—I am as free as the wind at Martinmas, that pays neither land-rent nor annual; all is explained—all settled with the honest

old drivellers yonder of Auld Reekie—pooh! pooh! they dared not keep me a week of days in durance. A certain person has better friends among them than you wot of, and can serve a friend when it is least likely."

"Pshaw!" answered Hayston, who perfectly knew and thoroughly despised the character of this man, "none of your cogging gibberish— tell me truly, are you at liberty and in safety?"

"Free and safe as a whig baillie on the causeway of his own burgh, or a canting presbyterian minister in his own pulpit—and I came to tell you that you need not remain in hiding any longer."

"Then I suppose you call yourself my friend, Captain Craigengelt?" said Bucklaw.

"Friend!" replied Craigengelt, "my cock of the pit? why, I am thy very Achates, man, as I have heard scholars say—hand and glove— bark and tree—thine to life and death."

"I'll try that in a moment," said Bucklaw. "Thou art never without money, however thou comest by it.—Lend me two pieces to wash the dust out of these honest fellows' throats, in the first place, and then"——

"Two pieces?—twenty are at thy service, my lad—and twenty to back them."

"Aye—say you so?" said Bucklaw, pausing, for his natural penetration led him to suspect some extraordinary motives lay couched under such an excess of generosity. "Craigengelt, you are either an honest fellow in right good earnest, and I scarce know how to believe that—or you are cleverer than I took you for, and I scarce know how to believe that neither."

"*L'un n'empêche pas l'autre*," said Craigengelt, "touch and try—the gold is good as ever was weighed."

He put a quantity of gold pieces into Bucklaw's hand, which he thrust into his pocket without either counting or looking at them, only observing he was so circumstanced that he must enlist, though the devil offered the press-money; and then turning to the huntsmen, he called out, "Come along, my lads—all is at my cost."

"Long life to Bucklaw!" shouted the men of the chase.

"And d——n to him that takes his share of the sport, and leaves the hunters as dry as a drum-head," added another, by way of corollary.

"The house of Ravenswood was ance a gude and an honourable house in this land," said an old man, "but it's lost its credit this day, and the Master has shewn himself no better than a greedy cullion."

And with this conclusion, which was unanimously agreed to by all who heard it, they rushed tumultuously into the house of entertainment, where they revelled till a late hour. The jovial temper of Bucklaw seldom permitted him to be nice in the choice of his associates; and on the present occasion, when his joyous debauch received additional zest from the intervention of an unusual space of sobriety, and almost abstinence, he was as happy in leading the revels, as if his comrades had been sons of princes. Craigengelt had his own purposes, in fooling him up to the top of his bent; and having some low humour, much impudence, and the power of singing a good song, understanding besides thoroughly the disposition of his regained associate, he readily succeeded in involving him bumper-deep in the festivity of the meeting.

A very different scene was in the meantime passing in the tower of Wolfscrag. When the Master of Ravenswood left the court-yard, too much busied with his own perplexed reflections to pay attention to the manœuvres of Caleb, he ushered his guests into the great hall of the castle.

The indefatigable Balderstone, who, from choice or habit, worked on from morning to night, had, by degrees, cleared this desolate apartment of the confused reliques of the funeral banquet, and restored it to some order. But not all his skill and labour, in disposing to advantage the little furniture which remained, could remove the dark and disconsolate appearance of those ancient and disgarnished walls. The narrow windows, flanked by deep indentures into the wall, seemed formed rather to exclude than to admit the cheerful light; and the heavy and gloomy appearance of the thunder-sky added still further to the obscurity.

As Ravenswood, with the grace of a gallant of that period, but not without a certain stiffness and embarrassment of manner, handed the young lady to the upper end of the apartment, her father remained standing more near to the door, as if about to disengage himself from his hat and cloak. At this moment the clang of the portal was heard, a sound at which the stranger started, stepped hastily to the window, and looked with an air of alarm at Ravenswood, when he saw that the gate of the court was shut, and his domestics excluded.

"You have nothing to fear, sir," said Ravenswood, gravely; "this roof retains the means of giving protection, though not welcome. Methinks," he added, "it is time that I should know who they are that have thus highly honoured my ruined dwelling?"

The young lady remained silent and motionless, and the father, to whom the question was more directly addressed, seemed in the situation of a performer who has ventured to take upon himself a part which he finds himself unable to perform, and who comes to a pause when it is most to be expected that he should speak. While he endeavoured to cover his embarrassment with exterior ceremonials of a well-bred demeanour, it was obvious, that in making his bow, one foot shuffled forward, as if to advance—the other backward, as with the purpose of escape—and as he undid the cape of his cloak, and raised his beaver from his face, his fingers fumbled as if the one had been linked with rusted iron, or the other had weighed a stone of lead. The darkness of the sky seemed to increase, as if to supply the want of those mufflings which he laid aside with such evident reluctance. The impatience of Ravenswood increased also in proportion to the delay of the stranger, and he appeared to labour under agitation, though probably from a very different cause. He laboured to restrain his desire to speak, while the stranger, to all appearance, was at a loss for words to express what he felt it necessary to say. At length Ravenswood's impatience broke the bounds he had imposed upon it.

"I perceive," he said, "that Sir William Ashton is unwilling to announce himself in the Castle of Wolfscrag."

"I had hoped it was unnecessary," said the Lord Keeper, relieved from his silence, as a spectre by the voice of the exorcizer; "and I am obliged to you, Master of Ravenswood, for breaking the ice at once, where circumstances—unhappy circumstances let me call them—rendered self-introduction peculiarly awkward."

"And I am not then," said the Master of Ravenswood, gravely, "to consider the honour of this visit as purely accidental."

"Let us distinguish a little," said the Keeper, assuming an appearance of ease which perhaps his heart was a stranger to; "this is an honour which I have eagerly desired for some time, but which I might never have obtained, save for the accident of the storm. My daughter and I are alike grateful for this opportunity of thanking the brave man, to whom she owes her life and I mine."

The hatred which divided the great families in the feudal times had lost little of its bitterness, though it no longer expressed itself in deeds of open violence. Not the feelings which Ravenswood had begun to entertain towards Lucy Ashton, not the hospitality due to his guests, were able entirely to subdue, though they warmly combatted, the deep passion which arose within him, at beholding his father's foe standing in the hall of the family of which he had in a great measure accelerated the ruin. His looks glanced from the father to the daughter with an irresolution, of which Sir William Ashton did not think it proper to await the conclusion. He had now disembarrassed himself of his riding-dress, and walking up to his daughter, he undid the fastening of her mask.

"Lucy, my love," he said, raising her, and leading her towards Ravenswood, "lay aside your mask, and let us express our gratitude to the Master openly and barefaced."

"If he will condescend to accept it," was all that Lucy uttered, but in a tone so sweetly modulated, and which seemed to imply at once a feeling and a forgiving of the cold reception to which they were exposed, that, coming from a creature so innocent and so beautiful, her words cut Ravenswood to the very heart for his harshness. He muttered something of surprise, something of confusion, and, ending with a warm and eager expression of his happiness at being able to afford her shelter under his roof, he saluted her, as the ceremonial of the time enjoined upon such occasions. Their cheeks had touched and were withdrawn from each other—Ravenswood had not quitted the hand which he had taken in kindly courtesy—a blush which attached more consequence by far than was usual to such ceremony still mantled on Lucy Ashton's beautiful cheek, when the apartment was suddenly illuminated by a flash of lightning, which seemed absolutely to swallow the darkness of the hall. Every object might have been for an instant seen distinctly. The slight and half-sinking form of Lucy Ashton, the well-proportioned and stately figure of Ravenswood, his dark features, and the fiery, yet irresolute expression of his eye,—the old arms and scutcheons which hung on the walls of the apartment, were for a second distinctly visible to the Keeper by a strong red brilliant glare of light. Its disappearance was almost instantly followed by a burst of thunder, for the storm-cloud was very near the castle; and the peal was so sudden and dreadful, that the old tower rocked to its foundation, and every inmate concluded it was falling upon them. Soot, which had not been disturbed for centuries, showered down the huge tunnelled chimneys—lime and dust flew in clouds from the wall; and whether the lightning had actually struck the castle, or whether through the violent concussion of the air, several heavy stones were hurled from the mouldering battlements into the roaring sea beneath. It seemed as if the ancient founder of the castle was bestriding the thunder-storm, and proclaiming his displeasure at the reconciliation of his descendant with the enemy of his house.

The consternation was general, and it required the efforts of both the Lord Keeper and Ravenswood to keep Lucy from fainting. Thus was the Master a second time engaged in the most delicate and dangerous of all tasks, that of affording support and assistance to a beautiful and helpless being, whose idea, as seen before in a similar situation, had already become a favourite to his imagination, both when awake and when slumbering. If the Genius of the House really condemned a union betwixt the Master and his fair guest, the means by which he expressed his sentiments were as unhappily chosen as if he had been a mere mortal. The train of little attentions, absolutely necessary to sooth the young lady's mind, and aid her in composing her spirits, necessarily threw the Master of Ravenswood into such an intercourse with her father, as was calculated, for the moment at least, to break down the barrier of feudal enmity which divided them. To express himself churlishly, or even coldly, towards an old man, whose daughter (and *such* a daughter) lay before them, overpowered with natural terror—and all this under his own roof—the thing was impossible; and by the time that Lucy, extending a hand to each, was able to thank them for their kindness, the Master felt that his sentiments of hostility towards the Lord Keeper were by no means predominant in his bosom.

The weather, her state of health, the absence of her attendants, all prevented the possibility of Lucy Ashton renewing her journey to Bittlebrain-House, which was full five miles distant; and the Master of Ravenswood could not but, in common courtesy, offer the shelter of his roof for the rest of the day and for the night. But a flash of less soft expression, a look much more habitual to his features, resumed predominance when he mentioned how meanly he was provided for the entertainment of his guests.

"Do not mention deficiencies," said the Lord Keeper, eager to interrupt him and prevent his resuming an alarming topic; "you are designed for the continent, and your house is probably for the present displenished. All this we understand; but if you mention inconvenience, you will oblige us to seek accommodations in the hamlet."

As the Master of Ravenswood was about to reply, the door of the hall opened, and Caleb Balderstone rushed in.

Chapter Eleven

> Let them have meat enough, woman—half a hen;
> There be old rotten pilchards—put them off too;
> 'Tis but a little new anointing of them,
> And a strong onion, that confounds the savour.
> *Love's Pilgrimage*

THE THUNDER-BOLT, which had stunned all who were within hearing of it, had only served to awaken the bold and inventive genius of the flower of Majors-Domo. Almost before the clatter had ceased, and while there was yet scarce an assurance whether the castle was standing or falling, Caleb exclaimed, "Heaven be praised!—this comes to hand like the boul of a pint-stoup." He then barred the kitchen-door in the face of the Lord Keeper's servant, whom he perceived returning from the parley at the gate, and muttering, "how the de'il came he in?—but de'il may care—Mysie, what are sitting shaking and greeting in the chimlay-nuik for? Come here—or stay where ye are, and skirl—it's a' ye'se guid for—I say, ye auld deevil, skirl—skirl as loud as ye can—louder—louder woman!—gar the gentles hear ye in the ha'—I have heard ye as far off as the Bass for a less matter. And stay—doun wi' that crockery——"

And with a sweeping blow, he threw down from a shelf some articles of pewter and earthen ware. He exalted his voice amid the clatter, shouting and roaring in a manner which changed Mysie's hysterical apprehensions of the thunder into fears that her old fellow-servant was gone distracted. "He has dung down a' the bits o' pigs too—the only thing we had left to haud a soup milk—and he has spilt the hatted kitt that was for the Master's dinner. Mercy save us, the auld man's ga'en wud wi' the thunner!"

"Haud your tongue, ye b——," said Caleb, in the impetuous and overbearing triumph of successful invention, "a's provided now—denner and a' thing—the thunner's done it a' in the clap of a hand!"

"Puir man! he's muckle astray," said Mysie, looking at him with a mixture of pity and alarm; "I wish he may ever come hame to himsell again."

"Here, ye auld doited deevil," said Caleb, still exulting in his extrication from a dilemma which seemed insurmountable; "keep the strange man out of the kitchen—swear the thunner come down the chimlay, and spoiled the best dinner ye ever dressed—Beef—bacon —kid—lark—leveret—wild-fowl—venison, and what not. Lay it on thick, and never mind expences. I'll awa' up to the ha'—make a' the confusion ye can—but be sure ye keep out the strange servant."

With these charges to his ally, Caleb posted up to the hall, but stopping to reconnoitre through an aperture, which time, for the convenience of many a domestic in succession, had made in the door, and perceiving the situation of Miss Ashton, he had prudence enough to make a pause, both to avoid adding to her alarm, and in order to secure attention to his account of the disastrous effects of the thunder.

But when he perceived that the lady was recovered, and heard the conversation turn upon the accommodation and refreshment which the castle afforded, he thought it time to burst into the room in the manner announced in the last chapter.

"Wull a wins!—wull a wins!—such a misfortune to befa' the House of Ravenswood, and I to live to see it!"

"What is the matter, Caleb?" said his master, somewhat alarmed in his turn; "has any part of the castle fallen?"

"Castle fa'an?—na, but the sute's fa'an, and the thunner's come right doun the kitchen-lumm, and the things are a' lying here awa', there awa', like the Laird o' Hotchpotch's lands—and wi' brave guests of honour and quality to entertain,"—a low bow here to Sir William Ashton and his daughter,—"and naething left in the house fit to present for dinner—or for supper either, for aught that I can see."

"I verily believe you, Caleb," said Ravenswood drily.

Balderstone here turned to his master a half-upbraiding, half imploring countenance, and edged towards him as he repeated, "It was nae grit matter of preparation; but just something added to your honour's ordinary course of fare—*petty cover*, as they say at the Louver—three courses and the fruit."

"Keep your intolerable nonsense to yourself, you old fool," said Ravenswood, mortified at his officiousness, yet not knowing how to contradict him, without the risk of giving rise to scenes yet more ridiculous.

Caleb saw his advantage, and resolved to improve it. But first, observing that the Lord Keeper's servant entered the apartment, and spoke apart with his master, he took the same opportunity to round a few words into Ravenswood's ear—"Haud your tongue for Heaven's sake, sir—if it's my pleasure to hazard my soul in telling lies for the honour of the family, it's nae business of yours—and if ye let me gang on quietly, I'se be moderate in my banquet; but if ye contradict me, de'il but I dress ye a dinner for a duke."

Ravenswood, in fact, thought it would be best to let his officious butler run on, who proceeded to enumerate upon his fingers,—"No muckle provision—might hae served four persons of honour,—first course, capons in white broth—roast kid—bacon with reverence—second course, roasted leverit—butter crabs—a veal florentine—third course, black-cock—it's black eneugh now wi' the sute—plumdamas—a tart—a flam—and some nonsense sweet things, and comfits—And that's a," he said, seeing the impatience of his master; "that's just a' was o't—forbye the apples and pears."

Miss Ashton had by degrees gathered her spirits, so far as to pay some attention to what was going on; and observing the restrained impatience of Ravenswood, contrasted with the peculiar determination of manner with which Caleb detailed his imaginary banquet, the whole struck her as so ridiculous, that, despite every effort to the contrary, she burst into a fit of incontrolable laughter, in which she was joined by her father, though with more moderation, and finally by the Master of Ravenswood himself, though conscious that the jest was at his own expence. Their mirth—for a scene which we read with little emotion often appears extremely ludicrous to the spectators—made the old vault ring again. They ceased—they renewed—they ceased—they renewed again their shouts of laughter! Caleb in the meantime stood his ground with a grave, angry, and scornful dignity, which greatly enhanced the ridicule of the scene, and the mirth of the spectators.

At length, when the noise, and nearly the strength of the laughers, was exhausted, he exclaimed, with very little ceremony, "The de'il's in the gentles! they breakfast sae lordly, that the loss of the best dinner ever cook pat fingers to, makes them as merry as if it were the best jeest in a' George Buchanan. If there was as little in your honours' wames, as there is in Caleb Balderstane's, less cackling wad serve ye on sic a gravaminous subject."

Caleb's blunt expression of resentment again awakened the mirth of the company, which, by the way, he regarded not only as an aggression upon the dignity of the family, but a special contempt of the eloquence with which he himself had summed up the extent of their supposed losses;—"a description of a dinner," as he said afterwards to Mysie, "that wad hae made a fu' man hungry, and them to sit there laughing at it."

"But," said Miss Ashton, composing her countenance as well as she could, "are all these delicacies so totally destroyed, that no scrap can be collected?"

"Collected, my leddy! what wad ye collect out of the sute and the ass? Ye may gang doun yoursell, and look into our kitchen—the cookmaid in the trembling exies—the gude vivers lying a' about—beef —capons, and white broth—florentine and flams—bacon wi' reverence, and a' the sweet confections and whim-whams; ye'll see them a', my leddy—that is," he said correcting himself, "ye'll no see ony of them now, for the cook has sweepit them up, as was weel her part; but ye'll see the white broth where it was spilt—I pat my finger in it, and it tastes as like sour-milk as ony thing else; if that isna the effect of thunner, I kenna what is.—This gentleman here couldna but hear the clash of our haill dishes, china and silver thegither."

The Lord Keeper's domestic, though a statesman's attendant, and of course trained to command his countenance upon all occasions, was somewhat discomposed by this appeal, to which he only answered by a bow.

"I think, Mr Butler," said the Lord Keeper, who began to be afraid lest the prolongation of this scene should anew displease Ravenswood,—"I think, that were you to retire with my servant Lockhard— he has travelled, and is quite accustomed to accidents and contingencies of every kind, and I hope betwixt you, you may find out some mode of supply at this emergency."

"His honour kens," said Caleb, who, however hopeless of himself of accomplishing what was desirable, would, like the high-spirited elephant, rather have died in the effort, than brooked the aid of a brother in commission; "his honour kens weel I need nae counsellor, where the honour of the house is concerned."

"I should be unjust if I denied it, Caleb," said his master; "but your art lies chiefly in making apologies, upon which we can no more dine, than upon the bill of fare of our thunder-blasted dinner. Now, possibly, Mr Lockhard's talent may consist in finding some substitute for that, which certainly is not, and has in all probability never been."

"Your honour is pleased to be facetious," said Caleb, "but I am sure, that at the warst, for a walk as far as Wolfshope, I could dine forty men,—no that the folk there deserve your honour's custom. They hae been ill advised in the matter of the duty-eggs and butter, I winna deny that."

"So go consult together," said the Master, "go down to the village, and do the best we can. We must not let our guests remain without refreshment, to save the honour of a ruined family. And here, Caleb—take my purse; I believe that will prove your best ally."

"Purse? purse, indeed?" quoth Caleb, indignantly flinging out of the room,—"what suld I do wi' your honour's purse, on your ain grund? I trust we are no to pay for our ain?"

The servants left the hall; and the door was no sooner shut, than the Lord Keeper began to apologize for the rudeness of his mirth; and Lucy to hope she had given no pain or offence to the kind-hearted faithful old man.

"Caleb and I must both learn, madam, to undergo with good humour, or at least with patience, the ridicule which every where attaches itself to poverty."

"You do yourself injustice, Master of Ravenswood, on my word of honour," answered his elder guest. "I believe I know more of your affairs than you do yourself, and I hope to shew that I am interested in them; and that—in short, that your prospects are better than you apprehend. In the meantime, I can conceive nothing so respectable, as the spirit which rises above misfortune, and prefers honourable privations to debt or to dependence."

Whether from fear of offending the delicacy, or awakening the pride of the Master, the Lord Keeper made these allusions with an appearance of fearful and hesitating reserve, and seemed to be afraid that he was intruding too far, in venturing to touch, however lightly, upon such a topic, even when the Master had led to it. In short, he appeared at once pushed on by his desire of appearing friendly, and held back by the fear of intrusion. It was no wonder that the Master of Ravenswood, little acquainted as he then was with life, should have given this consummate courtier credit for more sincerity than was probably to be found in a score of his cast. He answered, however, with reserve, that he was indebted to all who might think well of him; and, apologizing to his guests, he left the hall, in order to make such arrangements for their entertainment as circumstances admitted.

Upon consulting with old Mysie, the accommodations for the night were easily completed, as indeed they admitted of little choice. The Master surrendered his apartment for the use of Miss Ashton, and Mysie, (once a person of consequence) dressed in a black sattin gown which had belonged of yore to the Master's grandmother, and had figured in the court-balls of Henrietta Maria, went to attend her as lady's-maid. He next enquired after Bucklaw, and understanding he was at the Change-house with the huntsman and some companions, he desired Caleb to call there and acquaint him how he was circumstanced at Wolfscrag—to intimate to him it would be most convenient if he could find a bed in the hamlet, as the elder guest must necessarily be quartered in the secret chamber, the only spare bed-room which could be made fit to receive him. The Master saw no hardship in passing the night by the hall fire, wrapt in his campaign-cloak; and to Scottish domestics of the day, even of the highest rank, nay, to young men of family or fashion, on any pinch, clean straw, or a dry hay-loft, was always held good night-quarters.

For the rest, Lockhard had his master's orders to bring some venison from the inn, and Caleb was to trust to his wits for the honour of the family. The Master, indeed, a second time held out his purse; but, as it was in sight of the strange servant, the Butler thought himself obliged to decline what his fingers itched to clutch. "Couldna he hae slippit it gently into my hand?" said Caleb—"but his honour will never learn how to bear himsel in siccan cases."

Mysie, in the meantime, according to a uniform custom in remote places in Scotland, offered the strangers the produce of their little dairy, "till better meat was getting ready." And according to another custom, not yet wholly in desuetude, as the storm was now drifting off to leeward, the Master carried the Keeper to the top of his highest tower to admire a wide and waste extent of view, and to "weary for his dinner."

Chapter Twelve

"Now dame," quoth he, "Je vous dis sans doute,
Had I nought of a capon but the liver,
And of your white bread nought but a shiver,
And after that a roasted pigge's head,
(But I ne wold for me no beast were dead)
Then had I with you homely suffisaunce."
CHAUCER, *Sumner's Tale*

IT WAS not without some secret misgiving that Caleb set out upon his exploratory expedition. In fact, it was attended with a treble difficulty. He dared not tell his master the offence which he had that morning given to Bucklaw, (just for the honour of the family,)—he dared not acknowledge he had been too hasty in refusing the purse—and, thirdly, he was something apprehensive of unpleasant consequences upon his meeting Hayston under the impression of an affront, and probably by this time under the influence also of no small quantity of brandy.

Caleb, to do him justice, was as bold as any lion where the honour of the family of Ravenswood was concerned, but his was that considerate valour which does not delight in unnecessary risks. This, however, was a secondary consideration; the main point was to veil the indigence of the house-keeping at the Castle, and to make good his vaunt of the cheer which his resources could procure, without Lockhard's assistance, and without supplies from his master. This was as prime a point of honour with him, as with the generous elephant with whom we have already compared him, who, being over-tasked, broke his skull through the desperate exertions which he made to discharge his duty, when he perceived they were bringing up another to his assistance.

The village which they now approached had frequently afforded the distressed Butler resources upon similar emergencies; but his relations with it had been of late much altered.

It was a little hamlet which straggled along the side of a creek formed by the discharge of a small brook into the sea, and was hidden from the castle, to which it had been in former times an appendage, by the intervention of the shoulder of a hill forming a projecting headland. It was called Wolfshope, (i.e. Wolf's Haven) and the few inhabitants gained a precarious subsistence by manning two or three fishing boats in the herring season, and smuggling gin and brandy during the winter months. They paid a kind of hereditary respect to the lords of Ravenswood; but, in the difficulties of the family, most of the inhabit-

ants of Wolfshope had contrived to get feu-rights to their little possessions, their huts, kail-yards, and rights of commonty, so that they were
emancipated from the chains of feudal dependence, and free from the
various exactions with which, under every possible pretext, or without
pretext at all, the Scottish landlords of the period, themselves in great
poverty, were wont to harass their still poorer tenants at will. They
might be, on the whole, termed independent, a circumstance peculiarly galling to Caleb, who had been wont to exercise over them the
same sweeping authority in levying contributions which was exercised
in former times in England, when "the royal purveyors, sallying forth
from under the Gothic portcullis to purchase provisions with power
and prerogative, instead of money, brought home the plunder of an
hundred markets, and all that could be seized from a flying and hiding
country, and deposited their spoil in an hundred caverns." *

Caleb loved the memory and resented the downfall of that authority, which mimicked, on a petty scale, the grand contributions exacted
by the feudal sovereigns. And as he fondly flattered himself that awful
rule and right supremacy which assigned to the Barons of Ravenswood the first and most effective interest in all productions of nature
within five miles of their castle, only slumbered and was not departed
for ever, he used every now and then to give the recollection of the
inhabitants a little jog by some petty exaction. These were at first
submitted to, with more or less readiness, by the inhabitants of the
hamlet; for they had been so long used to consider the wants of the
Baron and his family as having a title to be preferred to their own, that
their actual independence did not convey to them an immediate sense
of freedom. They resembled a man that has been long fettered, who,
even at liberty, feels, in imagination, the grasp of the hand-cuffs still
binding his wrists. But the exercise of freedom is quickly followed
with the natural consciousness of its immunities, as the enlarged
prisoner, by the free use of his limbs, soon dispels the cramped feeling
they had acquired when bound.

The inhabitants of Wolfshope began to grumble, to resist, and at
length positively to refuse compliance with the exactions of Caleb
Balderstone. It was in vain he reminded them, that when the eleventh
Lord Ravenswood, called the Skipper, from his delight in naval matters, had encouraged the trade of their port by building the pier, (a
bulwark of stones rudely piled together), which protected the fishing-
boats from the weather, it had been matter of understanding, that he
was to have the first stone of butter after the calving of every cow
within the barony, and the first egg, thence called the Monday's egg,
laid by every hen on every Monday in the year.

*Burke's Speech on Economical Reform.—Works, vol. iii. p. 280.

The feuars heard and scratched their heads, coughed, sneezed, and being pressed for answer, rejoined with one voice, "they could not say;"—the universal refuge of a Scottish peasant, when pressed to admit a claim which his conscience owns, and his interest inclines him to deny.

Caleb, however, furnished the notables of Wolfshope with a note of the requisition of butter and eggs, which he claimed as arrears of the aforesaid subsidy, or kindly aid, payable as above mentioned; and having intimated that he would not be averse to compound the same for goods or money, if it was inconvenient to them to pay in kind, left them, as he hoped, to debate the mode of assessing themselves for that purpose. On the contrary, they met with a determined purpose of resisting the exaction, and were only undecided as to the mode of grounding their opposition, when the cooper, a very important person on a fishing station, and one of the Conscript Fathers of the village, observed, "That their hens had cackled mony a day for the Lords of Ravenswood, and it was time they suld cackle for those that gave them roosts and barley." An unanimous grin intimated the assent of the assembly. "And," continued the orator, "if it's your wull, I'll just tak a step as far as Dunse for Davie Dingwall the writer, that's come frae the North to settle amang us, and he'll pit this job to rights, I'se warrant him."

A day was accordingly fixed for holding a grand *palaver* at Wolfshope on the subject of Caleb's requisitions, and he was invited to attend at the hamlet for that purpose.

He went with open hands and empty stomach, trusting to fill the one on his master's account, and the other on his own score, at the expence of the feuars of Wolfshope. But, death to his hopes! as he entered the eastern end of the straggling village, the awful form of Davie Dingwall, a sly, dry, hard-fisted, shrewd country attorney, who had already acted against the family of Ravenswood, and was a principal agent of Sir William Ashton, trotted in at the western extremity, bestriding a leathern portmanteau stuffed with the feu-charters of the hamlet, and hoping he had not kept Mr Balderstone waiting, "as he was instructed and fully empowered to pay or receive, compound or compensate, and, in fine, to *agé* as accords, respecting all mutual and unsettled claims whatsoever, belonging or competent to the Honourable Edgar Ravenswood, commonly called Master of Ravenswood"——

"The *Right* Honourable Edgar *Lord Ravenswood*," said Caleb with great emphasis; for, though conscious he had little chance of advantage in the conflict to ensue, he was resolved not to sacrifice one jot of honour.

"Lord Ravenswood then," said the man of business; "we shall not quarrel with you about titles of courtesy—commonly called Lord Ravenswood, or Master of Ravenswood, heritable proprietor of the lands and barony of Wolfscrag, on the one part, and to John Whitefish and others, feuars in the town of Wolfshope, within the barony afore-said, on the other part."

Caleb was conscious from sad experience, that he would wage a very different strife with this mercenary champion, than with the individual feuars themselves, upon whose old recollections, predilec-tions, and habits of thinking, he might have wrought by an hundred indirect arguments, to which their deputy-representative was totally insensible. The issue of the debate proved the reality of his apprehen-sions. It was in vain he strained his eloquence and ingenuity, and collected into one mass all arguments arising from antique custom and hereditary respect, from the good deeds done by the Lord of Ravenswood to the community of Wolfshope in former days, and from what might be expected from them in future. The Writer stuck to the contents of his feu-charters—he could not see it—'twas not in the bond. And when Caleb, determined to try what a little spirit would do, deprecated the consequences of Lord Ravenswood with-drawing his protection from the burgh, and even hinted at his using active measures of resentment, the man of law sneered in his face.

"His clients," he said, "had determined to do the best they could for their own toun, and he thought Lord Ravenswood, since he was a lord, might have enough to do to look after his own castle. As to any threats of stouthrief, or oppression by strength of hand, or *via facti*, as the law termed it, he would have Mr Balderstone recollect, that new times were not as old times—that they lived on the south of the Forth, and far from the Hielands—that his clients thought themselves able to protect themselves; but should they find themselves mistaken, they would apply to the government for the protection of a corporal and four red-coats, who," said Mr Dingwall, "would be perfectly able to secure them against the Lord of Ravenswood, and all that he or his following could do by the strong hand."

If Caleb could have concentrated all the lightnings of aristocracy in his eye, to have struck dead this contemner of allegiance and privilege, he would have launched them at his head, without respect to the consequences. As it was, he was compelled to turn his course back-ward to the castle; and there he remained for full half a day invisible and inaccessible even to Mysie, sequestered in his own peculiar dun-geon, where he sat burnishing a single pewter-plate, and whistling Maggy Lauder six hours without intermission.

The issue of this unfortunate requisition had shut against Caleb all resources which could be derived from Wolfshope and its purlieus, the El Dorado, or Peru, from which, in all former cases of exigence, he had been able to extract some assistance. He had, indeed, in a manner vowed that the de'il should have him, if ever he put the print of his foot within its causeway again. He had hitherto kept his word; and, strange to tell, this secession had, as he intended, in some degree the effect of a punishment upon the refractory feuars. Mr Balderstone had been a thing in their eyes connected with a superior order of beings, whose presence used to grace their little festivities, whose advice they found useful on many occasions, and whose communication gave a sort of credit to their village. The place, they acknowledged, "didna look as it used to do, and should do, since Mr Caleb keepit the castle sae closely—but doubtless, touching the eggs and butter, it was a maist unreasonable demand, as Mr Dingwall had justly made manifest."

Thus stood matters betwixt the parties, when the old Butler, though it was gall and wormwood to him, found himself obliged either to acknowledge before a strange man of quality, and, what was much worse, before that stranger's servant, the total inability of Wolfscrag to produce a dinner, or he must trust to the compassion of the feuars of Wolfshope. It was a dreadful degradation, but necessity was equally imperious and lawless. With these feelings he entered the street of the village.

Willing to shake himself free of his companion as soon as possible, he directed Mr Lockhard to Luckie Sma'trash's change-house, where a din, proceeding from the revels of Bucklaw, Craigengelt, and their party, sounded half-way down the street, while the red glare from the window overpowered the grey twilight which was now settling down, and glimmered against a parcel of old tubs, kegs, and barrels, piled up in the cooper's yard, on the other side of the way.

"If you, Mr Lockhard," said the old Butler to his companion, "will be pleased to step to the change-house where that light comes from, and where, as I judge, they are now singing, 'Cauld Kail in Aberdeen,' ye may do your master's errand about the venison, and I will do mine about Bucklaw's bed, as I return frae getting the rest of the vivers.— It's no that the venison is actually needfu'," he added, detaining his colleague by the button, "to make up the dinner—but is a compliment to the hunters, ye ken—and, Mr Lockhard—if they offer a drink o' yill, or a cup o' wine, or a glass o' brandy, ye'll be a wise man to tak it, in case the thunner should hae soured ours at the castle,—whilk is ower muckle to be dreaded."

He then permitted Lockhard to depart; and with feet heavy as lead, and yet far lighter than his heart, stepped on through the unequal street of the straggling village, meditating on whom he ought to make his first attack. It was necessary he should find some one, with whom old acknowledged greatness should weigh more than recent independence, and to whom his application might appear an act of high dignity, relenting at once and soothing. But he could not recollect an inhabitant of a mind so constructed. "Our kail is like to be cauld eneugh too," he reflected, as the chorus of Cauld Kail in Aberdeen again reached his ears. The minister—he had got his presentation from the late lord, but they had quarrelled about tiends—The brewster wife—she had trusted long—and the bill was aye scored up—and unless the dignity of the family should actually require it, it would be a sin to distress a widow woman. None was so able—but, on the other hand, none was likely to be so unwilling to stand his friend upon the present occasion, as John Girder, the man of tubs and barrels already mentioned, who had headed the insurrection in the matter of the egg and butter subsidy.—"But a' comes o' taking folk on the right side, I trow," quoth Caleb to himself; "and I had ance the ill hap to say he was but a Johnie Newcome in our town-end—the carle bore the family an ill-will ever since. But he married a bonnie young quean, Jean Lightbody, auld Lightbody's daughter, him that was on the steading of Loupthedyke,—that was married himsel to Marion, that was about my lady in the family forty years syne—I hae had mony a day's daffing wi' Jean's mither, and they say she bides on wi' them— the carle has Jacobuses and Georgiuses baith, an' ane could get at them—and sure I am, it's doing him an honour him or his never deserved at our hand, the ungracious sumph; and if he loses by us a' thegither, he is e'en cheap o't, he can spare it brawly."

Shaking off irresolution, therefore, and turning at once upon his heel, Caleb walked hastily back to the cooper's house, lifted the latch without ceremony, and, in a moment, found himself behind the *hallan*, or partition, from which position he could, himself unseen, reconnoitre the interior of the *but*, or kitchen apartment, of the mansion.

Reverse of the sad menage at the Castle of Wolfscrag, a bickering fire roared up the cooper's chimney. His wife on the one side, in her pearlings and pudding-sleeves, put the last finishing touch to her holiday's apparel, while she contemplated a very handsome and good-humoured face in a broken mirror, raised upon the *bink* (the shelves on which the plates are disposed,) for her special accommodation. Her mother, old Luckie Loupthedyke, "a canty carline" as was within twenty miles of her, according to the unanimous report of her *cummers*, or gossips, sat by the fire in full glory of a grogram gown, lammer beads, and a clean cockernony, whiffing a snug pipe of tobacco, and superintending the affairs of the kitchen. For—sight more interesting to the anxious heart and craving entrails of the desponding Seneschal, than either buxom dame or canny cummer,—there bubbled on the aforesaid bickering fire, a huge pot, or rather cauldron, steaming with beef and brewis; while before it revolved two spits, turned by two of the cooper's apprentices who sat in the opposite corners of the chimney; the one loaded with a quarter of mutton, while the other was graced with a fat goose and a brace of wild ducks. The sight and scent of such a land of plenty almost wholly overcame the drooping spirits of Caleb. He turned, for a moment's space, to reconnoitre the *ben*, or parlour end of the house, and there saw a sight scarce less affecting to his feelings;—a large round table, covered for ten or twelve persons, *decored* (according to his own favourite term,) with *napery* as white as snow; grand flagons of pewter, intermixed with one or two silver cups, containing, as was probable, something worthy the brilliancy of their outward appearance; clean trenchers, cutty spoons, knives and forks, sharp, burnished, and prompt for action, which lay all displayed as for an especial festival.

"The deil's in the pedling tub-coopering carle," thought Caleb, in all the envy of astonishment; "it's a shame to see the like o' them gusting their gabs at sic a rate. But if some o' that gude cheer does not find it's way to Wolfscrag this night, my name is not Caleb Balderstone."

So resolving, he entered the apartment, and, in all courteous greeting, saluted both the mother and daughter. Wolfscrag was the court of the barony, Caleb prime minister at Wolfscrag; and it has ever been remarked, that though the masculine subject who pays the taxes, sometimes growls at the courtiers by whom they are imposed, the said courtiers continue, nevertheless, welcome to the fair sex, to whom they furnish the newest small-talk and the earliest fashions. Both the dames were, therefore, at once about old Caleb's neck, setting up their throats together by way of welcome.

"Aye, sirs, Mr Balderstone, and is this you?—A sight of you is gude for sair een—sit doun—sit doun—the gudeman will be blythe to see you—Ye nar saw him sae cadgy in your life; but we are to christen our bit wean the night, as ye will hae heard, and doubtless ye will stay and see the ordinance—we hae killed a wether, and ane o' our lads has been out wi' his gun at the moss—ye used to like wild-fowl."

"Na—na—gudewife," said Caleb, "I just keekit in to wish ye joy, and I wad been glad to hae spoken wi' the gudeman, but——" moving, as if to go away.

"The ne'er a fit ye's gang," said the elder dame, laughing and holding him fast, with a freedom which belonged to their old acquaintance; "wha kens what it may bring to the bairn, if ye owerlook it in that gate?"

"But I'm in a preceese hurry, gudewife," said the Butler, suffering himself to be dragged to a seat without much resistance; "and as to eating"—for he observed the mistress of the dwelling bustling about to place a trencher for him—"as for eating—lack-a-day, we a' are just killed up yonder wi' eating frae morning to night—it's shamefu' epicurism; but that's what we hae gotten frae the English pock-puddings."

"Hout—never mind the Southron pock-puddings," said Luckie Lightbody; "try our puddings, Mr Balderstone—there is black pudding and white-hass—try whilk ye like best."

"Baith gude—baith excellent—canna be better; but the very smell is eneugh for me that hae dined sae lately (the faithful wretch had fasted since day-break.) But I wadna affront your housewifeskap, gudewife; and, wi' your permission, I'se e'en pit them in my napkin, and eat them to my supper at e'en, for I am wearied of Mysie's pastry and nonsense—ye ken landward dainties aye pleased me best, Marion —and landward lasses too—(looking at the cooper's wife)—Ne'er a bit but she looks far better than when she married John, and then she was the bonniest lass in our parochine and the neest till it.—But gawsie cow, goodly calf."

The women smiled at the compliment each to herself, and they smiled again to each other as Caleb wrapt up the puddings in a towel which he had brought with him, as a dragoon carries his foraging bag to receive what may fall.

"And what news at the Castle?" quo' the gudewife.

"News?—the bravest news ye ever heard—the Lord Keeper's up yonder wi' his fair daughter, just ready to fling her at my lord's head, if he winna tak her out o' his arms; and I'se warrant he'll stitch our auld lands of Ravenswood to her petticoat tail."

"Eh! sirs—aye!—and will he hae her?—and is she weel-favoured? —and what's the colour o' her hair?—and does she wear a habit or a railly?" were the questions which the females showered upon the Butler.

"Hout tout!—it wad tak a man a day to answer a' your questions, and I hae hardly a minute. Whare's the gude-man?"

"Awa' to fetch the minister," said Mrs Girder, "precious Mr Peter Bidethebent frae the Mosshead—the honest man has the rheumatics wi' lying in the hills in the persecution."

"Aye!—a whig and a mountain-man nae less," said Caleb, with a peevishness he could not suppress; "I hae seen the day, Luckie, when worthy Mr Cuffcushion and the Service-book would hae served your turn (to the elder dame,) or ony honest woman in like circumstances."

"And that's true too," said Mrs Lightbody, "but what can a body do?—Jean maun baith sing her psalm and busk her cockernony the gate the gudeman likes, and nae ither gate, for he's maister and mair at hame, I can tell ye, Mr Balderstone."

"Aye, and does he guide the gear too?" said Caleb, to whose projects masculine rule boded little good.

"Ilka penny o't—but he'll dress her as dink as a daisy, as ye see—sae she has little reason to complain—where there's ane better aff there is ten waur."

"Aweel, gudewife," said Caleb, crest-fallen, but not beaten off, "that wasna the way ye guided your gudeman; but ilka land has it's ain lauch. I maun be ganging—I just wanted to round into the gudeman's lug, that I heard them say up bye yonder, that Peter Puncheon that was cooper to the Queen's stores at the Timmer Burse at Leith, is dead—sae I thought that maybe a word frae my lord to the Lord Keeper might hae served John; but since he's frae hame"——

"O but ye maun stay his hame-coming," said the dame—"I aye telled the gudeman ye meant weel be him; but he taks the tout at every bit lippening word."

"Aweel, I'll stay the last minute I can."

"And so," said the handsome young spouse of Mr Girder, "ye think this Miss Ashton is weel-favoured—troth, and sae she should, to set up for our young lord, wi' a face, and a hand, and a seat on his horse, that might be a king's son—d'ye ken he aye glowers up at my window, Mr Balderstone, when he chaunces to ride thro' the town, sae I hae a right to ken what like he is, as weel as ony body."

"I ken that brawly," said Caleb, "for I have heard his lordship say the cooper's wife had the blackest e'e in the barony; and I said, Weel may that be, my lord, for it was her mither's afore her, as I ken to my cost—Eh, Marion? Ha, ha, ha!—Ah! these were merry days!"

"Hout awa, daft carle," said the old dame, "to speak sic daffing to young folk.—But, Jean—fie, woman, dinna hear the bairn greet? I'se warrant it's that weary weid has come ower it again."

Up got mother and grandmother, and scoured away, jostling each other as they ran, into some remote corner of the tenement, where the young hero of the evening was deposited. When Caleb saw the coast fairly clear, he took an invigorating pinch of snuff, to sharpen and confirm his resolution.

"Cauld be my cast," thought he, "if either Bidethebent or Girder taste that broche of wild-fowl this evening;" and then addressing the elder turnspit, a boy of about eleven years old, and putting a penny into his hand, he said, "Here is twal pennies,* my man; carry that ower to

* Monetæ Scoticæ scilicet.

Mrs Sma'trash, and bid her fill my mill wi' snishing, and I'll turn the broche for ye in the meantime—and she will gi'e ye a ginge-bread snap for your pains."

No sooner was the elder boy departed on this mission, than Caleb, looking the remaining turnspit gravely and steadily in the face, removed from the fire the spit bearing the wild-fowl of which he had undertaken the charge, clapped his hat on his head, and fairly marched off with it. He stopped at the door of the Change-house only to say, in a few brief words, that Mr Hayston of Bucklaw was not to expect a bed that evening in the castle.

If this message was too briefly delivered by Caleb, it became absolute rudeness when conveyed through the medium of a suburb landlady; and Bucklaw was, as a more calm and temperate man might have been, highly incensed. Captain Craigengelt proposed, with the unanimous applause of all present, that they should course the old fox (meaning Caleb) ere he got to cover, and toss him in a blanket. But Lockhard intimated with authority to his master's servants, and those of Lord Bittlebrain, that the slightest impertinence to the Master of Ravenswood's domestic would give Sir William Ashton the highest offence. And having so said, in a tone sufficient to prevent any aggression on their part, he left the public-house, taking along with him two servants loaded with such provisions as he had been able to procure, and overtook Caleb just as he had cleared the village.

Chapter Thirteen

> Should I take aught of you?—'tis true I begged now;
> And what is worse than that, I stole a kindness;
> And, what is worst of all, I lost my way in't.
> *Wit without Money*

THE FACE of the little boy, sole witness to Caleb's infringement upon the laws at once of property and hospitality, would have made a good picture. He sate motionless, as if he had witnessed some of the spectral appearances which he had heard told of in a winter's evening; and as he forgot his own duty, and allowed his spit to stand still, he added to the misfortunes of the evening, by suffering the mutton to burn as black as a coal. He was first recalled from his trance of astonishment by a hearty cuff, administered by Dame Lightbody, who (in whatever other respects she might conform to her name) was a woman strong of person, and expert in the use of her hands, as some say her deceased husband had known to his cost.

"What gar'd ye let the roast burn, ye ill-clackit gude-for-nought?"

"I dinna ken," said the boy.

"And where's that ill-deedy gett, Giles?"

"I dinna ken," blubbered the astounded declarant.

"And where's Mr Balderstone?—and abune a', and in the name of council and kirk-session, that I suld say sae, where is the broche wi' the wild-fowl?"

As Mrs Girder here entered, and joined her mother's exclamations, screaming into one ear while the old lady deafened the other, they succeeded in so utterly confounding the unhappy urchin, that he could not for some time tell his story at all, and it was only when the elder boy returned that the truth began to dawn on their minds.

"Weel, sirs!" said Mrs Lightbody, "wha wad hae thought o' Caleb Balderstone playing an auld acquaintance sic a pliskie!"

"O, weary on him!" said the spouse of Mr Girder; "and what am I to say to the gudeman?—he'll brain me, if there wasna anither woman in a' Wolfshope."

"Hout tout, silly quean," said the mother; "na, na—it's come to muckle, but it's no come to that neither; for an he brain you he maun brain me, and I have gar'd his betters stand aback—hands aff is fair play—we maunna head a bit flyting."

The tramp of horses now announced the arrival of the cooper, with the minister. They had no sooner dismounted than they made for the kitchen fire, for the evening was cool after the thunder-storm, and the roads wet and dirty. The young gudewife, strong in the charms of her Sunday gown and biggonets, threw herself in the way of receiving the first attack, while her mother, like the veteran division of the Roman legion, remained in the rear, ready to support her in case of necessity. Both hoped to protract the discovery of what had happened—the mother by interposing her bustling person betwixt Mr Girder and the fire, and the daughter by the extreme cordiality with which she received the minister and her husband, and the anxious fears she expressed lest they should have "gotten cauld."

"Cauld?" quoth the husband surlily, for he was not of that class of lords and masters whose wives are viceroys over them—"we'll be cauld aneugh, I think, if ye dinna let us in to the fire."

And so saying, he burst his way through both lines of defence; and, as he had a careful eye over his property of every kind, he perceived at one glance the absence of the spit with its savoury burthen. "What the de'il, woman"——

"Fye for shame!" exclaimed both the women; "and before Mr Bidethebent!"

"I stand reproved," said the cooper, "but"——

"The taking in our mouths the name of the great enemy of our souls," said Mr Bidethebent——

"I stand reproved," said the cooper.

"Is an exposing ourselves to his temptations, and an inviting, or, in some sort, a compelling, of him to lay aside his other trafficking with unhappy persons, and wait upon those in whose mouth his name is frequent."

"Weel, weel, Mr Bidethebent, can a man do mair than stand reproved?" said the cooper; "but just let me ask the women what for they hae dished the wild-fowl before we came."

"They are no dished, John," said his wife; "but—but an accident"——

"What accident?" said Girder, with flashing eyes—"Nae ill come ower them, I trust? Uh?"

His wife, who stood much in awe of him, durst not reply, but her mother bustled up to her support.—"I gied them to an acquaintance of mine, John Girder; and what about it now?"

Her excess of assurance struck Girder mute for an instant.—"And *ye* gied the wild-fowl, the best end of our christening dinner, to a friend of yours, ye auld rudas! and what was his name, I pray ye?"

"Worthy Mr Caleb Balderstane, frae Wolfscrag," answered Marion, quite prepared for battle.

Girder's wrath foamed over all restraint. If there was a circumstance which could have added to the resentment he felt, it was that this extravagant donation had been made in favour of our friend Caleb, towards whom, for reasons to which the reader is no stranger, he nourished a decided resentment. He raised his riding wand against the elder matron, but she stood firm, collected in herself, and undauntedly brandished the iron ladle with which she had just been *flambing (anglice*, basting) the roast of mutton. Her weapon was certainly the better, and her arm not the weakest of the two; so that John thought it safest to turn short off upon his wife, who had by this time hatched a sort of hysterical whine, which greatly moved the minister, who was in fact as simple and kind-hearted a creature as ever breathed.—"And you, ye thowless jadd, to sit still and see my substance disponed upon to an idle, drucken, reprobate, worm-eaten serving-man, just because he kittles the lugs o' a silly auld wife wi' useless clavers, and every twa words a lie?—I'll gar you as gude"——

Here the minister interposed, both by voice and action, while Dame Lightbody threw herself in front of her daughter, and flourished her ladle.

"Am I no to chastise my ain wife?" said the cooper, very indignantly.

"Ye may chastise your ain wife if ye like," answered Dame Lightbody; "but ye shall never lay finger on my daughter, and that ye may found upon."

"For shame, Mr Girder," said the clergyman; "this is what I little expected to have seen of you, that ye suld give rein to your sinful passions against your nearest and your dearest; and this night too, when ye are called to the most solemn duty of a Christian parent—and a' for what? for a redundancy of creature comforts, as worthless as they are unneedful."

"Worthless!" exclaimed the cooper—"a better guse ne'er walked on stubble; twa finer dentier wild-deucks ne'er wat a feather."

"Be it so, neighbour," rejoined the minister; "but see what superfluities are yet revolving before your fire. I have seen the day when ten of the bannocks that stand upon that board would have been an acceptable dainty to as many men, that were starving in hills and hags, and caves of the earth, for the Gospel's sake."

"And that's what vexes maist of a'," said the cooper, anxious to get some one to sympathise with his not altogether causeless anger; "an the quean had gi'en it to ony suffering sant, or to ony body ava but that reaving, lying, oppressing tory villain, that rade in the wicked troop of militia when it was commanded out against Argyle by the auld tyrant Allan Ravenswood, that is gane to his place, I wad the less hae minded it. But to gie the principal part o' the feast to the like o' him!"——

"Aweel, John," said the minister, "and dinna ye see a high judgment in this?—The seed of the righteous are not seen begging their bread—think of the son of a powerful oppressor being brought to the pass of supporting his household from your fullness."

"And besides," said the wife, "it wasna for Lord Ravenswood neither, an he wad hear but a body speak—it was to help to entertain the Lord Keeper, as they ca' him, that's up yonder at Wolfscrag."

"Sir William Ashton at Wolfscrag!" ejaculated the astonished man of hoops and staves.

"And hand and glove wi' Lord Ravenswood," added Dame Lightbody.

"Doited ideot!—that auld clavering sneck-drawer wad gar ye trow the moon is made of green cheese.—Lord Keeper and Ravenswood! they are cat and dog, hare and hound."

"I tell ye they are man and wife, and gree better than some others," retorted the mother-in-law; "forbye, Peter Puncheon, that's cooper to the Queen's stores, is dead, and the place is to fill, and"——

"Od guide us, wull ye haud your skirling tongues," said Girder—for we are to remark, that this explanation was given like a catch for two voices, the younger dame taking up, and repeating, in a higher tone, the words as fast as they were uttered by her mother.

"The gudewife says naething but what's true, maister," said Girder's foreman, who had come in during the fray. "I saw a' the Lord

Keeper's servants drinking and driving ower at Luckie Sma'trash's, ower by yonder."

"And is their maister up at Wolfscrag?" said Girder.

"Ay, troth is he," replied his man of confidence.

"An friends wi' Ravenswood?"

"It's like sae," answered the foreman, "since he is putting up wi' him."

"And Peter Puncheon is dead?"

"Ay, ay—he has leaked out at last, the auld carle," said the foreman; "mony a dribble o' brandy has gaen through him in his day.— But as for the broche and the wild-fowl, the saddle's no aff your mare yet, maister, and I could follow and bring it back, for Mr Balderstone's no far aff the town yet."

"Do sae, Will—and come here—I'll tell ye what to do when ye owertake him."

He relieved the females of his presence, and gave Will his private instructions.

"A bonnie-like thing," said the mother-in-law on his return, "to send the innocent lad after an armed man, when ye ken Mr Balderstane aye wears a rapier."

"I trust," said the minister, "ye hae reflected weel on what ye have done, least you should minister cause of strife, of which it is my duty to say, he who affordeth matter is no manner guiltless."

"Never fash your beard, Mr Bidethebent—ane canna get their breath out here between wives and ministers—I ken best how to turn my ain cake.—Jean, serve up the dinner, and nae mair about it."

Nor did he again allude to the deficiency in the course of the evening.

Meantime, the foreman, mounted on his master's steed, and charged with his special orders, pricked swiftly forth in pursuit of the marauder Caleb. That personage, it may be imagined, did not linger by the way. He intermitted even his dearly-beloved chatter, for the purpose of making more haste—only assuring Mr Lockhard that he had made the purveyor's wife give the wild-fowl a few turns before the fire, in case that Mysie, who had been so much alarmed by the thunder, should not have her kitchen-grate in full splendour. Meanwhile, alleging the necessity of being at Wolfscrag as soon as possible, he pushed on so fast that his companions could scarce keep up with him. He began already to think he was safe from pursuit, having gained the summit of the swelling eminence which divides Wolfscrag from the village, when he heard the distant tread of a horse, and a voice which shouted at intervals, "Mr Caleb—Mr Balderstone—Mr Caleb Balderstone—hollo—bide a wee!"

Caleb, it may be well believed, was in no hurry to acknowledge the summons. First, he would not hear it, and faced his companions down, that it was the echo of the wind; then he said it was not worth stopping for; and, at length, halting reluctantly, as the figure of the horseman appeared through the shades of the evening, he bent up his whole soul to the task of defending his prey, threw himself into an attitude of dignity, advanced the spit, which in his grasp "might seem both spear and shield," and firmly resolved to die rather than surrender it.

What was his astonishment, when the cooper's foreman, riding up and addressing him with respect, told him, "his master was sorry he was absent when he came to his dwelling, and grieved that he could not tarry the christening dinner, and that he had ta'en the freedom to send a sma' rundlet of sack, and ane anker of brandy, as he understood there were guests at the castle, and that they were short of preparation."

I have heard somewhere a story of an elderly gentleman, who was pursued by a bear that had gotten loose from its muzzle; until, completely exhausted and in a fit of desperation, he faced round upon Bruin and lifted his cane, at the sight of which the instinct of discipline prevailed, and the animal, instead of tearing him to pieces, rose up upon his hind-legs, and instantly began to shuffle a saraband. Not less than the joyful surprise of the senior, who had supposed himself in the extremity of peril from which he was thus unexpectedly relieved, was that of our excellent friend Caleb, when he found the pursuer intended to add to his prize, instead of bereaving him of it. He recovered his latitude, however, instantly, so soon as the foreman, stooping from his nag, where he sate perched betwixt the two barrels, whispered in his ear,—"If ony thing about Peter Puncheon's place could be airted their way, John Girder wad mak it better to the Master of Ravenswood than a pair of new gloves; and that he wad be blythe to speak wi' Master Balderstane on that head, and he wad find him as pliant as a hoop-willow in a' that he could wish of him."

Caleb heard all this without rendering any answer, except that of all great men from Louis XIV. downward, namely, "we will see about it;" and then added aloud, for the edification of Mr Lockhard,—"Your master has acted with becoming civility and attention in forwarding the liquors, and I will not fail to represent it properly to my Lord Ravenswood. And, my lad," he said, "you may ride on the castle, and if none of the servants are returned, whilk is to be dreaded, as they make day and night of it when they are out of sight, ye may put them into the porter's lodge, whilk is on the right hand of the great entry—the porter has got leave to go to see his friends, sae ye will meet no ane to steer ye."

The foreman, having received his orders, rode on; and having deposited the casks in the deserted and ruinous porter's lodge, he returned unquestioned by any one. Having thus executed his master's commission, and doffed his bonnet to Caleb and his company as he repassed them in his way to the village, he returned to have his share of the christening festivity.

Chapter Fourteen

As, to the Autumn breeze's bugle-sound,
Various and vague the dry leaves dance their round;
Or, from the garner-door, on æther borne,
The chaff flies devious from the winnow'd corn;
So vague, so devious, at the breath of heaven,
From their fix'd aim are mortal counsels driv'n.
Anonymous

WHEN CALEB had mustered and marshalled his dishes of divers kinds, a more royal provision had not been seen in Wolfscrag, since the funeral feast of its deceased lord. Great was the glory of the serving-man, as he *decored* the old oaken table with a clean cloth, and arranged upon it carbonaded venison and roasted wild-fowl, with a glance, every now and then, as if to upbraid the incredulity of his master and his guests; and with many a story, more or less true, was Lockhard that evening regaled concerning the ancient grandeur of Wolfscrag, and the sway of its Barons over the country in their neighbourhood.

"A vassal scarce held a calf or a lamb was his ain, till he had first asked if the Lord of Ravenswood was pleased to accept it; and they were obliged to ask the lord's consent before they married in these days, and mony a merry tale they tell about that right as weel as others. And although," said Caleb, "these times are not like the gude auld times, when authority had its due, yet, true it is, Mr Lockhard, and you yoursell may partly have remarked, that we of the House of Ravenswood do our devoir in keeping up, by all just and lawful exertion of our baronial authority, that due and fitting connection betwixt superior and vassal, whilk is in some danger of falling into desuetude, owing to the general license and misrule of these present unhappy times."

"Umph!" said Mr Lockhard; "and if I may enquire, Mr Balderstone, pray do you find your people at the village yonder amenable? for I must needs say, that at Ravenswood Castle, now pertaining to my

master, the Lord Keeper, ye have not left behind ye the most compliant set of tenantry."

"Ah! but Mr Lockhard," replied Caleb, "ye must consider there
has been a change of hands, and the auld lord might expect twa turns
frae them, when the new comer canna get ane. A dour and fractious
set they were, thae tenants of Ravenswood, and ill to live wi' whan they
dinna ken their master—and if your master put them mad ance, the
whole country will not put them down."

"Troth," said Mr Lockhard, "an such be the case, I think the wisest
thing for us a' wad be to hammer up a match between your young lord
and our winsome young leddy up bye there; and Sir William might
just stitch your auld barony to her gown-sleeve, and he wad sune
crinkle another out o' somebody else, sic a lang head as he has."

Caleb shook his head.—"I wish," he said, "I wish that may answer,
Mr Lockhard. There are auld prophecies about this house I wad like
ill to see fulfilled wi' my auld e'en, that hae seen evil aneugh already."

"Pshaw! never mind freits," said his brother butler; "if the young
folk liked ane anither, they wad make a winsome couple. But, to say
truth, there is a leddy sits in our hall-nook, maun have her hand in that
as weel as in every other job. But there's no harm in drinking to their
healths, and I will fill Mrs Mysie a cup of Mr Girder's canary."

While they thus enjoyed themselves in the kitchen, the company in
the hall were not less pleasantly engaged. So soon as Ravenswood had
determined upon giving the Lord Keeper such hospitality as he had to
offer, he deemed it incumbent on him to assume the open and courteous brow of a well-pleased host. It has been often remarked, that when
a man commences by acting a character, he frequently ends by adopting it in good earnest. In the course of an hour or two, Ravenswood, to
his own surprise, found himself in the situation of one who frankly
does his best to entertain welcome and honoured guests. How much
of this change in his disposition was to be ascribed to the beauty and
simplicity of Miss Ashton, to the readiness with which she accommodated herself to the inconveniencies of her situation—how much
to the smooth and plausible conversation of the Lord Keeper,
remarkably gifted with those words which win the ear, must be left to
the reader's ingenuity to conjecture. But Ravenswood was insensible
to neither.

The Lord Keeper was a veteran statesman, well acquainted with
courts and cabinets, and intimate with all the various turns of public
affairs during the last eventful years of the seventeenth century. He
could talk, from his own knowledge, of men and events, in a way which
failed not to win attention, and had the peculiar art, while he never
said a word which committed himself, at the same time to persuade

the hearer that he was speaking without the least shadow of scrupulous caution or reserve. Ravenswood, in spite of his prejudices and real grounds of resentment, felt himself at once amused and instructed in listening to him, while the statesman, whose awkward feelings had at first so much impeded his first efforts to make himself known, had now regained all the ease and fluency of a silver-tongued lawyer of the very highest order.

His daughter did not speak much, but she smiled, and she sang; and what she did say argued a submissive gentleness, and a desire to give pleasure, which, to a proud man like Ravenswood, was more fascinating than the most brilliant wit. Above all, he could not but observe, that, whether from gratitude or from some other motive, he himself, in his deserted and unprovided hall, was as much the object of respectful attention to his guests, as he would have been when surrounded by all the appliances and means of hospitality proper to his high birth. All deficiencies passed unobserved, or, if they did not escape notice, it was to praise the substitutes which Caleb had contrived to supply the want of the usual accommodations. Where a smile was unavoidable, it was a very good-humoured one, and often coupled with some well-turned compliment, to shew how much the guests esteemed the merit of their noble host, how little they thought of the inconveniencies with which they were surrounded. I am not sure whether the pride of being found to outbalance, in virtue of his own personal merit, all the disadvantages of fortune, did not make as favourable an impression upon the haughty heart of the Master of Ravenswood, as the conversation of the father and the beauty of Lucy Ashton.

The hour of repose arrived. The Keeper and his daughter retired to their apartments, which were "decored" more properly than could have been anticipated. In making the necessary arrangements, Mysie had indeed enjoyed the assistance of a gossip who had arrived from the village upon an exploratory expedition, but had been arrested by Caleb, and impressed into the domestic drudgery of the evening. So that, instead of returning home to describe the dress and person of the grand young lady, she found herself compelled to be active in the domestic economy of Wolfscrag.

According to the custom of the time, the Master of Ravenswood attended the Lord Keeper to his apartment, followed by Caleb, who placed on the table, with all the ceremonial due to torches of wax, two rudely formed tallow-candles, such as in these days were only used by the peasantry, hooped in paltry clasps of wire, which served for candlesticks. He then disappeared, and presently entered with two earthen flagons, (the china, he said, had been little used since my lady's time,) one filled with canary wine, the other with brandy. The canary sack, unheeding all probabilities of detection, he declared had been twenty years in the cellars of Wolfscrag, "though it was not for him to speak before their honours; the brandy,—it was weel ken'd liquor, as mild as mead, and as strong as Sampson—it had been in the house ever since the memorable revel, in which auld Mickletale had been slain at the head of the stair by Jamie of Jenklebrae, on account of the honour of the worshipful Lady Muirend, wha was in some sort an ally of the family; natheless"——

"But to cut that matter short, Mr Caleb," said the Keeper, "perhaps you will favour me with a ewer of water."

"God forbid your lordship should drink water in this family, to the disgrace of so honourable an house!"

"Nevertheless, if his lordship have a fancy," said the Master, smiling, "I think you might indulge him; for, if I mistake not, there has been water drank here at no distant date, and with good relish too."

"To be sure, if his lordship has a fancy," said Caleb; and re-entering with a jug of pure element—"He will scarce find such water ony where as is drawn frae the well at Wolfscrag—nevertheless"——

"Nevertheless, we must leave the Lord Keeper to his repose in this poor chamber of ours," said the Master of Ravenswood, interrupting his talkative domestic, who immediately turning to the door-way, with a profound reverence, prepared to usher his master from the secret chamber.

But the Lord Keeper prevented his host's departure.—"I have but one word to say to the Master of Ravenswood, Mr Caleb, and I fancy he will excuse your waiting."

With a second reverence, lower than the former, Caleb withdrew—and his master stood motionless, expecting, with considerable embarrassment, what was to close the events of a day fraught with unexpected incidents.

"Master of Ravenswood," said Sir William Ashton, with some embarrassment, "I hope you understand the Christian law too well to suffer the sun to set upon your anger."

The Master blushed, and replied, "He had no occasion that evening to exercise the duty enjoined him by his Christian faith."

"I should have thought otherwise," said his guest, "considering the various subjects of dispute and litigation which have unhappily occurred more frequently than was desirable or necessary betwixt the late honourable lord, your father, and myself."

"I could wish, my lord," said Ravenswood, agitated by suppressed emotion, "that reference to these circumstances should be made any where rather than under my father's roof."

"I should have felt the delicacy of this appeal at another time," said Sir William Ashton, "but now I must proceed with what I meant to say. —I have suffered too much in my own mind from the false delicacy which prevented my soliciting with earnestness, what indeed I frequently requested, a personal communing with your father—much distress of mind to him and to me might have been prevented."

"It is true," said Ravenswood, after a moment's reflection; "I have heard my father say your lordship had proposed a personal interview."

"Proposed, my dear Master? I did indeed propose it, but I ought to have begged, entreated, beseeched it. I ought to have torn away the veil which interested persons had stretched betwixt us, and shewn myself as I was, willing to sacrifice a considerable part even of my legal rights in order to conciliate feelings so natural as his must be allowed to have been. Let me say for myself, my young friend, for so I will call you, that had your father and I spent the same time together which my good fortune has allowed me to-day to pass in your company, it is possible the land might yet have enjoyed one of the most respectable of its ancient nobility, and I should have been spared the pain of parting in enmity from a person whose general character I so much admired and honoured."

He put his handkerchief to his eyes. Ravenswood also was moved, but awaited in silence the progress of this extraordinary communication.

"It is necessary," continued the Lord Keeper, "and proper that you should understand, that there have been many points betwixt us, in which, although I judged it proper that there should be an exact ascertainment of my legal rights by the decree of a court of justice, yet it was never my intention to press them beyond the verge of equity."

"My lord," said the Master of Ravenswood, "it is unnecessary to press this topic farther. What the law will give you, or has given you, you enjoy—or you shall enjoy; neither my father, nor I myself, would have received any thing on the footing of favour."

"Favour? no, you misunderstand me," resumed the Keeper; "or rather you are no lawyer. A right may be good in law, and ascertained to be so, which yet a man of honour may not in every case care to avail himself of."

"I am sorry for it, my lord," said the Master.

"Nay, nay," retorted his guest, "you speak like a young council; your spirit goes before your wit. There are many things still open for decision betwixt us. Can you blame me, an old man desirous of peace, and in the castle of a young nobleman who has saved my daughter's life and my own, that I am desirous, anxiously desirous, that these should be settled on the most liberal principle?"

The old man kept fast hold of the Master's passive hand as he spoke, and made it impossible for him, be his predetermination what it would, to return any other than an acquiescing reply; and wishing his guest good night, he referred farther conference until the next morning.

Ravenswood hurried into the hall where he was to spend the night, and for a time traversed its stony floor with a disordered and rapid pace. His mortal foe was under his roof, yet his sentiments towards him were neither those of a feudal enemy nor of a true Christian. He felt as if he could neither forgive him in the one character, or follow forth his vengeance in the other, but that he was making a base and dishonourable composition betwixt his resentment against the father and his affection for the daughter. He cursed himself, as he hurried to and fro in the pale moonlight, and more ruddy gleams of the expiring wood-fire. He threw open and shut the latticed windows with violence, as if alike impatient of the admission and exclusion of the free air. At length, however, the torrent of passion foamed off its madness, and he threw himself into the chair, which he proposed as his place of repose for the night.

"If, in reality,"—such were the calmer thoughts that followed the first tempest of his passion—"If, in reality, this man desired no more than the law allows him—if he is willing to adjust even his acknowledged rights upon an equitable footing, what could be my father's cause of complaint? What is mine?—Those from whom we won our ancient possessions fell under the sword of my ancestors, and left lands and livings to the conquerors. We sink under the force of the law, now too powerful for the Scottish chivalry. Let us parley with the victors of the day, as if we had been besieged in our fortress and without hope of relief. This man may be other than I have thought him; and his daughter—but I have resolved not to think upon her."

He wrapt his cloak around him, fell asleep, and dreamed of Lucy Ashton till day-light gleamed through the lattices.

END OF VOLUME FIRST

THE
BRIDE OF LAMMERMOOR

Chapter One

We worldly men, when we see friends and kinsmen
Past hope sunk in their fortunes, lend no hand
To lift them up, but rather set our feet
Upon their heads to press them to the bottom,
As I must yield with you I practised it;
But now I see you in a way to rise,
I can and will assist you.—
New Way to Pay Old Debts

THE LORD KEEPER carried with him to a couch, harder than he was accustomed to stretch himself upon, the same ambitious thoughts and political perplexities, which drive sleep from the softest down that ever spread a bed of state. He had sailed long enough amid the contending tides and currents of the time to be sensible of their peril, and of the necessity of trimming his vessel to the prevailing wind, if he would have her escape suffering in the storm. The nature of his talents, and a timorousness of disposition connected with them, had made him assume the pliability of the versatile old Earl of Wiltshire, who explained the art by which he kept his ground during all the changes of state, from the reign of Henry VIII. to that of Elizabeth, by the frank avowal, that he was born of the willow, not of the oak. It had accordingly been Sir William Ashton's policy on all occasions to watch the changes in the political horizon, and, ere yet the conflict was decided, to negociate some interest for himself with the party most likely to prove victorious. His time-serving disposition was well known, and excited the contempt of the more daring leaders of both factions in the state. But his talents were of a useful and practical kind, and his legal knowledge held in high estimation; and they so far counter-balanced other deficiencies, that those in power were glad to use and to reward, though without trusting or respecting him.

The Marquis of A—— had used his utmost influence to effect a change in the Scottish cabinet, and his schemes had been of late so well laid and so ably supported, that there appeared a very great chance of his proving ultimately successful. He did not, however, feel so strong or so confident as to neglect any means of drawing recruits to his standard. The acquisition of the Lord Keeper was deemed of some importance, and a friend, perfectly acquainted with his circumstances and character, became responsible for his conversion.

When this gentleman arrived at Ravenswood Castle upon a visit, the real purpose of which was disguised under general courtesy, he found the prevailing fear, which at present beset the Lord Keeper, was that of danger to his own person from the Master of Ravenswood. The language which the blind sybil, old Alice, had used; the sudden appearance of the Master armed, and within his precincts, immediately after he had been warned against danger from him; his cold and haughty return to the acknowledgments with which he loaded him for his timely protection, had all made a strong impression on his imagination.

So soon as the Marquis's political agent found how the wind sate, he began to insinuate fears and doubts of another kind, scarce less calculated to affect the Lord Keeper. He enquired with seeming interest, whether the proceedings in Sir William's complicated litigation with the Ravenswoods were out of court, and settled without the possibility of appeal? The Lord Keeper answered in the affirmative; but his interrogator was too well informed to be imposed upon. He pointed out to him, by unanswerable arguments, that some of the most important points which had been decided in his favour against the House of Ravenswood, were liable to be reviewed by the Estates of the Scottish Parliament, upon an appeal from the party injured, or, as it was technically termed, "a protestation for remeid in law."

The Lord Keeper, after he had for some time disputed the regularity of such a procedure, was compelled, at length, to comfort himself with the improbability of the young Master of Ravenswood finding friends in parliament, capable of stirring in so weighty an affair.

"Do not comfort yourself with that false hope," said his wily friend; "it is possible, that in the next sessions of parliament, young Ravenswood may find more friends and favour even than your lordship."

"That would be a sight worth seeing," said the Keeper scornfully.

"And yet," said his friend, "such things have been seen ere now, and in our own time—there are many at the head of affairs even now, that a few years agone were under hiding for their lives; and many a man dining on plate of silver, that was fain to eat his crowdy without a bicker; and many a high head has been brought full low among us in as short a space. Scott of Scotstarvet's 'Staggering State of Scots Statesmen,' of which curious memoir you shewed me a manuscript, has been out-staggered in our time."

The Lord Keeper answered with a deep sigh, "that these were no new sights in Scotland, and had been witnessed long before the time of the satirical author he had quoted. It was many a long year," he said, "since Fordun had quoted, as an ancient proverb, *'neque dives, neque fortis, sed nec sapiens Scotus, prædominante invidia, diu durabit in terra.'* "

"And be assured, my esteemed friend," was the answer, "that even your long services to the state, and deep legal knowledge, will not save you, or render your estate stable, if the Marquis of A—— comes in with a parliament according to his will. You know that Lord Ravenswood that is deceased was his near ally, his lady being fifth in descent from the Knight of Tillibardine; and I am well assured that he will take young Ravenswood by the hand, and be his very good lord and kinsman. Why suld he not?—he is an active and stirring young fellow, able to help himself with tongue and hands; and it is such as he that find friends among their kindred, and not those unarmed and unable Mephebosheths, that are sure to be a burthen to every one that takes them up. And so, if these Ravenswood cases be called over the coals in parliament, you will find that the Marquis will have a crow to pluck with you."

"That would be an evil requital," said the Lord Keeper, "for my long services to the state, and the ancient respect in which I have held his lordship's honourable family and person."

"Aye, but," rejoined the agent of the Marquis, "it is in vain to look back on past service and auld respect, my lord—it will be present service and immediate proofs of regard, which, in these sliddery times, will be expected by a man like the Marquis."

The Lord Keeper now saw the full drift of his friend's argument, but he was too cautious to return any positive answer.

"He knew not," he said, "the service which the Lord Marquis could expect from one of his limited abilities, that had not always stood at his command, always saving and reserving his duty to his king and country."

Having thus said nothing, while he seemed to say every thing, for the exception was calculated to cover whatever he might afterwards think proper to bring under it, Sir William Ashton changed the conversation, nor did he again permit it to be introduced. His guest departed, without having brought the wily old statesman the length of committing himself, or pledging himself to any future line of conduct, but with the certainty that he had alarmed his fears in a most sensible point, and laid a foundation for future and further treaty.

When he rendered an account of his negociation to the Marquis, they both agreed that the Keeper ought not to be permitted to relapse into security, and that he should be plied with new subjects of alarm, especially during the absence of his lady. They were well aware that her proud, vindictive, and predominating spirit, would be likely to supply him with the courage in which he was deficient—that she was immovably wedded to the party now in power, with whom she maintained a close correspondence and alliance, and that she hated, without fearing, the Ravenswood family, whose more ancient dignity threw discredit on the newly acquired grandeur of her husband, to such a degree that she would have periled the interest of her own house, to have the prospect of altogether crushing that of her enemy.

But Lady Ashton was now absent. The business which had long detained her in Edinburgh, had afterwards induced her to travel to London, not without the hope that she might contribute her share to disconcert the intrigues of the Marquis at court, for she stood high in favour with the celebrated Sarah, Duchess of Marlborough, to whom, in point of character, she bore considerable resemblance. It was necessary to press her husband hard before her return; and, as a preparatory step, the Marquis wrote to the Master of Ravenswood the letter which we rehearsed in a former chapter. It was cautiously worded, so as to leave it in the power of the writer hereafter to take as deep, or as slight an interest in the fortunes of his kinsman, as the progress of his own schemes might require. But however unwilling, as a statesman, the Marquis might be to commit himself, or assume the character of a patron, while he had nothing to give away, it must be said to his honour, that he felt a strong inclination effectually to befriend the Master of Ravenswood, as well as to use his name as a means of alarming the terrors of the Lord Keeper.

As the messenger who carried this letter was to pass near the house of the Lord Keeper, he had it in direction, that in the village adjoining to the park gate of the castle, his horse should lose a shoe, and that, while it was replaced by the smith of the place, he should express the utmost regret for the necessary loss of time, and in the vehemence of his impatience, give it to be understood, that he was bearing a message from the Marquis of A—— to the Master of Ravenswood, upon a matter of life and death.

This news, with exaggerations, was speedily carried from various quarters to the ears of the Lord Keeper, and each reporter dwelt upon the extreme impatience of the courier, and the surprising short time in which he had executed his journey. The anxious statesman heard in silence; but in private Lockhard received orders to watch the courier on his return, to way-lay him in the village, to fill him drunk if possible, and to use all means, fair or foul, to learn the contents of the letters of which he was the bearer. But as if this plot had been foreseen, the messenger returned by a different and distant road, and thus escaped the snare that was laid him.

After he had been in vain expected for some time, Mr Dingwall had orders to make especial enquiries among his clients of Wolfshope, whether such a domestic belonging to the Marquis of A—— had actually arrived at the neighbouring castle. This was easily ascertained; for Caleb had been in the village one morning by five o'clock, to borrow "twa chappins of ale and a kipper" for the messenger's refreshment, and the poor fellow had been ill for twenty-four hours at Luckie Sma'trash's, in consequence of dining upon "saut saumon and sour drink." So that the existence of a correspondence betwixt the Marquis and his distressed kinsman, which Sir William Ashton had sometimes treated as a bug-bear, was proved beyond the possibility of further doubt.

The alarm of the Lord Keeper became very serious. Since the Claim of Right, the power of appealing from the decisions of the civil court to the estates of parliament, which had formerly been held incompetent, had in many instances been claimed, and in some allowed, and he had no small reason to apprehend the issue, if the Scottish parliament should be disposed to act upon the protestation of the Master of Ravenswood "for remeid in law." It would resolve into an equitable claim, and be decided, perhaps, upon the broad principles of justice, which were not quite so favourable to the Lord Keeper as those of strict law. Meanwhile, every report which reached him seemed to render the success of the Marquis's intrigues the more probable, and the Lord Keeper began to think it indispensible, that he should look round for some kind of protection against the coming storm. The timidity of his temper induced him to adopt measures of compromise and conciliation. The affair of the wild bull, properly managed, might, he thought, be made to facilitate a personal communication and reconciliation betwixt the Master and himself. He would then learn, if possible, what his own ideas were of the extent of his rights, and the means of reinforcing them; and perhaps matters might be brought to a compromise, where one party was wealthy, and the other so very poor. A reconciliation with Ravenswood was like to give him an opportunity to play his own game with the Marquis of A——. "And besides," said he to himself, "it will be an act of generosity to raise up the heir of this distressed family; and if he is to be warmly and effectually friended by the new government, who knows but my virtue may prove its own reward?"

Thus thought Sir William Ashton, covering with no unusual self-delusion his interested views with a hue of virtue; and having attained this point, his fancy strayed still farther. He began to bethink himself, "that if Ravenswood was to have a distinguished place of power and trust—and if such a union would sopite the heavier part of his unadjusted claims—there might be worse matches for his daughter Lucy—the Master might be reponed against the attainder—Lord Ravenswood was an ancient title, and the alliance would, in some measure, legitimate his own possession of the greater part of the Master's spoils, and make the surrender of the rest a subject of less bitter regret."

With these mingled and multifarious plans occupying his head, the Lord Keeper availed himself of my Lord Bittlebrain's repeated invitation to his residence, and thus came within a very few miles of Wolfscrag. Here he found the lord of the mansion absent, but was courteously received by the lady, who expected her husband's immediate return. She expressed her particular delight at seeing Miss Ashton, and appointed the hounds to be taken out for the Lord Keeper's special amusement. He readily embraced the proposal, as giving him an opportunity to reconnoitre Wolfscrag, and perhaps to make some acquaintance with the owner, if he should be tempted from his desolate mansion by the chase. Lockhard had his orders to endeavour on his part to make some acquaintance with the inmates of the castle, and we have seen how he played his part.

The accidental storm did more to further the Lord Keeper's plan of forming a personal acquaintance with young Ravenswood, than his most sanguine expectations could have anticipated. His fear of the young nobleman's personal resentment had greatly decreased, since he considered him as formidable from his legal claims, and the means he might have of enforcing them. But although he thought, not unreasonably, that only desperate circumstances drove men on desperate measures, it was not without a secret terror, which shook his heart within him, that he first felt himself enclosed within the desolate tower of Wolfscrag; a place so well fitted, from solitude and strength, to be a scene of violence and vengeance. The stern reception at first given to them by the Master of Ravenswood, and the difficulty he felt in explaining to that injured nobleman what guests were under the shelter of his roof, did not sooth these alarms; so that when Sir William Ashton heard the door of the court-yard shut behind him with violence, the words of Alice rung in his ears, "that he had driven on matters too hardly with so fierce a race as those of Ravenswood, and that they would bide their time to be avenged."

The subsequent frankness of the Master's hospitality, as their acquaintance increased, abated the apprehensions these recollections were calculated to excite; and it did not escape Sir William Ashton, that it was to Lucy's grace and beauty he owed the change in their host's behaviour.

All these thoughts thronged upon him when he took possession of the secret chamber. The iron lamp, the unfurnished apartment, more resembling a prison than a place of ordinary repose, the hoarse and ceaseless sound of the waves rushing against the base of the rock on which the castle was founded, saddened and perplexed his mind. To his own successful machinations, the ruin of this family had been in a great measure owing, but his disposition was crafty and not cruel; so that actually to witness the desolation and distress he had himself occasioned, was as painful to him as it would be to the humane mistress of a family to superintend in person the execution of the lambs and poultry which are killed by her own directions. At the same time, when he thought of the alternative, of restoring to Ravenswood a large proportion of his spoils, or of adopting, as an ally and member of his own family, the heir of this impoverished house, he felt as the spider may be supposed to do, when his whole web, the intricacies of which had been planned with so much artifice, is destroyed by the chance sweep of a broom. And then, if he should commit himself too far in this matter, it gave rise to a perilous question, which many a good husband, when under temptation to act as a free agent, has asked himself without being able to return a satisfactory answer; "What will my wife—what will Lady Ashton say?" On the whole, he came at length to the resolution in which minds of a weaker cast so often take refuge. He resolved to watch events, to take advantage of circumstances as they occurred, and regulate his conduct accordingly. In this spirit of temporizing policy, he at length composed his mind to rest.

Chapter Two

> "A slight note I have about me for you, for the delivery of which you must excuse me. It is an office that friendship calls upon me to do, and no way offensive to you, since I desire nothing but right upon both sides."
>
> *King and no King*

WHEN Ravenswood and his guest met in the morning, the gloom of the Master's spirit had in part returned. He, also, had passed a night rather of reflection than of slumber; and the feelings which he could not but entertain towards Lucy Ashton, had to support a severe conflict against those which he had so long nourished against her father. To clasp in friendship the hand of the enemy of his house, to entertain him under his roof, to exchange with him the courtesies and the kindness of domestic familiarity, was a degradation which his proud spirit could not be bent to without a struggle.

But the ice being once broken, the Lord Keeper resolved it should not have time again to freeze. It had been part of his plan to stun and confuse Ravenswood's ideas, by a complicated and technical statement of the matters which had been in debate betwixt their families, justly thinking it would be difficult for a youth of his age to follow the expositions of a practical lawyer, concerning actions of compt and reckoning, and of multiplepoinding, and adjudication and wadsets, proper and improper, and poindings of the ground and declarators of expiry of the legal. Thus, thought Sir William, I shall have all the grace of appearing perfectly communicative, while my party will derive very little advantage from any thing I may tell him. He therefore took Ravenswood aside into the deep recess of a window in the hall, and resuming the discourse of the preceding evening, expressed a hope that his young friend would assume some patience, in order to hear him enter into a minute and explanatory detail of those unfortunate circumstances, in which his late honourable father had stood at variance with the Lord Keeper. The Master of Ravenswood coloured highly, but was silent; and the Lord Keeper, though not greatly approving the sudden heightening of his auditor's complexion, commenced the history of a bond for twenty thousand marks, advanced by his father to the father of Allan Lord Ravenswood, and was proceeding to detail the executorial proceedings by which this large sum had been rendered a *debitum fundi*, when he was interrupted by the Master.

"It is not in this place," he said, "that I can hear Sir William Ashton's explanation of the matters in question between us. It is not here, where my father died of a broken heart, that I can with decency or temper investigate the cause of his distress. I might remember that I was a son, and forget the duties of a host. A time, however, there must come, when these things shall be discussed in a place and in a presence where both of us will have equal freedom to speak and to hear."

"Any time," the Lord Keeper said, "any place was alike to those who sought nothing but justice. Yet it would seem he was, in fairness, entitled to some premonition respecting the grounds on which the Master proposed to impugn the whole train of legal proceedings, which had been so well and ripely advised in the only courts competent."

"Sir William Ashton," answered the Master with warmth, "the lands of Ravenswood which you now occupy were granted to my remote ancestor for services done with his sword against the English invaders. How they have glided from us by a train of proceedings that

seem to be neither sale, nor mortgage, nor adjudication for debt, but a
non-descript and entangled mixture of all these rights—how annual-
rent has been accumulated upon principal, and no nook or coign of
legal advantage left unoccupied, until our interest in our hereditary
property seems to have melted away like an icicle in thaw—all this you
understand better than me. I am willing, however, to suppose, from
the frankness of your conduct towards me, that I may in a great
measure have mistaken your character, and that things may have
appeared right and fitting to you, a skilful and practised lawyer, which
to my ignorant understanding seem very little short of injustice and
gross oppression."

"And you, my dear Master," answered Sir William, "you, permit
me to say, have been equally misrepresented to me. I was taught to
believe you a fierce, imperious, hot-headed youth, ready, at the slightest provocation, to throw your sword into the scales of justice, and to
appeal to those rude and forcible measures from which civil polity has
long protected the people of Scotland. Then, since we were mutually
mistaken in each other, why should not the young nobleman be willing
to listen to the old lawyer, while, at least, he explains the points of
difference betwixt them?"

"No, my lord," answered Ravenswood; "it is in the Estates of the
nation, in the supreme Court of Parliament, that we must parley
together. The belted lords and knights of Scotland, her ancient peers
and baronage, must decide, if it is well that a house, not the least noble
of their number, shall be stripped of their possessions, the reward of
the patriotism of generations, as the pawn of a wretched mechanic
becomes forfeit to the usurer the instant the hour of redemption has
passed away. If they yield to the grasping severity of the creditor, and
to the gnawing usury that eats into our lands as moths into raiment, it
will be of more evil consequence to them and their posterity than to
Edgar Ravenswood—I shall still have my sword and my cloak, and can
follow the profession of arms wherever a trumpet shall sound."

As he pronounced these words, in a firm yet melancholy tone, he
raised his eyes, and suddenly encountered those of Lucy Ashton,
who had stolen unawares on their interview, and observed her looks
fastened on them with an expression of enthusiastic interest and
admiration, which had rapt her for the moment beyond the fear of
discovery. The noble form and fine features of Ravenswood, fired
with the pride of birth and sense of internal dignity—the mellow
and expressive tones of his voice, the desolate state of his fortunes,
and the indifference with which he seemed to endure and to dare
the worst that might befall, rendered him a dangerous object of
contemplation for a maiden already too much disposed to dwell

upon recollections connected with him. When their eyes encountered each other, both blushed deeply, conscious of some strong internal emotion, and shunned again to meet each other's look.

Sir William Ashton had, of course, closely watched the expression of their countenances. "I need fear," thought he to himself, "neither Parliament nor protestation; I have an effectual mode of reconciling myself with this hot-tempered young fellow, in case he shall become formidable. The present object is, at all events, to avoid committing ourselves. The hook is fixed; we will not strain the line too soon, and we will reserve the privilege of slipping it loose, if we do not find the fish worth landing."

In this selfish and cruel calculation upon the supposed attachment of Ravenswood to Lucy, he was so far from considering the pain he might give to the former, by thus dallying with his affections, that he did not even think upon the risk of involving his own daughter in the perils of an unfortunate passion; as if her predilection, which could not escape his attention, were like the flame of a taper, which might be lighted or extinguished at pleasure. But Providence had prepared a dreadful requital for this keen observer of human passions, who had spent his life in securing advantages to himself by artfully working upon the passions of others.

Caleb Balderstone now came to announce that breakfast was prepared; for in these days of substantial feeding, the reliques of the supper amply furnished forth the morning meal. Neither did he forget to present to the Lord Keeper, with great reverence, a morning-draught in a large pewter cup, garnished with leaves of parsley and scurvy-grass. He craved pardon, of course, for having omitted to serve it in the great silver standing cup as behoved, being that it was at present in a silversmith's in Edinburgh, for the purpose of being overlaid with gilt.

"In Edinburgh sure enough," said Ravenswood; "but in what place, or for what purpose, Caleb, I am afraid neither you nor I know."

"Aweel!" said Caleb peevishly, "there's a man standing at the gate already this morning—that's ae thing that I ken—Does your honour ken whether ye will speak wi' him or no?"

"Does he wish to speak with me, Caleb?"

"Less will no serve him," said Caleb; "but ye had best take a visie of him through the wicket before opening the gate—its no every ane we suld let into this castle."

"What! do you suppose him to be a messenger come to arrest me for debt?" said Ravenswood.

"A messenger—your honour for debt—and in your Castle of Wolfscrag!—your honour is jesting wi' auld Caleb this morning."

However, he whispered in his ear as he followed him out, "I would be loth to do ony decent man a prejudice in your honour's gude opinion; but I wad take twa looks of that chield before I let him within these walls."

It was no officer of the law, however, but no less a person than Captain Craigengelt, with his nose as red as a comfortable cup of brandy could make it, his laced cocked-hat set a little aside upon the top of his black riding periwig, a sword by his side, and pistols at his holsters, and his person arrayed in a riding suit, laid over with tarnished lace,—the very moral of one who would say, Stand, to a true man.

When the Master had recognized him, he ordered the gates to be opened. "I suppose," he said, "Captain Craigengelt, there are no such weighty matters betwixt you and me, but what may be discussed in this place. I have company in the castle at present, and the terms upon which we last parted must excuse my asking you to make part of them."

Craigengelt, although the very perfection of impudence, was somewhat abashed by this unfavourable reception. "He had no intention," he said, "to force himself upon the Master of Ravenswood's hospitality—he was in the honourable service of bearing a message to him from a friend, otherwise the Master of Ravenswood should not have had reason to complain of this intrusion."

"Let it be short, sir," said the Master, "for that will be the best apology. Who is the gentleman who is so fortunate as to have your services as a messenger?"

"My friend Mr Hayston of Bucklaw, sir" answered Craigengelt, with conscious importance, and that confidence which the acknowledged courage of his principal inspired, "who conceives himself to have been treated by you with something much short of the respect which he had reason to demand, and therefore is resolved to exact satisfaction. I bring with me," said he, taking a piece of paper out of his pocket, "the precise length of his sword; and he requests you will meet him, accompanied with a friend, and equally armed, at any place within a mile of the castle, when I shall give attendance as umpire or second on his behoof."

"Satisfaction—and equal arms!" repeated Ravenswood, who, the reader will recollect, had no reason whatever to suppose he had given the slightest offence to his late inmate—"upon my word, Captain Craigengelt, either you have invented the most improbable falsehood that ever came into the mind of such a person, or your morning-draught has been somewhat of the strongest. What could persuade Bucklaw to send me such a message?"

"For that, sir," replied Craigengelt, "I am desired to refer you to what, in duty to my friend, I am to term your inhospitality in excluding him from your house, without reasons assigned."

"It is impossible," replied the Master; "he cannot be such a fool as to interpret actual necessity as an insult. Nor do I believe, that, knowing my opinion of you, captain, he would have employed the services of so slight and inconsiderable a person as yourself upon such an errand, as I certainly could expect no man of honour to act with you in the office of umpire."

"I slight and inconsiderable!" said Craigengelt, raising his voice, and laying his hand on his cutlass; "if it were not that the quarrel of my friend craves the precedence, and is in dependence before my own, I would give you to understand"——

"I can understand nothing upon your explanation, Captain Craigengelt—be satisfied of that, and oblige me with your departure."

"D——n!" muttered the bully; "and is this the answer which I am to carry back to an honourable message?"

"Tell the Laird of Bucklaw," answered Ravenswood, "if you are really sent by him, that when he sends me his cause of grievance by a person fitting to carry such an errand betwixt him and me, I will either explain it or maintain it."

"Then, Master, you will at least cause to be returned to Hayston, by my hands, his property which is remaining in your possession."

"Whatever property Bucklaw may have left behind him, sir," replied the Master, "shall be returned to him by my servant, as you do not shew me any credentials from him which entitle you to receive it."

"Well, Master," said Captain Craigengelt, with malice which even his fear of the consequences could not suppress; "you have this morning done me egregious wrong and dishonour, but far more to yourself. A castle indeed?" he continued, looking around him; "why this is worse than a *coupe-gorge* house, where they receive travellers to plunder them of their property."

"You insolent rascal," said the Master, raising his cane, and making a grasp at the captain's bridle, "if you do not depart without uttering another syllable, I will batoon you to death."

At the motion of the Master towards him, the bully turned so sharply round, that with some difficulty he escaped throwing down his horse, whose hoofs struck fire from the rocky pavement in every direction. Recovering him, however, with the bridle, he pushed for the gate, and rode sharply back again in the direction of the village.

As Ravenswood turned round to leave the court-yard after this dialogue, he found that the Lord Keeper had descended from the hall, and witnessed, though at the distance prescribed by politeness, his interview with Craigengelt.

"I have seen," said the Lord Keeper, "that gentleman's face, and at no great distance of time—his name is Craig—Craig—something, is it not?"

"Craigengelt is the fellow's name," said the Master, "at least that by which he passes at present."

"Craig-in-guilt," said Caleb, punning upon the word *craig*, which in Scotch signifies throat; "if he is Craig-in-guilt just now, he is as likely to be Craig-in-peril as ony chield I ever saw—the loon has woodie written on his very visnomy, and I wad wage twa and a plack that hemp plaits his cravat yet."

"You understand physiognomy, good Mr Caleb," said the Keeper, smiling; "I assure you the gentleman has been near such a consummation before now; for I most distinctly recollect, that, upon occasion of a journey which I made about a fortnight ago to Edinburgh, I saw Mr Graigengelt, or whatever his name is, undergo a severe examination before the Privy Council."

"Upon what account?" said the Master of Ravenswood, with some interest.

The question led immediately to a tale which the Lord Keeper had been very anxious to introduce, when he could find a graceful and fitting opportunity. He took hold of the Master's arm, and led him back towards the hall. "The answer to your question," he said, "though it is a ridiculous business, is only fit for your own ear."

As they entered the hall, he again took the Master apart into one of the recesses of the window, where it will be easily believed Miss Ashton did not venture again to intrude upon their conference.

Chapter Three

——Here is a father now,
Will truck his daughter for a foreign venture,
Make her the stop-gap to some cankered feud,
Or fling her o'er, like Jonah, to the fishes,
To appease the sea at highest.
Anonymous

THE LORD KEEPER opened his communication with an appearance of unconcern, marking, however, very carefully, the effect of his communication upon young Ravenswood.

"You are aware," he said, "my young friend, that suspicion is the natural vice of our unsettled times, and exposes the best and wisest of us to the impositions of artful rascals. If I had been disposed to listen to such the other day, or if I had been the wily politician which you have been taught to believe me, you, Master of Ravenswood, instead of being at freedom, and with full liberty to solicit and act against me as you please, in defence of what you suppose to be your right, would have been in the Castle of Edinburgh, or some other state prison; if you had escaped that destiny, it must have been by flight to a foreign country, and at the risk of a sentence of fugitation."

"My Lord Keeper," said the Master, "I think you would not jest on such a subject—yet it seems impossible you can be in earnest."

"Innocence," said the Lord Keeper, "is also confident, and sometimes, though very excusably, presumptuously so."

"I do not understand," said Ravenswood, "how a consciousness of innocence can be, in any case, accounted presumptuous."

"Imprudent, at least, it may be called," said Sir William Ashton, "since it is apt to lead us into the mistake of supposing that sufficiently evident to others, of which, in fact, we are only conscious ourselves. I have known a rogue, for this very reason, make a better defence than an innocent man could have done in the same circumstances of suspicion. Having no consciousness of innocence to support him, such a fellow applies himself to all the advantages which the law will afford him, and sometimes (if his counsel be men of talent,) succeeds in compelling his judges to receive him as innocent. I remember the celebrated case of Sir Coolie Condiddle of Condiddle, who was tried for theft under trust, of which all the world knew him guilty, and yet was not only acquitted, but lived to sit in judgment on honester folks."

"Allow me to beg you will return to the point," said the Master; "you seemed to say that I had suffered under some suspicion."

"Suspicion, Master?—ay, truly—And I can shew you the proofs of it; if I happen only to have them with me.—Here, Lockhard"—His attendant came—"Fetch me the little private mail with the padlocks, that I recommended to your particular charge—d'ye hear?"

"Yes, my lord." Lockhard vanished; and the Keeper continued as if half speaking with himself.

"I think the papers are with me—I think so—for as I was to be in this country, it was natural for me to bring them with me—I have them, however, at Ravenswood Castle—that I am sure of—so perhaps you might condescend"——

Here Lockhard entered, and put the leathern scrutoire, or mailbox, into his hands. The Keeper produced one or two papers, respecting the information laid before the Privy Council, concerning the riot, as it was termed, at the funeral of Allan Lord Ravenswood, and the active share he had himself taken in quashing the proceedings against the Master. These documents had been selected with care, so as to irritate the natural curiosity of Ravenswood upon such a subject, without gratifying it, yet to shew that Sir William Ashton had acted upon that trying occasion the part of an advocate and peace-maker betwixt him and the jealous authority of the day. Having furnished his host with such subjects for examination, the Lord Keeper turned to the breakfast-table, and entered into light conversation, addressed partly to old Caleb, whose resentment against the usurper of the Castle of Ravenswood began to be softened by his familiarity, and partly to his daughter.

After perusing the papers, the Master of Ravenswood remained for a minute or two with his hand pressed against his brow, in deep and profound meditation. He then again ran his eye hastily over the papers, as if desirous of discovering in them some deep purpose, or some mark of fabrication, which had escaped him at first perusal. Apparently the second reading confirmed the opinion which had pressed upon him at the first, for he started from the stone-bench on which he was sitting, and, going to the Lord Keeper, took his hand, and, strongly pressing it, asked him pardon repeatedly for the injustice he had done him, when it appeared he was experiencing, at his hands, the benefit of protection to his person, and vindication to his character.

The statesman received these acknowledgments at first with well-feigned surprise, and then with an affectation of frank cordiality. The tears began already to start in Lucy's blue eyes at viewing this unexpected and moving scene. To see the Master, late so haughty and reserved, and whom she had always supposed the injured person, supplicating her father for forgiveness, was a change at once surprising, flattering, and affecting.

"Dry your eyes, Lucy," said her father; "why should you weep, because your father, although a lawyer, is discovered to be a fair and honourable man?—What have you to thank, my dear Master," he continued, addressing Ravenswood, "that you would not have done in my case? '*Suum cuique tribuito*,' was the Roman justice, and I learned it when I studied Justinian. Besides, have you not overpaid me a thousand times in saving the life of this dear child?"

"Yes," answered the Master, in all the remorse of self-accusation; "but the little service *I* did was an act of mere brutal instinct; *your* defence of my cause, when you knew how ill I thought of you, and how much I was disposed to be your enemy, was an act of generous, manly, and considerate wisdom."

"Pshaw!" said the Lord Keeper, "each of us acted in our own way; you as a gallant soldier, I as an upright judge and privy-councillor. We could not, perhaps, have changed parts—at least I should have made a very sorry *Tauridor*, and you, my good Master, though your cause is so excellent, might have pleaded it perhaps worse yourself, than I who acted for you before the council."

"My generous friend!" said Ravenswood; and with that brief word, which the Keeper had often lavished on him, but which he himself now pronounced for the first time, he gave to his feudal enemy the full confidence of an haughty but honourable heart. He had been remarked among his contemporaries for sense and acuteness, as well as for his reserved, pertinacious, and irascible character. His prepossessions accordingly, however obstinate, were of a nature to give way before love and gratitude; and the real charms of the daughter, joined to the supposed services of the father, cancelled in his memory the vows of vengeance which he had taken so deeply on the eve of his father's funeral. But they had been heard and registered in the book of fate.

Caleb was present at this extraordinary scene, and he could conceive no other reason for a proceeding so extraordinary than an alliance betwixt the houses, and Ravenswood Castle assigned for the young lady's dowry. As for Lucy, when Ravenswood uttered the most passionate excuses for his ungrateful negligence, she could but smile through her tears, and, as she abandoned her hand to him, assure him, in broken accents, of the delight with which she beheld the complete reconciliation between her father and her deliverer. Even the statesman was moved and affected by the fiery, unreserved, and generous self-abandonment with which the Master of Ravenswood renounced his feudal enmity, and threw himself without hesitation upon his forgiveness. His eyes glistened as he looked upon a couple who were obviously becoming attached, and who seemed made for each other. He thought how high the proud and chivalrous character of Ravenswood might arise under many circumstances, in which *he* felt himself "over-crowed," to use a phrase of Spencer, and kept under, by his brief pedigree, and timidity of disposition. Then his daughter—his favourite child—his constant play-mate—seemed formed to live happy in union with such a commanding spirit as Ravenswood; and even the fine, delicate, fragile form of Lucy Ashton seemed to require the support of the Master's muscular strength and masculine character. And it was not merely during a few moments that Sir William Ashton looked upon their marriage as a probable and even desirable event, for a full hour intervened ere his imagination was crossed by recollection of the Master's poverty, and the certain displeasure of Lady Ashton. It is certain, that the very unusual flow of kindly feeling into which the Lord Keeper had been thus surprised, was one of the circumstances which gave much tacit encouragement to the attachment between the Master and his daughter, and led both the lovers distinctly to believe that it was a connection which would be most agreeable to him. He himself was supposed to have admitted this effect, when, long after the catastrophe of their love, he used to warn his hearers against permitting their feelings to obtain an ascendancy over their judgment, and affirm that the greatest misfortune of his life was owing to a very temporary predominance of sensibility over self-interest. It must be owned, if such was the case, he was long and severely punished for an offence of very brief duration.

After some pause, the Lord Keeper resumed the conversation.— "In your surprise at finding me an honester man than you expected, you have lost your curiosity about this Craigengelt, my good Master; and yet your name was brought in in the course of that matter too."

"The scoundrel!" said Ravenswood; "my connection with him was of the most temporary nature possible; and yet I was very foolish to hold any communication with him at all.—What did he say of me?"

"Enough," said the Keeper with a smile, "to excite the very loyal terrors of some of our sages, who are for proceeding against men on mere grounds of suspicion or mercenary information—Some nonsense about your proposing to enter into the service of France, or of the Pretender, I don't recollect which, but which the Marquis of A——, one of your best friends, and another person, one of your worst and most interested enemies, could not, some how, be brought to listen to."

"I am obliged to my honourable friend—and yet"—shaking the Lord Keeper's hand—"and yet I am still more obliged to my honourable enemy."

"*Inimicus amicissimus*," said the Lord Keeper, returning the pressure; "but this gentleman—this Mr Hayston of Bucklaw. I am afraid the poor young man—I heard the fellow mention his name—is under very bad guidance."

"He is old enough to govern himself," answered the Master.

"Old enough, perhaps, but scarce wise enough, if he has chosen this fellow for his *fidus Achates*. Why, he lodged an information against him—that is, such a consequence must have ensued from his examination, had we not looked rather at the character of the witness than the tenor of his evidence."

"Mr Hayston of Bucklaw," said the Master, "is, I believe, a most honourable man, and capable of nothing that is mean or disgraceful."

"Capable of much that is unreasonable though, that you must needs allow, Master. Death will soon put him in possession of a fair estate, if he hath it not already. Old Lady Girnington—an excellent person, excepting that her inveterate ill-nature rendered her intolerable to the whole world—is probably dead by this time. Six heirs portioners have successively died to make her rich. I know the estates well; they march with my own—a noble property."

"I am glad of it," said Ravenswood, "and should be more so, were I confident that Bucklaw would change his company and habits with his fortunes. This appearance of Craigengelt, acting in the capacity of his friend, is a most vile augury for his future respectability."

"He is a bird of evil omen, to be sure," said the Keeper, "and croaks of jail and gallow-tree.—But I see Mr Caleb grows impatient for our return to breakfast."

Chapter Four

Sir, stay at home and take an old man's council;
Seek not to bask you by a stranger's hearth;
Our own blue smoke is warmer than their fire.
Domestic food is wholesome, though 'tis homely,
And foreign dainties poisonous, though tasteful.
                                    The French Courtezan

THE MASTER of Ravenswood took an opportunity to leave his guests to prepare for their departure, while he himself made the brief arrangements necessary previous to his absence from Wolfscrag for a day or two. It was necessary to communicate with Caleb on this occasion, and he found that faithful servitor in his sooty and ruinous den, greatly delighted with the departure of their visitors, and computing how long, with good management, the provisions which had been unexpended might furnish forth the Master's table. "He's nae belly-god, that's ae blessing; and Bucklaw's gane, that could have eaten a horse behind the saddle. Cresses or water-purpie, and a bit cake, can serve the Master for breakfast as weel as Caleb—than for dinner—there's no muckle left on the spule-bane—it will brander though—it will brander very weel."

His triumphant calculations were interrupted by the Master, who communicated to him, not without some hesitation, his purpose to ride with the Lord Keeper as far as Ravenswood Castle, and to remain there for a day or two."

"The mercy of Heaven forbid!" said the old serving-man, turning as pale as the table-cloth which he was folding up.

"And why, Caleb?" said his master, "why should the mercy of Heaven forbid my returning the Lord Keeper's visit?"

"Oh, sir!" replied Caleb—"O Mr Edgar! I am your servant, and it ill becomes me to speak—but I am an auld servant—have served baith your father and goodsire, and mind to hae seen Lord Randal, your great-grandsire—but that was when I was a bairn."

"And what of all this, Balderstone?" answered the Master; "what can it possibly have to do with my paying some ordinary civility to a neighbour?"

"O Mr Edgar!"—answered the Butler, "your ain conscience tells you it isna for your father's son to be neighbouring wi' the like o' him —it is no for the credit of the family. An he were anes come to terms, and to gi'e ye back your ain, e'en though you suld honour his house wi' your alliance, I suldna say nae—for the young leddy is a winsome sweet creature—But keep your ain state wi' them—I ken the race o' them weel—they will think the mair o' ye."

"Why, now, you go farther than I do, Caleb," said the Master, drowning a certain degree of consciousness in a forced laugh; "you are for marrying me into a family that you will not allow me to visit— how's this?—and you look as pale as death besides."

"O, sir," repeated Caleb again, "you would but laugh if I tauld it; but Thomas the Rhymer, whose tongue couldna lie, spoke the word of your house that will e'en prove ower true if you go to Ravenswood this day—O that it should e'er have been fulfilled in my time!"

"And what is it, Caleb?" said Ravenswood, wishing to sooth the fears of his old servant.

Caleb replied, "he had never repeated the lines to living mortal— they were told to him by an auld priest that had been confessor to Lord Allan's father when the family were catholic. But mony a time," he said, "I hae soughed thae dark words ower to mysell, and, well-a-day! little did I think of their coming round this day."

"Truce with your nonsense, and let me hear the doggrel which has put it into your head," said the Master impatiently.

With a quivering voice, and a cheek pale with apprehension, Caleb faultered out the following lines:—

> "When the last Laird of Ravenswood to Ravenswood shall ride,
> And wooe a dead maiden to be his bride,
> He shall stable his steed on the Kelpie's flow,
> And his name shall be lost for evermoe!"

"I know the Kelpie's flow well enough; I suppose, at least, you mean the quick-sand betwixt this tower and Wolfshope; but why any man in his senses should stable a steed there"——

"O, never speer ony thing about that, sir—God forbid we should ken what the prophecy means—but just bide you at hame, and let the strangers ride to Ravenswood by themselves. We have done aneugh for them; and to do mair, would be mair against the credit of the family than in its favour."

"Well, Caleb," said the Master, "I give you the best possible credit for your good advice on this occasion; but as I do not go to Ravenswood to seek a bride, dead or alive, I hope I shall chuse a better stable for my horse than the Kelpie's quick-sand, especially as I have always had a particular dread of it since the patrole of dragoons were lost there ten years since. My father and I saw them from the tower struggling amid the advancing tide and lost long before any help could reach them."

"And they deserved it weel, the Southron loons," said Caleb; "what had they ado capering on our sands, and hindering a wheen honest folk frae bringing in a drap brandy? I hae seen them that busy, that I wad hae fired the auld culverin, and the demisaker that's on the south bartizan at them, only I was feared they might burst in the ganging off."

Caleb's brain was now fully engaged with abuse of the English soldiery and excisemen, so that his master found no great difficulty in escaping from him and rejoining his guests. All was now ready for their departure; and one of the Lord Keeper's grooms having saddled the Master's steed, they mounted in the court-yard.

Caleb had, with much toil, opened the double doors of the outward gate, and stationed himself, endeavouring, by the reverential, and, at the same time, consequential air which he assumed, to supply, by his own gaunt, wasted, and thin person, the absence of a whole baronial establishment of porters, warders, and liveried menials.

The Keeper returned his deep reverence with a cordial farewell, stooping at the same time from his horse, and sliding into the Butler's hand the remuneration, which in these days was always given by a departing guest to the domestics of the family where he had been entertained. Lucy smiled on the old man with her usual sweetness, bade him adieu, and deposited her guerdon with a grace of action, and a gentleness of accent, which would not have failed to have won the faithful retainer's heart, but for Thomas the Rhymer, and the successful law-suit against his master. As it was, he might have adopted the language of the Duke, in *As You Like It*—

> Thou wouldst have better pleased me with this deed,
> If thou hadst told me of another father.——

Ravenswood was at the lady's bridle-rein, encouraging her timidity, and guiding her horse carefully down the rocky path which led to the moor, when one of the servants announced from the rear that Caleb was calling loudly after them, desiring to speak with his master. Ravenswood felt it would look singular to neglect this summons, although inwardly cursing Caleb for his impertinent officiousness; therefore he was compelled to relinquish to Mr Lockhard the agreeable duty in which he was engaged, and to ride back to the gate of the

court-yard. Here he was beginning, somewhat peevishly, to ask Caleb
the cause of his clamour, when the good old man exclaimed, "Whisht,
sir! whisht, and let me speak just ae word that I couldna say afore frem
folk—there"—(putting into his lord's hand the money he had just
received)—"there's three gowd pieces—and ye'll want siller up-bye
yonder—but stay, whisht now!"—for the Master was beginning to
exclaim against this transference—"never say a word, but just see to
get them changed in the first town ye ride through, for they are bran
new frae the mint, and kenspeckle a wee bit."

"You forget, Caleb," said his master, striving to force back the
money upon his servant, and extricate the bridle from his hold—"You
forget that I have some gold pieces left of my own. Keep these to
yourself, my old friend; and, once more, good day to you. I assure you
I have plenty. You know you have managed that our living should cost
us little or nothing."

"Aweel," said Caleb, "these will serve for you another time; but see
ye hae aneugh, for, doubtless, for the credit of the family, there maun
be something gi'en to the servants, and ye maun hae something to mak
a show with when they say, Master, will you bet a broad piece? Then
ye maun tak out your purse, and say, I carena if I do; and tak care no to
agree on the articles of the wager, and just put up your purse again,
and"——

"This is intolerable, Caleb—I really must be gone."

"And you will go, then?" said Caleb, loosening his hold upon the
Master's cloak, and changing his didactic into a pathetic and mournful
tone—"And you *will* go, for a' I have told you about the prophecy, and
the dead bride, and the Kelpie's quick-sand—Aweel! a wilful man
maun hae his way—he that will to Cupar maun to Cupar—but pity of
your life, sir, if ye be fowling or shooting in the Park—beware of
drinking at the Mermaiden's well——He's gane! he's down the path,
arrow-flight after her!—The head is as clean ta'en aff the Ravenswood family this day, as I wad chap the head aff a sybo!"

The old Butler looked long after his master, often clearing away the
dew as it rose to his eyes, that he might, as long as possible, distinguish
his stately form from those of the other horsemen. "Close to her
bridle-rein—ay, close to her bridle-rein!—Wisely saith the holy man,
'By this also ye may know that woman hath dominion over all men;'—
and without this lass would not our ruin have been altogether fulfilled."

With an heart fraught with such sad auguries did Caleb return to his
necessary duties at Wolfscrag, so soon as he could no longer distinguish the object of his anxiety among the groupe of riders, which
diminished in the distance.

In the mean time the party pursued their route joyfully. Having once taken his resolution, the Master of Ravenswood was not of a character to hesitate or pause upon it. He abandoned himself to the pleasure he felt in Miss Ashton's company, and displayed an assiduous gallantry, which approached as nearly to gaiety as the temper of his mind and state of his family permitted. The Lord Keeper was much struck by his depth of observation, and the unusual improvement which he had derived from his studies. Of these accomplishments Sir William Ashton's profession and habits of society rendered him an excellent judge; and he well knew how to appreciate what he did not quite so well comprehend, being a quality to which he himself was a total stranger, the brief and decided dauntlessness of the Master of Ravenswood's disposition, who seemed equally a stranger to doubt and to fear. In his heart the Lord Keeper rejoiced at having conciliated an adversary so formidable, while, with a mixture of pleasure and anxiety, he anticipated the great things his young companion might achieve, were the breath of court-favour to fill his sails.

"What could she desire," he thought, his mind always conjuring up opposition in the person of Lady Ashton to his now prevailing wish—"What could the woman desire in a match, more than the sopiting of a very dangerous claim, and the alliance of a son-in-law, noble, brave, well-gifted, and highly-connected—sure to float whenever the tide sets his way—strong, exactly where we are weak, in pedigree and in the temper of a swordsman?—Sure no reasonable woman would hesitate—but, alas!"—Here his argument was stopped by the consciousness that Lady Ashton was not always reasonable, in his sense of the word. "To prefer some clownish Merse laird to the gallant young nobleman, and to the secure possession of Ravenswood upon terms of easy compromise—it would be the act of a madwoman!"

Thus pondered the veteran politician, until they reached Bittlebrain House, where it had been previously settled they were to dine and repose themselves, and prosecute their journey in the afternoon.

They were received with an excess of hospitality; and the most marked attention was offered to the Master of Ravenswood, in particular, by their noble entertainers. The truth was, that Lord Bittlebrain had obtained his peerage by a good deal of plausibility, an art of building up a character for wisdom upon a very trite style of commonplace eloquence, a steady observation of the changes of the times, and the power of rendering certain political services to those who could best reward them. His lady and he not feeling quite easy under their new honours, to which use had not adapted their feelings, were very desirous to procure the fraternal countenance of those who were born denizens of the regions into which they had been exalted from a lower sphere. The extreme attention which they paid to the Master of Ravenswood, had its usual effect in exalting his importance in the eyes of the Lord Keeper, who, although he had a reasonable degree of contempt for Lord Bittlebrain's general parts, entertained a high opinion of the acuteness of his judgment in matters of self-interest.

"I wish Lady Ashton had seen this," was his internal reflection; "no man knows so well as Bittlebrain on which side his bread is buttered; and he fawns on the Master like a beggar's messan on a cook. And my lady, too, bringing forward her beetle-browed misses to skirl and play upon the virginals, as if she said, pick and chuse. They are no more comparable to Lucy than a crow is to a cygnet, and so they may carry their black brows to a farther market."

The entertainment being ended, our travellers, who had still to measure the longest part of their journey, resumed their horses; and after the Lord Keeper, the Master, and the domestics, had drunk *dochan dorroch*, or the stirrup-cup, in the liquors adapted to their various ranks, the cavalcade resumed its progress.

It was dark by the time they entered the avenue at Ravenswood Castle, a long straight line leading directly to the front of the house, flanked with huge elm-trees, which sighed to the night-wind, as if they compassionated the heir of their ancient proprietors, who now returned to their shades in the society, and almost in the retinue, of their new master. Some feelings of the same kind oppressed the mind of the Master himself. He gradually became silent, and dropped a little behind the lady, at whose bridle-rein he had hitherto waited with such devotion. He well recollected the period, when, at the same hour in the evening, he had accompanied his father, as that nobleman left, never again to return to it, the mansion from which he derived his name and title. The extensive front of the old castle, on which he remembered having often looked back, was then "as black as mourning weed." The same front now glanced with many lights, some throwing far forward into the night a fixed and stationary blaze, and others hurrying from one window to another, intimating the bustle and busy preparation preceding their arrival, which had been intimated by an avant-courier. The contrast pressed so strongly upon the Master's heart, as to awaken some of the sterner feelings with which he had been accustomed to regard the new lord of his paternal domain, and to impress his countenance with an air of severe gravity, when, alighted from his horse, he stood in the hall no longer his own, surrounded by the numerous menials of its present owner.

The Lord Keeper, when about to welcome him with the cordiality which their late intercourse seemed to render proper, became aware of the change, refrained from his purpose, and only intimated the ceremony of reception by a deep reverence to his guest, seeming thus delicately to share the feelings which predominated on his brow.

Two upper domestics, bearing each a huge pair of silver candlesticks, now marshalled the company into a large saloon or with-drawing room, where new alterations impressed upon Ravenswood the superior wealth of the present inhabitants of the castle. The mouldering tapestry, which, in his father's time, had half covered the walls of this stately apartment, and half streamed from them in tatters, had given place to a complete finishing of wainscot, the cornice of which, as well as the frames of the various copartments, were ornamented with festoons of flowers and with birds, which, though carved in oak, seemed, such was the art of the chisel, actually to swell their throats, and flutter their wings. Several old family portraits of armed heroes of the house of Ravenswood, together with a suit or two of old armour, and some military weapons, had given place to those of King William and Queen Mary, of Sir Thomas Hope and Lord Stair, two distinguished Scottish lawyers. The pictures of the Lord Keeper's father and mother were also to be seen; the latter, sour, shrewish, and solemn, in her black hood and close pinners, with a book of devotion in her hand; the former, exhibiting beneath a black silk Geneva cowl, or scull-cap, which sate as close to the head as if it had been shaven, a pinched, peevish, puritanical set of features, terminating in a hungry, reddish, peaked beard, forming on the whole a countenance, in the expression of which the hypocritic seemed to contend with the miser or the knave. And it is to make room for such as these, thought Ravenswood, that my ancestors have been torn from the walls which they erected. He looked at them again, and, as he looked, the recollection of Lucy Ashton (for she had not entered the apartment with them) seemed less lovely in his imagination. There were also two or three Dutch drolleries, as the pictures of Ostade and Teniers were then termed, with one good painting of the Italian school. There was, besides, a noble full-length of the Lord Keeper in his robes of office, placed beside his lady in silk and ermine, a haughty beauty, bearing in her looks all the pride of the House of Douglas, from which she was descended. The painter, notwithstanding his skill, overcome by the reality, or, perhaps, from a suppressed sense of humour, had not been able to give the husband on the canvass that air of awful rule and right supremacy, which indicates the full possession of domestic authority. It was obvious, at the first glance, that, despite mace and gold frogs, the Lord Keeper was somewhat hen-pecked. The floor of this fine saloon was laid with rich carpets, huge fires blazed in the double chimnies, and ten silver sconces reflecting, with their bright plates, the lights which they supported, made the whole scene as brilliant as day.

"Would you chuse any refreshment, Master?" said Sir William Ashton, not unwilling to break the awkward silence.

He received no answer, the Master being so busily engaged in marking the various changes which had taken place in the apartment, that he scarcely heard the Lord Keeper address him. A repetition of the offer of refreshment, with the addition, that the family meal would be presently ready, compelled his attention, and reminded him, that he acted a weak, perhaps even a ridiculous part, in suffering himself to be overcome by the circumstances in which he found himself. He compelled himself, therefore, to enter into conversation with Sir William Ashton, with as much appearance of indifference as he could well command.

"You will not be surprised, Sir William, that I am interested in the changes you have made for the better in this apartment. In my father's time, after our misfortunes compelled him to live in retirement, it was little used, except by me as a play-room, when the weather would not permit me to go abroad. In that recess was my little work-shop, where I treasured the few carpenter's tools which old Caleb procured for me, and taught me how to use—there, in yonder corner, under that handsome silver sconce, I kept my fishing-rods, and hunting poles, bows, and arrows."

"I have a young *birkie*," said the Lord Keeper, willing to change the tone of the conversation, "of much the same turn—He is never happy, save when he is in the field—I wonder he is not here.—Here, Lockhard—send William Shaw for Mr Henry—I suppose he is, as usual, tied to Lucy's apron-string—that foolish girl, Master, draws the whole family after her at her pleasure."

Even this allusion to his daughter, though artfully thrown out, did not recal Ravenswood from his own topic.

"We were obliged to leave," he said, "some armour and portraits in this apartment—may I ask where they have been removed to?"

"Why," answered the Keeper, with some hesitation, "the room was fitted in our absence—and *cedant arma togæ*, is the maxim of lawyers you know—I am afraid it has been here somewhat too literally complied with. I hope—I believe they are safe—I am sure I gave orders—may I hope that when they are recovered and put in proper order, you will do me the honour to accept them at my hand, as an atonement for their accidental derangement?"

The Master of Ravenswood bowed stifly, and, with folded arms, again resumed his survey of the room.

Henry, a spoilt boy of fifteen, burst into the room, and ran up to his father. "Think of Lucy, papa; she has come home so cross and so fractious, that she will not go down to the stable to see my new poney, that Bob Wilson brought from the Mull of Galloway."

"I think you were very unreasonable to ask her," said the Keeper.

"Then you are as cross a patch as she is," answered the boy; "and when mamma comes home she'll claw up both your mittens."

"Hush your impertinence, you little forward imp," said his father; "where's your tutor?"

"Gone to a wedding at Dunbar—I hope he'll get a haggis to his dinner;" and he began to sing the old Scottish song,

> "There was a haggis in Dunbar,
> Fal de ral, &c.
> Mony better and few waur,
> Fal de ral," &c.

"I am much obliged to Mr Cordery for his attention," said the Lord Keeper; "and pray who has had charge of you while I was away, Mr Henry?"

"Norman and Bob Wilson—forbye my own self."

"A groom and a game-keeper, and your own silly self—proper guardians for a young advocate!—Why, you will never know any statutes but those against shooting red-deer, killing salmon, and"——

"And speaking of red-game," said the young scape-grace, interrupting his father without scruple or hesitation, "Norman has shot a buck, and I shewed the branches to Lucy, and she says they have but eight tynes, and she says that you killed a deer with Lord Bittlebrain's hounds, when you were west away, and do ye know she says it had ten tynes—is it true?"

"It may have had twenty, Henry, for what I know; but if you go to that gentleman he can tell you all about it—Go speak to him, Henry—it is the Master of Ravenswood."

While they conversed thus, the father and son were standing by the fire; and the Master having walked towards the upper end of the apartment, stood with his back towards them, apparently engaged in examining one of the paintings. The boy ran up to him, and pulled him by the skirt of the cloak with the freedom of a spoilt child, saying, "I say, sir—if you please to tell me"——but when the Master turned round, and Henry saw his face, he became suddenly and totally disconcerted—walked two or three steps backward, and still gazed on the Master with an air of fear and wonder, which had totally banished from his features their usual expression of pert vivacity.

"Come to me, young gentleman," said the Master, "and I will tell you all I know about the hunt."

"Go to the gentleman, Henry," said his father, "you are not used to be so shy."

But neither invitation nor exhortation had any effect on the boy. On the contrary, he turned round as soon as he had completed his survey of the Master, and walking as cautiously as if he had been treading upon eggs, he glided back to his father, and pressed as close to him as possible. Ravenswood, to avoid hearing the dispute betwixt the father and the over-indulged boy, thought it most polite to turn his face once more towards the pictures, and pay no attention to what they said.

"Why do you not speak to the Master, you little fool?" said the Lord Keeper.

"I am afraid," said Henry, in a very low tone.

"Afraid, you goose!" said his father, giving him a slight shake by the collar. "What makes you afraid?"

"What makes him so like the picture of Sir Malise Ravenswood, then?" said the boy, whimpering.

"What picture, you natural?" said his father. "I used to think you only a scape-grace, but I believe you turn out a born ideot."

"I tell you it is the picture of old Malise of Ravenswood, and he is as like it as if he had loupen out of the canvas; and it is up in the old Baron's hall that the maids launder the clothes in, and it has armour and not a coat like the gentleman, and he has whiskers and not a beard like the picture, and it has another kind of thing about the throat and no band-strings as he has, and"——

"And why should not the gentleman be like his ancestor, you silly boy?" said the Lord Keeper.

"Ay; but if he is come to chase us all out of the castle," said the boy, "and has twenty men at his back in disguise—and is come to say, with a hollow voice, *I bide my time*,—and is to kill you on the hearth as Malise did the other man, and whose blood is still to be seen!"

"Hush! nonsense!" said the Lord Keeper, not himself much pleased to hear these disagreeable coincidences forced on his notice. "Master, here comes Lockhard to say dinner is served."

And, at the same instant, Lucy entered at another door, having changed her dress since her return. The exquisite feminine beauty of the countenance, now shaded only by a profusion of sunny tresses; the sylph-like form disencumbered of her heavy riding-skirt, and mantled in azure silk; the grace of her manner and of her smile, cleared, with a celerity which surprised the Master himself, all the gloomy and unfavourable thoughts which had for some time over-clouded his fancy. In those features, so simply sweet, he could trace no alliance with the pinched visage of the peak-bearded black-capped puritan, or his starched withered spouse, with the craft expressed in the Lord Keeper's countenance, or the haughtiness which predominated in that of his lady; and, while he gazed on Lucy Ashton, she seemed to be an angel descended on earth, unallied to the coarser mortals among whom she deigned to dwell for a season. Such is the power of beauty over a youthful and enthusiastic fancy.

Chapter Five

————I do too ill in this,
And must not think but that a parent's plaint
Will move the heavens to pour forth misery
Upon the head of disobediency.
Yet reason tells us, parents are o'erseen,
When with too strict a rein they do hold in
Their child's affection, and controul that love,
Which the high powers divine inspire them with.
The Hog hath lost his Pearl

THE FEAST of Ravenswood Castle was as remarkable for its profusion, as that of Wolfscrag had been for its ill-veiled penury. The Lord Keeper might feel internal pride at the contrast, but he had too much *tact* to suffer it to appear. On the contrary, he appeared to remember with pleasure what he called Mr Balderstone's bachelor meal, and to be rather disgusted than pleased with the display around his own groaning board.

"We do these things," he said, "because others do them—but I was bred a plain man at my father's frugal table, and I should like well would my wife and family permit me to return to my sowens and my poor-man-of-mutton."

This was a little over-stretched. The Master only answered, "That different ranks—I mean," said he, correcting himself, "different degrees of wealth, required a different style of house-keeping."

This dry remark put a stop to farther conversation on the subject, nor is it necessary to record that which was substituted in its place. The evening was spent with freedom, and even cordiality; and Henry had so far overcome his first apprehensions, that he had settled a party for coursing a stag with the representative and living resemblance of grim Sir Malisius of Ravenswood, called the Revenger. The next morning was the appointed time—it rose upon active sportsmen and successful sport. The banquet came in course; and a pressing invitation to tarry yet another day was given and accepted. This Ravenswood had resolved should be the last of his stay; but he recollected he had not yet visited the ancient and devoted servant of his house, old Alice, and it was but kind to dedicate one morning to the gratification of so ancient an adherent.

To visit Alice, therefore, a day was devoted, and Lucy was the Master's guide upon the way. Henry, it is true, accompanied them, and took from their walk the air of a *tête-à-tête*, while, in reality, it was little else, considering the variety of circumstances which occurred to prevent the boy from giving the least attention to what passed between his companions. Now a rook settled on a branch within shot—anon a hare crossed their path, and Henry and his greyhound went astray in pursuit of it—then he had to hold a long conversation with the forester, which detained him a while behind his companions—and again he went to examine the earth of a badger, which carried him on a good way before them.

The conversation betwixt the Master and his sister, meanwhile, took an interesting, and almost a confidential turn. She could not help mentioning her sense of the pain he must feel in visiting scenes so well known to him, bearing now an aspect so different; and so gently was her sympathy expressed, that Ravenswood felt it for a moment as a full requital of all his misfortunes. Some such sentiment escaped him, which Lucy heard with more of confusion than displeasure; and she may be forgiven the imprudence of listening to such language, considering that the situation in which she was placed by her father seemed to authorise Ravenswood to use it. Yet she made an effort to turn the conversation, and she succeeded; for the Master also had advanced further than he intended, and his conscience had instantly checked him when he found himself on the verge of speaking of love to the daughter of Sir William Ashton.

They now approached the hut of old Alice, which had of late been rendered more comfortable, and presented an appearance less picturesque, perhaps, but far neater than before. The old woman was on her accustomed seat beneath the weeping birch, basking, with the listless enjoyment of age and infirmity, in the beams of the autumn sun. At the arrival of her visitors she turned her head towards them. "I hear your step, Miss Ashton," she said, "but the gentleman who attends you is not my lord, your father."

"And why should you think so, Alice?" said Lucy; "or how is it possible for you to judge so accurately by the sound of a step, on the firm earth, and in the open air?"

"My hearing, my child, has been sharpened by my blindness, and I can now judge of the slightest sounds, which formerly reached my ears as unheeded as they now approach yours. Necessity is a stern, but an excellent school-mistress, and she that has lost her sight must collect her information from other sources."

"Well, you hear a man's step, I grant it," said Lucy; "but why, Alice, may it not be my father's?"

"The pace of age, my love, is timid and cautious—the foot takes leave of the earth slowly, and is planted down upon it with hesitation; it is the hasty and determined step of youth that I now hear, and—could I give credit to so strange a thought—I should say it was the step of a Ravenswood."

"This is indeed," said Ravenswood, "an acuteness of organ which I could not have credited had I not witnessed it.—I am indeed the Master of Ravenswood, Alice—the son of your old master."

"You?" said the old woman with almost a scream of surprise—"you the Master of Ravenswood—here—in this place, and thus accompanied?—I cannot believe it—let me pass my old hand over your face, that my touch may bear witness to my ears."

The Master sate down beside her on the earthen bank, and permitted her to touch his features with her trembling hand.

"It is he indeed!" she said, "it is the features as well as the voice of Ravenswood—the high lines of pride, as well as the bold and haughty tone—but what do you here, Master of Ravenswood?—what do you in your enemy's domain, and in company with his child?"

As old Alice spoke, her face kindled, as probably that of an ancient feudal vassal might have done, in whose presence his youthful liege-lord had shewed some symptom of degenerating from the spirit of his ancestors.

"The Master of Ravenswood," said Lucy, who liked not the tone of this expostulation, and was desirous to abridge it, "is upon a visit to my father."

"Indeed?" said the old blind woman, in an accent of surprise.

"I knew," continued Lucy, "I should do him a pleasure by conducting him to your cottage."

"Where, to say the truth, Alice," said Ravenswood, "I expected a more cordial reception."

"It is most wonderful," said the old woman, muttering to herself; "but the ways of Heaven are not like our ways, and its judgments are brought about by means far beyond our fathoming.—Hearken, young man," she said; "your fathers were implacable, but they were honourable foes; they sought not to ruin their enemies under the mask of hospitality. What have you to do with Lucy Ashton?—why should your steps move in the same foot-path with her's?—why should your voice sound in the same chord and time with those of Sir William Ashton's daughter?—Young man, he who aims at revenge by dishonourable means"——

"Be silent, woman!" said Ravenswood sternly; "is it the devil that prompts your voice?—know that this young lady has not on earth a friend, who would venture farther to save her from injury or from insult."

"And is it even so?" said the old woman, in an altered but melancholy tone—"then God help you both!"

"Amen! Alice," said Lucy, who had not comprehended the import of what the blind woman had hinted, "and send you your senses, Alice, and your good-humour: if you hold this mysterious language instead of welcoming your friends, they will think of you as other people do."

"And how do other people think?" said Ravenswood, for he also began to think the old woman spoke with incoherence.

"They think," said Henry Ashton, who came up at that moment, and whispered into Ravenswood's ear, "that she is a witch that should have been burned with them that suffered at Haddington."

"What is that you say?" said Alice, turning towards the boy, her sightless visage inflamed with passion, "that I am witch, and ought to have suffered with the helpless old wretches who were murdered at Haddington?"

"Hear to that now," again whispered Henry, "and me whispering lower than a wren cheeps."

"If the usurer, and the oppressor, and the grinder of the poor man's face, and the remover of ancient land-marks, and the subverter of ancient houses, were at the same stake with me, I could say, light the fire, in God's name!"

"This is dreadful," said Lucy; "I have never seen the poor deserted woman in this state of mind; but age and poverty can ill bear reproach. —Come, Henry, we will leave Alice for the present—she wishes to speak with the Master alone—we will walk homeward, and rest us," she added, looking at Ravenswood, "by the Mermaiden's Well."

"And Alice," said the boy, "if you know of any hare that comes through among the deer, and makes them drop their calves out of season, you may tell her, with my compliments to command, that if Norman has not got a silver bullet ready for her, I'll lend him one of my doublet-buttons on purpose."

Alice made no answer till she was aware that they were out of hearing. She then said to Ravenswood, "And you, too, are angry with me for my love?—it is just that strangers should be offended, but you, too, are angry."

"I am not angry, Alice," said the Master, "only surprised that you, whose good sense I have heard so often praised, should give way to offensive and unfounded suspicions."

"Offensive?" said Alice—"Ay, truth is ever offensive—but, surely, not unfounded."

"I tell you, dame, most groundless," replied Ravenswood.

"Then the world has changed its wont, and Ravenswoods their hereditary temper, and the eyes of old Alice's understanding are yet more blind than those of her countenance. When did a Ravenswood seek the house of his enemy, but with the purpose of revenge?—And hither you are come, Edgar Ravenswood, either in fatal anger, or in still more fatal love."

"In neither," said Ravenswood, "I give you mine honour—I mean, I assure you."

Alice could not see his blushing cheek, but she noticed his hesitation, and that he retracted the pledge which he seemed at first disposed to attach to his denial.

"It is so, then," she said, "and therefore she is to tarry by the Mermaiden's Well! Often has it been called a place fatal to the race of Ravenswood—often has it proved so—but never was it likely to verify old sayings so much as on this day."

"You drive me to madness, Alice," said Ravenswood; "you are more silly and more superstitious than old Balderstone. Are you such a wretched Christian as to suppose I should maintain war with the Ashton family, as was the sanguinary custom in elder times? or do you suppose me so foolish, that I cannot walk by a young lady's side without plunging headlong in love with her?"

"My thoughts," replied Alice, "are my own; and if my mortal sight is closed to objects present with me, it may be I can look with the more steadiness into future events. Are you prepared to sit lowest at the board which was once your father's, owned unwillingly as a connection and ally of his proud successor?—are you ready to live on his bounty—to follow him in the bye-paths of intrigue and chicane, which none can better point out to you—to gnaw the bones of his prey when he has devoured the substance?—can you say as Sir William Ashton says—think as he thinks—vote as he votes, and call your father's murtherer your worshipful father-in-law and revered patron? —Ravenswood, I am the oldest servant of your house, and I would rather see you shrouded and coffined."

The tumult in Ravenswood's mind was uncommonly great; she struck upon and awakened a chord which he had for some time successfully silenced. He strode backwards and forwards through the little garden with a hasty pace; and at length checking himself, and stopping right opposite to Alice, he exclaimed, "Woman! on the verge of the grave, dare you urge the son of your master to blood and to revenge?"

"God forbid!" said Alice solemnly; "and therefore I would have you depart these fatal bounds, where your love, as well as your hatred, threatens sure mischief, or at least disgrace, both to yourself and others. I would shield, were it in the power of this withered hand, the Ashtons from you and you from them, and both from your own passions. You can have nothing—ought to have nothing, in common with them—Begone from among them; and if God has destined vengeance on the oppressor's house, do not you be the instrument."

"I will think on what you have said, Alice," said Ravenswood more composedly. "I believe you mean truly and faithfully by me, but you urge the freedom of an ancient domestic somewhat too far. But farewell; and if Heaven afford me better means, I will not fail to contribute to your comfort."

He attempted to put a piece of gold into her hand, which she refused to receive; and, in the slight struggle attending his wish to force it upon her, it dropped to the earth.

"Let it remain an instant on the ground," said Alice, as the Master stooped to raise it; "and believe me, that piece of gold is an emblem of her whom you love; she is as precious, I grant, but you must stoop even to abasement before you can win her. For me, I have as little to do with gold as with earthly passions; and the best news which the world has in store for me is, that Edgar Ravenswood is an hundred miles distant from the seat of his ancestors, with the determination never again to review it."

"Alice," said the Master, who began to think this earnestness had some more secret cause than arose from any thing that the blind woman could have gathered from this casual visit, "I have heard you praised by my mother for your sense, acuteness, and fidelity. You are no fool to start at shadows, or to dread old superstitious saws, like Caleb Balderstone; tell me distinctly where my danger lies, if you are aware of any which is tending towards me. If I know myself, I am free from all such views respecting Miss Ashton as you impute to me. I have necessary business to settle with Sir William—that arranged, I shall depart; and with as little wish, as you may easily believe, to return to a place full of melancholy subjects of reflection, as you have to see me here."

Alice bent her sightless eyes upon the ground, and was for a moment plunged in deep meditation. "I will speak the truth," she said at length, raising up her head—"I will tell you the source of my apprehensions, whether my candour be for good or evil—Lucy Ashton loves you, Lord of Ravenswood!"

"It is impossible," said the Master.

"A thousand circumstances have proved it to me. Her thoughts have turned on no one else since you saved her from death, and that my experienced judgment has won from her own conversation.

Having told you this—if you are indeed a gentleman and your father's son—you will make it a motive for flying from her presence—if her passion receives no countenance from your presence it will die like a lamp, for want of that the flame should feed upon; but, if you remain here, her destruction, or yours, or that of both, will be the inevitable consequences of her misplaced attachment. I tell you this secret unwillingly, but it could not have been hid long from your own observation; and it is better you learn it from mine. Depart, Master of Ravenswood—you have my secret. If you remain an hour under Sir William Ashton's roof without the resolution to marry his daughter, you are a villain—if with the purpose of allying yourself with him, you are an infatuated and predestined fool."

So saying, the old blind woman arose, assumed her staff, and, tottering to her hut, entered it and closed the door, leaving Ravenswood to his own reflections.

Chapter Six

Lovelier in her own retired abode
——than Naiad by the side
Of Grecian brook — or Lady of the Mere
Lone sitting by the shores of old romance.
WORDSWORTH

THE meditations of Ravenswood were of a very mixed complexion. He saw himself at once in the very dilemma which he had for some time felt apprehensive he might be placed in. The pleasure he felt in Lucy's company had indeed approached to fascination, yet it had never altogether surmounted his internal reluctance to wed with the daughter of his father's foe; and even in forgiving Sir William Ashton the injuries which his house had received, and giving him credit for the kind intentions he professed to entertain, he could not bring himself to contemplate as possible an alliance betwixt their houses. But he felt that Alice spoke truth, and that his honour now required he should take an instant leave of Ravenswood Castle, or become a suitor of Lucy Ashton. The possibility of being rejected, too, should he make advances to her wealthy and powerful father—to sue for the hand of an Ashton and be refused—this were a consummation too disgraceful. "I wish her well," he said to himself, "and for her sake I forgive the injuries her father has done to my house; but I will never—no, never see her more!"

With one bitter pang he adopted the resolution, just as he came to where two paths parted; the one to the Mermaiden's Fountain, where he knew Lucy waited him, the other leading to the castle by another and more circuitous road. He paused an instant when about to take the latter path, thinking what apology he should make for conduct which must needs seem extraordinary, and had just muttered to himself, "Sudden news from Edinburgh—any pretext will serve—only let me dally no longer here," when young Henry came flying up to him, half out of breath—"Master, Master—you must give Lucy your arm back to the castle, for I cannot give her mine; for Norman is waiting for me, and I am to go with him to make his ring-walk, and I would not stay away for a gold Jacobus, and Lucy is afraid to walk home alone, though all the wild nowt have been shot, and so you must come away directly."

Betwixt two scales equally loaded, a feather's weight will turn the scale. "It is impossible for me to leave the young lady in the wood alone," said Ravenswood; "to see her once more can be of little consequence, after the frequent meetings we have had—I ought too, in courtesy, to apprize her of my intention to quit the castle."

And having thus satisfied himself that he was taking not only a wise, but an absolutely necessary step, he took the path to the fatal fountain. Henry no sooner saw him on the way to join his sister, than he was off like lightning in another direction, to enjoy the society of the forester in their congenial pursuits. Ravenswood, not allowing himself to give a second thought to the propriety of his own conduct, walked with a quick step towards the stream, where he found Lucy seated alone by the ruin.

She sate upon one of the disjointed stones of the ancient fountain, and seemed to watch the progress of its current, as it bubbled forth to day-light, in gay and sparkling profusion, from under the shadow of the ribbed and darksome vault with which veneration, or perhaps remorse, had canopied its source. To a superstitious eye, Lucy Ashton, folded in her plaiden mantle, with her long hair, escaping partly from the snood and falling upon her silver neck, might have suggested the idea of the murdered Nymph of the Fountain. But Ravenswood only saw a female exquisitely beautiful, and rendered yet more so in his eyes—how could it be otherwise—by having placed her affections on him. As he gazed on her, he felt his fixed resolution melting like wax in the sun, and hastened, therefore, from his concealment in the neighbouring thicket. She saluted him, but did not arise from the stone on which she was seated.

"My mad-cap brother," she said, "has left me, but I expect him back in a few minutes—for fortunately, as every thing, at least any thing, pleases him for a minute, nothing has charms for him much longer."

Ravenswood did not feel the power of informing Lucy that her brother meditated a distant excursion, and would not return in haste. He sate himself down on the grass, at some little distance from Miss Ashton, and both were silent for a short space.

"I like this spot," said Lucy at length, as if she had found the silence embarrassing; "the bubbling murmur of the clear fountain, the waving of the trees, the profusion of grass and wild-flowers, that rise among the ruins, make it like a scene in romance. I think, too, I have heard it is a spot connected with the legendary lore which I love so well."

"It has been thought," answered Ravenswood, "a fatal spot to our family, and I have some reason to term it so, for it was here I first saw Miss Ashton—and it is here I must take my leave of her for ever."

The blood, which the first part of this speech called into Lucy's cheeks, was speedily expelled by its conclusion.

"To take leave of us, Master!" she exclaimed; "what can have happened to hurry you away?—I know Alice hates—I mean dislikes my father—and I hardly understood her humour to-day, it was so mysterious. But I am certain my father is sincerely grateful for the high service you rendered us. Let me hope that having won your friendship hardly, we shall not lose it lightly."

"Lose it, Miss Ashton?—no—wherever my fortune calls me— whatever she inflicts upon me—it is your friend—your sincere friend, who acts or suffers. But there is a fate on me, and I must go, or I shall add the ruin of others to my own."

"Yet do not go from us, Master," said Lucy; and she laid her hand, in all simplicity and kindness, upon the skirt of his cloak, as if to detain him—"You shall not part from us—My father is powerful! he has friends that are more so than himself—do not go till you see what his gratitude will do for you. Believe me, he is already labouring in your behalf with the Council."

"It may be so," said the Master, proudly; "yet it is not to your father, Miss Ashton, but to my own exertions, that I ought to owe success in the career on which I am about to enter. My preparations are already made—a sword and a cloak, a bold heart and a determined hand."

Lucy covered her face with her hands, and the tears, in spite of her, forced their way between her fingers. "Forgive me," said Ravenswood, taking her right hand, which, after slight resistance, she yielded to him, still continuing to shade her face with the left—"I am too rude —too rough—too intractable to deal with any being so soft and gentle as you are. Forget that so stern a vision has crossed your path of life— and let me pursue mine, sure that I can meet with no worse misfortune after the moment it divides me from your side."

Lucy wept on, but her tears were less bitter. Each attempt which the Master made to explain his purpose of departure, only proved a new evidence of his desire to stay; until, at length, instead of bidding her farewell, he gave his faith to her for ever, and received her troth in return. The whole passed so suddenly, and arose so much out of the immediate impulse of the moment, that ere the Master of Ravenswood could reflect upon the consequences of the step which he had taken, their lips, as well as their hands, had pledged the sincerity of their affection.

"And now," he said, after a moment's consideration, "it is fit I should speak to Sir William Ashton—he must know of our engagement. Ravenswood must not seem to dwell under his roof, to solicit clandestinely the affections of his daughter."

"You would not speak to my father on the subject," said Lucy, doubtingly; and then added more warmly, "O do not—do not!—let your lot in life be determined, your station and purpose ascertained, before you address my father. I am sure he loves you—I think he will consent—but then my mother——"

She paused, ashamed to express the doubt she felt how far her father dared to form any positive resolution on this most important subject, without the consent of his lady.

"Your mother, my Lucy?" replied Ravenswood; "she is of the house of Douglas, a house that has intermarried with mine, even when its glory and power were at the highest—What could your mother object to my alliance?"

"I did not say object," said Lucy; "but she is jealous of her rights, and may claim a mother's title to be consulted in the first instance."

"Be it so," replied Ravenswood; "London is distant, but a letter will reach it and receive an answer within a fortnight—I will not press on the Lord Keeper for an instant reply to my proposal."

"But," hesitated Lucy, "were it not better to wait—to wait a few weeks—were my mother to see you—to know you—I am sure she would approve; but you are unacquainted personally, and the ancient feud between the families"——

Ravenswood fixed upon her his keen dark eyes, as if he was desirous of penetrating into her very soul.

"Lucy," he said, "I have sacrificed to you projects of vengeance long nursed, and sworn to with ceremonies little better than heathen—I sacrificed them to your image, ere I knew the worth which it represented. In the evening that succeeded my poor father's funeral, I cut a lock from my hair, and, as it consumed in the fire, I swore that my rage and revenge should pursue his enemies, until they shrivelled before me like that scorched-up symbol of annihilation."

"It was a deadly sin," said Lucy, turning pale, "to make a vow so fatal."

"I acknowledge it," said Ravenswood, "and it had been a worse crime to keep it. It was for your sake that I abjured these purposes of vengeance, though I scarce knew that such was the argument by which I was conquered, until I saw you once more, and became conscious of the influence you possessed over me."

"And why do you now," said Lucy, "recall sentiments so terrible—sentiments so inconsistent with those you profess for me—with those your importunity has prevailed on me to acknowledge?"

"Because I would impress on you the price at which I have bought your love—the right I have to expect your constancy. I say not that I have bartered for it the honour of my house—its last remaining possession—but though I say it not, and think it not, I cannot conceal from myself that the world may do both."

"If such are your sentiments," said Lucy, "you have played a cruel game with me—but it is not too late to give it over—take back the faith and troth which you could not plight to me without suffering abatement of honour—let what is passed be as if it had not been—forget me and I will endeavour to forget myself."

"You do me injustice," said the Master of Ravenswood; "by all I hold true and honourable, you do me the extremity of injustice—if I mentioned the price at which I have bought your love, it is only to shew how much I prize it, to bind our engagement by a still firmer tie, and to shew, by what I have done to attain this station in your regard, how much I must suffer should you ever break your faith."

"And why, Ravenswood," answered Lucy, "should you think that possible?—why should you urge me with even the mention of infidelity?—Is it because I ask you to delay applying to my father for a little space of time? Bind me by what vows you please; if vows are unnecessary to secure constancy, they may yet prevent suspicion."

Ravenswood pleaded, apologized, and even kneeled, to appease her displeasure; and Lucy, as placable as she was single-hearted, readily forgave the offence which his doubts had implied. The dispute thus agitated, however, ended by the lovers going through an emblematic ceremony of their troth-plight of which the vulgar still preserve some traces. They broke betwixt them the thin broad-piece of gold which Alice had refused to receive from Ravenswood.

"And never shall this leave my bosom," said Lucy, as she hung the piece of gold around her neck, and concealed it with her handkerchief, "until you, Edgar Ravenswood, ask me to resign it to you—and, while I wear it, never shall that heart acknowledge another love than you."

With like protestations, Ravenswood placed his portion of the coin opposite to his heart. And now, at length, it struck them, that time had hurried fast on during their interview, and their absence at the castle would be subject of remark, if not of alarm. As they arose to leave the fountain which had been witness of their mutual engagement, an arrow whistled through the air, and struck a raven perched on the sere branch of an old oak, near to where they had been seated. The bird fluttered a few yards, and dropped at the feet of Lucy, whose dress was stained with some spots of its blood.

Miss Ashton was much alarmed, and Ravenswood, surprised and angry, looked everywhere for the marksman, who had given them a proof of his skill as little expected as desired. He was not long of discovering himself, being no other than Henry Ashton, who came running up with a cross-bow in his hand.

"I knew I should startle you," he said; "and do you know you looked so busy that I thought it would have fallen souse on your heads before you were aware of it—What was the Master saying to you, Lucy?"

"I was telling your sister what an idle lad you were, keeping us waiting here for you so long," said Ravenswood, to save Lucy's confusion.

"Waiting for me? Why, I told you to see Lucy home, and that I was to go to make the ring-walk with old Norman in the Hayberry thicket, and you may be sure that would take a good hour, and we have all the deer's marks and fewmishes got, while you were sitting here with Lucy like a lazy loon."

"Well, well, Mr Henry," said Ravenswood; "but let us see how you will answer to me for killing the raven. Do you know the ravens are all under the protection of the Lords of Ravenswood, and, to kill one in their presence, is such bad luck that it deserves the stab?"

"And that's what Norman said," replied the boy; "he came as far with me as within a flight-shot of you, and he said he never saw a raven sit still so near living folks, and he wished it might be for good luck; for the raven is one of the wildest birds that flies, unless it be a tame one— and so I crept on and on, till I was within three score yards of him, and then whiz went the bolt, and there he lies, faith! Was it not well shot? —and, I dare say, I have not shot in a cross-bow—not ten times, maybe."

"Admirably shot indeed," said Ravenswood; "and you will be a fine marksman if you practise hard."

"That's what Norman says," answered the boy; "but I am sure it is not my fault if I do not practise enough; for, of free will, I would do little else, only my father and tutor are angry sometimes, and only Miss Lucy there gives herself airs about my being busy, for all she can sit idle by a well-side the whole day when she has a handsome young gentleman to prate wi'. I have known her do so twenty times, if you will believe me."

The boy looked at his sister as he spoke, and, in the midst of his mischievous chatter, had the sense to see that he was really inflicting pain upon her, though without being able to comprehend the cause or the amount.

"Come now, Lucy," he said, "don't greet; and if I have said any thing beside the mark, I'll deny it again—and what does the Master of Ravenswood care if you had a hundred joes—so ne'er put fingers in your eye about it."

The Master was, for the moment, scarce satisfied with what he heard; yet his good sense naturally regarded it as the chatter of a spoiled boy, who strove to mortify his sister in the point which seemed most accessible for the time. But, although of a temper equally slow in receiving impressions, and obstinate in retaining them, the prattle of Henry served to nourish in his mind some vague suspicion, that his present engagement might only end in his being exposed like a vanquished enemy in a Roman triumph, a captive attendant on the car of a victor, who meditated only the satiating his pride at the expense of the vanquished. There was, we repeat it, no real ground whatever for such an apprehension, nor could he be said seriously to entertain such for a moment. Indeed it was impossible to look at the clear blue eye of Lucy Ashton, and entertain the slightest permanent doubt concerning the sincerity of her disposition. Still, however, conscious pride and conscious poverty combined to render a mind suspicious, which, in more fortunate circumstances, would have been a stranger to that as well as to other meanness.

They reached the castle, where Sir William Ashton, who had been alarmed by the length of their stay, met them in the hall.

"Had Lucy," he said, "been in any other company than that of one who had shewn he had so complete power of protecting her, he confessed he should have been very uneasy, and would have dispatched persons in quest of them. But, in the company of the Master of Ravenswood, he knew his daughter had nothing to dread."

Lucy commenced some apology for their long delay, but, conscience-struck, became confused as she proceeded; and when Ravenswood, coming to her assistance, endeavoured to render the explanation complete and satisfactory, he only involved himself in the same disorder, like one who, endeavouring to extricate his companion from a slough, entangles himself in the same tenacious swamp. It cannot be supposed that the confusion of the two youthful lovers escaped the observation of the wily lawyer, accustomed, by habit and profession, to trace human nature through all her windings. But it was not his present policy to take any notice of what he observed. He desired to hold the Master of Ravenswood bound, but that he himself should be free; and it did not occur to him that his plan might be defeated by Lucy's returning the passion which he wished she might inspire. If she should adopt some romantic feelings towards Ravenswood, in which circumstances, or the positive and absolute opposition of Lady Ashton, might render it unadvisable to indulge her, the Lord Keeper conceived they might be easily superseded and annulled by a journey to Edinburgh, or even to London, a new set of Brussels lace, and the soft whispers of half a dozen of lovers, anxious to replace him whom it was convenient she should renounce. This was his provision for the worst view of the case. But, according to its more probable issue, any passing favour she might entertain for the Master of Ravenswood, might require encouragement rather than repression.

This seemed the more likely, as he had that very morning, since their departure from the castle, received a letter, the contents of which he hastened to communicate to Ravenswood. A foot-post had arrived with a packet to the Lord Keeper from that friend whom we have already mentioned, who was labouring hard under-hand to consolidate a band of patriots, at the head of whom stood Sir William's greatest terror, the active and ambitious Marquis of A——. The success of this convenient friend had been such, that he had obtained from Sir William, not indeed a directly favourable answer, but certainly a most patient hearing. This he had reported to his principal, who had replied with the ancient French adage, "*Château qui parle, et femme qui écoute, l'un et l'autre va se rendre.*" A statesman who hears you propose a change of measures without reply, was, according to the Marquis's opinion, in the situation of the fortress which parleys, and the lady who listens, and he resolved to press the siege of the Lord Keeper.

The packet, therefore, contained a letter from his friend and ally, and another from himself to the Lord Keeper, frankly offering an unceremonious visit. They were crossing the country to go to the southward—the roads were indifferent—the accommodation of the inns as execrable as possible—the Lord Keeper had been long acquainted intimately with one of his correspondents, and though more slightly known to the Marquis, had yet enough of his Lordship's acquaintance to render the visit sufficiently natural, and to shut the mouths of those who might be disposed to impute it to a political intrigue. He instantly accepted the offered visit, determined, however, that he would not pledge himself an inch farther for the furtherance of their views than *reason* (by which he meant his own self-interest) should plainly point out to him as proper.

Two circumstances particularly delighted him; the presence of Ravenswood, and the absence of his own lady. By having the former under his roof, he conceived he might be able to quash all such hazardous and hostile proceedings as he might otherwise have been engaged in, under the patronage of the Marquis; and Lucy, he foresaw, would make, for his immediate purpose of delay and procrastination, a much better mistress of his family than her mother, who would, he was sure, in some shape or other, contrive to disconcert his political schemes by her proud and implacable temper.

His anxious solicitations that the Master would stay to receive his kinsman, were of course readily complied with, since the *éclaircissement* which had taken place at the Mermaiden's Fountain had removed all wish for sudden departure. Lucy and Lockhard had, therefore, orders to provide all things necessary in their different departments, for receiving the expected guests, with a pomp and display of luxury very uncommon in Scotland at that remote period.

Chapter Seben

> *Marall.* Sir, the man of honour's come,
> Newly alighted——
>   *Overreach.* In without reply,
> And do as I command.—
> Is the loud music I gave order for
> Ready to receive him?—
>   *New Way to Pay Old Debts*

SIR WILLIAM ASHTON, although a man of sense, legal information, and great practical knowledge of the world, had yet some points of character which corresponded better with the timidity of his disposition and the supple arts by which he had risen in the world, than to the degree of eminence which he had attained; as they tended to shew an original mediocrity of understanding, however highly it had been cultivated, and a native meanness of disposition, however carefully veiled. He loved the ostentatious display of his wealth, less as a man to whom habit has made it necessary, than as one to whom it is still delightful from its novelty. The most trivial details did not escape him; and Lucy soon learned to watch with apprehension the flush of scorn which crossed Ravenswood's cheek, when he heard her father gravely arguing with Lockhard, nay, even with the old housekeeper, upon circumstances which, in families of rank, are left uncared for, because it is supposed impossible they can be neglected.

"I could pardon Sir William," said Ravenswood one evening after he had left the room, "some general anxiety upon this occasion, for the

Marquis's visit is an honour, and should be received as such. But I am worn out by these miserable minutiæ of the butchery, and the larder, and the very hen-coop—they drive me beyond my patience; I would rather endure the poverty of Wolfscrag, than be pestered with the wealth of Ravenswood Castle."

"And yet," said Lucy, "it was by attention to these minutiæ that my father acquired the property"——

"Which my ancestors sold for lack of it," answered Ravenswood. "Be it so; a porter still bears but a burthen, though the burthen be of gold."

Lucy sighed; she perceived too plainly that her lover held in scorn the manners and habits of a father, to whom she had long looked up as her best and most partial friend, whose fondness had often consoled her for her mother's contemptuous harshness.

The lovers soon discovered that they differed upon other and no less important topics. Religion, the mother of peace, was, in these days of discord, so much misconstrued and mistaken, that her rites and forms were the subject of the most opposite opinions and the most hostile animosities. The Lord Keeper, being a whig, was, of course, a presbyterian, and had found it convenient, at different periods, to express greater zeal for the kirk, than perhaps he really felt. His family, equally of course, were trained under the same institution. Ravenswood, as we know, was a high-church man, or episcopalian, and frequently objected to Lucy the fanaticism of some of her communion, while she intimated, rather than expressed, horror at the latitudinarian principles which she had been taught to think connected with the prelatical form of church-government.

Thus, although their mutual affection seemed to increase rather than to be diminished, as their characters opened more fully on each other, the feelings of each were mingled with some less agreeable ingredients. Lucy felt a secret awe, amid all her affection for Ravenswood. His soul was of an higher, prouder character, than those with whom she had hitherto mixed in intercourse; his ideas were more fierce and free; and he contemned many of the opinions which had been inculcated upon her, as chiefly demanding her veneration. On the other hand, Ravenswood saw in Lucy a soft and flexible character, which, in his eyes at least, seemed too susceptible of being moulded to any form by those with whom she lived. He felt that his own temper required a partner of a more independent spirit, who could set sail with him on his course of life, as resolved as himself to dare indifferently the storm and the favouring breeze. But Lucy was so beautiful, so devotedly attached to him, of a temper so exquisitely soft and kind, that, while he could have wished it were possible to inspire her with a greater degree of firmness and resolution, and while he sometimes became impatient of the extreme fear which she expressed of their attachment being prematurely discovered, he felt that the softness of a mind, amounting almost to feebleness, rendered her even dearer to him, as a being who had voluntarily clung to him for protection, and made him the arbiter of her fate for weal or woe. His feelings towards her at such moments, were those which have been since so beautifully expressed by our immortal Joanna Baillie:

> ——————Thou sweetest thing,
> That e'er did fix its lightly-fibred sprays
> To the rude rock, ah! would'st thou cling to me?
> Rough and storm-worn I am—yet love me as
> Thou truly dost, I will love thee again
> With true and honest heart, though all unmeet
> To be the mate of such sweet gentleness.

Thus the very points in which they differed, seemed, in some measure, to ensure the continuance of their mutual affection. If, indeed, they had so fully appreciated each other's character before the burst of passion in which they hastily pledged their faith to each other, Lucy might have feared Ravenswood too much ever to have loved him, and he might have construed her softness and docile temper as imbecility, rendering her unworthy of his regard. But they stood pledged to each other; and Lucy only feared that her lover's pride might one day teach him to regret his attachment, Ravenswood that a mind so ductile as Lucy's might, in absence or difficulties, be induced, by the entreaties or influence of those around her, to renounce the engagement she had formed.

"Do not fear it," said Lucy, when, upon one occasion, a hint of such suspicion escaped her lover; "the mirrors which receive the reflection of all successive objects are framed of hard materials like glass or steel —the softer substances, when they receive an impression, retain it undefaced."

"This is poetry, Lucy," said Ravenswood; "and in poetry there is always fallacy, and sometimes fiction."

"Believe me then, once more, in honest prose," said Lucy, "that, though I will never wed man without the consent of my parents, yet neither force nor persuasion shall dispose of my hand till you renounce the right I have given you to it."

The lovers had ample time for such explanations. Henry was now more seldom their companion, being either a most unwilling attendant upon the lessons of his tutor, or a forward volunteer under the instructions of the foresters or grooms. As for the Keeper, his mornings were spent in his study, maintaining correspondences of all kinds, and balancing in his anxious mind the various intelligence which he collected from every quarter concerning the expected change in Scottish politics, and the probable strength of the parties who were about to struggle for power. At other times he busied himself about arranging, and countermanding, and then again arranging, the preparations which he judged necessary for the reception of the Marquis of A——, whose arrival had been twice delayed by some necessary cause of detention.

In the midst of all these various avocations, political and domestic, he seemed not to observe how much his daughter and his guest were thrown into each other's society, and was censured by many of his neighbours, according to the fashion of neighbours in all countries, for suffering such an intimate connection to take place betwixt two young persons. The only natural explanation was, that he designed them for each other; while, in truth, his only motive was to temporize and procrastinate, until he should discover the real extent of the interest which the Marquis took in Ravenswood's affairs, and the power which he was likely to possess of advancing them. Until these points should be made both clear and manifest, the Lord Keeper resolved that he would do nothing to commit himself, either in one shape or other, and, like many cunning persons, he over-reached himself deplorably.

Amongst those who had been disposed to censure, with the greatest severity, the conduct of Sir William Ashton, in permitting the prolonged residence of Ravenswood under his roof, and his constant attendance on Miss Ashton, was the new Laird of Girnington, and his faithful squire and bottle-holder, personages formerly well known to us by the names of Hayston of Bucklaw, and his companion Captain Craigengelt. The former had already succeeded to the extensive property of his long-lived grand-aunt, and to considerable wealth besides, which he had employed in redeeming his paternal acres, (by the title appertaining to which he still chose to be designated,) notwithstanding Captain Craigengelt had proposed to him a most advantageous mode of vesting the money in Law's scheme, which was just then set abroach, and offered his services to travel express to Paris for the purpose. But Bucklaw had so far derived wisdom from adversity, that he would listen to no proposal which Craigengelt could invent, having a tendency to risk his newly-acquired independence. He that had once eat pease-bannocks, drunk sour wine, and slept in the secret chamber at Wolfscrag, would, he said, prize good cheer and a soft bed as long as he lived, and take special care never to need such hospitality again.

Craigengelt, therefore, found himself disappointed in the first hopes he had entertained of "making a good hand of the Laird of Bucklaw." Still, however, he reaped many advantages from his friend's good fortune. Bucklaw, who had never been at all scrupulous in chusing his companions, was accustomed to, and entertained by a fellow, whom he could either laugh with or laugh at as he had a mind, who would take, according to Scottish phrase, "the bit and the buffet," understood all sports, whether without or within doors, and, when the Laird had a mind for a bottle of wine, (no infrequent circumstance,) was always ready to save him from the scandal of getting drunk by himself. Upon these terms Craigengelt was the frequent, almost the constant, inmate of the house of Girnington.

In no time, and under no possibility of circumstances, could good have been derived from such an intimacy, however its bad consequences might be qualified by the thorough knowledge which Bucklaw possessed of his dependant's character, and the high contempt in which he held it. But as circumstances stood, this evil communication was particularly liable to corrupt what good principles nature had implanted in the patron.

Craigengelt had never forgiven the scorn with which Ravenswood had torn the mask of courage and honesty from his countenance; and to exasperate Bucklaw's resentment against him, was the safest mode of revenge which occurred to his cowardly, yet cunning and malignant disposition.

He brought up, on all occasions, the story of the challenge which Ravenswood had declined to accept, and endeavoured, by every possible insinuation, to make his patron believe that his honour was concerned in bringing that matter to an issue by a personal discussion with Ravenswood. But respecting this subject, Bucklaw imposed on him, at length, a peremptory command of silence.

"I think," he said, "the Master has treated me unlike a gentleman, and I see no right he had to send me back a cavalier answer when I demanded the satisfaction of one—But he gave me my life once—and, in looking this matter over at present, I put myself but on equal terms with him—should he cross me again, I shall consider the old accompt as balanced, and his Mastership will do well to look to himself."

"That he should," re-echoed Craigengelt; "for when you are in practice, Bucklaw, I would bet a magnum you are through him before the third pass."

"Then you know nothing of the matter," said Bucklaw, "and you never saw him fence."

"I know nothing of the matter? a good jest, I promise you—and though I never saw Ravenswood fence, have I not been at Monsieur Sagoon's school, who was the first *maitre d'armes* at Paris; and have I not been at Seignor Poco's at Florence, and Meinherr Durchstossen at Vienna, and have I not seen all their play?"

"I don't know whether you have or not," said Bucklaw; "but what about it, though you had?"

"Only that I will be d—d if ever I saw French, Italian, or High-Dutchman ever make foot, hand, and eye, keep time half so well as you, Bucklaw."

"I believe you lie, Craigie," said Bucklaw; "however, I can hold my own, both with single rapier, back-sword, sword and dagger, broad-sword, or case of faulchions—and that's as much as any gentleman need know of the matter."

"And the double of what ninety-nine out of a hundred knows," said Craigengelt; "they learn to change a few thrusts with the small sword, and then, forsooth, they understand the noble art of defence! Now, when I was at Rouen in the 1695, there was the Chevalier de Chapon and I went to the Opera, where we found three bits of English birkies"——

"Is it a long story you are going to tell?" said Bucklaw, yawning.

"Just as you like," answered the parasite, "for we made short work of it."

"Then I like it short," said Bucklaw; "is it serious or merry?"

"Devilish serious, I assure you, and so they found it; for the chevalier and I"——

"Then I don't like it at all," said Bucklaw; "so fill a brimmer of my auld auntie's claret, rest her heart! And, as the Hïelandman says, *Skioch doch na skiaill*."*

"That was what tough old Sir Evan Dhu used to say to me when I was out with the metall'd lads in 1689. 'Craigengelt,' he used to say, 'you are as pretty a fellow as ever held steel in his grip, but you have one fault.'"

"If he had known you as long as I have done," said Bucklaw, "he would have found out some—twenty more; but hang long stories, give us your toast, man."

Craigengelt rose, went a tiptoe to the door, peeped out, shut it carefully, came back again—clapped his tarnished gold-laced hat on one side of his head, took his glass in one hand, and touching the hilt of his hanger with the other, named, "The King over the water."

"I tell you what it is, Captain Craigengelt," said Bucklaw; "I shall keep my mind to myself on these subjects, having too much respect for the memory of my venerable aunt Girnington to put her lands and tenements in the way of committing treason against established

---

* "Cut a tale with a drink;" equivalent to the English adage of "boon companions, don't preach over your liquor."

authority. Bring you King James to Edinburgh, Captain, with thirty thousand men at his back, and I'll tell you what I think about his title; but as for running my neck into a noose, and my good broad lands into the statutory penalties, 'in that case, made and provided,' rely upon it you will find me no such fool. So when you mean to vapour with your hanger and your dram-cup in support of treasonable toasts, you must find your liquor and company elsewhere."

"Well, then," said Craigengelt, "name the toast yourself, and be it what it like, I'll pledge you if it were a mile to the bottom."

"And I'll give you a toast that deserves it, my boy," said Bucklaw; "what say you to Miss Lucy Ashton?"

"Up with it," said the Captain, as he tossed off his brimmer, "the bonniest lass in Lothian—What a pity the old sneck-drawing whiga-more, her father, is about to throw her away upon that rag of pride and beggary, the Master of Ravenswood."

"That's not quite so clear," said Bucklaw, in a tone, which, though it seemed indifferent, excited his companion's eager curiosity; and not that only, but also his hope of working himself into some sort of confidence, which might make him necessary to his patron, being by no means satisfied to rest on mere sufferance, if he could form, by art or industry, a more permanent title to his favour.

"I thought," said he, after a moment's pause, "that was a settled matter—they are continually together, and nothing else is spoken of betwixt Lammerlaw and Traprain."

"They may say what they please," replied his patron, "but I know better, and I'll give you Miss Lucy Ashton's health again, my boy."

"And I would drink it on my knee," said Craigengelt, "if I thought the girl had the spirit to jilt that d—d son of a Spaniard."

"I am to request you will not use the word jilt and Miss Ashton's name together," said Bucklaw, gravely.

"Discard, my lad of acres—by Jove, I meant to say discard," replied Craigengelt, "and I hope she'll discard him like a small card at piquet, and take in the king of hearts, my boy—But yet——"

"But what?" said his patron.

"But yet I know for certain they are hours together alone, and in the woods and the fields."

"That's her foolish father's dotage—that will be soon put out of the lass's head, if it ever gets into it," answered Bucklaw. "And now fill your glass again, Captain, I am going to make you happy—I am going to let you into a secret—a plot—a noosing plot—only the noose is but typical."

"A marrying matter?" said Craigengelt, and his jaw fell as he asked the question; for he suspected that matrimony would render his situation at Girnington much more precarious than during the jolly days of his patron's bachelorhood.

"Ay, a marriage, man," said Bucklaw; "but wherefore droops thy mighty spirit, and why grow the rubies on thy cheek so pale? The board will have a corner, and the corner will have a trencher, and the trencher will have a glass beside it; and the board-end shall be filled, and the trencher and the glass shall be replenished for thee, if all the petticoats in Lothian had sworn the contrary—what, man! I am not the boy to put myself into leading strings."

"So says many an honest fellow," said Craigengelt, "and some of my special friends: but, curse me if I know the reason, the women could never bear me, and always contrived to trundle me out of favour before the honey-moon was over."

"If you could have kept your ground till that was over, you might have made good your position," said Bucklaw.

"But I never could," answered the dejected parasite; "there was my Lord Castle-Cuddy—we were hand and glove—I rode his horses—borrowed money, both for him and from him—trained his hawks, and taught him how to lay his bets; and when he took a fancy of marrying, I married him to Katie Glegg, whom I thought myself as sure of as man could be of woman. Egad, she had me out of the house, as if I had run on wheels, within the first fortnight."

"Well!" replied Bucklaw, "I think I have nothing of Castle-Cuddy about me, or Lucy of Katie Glegg—but you see the thing will go on whether you like it or no—the only question is, will you be useful?"

"Useful?—and to thee, my lad of lands, my darling boy, whom I would tramp bare-footed through the world for?—name time, place, mode, and circumstance, and see if I will not be useful in all uses that can be devised."

"Why, then, you must ride two hundred miles for me," said the patron.

"A thousand, and call them a flea's leap," answered the dependent; "I'll cause saddle my horse directly."

"Better stay till you know where you are to go, and what you are to do," quoth Bucklaw. "You know I have a kinswoman in Northumberland, Lady Blenkinsop by name, whose old acquaintance I had the misfortune to lose in the period of my poverty, but the light of whose countenance shone forth upon me when the sun of my prosperity began to arise."

"D—n all such double-faced bitches," exclaimed Craigengelt, heroically; "this I will say for John Craigengelt, that he is his friend's friend through good report and bad report, poverty and riches; and you know something of that yourself, Bucklaw."

"I have not forgot your merits," said his patron; "I do remember, that, in my extremities, you had a mind to *crimp* me for the service of the French king, or of the Pretender; and, moreover, that you afterwards lent me a score of pieces, when, as I firmly believe, you had heard the news that old Lady Girnington had a touch of the dead palsy —but don't be down-cast, John; I believe, after all, you like me very well in your way, and it is my misfortune to have no better counsellor at present.—To return to this Lady Blenkinsop, you must know she is a close confederate of Duchess Sarah."

"What, of Sall Jennings!" exclaimed Craigengelt; "then she must be a good one."

"Hold your tongue, and keep your Tory rants to yourself, if it be possible," said Bucklaw; "I tell you, that through the Duchess of Marlborough has this Northumbrian cousin of mine become a crony of Lady Ashton, the Keeper's wife, or, I may say, the Lord Keeper's Lady Keeper, and she has favoured Lady Blenkinsop with a visit on her return from London, and is just now at her old mansion-house on the banks of the Wansbeck. Now, sir, as it has been the use and wont of these ladies to consider their husbands as of no importance in the management of their own families, it has been their present pleasure, without consulting Sir William Ashton, to put on the *tapis* a matrimonial alliance, to be concluded between Lucy Ashton and my own right honourable self, Lady Ashton acting as self-constituted plenipotentiary on the part of her daughter and husband, and Mother Blenkinsop, equally unaccredited, doing me the honour to be my representative. You may suppose I was a little astonished when I found that a treaty, in which I was so considerably interested, had advanced a good way before I was even consulted."

"Capot me if I think that was according to the rules of the game," said his confidant; "and pray, what answer did you return?"

"Why, my first thought was to send the treaty to the devil, and the negociators along with it, for a couple of meddling old women; my next was to laugh very heartily; and my third and last was a settled opinion that the thing was reasonable, and would suit me well enough."

"Why, I thought you had never seen the wench but once—and then she had her riding-mask on. I am sure you told me so."

"Ay—but I liked her very well then. And Ravenswood's dirty usage of me—shutting me out of doors to dine with the lacqueys, because he had the Lord Keeper, forsooth, and his daughter, to be guests in his beggarly castle of starvation—D—n me, Craigengelt, if I ever forgive him till I play him as good a trick."

"No more you should, if you are a lad of mettle," said Craigengelt, the matter now taking a turn in which he could sympathize; "and if you carry this wench from him, it will break his heart."

"That it will not," said Bucklaw; "his heart is all steeled over with reason and philosophy—things that you, Craigie, know nothing about more than myself, God help me—But it will break his pride though, and that's what I am driving at."

"Distance me," said Craigengelt, "but I know the reason now of his unmannerly behaviour at his old tumble-down tower yonder—ashamed of your company?—no, no! Gad, he was afraid you would cut in and carry off the girl."

"Eh! Craigengelt?" said Bucklaw—"do you really think so?—but no, no!—he is a devilish deal prettier man than I am."

"Who—he?" exclaimed the parasite—"he is as black as the crook; and for his size—he's a tall fellow, to be sure—but give me a tight, stout, middle-sized"——

"Plague on thee!" said Bucklaw, interrupting him, "and on me for listening to you!—you would say as much if I were hunch-backed. But as to Ravenswood—he has kept no terms with me—I'll keep none with him. If I can win this girl from him"——

"Win her?—'sblood, you shall win her, point, quint, and quatorze, my king of trumps—you shall pique, repique, and capot him."

"Prithee, stop thy gambling cant for one instant," said Bucklaw. "Things have come thus far, that I have entertained the proposal of my kinswoman, agreed to the terms of jointure, amount of fortune, and so forth, and that the affair is to go forward when Lady Ashton comes down, for she takes her daughter and her son in her own hand. Now, they want me to send up a confidential person with some writings."

"By this good wine, I'll ride to the end of the world—the very gates of Jericho—and the judgment-seat of Prester John, for thee," ejaculated the Captain.

"Why, I believe you would do something for me, and a great deal for yourself. Now, any one could carry the writings; but you will have a little more to do; you must contrive to drop out before my Lady Ashton, just as if it were a matter of little consequence, the residence of Ravenswood at her husband's house, and his close intercourse with Miss Ashton; and you may tell her, that all the country talks of a visit from the Marquis of A——, as it is supposed, to make up the match betwixt Ravenswood and her daughter. I should like to hear what she says to all this; for, rat me, if I have any idea of starting for the plate at all if Ravenswood is to win the race, and he has odds against me already."

"Never a bit—the wench has too much sense—and in that belief I drink her health a third time; and, were time and place fitting, I would drink it on bended knees, and he that would not pledge me, I would make his guts garter his stockings."

"Hark ye, Craigengelt; as you are going into the society of women of rank," said Bucklaw, "I'll thank you to forget your strange black-guard oaths and damme's—I will write to them, though, that you are a blunt untaught fellow."

"Ay, ay," replied Craigengelt; "a plain, blunt, honest, down-right soldier."

"Not too honest, or too much of the soldier neither; but, such as thou art, it is my luck to need thee, for I must have spurs put to Lady Ashton's motions."

"I'll dash them up to the rowel-heads," said Craigengelt; "she shall come here at the gallop, like a cow chased by a whole nest of hornets, and her tail twisted over her rump like a cork-screw."

"And heark ye, Craigie," said Bucklaw; "your boots and doublet are good enough to drink in, as the man says in the play, but they are somewhat too greasy for tea-table service—prithee, get thyself a little better rigged-out, and here is to pay all charges."

"Nay, Bucklaw—on my soul, man—you use me ill—however," added Craigengelt, pocketting the money, "if you will have me so far indebted to you, I must be conforming."

"Well, horse and away!" said the patron, "so soon as you have got your riding livery in trim—you may ride the black crop-ear—and hark ye, I'll make you a present of him to boot."

"I drink to the good luck of my mission," answered the ambassador, "in a half-pint bumper."

"I thank ye, Craigie, and I pledge you—I see nothing against it but the father or the girl taking a tantrum, and I am told the mother can wind them both round her little finger. Take care not to affront her with any of your jacobite jargon."

"O ay, true—she is a whig, and a friend of old Sall of Marlborough—thank my stars, I can hoist any colours at a pinch. I have fought as hard under John Churchill as ever I did under Dundee or the Duke of Berwick."

"I verily believe you, Craigie," said the lord of the mansion; "but, Craigie, do you, pray, step down to the cellar and fetch us up a bottle of the Burgundy 1678—it is in the fourth bin from the right-hand turn—And I say, Craigie—you may fetch up a half-dozen whilst you are about it—Egad, we'll make a night on't."

Chapter Eight

And soon they spied the merry-men green,
And eke the coach and four.
Duke upon Duke

CRAIGENGELT set forth on his mission, so soon as his equipage was complete, prosecuted his journey with all diligence, and accomplished his commission with all the dexterity for which Bucklaw had given him credit. As he arrived with credentials from Mr Hayston of Bucklaw, he was extremely welcome to both ladies; and those who are prejudiced in favour of a new acquaintance can, for a time at least, discover excellencies in his very faults, and perfections in his deficiencies. Although both ladies were accustomed to good society, yet, being predetermined to find out an agreeable and well-behaved gentleman in Mr Hayston's friend, they succeeded wonderfully in imposing on themselves. It is true that Craigengelt was now handsomely dressed, and that was a point of no small consequence. But independent of outward shew, his blackguard impudence of address was construed into honourable bluntness, becoming his supposed military profession; his hectoring passed for courage, and his sauciness for wit. Lest, however, any one should think this a violation of probability, we must add, in fairness to the two ladies, that their discernment was greatly blinded, and their favour propitiated, by the opportune arrival of Captain Craigengelt, in the moment when they were longing for a third hand to make a party at tredille, in which, as in all games, whether of chance or skill, that worthy person was a great proficient.

When he found himself established in favour, his next point was how best to use it for the furtherance of his patron's views. He found Lady Ashton prepossessed strongly in favour of the motion, which Lady Blenkinsop, partly from regard to her kinsman, partly from the spirit of match-making, had not hesitated to propose to her; so that his task was an easy one. Bucklaw, reformed from his prodigality, was just the sort of husband whom she desired to have for her Shepherdess of Lammermoor; and while the marriage gave her fortune, and a gentleman for her husband, Lady Ashton was of opinion that her destinies would be fully and most favourably accomplished. It so chanced, also, that Bucklaw, among his new acquisitions, had gained the management of a little separate interest in a neighbouring county, where the Douglas family originally held large possessions. It was one of the bosom-hopes of Lady Ashton, that her eldest son, Sholto, should represent this county in the British Parliament, and she saw this alliance with Bucklaw as a circumstance which might be highly favourable to her wishes.

Craigengelt, who in his way by no means wanted sagacity, no sooner discovered in what quarter the wind of Lady Ashton's wishes sate, than he trimmed his course accordingly. "There was little to prevent Bucklaw himself from setting up for the county—he must carry the heat—must walk the course. Two cousins-german—six more distant kinsmen, his factor and his chamberlain, were all hollow votes—and the Girnington interest had always carried, betwixt love and fear, about as many more—But Bucklaw cared no more about riding the first horse, and that sort of thing, than he, Craigengelt, did about a game at birkie—it was a pity his interest was not in good guidance."

All this Lady Ashton drank in with willing and attentive ears, resolving internally to be herself the person who should take the management of the political influence of her destined son-in-law, for the benefit of her eldest born, Sholto, and all other parties concerned.

When he found her ladyship thus favourably disposed, the Captain proceeded, to use his employer's phrase, to set spurs to her resolution, by hinting at the situation of matters at Ravenswood Castle, the long residence which the heir of that family had made with the Lord Keeper, and the reports which (though he would be d—d ere he gave credit to any of them) had been idly circulated in the neighbourhood. It was not the Captain's cue to appear himself to be uneasy on the subject of these rumours; but he easily saw from Lady Ashton's flushed cheek, hesitating voice, and flashing eye, that she had caught the alarm which he intended to communicate. She had not heard from her husband so often or so regularly as she thought him bound in duty to have written, and of this very interesting intelligence, concerning his visit to the Tower of Wolfscrag, and the guest, whom, with such cordiality, he had received at Ravenswood Castle, he had suffered his lady to remain altogether ignorant, until she now learned it by the chance information of a stranger. Such concealment approached, in her apprehension, to a misprision, at least, of treason, if not to actual rebellion against matrimonial authority; and in her inward soul did she swear to take vengeance on the Lord Keeper, as on a subject detected in meditating revolt. Her indignation burned the more fiercely, as she found herself obliged to suppress it in presence of Lady Blenkinsop, the kinswoman, and of Craigengelt, the confidential friend of Bucklaw, of whose alliance she now became trebly desirous, since it occurred to her alarmed imagination, that her husband might, in his policy or timidity, prefer that of Ravenswood.

The Captain was engineer enough to discover that the train was fired; and therefore heard, in the course of the same day, without the least surprise, that Lady Ashton had resolved to abridge her visit to Lady Blenkinsop, and set forth with the peep of morning on her return to Scotland, using all the dispatch which the state of the roads, and the mode of travelling, would possibly permit.

Unhappy Lord Keeper!—little was he aware what a storm was travelling towards him in all the speed with which an old-fashioned coach and six could possibly achieve its journey. He, like Don Gayferos, "forgot his lady fair and true," and was only anxious about the expected visit of the Marquis of A——. Soothfast tidings had assured him that this nobleman was at length, and without fail, to honour his castle at one after noon, being a late dinner-hour; and much was the bustle in consequence of the annunciation. The Lord Keeper traversed the chambers, held consultation with the butler in the cellars, and even ventured, at the risk of a *démêlée* with a cook, of a spirit lofty enough to scorn the admonitions of Lady Ashton herself, to peep into the kitchen. Satisfied, at length, that every thing was in as active a train of preparation as was possible, he summoned Ravenswood and his daughter to a walk upon the terrace, for the purpose of watching, from that commanding position, the earliest symptoms of his Lordship's approach. For this purpose, with slow and idle step, he paraded the terrace, which, flanked with a heavy stone battlement, stretched in front of the castle upon a level with the first storey; while visitors found access to the court by a projecting gate-way, the bartizan or flat-leaded roof of which was accessible from the terrace by an easy flight of low and broad steps. The whole bore a middle resemblance to a castle and a nobleman's seat; and though calculated, in some respects, for defence, evinced that it had been constructed under a sense of the power and security of the ancient Lords of Ravenswood.

This pleasant walk commanded a beautiful and extensive view. But what was most to our present purpose, there were seen from the terrace two roads, one leading from the east, and one from the westward, which, crossing a ridge opposed to the eminence on which the castle stood, at different angles, gradually approached each other, until they joined not far from the gate of the avenue. It was to the westward approach that the Lord Keeper, from a sort of fidgetty anxiety, his daughter, from complaisance to him, and Ravenswood, though feeling some symptoms of internal impatience, out of complaisance to his daughter, directed their eyes to see the precursors of the Marquis's approach.

These were not long of presenting themselves. Two running footmen, dressed in white, with black jockey-caps, and long staffs in their hand, headed the train; and such was their agility, that they found no difficulty in keeping the necessary advance, which the etiquette of their station required, before the carriage and horsemen. Onwards they came at a long swinging trot, arguing unwearied speed in their long-breathed calling. Such running footmen are often alluded to in old plays, (I would particularly instance "Middleton's Mad World my Masters,") and perhaps may be still remembered by some old persons in Scotland, as part of the retinue of the ancient nobility when travelling in full ceremony.* Behind these glancing meteors, who footed it as if the Avenger of Blood had been behind them, came a cloud of dust, raised by riders who preceded, attended, or followed, the state-carriage of the Marquis.

The privilege of nobility, in these days, had something in it impressive on the imagination. The dresses and liveries and number of their attendants, their style of travelling, the imposing, and almost warlike air of the armed men who surrounded them, placed them far above the laird, who travelled with his brace of footmen; and as to rivalry from the mercantile part of the community, they would as soon have thought of emulating the state equipage of the Sovereign. At present it is different; and I myself, Peter Pattieson, in a late journey to Edinburgh, had the honour, in the mail-coach phrase, to "change a leg" with a peer of the realm. It was not so in the days of which I write; and the Marquis's approach, so long expected in vain, now took place in the full pomp of ancient aristocracy. Sir William Ashton was so much interested in what he beheld, and in considering the ceremonial of reception in case any circumstance had been omitted, that he scarce heard his son Henry exclaim, "there is another coach and six coming down the east road, papa—will they both belong to the Marquis of A——?"

---

*Hereupon I, Jedidiah Cleishbotham, crave leave to remark, *primo*, which signifies, in the first place, that, having in vain enquired at the Circulating Library in Gandercleugh, albeit it aboundeth in similar vanities, for this samyn Middleton and his Mad World, it was at length shewn unto me amongst other ancient fooleries carefully compiled by one Dodsley, who, doubtless, hath his reward for neglect of precious time; and having misused so much of mine as was necessary for the purpose, I therein found that a play-man is brought in as a footman, whom a knight is made to greet facetiously with the epithet of "linen stocking, and three-score miles a day."

Secundo, (which is secondly in the vernacular,) under Mr Pattieson's favour, some men not altogether so old as he would represent them, do remember this species of menial, or fore-runner. In evidence of which, I, Jedidiah Cleishbotham, though mine eyes yet do me good service, remember me to have seen one of this tribe clothed in white, and bearing a staff, who ran daily before the state-coach of the umquhile John, Earl of Hopeton, father of this Earl, Charles, that now is; unto whom it may be justly said, that Renown playeth the part of a running footman, or precursor; and, as the poet singeth—

> Mars standing by asserts his quarrel,
> And Fame flies after with a laurel.

J.C.

At length, when the youngster had fairly compelled his attention by pulling his sleeve,

> He turned his eyes, and, as he turn'd, survey'd
> An awful vision.—

Surely enough, another coach and six, with four servants or out-riders in attendance, was descending the hill from the eastward, at such a pace as made it doubtful which of the carriages thus approaching from distant quarters should first reach the gate at the extremity of the avenue. The one coach was green, the other blue; and not the green and blue chariots in the Circus of Rome or Constantinople excited more turmoil among the citizens than this double apparition occasioned in the mind of the Lord Keeper. We all remember the terrible exclamation of the dying profligate, when a friend, to destroy what he supposed the hypochondriac idea of a spectre appearing in a certain shape at a given hour, placed before him a person dressed up in the manner he described. "*Mon Dieu!*" said the expiring sinner, who, it seems, saw both the real and polygraphic apparition—"*Il y en est deux!*"

The surprise of the Lord Keeper was scarce less unpleasing at the duplication of the expected arrival; his mind misgave him strangely. There was no neighbour who would have approached so unceremoni-ously, at a time when ceremony was held in such respect. It must be Lady Ashton, said his conscience, and followed up the hint with an anxious anticipation of the purpose of her sudden and unannounced return. He felt that he was caught "in the manner." That the company in which she had so unluckily surprised him was likely to be highly distasteful to her, there was no question; and the only hope which remained for him was her high sense of dignified propriety, which, he trusted, might prevent a public explosion. But so active were his doubts and fears, as altogether to derange his purposed ceremonial for the reception of the Marquis.

These feelings of apprehension were not confined to Sir William Ashton. "It is my mother—it is my mother," said Lucy, turning as pale as ashes, and clasping her hands together as she looked at Ravens-wood.

"And if it be Lady Ashton," said her lover to her in a low tone, "what can be the occasion of such alarm?—Surely the return of a lady to the family from which she has been so long absent, should excite other sensations than those of fear and dismay."

"You do not know my mother," said Miss Ashton, in a tone almost breathless with terror; "what will she say when she sees you in this place!"

"My stay is too long," said Ravenswood somewhat haughtily, "if her

displeasure at my presence is like to be so formidable. My dear Lucy,"
he resumed, in a tone of soothing encouragement, "you are too child-
ishly afraid of Lady Ashton; she is a woman of family—a lady of
fashion—a person who must know the world, and what is due to her
husband and her husband's guests."

Lucy shook her head; and, as if her mother, still at the distance of
half a mile, could have seen and scrutinized her deportment, she
withdrew herself from beside Ravenswood, and, taking her brother
Henry's arm, led him to a different part of the terrace. The Keeper
also shuffled down towards the portal of the great gate, without inviting Ravenswood to accompany him, and thus he remained standing
alone on the terrace, deserted and shunned, as it were, by the inhabitants of the mansion.

This suited not the mood of one who was proud in proportion to his
poverty, and who thought that, in sacrificing his deep-rooted resent-
ments so far as to become Sir William Ashton's guest, he conferred a
favour, and received none. "I can forgive Lucy," he said to himself;
"she is young, timid, and conscious of an important engagement
assumed without her mother's sanction; yet she should remember
with whom it has been assumed, and leave me no reason to suspect
that she is ashamed of her choice. For the Keeper, sense, spirit, and
expression seem to have left his face and manner since he had the first
glimpse of Lady Ashton's carriage. I must watch how this is to end;
and, if they give me reason to think myself an unwelcome guest, my
visit is soon abridged."

With these suspicions floating on his mind he left the terrace, and,
walking towards the stables of the castle, gave directions that his horse
should be kept in readiness, in case he should have occasion to ride
abroad.

In the meanwhile the drivers of the two carriages, the approach of
which had occasioned so much dismay at the castle, had become
aware of each other's presence as they approached upon different
lines to the head of the avenue, as a common centre. Lady Ashton's
driver and postillions instantly received orders to get foremost, if
possible, her ladyship being desirous of dispatching her first interview
with her husband before the arrival of these guests, whoever they
might happen to be. On the other hand, the coachman of the Marquis,
conscious of his own dignity and that of his master, and observing the
rival charioteer was mending his pace, resolved, like a true brother of
the whip, whether ancient or modern, to vindicate his right of precedence. So that, to increase the confusion of the Lord Keeper's understanding, he saw the short time which remained for consideration
abridged by the haste of the contending coachmen, who, fixing their

eyes sternly on each other, and applying the lash smartly to their horses, began to thunder down the descent with emulous rapidity, while the horsemen who attended them were forced to put on to a hand gallop.

Sir William's only chance now remaining was the possibility of an overturn, and that his lady or visitor might break their necks. I am not aware that he formed any distinct wish on the subject, but I have no reason to think that his grief in either case would have been altogether inconsolable. This chance, however, also disappeared; for Lady Ashton, though insensible to fear, began to see the ridicule of running a race with a visitor of distinction, the goal being the portal of her own castle, and commanded her coachman, as they approached the avenue, to slacken his pace, and allow precedence to the stranger's equipage, a command which he gladly obeyed, as coming in time to save his honour, the horses of the Marquis's carriage being better, or, at least, fresher than his own. He restrained his speed, therefore, and suffered the green coach to enter the avenue, with all its retinue, which pass it occupied with the speed of a whirlwind. The Marquis's laced charioteer no sooner found the *pas d'avance* was granted to him, than he resumed a more deliberate pace, at which he advanced under the embowering shade of the lofty elms, surrounded by all the attendants; while the carriage of Lady Ashton followed still more slowly at some distance.

In the front of the castle, and beneath the portal which admitted guests into the inner court, stood Sir William Ashton, much perplexed in mind, his younger son and daughter beside him, and in their rear a train of attendants of various ranks, in and out of livery. The nobility and gentry of Scotland, at this period, were remarkable even to extravagance for the number of their servants, whose services were easily purchased in a country where men were numerous in proportion to the means of employing them.

The manners of a man, trained like Sir William Ashton, are too much at his command to remain long disconcerted with the most adverse concurrence of circumstances. He received the Marquis, as he alighted from his equipage, with the usual compliments of welcome; and, as he ushered him into the great hall, expressed his hope that his journey had been pleasant. The Marquis was a tall, well-made man, with a thoughtful and intelligent countenance, and an eye, in which the fire of ambition had for some years replaced the vivacity of youth; a bold, proud expression of countenance, yet chastened by habitual caution, and the desire which, as the head of a party, he necessarily entertained of acquiring popularity. He answered with courtesy the courteous enquiries of the Lord Keeper, and was formally presented to Miss Ashton, in the course of which ceremony Sir William gave the first symptom of what was chiefly occupying his mind, by introducing her as "his wife, Lady Ashton."

Lucy blushed; the Marquis looked surprised at the extremely juvenile appearance of his hostess, and the Lord Keeper with difficulty rallied himself so far as to explain. "I should have said my daughter, my lord; but the truth is, that I saw Lady Ashton's carriage enter the avenue shortly after your lordship's, and"——

"Make no apology, my lord," replied his noble guest; "let me entreat you will wait on your lady, and leave me to cultivate Miss Ashton's acquaintance. I am shocked my people should have taken precedence of our hostess at her own gate; but your lordship is aware, that I supposed Lady Ashton was still in the south. Let me entreat you will waive ceremony, and hasten to welcome her."

This was precisely what the Lord Keeper longed to do; and he instantly profited by his lordship's obliging permission. To see Lady Ashton, and encounter the first burst of her displeasure in private, might prepare her, in some degree, to receive her unwelcome guests with due decorum. As her carriage, therefore, stopped, the arm of the attentive husband was ready to assist Lady Ashton in dismounting. Looking as if she saw him not, she put his arm aside, and requested that of Captain Craigengelt, who stood by the coach with his laced hat under his arm, having acted as *cavaliere servente*, or squire in attendance, during the journey. Taking hold of this respectable person's arm as if to support her, Lady Ashton traversed the court, uttering a word or two by way of direction to the servants, but not one to Sir William, who in vain endeavoured to attract her attention, as he rather followed than accompanied her into the hall, in which they found the Marquis in close conversation with the Master of Ravenswood: Lucy had taken the first opportunity of escaping. There was embarrassment on every countenance except that of the Marquis of A——, for even Craigengelt's impudence was hardly able to veil his fear of Ravenswood, and the rest felt the awkwardness of the position in which they were thus unexpectedly placed.

After waiting a moment to be presented by Sir William Ashton, the Marquis resolved to introduce himself. "The Lord Keeper," he said, bowing to Lady Ashton, "has just introduced to me his daughter as his wife—he might very easily present Lady Ashton as his daughter, so little does she differ from what I remember her some years since— Will she permit an old acquaintance the privilege of a guest?"

He saluted the lady with too good a grace to apprehend a repulse, and then proceeded—"This, Lady Ashton, is a peace-making visit, and therefore I presume to introduce my cousin, the young Master of

Ravenswood, to your favourable notice."

Lady Ashton could not chuse but courtsy; but there was in her obeisance an air of haughtiness approaching to contemptuous repulse. Ravenswood could not chuse but bow; but his manner returned the scorn with which he had been greeted.

"Allow me," she said, "to present to your lordship *my* friend." Craigengelt, with the forward impudence which men of his cast mistake for ease, made a sliding bow to the Marquis, which he graced by a flourish of his gold-laced hat. The lady turned to her husband—"You and I, Sir William," she said, and these were the first words she had addressed to him, "have acquired new acquaintances since we parted —let me introduce the acquisition I have made to mine—Captain Craigengelt."

Another bow, and another flourish of the gold-laced hat, which was returned by the Lord Keeper without intimation of former recognition, and with that sort of anxious readiness, which intimated his wish, that peace and amnesty should take place betwixt the contending parties, including the auxiliaries on both sides. "Let me introduce you to the Master of Ravenswood," said he to Captain Craigengelt, following up the same amicable system. But the Master drew up his tall form to the full extent of his height, and without so much as looking towards the person thus introduced to him, he said, in a marked tone, "Captain Craigengelt and I are already perfectly acquainted with each other."

"Perfectly—perfectly," replied the Captain, in a mumbling tone, like that of a double echo, and with a flourish of his hat, the circumference of which was greatly abridged, compared with those which had so cordially graced his introduction to the Marquis and the Lord Keeper.

Lockhard, followed by three menials, now entered with wine and refreshments, which it was the fashion to offer as a whet before dinner; and when they were placed before the guests, Lady Ashton made an apology for withdrawing her husband from them for some minutes upon business of special import. The Marquis, of course, requested her ladyship would lay herself under no restraint; and Craigengelt, bolting with speed a second glass of racy canary, hastened to leave the room, feeling no great pleasure in the prospect of being left alone with the Marquis of A—— and the Master of Ravenswood; the presence of the former holding him in awe, and that of the latter in bodily terror. Some arrangements about his horse and baggage formed the pretext for his sudden retreat, in which he persevered, although Lady Ashton gave Lockhard orders to be careful most particularly to accommodate Captain Craigengelt with all the attendance which he could possibly require. The Marquis and the Master of Ravenswood were thus left to communicate to each other their remarks upon the reception which they had met with, while Lady Ashton led the way, and her lord followed somewhat like a condemned criminal, to her ladyship's undressing-room.

So soon as they had both entered, her ladyship gave way to that fierce audacity of temper, which she had with difficulty suppressed, out of respect to appearances. She shut the door behind the alarmed Lord Keeper, took the key out of the spring-lock, and with a countenance which years had not bereft of its haughty charms, and eyes which spoke at once resolution and resentment, she addressed her astonished husband in these words:—"My lord, I am not greatly surprised at the connections you have been pleased to form during my absence —they are entirely in conformity to your birth and breeding; and if I did expect any thing else, I heartily own my error, and that I merit, by having done so, the disappointment you had prepared for me."

"My dear Lady Ashton—my dear Eleanor," said the Lord Keeper, "listen to reason for a moment, and I will convince you I have acted with all the regard due to the dignity, as well as the interest of my family."

"To the interest of your family I conceive you perfectly capable of attending," returned the indignant lady, "and even to the dignity of *your* family also—But as mine happens to be inextricably involved with it, you will excuse me if I chuse to give my own attention so far as that is concerned."

"What would you have, Lady Ashton?" said the husband—"What is it that displeases you? Why is it, that on your return after so long an absence, I am arraigned in this manner?"

"Ask your own conscience, Sir William, what has prompted you to become a renegade to your political party and opinions, and, for what I know, to be on the point of marrying your only daughter to a beggarly jacobite bankrupt, the inveterate enemy of your family to the boot."

"Why, what, in the name of common sense and common civility, would you have me do, madam?" answered her husband—"Is it possible for me, with ordinary decency, to turn a young gentleman out of my house, who saved my daughter's life and my own, but the other morning as it were?"

"Saved your life! I have heard of that story," said the lady—"the Lord Keeper was scared by a dun cow, and he takes the young fellow who killed her for Guy of Warwick—any butcher from Haddington may soon have an equal claim on your hospitality."

"Lady Ashton," stammered the Keeper, "this is intolerable—and when I am desirous, too, to make you easy by any sacrifice—if you would but tell me what you would be at."

"Go down to your guests," said the imperious dame, "and make your apology to Ravenswood, that the arrival of Captain Craigengelt and some other friends, renders it impossible for you to offer him lodgings at the castle—I expect young Mr Hayston of Bucklaw."

"Good Heavens, madam!" ejaculated her husband—"Ravenswood to give place to Craigengelt, a common gambler and an informer!—it was all I could do to forbear desiring the fellow to get out of my house, and I was much surprised to see him in your ladyship's train."

"Since you saw him there, you might be well assured," answered this meek helpmate, "that he was proper society. As to this Ravenswood, he only meets with the treatment which, to my certain knowledge, he gave to a much valued friend of mine, who had the misfortune to be his guest some time since. But take your resolution; for, if Ravenswood does not quit the house, I will."

Sir William Ashton paced up and down the apartment in the most distressing agitation; fear, and shame, and anger contending against the habitual deference he was in the use of rendering to his lady. At length it ended, as is usual with timid minds placed in such circumstances, in his adopting a *mezzo-termine*, a middle measure.

"I tell you frankly, madam, I neither can nor will be guilty of the incivility you propose to the Master of Ravenswood—he has not deserved it at my hand. If you will be so unreasonable as to insult a man of quality under your own roof, I cannot prevent you, but I will not at least be the agent in such a preposterous proceeding."

"You will not?" asked the lady.

"No, by Heavens, madam," her husband replied; "ask me anything congruent with common decency, as to drop his acquaintance by degrees, or the like—but to bid him leave my house, is what I will not, and cannot consent to."

"Then the task of supporting the honour of the family will fall on me, as it has often done before," said the lady.

She sat down, and hastily wrote a few lines. The Lord Keeper made another effort to prevent her taking a step so decisive, just as she opened the door to call her female attendant from the anti-room. "Think what you are doing, Lady Ashton—you are making a mortal enemy of a young man, who is like to have the means of harming us"——

"Did you ever know a Douglas who feared an enemy?" answered the lady contemptuously.

"Ay, but he is as proud and vindictive as an hundred Douglasses, and an hundred devils to boot. Think of it for a night only."

"Not for another moment," answered the lady;—"here, Mrs

Patullo, give this billet to young Ravenswood."

"To the Master, madam?" said Mrs Patullo.

"Ay, to the Master, if you call him so."

"I wash my hands of it entirely," said the Keeper; "and I shall go down into the garden, and see that Jardine gathers the winter fruit for the dessert."

"Do so," said the lady, looking after him with looks of infinite contempt; "and thank God that you leave one behind you as fit to protect the honour of the family, as you are to look after pippins and pears."

The Lord Keeper remained long enough in the garden to give her ladyship's mine time to explode, and to let, as he thought, at least the first violence of Ravenswood's displeasure blow over. When he entered the hall, he found the Marquis of A—— giving orders to some of his attendants. He seemed in high displeasure, and interrupted an apology which Sir William had commenced, for having left his lordship alone.

"I presume, Sir William, you are no stranger to this singular billet with which my kinsman of Ravenswood (an emphasis on the word *my*) has been favoured by your lady—and, of course, that you are prepared to receive my adieus—My kinsman is already gone, having thought it unnecessary to offer any on his part, since all former civilities have been cancelled by this singular insult."

"I protest, my lord," said Sir William, holding the billet in his hand, "I am not privy to the contents of this letter. I know Lady Ashton is a warm-tempered and prejudiced woman, and I am sincerely sorry for any offence that has been given or taken; but I hope your lordship will consider that a lady"——

"Should bear herself towards persons of a certain rank with the breeding of one," said the Marquis, completing the half-uttered sentence.

"True, my lord," said the unfortunate Keeper; "but Lady Ashton is still a woman"——

"And as such, methinks," said the Marquis, again interrupting him, "should be taught the duties which correspond to her station. But here she comes, and I will learn from her own mouth the reason of this extraordinary and unexpected affront offered to my near relation, while both he and I were her ladyship's guests."

Lady Ashton accordingly entered the apartment at this moment. Her dispute with Sir William, and a subsequent interview with her daughter, had not prevented her from attending to the duties of her toilette. She appeared in full dress; and, from the character of her countenance and manner, well became the splendour with which ladies of quality then appeared on such occasions.

The Marquis of A—— bowed haughtily, and she returned the salute with equal pride and distance of demeanour. He then took from the passive hand of Sir William Ashton the billet he had given him the moment before he approached the lady, and was about to speak, when she interrupted him. "I perceive, my lord, you are about to enter upon an unpleasant subject. I am sorry any such should have occurred at this time, to interrupt, in the slightest degree, the respectful reception due to your lordship—but so it is.—Mr Edgar Ravenswood, for whom I have addressed the billet in your lordship's hand, has abused the hospitality of this family, and Sir William Ashton's softness of temper, in order to seduce a young person into engagements without her parents' consent, and of which they never can approve."

Both gentlemen answered at once,—"My kinsman is incapable"——said the Lord Marquis.

"I am confident that my daughter Lucy is still more incapable"——said the Lord Keeper.

Lady Ashton at once interrupted, and replied to them both,—"My Lord Marquis, your kinsman, if Mr Ravenswood has the honour to be so, has made this attempt privately to secure the affections of this young and inexperienced girl.—Sir William Ashton, your daughter has been simple enough to give more encouragement than she ought to have done to so very improper a suitor."

"And I think, madam," said the Lord Keeper, losing his accustomed temper and patience, "that if you had nothing better to tell us, you had better have kept this family secret to yourself also."

"You will pardon me, Sir William," said the lady, calmly; "the noble Marquis has a right to know the cause of the treatment I have found it necessary to use to a gentleman whom he calls his blood-relation."

"It is a cause," muttered the Lord Keeper, "which has emerged since the effect has taken place; for, if it exists at all, I am sure she knew nothing of it when her letter to Ravenswood was written."

"It is the first time that I have heard of this," said the Marquis; "but since your ladyship has tabled a subject so delicate, permit me to say, that my kinsman's birth and connections entitled him to a patient hearing, and, at least, a civil refusal, even in case of his being so ambitious as to raise his eyes to the daughter of Sir William Ashton."

"You will recollect, my lord, of what blood Miss Lucy Ashton is come by the mother's side," said the lady.

"I do remember your descent—from a younger branch of the house of Angus," said the Marquis—"and your ladyship—forgive me, lady —ought not to forget that the Ravenswoods have thrice intermarried with the main branch. Come, madam—I know how matters stand—

old and long-fostered prejudices are difficult to get over—I make every allowance for them—I ought not, and I would not have suffered my kinsman to depart alone, expelled, in a manner, from this house—but I had hopes of being a mediator. I am still unwilling to leave you in anger—and shall not set forward till after noon, as I rejoin the Master of Ravenswood upon the road a few miles from hence. Let us talk over this matter more coolly."

"It is what I anxiously desire, my lord," said Sir William Ashton, eagerly. "Lady Ashton, we will not permit my Lord of A—— to leave us in displeasure. We must compel him to tarry dinner at the castle."

"The castle," said the lady, "and all that it contains, are at the command of the Marquis, so long as he chuses to honour it with his residence—but touching the farther discussion of this disagreeable topic"——

"Pardon me, good madam," said the Marquis; "but I cannot allow you to express any hasty resolution on a subject so important. I see that more company is arriving; and since I have the good fortune to renew my former acquaintance with Lady Ashton, I hope she will give me leave to avoid perilling what I prize so highly upon any disagreeable subject of discussion—at least, till we have talked over more agreeable topics."

The lady smiled, curtsied, and gave her hand to the Marquis, by whom, with all the formal gallantry of the time, which did not permit the guest to tuck the lady of the house under the arm, as a rustic does his sweetheart at a wake, she was ushered to the eating-room.

Here they were joined by Bucklaw, Craigengelt, and other neighbours, whom the Lord Keeper had previously invited to meet the Marquis of A——. An apology, founded upon a slight indisposition, was alleged as an excuse for the absence of Miss Ashton, whose seat appeared unoccupied. The entertainment was splendid to profusion, and was protracted till a late hour.

Chapter Nine

Such was our fallen father's state,
    Yet better than mine own;
He shared his exile with his mate,
    I'm banished forth alone.
                    WALLER

I WILL NOT attempt to describe the mixture of indignation and regret with which Ravenswood left the seat which had belonged to his ancestors. The terms in which Lady Ashton's billet was couched rendered it impossible for him, without being deficient in that spirit of which he perhaps had too much, to remain an instant longer within its walls. The Marquis, who had his share in the affront, was, nevertheless, still willing to make some efforts at conciliation. He therefore suffered his kinsman to depart alone, making him promise, however, that he would wait for him at the small inn called the Tod's-hole, situated, as our readers may be pleased to recollect, half way betwixt Ravenswood Castle and Wolfscrag, and about five Scottish miles distant from each. Here the Marquis proposed to join the Master of Ravenswood, either that night or the next morning. His own feelings would have induced him to have left the castle directly, but he was loth to forfeit, without at least one effort, the advantages which he had proposed from his visit to the Lord Keeper; and in consideration of the circumstances in which he stood with Lucy the Master of Ravenswood was, even in the very heat of his resentment, unwilling to foreclose any chance of reconciliation which might arise out of the partiality which Sir William Ashton had shewn towards him, as well as the intercessory arguments of his noble kinsman. He himself departed without a moment's delay, farther than was necessary to make this arrangement.

At first he spurred his horse at a quick pace through an avenue of the park, as if, by rapidity of motion, he could stupify the confusion of feelings with which he was assailed. But as the road grew wilder and more sequestered, and when the trees had hidden the turrets of the castle, he gradually slackened his pace, as if to indulge those painful reflections which he had in vain endeavoured to repress. The path in which he found himself led him to the Mermaiden's Fountain, and to the cottage of Alice; and the fatal influence which superstitious belief attached to the former spot, as well as the admonitions which had been in vain offered to him by the inhabitant of the latter, forced themselves upon his memory. "Old saws speak truth," he said to himself; "and the Mermaiden's Well has indeed witnessed the last act of rashness of the heir of Ravenswood.—Alice spoke well," he continued, "and I am in the situation which she foretold—or rather I am more deeply dishonoured—not the dependent and ally of the destroyer of my father's house, as the old sybil presaged, but the degraded wretch, who has aspired to hold that subordinate character, and has been rejected with disdain."

We are bound to tell the tale as we have received it; and, considering the distance of the time, and propensity of those through whose mouths it has passed to the marvellous, this would not be a Scottish story, unless it manifested a tinge of Scottish superstition. As Ravenswood approached the solitary fountain, he is said to have met with the following singular adventure:—His horse, which was moving slowly forward, suddenly interrupted its steady and composed pace, snorted, reared, and, though urged by the spur, refused to proceed, as if some object of terror had suddenly presented itself. On looking to the fountain, Ravenswood discerned a female figure, dressed in a white, or rather greyish mantle, placed in the very spot on which Lucy Ashton had reclined while listening to his fatal tale of love. His immediate impression was, that she had conjectured by which path he would traverse the park on his departure, and placed herself at this well-known and sequestered place of rendezvous, to indulge her own sorrow and his in a parting interview. In this belief he jumped from his horse, and, making its bridle fast to a tree, walked hastily towards the fountain, pronouncing eagerly, yet under his breath, the words, "Miss Ashton!—Lucy!"

The figure turned as he addressed it, and displayed to his wondering eyes the features, not of Lucy Ashton, but of old blind Alice. The singularity of her dress, which rather resembled a shroud than the garment of a living woman—the appearance of her person, larger, as it struck him, than it usually seemed to be—above all, the strange circumstance of a blind and decrepit person being found at a distance from her habitation, (considerable if her infirmities be taken into account,) combined to impress him with a feeling of wonder approaching to fear. As he approached her, she rose up from her seat, held her shrivelled hand up as if to prevent his coming more near, and her withered lips moved fast, although no sound issued from them; and as, after a moment's pause, he again advanced towards her, Alice, or her apparition, moved or glided backwards towards the thicket, still keeping her face turned towards him. The trees soon hid her from his sight; and, yielding to the strong and terrific impression that the form which he had seen was not of this world, the Master of Ravenswood remained rooted to the ground whereon he had stood when he caught his last view of her. At length, summoning up his courage, he advanced to the spot on which the figure had seemed to be seated; but neither was there pressure of the grass, nor any other circumstance, to induce him to believe that what he had seen was real and substantial.

Full of those strange thoughts and confused apprehensions which awake in the bosom of one who conceives he has witnessed some preternatural appearance, the Master of Ravenswood walked back towards his horse, frequently however looking behind him, not without apprehension, as if expecting that the vision would re-appear. But the apparition, whether it was real, or whether it was the creation of a heated and agitated imagination, returned not again; and he found his horse sweating and terrified, as if experiencing that agony of fear, with which the presence of a supernatural being is supposed to agitate the brute creation. The Master mounted, and rode slowly forward, soothing his horse from time to time, while the animal seemed internally to shrink and shudder, as if expecting some new object of fear at the opening of every glade. The rider, after a moment's consideration, resolved to investigate the matter further. "Can my eyes have deceived me," he said, "and deceived me for such a space of time?—Or are this woman's infirmities but feigned, in order to excite compassion?— And even then, her motion resembled not that of a living and existing person. Must I adopt the popular creed, and think that the unhappy being has formed a league with the powers of darkness?—I am determined to be resolved—I will not brook imposition even from my own eyes."

In this uncertainty he rode up to the little wicket of Alice's garden. Her seat beneath the birch-tree was vacant, though the day was pleasant, and the sun was high. He approached the hut, and heard from within the sobs and wailing of a female. No answer was returned when he knocked, so that, after a moment's pause, he lifted the latch and entered. It was indeed a house of solitude and sorrow. Stretched upon her miserable pallet lay the corpse of the last retainer of the house of Ravenswood who still abode on their paternal domains. Life had but shortly departed; and the little girl by whom she had been attended in her last moments was wringing her hands and sobbing, betwixt childish fear and sorrow, over the body of her mistress.

The Master of Ravenswood had some difficulty to compose the terrors of the poor child, whom his unexpected appearance had at first rather appalled than comforted; and when he succeeded, the first expression which the girl used intimated that "he had come too late." Upon enquiring the meaning of this expression, he learned that the deceased, upon the first attack of the mortal agony, had sent a peasant to the castle to beseech an interview of the Master of Ravenswood, and had expressed the utmost impatience for his return. But the messengers of the poor are tardy and negligent: the fellow had not reached the castle, as was afterwards learned, until Ravenswood had left it, and had then found too much amusement among the retinue of the strangers to return in any haste to the cottage of Alice. Meantime her anxiety of mind seemed to increase with the agony of her body; and, to use the phrase of Babie, her only attendant, "she prayed powerfully that she might see her master's son once more, and renew her warning." She died just as the clock in the distant village church tolled one; and Ravenswood remembered, with internal shuddering, that he had heard the chime sound through the wood just before he had seen what he was now much disposed to consider as the spectre of the deceased.

It was necessary, as well from his respect to the departed as in common humanity to her terrified attendant, that he should take some measures to relieve the girl from her distressing situation. The deceased, he understood, had expressed a desire to be buried in a solitary church-yard near the little inn of the Tod's-hole, called the Hermitage, or more commonly Armitage, in which lay interred some of the Ravenswood family, and many of their followers. Ravenswood conceived it his duty to gratify this predilection, so commonly found to exist among the Scottish peasantry, and dispatched Babie to the neighbouring village to procure the assistance of some females, assuring her that, in the meanwhile, he would himself remain with the dead body, which, as in Thessaly of old, it is accounted highly unfit to leave without a watch.

Thus, in the course of a quarter of an hour, or little more, he found himself sitting, a solitary guard over the inanimate corse of her, whose dismissed spirit, unless his eyes had strangely deceived him, had so shortly before manifested itself before him. Notwithstanding his natural courage, the Master was considerably affected by a concurrence of circumstances so extraordinary. "She died expressing her eager desire to see me. Can it be, then,"—was his natural course of reflection—"can strong and earnest wishes, formed during the last agony of nature, survive its catastrophe, surmount the awful bounds of the spiritual world, and place before us its inhabitants in the hues and colouring of life?—And why was that manifested to the eye which could not unfold its tale to the ear?—and wherefore should a breach be made in the laws of nature, yet its purpose remain unknown?— Vain questions, which only Death, when it shall make me like the pale and withered form before me, can ever resolve."

He laid a cloth, as he spoke, over the lifeless face, upon whose features he felt unwilling any longer to dwell. He then took his place in an old carved oaken chair, ornamented with his own armorial bearings, which Alice had contrived to appropriate to her own use in the pillage which took place amongst creditors, officers, domestics, and messengers of the law, when his father left Ravenswood Castle for the last time. Thus seated, he banished, as much as he could, the superstitious feelings which the late incident naturally inspired. His own were sad enough, without the exaggerations of supernatural terror, since he found himself transferred from the situation of a successful lover of Lucy Ashton, and an honoured and respected friend of her father, into the melancholy and solitary guardian of the abandoned and forsaken corpse of a common pauper.

He was relieved, however, of his sad office sooner than he could reasonably have expected, from the distance betwixt the hut of the deceased and the village, and the age and infirmities of three old women, who came from thence, in military phrase, to relieve guard upon the body of the defunct. On any other occasion the speed of these reverend sybils would have been much more moderate, for the first was eighty years of age and upwards, the second was paralytic, and the third lame of a leg from some accident. But the burial duties rendered to the deceased, are, to the Scottish peasant of either sex, a labour of love. I know not whether it is from the temper of the people, grave and enthusiastic as it certainly is, or from the recollection of the ancient catholic opinions, when the funeral rites were always considered as a period of festival to the living; but feasting, good cheer, and even inebriety, were, and are, the frequent accompaniments of a Scottish old-fashioned burial. What the funeral feast, or *dirgie*, as it is called, was to the men, the gloomy preparations of the dead body for the coffin were to the women. To streight the contorted limbs upon a board used for that melancholy purpose, to array the corpse in clean linen, and over that in its woollen shroud, were operations committed always to the old matrons of the village, and in which they found a singular and gloomy delight.

The old women paid the Master their salutations with a ghastly smile, which reminded him of the meeting betwixt Macbeth and the witches on the blasted heath of Forres. He gave them some money, and recommended to them the charge of the dead body of their contemporary, an office which they willingly undertook; intimating to him at the same time that he must leave the hut, in order that they might begin their mournful duties. Ravenswood readily agreed to depart, only tarrying to recommend to them due attention to the body, and to receive information where he was to find the sexton, or beadle, who had in charge the deserted church-yard of the Armitage, in order to prepare matters for the reception of old Alice in the place of repose which she had selected for herself.

"Ye'll no be pinched to find out Johnie Mortsheugh," said the eldest sybil, and still her withered cheek bore a grisly smile—"he dwells near the Tod's-hole, an house of entertainment where there has been mony a blithe birling—for death and drink-draining are near neighbours to ane anither."

"Ay! and that's e'en true, cummer," said the lame hag, propping herself with a crutch which supplied the shortness of her left leg, "for I mind when the father of this Master of Ravenswood that is now standing before us, sticked young Blackhall with his whinger, for a wrang word said ower their wine, or brandy, or what not—He gaed in as light as a lark, and he came out with his feet foremost. I was at the winding of the corpse; and when the bluid was washed off, he was a bonnie bouk of man's body."

It may be easily believed that this ill-timed anecdote hastened the Master's purpose of quitting a company so evil-omened and so odious. Yet, while walking to the tree to which his horse was tied, and busying himself with adjusting the girths of the saddle, he could not avoid hearing, through the hedge of the little garden, a conversation respecting himself, betwixt the lame woman and the octogenarian sybil. The pair had hobbled into the garden to gather rosemary, southern-wood, rue, and other plants proper to be strewed on the body, and burned by way of fumigation in the chimney of the cottage. The paralytic wretch, almost exhausted by the journey, was left guard upon the corpse, least witches or fiends might play their sport with it.

The following low croaking dialogue was necessarily overheard by the Master of Ravenswood:—"That's a fresh and a full-grown hemlock, Ailsie Gourlay—mony a cummer lang syne wad hae sought nae better horse to flee over hill and how, through mist and moonlight, and light doun in the King of France's cellar."

"Ay, cummer! but the very de'il has turned as hard-hearted now as the Lord Keeper, and the grit folk that hae breasts like whin-stane. They prick us and they pine us, and they pit us on the pinny-winkles for witches; and, if I say my prayers backwards ten times ower, Satan will never gi'e me amends o' them."

"Did ye ever see the foul thief?" asked her neighbour.

"Na!" replied the other spokeswoman; "but I trow I hae dreamed of him mony a time, and I think the day will come they will burn me for't. But ne'er mind, cummer! we hae this dollar of the Master's, and we'll send doun for bread and for aill, and tobacco, and a drap brandy to burn, and a wee pickle saft sugar—and be there de'il or nae de'il, lass, we'se hae a merry night o't."

Here her leathern chops uttered a sort of cackling ghastly laugh, resembling, to a certain degree, the cry of the screech-owl.

"He is a frank man, and a free-handed man, the Master," said Annie Winnie, "and a comely personage—broad in the shouthers, an' narrow around the lungies—he wad mak a bonnie corpse—I wad like to hae the streaking and winding o' him."

"It is written on his brow, Annie Winnie," returned the octogenarian, her companion, "that hand of woman, or of man either, will never straught him—dead-deal will never be laid to his back—make you your market of that, for I hae it frae a sure hand."

"Will it be his lot to die on the battle-ground than, Ailsie Gourlay? —will he die by the sword or the ball, as his furbeirs hae dune before him mony ane o' them?"

"Ask nae mair questions about it—he'll no be graced sae far," replied the sage.

"I ken ye are wiser than ither folk, Ailsie Gourlay—But wha tell'd ye this?"

"Fashna your thumb about that, Annie Winnie," answered the sybil —"I hae it frae a hand sure aneugh."

"But ye said ye never saw the foul thief," reiterated her inquisitive companion.

"I hae it frae as sure a hand," said Ailsie, "and from them that spaed his fortune before the sark gaed ower his head."

"Hark! I hear his horse-feet riding off," said the other; "they dinna sound as if good luck was wi' them."

"Mak haste, sirs," cried the paralytic hag from the cottage, "and let us do what is needfu', and say what is fitting; for, if the dead corpse binna straughted, it will girn and thraw, and that will fear the best of us."

Ravenswood was now out of hearing. He despised most of the ordinary prejudices about witchcraft, omens, and vaticination, to which his age and country still gave such implicit credit, that to express a doubt of them, was accounted a crime equal to the unbelief of Jews or Saracens. He knew also that the prevailing belief concerning witches, operating upon the hypochondriac habits of those whom age, infirmity, and poverty rendered liable to suspicion, and enforced by the fear of death, and the pangs of the most cruel tortures, often extorted those confessions which encumber and disgrace the criminal records of Scotland during the seventeenth century. But the vision of that morning, whether real or imaginary, had impressed his mind with a superstitious feeling which he in vain endeavoured to shake off. The nature of the business which awaited him at the little inn, called Tod's-hole, where he soon after arrived, was not of a kind to restore his spirits.

It was necessary he should see Mortsheugh, the sexton of the old burial-ground at Armitage, to arrange matters for the funeral of Alice; and as the man dwelt near the place of her late residence, the Master, after a slight refreshment, walked towards the place where the body of Alice was to be deposited. It was situated in the nook formed by the eddying sweep of a stream, which issued from the adjoining hills. A rude cavern in an adjacent rock, which, in the interior, was cut into the shape of a cross, formed the hermitage, where some Saxon saint had in ancient times done penance, and given name to the place. The rich Abbey of Coldinghame had, in latter days, established a chapel in the neighbourhood, of which no vestige was now visible, though the church-yard which surrounded it, was still, as upon the present occasion, used for the interment of particular persons. One or two shattered yew-trees still grew within the precincts of that which had once been holy ground. Warriors and barons had been buried there of old, but their names were forgotten, and their monuments demolished. The only sepulchral memorials which remained, were the upright head-stones which mark the grave of persons of an inferior rank. The abode of the sexton was a solitary cottage adjacent to the ruined wall of the cemetery, but so low, and having its thatch, which nearly reached the ground, covered with such a crop of grass, fog, and house leeks, that it resembled an overgrown grave. On enquiry, however, Ravenswood found that the man of the last mattock was absent at a bridal, being fiddler as well as grave-digger to the vicinity. He therefore retired to the little inn, leaving a message that early next morning he would again call for the person, whose double occupation connected him at once with the house of mourning and the house of feasting.

An outrider of the Marquis arrived at Tod's-hole shortly after, with a message intimating that his master would join Ravenswood at that place on the following morning; and the Master, who would otherwise have proceeded to his old retreat at Wolfscrag, remained there accordingly, to give the meeting to his noble kinsman.

Chapter Ten

Hamlet. Has this fellow no feeling of his business—he sings at grave making.
Horatio. Custom hath made it in him a property of easiness.
Hamlet. 'Tis e'en so, the hand of little employment hath the daintier sense.
                                            SHAKESPEARE

THE sleep of Ravenswood was broken by ghastly and agitating visions, and his waking intervals disturbed by melancholy reflections on the past, and painful anticipations of the future. He was perhaps the only traveller who ever slept in that miserable kennel without complaining of his lodgings, or feeling inconvenience from their deficiencies. It is when "the mind is free the body's delicate." Morning, however, found him an early riser, in hopes that the fresh air of the dawn might afford the refreshment which night had refused him. He took his way towards the solitary burial-ground, which lay about half a mile from the inn.

The thin blue smoke, which already began to curl upward, and to distinguish the cottage of the living from the habitation of the dead, apprized him that its inmate had returned and was stirring. Accordingly, on entering the little church-yard, he saw the old man labouring in a half-made grave. My destiny, thought Ravenswood, seems to lead me to scenes of fate and of death; but these are childish thoughts, and they shall not master me. I will not again suffer my imagination to beguile my senses.—The old man rested on his spade as the Master approached him, as if to receive his commands, and as he did not immediately speak, the sexton opened the discourse in his own way.

"Ye will be a wedding customer, sir, I'se warrant."

"What makes you think so, friend?" replied the Master.

"I live by twa trades, sir," replied the blythe old man; "fiddle, sir, and shovel; filling the world, and emptying of it—bridals and burials; and I suld ken baith cast of customers by head-mark in thirty years practice."

"You are mistaken, however, this morning," replied Ravenswood.

"Am I?" said the old man, looking keenly at him, "troth and it may be; since, for as brent as your brow is, there is something sitting upon it this day, that is as near akin to death as to wedlock—weel—weel—the pick and shool are as ready to your order as bow and fiddle."

"I wish you," said Ravenswood, "to look after the decent interment of an old woman, Alice Gray, who lived at the Craig-foot in Ravenswood Park."

"Alice Gray! blind Alice!" said the sexton; "and is she gane at last? that is another jow of the bell to bid me be ready. I mind when Habbie Gray brought her down to this land; a likely lass she was then, and looked ower her southland nose at us a'. I trow her pride got a down-come—and is she e'en gane?"

"She died yesterday," said Ravenswood; "and desired to be buried here, beside her husband; you will know where he lies, no doubt."

"Ken where he lies?" answered the sexton, with national indirection of response, "I ken where a' body lies, that lies here—but grave? —Lord help us—it's no an ordinar grave will haud her in, if a's true that folks said of Alice in her auld days—And if I gae to six feet deep, and a warlock's grave shouldna be an inch mair ebb, or her ain witch cummers would soon whirl her out of her shroud for a' their auld acquaintance—And be't six feet, or be't three, wha's to pay the making o't, I pray ye?"

"I shall pay that, my friend, and all other reasonable charges."

"Reasonable charges?" said the sexton; "ou, there is ground-mail, and bell-siller, (though the bell is broken nae doubt) and the kist, and my day's wark, and my bit fee, and sum brandy and aill to the drigie—I am no thinking that you can inter her, to ca' decently, under saxteen pund Scots."

"There is the money, my friend," said Ravenswood, "and some-thing over. Be sure you know the grave."

"Ye'll be ane o' her English relations, I'se warrand," said the hoary man of skulls; "I hae heard she married far below her station. It was very right to let her bite on the bridle when she was living, and its very right to gie her a decent burial now she's dead, for that's a matter o' credit to yoursell rather than to her. Folk may let their kindred shift for themsells when they are alive, and can bear the burthen of their ain misdoings; but its an unnatural thing to let them be buried like dogs, when a' the discredit gangs to the kindred: what kens the dead corse about it?"

"You would not have people neglect their relations on a bridal occasion neither," said Ravenswood, who was amused with the pro-fessional limitation of the grave-digger's philanthropy.

The old man cast up his sharp grey eye with a shrewd smile, as if he understood the jest, but instantly continued with his former gravity,—"Bridals—wha wad neglect bridals that had ony regard for plenishing the earth? To be sure, they suld be celebrated with all manner of gude cheer, and meeting of friends, and musical instruments, harp, sack-but, and psaltery; or gude fiddle and pipes, when these auld-warld instruments of melody are hard to be compassed."

"The presence of the fiddle, I dare say," replied Ravenswood, "would atone for the absence of all the others."

The sexton again looked sharply up at him, as he answered, "Nae doubt, nae doubt—if it were weel played;—but yonder," he said, as if to change the discourse, "is Halbert Gray's lang hame, that ye were speering after, just the third bourock beyond the muckle through-stane that stands on sax legs yonder, abune some ane of the Ravens-woods; for there is mony of their kin and followers lie here, de'il lift them! though it isna just their main burial-place."

"They are no favourites then of yours these Ravenswoods," said the Master, not much pleased with the passing benediction which was thus bestowed on his family and name.

"I ken na wha should favour them," said the grave-digger; "when they had lands and power, they were ill guides of them baith, and now their head's down, there's few care how lang they may be of lifting it again."

"Indeed!" said Ravenswood, "I never heard that this unhappy fam-ily deserved ill-will at the hands of their country. I grant their poverty —if that renders them contemptible."

"It will gang a far way till't," said the sexton of Hermitage, "ye may tak my word for that—at least, I ken naething else that suld mak mysell contemptible, and folk are far frae respecting me as they wad do if I lived in a twa-lofted sclated house. But as for the Ravenswoods, I hae seen three generations of them, and de'il ane to mend other."

"I thought they had enjoyed a fair character in the country," said their descendant.

"Character! Ou ye see, sir," said the sexton, "as for the auld gude-sire body of a lord, I lived on his land when I was a swanking young chield, and could hae blawn the trumpet wi' ony body, for I had wind eneugh then—and as for this trumpeter Marine that I have heard play afore the Lords of the Circuit, I wad hae made nae mair o' him than of a bairn and a bawbee whistle—I defy him to hae play'd 'Boot and saddle,' or 'Horse and away,' or 'Gallants, come trot,' with me—he has na the tones."

"But what is all this to old Lord Ravenswood, my friend?" said the Master, who, with an anxiety not unnatural in his circumstances, was desirous of prosecuting the musician's first topic—"What had his memory to do with the degeneracy of the trumpet music?"

"Just this, sir," answered the sexton, "that I lost my wind in his service. Ye see I was trumpeter at the castle, and had allowance for blawing at break of day, and at dinner-time, and other whiles when there was company about, and it pleased my lord; and when he raised his troop of militia to caper awa' to Bothwell Brigg against thae wrang-headed wastland whigs, I behuved, reason or nane, to munt on a horse and caper awa' wi' them."

"And very reasonable," said Ravenswood; "you were his servant and vassal."

"Servitor, say ye?" replied the sexton, "and so I was—but it was to blaw folk to their warm dinner, or at the warst to a decent kirk-yard, and no to skreigh them awa' to a bluidy brae side, where there was de'il a bedral but the hooded craw. But bide ye—ye shall hear what came o't, and how far I am bund to be bedesman to the Ravenswoods. —Till't, ye see, we gae't on a braw simmer morning, twenty-fourth of June, sixteen hundred and se'enty-nine, of a' days of the month and year—Drums beat, guns rattled, horses kicked and trampled—Hackstoun of Rathillet keepit the brigg wi' musket and carabine and pike, sword and scythe for what I ken, and we horse were ordered doun to cross at the ford,—I hate fords at a' times, let abe when there's thousands of armed men on the other side. There was auld Ravenswood brandishing his Andrea Ferrara at the head, and crying to hus to come on and buckle to, as if we were ganging to a fair,—there was Caleb Balderstane, that is living yet, flourishing in the rear, and swearing Gog and Magog, he would put steel through the guts of ony man that turned bridle—there was young Allan Ravenswood, that was then Master, wi' a bended pistol in his hand,—it was a mercy it gaed na aff,—crying to me, that had scarce as much wind left as served the necessary purpose of my ain lungs, 'Sound, ye poltroon! Sound, you damned cowardly villain, or I will blow your brains out!' and, to be sure, I blew sic points of war, that the scraugh of a clockin-hen was music to them."

"Well, sir, cut all this short," said Ravenswood.

"Short!—I had been like to be cut short mysell, in the flour of my youth, as scripture says; and that's the very thing that I compleen o'.—Weel! in to the water we behoved a' to splash, heels ower head, sit or fa'—ae horse driving on anither, as is the way o' brute beasts, and riders that hae as little sense,—the very bushes on the ither side were ableeze, wi' the flashes of the whigs' guns; and my horse had just taen the grund, when a blackavised westland carle—I wad mind the face o' him a hundred years syne,—an ee like a wild falcon's, and a beard as broad as my shool, clapped the end o' his lang black gun within a quarters length of my lug!—by the grace of Mercy, the horse swarvit round, and I fell aff at the tae side as the ball whistled bye at the tither, and the fell auld lord took the whig such a swauk wi' his broadsword that he made twa pieces o' his head, and down fell the lurdane wi' a' his bowk abune me."

"You were rather obliged to the old lord, I think," said Ravenswood.

"Was I? my sartie! first for bringing me into jeopardy, would I nould I—and then for whomling a chield on the tap of me, that dung the very wind out of my body—I hae been short-breathed ever since, and canna gang twenty yards without peghing like a miller's aiver."

"You lost then your place as trumpeter," said Ravenswood.

"Lose it—to be sure I lose it," replied the sexton, "for I couldna plaid whew upon a dry humlock;—but I might hae dune weel eneugh, for I keepit the wage and the free house, and little to do but play on the fiddle to them, but for this Allan Lord Ravenswood, that's far waur than ever his father was."

"What," said the Master, "did my father—I mean did his father's son—this last Lord Ravenswood, deprive you of what the bounty of his father allowed you?"

"Ay, troth did he," answered the old man; "for he loot his affairs gang to the dogs, and let in this Sir William Ashton on huz, that will gi'e naething for naething, and just ruined me and a' the puir creatures that had bite and soup at the castle, and a hole to put our heads in, when things were in the auld way."

"If Lord Ravenswood protected his people, my friend, while he had the means of doing so, I think they might spare his memory," replied Ravenswood.

"Ye are welcome to your ain opinion, sir," said the sexton; "but ye winna persuade me that he did his duty, either to himsel or to huz poor dependent creatures, in guiding us the gate he has done—he might hae gi'en us life-rent tacks of our bits o' houses and yards—and me, that's an auld man, living in yon miserable cabin, that's fitter for the dead than the quick, and killed wi' rhematise, and John Smith in my dainty bit mailing, and his window glazen, and a' because Ravenswood guided his gear like a fule."

"It is but too true," said Ravenswood, conscience-struck; "the penalties of extravagance extend far beyond the prodigal's own sufferings."

"However," said the sexton, "this young man Edgar is like to avenge my wrangs on the haill of his kindred."

"Indeed," said Ravenswood; "why should you suppose so?"

"They say he is about to marry the daughter of Leddy Ashton; and let her leddyship get his head anes under her oxter, and see you if she winna gi'e his neck a thraw. Sarra a bit if I were him—Let her alane for hauding a' thing in het water that draws near her—sae the warst wish I shall wish the lad is, that he may take his ain creditable gate o't, and ally himsel wi' his father's enemies, that have wrang his broad lands and my bonnie kail-yard from the lawful owners thereof."

Cervantes acutely remarks, that flattery is pleasing even from the mouth of a madman; and censure, as well as praise, often affects us, while we despise the opinions and motives on which it is founded and expressed. Ravenswood, abruptly reiterating his command that Alice's funeral should be attended to, flung away from the sexton, under the painful impression that the great, as well as the small vulgar, would think of his engagement with Lucy like this ignorant and selfish peasant.

"And I have stooped to subject myself to these calumnies, and am rejected notwithstanding. Lucy, your faith must be as true and perfect as the diamond, to compensate for the dishonour which men's opinions, and the conduct of your mother, attach to the heir of Ravenswood."

As he raised his eyes, he beheld the Marquis of A——, who, having arrived at the Tod's-hole, had walked forth to seek for his kinsman.

After mutual greetings, the Marquis made some apology for not coming forwards on the preceding evening. "It was his wish," he said, "to have done so, but he had come to the knowledge of some matters which induced him to delay his purpose. I find," said he, "there has been a love affair here, kinsman; and though I might blame you for not having communicated with me, as being in some degree the chief of your family"——

"With your lordship's permission," said Ravenswood, "I am deeply grateful for the interest you are pleased to take in me—but *I* am the chief and head of my family."

"I know it—I know it," said the Marquis; "in a strict heraldic and genealogical sense, you certainly are so—What I mean is, that being in some measure under my guardianship"——

"I must take the liberty to say, my lord," answered Ravenswood— and the tone in which he interrupted the Marquis boded no long duration to the friendship of the noble relatives, when he himself was fortunately interrupted by the little sexton, who came puffing after them, to ask if their honours would chuse music at the change-house to make up for short cheer.

"We want no music," said the Master, abruptly.

"Your honour disna ken what ye're refusing, than," said the fiddler, with the importunate freedom of his profession. "I can play, 'Will't thou do't again,' and 'the Auld Man's Mear's Dead,' sax times better than ever Pattie Birnie. I'll get my fiddle in the turning of a coffin-screw."

"Take yourself away, sir," said the Marquis.

"And if your honour be a north-country gentleman," said the per-severing minstrel, "whilk I wad judge from your tongue, I can play, 'Liggeram Cosh,' and 'Mullin Dhu,' and 'the Cummers of Athole.'"

"Take yourself away, friend; you interrupt our conversation."

"Or if, under your honour's favour, ye should happen to be a thought *honest*, I can play, (this in a low and confidential tone,) 'Killiecrankie,' and 'the King shall hae his ain,' and 'the Auld Stuarts back again,'—and the wife at the change-house is a decent discreet body, neither kens nor cares what toasts are drucken, and what tunes are played in her house—she's deaf to a' thing but the clink o' the siller."

The Marquis, who was sometimes suspected of jacobitism, could not help laughing as he threw the fellow a dollar, and bid him go play to the servants if he had a mind, and leave them at peace.

"Aweel, gentlemen," said he, "I am wishing your honours gude day —I'll be a' the better of the dollar, and ye'll be the waur of wanting the music, I'se tell ye—But I'se gang hame, and finish the grave in the tuning o' a fiddle-string, and then get my bread-winner, and awa' to your folk, and see if they hae better lugs than their masters."

Chapter Eleven

True love, an' thou be true,
    Thou has ane kittle part to play;
For fortune, fashion, fancy, and thou,
    Maun strive for many a day.

I've kenn'd by mony a friend's tale,
    Far better by this heart of mine,
What time and change of fancy avail
    A true love-knot to untwine.
                        HENDERSOUN

"I WISHED to tell you, my good kinsman," said the Marquis, "now that we are quit of this impertinent fiddler, that I had tried to discuss this love affair of yours with Sir William Ashton's daughter. I never saw the young lady, but for a few minutes to-day; so, being a stranger to her personal merits, I pay a compliment to you, and offer her no offence, in saying you might do better."

"My lord, I am much indebted for the interest you have taken in my affairs," said Ravenswood. "I did not intend to have troubled you in any matter concerning Miss Ashton. As my engagement with that young lady has reached your lordship, I can only say, that you must necessarily suppose that I was aware of the objections to my marrying into her father's family, and of course must have been completely satisfied with the reasons by which these objections are over-balanced, since I have proceeded so far in the matter."

"Nay, Master, if you had heard me out," said his noble relation, "you might have spared that observation; for, without questioning that you had reasons which seemed to you to counterbalance every other obstacle, I set myself, by every means that it became me to use towards the Ashtons, to persuade them to meet your views."

"I am obliged to your lordship for your unsolicited intercession," said Ravenswood, "especially as I am sure your lordship would never carry it beyond the bounds which it became me to use."

"Of that," said the Marquis, "you may be confident; I myself felt the delicacy of the matter too much to place a gentleman nearly connected with my house in a degrading or dubious situation with these Ashtons. But I pointed out all the advantages of their marrying their daughter into a house so honourable, and so nearly related with the first in Scotland; I explained the exact degree of relationship in which the Ravenswoods stand to ourselves; and I even hinted how political matters were like to fudge, and what cards would be trumps next parliament. I said I regarded you as a son—or a nephew, or so—rather than as a more distant relation; and that I made your affair entirely my own."

"And what was the issue of your lordship's explanation?" said Ravenswood, in some doubt whether he should resent or express gratitude for his interference.

"Why, the Lord Keeper would have listened to reason," said the Marquis; "he is rather unwilling to leave his place, which, in the present view of a change, must vaik; and, to say truth, he seemed to have a liking for you, and to be sensible of the general advantages to be attained by such a match. But his lady, who is tongue of the trump, Master,"——

"What of Lady Ashton, my lord?" said Ravenswood; "let me know the issue of this extraordinary conference—I can bear it."

"I am glad of that, kinsman," said the Marquis, "for I am ashamed to tell you half what she said—it is enough—her mind is made up—and the mistress of a first-rate boarding-school could not have rejected with more haughty indifference the suit of a half-pay Irish officer, beseeching permission to wait upon the heiress of a West Indian planter, than Lady Ashton spurned every proposal of mediation which it could at all become me to offer in behalf of you, my good kinsman. I cannot guess what she means. A more honourable connection she could not form, that's certain. As for money and land, that uses to be her husband's business rather than her's; and I really think she hates you for having the birth that her husband wants, and perhaps for wanting the lands that her goodman has. But I should only vex you to say more about it—here we are at the change-house, and if the things have been dressed which I took the precaution of sending forward, we shall have an indifferent good nooning of it."

The Master of Ravenswood paused ere they entered the cottage, which reeked through all its crevices, and they were not few, from the exertions of the Marquis's travelling-cooks to supply good cheer, and spread, as it were, a table in the wilderness.

"My Lord Marquis," said Ravenswood, "I already mentioned that accident has put your lordship in possession of a secret, which, with my consent, should have remained one even to you, my kinsman, for some time. Since the secret was to part from my own custody, and that of the only person besides who was interested in it, I am not sorry it should have reached your lordship's ears, as being fully aware that you are my noble kinsman and friend."

"You may believe it is safely lodged with me, Master of Ravenswood," said the Marquis; "but I should have liked well to hear you say, that you renounced the idea of an alliance, which you can hardly pursue without a certain degree of degradation."

"Of that, my lord, I shall judge," answered Ravenswood—"and I hope with delicacy as sensitive as any of my friends. But I have no engagement with Sir William and Lady Ashton. It is with Miss Ashton alone that I have entered upon the subject, and my conduct in the matter shall be entirely ruled by her's. If she continues to prefer me in my poverty to the wealthier suitors whom her friends recommend, I may well sacrifice to her sincere affection, I may well surrender to her, the less tangible and less palpable advantage of birth, and the deep-rooted prejudices of family hatred. If Miss Lucy Ashton should change her mind on a subject of such delicacy, I trust my friends will be silent on my disappointment, and I shall know how to make my enemies so."

"Spoke like a gallant young nobleman," said the Marquis; "for my part I have that regard for you, that I should be sorry the thing went on. This Sir William Ashton was a pretty enough petty-fogging kind of a lawyer twenty years since, and betwixt brattling at the bar, and leading in committees of Parliament, has got well on—the Darien matter lent him a lift, for he had good intelligence and sound views, and sold out in time—but the best work is had out of him. No Scotch government will take him at his own, or rather his wife's extravagant valuation; and betwixt his indecision and her insolence, from all I can guess, he will outsit his market, and be had cheap when no one will bid for him. I say nothing of Miss Ashton; but I assure you, a connection with her father will be neither useful nor ornamental, beyond what part of your father's spoils he may be prevailed upon to disgorge by way of tocher-good—and take my word for it, you will get more if you have spirit to bell the cat with him in the Scots Parliament.—And I will be the man, cousin," continued his lordship, "will uncase the fox for you, and make him rue the day that ever he refused a composition too honourable for him, and proposed by me on the behalf of a kinsman."

There was something in all this that, as it were, overshot the mark. Ravenswood could not disguise from himself that his noble kinsman had more reasons for taking offence at the reception of his suit, than regarded his interest and honour, yet he could neither complain nor be surprised that it should be so. He contented himself therefore with repeating, that his attachment was to Miss Ashton personally; that he desired neither wealth nor aggrandizement from her father's means and influence, and that nothing should prevent his keeping his engagement, excepting her own express desire that it should be relinquished—and he requested as a favour that the matter might be no more mentioned betwixt them at present, assuring the Marquis of A—— that he should be his confident in its progress or its interruption.

The Marquis soon had more agreeable, as well as more interesting subjects on which to converse. A foot-post, who had followed him from Edinburgh to Ravenswood Castle, and had traced his steps to the Tod's-hole, brought him a packet laded with good news. The political calculations of the Marquis had proved just, both in London and at Edinburgh, and he saw almost within his grasp, the pre-eminence for which he had panted.—The refreshments which his servants had prepared were now put on the table, and an epicure would perhaps have enjoyed them with additional zest, from the contrast which such fare afforded to the miserable cabin in which it was served up.

The turn of conversation corresponded with and added to the social feelings of the company. The Marquis expanded with pleasure on the power which probable incidents were like to assign to him, and on the use which he hoped to make of it in serving his kinsman Ravenswood. Ravenswood could but repeat the gratitude which he really felt, even when he considered the topic as too long dwelt upon. The wine was excellent, notwithstanding its having been brought in a runlet from Edinburgh; and the habits of the Marquis, when engaged with such good cheer, were somewhat sedentary. And so it fell out that they delayed their journey two hours later than was their original purpose.

"But what of that, my good young friend?" said the Marquis; "your castle of Wolfscrag is but at five or six miles distance, and will afford the same hospitality to your kinsman of A——, that it gave to this same Sir William Ashton."

"Sir William took the castle by storm, my lord," said Ravenswood, "and, like many a victor, had little reason to congratulate himself on his conquest."

"Well, well!" said Lord A——, whose dignity was something relaxed by the wine he had drunk,—"I see I must bribe you to harbour me—come, pledge me in our last bumper to the last young lady that slept at Wolfscrag, and liked her quarters—my bones are not so tender as hers, and I am resolved to occupy her apartment to-night, that I may judge how hard the couch is that love can soften."

"Your lordship may chuse what penance you please," said Ravenswood; "but I assure you, I should expect my old servant to hang himself, or throw himself from the battlements, should your lordship visit him so unexpectedly—I do assure you, we are totally and literally unprovided."

But his declaration only brought from his noble patron an assurance of his own total indifference as to every species of accommodation, and his determination to see the tower of Wolfscrag. His ancestor, he said, had been feasted there, when he went forward with

the then Lord Ravenswood to the fatal battle of Flodden, in which
they both fell. Thus hard pressed, the Master offered to ride forward
to get matters put in such preparation, as time and circumstances
admitted; but the Marquis protested, his kinsman must afford him his
company, and would only consent that an avant-courier should carry
to the destined Seneschal, Caleb Balderstone, the unexpected news
of this invasion.

The Master of Ravenswood soon after accompanied the Marquis
in his carriage, as the latter had proposed; and when they became
better acquainted in the progress of the journey, his noble relation
explained the very liberal views which he entertained for his kinsman's
preferment, in case of the success of his own political schemes. They
related to a secret, and highly important commission beyond sea,
which could only be entrusted to a person of rank, talent, and perfect
confidence, and which, as it required great trust and reliance on the
envoy employed, could not but prove both honourable and advantageous to him. We need not enter into the nature and purpose of this
commission, farther than to acquaint our readers that it was highly
acceptable to the Master of Ravenswood, who hailed with pleasure the
prospect of emerging from his present state of indigence and inaction,
into independence and honourable exertion.

While he listened thus eagerly to the details with which the Marquis
now thought it necessary to entrust him, the messenger who had been
dispatched to the Tower of Wolfscrag, returned with Caleb Balderstone's humble duty, and an assurance, that "a' should been in seemly
order, sic as the hurry of time permitted, to receive their lordships as it
behoved."

Ravenswood was too well accustomed with his Seneschal's mode of
acting and speaking, to hope much from this confident assurance. He
knew that Caleb acted upon the principle of the Spanish generals, in
the campaign of ——, who, much to the perplexity of the Prince of
Orange, their commander in chief, used to report their troops as full
in number, and possessed of all necessary points of equipment, not
considering it consistent with their dignity, or the honour of Spain, to
confess any deficiency either in men or munition, until the want of
both was unavoidably discovered in the day of battle. Accordingly,
Ravenswood thought it necessary to give the Marquis some hint, that
the fair assurance which they had just received from Caleb, did not by
any means ensure them against a very indifferent reception.

"You do yourself injustice, Master," said the Marquis, "or you
wish to surprise me agreeably. From this window I see a great light
in the direction where, if I remember aright, Wolfscrag lies; and, to
judge from the splendour which the old tower sheds around it, the

preparations for our reception must be of no ordinary description. I remember your father putting the same deception on me, when we went to the tower for a few days hawking, about twenty years since, and yet we spent our time as jollily at Wolfscrag as at my own hunting seat at B——."

"Your lordship, I fear, will find the faculty of the present proprietor to entertain his friends greatly abridged," said Ravenswood; "the will, I need hardly say, remains the same. But I am as much at a loss as your lordship to account for so strong and brilliant a light as is now glaring above Wolfscrag—The windows of the tower are few and narrow, and those of the lower story are hidden from us by the walls of the court.— I cannot conceive that any illumination of an ordinary nature could afford such a blaze of light."

The mystery was soon explained; for the cavalcade almost instantly halted, and the voice of Caleb Balderstone was heard at the coach window, exclaiming, in accents broken by grief and fear, "Och, gentlemen—Och, my gude lords—Och, haud to the right!—Wolfscrag's burning, bower and ha'—a' the rich plenishing outside and inside— a' the fair graith, pictures, tapestries, needle-wark, hangings, and other decorements,—a' in a bleeze, as if they were nae mair than sae mony peats, or as muckle pease strae. Haud to the right, gentlemen, I implore ye—there is some sma' provision making at Lucky Sma'trash's—but O, wae for this night, and wae for me that lives to see it!"——

Ravenswood was at first stunned by this new and unexpected calamity; but after a moment's recollection, he sprang from the carriage, and hastily bidding his noble kinsman good night, was about to ascend the hill towards his castle, the broad and full conflagration of which now flung forth a high column of red light, that flickered far to seaward upon the dashing waves of the ocean.

"Take a horse, Master," exclaimed the Marquis, greatly affected by this additional misfortune, so unexpectedly heaped upon his young protégé; "and give me my ambling palfrey, and haste forward, you knaves, and see what can be done to save or to extinguish—ride, you knaves, for your lives."

The attendants bustled together, and began to strike their horses with the spur, and call upon Caleb to shew them the road. But the voice of that careful Seneschal was heard above the tumult, "O stop— sirs, stop—turn bridle, for the luve of mercy—add not loss of lives to loss of warld's gear.—Thirty barrels of powther landed out of a Dunkirk dogger in the auld Lord's time—a' in the vau'ts of the auld tower, —the fire canna be far aff it, I trow—Lord's sake, to the right, lads— to the right—lets pit the hill atween us and peril,—a wap wi' a corner-stane o' Wolfscrag wad defy the doctor."

It will readily be supposed that this annunciation hurried the Marquis and his attendants into the route which Caleb prescribed, dragging Ravenswood along with them, although there was much in the matter which he could not possibly comprehend. "Gun-powder!" he exclaimed, laying hold of Caleb, who in vain endeavoured to escape from him, "what gun-powder?—how any quantity of powder could be in Wolfscrag without my knowledge, I cannot possibly comprehend."

"But I can," interrupted the Marquis, whispering him, "I can comprehend it thoroughly—for God's sake, ask him no more questions at present."

"There it is now," said Caleb, extricating himself from his master, and adjusting his dress, "your honour will believe his lordship's honourable testimony—His lordship minds weel, how, in the year that him they ca'd King Willie died"——

"Hush! hush, my good friend!" said the Marquis; "I shall satisfy your master upon that subject."

"And the people at Wolfshope—" said Ravenswood, "did none of them come to your assistance before the flame got so high?"

"Aye did they, mony ane of them, the rapscallions," said Caleb; "but truly I was in nae hurry to let them into the tower, where there was so much plate and valuables."

"Confound you for an impudent liar," said Ravenswood; "there was not a single ounce"——

"Forbye," said the Butler, most irreverently raising his voice to a pitch which drowned his master, "the fire made fast on us, owing to the store of tapestry and carved timmer in the banqueting ha', and the loons ran like scauded rats so sune as they heard of the gunpowther."

"I do entreat," said the Marquis to Ravenswood, "you will ask him no more questions."

"Only one, my lord—what has become of poor Mysie?"

"Mysie?" said Caleb—"I hadna time to look about ony Mysie—she's in the tower, I'se warrant, biding her awful doom."

"By heaven!" said Ravenswood, "I do not understand all this—the life of a faithful old creature is at stake—my lord, I will be withheld no longer—I will at least ride up, and see whether the danger is so imminent as this old fool pretends."

"Weel, then, as I live by bread," said Caleb, "Mysie is weel and safe. I saw her out of the castle before I left it mysell—was I ganging to forget an auld fellow-servant?"

"What made you tell me the contrary this moment?" said his master.

"Did I say otherwise?" answered Caleb; "then I maun hae been dreaming surely, or this awsome night has turned my judgment—but safe she is, and ne'er a living soul in the castle—a' the better for them, they wad get an unco heezy."

The Master of Ravenswood, upon this assurance being solemnly reiterated, and notwithstanding his extreme wish to witness the last explosion, which was to ruin to the ground the mansion of his fathers, suffered himself to be dragged onward towards the village of Wolfshope, where not only the change-house, but that of our own well-known friend the cooper, were all prepared for reception of himself and his noble guest, with a liberality of provision which requires some explanation.

We omitted to mention in its place, that Lockhard having fished out the truth concerning the mode in which Caleb had obtained the supplies for his banquet, the Lord Keeper, amused with the incident, and desirous at the time to gratify Ravenswood, had recommended the cooper of Wolfshope to the official situation under government, the prospect of which had reconciled him to the loss of his wild-fowl. Mr Girder's preferment had occasioned a pleasing surprise to old Caleb; for when, some days after his master's departure, he found himself absolutely compelled, by some necessary business, to visit the fishing hamlet, and was gliding like a ghost past the door of the cooper, for fear of being summoned to give some account of the progress of solicitation in his favour, or, more probably, that the inmates might upbraid him with the false hope he had held out upon the subject, he heard himself, not without some apprehension, summoned at once in treble, tenor, and bass,—a trio performed by the voices of Mrs Girder, old Dame Loupthedike, and the goodman of the dwelling —"Mr Caleb—Mr Caleb—Mr Caleb Balderstone! I hope ye arena ganging dry-lipped by our door, and we sae mickle indebted to you?"

This might be said ironically as well as in earnest. Caleb augured the worst, turned a deaf ear to the trio aforesaid, and was moving doggedly on, his ancient castor pulled over his brows, and his eyes bent on the ground, as if to count the flinty pebbles with which the rude foot-path was causewayed. But on a sudden he found himself surrounded on his progress, like a stately merchantman in the Gut of Gibraltar, (I hope the ladies will excuse the tarpaulin phrase,) by three Algerine gallies.

"God guide us, Mr Balderstone!" said Mrs Girder.

"Wha wad hae thought it of an auld and kenn'd friend!" said the mother.

"No sae mickle as stay to receive our thanks," said the cooper himself, "and frae the like o' me that seldom offer them. I am sure I hope there is nae ill seed sawn between us, Mr Balderstane—Ony man that has said to ye, I am no gratefu' for the situation of Queen's cooper, let me hae a whample at him wi' mine eatche*—that's a'."

"My good friends—my dear friends," said Caleb, still doubting how the certainty of the matter might stand, "what needs a' this ceremony?—Ane tries to serve their friends, and sometimes they may happen to prosper, and sometimes to misgi'e—naething I care to be fashed wi' less than thanks—I never could bide them."

"Faith, Mr Balderstone, ye suld hae been fashed wi' few o' mine," said the downright man of staves and hoops, "if I had had only your gude-will to thank ye for—I suld e'en hae set the guse, and the wild-deukes, and the runlet of sack, to balance that account. Gude-will, man, its a geizen'd tub, that hauds in nae liquor—but gude deed's like the cask, tight, round, and sound, that will haud liquor for the king."

"Have ye no heard of our letter," said the mother-in-law, "making John the Queen's cooper for certain?—and scarce a chield that had ever hammered girth upon tub but was applying for it?"

"Have I heard!!!" said Caleb, (who now found how the wind set,) with an accent of strong contempt at the doubt expressed—"Have I heard, quo' she!!!"—and as he spoke, he changed his shambling, skulking, dodging pace, into a manly and authoritative step, re-adjusted his cocked hat, and suffered his brow to emerge from it in all the pride of aristocracy, like the sun from beneath a cloud.

"To be sure, he canna but hae heard," said the good woman.

"Ay, to be sure it's impossible but I should," said Caleb; "and sae I'll be the first to kiss ye, joe, and wish you, cooper, much joy of your preferment, naething doubting that ye ken wha are your friends, and have helped ye, and can help ye. I thought it right to look a wee strange upon it at first," added Caleb, "just to see if ye were made of the right mettle—but ye ring true, lad, ye ring true."

So saying, with a most lordly air he kissed the women, and abandoned his hand, with an air of serene patronage, to the hearty shake of Mr Girder's horn-hard palm. Upon this complete, and to Caleb most satisfactory information, he did not, it may readily be believed, hesitate to accept an invitation to a solemn feast, to which were invited, not only all the *notables* of the village, but even his ancient antagonist, Mr Dingwall himself. At this festivity he was, of course, the most welcome and most honoured guest; and so well did he ply the company with stories of what he could do with his master, his master with the Lord Keeper, the Lord Keeper with the Council, and the Council with the Queen, that before the company dismissed, (which was, indeed, rather at an early hour than a late one,) every man of note in the village was ascending to the top-gallant of some ideal preferment by the

*Anglice, adze.

ladder of ropes which Caleb had presented to their imagination. Nay, the cunning Butler regained in that moment, not only all the influence he possessed formerly over the villagers, when the baronial family which he served were at their proudest, but acquired even an accession of importance. The writer—the very attorney himself—such is the thirst of preferment—felt the force of the attraction, and taking an opportunity to draw Caleb into a corner, spoke, with affectionate regret, of the declining health of the sheriff-clerk of the county.

"An excellent man—a most valuable man, Mr Caleb—but fat sall I say!—we are puir feckless bodies—here the day, and awa' by cock-screech the morn—and if he failzies, there maun be sumbody in his place—and gif that ye could airt it my way, I suldna be thankless, man—a gluve stuffed wi' gowd nobles—an' hark ye, man, something canny till yoursell—and the Wolfshope carles to settle kindly wi' the Master of Ravensweed—that is, Lord Ravensweed—God bless his lordship."

A smile, and a hearty squeeze by the hand, was the suitable answer to this overture, and Caleb made his escape from the jovial party, in order to avoid committing himself by any special promises.

"The Lord be gude to me," said Caleb, when he found himself in the open air, and at liberty to give vent to the self-exultation with which he was, as it were, distended; "did ever ony man see sic a set of green-gaislings!—The very pick-maws and solan-geese out by yonder at the Bass hae ten times their sense—God, an' I had been the Lord High Commissioner to the Estates o' Parliament, they couldna hae beflumm'd me mair—and, to speak Heaven's truth, I could hardly hae beflumm'd them better neither. But the writer—ha! ha! ha!—mercy on me, that I suld live in my auld days to gi'e the gang-bye to the very writer! Sheriff clerk!!!—But I hae an auld account to settle wi' the carle; and to make amends for bye-ganes, the office shall just cost him as much time-serving and tide-serving, as if he were to get it in gude earnest—of whilk there is sma' appearance, unless the Master learns mair the ways of this warld, whilk it is muckle to be doubted that he never will."

Chapter Twelve

Why flames yon far summit—why shoot to the blast
Those embers, like stars from the firmament cast?—
'Tis the fire-shower of ruin, all dreadfully driven
From thine eyrie, that beacons the darkness of Heaven.
                                        CAMPBELL

THE circumstances announced in the conclusion of the last chapter, will account for the ready and cheerful reception of the Marquis of A—— and the Master of Ravenswood in the village of Wolfshope. In fact, Caleb had no sooner announced the conflagration of the tower, than the whole hamlet were upon foot to hasten to extinguish the flames. And although that zealous adherent diverted their zeal by intimating the formidable contents of the subterranean apartments, yet the check only turned their assiduity into another direction. Never had there been such slaughtering of capons, and fat geese, and barn-door fowls,—never such boiling of *reested* hams,—never such making of car-cakes and sweet scones, Selkirk bannocks, cookies, and petti-coat-tails, delicacies little known to the present generation. Never had there been such tapping of barrels, and such uncorking of grey-beards, in the village of Wolfshope. All the inferior houses were thrown open for the reception of the Marquis's dependants, who came, it was thought, as precursors of the shower of preferment, which hereafter was to leave the rest of Scotland dry, in order to distil its rich dews on the village of Wolfshope under Lammermoor. The minister put in his claim to have the guests of distinction lodged at the Manse, having his eye, it was thought, upon a neighbouring prefer-ment, where the incumbent was sickly; but Mr Balderstone destined that honour to the cooper, his wife, and wife's mother, who danced for joy at the preference thus assigned them.

Many a beck and many a bow welcomed these noble guests to as good entertainment as persons of such a rank could set before such visitors; and the old dame, who had formerly lived in Ravenswood Castle, and knew, as she said, the ways of the nobility, was no ways wanting in arranging matters, as well as circumstances permitted, according to the etiquette of the times. The cooper's house was so roomy, that each guest had his separate retiring room, to which they were ushered with all due ceremony, while the plentiful supper was in the act of being placed upon the table.

Ravenswood no sooner found himself alone, than, impelled by a thousand feelings, he left the apartment, the house, and the village, and hastily retraced his steps to the brow of the hill, which rose betwixt the village, and screened it from the tower, in order to view the final fall of the house of his fathers. Some idle boys from the hamlet were taking the same direction out of curiosity, having first witnessed the arrival of the coach-and-six and its attendants. As they ran one by one past the Master, calling to each other to "come and see the auld tower blaw up in the lift like the peelings of an ingan," he could not but feel himself moved with indignation. "And those are the sons of my father's vassals," he said—"of men bound, both by law and gratitude, to follow our steps through battle, and fire, and flood; and now the destruction of their liege-lord's house is but a holiday's sight to them!"

These exasperating reflections were partly expressed in the acrimony with which he exclaimed, on feeling himself pulled by the cloak, —"What do ye want, ye dog?"

"I am a dog, and an auld dog too," answered Caleb, for it was he who had taken the freedom,—"and I am like to get a dog's wages—but it does not signification a pinch of sneeshing, for I am ower auld a dog to learn new tricks, or to follow a new master."

As he spoke, Ravenswood attained the ridge of the hill from which Wolfscrag was visible; the flames had entirely sunk down, and to his great surprise, there was only a dusky reddening upon the clouds immediately over the castle, which seemed the reflection of the embers of the sunken fire.

"The place cannot have blown up," said the Master; "we must have heard the report—if a quarter of the gunpowder was there you tell me of, it would have been heard twenty miles off."

"It's very like it wad," said Balderstone, composedly.

"Then the fire cannot have reached the vaults——"

"It's like no," answered Caleb, with the same impenetrable gravity.

"Hark ye, Caleb," said his master, "this grows a little too much for my patience. I must go and examine how matters stand at Wolfscrag myself."

"Your honour is ganging to gang nae sic gate," said Caleb, firmly.

"And why not?" said Ravenswood, sharply; "who or what shall prevent me?"

"Even I mysel," said Caleb, with the same determination.

"You, Balderstone?" replied the Master, "you are forgetting yourself, I think."

"But I think no," said Balderstone; "for I can just tell you a' about the castle on this know-head as weel as if you were at it. Only dinna pit yoursel into a kippage, and expose yoursel before the weans, or before the Marquis, when ye gang down bye."

"Speak out, you old fool," replied his master, "and let me know the best and the worst at once."

"Ou, the best and warst is just that the tower is standing hail and fear, as safe and as empty as when ye left it."

"Indeed!—and the fire?" said Ravenswood.

"Not a gleed of fire, then, except the bit kindling peat, and maybe a spunk in Mysie's cutty-pipe," replied Caleb.

"But the flame?" demanded Ravenswood; "the broad blaze which might have been seen ten miles off—what occasioned that?"

"Hout awa! it's an auld saying and a true,—

> Little's the light
> Will be seen far in a mirk night.

A wheen fern and horse litter that I fired in the court-yard, after sending back the loun of a footman; and, to speak Heaven's truth, the next time that ye send or bring ony body here before we are blessed wi' better provision, let them be gentles allenarly, without ony fremd servants, like that chield Lockhard, to be gledging and gleeing about, and looking upon the wrang side of ane's housekeeping, to the discredit of the family, and forcing ane to damn their souls wi' telling ae lee after another faster than I can count them—I wad rather set fire to the tower in gude earnest, and burn it ower my ain head into the bargain, or I see the family dishonoured in the sort."

"Upon my word, I am infinitely obliged by the proposal, Caleb," said his master, scarce able to restrain his laughter, though rather angry at the same time. "But the gunpowder?—is there such a thing in the tower?—the Marquis seemed to know of it."

"The pouther—ha! ha! ha!—the Marquis—ha! ha! ha!" replied Caleb; "if your honour were to brain me, I behooved to laugh—the Marquis—the pouther—was it there? ay, it was there. Did he ken o't? —my certie! the Marquis kenn'd o't, and it was the best of the game; for, when I couldna pacify your honour wi' a' that I could say, I aye threw out a word mair about the gunpouther, and garr'd the Marquis tak the job in his ain hand."

"But you have not answered my question," said the Master impatiently; "how came the powder there, and where is it now?"

"Ou, it came there, an ye maun needs ken," said Caleb, looking mysteriously, and whispering, "when there was like to be a wee bit rising here; and the Marquis, and a' the great lords of the north, were a' in it, and mony a gudely gun and broadsword were ferried ower frae Dunkirk forbye the pouther—awfu' wark we had getting them into the tower under cloud o' night, for ye maun think it wasna every body could be trusted wi' sae kittle jobs—But if ye will gae hame to your supper, I will tell you a' about it as ye gang down."

"And these wretched boys," said Ravenswood, "is it your pleasure they are to sit there all night, to wait for the blowing up of a tower that is not even on fire?"

"Surely not, if it is your honour's pleasure that they suld gang hame; although," added Caleb, "it wadna do them a grain's damage—they wad screigh less the next day, and sleep the sounder at e'en—But just as your honour likes."

Stepping accordingly towards the urchins who manned the knolls near which they stood, Caleb informed them, in an authoritative tone, that their Honours Lord Ravenswood and the Marquis of A—— had given orders that the tower was not to blow up till next day at noon. The boys dispersed upon this comfortable assurance. One or two, however, followed Caleb for more information, particularly the urchin whom he had cheated while officiating as turnspit, who screamed, "Mr Balderstone! Mr Balderstone! than the castle's gane out like an auld wife's spunk!"

"To be sure it is, callant," said the Butler; "do ye think the castle of as great a lord as Lord Ravenswood wad continue in a bleeze, and him standing looking on wi' his ain very een?—It's aye right," continued Caleb, shaking off his ragged page, and closing in to his master, "to train up weans, as the wise man says, in the way they should go, and aboon a' to teach them respect to their superiors."

"But all this while, Caleb, you have never told me what became of the arms and powder," said Ravenswood.

"Why, as for the arms," said Caleb, "it was just like the bairns' rhyme—

> Some gaed east, and some gaed west,
> And some gaed to the craw's nest;

and I'll no say but some o' them may make themselves heard in the field yet unless times be a' the quieter. And for the pouther, I e'en changed it, as occasion served, with the skippers o' Dutch luggers and French vessels, for gin and brandy, and it served the house mony a year—a gude swap too, between what cheereth the soul of man and that which dingeth it clean out of the body; forbye, I keepit a wheen pounds of it for yoursell when ye wanted to take the pleasure o' shooting—whiles, in these latter days, I wad hardly hae kenn'd else whar to get pouther for your pleasure. And now that your anger is ower, sir, wasna that weel managed o' me, and arena ye far better sorted doun yonder than ye could hae been in your ain auld ruins up bye yonder, as the case stands wi' us now?—the mair's the pity."

"I believe you may be right, Caleb; but, before burning down my castle, either in jest or in earnest," said Ravenswood, "I think I had a right to be in the secret."

"Fie for shame, your honour!" replied Caleb; "it fits an auld carle like me weel eneugh to tell lees for the credit of the family, but it wadna beseem the like o' your honour's sell; besides, young folk are no judicious—they cannot make the maist of a bit figment. Now this fire—for a fire it sall be, if I suld burn the auld stable to make it mair feasible—this fire, besides that it will be an excuse for asking ony thing we want through the country, or doun at the haven—this fire will settle mony things on an honourable footing for the family's credit, that cost me telling twenty daily lees to a wheen idle chaps and queans, and, what's waur, without gaining credence."

"That was hard indeed, Caleb; but I do not see how this fire should help your veracity or your credit."

"There it is now," said Caleb; "wasna I saying that young folk had a green judgement?—How suld it help me, quotha?—it will be a credit-able apology for the honour of the family for this score of years to come, if it is weel guided. Where's the family pictures? says ae med-dling body—the great fire at Wolfscrag, answers I. Where's the family plate? says another—the great fire, says I; wha was to think of plate when life and limb were in danger?—Where's the wardrobe and the linens?—where's the tapestries and the decorements?—beds of state, twilts, pands and testors, napery and broidered work?—The fire —the fire—the fire. Guide the fire weel, and it will serve ye for a' that ye suld have and have not—and, in some sort, a gude excuse is better than the things themselves; for they maun crack and wear out, and be consumed by time, whereas a gude offcome, prudently and creditably handled, may serve a nobleman and his family, Lord kens how lang!"

Ravenswood was too well acquainted with his Butler's pertinacity and self-opinion, to dispute the point with him any further. Leaving Caleb, therefore, to the enjoyment of his own successful ingenuity, he returned to the hamlet, where he found the Marquis and the good women of the mansion under some anxiety—the former on account of his absence, the others for the discredit their cookery might sustain by the delay of the supper. All were now at ease, and heard with pleasure that the fire at the castle had burned out of itself without reaching the vaults, which was the only information that Ravenswood thought it proper to give in public concerning the event of his Butler's stratagem.

They sat down to an excellent supper. No invitation could prevail on Mr and Mrs Girder, even in their own house, to sit down at table with guests of such high quality. They remained standing in the apart-ment, and acted the part of respectful and careful attendants on the company. Such were the manners of the time. The elder dame, con-fident through her age and connection with the Ravenswood family, was less scrupulously ceremonious. She played a mixed part betwixt that of the hostess of an inn, and the mistress of a private house, who receives guests above her own degree. She recommended, and even pressed what she thought best, and was herself easily entreated to take a moderate share of the good cheer, in order to encourage her guests by her own example. Often she interrupted herself, to express her regret that "my Lord did not eat—that the Master was pyking a bare bane—that, to be sure, there was naething there fit to set before their honours—that Lord Allan, rest his saul, used to like a pouthered guse, and said it was Latin for a tass o' brandy—that the brandy came frae France direct; for, for a' the English laws and gaugers, the Wolfshope brigs hadna forgotten the gate to Dunkirk."

Here the cooper admonished his mother-in-law with his elbow, which procured him the following special notice in the progress of her speech.

"Ye needna be dunshin that gate, John," continued the old lady; "naebody says that ye ken whar the brandy comes from; and it wadna be fitting ye should, and you the queen's cooper; and what signifies't," continued she, addressing Lord Ravenswood, "to king, queen, or keiser, whar an auld wife like me buys her pickle sneeshin, or her drap brandy-wine, to haud her heart up?"

Having thus extricated herself from her supposed false step, Dame Loupthedyke proceeded, during the rest of the evening, to supply, with great animation, and very little assistance from her guests, the funds necessary for the support of the conversation, until, declining any further circulation of their glass, her guests requested her permission to retire to their apartments.

The Marquis occupied the chamber of dais, which, in every house above the rank of a mere cottage, was kept sacred for such high occasions as the present. The modern finishing with plaister was then unknown, and tapestry was confined to the houses of the nobility and superior gentry. The cooper, therefore, who was a man of some vanity, as well as some wealth, had imitated the fashion observed by the inferior landholders and clergy, who usually garnished their state apartments with hangings of a sort of stamped leather, manufactured in the Netherlands, garnished with trees and animals executed in copper foil, and with many a pithy sentence of morality, which, although couched in Low Dutch, were perhaps as much attended to in practice as if written in broad Scotch. The whole had somewhat of a gloomy aspect; but the fire, composed of old pitch-barrel staves, blazed merrily up the chimney; the bed was decorated with linen of most fresh and dazzling whiteness, which had never before been used, and might, perhaps, have never been used at all, but for this high occasion. On the toilette beside, stood an old-fashioned mirror, in a fillagree frame, part of the dispersed finery of the neighbouring castle. It was flanked by a long-necked bottle of Florence wine, by which stood a glass nearly as tall, resembling in shape that which Teniers usually places in the hands of his own portrait, when he paints himself as mingling in the revels of a country village. To counterbalance those foreign centinels, there mounted guard on the other side of the mirror two stout warders of Scottish lineage; a jug, namely, of double ale, which held a Scotch pint, and a quegh or bicker of ivory and ebony, hooped with silver, the work of John Girder's own hands, and the pride of his heart. Besides these preparations against thirst, there was a goodly diet-loaf, or sweet cake; so that, with such auxiliaries, the apartment seemed victualled against a siege of two or three days.

It only remains to say, that the Marquis's valet was in attendance, displaying his master's brocaded night-gown, and richly embroidered velvet cap, lined and faced with Brussels lace, upon a huge leathern easy chair, wheeled round so as to have the full advantage of the comfortable fire which we have already mentioned. We therefore commit that eminent person to his night's repose, trusting he profited by the ample preparations made for his accommodation,—preparations which we have mentioned in detail, as illustrative of ancient Scottish manners.

It is not necessary we should be equally minute in describing the sleeping apartment of the Master of Ravenswood, which was that usually occupied by the goodman and goodwife themselves. It was comfortably hung with a sort of warm-coloured worsted, manufactured in Scotland, approaching in texture to what is now called shaloon. A staring picture of John Girder himself ornamented this dormitory, painted by a starving Frenchman, who had, God knows how or why, strolled over from Flushing or Dunkirk to Wolfshope in a smuggling dogger. The features were, indeed, those of the stubborn, opinionative, yet sensible artizan, but Monsieur had contrived to throw a French grace into the look and manner, so utterly inconsistent with the dogged gravity of the original, that it was impossible to look at it without laughing. John and his family, however, piqued themselves not a little upon this picture, and were proportionably censured by the neighbourhood, who pronounced that the cooper, in sitting for the same, and yet more in presuming to hang it up in his bed-chamber, had exceeded his privilege as the richest man of the village; at once stept beyond the bounds of his own rank, and encroached upon those of the superior orders; and, in fine, had been guilty of a very over-weening act of vanity and presumption. Respect for the memory of my deceased friend, Mr Richard Tinto, has obliged me to treat this matter at some length; but I spare the reader his prolix, though curious observations, as well upon the character of the French school, as upon the state of painting in Scotland, at the beginning of the eighteenth century.

The other preparations of the Master's sleeping apartment, were similar to those in the chamber of dais.

At the usual early hour of that period, the Marquis of A—— and his kinsman prepared to resume their journey. This could not be done without an ample breakfast, in which cold meat and hot meat, and oatmeal flummery, wine and spirits, and milk varied by every possible mode of preparation, evinced the same desire to do honour to their guests, which had been shewn by the hospitable owners of the mansion upon the evening before. All the bustle of preparation for departure now resounded through Wolfshope. There was paying of bills and shaking of hands, and saddling of horses, and harnessing of carriages, and distributing of drink-money. The Marquis left a broad piece for the gratification of John Girder's household, which he, the said John, was for some time disposed to convert to his own use; Dingwall the writer assuring him he was justified in so doing, seeing he was the disburser of those expences which were the occasion of the gratification. But, notwithstanding this legal authority, John could not find in his heart to dim the splendour of his late hospitality, by pocketing any thing in the nature of a gratuity. He only assured his menials he would consider them as a damned ungrateful pack, if they bought a gill of brandy elsewhere than out of his own stores; and as the drink-money was likely to go to its legitimate use, he comforted himself that, in this manner, the Marquis's donative would, without any impeachment of credit and character, come ultimately into his own exclusive possession.

While arrangements were making for departure, Ravenswood made blythe the heart of his ancient butler, by informing him, cautiously however, for he knew Caleb's warmth of imagination, of the probable change which was about to take place in his fortunes. He deposited with Balderstone, at the same time, the greater part of his slender funds, with an assurance which he was obliged to reiterate more than once, that he himself had sufficient supplies in certain prospect. He, therefore, enjoined Caleb, as he valued his favour, to desist from all further manœuvres against the inhabitants of Wolfshope, their cellars, poultry, yards, and substance whatsoever. In this prohibition, the old domestic acquiesced more readily than his master expected.

"It was doubtless," he said, "a shame, a discredit, and a sin, to harry the puir creatures, when the family were in circumstances to live honourably on their ain means; and there might be wisdom," he said, "in giving them a whiles breathing time, at any rate, that they might be the more readily brought forwards upon his honour's future occasions."

This matter being settled, and having taken an affectionate farewell of his old domestic, the Master rejoined his noble relative, who was now ready to enter his carriage. The two landladies, old and young, in all kindly greeting, stood simpering at the door of their house, as the coach and six, followed by its train of clattering horsemen, thundered out of the village. John Girder also stood upon his threshold, now looking at his honoured right hand, which had been so lately shaken by a marquis and a lord, and now giving a glance into the interior of his mansion, which manifested all the disarray of the late revel, as if balancing the distinction which he had attained with the expences of the entertainment.

At length he opened his oracular jaws. "Let every man and woman here set about their ain business, as if there was nae sic thing as marquis or master, duke or drake, laird or lord, in this world. Let the house be redd up, the broken meat set bye, and if there is ony thing totally uneatable, let it be gien to the puir folk; and gudemother and wife, I hae just ae thing to entreat ye, that ye will never speak to me a single word, good or bad, anent a' this nonsense wark, but keep a' your cracks about it to yoursells and your kimmers, for my head is weel nigh dung donnart wi' it already."

As John's authority was tolerably absolute, all departed to their usual occupations, leaving him to build castles in the air, if he had a mind, upon the court-favour which he had acquired by the expenditure of his worldly substance.

Chapter Thirteen

> Why, now I have Dame Fortune by the forelock,
> And if she scapes my grasp, the fault is mine;
> He that hath buffetted with stern adversity,
> Best knows to shape his course to favouring breezes.
> *Old Play*

OUR TRAVELLERS reached Edinburgh without any farther adventure, and the Master of Ravenswood, as had been previously settled, took up his abode with his noble friend.

In the mean time, the political crisis which had been expected, took place, and the Tory party obtained, in the Scottish councils of Queen Anne, a short-lived ascendency, of which it is not our business to trace either the cause or consequences. Suffice it to say, that it affected the different political parties according to the nature of their principles. In

England, many of the High Church party, with Harley, afterwards Earl of Oxford, at their head, affected to separate their principles from those of the Jacobites, and, on that account, obtained the denomination of Whimsicals. The Scottish High Church party, on the contrary, or, as they termed themselves, the Cavaliers, were more consistent, if not so prudent, in their politics, and viewed all the changes now made, as preparatory to calling to the throne, upon the queen's demise, her brother, the Chevalier St George. Those who had suffered in his service, now entertained the most unreasonable hopes, not only of indemnification, but of vengeance upon their political adversaries, while families attached to the Whig interest, saw nothing before them but a renewal of the hardships they had undergone during the reigns of Charles the Second and his brother, and a retaliation of the confiscations which had been inflicted upon the Jacobites during that of King William.

But the most alarmed at the change of system, was that prudential set of persons, some of whom are found in all governments, but who abound in a provincial administration like that of Scotland during the period, and who are what Cromwell called waiters upon providence, or, in other words, uniform adherents to the party who are uppermost. Many of these hastened to read their recantation to the Marquis of A——; and, as it was easily seen, that he took a deep interest in the affairs of his kinsman, the Master of Ravenswood, they were the first to suggest measures for retrieving at least a part of his property, and for restoring him in blood against his father's attainder.

Old Lord Turntippet professed to be one of the most anxious for the success of these measures; for "it grieved him to the very saul," he said, "to see so brave a young gentleman, of sic auld and undoubted nobility, and, what was mair than a' that, a bluid-relation of the Marquis of A——, the man whom," he swore, "he honoured most upon the face of the yearth, brought to so severe a pass. For his ain puir peculiar," as he said, "and to contribute something to the rehabitation of sae auld ane house," the said Turntippet sent in three family pictures lacking the frames, and six high-backed chairs, with worked Turkey cushions, having the crest of Ravenswood broidered thereon, without charging a penny either of the principal or interest they had cost him, when he bought them, sixteen years before, at a roup of the furniture of Lord Ravenswood's lodgings in the Canongate.

Much more to Lord Turntippet's dismay than to his surprise, although he affected to feel more of the latter than the former, the Marquis received his gift very drily, and observed, that his lordship's restitution, if he expected it to be received by the Master of Ravenswood and his friends, must comprehend a pretty large farm, which having been mortgaged to Turntippet for a very inadequate sum, he had contrived, during the confusion of the family affairs, and by means well understood by the lawyers of that period, to acquire to himself in absolute property.

The old time-serving lord winced excessively under this requisition, protesting to God, that he saw no occasion the lad could have for the instant possession of the land, seeing he would doubtless now recover the bulk of his estate from Sir William Ashton, to which he was ready to contribute by every means in his power, as was just and reasonable; and finally declaring, that he was willing to settle the land on the young gentleman, after his own natural demise.

But all these excuses availed nothing, and he was compelled to disgorge the property, on receiving back the sum for which it had been mortgaged. Having no other means of making peace with the higher powers, he returned home sorrowful and malcontent, complaining to his confidants, "that every mutation or change in the state had hitherto been productive of some sma' advantage to him in his ain quiet affairs; but that the present had (pize upon it!) cost him one of the best pen-feathers o' his wing."

Similar measures were threatened against others who had profited by the wreck of the fortune of Ravenswood; and Sir William Ashton, in particular, was menaced with a parliamentary reversal of the judicial sentences under which he held the Castle and Barony of Ravenswood. With him, however, the Master, as well for Lucy's sake as on account of the hospitality he had received from him, felt himself under the necessity of proceeding with great candour. He wrote to the late Lord Keeper, for he no longer held that office, stating frankly the engagement which existed between him and Miss Ashton, requesting his permission for their union, and assuring him of his willingness to put the settlement of all matters between them upon such a footing, as Sir William himself should think favourable.

The same messenger was charged with a letter to Lady Ashton, deprecating any cause of displeasure which the Master might unintentionally have given her, enlarging upon his attachment to Miss Ashton, and the length to which it had proceeded, and conjuring the lady, as a Douglas in nature as well as in name, generously to forget ancient prejudices and misunderstandings; and to believe that the family had acquired a friend, and she herself a respectful and attached humble servant, in him who subscribed himself Edgar, Master of Ravenswood.

A third letter Ravenswood addressed to Lucy, and the messenger was instructed to find some secret and secure means of delivering it into her own hands. It contained the strongest protestations of continued affection, and dwelt upon the approaching change of the writer's fortunes as chiefly valuable, by tending to remove the impediments to their union. He related the steps he had taken to overcome the prejudices of her parents, and especially of her mother, and expressed his hope they might prove effectual. If not, he still trusted that his absence from Scotland upon an important and honourable mission might give time for prejudices to die away; while he hoped and trusted Miss Ashton's constancy, on which he had the most implicit reliance, would baffle any effort that might be used to divert her attachment. Much more there was, which, however interesting to the lovers themselves, would afford the reader neither interest nor information. To each of these three letters the Master of Ravenswood received an answer, but by different means of conveyance, and certainly couched in very different styles.

Lady Ashton answered his letter by his own messenger, who was not allowed to remain at Ravenswood a moment longer than she was engaged in penning these lines. "For the hand of Mr Ravenswood of Wolfscrag, these:

"SIR UNKNOWN,

"I have received a letter, signed Edgar, Master of Ravenswood, concerning the writer whereof I am uncertain, seeing that the honours of such a family were forfeited for high treason in the person of Allan, late Lord Ravenswood. Sir, if you shall happen to be the person so subscribing yourself, you will please to know, that I claim the full interest of a parent in Miss Lucy Ashton, which I have disposed of irrevocably in behalf of a worthy person. And, sir, were this otherwise, I would not listen to a proposal from you, or any of your house, seeing their hand has been uniformly held up against the freedom of the subject, and the immunities of God's kirk. Sir, it is not a flightering blink of prosperity which can change my constant opinion in this regard, seeing it has been my lot before now, like holy David, to see the wicked great in power, and flourishing like a green bay tree; nevertheless I passed, and they were not, and the place thereof knew them no more. Wishing you to lay these things to your heart for your own sake, so far as they may concern you, I pray you to take no farther notice of her, who desires to remain your unknown servant,

"MARGARET DOUGLAS,
"otherwise ASHTON."

About two days after he had received this very unsatisfactory epistle, the Master of Ravenswood, while walking up the High-street of Edinburgh, was jostled by a person, in whom, as the man pulled off his hat to make an apology, he recognized Lockhard, the confidential domestic of Sir William Ashton. The man bowed, slipt a letter into his hand, and disappeared. The packet contained four close-written folios, from which, however, as is sometimes incident to the compositions of great lawyers, little could be extracted, excepting that the writer felt himself in a very puzzling predicament.

Sir William spoke at length of his high value and regard for his dear young friend, the Master of Ravenswood, and of his very extreme high value and regard for the Marquis of A——, his very dear old friend;—he trusted that any measures that they might adopt, in which he was concerned, would be carried on with due regard to the sanctity of decreets, and judgments obtained *in foro contentioso;* protesting, before men and angels, that if the law of Scotland, as declared in her established courts, were to undergo a reversal in any popular assembly, the evils which would thence arise to the public, would inflict a greater wound upon his heart, than any loss he might himself sustain by such irregular proceedings. He flourished much on generosity and forgiveness of mutual injuries, and hinted at the mutability of human affairs, always favourite topics with the weaker party in politics. He pathetically lamented, and gently censured, the haste which had been used in depriving him of his situation of Lord Keeper, which his experience had enabled him to fill with some advantage to the public, without so much as giving him an opportunity of explaining how far his own views of general politics might essentially differ from those now in power. He was convinced the Marquis of A—— had as sincere intentions towards the public, as himself or any man; and if, upon a conference, they could have agreed upon the measures by which it was to be pursued, his experience and his interest should have gone to support the present administration. Upon the engagement betwixt Ravenswood and his daughter, he spoke in a dry and confused manner. He regretted so premature a step as the engagement of the young people should have been taken, and conjured the Master to remember he had never given any encouragement thereunto; and observed, that, as a transaction *inter minores,* and without concurrence of his daughter's natural curators, the engagement was inept, and void in law. This precipitate measure, he added, had produced a very bad effect upon Lady Ashton's mind, which it was impossible at present to remove. Her son, Colonel Douglas Ashton, had embraced her prejudices in their fullest extent, and it was impossible for Sir William to adopt a course disagreeable to them, without a fatal and irreconcileable breach in his family; which was not at present to be thought of. Time, the great physician, he hoped would mend all.

In a postscript, Sir William said something more explicitly, that rather than the law of Scotland should sustain a severe wound through his sides, by a parliamentary reversal of the judgment of her supreme courts, in the case of the Barony of Ravenswood, he himself would extra-judicially consent to considerable sacrifices.

From Lucy Ashton, by some unknown conveyance, the Master received the following lines:—"I received your's, but it was at the utmost risk; do not attempt to write again till better times. I am sore beset, but I will be true to my word, while the exercise of my reason is vouchsafed to me. That you are happy and prosperous is some consolation, and my situation requires it all." The note was signed L. A.

This letter filled Ravenswood with the most lively alarm. He made many attempts, notwithstanding her prohibition, to convey letters to Miss Ashton, and even to obtain an interview; but his attempts were frustrated, and he had only the mortification to learn that anxious and effectual precautions had been taken to prevent the possibility of their correspondence. The Master was more distressed by these circumstances, as it became impossible to delay his departure from Scotland, upon the important mission which had been confided to him. Before his departure, he put Sir William Ashton's letter into the hands of the Marquis of A——, who observed with a smile, that Sir William's day of grace was past, and that he had now to learn which side of the hedge the sun had got to. It was with the greatest difficulty that Ravenswood extorted from the Marquis a promise, that he would compromise the proceedings in parliament, providing Sir William should be disposed to acquiesce in a union between him and Lucy Ashton.

"I would hardly," said the Marquis, "consent to your throwing away your birth-right in this manner, were I not perfectly confident that Lady Ashton, or Lady Douglas, or whatever she calls herself, will, as Scotchmen say, keep her threep; and that her husband dares not contradict her."

"But yet," said the Master, "I trust your Grace will consider my engagement as sacred."

"Believe my word of honour," said the Marquis, "I would be a friend even to your follies; and having thus told you *my* opinion, I will endeavour, as occasion offers, to serve you according to your own."

The Master of Ravenswood could but thank his generous kinsman and patron, and leave him full power to act in all his affairs. He departed from Scotland upon his mission, which, it was supposed, might detain him upon the continent for some months.

END OF VOLUME SECOND

THE
BRIDE OF LAMMERMOOR

Chapter One

Was ever woman in this humour wooed?—
Was ever woman in this humour won?—
I'll have her.——

Richard the Third

TWELVE months had past away since the Master of Ravenswood's departure for the continent, and, although his return to Scotland had been expected in a much shorter space, yet the affairs of his mission, or, according to a prevailing report, others of a nature personal to himself, still detained him abroad. In the mean time, the altered state of affairs in Sir William Ashton's family may be gathered from the following conversation which took place betwixt Bucklaw and his confidential bottle-companion and dependent, the noted Captain Craigengelt.

They were seated on either side of the huge sepulchral-looking freestone chimney in the low hall at Girnington. A wood fire blazed merrily in the grate; a round oaken table, placed between them, supported a stoup of excellent claret, two rummer glasses, and other good cheer; and yet, with all these appliances and means to boot, the countenance of the patron was dubious, doubtful, and unsatisfied, while the invention of his dependent was taxed to the utmost, to parry what he most dreaded, a fit, as he called it, of the sullens on the part of his protector. After a long pause, only interrupted by the devil's tatoo, which Bucklaw kept beating against the hearth with the toe of his boot, Craigengelt at last ventured to break silence. "May I be double distanced," said he, "if ever I saw a man in my life have less the air of a bridegroom! Cut me out of feather, if you have not more the look of a man condemned to be hanged."

"My kind thanks for the compliment," replied Bucklaw; "but I suppose you think upon the predicament in which you yourself are most likely to be placed;—and pray, Captain Craigengelt, if it please your worship, why should I look merry, when I'm sad, and devilish sad too?"

"And that's what vexes me," said Craigengelt. "Here is this match, the best in the whole country, and which you were so anxious about, is on the point of being concluded, and you are as sulky as a bear that's lost its whelps."

"I do not know," answered the laird, doggedly, "whether I should conclude it or not, if it was not that I am too far forwards to leap back."

"Leap back!" exclaimed Craigengelt, with a well-assumed air of astonishment, "that would be playing the back-game with a witness! Leap back! Why, is not the girl's fortune"——

"The young lady's, if you please," said Hayston, interrupting him.

"Well, well, no disrespect meant—Will Miss Ashton's tocher not weigh against any in Lothian?"

"Granted," answered Bucklaw; "but I care not a penny for her tocher, I have enough of my own."

"And the mother, that loves you like her own child?"

"Better than some of her children, I believe," said Bucklaw, "or there would be little love wared on the matter."

"And Colonel Sholto Douglas Ashton, who desires the match above all earthly things?"

"Because," said Bucklaw, "he expects to carry the county of —— through my interest."

"And the father, who is as keen to see the match concluded, as ever I have been to win a main?"

"Aye," said Bucklaw, in the same disparaging manner, "it lies with Sir William's policy to secure the next best match, since he cannot barter his child to save the great Ravenswood estate, which Parliament are about to wrench out of his clutches."

"What say you to the young lady herself?" said Craigengelt; "the finest young woman in all Scotland, one that you used to be so fond of when she was cross, and now she consents to have you, and gives up her engagement with Ravenswood, you are for jibbing—I must say, the devil's in ye, when ye neither know what you would have, nor what you would want."

"I'll tell you my meaning in a word," answered Bucklaw, getting up and walking through the room; "I want to know what the devil is the cause of Miss Ashton's changing her mind so suddenly."

"And what need you care," said Craigengelt, "since the change is in your favour?"

"I'll tell you what it is," returned his patron, "I never knew much of that sort of fine ladies, and I believe they may be as capricious as the devil; but there is something in Miss Ashton's change, a devilish deal too sudden, and too serious for a mere flisk of her own. I'll be bound Lady Ashton understands every machine for breaking in the human mind, and there are as many as there are cannon-bits, martingals, and cavessons for young colts."

"And if that were not the case," said Craigengelt, "how the devil should we ever get them into training at all?"

"And that's true too," said Bucklaw, suspending his march through the dining-room, and leaning upon the back of a chair.—"And besides, here's Ravenswood in the way still; do you think he'll give up Lucy's engagement?"

"To be sure he will," answered Craigengelt; "what good can it do him to refuse, since he wishes to marry another woman, and she another man?"

"And you believe seriously," said Bucklaw, "that he is going to marry the foreign lady we heard of?"

"You heard yourself," answered Craigengelt, "what Captain Westenho said about it, and the great preparation made for their blythsome bridal."

"Captain Westenho," replied Bucklaw, "has rather too much of your own cast about him, Craigie, to make what Sir William would call a 'famous witness.' He drinks deep, plays deep, swears deep, and I suspect can lie and cheat a little into the bargain. Useful qualities, Craigie, if kept in their proper sphere, but which have a little too much of the freebooter to make a figure in a court of evidence."

"Well then," said Craigengelt, "will you believe Colonel Douglas Ashton, who heard the Marquis of A—— say in a public circle, but not aware that he was within ear-shot, that his kinsman had made a better arrangement for himself than to give his father's land for the pale-cheeked daughter of a broken down fanatic, and that Bucklaw was welcome to the wearing of Ravenswood's shaughled shoes."

"Did he say so, by heavens!" cried Bucklaw, breaking out into one of those incontroulable fits of passion to which he was constitutionally subject,—"if I had heard him, I would have tore the tongue out of his throat before all his peats and minions, and Highland bullies into the bargain. Why did not Ashton run him through the body?"

"Capote me if I know," said the Captain. "He deserved it sure enough, but he is an old man, and a minister of state, and there would be more risk than credit in meddling with him. You had more need to think of making up to Miss Lucy Ashton the disgrace that's like to fall upon her, than of interfering with a man too old to fight, and on too high a stool for your hand to reach him."

"It *shall* reach him though one day," said Bucklaw, "and his kinsman Ravenswood to boot. In the mean time, I'll take care Miss Ashton receives no discredit for the slight they have put upon her. It's an awkward job, however, and I wish it was ended; I scarce know how to talk to her,—but fill a bumper, Craigie, and we'll drink her health. It grows late, and a night-cowl of good claret is worth all the considering caps in Europe."

Chapter Two

It was the copy of our conference.
In bed she slept not, for my urging it;
At board she fed not, for my urging it;
Alone, it was the subject of my theme;
In company, I often glanced at it.
Comedy of Errors

THE NEXT morning saw Bucklaw, and his faithful Achates, Craigengelt, at Ravenswood Castle. They were most courteously received by the knight and his lady, as well as by their son and heir, Colonel Ashton. After a good deal of stammering and blushing,—for Bucklaw, notwithstanding his audacity in other matters, had all the sheepish bashfulness common to those who have lived little in respectable society,—he contrived at length to explain his wish to be admitted to a conference with Miss Ashton upon the subject of their approaching union. Sir William and his son looked at Lady Ashton, who replied with the greatest composure, "that Lucy would wait upon Mr Hayston directly. I hope," she added with a smile, "that as Lucy is very young, and has been lately trepanned into an engagement, of which she is now heartily ashamed, our dear Bucklaw will excuse her wish, that I should be present at their interview?"

"In truth, my dear lady," said Bucklaw, "it is the very thing that I would have desired on my own account; for I have been so little accustomed to what is called gallantry, that I shall certainly fall into some cursed mistake, unless I have the advantage of your ladyship as an interpreter."

It was thus that Bucklaw, in the perturbation of his embarrassment upon this critical occasion, forgot the just apprehensions he had entertained of Lady Ashton's overbearing ascendancy over her daughter's mind, and lost an opportunity of ascertaining, by his own investigation, the real state of Lucy's feelings.

The other gentlemen left the room, and in a short time, Lady Ashton, followed by her daughter, entered the apartment. She appeared, as he had seen her on former occasions, rather composed than agitated; but a nicer judge than he could scarce have determined, whether her calmness was that of despair, or of indifference. Bucklaw was too much agitated by his own feelings minutely to scrutinise those of the lady. He stammered out an unconnected address, confounding together the two or three topics to which it related, and stopt short before he brought it to any regular conclusion. Miss Ashton listened, or looked as if she listened, but returned not a single word in answer, continuing to fix her eyes on a small piece of embroidery, on which, as if by instinct or habit, her fingers were busily employed. Lady Ashton sat at some distance, almost screened from notice by the deep embrasure of the window in which she had placed her chair. From this she whispered in a tone of voice, which, though soft and sweet, had something in it of admonition, if not command,—"Lucy, my dear, remember—have you heard what Bucklaw has been saying?"

The idea of her mother's presence seemed to have slipped from the unhappy girl's recollection. She started, dropped her needle, and repeated hastily, and almost in the same breath, the contradictory answers, "Yes, madam—no, my lady—I beg pardon—I did not hear."

"You need not blush, my love, and still less need you look so pale and frightened," said Lady Ashton, coming forward; "we know that maidens' ears must be slow in receiving a gentleman's language; but you must remember Mr Hayston speaks on a subject on which you have long since agreed to give him a favourable hearing. You know how much your father and I have our hearts set upon an event so desirable."

In Lady Ashton's voice, a tone of impressive, and even stern inuendo was sedulously and skilfully concealed, under an appearance of the most affectionate maternal tenderness. The manner was for Bucklaw, who was easily enough imposed upon; the matter of the exhortation was for the terrified Lucy, who well knew how to interpret her mother's hints, however skilfully their real purport might be veiled from general observation.

Miss Ashton sat upright in her chair, cast round her a glance, in which fear was mingled with a still wilder expression, but remained perfectly silent. Bucklaw, who had in the mean time paced the room to and fro, until he had recovered his composure, now stopped within two or three yards of her chair, and broke out as follows:—"I believe I have been a d—d fool, Miss Ashton; I have tried to speak to you as people tell me young ladies like to be talked to, and I don't think you comprehend what I have been saying; and no wonder, for d—n me if I understand it myself! But, however, once for all, and in broad Scotch, your father and mother like what is proposed, and if you can take a plain young fellow for your husband, who will never cross you in any

thing you have a mind to, I will place you at the head of the best
establishment in the three Lothians; you shall have Lady Girnington's lodging in the Canongate of Edinburgh, go where you please, do
what you please, and see what you please, and that's fair. Only I must
have a corner at the board end for a worthless old play-fellow of mine,
whose company I would rather want than have, if it were not that the
d—d fellow has persuaded me that I can't do without him; and so I
hope you won't except against Craigie, although it might be easy to
find much better company."

"Now, out upon you, Bucklaw," said Lady Ashton, again interposing,—"how can you think Lucy can have any objection to that blunt,
honest, good-natured creature, Captain Craigengelt?"

"Why, madam," replied Bucklaw, "as to Craigie's sincerity, honesty, and good-nature, they are, I believe, pretty much upon a par—
but that's neither here nor there—the fellow knows my ways, and has
got useful to me, and I cannot well do without him, as I said before.
But all this is nothing to the purpose; for, since I have mustered up
courage to make a plain proposal, I would fain hear Miss Ashton, from
her own lips, give me a plain answer."

"My dear Bucklaw," said Lady Ashton, "let me spare Lucy's bashfulness. I tell you, in her presence, that she has already consented to
be guided by her father and me in this matter.—Lucy, my love," she
added, with that singular combination of suavity of tone and pointed
energy which we have already noticed—"Lucy, my dearest love!
speak for yourself, is it not as I say?"

Her victim answered in a tremulous and hollow voice—"I *have*
promised to obey you,—but upon one condition."

"She means," said Lady Ashton, turning to Bucklaw, "she expects
an answer to the demand which she has made upon the man at Vienna,
or Ratisbon, or Paris,—or where is he—the restitution of the engagement in which he had the art to involve her. You will not, I am sure, my
dear friend, think it is wrong that she should feel much delicacy upon
this head; indeed, it concerns us all."

"Perfectly right—quite fair," said Bucklaw, half humming, half
speaking the end of the old song—

> "It is best to be off wi' the old love
> Before you be on wi' the new.

But I thought," said he, pausing, "you might have had an answer six
times told from Ravenswood. D—n me if I have not a mind to go and
fetch one myself, if Miss Ashton will honour me with the commission."

"By no means," said Lady Ashton, "we have had the utmost difficulty of preventing Douglas, (for whom it would be more proper,)

from taking so rash a step; and do you think we could permit you, my good friend, almost equally dear to us, to go to a desperate man upon an errand so desperate? In fact, all the friends of the family are of opinion, and my dear Lucy herself ought so to think, that, as this unworthy person has returned no answer to her letter, silence must on this, as in other cases, be held to give consent, and a contract must be supposed to be given up, when the party waives insisting upon it. Sir William, who should know best, is clear upon this subject; and therefore, my dear Lucy"——

"Madam," said Lucy, with unwonted energy, "urge me no farther —if this unhappy engagement be restored, I have already said you shall dispose of me as you will—till then I should commit a heavy sin in the sight of God and man, in doing what you require."

"But, my love, if this man remains obstinately silent"——

"He will *not* be silent," answered Lucy; "it is six weeks since I sent him a double of my former letter by a sure hand."

"You have not—you could not—you durst not," said Lady Ashton, with violence inconsistent with the tone she had intended to assume; but, instantly correcting herself, "My dearest Lucy," said she, in her sweetest tone of expostulation, "how could you think of such a thing?"

"No matter," said Bucklaw; "I respect Miss Ashton for her sentiments, and I only wish I had been her messenger myself."

"And pray how long, Miss Ashton," said her mother ironically, "are we to wait the return of your Pacolet—your fairy messenger—since our humble couriers of flesh and blood could not be trusted in this matter?"

"I have numbered weeks, days, hours, and minutes," said Miss Ashton; "within another week I shall have an answer, unless he is dead. Till that time, sir," she said, addressing Bucklaw, "let me be thus far beholden to you, that you will beg my mother to forbear me upon this subject."

"I will make it my particular entreaty to Lady Ashton," said Bucklaw; "by my honour, madam, I respect your feelings, and although the prosecution of this affair be rendered dearer to me than ever, yet, as I am a gentleman, I would renounce it, were it so urged as to give you a moment's pain."

"Mr Hayston, I think, cannot apprehend that," said Lady Ashton, looking pale with anger, "when the daughter's happiness lies in the bosom of the mother. Let me ask you, Miss Ashton, in what terms your last letter was couched?"

"Exactly in the same, madam," answered Lucy, "which you dictated on a former occasion."

"When eight days have elapsed then," said her mother, resuming her tone of tenderness, "we shall hope, my dearest love, that you will end this suspense."

"Miss Ashton must not be hurried, madam," said Bucklaw, whose bluntness of feeling did not by any means arise from want of good-nature—"messengers may be stopped or delayed. I have known a day's journey broke by the casting of a fore-shoe—Stay, let me see my calendar—the 20th day from this is St Jude's, and the day before I must be at Caverton Edge to see the match between the Laird of Kittlegirth's black mare, and Johnston the meal-monger's four-year old colt; but I can ride all night, or Craigie can bring me word how the match goes; and I hope, in the mean time, as I shall not myself distress Miss Ashton with any further importunity, that your ladyship yourself, and Sir William, and Colonel Douglas, will have the goodness to allow her uninterrupted time for making up her mind."

"Sir," said Miss Ashton, "you are generous."

"As for that, madam," answered Bucklaw, "I only pretend to be a plain good-humoured young fellow, as I said before, who will willingly make you happy if you will permit him, and shew him how to do so."

Having said this, he saluted her with more emotion than was consistent with his usual train of feeling, and took his leave; Lady Ashton, as she accompanied him out of the apartment, assuring him, that her daughter did full justice to the sincerity of his attachment, and requesting him to see Sir William before his departure, "since," as she said, with a glance reverting towards Lucy, "against St Jude's day, we must all be ready to *sign and seal*."

"To sign and seal!" echoed Lucy in a muttering tone, as the door of the apartment closed—"To sign and seal—to do and die!" and clasping her extenuated hands together, she sunk back on the easy chair she occupied, in a state resembling stupor.

From this she was shortly after awakened by the boisterous entry of her brother Henry, who clamorously reminded her of a promise to give him two yards of carnation ribbon to make knots to his new garters. With the most patient composure Lucy arose, and, opening a little ivory-cabinet, sought out the ribbon the lad wanted, measured it accurately, cut it off into proper lengths, and knotted it into the fashion his boyish whim required.

"Dinna shut the cabinet yet," said Henry, "for I must have some of your silver-wire to fasten the bells to my hawk's jesses, and yet the new falcon's not worth them neither; for do you know, after all the plague we had to get her from an eyery, all the way at Posso, in Mannor Water, she's going to prove, after all, nothing better than a rifler—she just wets her singles in the blood of the partridge, and then breaks away, and lets her fly; and what good can the poor bird do after that,

you know, except pine and die in the first heather-cow or whin-bush
she can crawl into?"

"Right, Henry—right, very right," said Lucy, mournfully, holding
the boy fast by the hand, after she had given him the wire that he
wanted; "but there are more riflers in the world than your falcon, and
more wounded birds that seek but to die in quiet, that can find neither
brake nor whin-bush to hide their heads in."

"Ah! that's some speech out of your romances," said the boy; "and
Sholto says they have turned your head; but I hear Norman whistling
to the hawk—I must go fasten on the jesses."

And he scampered away with the thoughtless gaiety of boyhood,
leaving his sister to the bitterness of her own reflections.

"It is decreed," she said, "that every living creature, even those who
owe me most kindness, are to shun me, and leave me to those by whom
I am beset. It is just it should be thus—alone and uncounselled,
I involved myself in these perils—alone and uncounselled, I must
extricate myself or die."

Chapter Three

——— what doth ensue
But moody and dull melancholy,
Kinsman to grim and comfortless despair,
And at her heels a huge infectious troop
Of pale distemperatures and foes to life.
                    Comedy of Errors

AS SOME vindication of the ease with which Bucklaw, (who otherwise, as he termed himself, was really a very good-humoured fellow,)
resigned his judgment to the management of Lady Ashton, while
paying his addresses to her daughter, the reader must call to mind the
strict domestic discipline, which, at this period, was exercised over the
females of a Scottish family.

The manners of the country in this, as in many other respects,
coincided with those of France before the revolution. Young women
of the higher ranks seldom mingled in society until after marriage,
and, both in law and fact, were held to be under the strict tutelage of
their parents, who were too apt to enforce the views for their settlement in life, without paying any regard to the inclination of the parties
chiefly interested. On such occasions, the suitor expected little more
from his bride than a silent acquiescence in the will of her parents;
and as few opportunities of acquaintance, far less of intimacy,
occurred, he made his choice by the outside, as the lovers in the
Merchant of Venice select the casket, contented to trust to chance the

issue of the lottery, in which he had hazarded a venture.

It was not therefore surprising, such being the general manners of the age, that Mr Hayston of Bucklaw, whom dissipated habits had detached from good society, should not attend particularly to those feelings in his elected bride, to which many men of more sentiment, experience, and reflection, would, in all probability, have been equally indifferent. He knew what all accounted the principal point, that her parents and friends, namely, were decidedly in his favour, and that there existed most powerful reasons for their predilection.

In truth, the conduct of the Marquis of A——, since Ravenswood's departure, had been such as almost to bar the possibility of his kinsman's union with Lucy Ashton. The Marquis was Ravenswood's sincere, but misjudging friend; or rather, like many friends and patrons, he consulted what he considered to be his relation's true interest, although he knew that in doing so he run counter to his inclinations.

The Marquis drove on, therefore, with the plenitude of ministerial authority, an appeal in the Scottish Parliament against those judgments of the courts of law, by which Sir William became possessed of Ravenswood's hereditary property. As this measure was enforced with all the authority of power, it was exclaimed against by the members on the opposite side, as an interference with the civil judicature of the country, equally new, arbitrary, and tyrannical. And if it thus affected even strangers connected with them only by political party, it may be guessed what the Ashton family themselves said and thought under so cross a dispensation. Sir William, still more worldly-minded than he was timid, was reduced to despair by the loss by which he was threatened. His son's haughtier spirit was exalted into rage, at the idea of being deprived of his expected patrimony. But to Lady Ashton's yet more vindictive temper, the conduct of Ravenswood, or rather of his patron, appeared to be an offence challenging the deepest and most immortal revenge. Even the quiet and confiding temper of Lucy herself, swayed by the opinions expressed by all around her, could not but consider the conduct of Ravenswood as precipitate, and even unkind. "It was my father," she repeated with a sigh, "who welcomed him to this place, and encouraged, or at least allowed, the intimacy between us. Should he not have remembered this, and requited it with at least some moderate degree of procrastination in the assertion of his own alleged rights? I would have forfeited for him double the value of these lands, which he pursues with an ardour that shows he has forgotten how much I am implicated in the matter."

Lucy, however, could only murmur these things to herself, unwilling to increase the prejudices against her lover entertained by all around her, who exclaimed against the steps pursued on his account, as illegal, vexatious, and tyrannical, resembling the worst measures in the worst times of the worst Stuarts. As a natural consequence, every means was resorted to, and every argument urged, to induce her to break off her engagement with Ravenswood, as being scandalous, shameful, and sinful, formed with the mortal enemy of her family, and calculated to add bitterness to the distress of her parents.

Lucy's spirit, however, was high; and although unaided and alone, she could have borne much—she could have endured the repinings of her father—his murmurs against what he called the tyrannical usage of the ruling party—his ceaseless charges of ingratitude against Ravenswood—his endless lectures on the various means by which contracts may be voided and annulled—his quotations from the civil, the municipal, and the canon law—and his prelections upon the *patria potestas*.

She might have borne also in patience, or repelled with scorn, the bitter taunts and occasional violence of her brother Colonel Ashton, and the impertinent and intrusive interference of other friends and relations. But it was beyond her power effectually to withstand or elude the constant and unceasing persecution of Lady Ashton, who, laying every other wish aside, had bent the whole efforts of her powerful mind to break her daughter's contract with Ravenswood, and to place a perpetual bar between the lovers, by effecting Lucy's union with Bucklaw. Far more deeply skilled than her husband in the recesses of the human heart, she was aware, that in this way she might strike a blow of deep and decisive vengeance upon one, whom she esteemed as her mortal enemy; nor did she hesitate at raising her arm, although she knew that the wound must be dealt through the bosom of her daughter. With this stern and fixed purpose, she sounded every depth and shallow of her daughter's soul, assumed alternately every disguise of manner which could serve her purpose, and prepared at leisure every species of dire machinery, by which the human mind can be wrenched from its settled purpose. Some of these were of an obvious description, and require only to be cursorily mentioned; others were characteristic of the time, the country, and the persons engaged in this singular drama.

It was of the last consequence, that all intercourse betwixt the lovers should be stopped, and, by dint of gold and authority, Lady Ashton contrived to possess herself of such a complete command of all who were placed around her daughter, that, in fact, no leaguered fortress was ever more completely blockaded; while, at the same time, to all outward appearance, Miss Ashton lay under no restriction. The verge of her parents' domains became, in respect to her, like the viewless and enchanted line drawn around a fairy castle, where nothing unpermitted can either enter from without, or escape from within. Thus every letter, in which Ravenswood conveyed to Lucy Ashton the indispensable reasons which detained him abroad, and more than one note which poor Lucy had addressed to him through what she thought a secure channel, fell into the hands of her mother. It could not be, but what the tenor of these intercepted letters, especially those of Ravenswood, should contain something to irritate the passions, and fortify the obstinacy, of her into whose hands they fell; but Lady Ashton's passions were too deep-rooted to require this fresh food. She burnt the papers as regularly as she perused them; and as they consumed into vapour and tinder, regarded them with a smile upon her compressed lips, and an exultation in her steady eye, which showed her confidence that the hopes of the writers should soon be rendered equally unsubstantial.

It usually happens that fortune aids the machinations of those who are prompt to avail themselves of every chance that offers. A report was wafted from the continent, founded, like others of the same sort, upon many plausible circumstances, but without any real basis, stating the Master of Ravenswood to be on the eve of marriage with a foreign lady of fortune and distinction. This was greedily caught up by both the political parties, who were at once struggling for power and for popular favour, and who seized, as usual, upon the most private circumstances in the lives of each other's partizans to convert them into subjects of political discussion.

The Marquis of A—— gave his opinion aloud and publicly, not indeed in the coarse terms ascribed to him by Captain Craigengelt, but in a manner sufficiently offensive to the Ashtons. "He thought the report," he said, "highly probable, and heartily wished it might be true. Such a match was fitter and far more creditable for a spirited young fellow, than a marriage with the daughter of an old whig lawyer, whose chicanery had so nearly ruined his father."

The other party, of course, laying out of view the opposition which the Master of Ravenswood received from Miss Ashton's family, cried shame upon his fickleness and perfidy, as if he had seduced the young lady into an engagement, and wilfully and causelessly abandoned her for another.

Sufficient care was taken that this report should find its way to Ravenswood Castle through every various channel, Lady Ashton being well aware, that the very reiteration of the same rumour from so many quarters could not but give it a semblance of truth. By some it was told as a piece of ordinary news, by some communicated as serious intelligence; now it was whispered to Lucy Ashton's ear in the tone of malignant pleasantry, and now transmitted to her as a matter of grave and serious warning.

Even the boy Henry was made the instrument of adding to his sister's torments. One morning he rushed into the room with a willow branch in his hand, which he told her had arrived that instant from Germany for her special wearing. Lucy, as we have seen, was remarkably fond of her younger brother, and at that moment his wanton and thoughtless unkindness seemed more keenly injurious than even the studied insults of her elder brother. Her grief, however, had no shade of resentment; she folded her arms about the boy's neck, and saying faintly, "Poor Henry! you speak but what they tell you," she burst into a flood of unrestrained tears. The boy was moved, notwithstanding the thoughtlessness of his age and character. "The devil take me," said he, "Lucy, if I fetch you any more of these tormenting messages again; for I like you better," said he, kissing away the tears, "than the whole pack of them; and you shall have my grey poney to ride on, and you shall canter him if you like, aye, and ride beyond the village too if you have a mind."

"Who told you," said Lucy, "that I am not permitted to ride where I please?"

"That's a secret," said the boy; "but you will find you can never ride beyond the village but your horse will cast a shoe, or fall lame, or the castle bell will ring, or something will happen to bring you back. But if I tell you more of these things, Douglas will not get me the pair of colours they have promised me, and so good morrow to you."

This dialogue plunged Lucy in still deeper dejection, as it tended to shew her plainly, what she had for some time suspected, that she was little better than a prisoner at large in her father's house. We have described her in the outset of our story as of a romantic disposition, delighting in tales of love and wonder, and readily identifying herself with the situation of those legendary heroines, with whose adventures, for want of better reading, her memory had become stocked. The fairy wand, with which in her solitude she had delighted to raise visions of enchantment, became now the rod of a magician, the bond slave of evil genii, serving only to invoke spectres at which the exorcist trembled. She felt herself the object of suspicion, of scorn, of dislike at least, if not of hatred, to her own family; and it seemed to her that she was abandoned by the very person on whose account she was exposed to the enmity of all around her. Indeed the evidence of Ravenswood's infidelity began to assume every day a more determined character.

A soldier of fortune of the name of Westenho, an old familiar of Craigengelt's, chanced to arrive from abroad about this time. The worthy Captain, though without any precise communication with

Lady Ashton, always acted most regularly and sedulously in support of her plans, and easily prevailed upon his friend, by dint of exaggeration of real circumstances, and coining of others, to give explicit testimony to the truth of Ravenswood's approaching marriage.

Thus beset on all hands, and in a manner reduced to despair, Lucy's temper gave way under the pressure of constant affliction and persecution. She became gloomy and abstracted, and, contrary to her natural and ordinary habit of mind, sometimes turned with spirit and even fierceness on those by whom she was long and closely annoyed. Her health also began to be shaken, and her hectic cheek and wandering eye gave symptoms of what is called a fever upon the spirits. In most mothers this would have moved compassion, but Lady Ashton, compact and firm of purpose, saw these waverings of health and intellect with no greater sympathy than that with which the hostile engineer regards the towers of a beleaguered city as they reel under the discharge of his artillery, or rather she considered these starts and inequalities of temper as symptoms of Lucy's expiring resolution; as the angler, by the throws and convulsive exertions of the fish which he has hooked, becomes aware that he soon will be able to land him. To accelerate the catastrophe in the present case, Lady Ashton had recourse to an expedient very consistent with the temper and credulity of those times, but which the reader will probably pronounce truly diabolical.

Chapter Four

In which a witch did dwell, in loathly weeds,
And wilful want, all careless of her needs;
So chusing solitary to abide,
Far from all neighbours, that her devilish deeds
And hellish arts from people she might hide,
And hurt far off, unknown, whomever she envied.
Fairy Queen

THE HEALTH of Lucy Ashton soon required the assistance of a person more skilled in the office of a sick nurse than the female domestics of the family. Ailsie Gourlay, sometimes called the Wise Woman of Bowden, was the person whom, for her own strong reasons, Lady Ashton selected as an attendant upon her daughter.

This woman had acquired a considerable reputation among the ignorant by the pretended cures which she performed, especially in *on-comes*, as the Scotch call them, or mysterious diseases which baffle the regular physician. Her pharmacopeia consisted partly of herbs selected in planetary hours, partly of words, signs, and charms, which sometimes, perhaps, produced a favourable influence upon the imagination of her patients. Such was the avowed profession of Lucky Gourlay, which, as may well be supposed, was looked upon with a suspicious eye, not only by her neighbours, but even by the clergy of the district. In private, however, she traded more deeply in the occult sciences; for, notwithstanding the dreadful punishments inflicted upon the supposed crime of witchcraft, there wanted not those who, steeled by want and bitterness of spirit, were willing to adopt the hateful and dangerous character, for the sake of the influence which its terrors enabled them to exercise in the vicinity, and the wretched emolument which they could extract by the practice of their supposed art.

Ailsie Gourlay was not indeed fool enough to acknowledge a compact with the Evil One, which would have been a swift and ready road to the stake and tar-barrel. Her fairy, she said, like Caliban's, was a harmless fairy. Nevertheless, she "spaed fortunes," read dreams, composed philtres, discovered stolen goods, and made and dissolved matches as successfully as if, according to the belief of the whole neighbourhood, she had been aided in these arts by Beelzebub himself. The worst of the pretenders to these sciences was, that they were generally persons who, feeling themselves odious to humanity, were careless of what they did to deserve the public hatred. Real crimes were often committed under pretence of magical imposture; and it somewhat relieves the disgust with which we read, in the criminal records, the conviction of these wretches, to be aware that many of them merit, as poisoners, suborners, and diabolical agents in secret domestic crimes, the severe fate to which they were condemned for the imaginary guilt of witchcraft.

Such was Ailsie Gourlay, whom, in order to attain the absolute subjugation of Lucy Ashton's mind, her mother thought it fitting to place near her person. A woman of less consequence than Lady Ashton had not dared to take such a step; but her high rank and strength of character set her above the censure of the world, and she was allowed to have selected for her daughter's attendant the best and most experienced sick nurse "and mediciner" in the neighbourhood, where an inferior person would have fallen under the reproach of calling in the assistance of a partner and ally of the great enemy of mankind.

The beldame caught her cue readily and by inuendo, without giving Lady Ashton the pain of distinct explanation. She was in many respects qualified for the part she played, which indeed could not be efficiently assumed without some knowledge of the human heart and passions. Dame Gourlay perceived that Lucy shuddered at her external appearance, which we have already described upon her appearance in the death-chamber of blind Alice; and while internally she hated the poor girl for the involuntary horror with which she perceived she was regarded, she commenced her operations by endeavouring to efface or overcome those prejudices which in her heart she resented as mortal offences. This was easily done, for the hag's external ugliness was soon balanced by a show of kindness and interest, to which Lucy had of late been little accustomed; her attentive services and real skill gained her the ear, if not the confidence, of her patient; and under pretence of diverting the solitude of a sick room, she soon led her attention captive by the legends in which she was well skilled, and to which Lucy's habits of reading and reflection induced her to "lend an attentive ear." Dame Gourlay's tales were at first of a mild and interesting character—

> Of fays that nightly dance upon the wold,
> And lovers doomed to wander and to weep,
> And castles high, where wicked wizzards keep
> Their captive thralls.

Gradually, however, they assumed a darker and more mysterious character, and became such as, told by the midnight lamp, and enforced by the tremulous tone, the quivering and livid lip, the uplifted skinny fore-finger, and the shaking head of the ugly blue-eyed hag, might have appalled a less credulous imagination, in an age more hard of belief. The old Sycorax saw her advantage, and gradually narrowed her magic circle around the devoted victim on whose spirit she practised. Her legends began to relate to the fortunes of the Ravenswood family, whose ancient grandeur and portentous authority, credulity had graced with so many superstitious attributes. The story of the fatal fountain was narrated at full length, and with formidable additions, by the ancient sybil. The prophecy, quoted by Caleb, concerning the dead bride, who was to be won by the last of the Ravenswoods, had its own mysterious commentary; and the singular circumstance of the apparition, seen by the Master of Ravenswood in the forest, having partly transpired through his hasty enquiries in the death chamber of old Alice, formed a theme for many exaggerations.

Lucy might have despised these tales, if they had been related concerning another family, or if her own situation had been less despondent. But circumstanced as she was, the idea that an evil fate hung over her attachment, became predominant over her other feelings, and the gloom of superstition darkened a mind, already sufficiently weakened by sorrow, distress, uncertainty, and an oppressive sense of desertion and desolation. Stories were told by her attendant so closely resembling her own in their circumstances, that she was gradually led to converse upon such tragic and mystical subjects with the beldame, whom she still regarded with involuntary shuddering. Dame Gourlay knew how to avail herself of this imperfect confidence. She directed Lucy's thoughts to the means of enquiring into futurity, —the surest mode, perhaps, of shaking the understanding and destroying the spirits. Omens were expounded, dreams were interpreted, and other tricks of jugglery perhaps resorted to, by which the pretended adepts of the period deceived and fascinated their deluded followers. I find it mentioned in the articles of dittay against Ailsie Gourlay, (——for it is some comfort to think that the old hag was tried, condemned, and burned on the top of North-Berwick-Law, by sentence of a commission from the Privy Council)——I find, I say, it was charged against her, among other offences, that she had, by the aid and delusions of Satan, shewn to a young person of quality, in a mirror glass, a gentleman then abroad, to whom the said young person was betrothed, and who appeared in the vision to be in the act of bestowing his hand upon another lady. But this and some other parts of the record appear to have been studiously left imperfect in names and dates, probably out of regard to the honour of the families concerned. If Dame Gourlay was able actually to play off such a piece of jugglery, it is clear she must have had better assistance to practise the deception, than her own skill or funds could supply. Meanwhile this mysterious visionary traffic had its usual effect, in unsettling Miss Ashton's mind. Her temper became unequal, her health decayed daily, her manners grew moping, melancholy, and uncertain. Her father, guessing partly at the cause of these appearances, and exerting a degree of authority unusual with him, made a point of banishing Dame Gourlay from the castle; but the arrow was shot, and was rankling barb-deep in the side of the wounded deer.

It was shortly after the departure of this woman, that Lucy Ashton, urged by her parents, announced to them, with a vivacity by which they were startled, "that she was conscious heaven and earth and hell had set themselves against her union with Ravenswood; still her contract," she said, "was a binding contract, and she neither would nor could resign it without the consent of Ravenswood. Let me be assured," she concluded, "that he will free me from my engagement, and dispose of me as you please, I care not how.—When the diamonds are gone, what signifies the casket?"

The tone of obstinacy with which this was said, her eyes flashing with unnatural light, and her hands firmly clenched, precluded the possibility of dispute; and the utmost length which Lady Ashton's art could attain, only got her the privilege of dictating the letter, by which her daughter required to know of Ravenswood whether he intended to abide by, or to surrender, what she termed, "their unfortunate engagement." Of this advantage Lady Ashton so far and so ingeniously availed herself, that, according to the wording of the letter, the reader would have supposed Lucy was calling upon her lover to renounce a contract which was contrary to the interests and inclinations of both. Not trusting even to this point of deception, Lady Ashton finally determined to suppress the letter altogether, in hopes that Lucy's impatience would induce her to condemn Ravenswood unheard and in absence. In this she was disappointed. The time, indeed, had long elapsed, when an answer should have been received from the continent. The faint ray of hope which still glimmered in Lucy's mind, was well nigh extinguished. But the idea never forsook her, that her letter might not have been duly forwarded. One of her mother's new machinations unexpectedly furnished her with the means of ascertaining what she most desired to know.

The female agent of hell having been dismissed from the castle, Lady Ashton, who wrought by all variety of means, resolved to employ, for working the same end on Lucy's mind, an agent of a very different character. This was no other than the Reverend Mr Bidethebent, a presbyterian clergyman, of the very strictest order and most rigid principles, whose aid she called in upon the principle of the tyrant in the tragedy:—

> I'll have a priest shall preach her from her faith,
> And make it sin not to renounce that vow,
> Which I'd have broken——

But Lady Ashton was mistaken in the agent she had selected. His prejudices, indeed, were easily enlisted on her side, and it was no difficult matter to make him regard with horror the prospect of a union betwixt the daughter of a God-fearing, professing, and presbyterian family of distinction, with the heir of a blood-thirsty prelatist and persecutor, the hands of whose fathers had been dyed to the wrists in the blood of God's saints. This resembled, in the divine's opinion, the union of a Moabitish stranger with a daughter of Zion. But with all the more severe prejudices and principles of his sect, Bidethebent possessed a sound judgment, and had learnt sympathy even in that very school of persecution, where the heart is so frequently hardened. In a private interview with Miss Ashton, he was deeply moved by her distress, and could not but admit the justice of her request to be permitted a direct communication with Ravenswood, upon the subject of their solemn contract. When she urged to him the great uncertainty under which she laboured, whether her letter had been ever forwarded, the old man paced the room with long steps, shook his grey head, rested repeatedly for a space on his ivory-headed staff, and after much hesitation, confessed that he thought her doubts so reasonable, that he would himself aid in the removal of them.

"I cannot but opine, Miss Lucy," he said, "that your worshipful lady mother hath in this matter an eagerness, whilk, although it ariseth doubtless from love to your best interests here and hereafter—for the man is of persecuting blood, and himself a persecutor, a cavalier or malignant, and a scoffer, who hath no inheritance in Jesse—nevertheless we are commanded to do justice unto all, and to fulfil our bond and covenant, as well to the stranger, as to him who is in brotherhood with us. Wherefore myself, even I myself, will be aiding unto the delivery of your letter to the man Edgar Ravenswood, trusting that the issue thereof may be your deliverance from the nets in which he hath sinfully engaged you. And that I may do in this neither more nor less than hath been warranted by your honourable parents, I pray you to transcribe, without increment or subtraction, the letter formerly expeded under the dictation of your right honourable mother; and I shall put it into such sure course of being delivered, that if, honoured young madam, you shall receive no answer, it will be necessary that you conclude that the man meaneth in silence to abandon that naughty contract, which, peradventure, he may be unwilling directly to restore."

Lucy eagerly embraced the expedient of the worthy divine. A new letter was written in the precise terms of the former, and consigned by Mr Bidethebent to the charge of Saunders Moonshine, a zealous elder of the church when on shore, and when on board his brig, as bold a smuggler as ever ran out a sliding bowsprit to the winds that blow betwixt Campvere and the east coast of Scotland. At the recommendation of his pastor, Saunders readily undertook that the letter should be securely conveyed to the Master of Ravenswood at the court where he now resided.

This retrospect became necessary to explain the conference betwixt Miss Ashton, her mother, and Bucklaw, which we have detailed in a preceding chapter.

Lucy was now like the sailor, who, while drifting through a tempestuous ocean, clings for safety to a single plank, his powers of grasping it becoming every moment more feeble, and the deep darkness of the night only chequered by the flashes of lightning, hissing as they show the white tops of the billows, in which he is soon to be engulphed.

Week crept away after week, and day after day. St Jude's day arrived, the last and protracted term to which Lucy had limited herself, and there was neither letter nor news of Ravenswood.

Chapter Five

How fair these names, how much unlike they look
To all the blurr'd subscriptions in my book!
The bridegroom's letters stand in row above,
Tapering, yet straight, like pine-trees in his grove;
While free and fine the bride's appear below,
As light and slender as her jessamines grow.
                                        CRABBE

ST JUDE'S day came, the term assigned by Lucy herself as the fur-
thest date of expectation, and, as we have already said, there were
neither letters from, nor news of, Ravenswood. But there were news
of Bucklaw, and of his trusty associate Craigengelt, who arrived early
in the morning for the completion of the proposed espousals, and for
signing the necessary deeds.

These had been carefully prepared under the revisal of Sir William
Ashton himself, it having been resolved, on account of the state
of Miss Ashton's health, as it was said, that none save the parties
immediately interested should be present when the parchments were
subscribed. It was further determined, that the marriage should be
solemnized upon the fourth day after signing the articles, a measure
adopted by Lady Ashton, in order that Lucy might have as little time
as possible to recede, or relapse into intractability. There was no
appearance, however, of her doing either. She heard the proposed
arrangement with the calm indifference of despair, or rather with an
apathy arising from the oppressed and stupified state of her feelings.
To an eye so unobserving as that of Bucklaw, her demeanour had little
more of reluctance than might suit the character of a bashful young
lady, however, he could not disguise from himself, who was complying
with the choice of her friends, rather than exercising any personal
predilection in his favour.

When the morning compliments of the bridegroom had been paid,
Miss Ashton was left for some time to herself; her mother remarking,
that the deeds must be signed before the hour of noon, in order that
the marriage might be happy.

Lucy suffered herself to be drest for the occasion, as the taste of her
attendants suggested, and was of course splendidly arrayed. Her dress
was composed of white satin and Brussels lace, and her hair arranged
with a profusion of jewels, whose lustre made a strange contrast to the
deadly paleness of her complexion, and to the trouble which dwelt in
her unsettled eye.

Her toilette was hardly finished, ere Henry appeared to conduct the passive bride to the state apartment, where all was prepared for signing the contract. "Do you know, sister," he said, "I am glad you are to have Bucklaw after all, instead of Ravenswood, who looked like a Spanish grandee come to cut our throats, and trample our bodies under foot. And I am glad the broad seas are between us this day, for I shall never forget how frightened I was when I took him for the picture of old Sir Malise walked out of the canvass. Tell me true, are you not glad to be fairly shot of him?"

"Ask me no questions, Henry," said his unfortunate sister; "there is little more can happen to make me either glad or sorry in this world."

"And that's what all young brides say," said Henry; "and so do not be cast down, Lucy, for you'll tell another tale a twelvemonth hence —and I am to be bride's-man, and ride before you to the kirk, and all our kith, kin, and ally, and all Bucklaw's, are to be mounted and in order—and I am to have a scarlet laced coat, and a feathered hat, and a sword-belt, double bordered with gold, and *point d'espagne*, and a dagger instead of a sword; and I should like a sword much better, but Douglas won't hear of it. All my things, and a hundred besides, are to come out from Edinburgh to-night with old Gilbert, and the sumpter mules—and I will bring them, and show them to you the instant they come."

The boy's chatter was here interrupted by the arrival of Lady Ashton, somewhat alarmed at her daughter's stay. With one of her sweetest smiles, she took Lucy's arm under her own, and led her to the apartment where her presence was expected.

There were only present, Sir William Ashton, and Colonel Douglas Ashton, the last in full regimentals—Bucklaw in bridegroom trim —Craigengelt freshly equipt from top to toe by the bounty of his patron, and bedizened with as much lace as might have become the stage dress of the Copper Captain, together with the Rev. Mr Bidethebent; the presence of a minister being, in strict presbyterian families, an indispensable requisite upon all occasions of unusual solemnity.

Wines and refreshments were placed on a table, on which the writings were displayed, ready for signature.

But before proceeding either to business or refreshment, Mr Bidethebent, at a signal from Sir William Ashton, invited the company to join him in a short extemporary prayer, in which he implored a blessing upon the contract now to be solemnized between the honourable parties then present. With the simplicity of his times and profession, which permitted strong personal allusions, he petitioned, that the wounded mind of one of these noble parties might be healed, in reward of her compliance with the advice of her right honourable parents; and that, as she had proved herself a child after God's commandment, by honouring her father and mother, she and her's might enjoy the promised blessing—length of days in the land here, and a happy portion hereafter in a better country. He prayed further, that the bridegroom might be weaned from those follies which seduce youth from the path of knowledge; that he might cease to take delight in vain and unprofitable company, scoffers, rioters, and those who sit late at the wine, (here Bucklaw winked to Craigengelt), and cease from the society that causeth to err. A suitable supplication in behalf of Sir William and Lady Ashton, and their family, concluded this religious address, which thus embraced every individual present, excepting Craigengelt, whom the worthy divine probably considered as past all hopes of grace.

The business of the day now went forward; Sir William Ashton signed the contract with legal solemnity and precision; his son, with military *non-chalance;* and Bucklaw, having subscribed as rapidly as Craigengelt could turn the leaves, concluded by wiping his pen on that worthy's new laced cravat.

It was now Miss Ashton's turn to sign the writings, and she was guided by her watchful mother to the table for that purpose. At her first attempt, she began to write with a dry pen, and when the circumstance was pointed out, seemed unable, after several attempts, to dip it in the massive silver ink-standish, which stood full before her. Lady Ashton's vigilance hastened to supply the deficiency. I have myself seen the fatal deed, and in the distinct characters in which the name of Lucy Ashton is traced on each page, there is only a very slight tremulous irregularity, indicating her state of mind at the time of the subscription. But the last signature is incomplete, defaced, and blotted; for while her hand was employed in tracing it, the hasty tramp of a horse was heard at the gate, succeeded by a step in the outer gallery, and a voice, which, in a commanding tone, bore down the opposition of the menials—the pen dropped from Lucy's fingers, as she exclaimed with a faint shriek—"He is come—he is come!"

Chapter Six

This by his tongue should be a Montague!
Fetch me my rapier, boy;
Now, by the faith and honour of my kin,
To strike him dead I hold it not a sin.
Romeo and Juliet

HARDLY had Miss Ashton dropped the pen, when the door of the apartment flew open, and the Master of Ravenswood entered the apartment.

Lockhard and another domestic, who had in vain attempted to oppose his passage through the gallery or anti-chamber, were seen standing on the threshold transfixed with surprise, which was instantly communicated to the whole party in the state-room. That of Colonel Douglas Ashton was mingled with resentment; that of Bucklaw, with haughty and affected indifference; the rest, even Lady Ashton herself, shewed signs of fear, and Lucy seemed petrified to stone by this unexpected apparition. Apparition it might well be termed, for Ravenswood had more the appearance of one returned from the dead, than of a living visitor.

He planted himself full in the middle of the apartment, opposite to the table at which Lucy was seated, on whom, as if she had been alone in the chamber, he bent his eyes with a mingled expression of deep grief and deliberate indignation. His dark-coloured riding cloak, displaced from one shoulder, hung around one side of his person in the ample folds of the Spanish mantle. The rest of his rich dress was travel-soil'd, and deranged by hard riding. He had a sword by his side, and pistols in his belt. His slouched hat, which he had not removed at entrance, gave an additional gloom to his dark features, which, wasted by sorrow, and marked by the ghastly look communicated by long illness, added to a countenance naturally somewhat stern and wild, a fierce and even savage expression. The matted and dishevelled locks of hair which escaped from under his hat, together with his fixed and unmoved posture, made his head more resemble that of a marble bust than of a living man. He said not a single word, and there was a deep silence in the company for more than two minutes.

It was broken by Lady Ashton, who in that space partly recovered her natural audacity. She demanded to know the cause of this unauthorised intrusion.

"That is a question, madam," said her son, "which I have the best right to ask—and I must request of the Master of Ravenswood to follow me, where he can answer it at leisure."

Bucklaw interposed, saying, "No man on earth should usurp his previous right in demanding an explanation from the Master.—Craigengelt," he added, in an under tone, "d—n ye, why do you stand staring as if you saw a ghost? fetch me my sword from the gallery."

"I will relinquish to no man," said Colonel Ashton, "my right of calling to account the man who has offered this unparalleled affront to my family."

"Be patient, gentlemen," said Ravenswood, turning sternly towards them, and waving his hand as if to impose silence on their altercation. "If you are as weary of your lives as I am, I will find time and place to pledge mine against one or both—at present I have no leisure for the disputes of triflers."

"Triflers!" echoed Colonel Ashton, half unsheathing his sword, while Bucklaw laid his hand on the hilt of that which Craigengelt had just reached him.

Sir William Ashton, alarmed for his son's safety, rushed between the young men and Ravenswood, exclaiming, "My son, I command you—Bucklaw, I entreat you—keep the peace, in the name of the queen and of the law."

"In the name of the law of God," said Bidethebent, advancing also with uplifted hands between Bucklaw, the Colonel, and the object of their resentment—"In the name of Him who brought peace on earth, and good will to mankind, I implore—I beseech—I command you to forbear violence towards each other. God hateth the blood-thirsty man—he who striketh with the sword, shall perish with the sword."

"Do you take me for a dog, sir," said Colonel Ashton, turning fiercely upon him, "or something more brutally stupid, to endure this insult in my father's house?—Let me go, Bucklaw! He shall account to me, or, by heaven, I will stab him where he stands."

"You shall not touch him here," said Bucklaw; "he once gave me my life, and were he the devil come to fly away with the whole house and generation, he shall have nothing but fair play."

The passions of the two young men thus counteracting each other, gave Ravenswood leisure to exclaim, in a stern and steady voice, "Silence!—let him who really seeks danger, take the fitting time when it is to be found; my mission here will be shortly accomplished. —Is *that*, madam, your hand?" he added in a softer tone, extending towards Miss Ashton her last letter.

A faultering "Yes," seemed rather to escape from her lips, than to be uttered as a voluntary answer.

"And is *this* also your hand?" extending towards her the mutual engagement.

Lucy remained silent. Terror, and a yet stronger and more con-

fused feeling, so utterly disturbed her understanding, that she probably scarcely comprehended the question that was put to her.

"If you design," said Sir William Ashton, "to found any legal claim
on that paper, sir, do not expect to receive any answer to an extrajudicial question."

"Sir William Ashton," said Ravenswood, "I pray you, and all who
hear me, that you will not mistake my purpose. If this young lady, of
her own free-will, desires the restoration of this contract, as her letter
would seem to imply—there is not a withered leaf which this autumn
wind strews on the heath, that is more valueless in my eyes. But I must
and will hear the truth from her own mouth—without this satisfaction
I will not leave this spot. Murder me by numbers you possibly may;
but I am an armed man,—I am a desperate man,—and I will not die
without ample vengeance. This is my resolution, take it as you may. I
WILL hear her determination from her own mouth—from her own
mouth, alone, and without witnesses, will I hear it. Now chuse," he
said, drawing his sword with the right hand, and, with the left, by the
same motion taking a pistol from his belt and cocking it, but turning
the point of one weapon and the muzzle of the other to the ground,—
"Chuse if you will have this hall floated with blood, or if you will grant
me the decisive interview with my affianced bride, which the laws of
God and the country alike entitle me to demand."

All recoiled at the sound of his voice, and the determined action by
which it was accompanied; for the ecstasy of real desperation seldom
fails to overpower the less energetic passions by which it may be
opposed. The clergyman was the first to speak. "In the name of God,"
said he, "receive an overture of peace from the meanest of his servants. What this honourable person demands, albeit it is urged with
over violence, hath yet in it something of reason. Let him hear from
Miss Lucy's own lips that she hath dutifully acceded to the will of her
parents, and repenteth her of her covenant with him; and when he is
assured of this, he will depart in peace unto his own dwelling, and
cumber us no more. Alas! the workings of the ancient Adam are
strong even in the regenerate—surely we should have long suffering
with those who, being yet in the gall of bitterness and bond of iniquity,
are swept forwards by the uncontroulable current of worldly passion.
Let then the Master of Ravenswood have the interview on which he
insisteth; it can but be as a passing pang to this honourable maiden,
since her faith is now irrevocably pledged to the choice of her parents.
Let it, I say, be thus—it belongeth to my functions to entreat your
honours' compliance with this healing overture."

"Never," answered Lady Ashton, whose rage had now overcome
her first surprise and terror—"never shall this man speak in private

with my daughter, the affianced bride of another. Pass from this room who will, I remain here. I fear neither his violence nor his weapons, though some," she said, glancing a look towards Colonel Ashton, "who bear my name, appear more moved by them."

"For God's sake, madam," answered the worthy divine, "add not fuel to firebrands. The Master of Ravenswood cannot, I am sure, object to your presence, the young lady's state of health being considered, and your maternal duty. I myself will also tarry; peradventure my grey hairs may turn away wrath."

"You are welcome to do so, sir," said Ravenswood; "and Lady Ashton is also welcome to remain, if she shall think proper; but let all others depart."

"Ravenswood," said Colonel Ashton, crossing him as he went out, "you shall account for this ere long."

"When you please," replied Ravenswood.

"But I," said Bucklaw, with a half smile, "have a prior demand on your leisure, a claim of some standing."

"Arrange it as you will," said Ravenswood; "leave me but this day in peace, and I will have no dearer employment on earth, to-morrow, than to give you all the satisfaction you can desire."

The other gentlemen left the apartment; but Sir William Ashton lingered.

"Master of Ravenswood," he said, in a conciliating tone, "I think I have not deserved that you should make this scandal and outrage in my family. If you will sheathe your sword, and retire with me into my study, I will prove to you, by the most satisfactory arguments, the inutility of your present irregular procedure"——

"To-morrow, sir—to-morrow—to-morrow, I will hear you at length," reiterated Ravenswood, interrupting him; "this day hath its own sacred and indispensable business."

He pointed to the door, and Sir William left the apartment.

Ravenswood sheathed his sword, uncocked and returned his pistol to his belt, walked deliberately to the door of the apartment, which he bolted—returned, raised his hat from his forehead, and, gazing upon Lucy with eyes in which an expression of sorrow overcame their late fierceness, spread his dishevelled locks back from his face, and said, "Do you know me, Miss Ashton?—I am still Edgar Ravenswood." She was silent; and he went on, with increasing vehemence—"I am still that Edgar Ravenswood, who, for your affection, renounced the dear ties by which injured honour bound him to seek vengeance. I am that Ravenswood, who, for your sake, forgave, nay, clasped hands in friendship with the oppressor and pillager of his house—the traducer and murderer of his father."

"My daughter," answered Lady Ashton, interrupting him, "has no occasion to dispute the identity of your person; the venom of your present language is sufficient to remind her, that she speaks with the mortal enemy of her father."

"I pray you to be patient, madam," answered Ravenswood; "my answer must come from her own lips.—Once more, Miss Lucy Ashton, I am that Ravenswood to whom you granted the solemn engagement, which you now desire to retract and cancel."

Lucy's bloodless lips could only faulter out the words, "It was my mother."

"She speaks truly," said Lady Ashton; "it was I, who, authorised alike by the laws of God and man, advised her, and concurred with her, to set aside an unhappy and precipitate engagement, and to annul it by the authority of Scripture itself."

"Scripture!" said Ravenswood, scornfully.

"Let him hear the text," said Lady Ashton, appealing to the divine, "on which you yourself, with cautious reluctance, declared the nullity of the pretended engagement insisted upon by this violent man."

The clergyman took his clasped Bible from his pocket, and read the following words: "*If a woman vow a vow unto the Lord, and bind herself by a bond, being in her father's house in her youth, and her father hear her vow and her bond, wherewith she hath bound her soul, and her father shall hold his peace at her, then all her vow shall stand.*"

"And was it not even so with us?" interrupted Ravenswood.

"Controul thy impatience, young man," answered the divine, "and hear what follows in the sacred text:—'*But if her father disallow her in the day that he heareth, not any of her vows, nor of her bonds, wherewith she hath bound her soul, shall stand. And the Lord shall forgive her, because her father disallowed her.*'"

"And was not," said Lady Ashton, fiercely and triumphantly breaking in,—"was not our's the case stated in holy writ?—Will this person deny, that the instant her parents heard of the vow, or bond, by which our daughter had bound her soul, we disallowed the same in the most express terms, and informed him by writing of our determination?"

"And is this all?" said Ravenswood, looking at Lucy—"Are you willing to barter sworn faith, the exercise of free-will, and the feelings of mutual affection, to this wretched hypocritical sophistry?"

"Hear him!" said Lady Ashton, looking to the clergyman—"hear the blasphemer!"

"May God forgive him," said Bidethebent, "and enlighten his ignorance!"

"Hear what I have sacrificed for you," said Ravenswood, still addressing Lucy, "ere you sanction what has been done in your name. The honour of an ancient family, the urgent advice of my best friends, have been in vain used to sway my resolution; neither the arguments of reason, nor the portents of superstition, have shaken my fidelity. The very dead have arisen to warn me, and their warning has been despised. Are you prepared to pierce my heart for its fidelity, with the very weapon which my rash confidence entrusted to your grasp?"

"Master of Ravenswood," said Lady Ashton, "you have asked what questions you thought fit. You see the total incapacity of my daughter to answer you. But I will reply for her, and in a manner which you cannot dispute. You desire to know whether Lucy Ashton, of her own free-will, desires to annul the engagement into which she has been trepanned. You have her letter under her own hand, demanding the surrender of it; and, in yet more full evidence of her purpose, here is the contract which she has this morning subscribed, in presence of this reverend gentleman, with Mr Hayston of Bucklaw."

Ravenswood gazed upon the deed, as if petrified. "And it was without fraud or compulsion," said he, looking towards the clergyman, "that Miss Ashton subscribed this parchment?"

"I vouch it upon my sacred character."

"This is, indeed, madam, an undeniable piece of evidence," said Ravenswood sternly; "and it will be equally unnecessary and dishonourable to waste another word in useless remonstrance or reproach. There, madam," he said, laying down before Lucy the signed paper and the broken piece of gold—"there are the evidences of your first engagement; may you be more faithful to that which you have just formed. I will trouble you to return the corresponding tokens of my ill-placed confidence—I ought rather to say of my egregious folly."

Lucy returned the scornful glance of her lover with a gaze, from which perception seemed to have been banished; yet she seemed partly to have understood his meaning, for she raised her hands as if to undo a blue ribbon which she wore around her neck. She was unable to accomplish her purpose, but Lady Ashton cut the ribbon asunder, and detached the broken piece of gold which Miss Ashton had till then worn concealed in her bosom. The written counterpart of the lovers' engagement she for some time had had in her own possession. With a haughty curtsey, she delivered both to Ravenswood, who was much softened when he took the piece of gold.

"And she could wear it thus," he said—speaking to himself— "could wear it in her very bosom—could wear it next to her heart— even when—but complaint avails not," he said, dashing from his eye the tear which had gathered in it, and resuming the stern composure of his manner. He strode to the chimney, and threw into the fire the paper and piece of gold, stamping upon the coals with the heel of his boot, as if to insure their destruction. "I will be no longer," he then said, "an intruder here—Your evil wishes, and your worse offices, Lady Ashton, I will only return, by hoping these will be your last machinations against your daughter's honour and happiness.—And to you, madam," he said, addressing Lucy, "I have nothing farther to say, except to pray to God that you may not become a world's wonder for this act of wilful and deliberate perjury."—Having uttered these words, he turned on his heel, and left the apartment.

Sir William Ashton, by entreaty and authority, had detained his son and Bucklaw in a distant part of the castle, in order to prevent their again meeting with Ravenswood; but as the Master descended the great staircase, Lockhard delivered him a billet, signed Sholto Douglas Ashton, requesting to know where the Master of Ravenswood would be heard of four or five days from hence, as the writer had business of weight to settle with him, so soon as an important family event had taken place.

"Say to Colonel Ashton," said Ravenswood, composedly, "I shall be found at Wolfscrag when his leisure serves him."

As he descended the outward stair which led from the terrace, he was a second time interrupted by Craigengelt, who, on the part of his principal, the Laird of Bucklaw, expressed a hope, that Ravenswood would not leave Scotland within ten days at least, as he had both former and recent civilities for which to express his gratitude.

"Tell your master," said Ravenswood fiercely, "to chuse his own time. He will find me at Wolfscrag, if his purpose is not forestalled."

"*My* master?" replied Craigengelt, encouraged by seeing Colonel Ashton and Bucklaw at the bottom of the terrace, "give me leave to say, I know of no such person upon earth, nor will I permit such language to be used to me."

"Seek your master, then, in hell!" exclaimed Ravenswood, giving way to the passion he had hitherto restrained, and throwing Craigengelt from him with such violence, that he rolled down the steps, and lay senseless at the foot of them—"I am a fool," he instantly added, "to vent my passion upon a caitiff so worthless."

He then mounted his horse, which at his arrival he had secured to a ballustrade in front of the castle, rode very slowly past Bucklaw and Colonel Ashton, raising his hat as he past each, and looking in their faces steadily while he offered this mute salutation, which was returned by both with the same stern gravity. Ravenswood walked on with equal deliberation until he reached the head of the avenue, as if to shew that he rather courted than avoided interruption. When he had passed the upper gate, he turned his horse, and looked at the castle

with a fixed eye; then set spurs to his good steed, and departed with
the speed of a demon dismissed by the exorcist.

Chapter Seven

"Who comes from the bridal chamber?"
It is Azrael, the angel of death.
            Thalaba

AFTER the dreadful scene that had taken place at the castle, Lucy
was transported to her own chamber, where she remained for some
time in a state of absolute stupor. Yet afterwards, in the course of
the ensuing day, she seemed to have recovered, not merely her
spirits and resolution, but a sort of flighty levity, that was foreign
to her character and situation, and which was at times checquered
by fits of deep silence and melancholy, and of capricious pettishness.
Lady Ashton became much alarmed, and consulted the family physicians. But as her pulse indicated no change, they could only say
that the disease was on the spirits, and recommended gentle exercise
and amusement. Miss Ashton never alluded to what had passed in
the state-room. It seemed doubtful even if she was conscious of it,
for she was often observed to raise her hands to her neck, as if in
search of the ribbon that had been taken from it, and mutter, in
surprise and discontent, when she could not find it, "It was the link
that bound me to life."

Notwithstanding all these remarkable symptoms, Lady Ashton was
too deeply pledged, to delay her daughter's marriage even in her
present state of health. It cost her much trouble to keep up the fair side
of appearances towards Bucklaw. She was well aware, that if he once
saw any reluctance on her daughter's part, he would break off the
treaty, to her great personal shame and dishonour. She therefore
resolved, that, if Lucy continued passive, the marriage should take
place upon the day that had been previously fixed, trusting that a
change of place, of situation, and of character, would operate a more
speedy and effectual cure upon the unsettled spirits of her daughter,
than could be attained by the slow measures which the medical men
recommended. Sir William Ashton's views of family aggrandisement,
and his desire to strengthen himself against the measures of the Marquis of A——, readily induced him to acquiesce in what he could not
have perhaps resisted if willing to do so. As for the young men,
Bucklaw and Colonel Ashton, they protested, that after what had
happened, it would be most dishonourable to postpone for a single
hour the time appointed for the marriage, as it would be generally

ascribed to their being intimidated by the intrusive visit and threats of Ravenswood.

Bucklaw would indeed have been incapable of such precipitation, had he been aware of the state of Miss Ashton's health, or rather of her mind. But custom, upon these occasions, permitted only brief and sparing intercourse between the bridegroom and the bride; a circumstance so well improved by Lady Ashton, that Bucklaw neither saw nor suspected.

On the eve of the bridal day, Lucy appeared to have one of her fits of levity, and surveyed with a degree of girlish interest the various preparations of dress, &c. &c., which the different members of the family had prepared for the occasion.

The morning dawned bright and cheerily. The bridal guests assembled in gallant troops from distant quarters. Not only the relations of Sir William Ashton, and the still more dignified connections of his lady, together with the numerous kinsmen and allies of the bridegroom, were present upon this joyful ceremony, gallantly mounted, arrayed, and caparisoned, but almost every presbyterian family of distinction, within fifty miles, made a point of attending upon an occasion which was considered as giving a sort of triumph over the Marquis of A——, in the person of his kinsman. Splendid refreshments awaited the guests on their arrival, and after it was finished, the cry was to horse. The bride was led forth betwixt her brother Henry and her mother. Her gaiety of the preceding day had given rise to a deep shade of melancholy, which, however, did not misbecome an occasion so momentous. There was a light in her eyes, and a colour in her cheek, which had not been kindled for many a day, and which, joined to her great beauty, and the splendour of her dress and jewels, occasioned her entrance to be greeted with an universal murmur of applause, in which even the ladies could not refrain themselves from joining. While the cavalcade were getting to horse, Sir William Ashton, a man of peace and of form, censured his son Henry for having begirt himself with a military sword of preposterous length, belonging to his brother, Colonel Ashton.

"If you must have a sword," he said, "upon such a peaceful occasion, why did you not use the short weapon sent from Edinburgh on purpose?"

The boy vindicated himself, by saying it was lost.

"You put it out of the way yourself, I suppose," said his father, "out of ambition to wear that thing that might have served Sir William Wallace—but never mind, get to horse now, and take care of your sister."

The boy did so, and was placed in the centre of the gallant train. At the time he was too full of his own appearance, his sword, his laced cloak, his feathered hat, and his managed horse, to pay much regard to any thing else; but he afterwards remembered to the hour of his death, that when the hand of his sister, by which she supported herself on the pillion behind him, touched his own, it felt as wet and cold as sepulchral marble.

Glancing wide over hill and dale, the fair bridal procession at last reached the parish church, which they nearly filled; for, besides domestics, above a hundred gentlemen and ladies were present upon the occasion. The marriage ceremony was performed, according to the rites of the presbyterian persuasion, to which Bucklaw of late had judged it proper to conform.

On the outside of the church, a liberal dole was distributed to the poor of the neighbouring parishes, under the direction of Johnny Mortsheugh, who had lately been promoted from his desolate quarters at the Hermitage, to fill the more eligible situation of sexton at the parish-church of Ravenswood. Dame Gourlay, with two of her contemporaries, the same who assisted at Alice's late-wake, seated apart upon a flat monument, or *through-stane*, sate enviously comparing the shares which had been allotted to them in dividing the dole.

"Johnny Mortsheugh," said Annie Winnie, "might hae minded auld lang syne, and thought of his auld kimmers, for as braw as he is with his new black coat. I hae gotten but five herring instead o' sax, and this disna look like a gude saxpennys, and I dare say this bit morsel o' beef is an unce lighter than ony that's been dealt round; and it's a bit o' the tenony hough, mair by token, that your's, Maggie, is out o' the back-sey."

"Mine, quo' she," mumbled the paralytic hag, "mine is half banes, I trow. If grit folk gie poor bodies ony thing for coming to their weddings and burials, it suld be something that wad do them gude, I think."

"Their gifts," said Ailsie Gourlay, "are dealt for nae love of us—nor for respect for whether we feed or starve. They wad gie us whinstanes for loaves, if it would serve their ain vanity, and yet they expect us to be as gratefu' as they ca' it, as if they served us for true love and likeing."

"And that's truly said," answered her companion.

"But, Ailsie Gourlay, ye're the auldest o' us three, did ye ever see a mair grand bridal?"

"I winna say that I have," answered the hag; "but I think soon to see as braw a burial."

"And that wad please me as weel," said Annie Winnie; "for there's as large a dole, and folk are no obliged to grin and laugh, and mak murgeons, and wish joy to these hellicat quality, that lord it ower us like brute beasts. I like to pack the dead dole in my lap, and rin ower my auld rhyme,—

> My loaf in my lap, my penny in my purse,
> Thou art ne'er the better, and I'm ne'er the worse."

"That's right, Annie," said the paralytic woman; "God send us a green Yule and a fat kirk-yard!"

"But I wad like to ken, Lucky Gourlay, for ye're the auldest and wisest amang us, whilk o' these revellers' turns it will be to be streekit first."

"D'ye see yon dandilly maiden," said Dame Gourlay, "a' glistenin' wi' goud and jewels, that they are mounting on the white horse behind that hare-brained callant in scarlet, wi' the lang sword at his side?"

"But that's the bride!" said her companion, her cold heart touched with some sense of compassion; "that's the very bride hersell! Eh, whow! sae young, sae braw, and sae bonnie—and is her time sae short?"

"I tell ye her winding sheet," said the sybil, "is up as high as her throat already, believe it wha list. Her sand has but few grains to run out, and nae wonder—they've been weel shaken. The leaves are withering fast on the trees, but she'll never see the Martinmas wind gar them dance in swirls like the fairy rings."

"Ye waited on her for a quarter," said the paralytic woman, "and got twa red pieces, or I am far beguiled."

"Ay, ay," answered Ailsie, with a bitter grin; "and Sir William Ashton promised me a bonnie red gown to the boot o' that—a stake, and a chain, and a tar-barrel, lass!—what think ye o' that for a pro-pine?—for being up early and doun late for fourscore nights and mair wi' his dwining daughter. But he may keep it for his ain lady, cum-mers."

"I hae heard a sough," said Annie Winnie, "as if Lady Ashton was nae canny body."

"D'ye see her yonder," said Dame Gourlay, "as she prances on her grey gelding out at the kirk-yard?—there's mair o' utter deevilry in that woman, as brave and fair-fashioned as she rides yonder, than in a' the Scotch witches that ever flew by moon-light ower North-Berwick Law."

"What's that ye say about witches, ye damned hags?" said Johnnie Mortsheugh; "are ye casting ye're cantraips in the very kirk-yard, to mischieve the bride and bridegroom? Get awa' hame, for if I tak my souple t'ye, I'll gar ye find the road faster than ye wad like."

"Eh! sirs!" answered Ailsie Gourlay; "bra' are we wi' our new black coat and our weel-pouthered head, as if we had never kenned hunger nor thirst oursells! and we'll be screwing up our bit fiddle, doubtless, in the ha' the night, amang a' the other elbo' jiggers for miles round—let's see if the pins haud, Johnnie—that's a', lad."

"I take ye a', gude people, to witness," said Mortsheugh, "that she threatens me wi' mischief, and forespeaks me. If onything but gude happens to me or my fiddle this night, I'll make it the blackest night's job she ever stirred in. I'll hae her before Presbytery and Synod—I'm half a minister mysel', now that I'm a bedral in an inhabited parish."

Although the mutual hatred betwixt these hags and the rest of mankind had steeled their hearts against all impressions of festivity, this was by no means the case with the multitude at large. The splendour of the bridal retinue—the gay dresses—the spirited horses—the blithesome appearance of the handsome women and gallant gentlemen assembled upon the occasion, had the usual effect upon the minds of the populace. The repeated shouts, of "Ashton and Bucklaw for ever!"—the discharge of pistols, guns, and muskettoons, to give what was called the bridal-shot, evinced the interest the people took in the occasion of the cavalcade, as they accompanied it upon their return to the castle. If there was here and there an elder peasant or his wife who sneered at the pomp of the upstart family, and remembered the days of the long-descended Ravenswoods, even they, attracted by the plentiful cheer which the castle that day afforded to rich and poor, held their way thither, and acknowledged, notwithstanding their prejudices, the influence of *l'Amphitrion où l'on dîne*.

Thus accompanied with the attendance both of rich and poor, Lucy returned to her father's house. Bucklaw used his privilege of riding next to the bride, but, new to such a situation, rather endeavoured to attract attention by the display of his person and horsemanship, than by any attempt to address her in private. They reached the castle in safety, amid a thousand joyous acclamations.

It is well known that the weddings of ancient days were celebrated with a festive publicity rejected by the delicacy of modern times. The marriage-guests upon the present occasion were regaled with a banquet of unbounded profusion, the relics of which, after the domestics had feasted in their turn, were distributed among the shouting crowd, with as many barrels of ale as made the hilarity without correspond to that within the castle. The gentlemen, according to the fashion of the times, indulged, for the most part, in deep draughts of the richest wines, while the ladies, prepared for the ball, which always closed a bridal entertainment, impatiently expected their arrival in the state gallery. At length the social party broke up at a late hour, and the gentlemen crowded into the saloon, and, enlivened by wine and the joyful occasion, laid aside their swords, and handed their impatient partners to the floor. The music already rung from the gallery, along the fretted roof of the ancient state apartment. According to strict etiquette, the bride ought to have opened the ball, but Lady Ashton, making an apology on account of her daughter's health, offered her own hand to Bucklaw as substitute for her daughter's.

But as Lady Ashton raised her head gracefully, expecting the strain at which she was to begin the dance, she was so much struck by an unexpected alteration in the ornaments of the apartment, that she was surprised into an exclamation,—"Who has dared to change the pictures?"

All looked up, and those who knew the usual state of the apartment, observed, with surprise, that the picture of Sir William Ashton's father was removed from its place, and in its stead that of old Sir Malise Ravenswood seemed to frown wrath and vengeance upon the party assembled below. The exchange must have been made while the apartments were empty, but had not been observed until the torches and lights in the sconces were kindled for the ball. The haughty and heated spirits of the gentlemen led them to demand an immediate enquiry into the cause of what they deemed an affront to their host and to themselves; but Lady Ashton, recovering herself, passed it over as the freak of a crazy wench who was maintained about the castle, and whose susceptible imagination had been observed to be much affected by the stories which Dame Gourlay delighted to tell concerning "the former family," so Lady Ashton named the Ravenswoods. The obnoxious picture was immediately removed, and the ball was opened by Lady Ashton with a grace and dignity which supplied the charms of youth, and almost verified the extravagant encomiums of the elder part of the company, who extolled her performance as far exceeding the dancing of the rising generation.

When Lady Ashton sat down, she was not surprised to find that her daughter had left the apartment, and she herself followed, eager to obviate any impression which might have been made upon her nerves by an incident so likely to affect them as the mysterious transposition of the portraits. Apparently she found her apprehensions groundless, for she returned in about an hour, and whispered the bridegroom, who extricated himself from the dancers, and vanished from the apartment. The instruments now played their loudest strains—the dancers pursued their exercise with all the enthusiasm inspired by youth, mirth, and high spirits, when a cry was heard so shrill and piercing, as at once to arrest the dance and the music. All stood motionless; but when the yell was again repeated, Colonel Ashton snatched a torch from the sconce, and demanding the key of the bridal-chamber from Henry, to whom, as bride's-man, it had been entrusted, rushed thither, followed by Sir William and Lady Ashton, and one or two others, near relations of the family. The bridal guests waited their return in stupified amazement.

Arrived at the door of the apartment, Colonel Ashton knocked and called, but received no answer, except stifled groans. He hesitated no longer to open the door of the apartment, in which he found opposition, from something which lay against it. When he had succeeded in opening it, the body of the bridegroom was found lying on the threshold of the bridal-chamber, and all around was flooded with blood. A cry of surprise and horror was raised by all present; and the company, excited by this new alarm, began to rush tumultuously towards the sleeping apartment. Colonel Ashton, first whispering to his mother,— "Search for her—she has murdered him!" drew his sword, planted himself in the passage, and declared he would suffer no man to pass excepting the clergyman, and a medical person present, related to the family. By their assistance, Bucklaw, who still breathed, was raised from the ground, and transported to another apartment, where his friends, full of suspicion and murmuring, assembled round him to learn the opinion of the surgeon.

In the mean while, Lady Ashton, her husband, and their assistants, in vain sought Lucy in the bridal bed and in the chamber. There was no private passage from the room, and they began to think that she must have thrown herself from the window, when one of the company, holding his torch lower than the rest, discovered something white in the corner of the great old-fashioned chimney of the apartment. Here they found the unfortunate girl, seated, or rather couched, like a hare upon its form—her head-gear dishevelled—her night-clothes torn and dabbled with blood—her eyes glazed, and her features convulsed into a wild paroxysm of insanity. When she saw herself discovered, she gibbered, made mouths, and pointed at them with her bloody fingers, with the frantic gestures of an exulting demoniac.

Female assistance was now hastily summoned; the unhappy bride was overpowered, not without the use of some force. As they carried her over the threshold, she looked down, and uttered the only articulate words that she had yet spoken, saying, with a sort of grinning exultation,—"So, you have ta'en up your bonnie bridegroom." She was by the shuddering assistants conveyed to another and more retired apartment, where she was secured as her situation required, and closely watched. The unutterable agony of the parents—the horror and confusion of all who were in the castle—the fury of contending passions between the friends of the different parties, passions augmented by previous intemperance, surpass description.

The surgeon was the first who obtained something like a patient hearing; he pronounced that the wound of Bucklaw, though severe and dangerous, was by no means fatal, but might readily be rendered so by disturbance and hasty removal. This silenced the numerous party of Bucklaw's friends, who had previously insisted that he should, at all rates, be transported from the castle to the nearest of their houses. They still demanded, however, that, in consideration of what had happened, four of their number should remain to watch over the sick-bed of their friend, and that a suitable number of their domestics, well armed, should also remain in the castle. This condition being acceded to on the part of Colonel Ashton and his father, the rest of the bridegroom's friends left the castle, notwithstanding the hour and the darkness of the night. The cares of the medical man were next employed in behalf of Miss Ashton, whom he pronounced to be in a very dangerous state. Farther medical assistance was immediately summoned. All night she remained delirious. On the morning, she fell into a state of absolute insensibility. The next evening, the physicians said, would be the crisis of her malady. It proved so, for although she awoke from her trance with some appearance of calmness, and suffered her night-clothes to be changed, or put in order, yet so soon as she put her hand to her neck, as if to search for the fatal blue ribbon, a tide of recollections seemed to rush upon her, which her mind and body were alike incapable of bearing. Convulsion followed convulsion, till they closed in death, without her being able to utter a word explanatory of the fatal scene.

The provincial judge of the district arrived the day after the young lady had expired, and executed, though with all possible delicacy to the afflicted family, the painful duty of enquiring into this fatal transaction. But there occurred nothing to explain the general hypothesis, that the bride, in a sudden fit of insanity, had stabbed the bridegroom at the threshold of the apartment. The fatal weapon was found in the chamber, smeared with blood. It was the same poniard which Henry should have worn upon the wedding-day, and which his unhappy sister had probably contrived to secrete upon the preceding evening, when it had been shewn to her among other articles of preparation for the wedding.

The friends of Bucklaw expected that upon his recovery he would throw some light upon this dark story, and eagerly pressed him with enquiries, which for some time he evaded under pretext of weakness. When, however, he had been transported to his own house, and was considered as in a state of convalescence, he assembled those persons, both male and female, who had considered themselves as entitled to press him on this subject, and returned them thanks for the interest they had expressed in his behalf, and their offers of adherence and support. "I wish you all," he said, "my friends, to understand, however, that I have neither story to tell, nor injuries to avenge. If a lady shall question me henceforward upon the incidents of that unhappy night, I shall remain silent, and in future consider her as desirous to break off her friendship with me. But if a gentleman shall ask me the same question, I shall regard the incivility as equivalent to an invitation to meet him in the Duke's Walk, and I expect that he will rule himself accordingly."

A declaration so decisive admitted no commentary; and it was soon after seen that Bucklaw had arisen from the bed of sickness a sadder and a wiser man than he had hitherto shewn himself. He dismissed Craigengelt from his society, but not without such a provision as, if well employed, might secure him against indigence, and against temptation.

Bucklaw afterwards went abroad, and never returned to Scotland; nor was he known ever to hint at the circumstances attending his fatal marriage. By many readers this may be deemed overstrained, romantic, and composed by the wild imagination of an author, desirous of gratifying the popular appetite for the horrible; but those who are read in the private family history of Scotland during the period in which the scene is laid, will readily discover, through the disguise of borrowed names and added incidents, the leading particulars of AN OWER TRUE TALE.

Chapter Eight

> Whose mind's so marbled, and his heart so hard,
> That would not, when this huge mishap was heard,
> To th' utmost note of sorrow set their song,
> To see a gallant, with so great a grace,
> So suddenly unthought on, so o'erthrown,
> And so to perish, in so poor a place,
> By too rash riding in a ground unknown!
> *Poem, in Nisbet's Heraldry*, Vol. II

WE HAVE anticipated the course of time to mention Bucklaw's recovery and fate, that we might not interrupt the detail of events which succeeded the funeral of the unfortunate Lucy Ashton. This melancholy ceremony was performed in the misty dawn of an autumnal morning, with as little attendance and ceremony as could possibly be dispensed with. A very few of the nearest relations attended her body to the same churchyard to which she had so lately been led as a bride, with as little free-will, perhaps, upon that former occasion, as could be now testified by her lifeless and passive remains. An aisle adjacent to the church had been fitted up by Sir William Ashton as a family cemetery; here, in a coffin bearing neither name nor date, were consigned to dust the remains of what was once lovely, beautiful, and innocent, though exasperated to phrenzy by a long tract of unremitting persecution.

While the mourners were busy in the vault, the three village hags, who, notwithstanding the unwonted earliness of the hour, had snuffed the carrion like vultures, were seated on the "through-stane," and engaged in their wonted unhallowed conference.

"Did not I say," said Dame Gourlay, "that the braw bridal would be followed by as braw a funeral?"

"I think," answered Dame Winnie, "there's little bravery at it; neither meat nor drink, and just a wheen silver tippences to the poor folk; it was little worth while to come sae far road for sae sma' profit, and us sae frail."

"Out, wretch!" replied Dame Gourlay, "can a' the dainties they could gi'e us be half sae sweet as this hour's vengeance? there they are that were capering on their prancing nags four days since, and they are now ganging as driegh and sober as oursells the day. They were a' glistening wi' gowd and silver; they are now as black as the crook; and Miss Lucy Ashton, that grudged when an honest woman came near her, a taed may sit on her coffin the day, and she never sconner when he croaks. And Lady Ashton has hell-fire burning in her breast by this time; and Sir William, wi' his gibbets, and his faggots, and his chains, how likes he the witcheries of his ain dwelling house?"

"And is it true then," mumbled the paralytic wretch, "that the bride was trailed out of her bed and up the chimlay by evil spirits, and that the bridegroom's face was wrung round ahint him?"

"Ye needna care wha did it, or how it was done," said Ailsie Gourlay; "but I'll uphaud it for nae sticket job, and that the lairds and ladies ken this day."

"And was it true," said Annie Winnie, "sin ye ken sae mickle about it, that the picture of auld Sir Malise Ravenswood came down on the ha' floor, and led out the brawl before them a'?"

"Na," said Ailsie; "but into the ha' came the picture—and I ken weel how it came there—to gi'e them a warning that pride would get a fa'—but there is as queer a ploy, cummers, as ony o' thae that's gaun on even now in the burial vault yonder—ye saw twal' mourners, wi' crape and cloke, gang down the steps pair and pair?"

"What should ail us to see them?" said the one old woman.

"I counted them," said the other, with the eagerness of a person to whom the spectacle had afforded too much interest to be viewed with indifference.

"But ye did not see," said Ailsie, exulting in her superior observation, "that there's a thirteenth amang them that they ken naething about; and, if auld freets say true, there's ane o' that company that'll no be lang for this world. But come awa, cummers; if we bide here, I'se warrant we get the wyte o' whatever ill comes of it, and that gude will come of it nane o' them need ever think to see."

And thus, croaking like the ravens when they anticipate pestilence, the ill-boding sybils withdrew from the church-yard.

In fact, the mourners, when the service of interment was ended, discovered that there was among them one more than the invited number, and the remark was communicated in whispers to each other. The suspicion fell upon a figure, which, muffled in the same deep mourning with the others, was reclined, almost in a state of insensibility, against one of the pillars of the sepulchral vault. The relatives of the Ashton family were expressing in whispers their surprise and displeasure at the intrusion, when they were interrupted by Colonel Ashton, who, in his father's absence, acted as principal mourner. "I know," he said in a whisper, "who this person is; he has, or shall soon have, as deep cause of mourning as ourselves—leave me to deal with him, and do not disturb the ceremony by unnecessary exposure." So saying, he separated himself from the group of his relations, and taking the unknown mourner by the cloak, he said to him, in a tone of suppressed emotion, "Follow me."

The stranger, as if starting from a trance at the sound of his voice, mechanically obeyed, and they ascended the broken ruinous stair which led from the sepulchre into the church-yard. The other mourners followed, but remained grouped together at the door of the vault, watching with anxiety the motions of Colonel Ashton and the stranger, who now appeared to be in close conference beneath the shade of a yew-tree, in the most remote part of the burial ground.

To this sequestered spot Colonel Ashton had guided the stranger, and then turning round, addressed him in a stern and composed tone —"I cannot doubt that I speak to the Master of Ravenswood." No answer was returned. "I cannot doubt," resumed the Colonel, trembling with rising passion, "that I speak to the murderer of my sister?"

"You have named me but too truly," said Ravenswood, in a hollow and tremulous voice.

"If you repent what you have done," said the Colonel, "may your penitence avail you before God; with me it shall serve you nothing. Here," he said, giving a paper, "is the measure of my sword, and a memorandum of the time and place of meeting. Sun-rise to-morrow morning, on the Links to the east of Wolfshope."

The Master of Ravenswood held the paper in his hand, and seemed irresolute. At length he spoke—"Do not," he said, "urge to farther desperation a wretch who is already desperate. Enjoy your life while you can, and let me seek my death from another."

"That you never, never shall," said Ashton. "You shall die by my hand, or you shall complete the ruin of my family by taking my life. If you refuse me my open challenge, there is no advantage I will not take of you, no indignity with which I will not load you, until the very name of Ravenswood shall be the sign of every thing that is dishonourable, as it is already of all that is villainous."

"That it shall never be," said Ravenswood, fiercely; "if I am the last who shall bear it, I owe it to those who once owned it, that the name shall be extinguished without infamy. I accept your challenge, time, and place of meeting. We meet, I presume, alone?"

"Alone we meet," said Colonel Ashton, "and alone will the survivor of us return from that place of rendezvous."

"Then God have mercy on the soul of him who falls!" said Ravenswood.

"So be it!" said Colonel Ashton; "so far can my charity reach even for the man I hate most deadly, and with the deepest reason. Now, break off, for we shall be interrupted. The links by the sea-shore to the east of Wolfshope—the hour sun-rise—our swords our only weapons."

"Enough," said the Master, "I will not fail you."

They separated; Colonel Ashton joining the rest of the mourners, and the Master of Ravenswood taking his horse, which was tied to a tree behind the church. Colonel Ashton returned to the castle with the funeral guests, but found a pretext for detaching himself from them in the evening, when, changing his dress to a riding habit, he rode to Wolfshope that night, and took up his abode in the little inn, in order that he might be ready for his rendezvous in the morning.

It is not known how the Master of Ravenswood disposed of the rest of that unhappy day. Late at night, however, he arrived at Wolfscrag, and aroused his old domestic, Caleb Balderstone, who had ceased to expect his return. Confused and flying rumours of the late tragical death of Miss Ashton, and of its mysterious cause, had already reached the old man, who was filled with the utmost anxiety, on account of the probable effect these events might produce upon the mind of his master.

The conduct of Ravenswood had nothing to alleviate his apprehensions. To the Butler's trembling entreaties, that he would take some refreshment, he at first returned no answer, and then suddenly and fiercely demanding wine, he drank, contrary to his habits, a very large draught. Seeing that his master would eat nothing, the old man affectionately entreated that he would permit him to light him to his chamber. It was not until the request was three or four times repeated, that

Ravenswood made a mute sign of compliance. But when Balderstone conducted him to an apartment which had been comfortably fitted up, and which, since his return, he had usually occupied, Ravenswood stopped short on the threshold.

"Not here," said he, sternly; "show me the room in which my father died. The room in which SHE slept the night they were at the castle."

"Who, sir?" said Caleb, too terrified to preserve his presence of mind.

"*She*, Lucy Ashton!—would you kill me, old man, by forcing me to repeat her name?"

Caleb would have said something of the disrepair of the chamber, but was silenced by the irritable impatience which was expressed in his master's countenance; he lighted the way trembling and in silence, placed the lamp on the table of the deserted room, and was about to attempt some arrangement of the bed, when his master bid him begone in a tone that admitted of no delay. The old man retired, not to rest, but to prayer; and from time to time crept to the door of the apartment, in order to find out whether Ravenswood had gone to repose. His measured heavy step upon the floor was only interrupted by deep groans; and the repeated stamps of the heel of his heavy boot, intimated too clearly, that the wretched inmate was abandoning himself at such moments to paroxysms of uncontrouled agony. The old man thought that the morning, for which he longed, would never have dawned; but time, whose course rolls on with equal current, however it may seem more rapid or more slow to mortal apprehension, brought the dawn at last, and spread a ruddy light on the broad verge of the glistening ocean. It was early in November, and the weather was serene for the season of the year. But an easterly wind had prevailed during the night, and the advancing tide rolled nearer than usual to the foot of the crags on which the castle was founded.

With the first peep of light, Caleb Balderstone again resorted to the door of Ravenswood's sleeping apartment, through a chink of which he observed him engaged in measuring the length of two or three swords which lay in a closet adjoining to the apartment. He muttered to himself, as he selected one of these weapons, "It is shorter—let him have this advantage as he has every other."

Caleb Balderstone knew too well, from what he witnessed, upon what enterprise his master was bound, and how vain all interference on his part must necessarily prove. He had but time to retreat from the door, so nearly was he surprised by his master suddenly coming out, and descending to the stables. The faithful domestic followed, and from the dishevelled appearance of his master's dress, and his ghastly looks, was confirmed in his conjecture that he had passed the night without sleep or repose. He found him busily engaged in saddling his horse, a service from which Caleb, though with faultering voice and trembling hands, offered to relieve him. Ravenswood rejected his assistance by a mute sign, and having led the animal into the court, was just about to mount him, when the old domestic's fear giving way to the strong attachment which was the principal passion of his mind, he flung himself suddenly at Ravenswood's feet, and clasped his knees, while he exclaimed, "Oh, sir! oh, master! kill me if you will, but do not go out on this dreadful errand. O! my dear master, wait but this day— the Marquis of A—— comes to-morrow, and a' will be remedied."

"You have no longer a master, Caleb," said Ravenswood, endeavouring to extricate himself; "why, old man, would you cling to a falling tower?"

"But I *have* a master," cried Caleb, still holding him fast, "while the heir of Ravenswood breathes—I am but a servant; but I was your father's—your grandfather's—I was born for the family—I have lived for them—I would die for them—Stay but at home, and all will be well!"

"Well? fool! well?" said Ravenswood; "vain old man, nothing hereafter in life will be well with me, and happiest is the hour that shall soonest close it."

So saying, he extricated himself from the old man's hold, threw himself on his horse, and rode out at the gate; but instantly turning back, he threw towards Caleb, who hastened to meet him, a heavy purse of gold.

"Caleb," he said, with a ghastly smile, "I make you my executor;" and again turning his bridle, he resumed his course down the hill.

The gold fell unheeded on the pavement, for the old man ran to observe the course which was taken by his master, who turned to the left down a small and broken path, which gained the sea-shore through a cleft in the rock, and led to a sort of cove, where, in former times, the boats of the castle were wont to be moored. Observing him take this course, Caleb hastened to the eastern battlement, which commanded the prospect of the whole sands, very near as far as the village of Wolfshope. He could easily see his master riding in that direction, as fast as the horse could carry him. The prophecy at once rushed on Balderstone's mind, that the Lord of Ravenswood should perish on the Kelpie's Flow, which lay half way betwixt the tower and the links or sand-knolls, to the north-east of Wolfshope. He saw him accordingly reach the fatal spot, but he never saw him pass further.

Colonel Ashton, frantic for revenge, was already in the field, pacing the turf with eagerness, and looking with impatience towards the tower for the arrival of his antagonist. The sun had now risen, and shewed its broad disk above the eastern sea, so that he could easily discern the horseman who rode towards him with a speed which argued impatience equal to his own. At once the figure became invisible, as if it had melted into the air. He rubbed his eyes, as if he had witnessed an apparition, and then hastened to the spot, near which he was met by Balderstone, who came from the opposite direction. No trace whatever of horse or rider could be discerned; it only appeared, that the late winds and high tides had greatly extended the usual bounds of the quicksand, and that the unfortunate horseman, as appeared from the hoof-tracks, in his precipitate haste, had not attended to keep on the firm sands on the foot of the rock, but had taken the shortest and most dangerous course. One only vestige of his fate appeared. A large sable feather had been detached from his hat, and the rippling waves of the rising tide wafted it to Caleb's feet. The old man took it up, dried it, and placed it in his bosom.

The inhabitants of Wolfshope were now alarmed, and crowded to the place, some on shore, and some in boats, but their searches availed nothing. The tenacious depths of the quicksand, as is usual in such cases, retained their prey.

Our tale draws to a conclusion. The Marquis of A——, alarmed at the frightful reports that were current, and anxious for his kinsman's safety, arrived on the subsequent day to mourn his loss; and, after renewing in vain a search for the body, returned to forget what had happened amid the bustle of politics and state affairs.

Not so Caleb Balderstone. If worldly profit could have consoled the old man, his age was better provided for than his earlier life had ever been; but life had lost to him its salt and its savour. His whole course of ideas, his feelings, whether of pride or of apprehension, of pleasure or of pain, had all arisen from his close connection with the family which was now extinguished. He held up his head no longer—forsook all his usual haunts and occupations, and seemed only to find pleasure in mopeing about those apartments in the old castle, which the Master of Ravenswood had last inhabited. He ate without refreshment, and slumbered without repose; and, with a fidelity sometimes displayed by the canine race, but seldom by human beings, he pined and died within a year after the catastrophe which we have narrated.

The family of Ashton did not long survive that of Ravenswood. Sir William Ashton survived his eldest son, the Colonel, who was slain in a duel in Flanders; and Henry, by whom he was succeeded, died unmarried. Lady Ashton lived to the verge of extreme old age, the only survivor of the group of unhappy persons, whose misfortunes were in a great degree owing to her implacability. That she might internally feel compunction, and reconcile herself with heaven whom she had offended, we will not, and we dare not deny; but to those around her, she did not evince the slightest symptom either of repentance or remorse. In all external appearance, she bore the same bold, haughty, unbending character, which she had displayed before these unhappy events. A splendid marble monument records her name, titles, and virtues, while her victims remain undistinguished by tomb or epitaph.

THE END

APPENDIX

SCOTT'S 'MAGNUM' INTRODUCTION TO
THE BRIDE OF LAMMERMOOR
from *The Waverley Novels*, 48 vols (Edinburgh, 1829–33), 13.237–55

The author, on a former occasion,* declined giving the real source from which he drew the tragic subject of this history, because, though occurring at a distant period, it might possibly be unpleasing to the feelings of the descendants of the parties. But as he finds an account of the circumstances given in the Notes to Law's Memorials,† by his ingenious friend Charles Kirkpatrick Sharpe, Esq., and also indicated in his reprint of the Rev. Mr Symson's poems, appended to the Description of Galloway, as the original of the Bride of Lammermoor, the author feels himself now at liberty to tell the tale as he had it from connexions of his own, who lived very near the period, and were closely related to the family of the Bride.

It is well known that the family of Dalrymple, which has produced, within the space of two centuries, as many men of talent, civil and military, and of literary, political, and professional eminence, as any house in Scotland, first rose into distinction in the person of James Dalrymple, one of the most eminent lawyers that ever lived, though the labours of his powerful mind were unhappily exercised on a subject so limited as Scottish Jurisprudence, on which he has composed an admirable work.

He married Margaret, daughter to Ross of Balniel, with whom he obtained a considerable estate. She was an able, politic, and high-minded woman, so successful in what she undertook, that the vulgar, no way partial to her husband or her family, imputed her success to necromancy. According to the popular belief, this Dame Margaret purchased the temporal prosperity of her family from the Master whom she served, under a singular condition, which is thus narrated by the historian of her grandson, the great Earl of Stair. 'She lived to a great age, and at her death desired that she might not be put under ground, but that her coffin should be placed upright on one end of it, promising, that while she remained in that situation, the Dalrymples

---

* See Introduction to the Chronicles of the Canongate.
† Law's Memorials, p. 226.

should continue in prosperity. What was the old lady's motive for such a request, or whether she really made such a promise, I cannot take upon me to determine; but it is certain her coffin stands upright in the aisle of the church of Kirkliston, the burial place of the family.'* The talents of this accomplished race were sufficient to have accounted for the dignities which many members of the family attained, without any supernatural assistance. But their extraordinary prosperity was attended by some equally singular family misfortunes, of which that which befell their eldest daughter was at once unaccountable and melancholy.

Miss Janet Dalrymple, daughter of the first Lord Stair, and Dame Margaret Ross, had engaged herself without the knowledge of her parents to the Lord Rutherford, who was not, acceptable to them either on account of his political principles, or his want of fortune. The young couple broke a piece of gold together, and pledged their troth in the most solemn manner; and it is said the young lady imprecated dreadful evils on herself should she break her plighted faith. Shortly after, a suitor who was favoured by Lord Stair, and still more so by his lady, paid his addresses to Miss Dalrymple. The young lady refused the proposal, and being pressed on the subject, confessed her secret engagement. Lady Stair, a woman accustomed to universal submission, (for even her husband did not dare to contradict her,) treated this objection as a trifle, and insisted upon her daughter yielding her consent to marry the new suitor, David Dunbar, son and heir to David Dunbar of Baldoon, in Wigtonshire. The first lover, a man of very high spirit, then interferred by letter, and insisted on the right he had acquired by his troth plighted with the young lady. Lady Stair sent him for answer, that her daughter, sensible of her undutiful behaviour in entering into a contract unsanctioned by her parents, had retracted her unlawful vow, and now refused to fulfil her engagement with him.

The lover, in return, declined positively to receive such an answer from any one but his mistress in person; and as she had to deal with a man who was both of a most determined character, and of too high condition to be trifled with, Lady Stair was obliged to consent to an interview between Lord Rutherford and her daughter. But she took care to be present in person, and argued the point with the disappointed and incensed lover with pertinacity equal to his own. She particularly insisted on the Levitical law, which declares, that a woman shall be free of a vow which her parents dissent from. This is the passage of Scripture she founded on:-

* Memoirs of John Earl of Stair, by an Impartial Hand. London, printed for C. Cobbet, p. 7.

'If a man vow a vow unto the Lord, or swear an oath to bind his soul with a bond; he shall not break his word, he shall do according to all that proceedeth out of his mouth.

'If a woman also vow a vow unto the Lord, and bind herself by a bond, being in her father's house in her youth;

'And her father hear her vow, and her bond wherewith she hath bound her soul, and her father shall hold his peace at her: then all her vows shall stand, and every bond wherewith she hath bound her soul shall stand.

'But if her father disallow her in the day that he heareth; not any of her vows, or of her bonds wherewith she hath bound her soul, shall stand: and the Lord shall forgive her, because her father disallowed her.' – Numbers, xxx. 2, 3, 4, 5.

While the mother insisted on these topics, the lover in vain conjured the daughter to declare her own opinion and feelings. She remained totally overwhelmed, as it seemed, – mute, pale, and motionless as a statue. Only at her mother's command, sternly uttered, she summoned strength enough to restore to her plighted suitor the piece of broken gold, which was the emblem of her troth. On this he burst forth into a tremendous passion, took leave of the mother with maledictions, and as he left the apartment, turned back to say to his weak, if not fickle mistress, 'For you, madam, you will be a world's wonder;' a phrase by which some remarkable degree of calamity is usually implied. He went abroad, and returned not again. If the last Lord Rutherford was the unfortunate party, he must have been the third who bore that title, and who died in 1685.

The marriage betwixt Janet Dalrymple and David Dunbar of Baldoon now went forward, the bride showing no repugnance, but being absolutely passive in every thing her mother commanded or advised. On the day of the marriage, which, as was then usual, was celebrated by a great assemblage of friends and relations, she was the same – sad, silent, and resigned, as it seemed, to her destiny. A lady, very nearly connected with the family, told the author that she had conversed on the subject with one of the brothers of the bride, a mere lad at the time, who had ridden before his sister to church. He said her hand, which lay on his as she held her arm round his waist, was as cold and damp as marble. But, full of his new dress, and the part he acted in the procession, the circumstance, which he long afterwards remembered with bitter sorrow and compunction, made no impression on him at the time.

The bridal feast was followed by dancing; the bride and bridegroom retired as usual, when of a sudden the most wild and piercing cries were heard from the nuptial chamber. It was then the custom, to prevent any coarse pleasantry which old times perhaps admitted, that the key of the nuptial chamber should be intrusted to the brideman. He was called upon, but refused at first to give it up, till the shrieks became so hideous that he was compelled to hasten with others to learn the cause. On opening the door, they found the bridegroom lying across the threshold, dreadfully wounded, and streaming with blood. The bride was then sought for: She was found in the corner of the large chimney, having no covering save her shift, and that dabbed in gore. There she sat grinning at them, mopping and mowing, as I heard the expression used; in a word, absolutely insane. The only words she spoke were, "Tak up your bonny bridegroom." She survived this horrible scene little more than a fortnight, having been married on the 24th of August, and dying on the 12th of September, 1669.

The unfortunate Baldoon recovered from his wounds, but sternly prohibited all enquiries respecting the manner in which he had received them. If a lady, he said, asked him any question upon the subject, he would neither answer her nor speak to her again while he lived; if a gentleman, he would consider it as a mortal affront, and demand satisfaction as having received such. He did not very long survive the dreadful catastrophe, having met with a fatal injury by a fall from his horse, as he rode between Leith and Holyrood-house, of which he died the next day, 28th March 1682. Thus a few years removed all the principal actors in this frightful tragedy.

Various reports went abroad on this mysterious affair, many of them very inaccurate, though they could hardly be said to be exaggerated. It was difficult at that time to become acquainted with the history of a Scottish family above the lower rank; and strange things sometimes took place there, into which even the law did not scrupulously enquire.

The credulous Mr Law says, generally, that the Lord President Stair had a daughter, who 'being married, the night she was *bride in*, [that is, bedded bride,] was taken from her bridegroom and *harled* [dragged] through the house, (by spirits, we are given to understand,) and soon afterwards died. Another daughter,' he says, 'was possessed by an evil spirit.'

My friend, Mr Sharpe, gives another edition of the tale. According to his information, it was the bridegroom who wounded the bride. The marriage, according to this account, had been against her mother's inclination, who had given her consent in these ominous words: 'You may marry him, but soon shall you repent it.'

I find still another account darkly insinuated in some highly scurrilous and abusive verses, of which I have an original copy. They are docketed as being written 'Upon the late Viscount Stair and his family, by Sir William Hamilton of Whitelaw. The marginals by William Dunlop, writer in Edinburgh, a son of the Laird of Househill, and nephew to the said Sir William Hamilton.' There was a bitter and personal quarrel and rivalry betwixt the author of this libel, a name which it richly deserves, and Lord President Stair; and the lampoon, which is written with much more malice than art, bears the following motto:-

'Stair's neck, mind, wife, sons, grandson, and the rest,
Are wry, false, witch, pests, parricide, possessed.'

This malignant satirist, who calls up all the misfortunes of the family, does not forget the fatal bridal of Baldoon. He seems, though his verses are as obscure as unpoetical, to intimate, that the violence done to the bridegroom was by the intervention of the foul fiend to whom the young lady had resigned herself, in case she should 'break her contract with her first lover. His hypothesis is inconsistent with the account given in the note upon Law's Memorials, but easily reconcilable to the family tradition.

'In al Stair's offspring we no difference know,
They doe the females as the males bestow;
So he of's daughter's marriage gave the ward,
Like a true vassal, to Glenuce's Laird;
He knew what she did to her suitor plight,
If she her faith to Rutherford should slight,
Which, like his own, for greed he broke outright.
Nick did Baldoon's posterior right deride,
And, as first substitute, did seize the bride;
Whate'er he to his mistress did or said,
He threw the bridegroom from the nuptial bed,
Into the chimney did so his rival maul,
His bruised bones ne'er were cured but by the fall.'*

One of the marginal notes ascribed to William Dunlop, applies to the above lines. 'She had betrothed herself to Lord Rutherford under horrid imprecations, and afterwards married Baldoon, his nevoy, and her mother was the cause of her breach of faith.'

The same tragedy is alluded to in the following couplet and note:-

'What train of curses that base brood pursues,
When the young nephew weds old uncle's spouse.'

The note on the word *uncle* explains it as meaning 'Rutherfoord, who should have married the Lady Baldoon, was Baldoon's uncle.' The poetry of this satire on Lord Stair and his family was, as already

* The fall from his horse, by which he was killed.

noticed, written by Sir William Hamilton of Whitelaw, a rival of Lord
Stair for the situation of President of the Court of Session; a person
much inferior to that great lawyer in talents, and equally ill-treated by
the calumny or just satire of his contemporaries, as an unjust and
partial judge. Some of the notes are by that curious and laborious
antiquary Robert Milne, who, as a virulent Jacobite, willingly lent a
hand to blacken the family of Stair.*

Another poet of the period, with a very different purpose, has left
an elegy, in which he darkly hints at and bemoans the fate of the
ill-starred young person, whose very uncommon calamity Whitelaw,
Dunlop, and Milne, thought a fitting subject for buffoonery and
ribaldry. This bard of milder mood was Andrew Symson, before the
Revolution minister of Kirkinner, in Galloway, and after his expulsion
as an Episcopalian, following the humble occupation of a printer in
Edinburgh. He furnished the family of Baldoon, with which he appears
to have been intimate, with an elegy on the tragic event in their family.
In this piece he treats the mournful occasion of the bride's death with
mysterious solemnity.

The verses bear this title – 'On the unexpected death of the virtuous
Lady Mrs Janet Dalrymple, Lady Baldoon, younger,' and afford us
the precise dates of the catastrophe, which could not otherwise have
been easily ascertained. 'Nupta August 12. Domum Ducta August 24.
Obiit September 12. Sepult. September 30, 1669.' The form of the
elegy is a dialogue betwixt a passenger and a domestic servant. The
first, recollecting that he had passed that way lately, and seen all around
enlivened by the appearance of mirth and festivity, is desirous to know
what had changed so gay a scene into mourning. We preserve the reply
of the servant as a specimen of Mr Symon's verses, which are not of
the first quality:-

───── 'Sir, 'tis truth you've told,
We did enjoy great mirth; but now, ah me!
Our joyful song's turn'd to an elegie.
A virtuous lady, not long since a bride,
Was to a hopeful plant by marriage tied,
And brought home hither. We did all rejoice,
Even for her sake. But presently our voice
Was turn'd to mourning for that little time
That she'd enjoy: She waned in her prime,

* I have compared the satire, which occurs in the first volume of the curious little
collection called a Book of Scottish Pasquils, 1827, with that which has a more full text,
and more extended notes, and which is in my own possession, by gift of Thomas
Thomson, Esq. Register-Depute. In the second Book of Pasquils, p. 72, is a most abusive
epitaph on Sir James Hamilton of Whitelaw.

> For Atropos, with her impartial knife,
> Soon cut her thread, and therewithal her life;
> And for the time we may it well remember,
> It being in unfortunate September;
> Where we must leave her till the resurrection,
> 'Tis then the Saints enjoy their full perfection.'*

Mr Symson also poured forth his elegiac strains upon the fate of the widowed bridegroom, on which subject, after a long and querulous effusion, the poet arrives at the sound conclusion, that if Baldoon had walked on foot, which it seems was his general custom, he would have escaped perishing by a fall from horseback. As the work in which it occurs is so scarce as almost to be unique, and as it gives us the most full account of one of the actors in this tragic tale which we have rehearsed, we will, at the risk of being tedious, insert some short specimens of Mr Symson's composition. It is entitled,—

'A Funeral Elegie, occasioned by the sad and much lamented death of that worthily respected, and very much accomplished gentleman, David Dunbar, younger of Baldoon, only son and apparent heir to the right worshipful Sir David Dunbar of Baldoon, Knight Baronet. He departed this life on March 28, 1682, having received a bruise by a fall, as he was riding the day preceding betwixt Leith and Holy-Rood-House; and was honourably interred in the Abbey church of Holy-Rood-House, on April 4, 1682.'

> 'Men might, and very justly too, conclude
> Me guilty of the worst ingratitude,
> Should I be silent, or should I forbear
> At this sad accident to shed a tear;
> A tear! said I? ah! that's a petit thing,
> A very lean, slight, slender offering,
> Too mean, I'me sure, for me, wherewith t'attend
> The unexpected funeral of my friend—
> A glass of briny tears charged up to th' brim,
> Would be too few for me to shed for him.'

The poet proceeds to state his intimacy with the deceased, and the constancy of the young man's attendance on public worship, which was regular, and has such effect upon two or three others that were influenced by his example,

---

* This elegy is reprinted in the appendix to a topographical work by the same author, entitled 'A Large Description of Galloway, by Andrew Symson, Minister of Kirkinner,' 8vo, Taits, Edinburgh, 1823. The reverend gentleman's elegies are extremely rare, nor did the author ever see a copy but his own, which is bound up with the Tripatriarchicon, a religious poem from the Biblical History, by the same author.

'So that my Muse 'gainst Priscian avers,
He, only he, *were* my parishioners;
Yes, and my only hearers.'

He then describes the deceased in person and manners, from which it
appears that more accomplishments were expected in the composition
of a fine gentleman in ancient than modern times:

'His body, though not very large or tall,
Was sprightly, active, yea and strong withal.
His constitution was, if right I've guess'd,
Blood mixt with choler, said to be the best.
In's gesture, converse, speech, discourse, attire,
He practis'd that which wise men still admire,
Commend, and recommend. What's that? you'l say;
'Tis this: He ever choos'd the middle way
'Twixt both th' extremes. Amost in ev'ry thing
He did the like, 'tis worth our noticing:
Sparing, yet not a niggard; liberal,
And yet not lavish or a prodigal,
As knowing when to spend and when to spare;
And that's a lesson which not many are
Acquainted with. He bashful was, yet daring
When he saw cause, and yet therein but sparing;
Familiar, yet not common, for he knew
To condescend, and keep his distance too.
He us'd, and that most commonly, to go
On foot; I wish that he had still done so.
Th' affairs of court were unto him well known:
And yet mean while he slighted not his own.
He knew full well how to behave at court,
And yet but seldome did thereto resort;
But lov'd the country life, choos'd to inure
Himself to past'rage and agriculture;
Proving, improving, ditching, trenching, draining,
Viewing, reviewing, and by those means gaining;
Planting, transplanting, levelling, erecting
Walls, chambers, houses, terraces; projecting
Now this, now that device, this draught, that measure,
That might advance his profit with his pleasure.
Quick in his bargains, honest in commerce,
Just in his dealings, being much averse
From quirks of law, still ready to refer
His cause t' an honest country arbiter.

He was acquainted with cosmography,
Arithmetic, and modern history;
With architecture and such arts as these,
Which I may call specifick sciences
Fit for a gentleman; and surely he
That knows them not, at least in some degree,
May brook the title, but he wants the thing,
Is but a shadow scarce worth noticing.
He learned the French, be t' spoken to his praise,
In very little more than forty days.'

Then comes the full burst of woe, in which, instead of saying much himself, the poet informs us what the ancients would have said on such an occasion:

'A heathen poet, at the news, no doubt,
Would have exclaimed, and furiously cry'd out
Against the fates, the destinies and starrs,
What! this the effect of planetarie warrs!
We might have seen him rage and rave, yea worse,
'Tis very like we might have heard him curse
The year, the month, the day, the hour, the place,
The company, the wager, and the race;
Decry all recreations, with the names
Of Isthmian, Pythian, and Olympick games;
Exclaim against them all both old and new,
Both the Nemæan and the Lethæan too:
Adjudge all persons under highest pain,
Always to walk on foot, and then again
Order all horses to be hough'd, that we
Might never more the like adventure see.'

Supposing our readers have had enough of Mr Sympson's verses, and finding nothing more in his poem worthy of transcription, we return to the tragic story.

It is needless to point out to the intelligent reader, that the witchcraft of the mother consisted only in the ascendancy of a powerful mind over a weak and melancholy one, and that the harshness with which she exercised her superiority in a case of delicacy, had driven her daughter first to despair, then to frenzy. Accordingly, the author has endeavoured to explain the tragic tale on this principle. Whatever resemblance Lady Ashton may be supposed to possess to the celebrated Dame Margaret Ross, the reader must not suppose that there was any idea of tracing the portrait of the first Lord Viscount Stair in the tricky and mean-spirited Sir William Ashton. Lord Stair, whatever might be his moral qualities, was certainly one of the first statesmen and lawyers of his age.

The imaginary castle of Wolf's Crag has been identified by some lover of locality with that of Fast Castle. The author is not competent to judge of the resemblance betwixt the real and imaginary scene, having never seen Fast Castle except from the sea. But fortalices of this description are found occupying, like ospreys' nests, projecting rocks, or promontories, in many parts of the eastern coast of Scotland, and the position of Fast Castle seems certainly to resemble that of Wolf's Crag as much as any other, while its vicinity to the mountain ridge of Lammermoor, renders the assimilation a probable one.

We have only to add, that the death of the unfortunate bridegroom by a fall from horseback, has been in the novel transferred to the no less unfortunate lover.

HISTORICAL NOTE

The Bride of Lammermoor transfers a story founded on a series of events which actually took place in 1669 to an historical setting shortly before the Union of Scotland and England in 1707.

The story was told, in one of its several versions, to Scott as a boy by his maternal great-aunt Margaret Swinton, who died in 1780, and it was also one of his mother's favourite tales.[1] He follows this oral narrative closely in his novel, with Lucy Ashton deriving from Janet Dalrymple, daughter of the eminent lawyer James Dalrymple (1619–95), first Viscount Stair from 1690. The Stairs of Kyle, Ayrshire, were a minor landowning family sympathetic to the Covenanting cause, who rose to prominence, like the Ashtons, during the Civil War. Janet had become engaged secretly to the third Lord Rutherfurd:[2] her parents' favoured suitor was Rutherfurd's nephew David Dunbar, of Baldoon, Wigtownshire. Scott's retelling of his source story in the Magnum Introduction (see Appendix) suggests that many of the most striking features of his own narrative derive from it.[3] Although he denied in that Introduction that he had modelled Sir William Ashton on Viscount Stair, both the Viscount and his son John were especially noted for brilliant pliability in an age of trimming.[4]

As well as the oral version heard in childhood, Scott was familiar with a number of other main versions of the story. One of these, a brief allusion in Robert Law's *Memorialls*, which Scott's friend Charles Kirkpatrick Sharpe published from manuscript in 1818, introduces a diabolical element into the story: 'The president had a daughter before this time, being married, the night she was bride in, she was taken out from her bridegroom and harled through the house, and afterward died'. Sharpe has a long note to the passage with variant traditions, which include the imputation of witchcraft to Lady Stair and a mention of 'her own violent turn towards conventicles'.[5] Accusations of diabolism are particularly fierce in a lampoon by Sir William Hamilton of Whitelaw, 'Satyre on the Familie of Stairs', which Scott himself intended to publish in the late 1820s: he was anticipated by James Maidment, who included it in his *A Book of Scottish Pasquils &c.* in 1827. Coleman Parsons has suggested that Scott's characterisation of the Ashtons was influenced by their portrayal in this lampoon, 'vacillating and two-faced' and 'domineering' respectively.[6] The Stair family also seem to have suggested (again by way of Margaret Swinton's narration) the charge against Ailsie Gourlay (241.9–17); furthermore, it is worthy of note that Eleanor, Viscountess Primrose (d. 1759), who married John, second Earl of Stair, Janet Dalrymple's nephew, is said to have seen her unfaithful first husband, then abroad, in a magic mirror.[7]

As Claire Lamont has shown,[8] Scott's chief modification of his source story, in which events move rapidly forward, is his introduction of the hiatus of Ravenswood's year abroad between the second and third volumes, during which intolerable psychological pressure is put on Lucy. Indeed, if the novel's time-scheme is to be analysed rigidly, this foreign assignment must have been preceded by some nine months in Edinburgh at the end of the second volume. The first two volumes occur in November and perhaps early December; after the hiatus the catastrophe centres on St Jude's day, 28 October. In the present text, following the first edition, the action takes place at some period between the accession of Queen Anne in March 1702 and the Union of May 1707. If the matter is pressed, the two years from November 1703 to October 1705 might be suggested. These encompass the brief Tory ascendancy referred to at 219.35–220.15, lasting from May 1704 with decreasing confidence for a year. A number of references to events shortly before 1702 or shortly after 1707 present no insuperable problems. Several utterances by Caleb, the villagers, and Sir William Ashton which might be taken to imply that William is still on the throne are (with one exception) certainly of a more general proverbial or automatic cast.[9] Caleb's complaint (140.8–10) about excise laws prohibiting the import of brandy may seem to anticipate post-Union 1707 legislation, but a similar law was in operation from 1701 to 1703.[10] The narrator's references to the ascendant Tories as the 'Whimsicals' (220.4), a term first recorded in 1714, and to Law's Scheme of 1717 (165.33), may seem authorial slips, but are better seen as adjustments of historical facts which bring period events within the scope of the fiction. In the former case it seems clear that the focus is earlier than 1714 because of the reference to 'Harley, afterwards Earl of Oxford': Harley, leader of the Tory compromisers in the interests of powerbroking, was created Earl in 1711.[11] Lady Ashton's hope that her son Sholto may take his place in the British Parliament (173.38–40) can reasonably be interpreted as a shrewd anticipation of the forthcoming Union.

Legally, probably the most significant feature of the pre-Union setting for the plot of the novel is the existence of a provision in the Claim of Right of 1689 for Scottish 'Subjects to protest for Remeed of Law to the King and Parliament, against sentences pronounced by the Lords of Session', together with a debate about the extent and applicability of this provision. Politically the period was immensely complex, with much jostling for position and shifting of allegiances: the novel alludes in particular to the ever-present threat of Jacobite uprising with French support, and to the absence of responsible government in a Scotland under delegated authority. In this environment the devious Sir William Ashton is able to flourish, for a while.

One of the novel's strongest links with actual history is in the character of the Marquis of A——, based on John Murray (1660–1724), second Marquis and first Duke of Atholl, who succeeded his father of the same name (1631–1703), as second Earl and first Marquis in 1703, when the dukedom was created. The father had led the Scottish Jacobites during the 1689 Revolution, but thereafter his opportunism led him to play an ambiguous, though powerful, role.[12] The son began as a supporter of King William, but by 1703 he was tending to Jacobitism and supported the increasingly powerful Tories in the years following. Apart from his caution (179.40–41), Scott's Marquis bears a close resemblance to his historical model.[13]

In a fine paragraph, James Anderson draws attention to the importance of the Gowrie Conspiracy as a pervasive influence on the Bride:

> The story ... is derived ... from a tragedy in the private life of a family of rank in the later 17th Century. But the novel has a basis in more general history as well: it is clearly connected with the Gowrie Conspiracy of 1600, to which Scott refers frequently in his historical writing—*Somers, Secret History, Provincial Antiquities, Grandfather*, and the "Lardner" *History*—so often in fact, that it would be surprising if the case produced no echo in the novels. King James VI, having exhausted his horse in the chase, visited, at his house in Perth, the Earl of Gowrie, whose father had been executed by the King's warrant; Sir William Ashton, having seen Ravenswood exhaust his horse in the chase, visited, at his house of Wolf's Crag, the Master of Ravenswood, whose father had been ruined and driven to his death by Ashton's chicanery. Logan of Restalrig, one of the conspirators, proposed to kidnap the King at Gowrie House and imprison him in his fortress of Fast Castle, on the Berwickshire coast: and behold, Wolf's Crag, though Scott would not admit its identification with Fast Castle, cannot in fact be anything else. The secret chamber, said Caleb, had not been used since the time of the Gowrie Conspiracy. The name of one of the lesser men in the conspiracy— [George] Craigengelt, the Gowrie cook, who, like Caleb, sent out for a fowl for the unexpected guest's dinner—is given to a petty intriguer in the novel. In a letter to Gowrie, Logan proposed a conference over a hattit kit; now, this old-fashioned Scotish sweet is mentioned nowhere in Scott's writings except in the *Bride*, where Caleb Balderstone's simulated thunderbolt spoils the hatted kit that was for the Master's dinner, just after Ashton and his daughter have entered Wolf's Crag. The Gowrie conspiracy developed into an obscure stabbing incident in a locked room: so did Lucy's marriage to Bucklaw, and in neither case has the whole truth about what happened ever been discovered. The Gowries were interested in magic and astrology; James VI was a notorious witch-hunter; and the *Bride of Lammermoor* is the supreme literary product of popular superstition, a story enacted beneath a brooding cloud, and pervaded by an evil fate.[14]

The geographical setting of the novel can easily be related generally to the actual map of the eastern Borders, but the detailed topography is essentially imaginary. None of the speculations about possible originals of Ravenswood Castle or Wolfscrag carry conviction,[15] and there is no point in trying to identify Wolfshope with any particular Berwickshire fishing community.[16]

Table of dates.

1660   Restoration of Charles II after the Commonwealth.

1662   In spite of having accepted, at his enthronement as King of
            Scots in 1651, the two Covenants guaranteeing Presbyter-
            ian government for Scotland, Charles II re-establishes epis-
            copacy. The Privy Council of Scotland requires ministers to
            take the oath of allegiance, to accept presentation to their
            charges by lay patrons, to submit themselves to their
            bishops, and to recognise holy days. Some 270 ministers
            refuse to conform, leave their parishes, and with the Coven-
            anters loyal to Presbyterianism begin to worship in open-air
            conventicles.

1679   Following the murder of Archbishop James Sharp on 3
            May, the Covenanters rout the Royalist forces at the battle
            of Drumclog on 1 June, but are defeated at Bothwell Bridge
            on 22 June.

1681   The Test Act and Oath requires all public officials *inter
            alia* to accept royal supremacy in the ordering of ecclesiast-
            ical as well as political affairs, and to renounce the Coven-
            ants.

1681–85   The 'killing time', marked by brutal persecution of the Cov-
            enanters.

1688   In the 'Glorious Revolution', the Protestant William and
            Mary of Orange replace the Roman Catholic James VII and
            II on the throne of England. James is supported in exile at
            Saint-Germain-en-Laye, France by Louis XIV.

1689   *11 April.* In the 'Claim of Right' the Scottish Convention of
            Estates complete the Revolution by declaring James VII to
            have forfeited the throne and offering it to William and
            Mary, stating the conditions upon which it wished them to
            govern.
            27 July. A Highland Jacobite army led by Claverhouse
            (Viscount Dundee) defeats government troops at Killie-
            krankie, but Claverhouse is himself killed.
            26 August. The Highlanders are defeated at Dunkeld,
            marking the end of effective armed resistance during Wil-
            liam's reign.

1690   The Church of Scotland becomes fully Presbyterian, and
            Episcopal services are restricted.

1694   Queen Mary dies.

1701   James VII and II dies, and his son James Francis assumes
            the title James VIII and III, but remains in exile until his
            death in 1766 in spite of several plots and uprisings in the
            period to 1745.

1702   William III dies and is succeeded by Queen Anne.

1707   The Act of Union.

NOTES

1   For a full account of the versions see Coleman O. Parsons, 'The Dalrymple Legend in *The Bride of Lammermoor*', *Review of English Studies*, 19 (1943), 51–58.

2   Caleb Balderstone is twice called Rutherford in the manuscript: 86.15, 94.26.

3   Scott did not feel able to reveal formally the source of his story until the Magnum because the current Lord Dalrymple had been involved in a protracted process involving matrimonial scandal between 1808 and 1820: see John W. Cairns, 'A Note on *The Bride of Lammermoor*: Why Scott did not Mention the Dalrymple Legend until 1830', *Scottish Literary Journal*, 20:1 (May 1993), 19–36.

4   William Ferguson, *Scotland 1689 to the Present*, Edinburgh History of Scotland, Vol. 4 (Edinburgh, 1968), 7.

5   *Memorialls; or, The Memorable Things that fell out within this Island of Brittain from 1638 to 1684* (Edinburgh, 1818), 225–27. Scott had advised Sharpe on this publication: *Letters*, 4.538–9 (11 October 1817). In his Prefatory Notice (lx), Sharpe mentions the nickname Annie Winnie applied to an alleged witch in 1644: compare 192.34 etc.

6   Parsons, 53.

7   Scott was to tell the story in 'My Aunt Margaret's Mirror' (1828): see his Magnum Introduction to that tale (41.294).

8   'Scott as Story-Teller: *The Bride of Lammermoor*', *Scottish Literary Journal*, 7:1 (May 1980), 113–26. Miss Lamont also notes (120): 'Scott brings the heroine's father out of the shadows to create the character of Sir William Ashton, a wily lawyer and politician whose success has been largely at the expense of the family of the lover, the Master of Ravenswood. The original story says that the lover was unacceptable to the girl's family "on account of his political principles, or his want of fortune". There is no suggestion that the two families had been in any way connected before. In the novel Scott adds the twist that the lover's loss of fortune has been the father's gain, and, furthermore, that the political circumstances that brought this about cannot be relied upon to continue. At the start of the novel the reader well versed in Scott might suppose that he is watching a representative of an old way of life being remorselessly supplanted by a new man; but he will not be entirely correct. In this novel the characters are not on a slide, but a see-saw.' Miss Lamont further suggests (122) that the development of the story may have been influenced by Scott's translation of the German ballad 'Der edle Möringer' as 'The Noble Moringer' during his composition of the *Bride*, 'the tale of a pilgrim who returned home on the day when his wife was about to marry another'.

9   88.21, 123.33–34, 209.13, and 216.18; the exception is at 209.40, which has been emended.

10   *Acts of the Parliament of Scotland*, 10.278, 11.112.

11   See for this and other relevant points Jane Millgate, 'Text and Context: Dating the Events of *The Bride of Lammermoor*', *Bibliotheck*, 9 (1979), 200–13 (204–5).

12   Ferguson, 3.

13 See for example the entry in the *Dictionary of National Biography*, and *The Lockhart Papers*, 2 vols (London, 1817), 1.72–74 (George Craigengelt appears at 2.151: Scott's character is called George in the manuscript).

14 James Anderson, *Sir Walter Scott and History* (Edinburgh, 1981), 69–70.

15 Fast Castle, on the Berwickshire coast N of St Abb's Head, is most often cited as the original of Wolfscrag, and Anderson's mention of its role in the Gowrie Conspiracy is suggestive; but Scott denied any specific identification in his Magnum Introduction to *Chronicles of the Canongate* (41.xxiii–xxiv: compare *Letters*, 11.331), and certainly the approach to the castle, steeply downhill, is quite unlike that in the novel. In the *Chronicles* Introduction, Scott suggests that 'the Kaim [fortress] of Urie' gave an idea for Wolfscrag. The tower in question, generally known as the Kaim of Mathers, from 1351 until 1650 a seat of the Barclays of Ury (Stonehaven), stands on a small promontory 2 km N of St Cyrus, Kincardineshire, and Scott probably visited it when he stayed at nearby Benholm in 1796 (*Letters*, 1.46). Much erosion has taken place since Scott's time, so that the only access to the surviving fragment of the tower is now by way of a very narrow isthmus, but (as with Fast Castle) the approach must always have been steeply downhill (for details see Andrew Jervise and James Gammack, *Memorials of Angus and the Mearns*, 2 vols (Edinburgh, 1886), 2.145). The Kaim of Mathers can have provided no more than a dramatic site (the story of the building of the Kaim, related in the *Minstrelsy*, 4.243, is hardly relevant to the *Bride*). Of the various suggested originals of Ravenswood Castle, the only one with any authorial backing is Crichton Castle, 16 km SE of Edinburgh: Scott approved the placing of a vignette of the castle on the title-page of Vol. 15 of the 1821 duodecimo *Novels and Tales* (MS 791, p. 69), but the splendid ruin bears no specific resemblance to the mansion in the novel.

16 The relationship of the *Bride* to previous works in the Gothic mode has been thoroughly explored by Fiona Robertson, the most significant documents being Horace Walpole's *The Castle of Otranto: A Gothic Story* (1765), Charles Robert Maturin's *The Milesian Chief: A Romance* (1812), and Scott's own drama *The Doom of Devorgoil*, written in 1817–18, but not published until 1830: see the notes to her World's Classics edition of the *Bride*; 'Castle Spectres: Scott, Gothic Drama, and the Search for the Narrator', *Scott in Carnival: Selected Papers from the Fourth International Scott Conference, Edinburgh, 1991*, ed. J. H. Alexander and David Hewitt (Aberdeen, 1993), 444–58; and *Legitimate Histories: Scott, Gothic, and the Authorities of Fiction* (Oxford, 1994). The pervasive presence of *Hamlet* is clear from the Explanatory Notes to the present edition, but Frank McCombie has demonstrated that Scott was particularly influenced by Charles Kemble's contemplative interpretation of the role of the Prince of Denmark: 'Scott, *Hamlet*, and *The Bride of Lammermoor*', *Essays in Criticism*, 25 (1975), 419–36.

EXPLANATORY NOTES

In these notes a comprehensive attempt is made to identify Scott's sources and all quotations, references, historical events, and historical personages, to explain proverbs, and to translate difficult or obscure language. (Phrases are explained in the notes while single words are treated in the glossary.) The notes are brief; they offer information rather than critical comment or exposition. When a quotation has not been recognised this is stated: any new information from readers will be welcomed. References are to standard editions, or to the editions Scott himself used. Thus proverbs are normally identified both by reference to the third edition of Ray's *A Compleat Collection of English Proverbs*, and to *The Oxford Dictionary of English Proverbs*. Books in the Abbotsford Library are identified by reference to the appropriate page of the *Catalogue of the Library at Abbotsford*. When quotations reproduce their sources accurately, the reference is given without comment. Verbal differences in the source are indicated by a prefatory 'see'. Biblical references are to the Authorised Version. Plays by Shakespeare are cited without authorial ascription, and references are to *William Shakespeare: The Complete Works*, edited by Peter Alexander (London and Glasgow, 1951, frequently reprinted).

The following publications are distinguished by abbreviations, or are given without the names of their authors, in the notes:

Cheviot   Andrew Cheviot, *Proverbs, Proverbial Expressions, and Popular Rhymes of Scotland* (Paisley and London, 1896).

Child   *The English and Scottish Popular Ballads*, ed. Francis James Child, 5 vols (Boston and New York, 1882–98).

CLA   [J. G. Cochrane], *Catalogue of the Library at Abbotsford* (Edinburgh, 1838).

The Faerie Queene   Edmund Spenser, *The Faerie Queene* (written 1579–96), ed. J. C. Smith, 2 vols (Oxford, 1909).

Kelly   James Kelly, *A Compleat Collection of Scotish Proverbs Explained and Made Intelligible to the English Reader* (London, 1721): *CLA*, 169.

Letters   *The Letters of Sir Walter Scott*, ed. H. J. C. Grierson and others, 12 vols (London, 1932–37).

Lockhart   J. G. Lockhart, *Memoirs of the Life of Sir Walter Scott, Bart.*, 7 vols (Edinburgh, 1837–38).

Magnum   Walter Scott, *Waverley Novels*, 48 vols (Edinburgh, 1829–33).

Minstrelsy   Walter Scott, *Minstrelsy of the Scottish Border*, ed. T. F. Henderson, 4 vols (Edinburgh, 1902).

ODEP   *The Oxford Dictionary of English Proverbs*, 3rd edn, rev. F. P. Wilson (Oxford, 1970).

OED   *The Oxford English Dictionary*, 12 vols (Oxford, 1933).

Percy   *Reliques of Ancient English Poetry*, [ed. Thomas Percy], 3 vols (London, 1765): compare *CLA*, 172.

Poetical Works   *The Poetical Works of Sir Walter Scott, Bart.*, ed. J. G. Lockhart, 12 vols (Edinburgh, 1833–34).

Prose Works   *The Prose Works of Sir Walter Scott, Bart.*, 28 vols (Edinburgh, 1834–36).

Ramsay   Allan Ramsay, *A Collection of Scots Proverbs* (1737), in *The Works of Allan Ramsay*, ed. Alexander M. Kinghorn and Alexander Law, Vol. 5

(Edinburgh and London: Scottish Text Society, 1972), 59–133.
Ray   J[ohn] Ray, *A Compleat Collection of English Proverbs*, 3rd edn (London, 1737): *CLA*, 169.
Tilley   Morris Palmer Tilley, *A Dictionary of the Proverbs in England in the Sixteenth and Seventeenth Centuries* (Ann Arbor, Michigan, 1950).
Turbervile   [George Turbervile,] *The Noble Art of Venerie or Hunting, etc.*, 2nd edn (London, 1611): *CLA*, 105.

All manuscripts referred to in the notes are in the National Library of Scotland. Information derived from the notes of the late Dr J. C. Corson is indicated by '(Corson)'. For legal matters the notes by Lord Normand (MS 23077) have been useful. Information derived from Fiona Robertson's World's Classics edition of *The Bride of Lammermoor* (Oxford and New York, 1991), or occasional reproduction of her formulations, is indicated by '(Robertson)' or '(from Robertson)'. The Dryburgh Edition, 25 vols (London, 1892–94), Vol. 8, and the edition by J. Harold Boardman (London, 1908) have also proved useful.

title-page   Jedidiah Cleishbotham   Jedidiah ('beloved of the Lord') is the name given to Solomon in 2 Samuel 12.25. 'Clashbottom' was a facetious name used by one of Joseph Train's corresponding 'Parish Clerks and Schoolmasters of Galloway', 'derived . . . from his using the Birch' (MS 3277, pp. 22–23); *clash* in Scots means 'strike' or 'flog'. For further discussion of the name and its origins, see *The Black Dwarf*, ed. Peter Garside, EEWN 4a (Edinburgh and New York, 1993), 129–30.
title-page   Parish-clerk   clerk to the kirk session, the lowest church court in the Presbyterian system. The position was very often given to the schoolmaster.
title-page   Gandercleugh   in Scots, *cleugh* is a gorge or ravine; hence, most obviously, 'goose-hollow'.
title-page   Hear, Land o' Cakes . . . prent it   Robert Burns, 'On the Late Captain Grose's Peregrinations thro' Scotland, collecting the Antiquities of that Kingdom' (1789), lines 1–6.
epigraph   for the translated passage, see *The Life and Exploits of the Ingenious Gentleman Don Quixote De La Mancha Translated from the Original Spanish of . . . Cervantes . . . by Charles Jarvis, Esq.*, 2 vols (London, 1742), 1.204. The incident occurs in Part 1, Bk 4, Ch. 5 (or Part 1, Ch. 32: 'Which treats of what befel Don Quixote's whole company in the inn').
3   motto   see 'The Gaberlunzie Man', in *Ancient and Modern Scottish Songs, Heroic Ballads, &c.*, ed. David Herd, 2nd edn, 2 vols (Edinburgh, 1776), 2.51: *CLA*, 171. 'To carry the gaberlunzie on' means 'to maintain the beggar or tinker'. Fortune-tellers would pretend to be dumb and use *cauk* ('chalk') and *keel* ('ruddle, red chalk') to make magic signs.
3.13   monstrari digito   Latin, *literally* to be pointed out with the finger; to become famous. See Persius (AD 34–62), 1.28.
3.16   Punch and his wife Joan   the usual modern name Judy for the wife in the celebrated puppet-show first appears in 1825.
3.18   Peter Pattieson   the fictitious schoolmaster (teacher of the lower classes at the Gandercleugh village school), author of the first and second series of *Tales of my Landlord* (*The Black Dwarf* and *The Tale of Old Mortality*, and *The Heart of Mid-Lothian*). These had been published anonymously, like all of Scott's novels before 1827, in 1816 and 1818. Jedidiah Cleishbotham explains in the Introduction to the first series that he merely transmitted the manuscript by his deceased young colleague to the publisher.
3.20   up to   back to.
3.29–31   "come in place as a lion" . . . roar ye as it were any nightingale   a double allusion to *A Midsummer Night's Dream*, echoing Lion's speech

(5.1.222–23) and slightly adapting part of Bottom's plea to be allowed to act the part of Lion (1.2.73–74). There is also a reference to *lion* as 'sought-after celebrity'.

4.6–8 imprisoned Sampson . . . Philistian lords and ladies see Judges 16.21–27.

4.10–11 the iron and earthen vessels 'Two Pots' by the Roman fabulist Avianus (fl. *c.* AD 400), fable 11. A brass pot promises not to harm an earthen one as they are swept down a river, but the earthen pot is worried that they may collide accidentally.

4.21 Parve . . . urbem the first line of *Tristia*, written by the Roman poet Ovid *c.* AD 8 during the early years of his exile from Rome, is followed by the line 'ei mihi, quod domino non licet ire tuo!' ('Little book, you go to Rome without me (I don't begrudge you that) but alas your master cannot go too!')

4.26 Tinto an Italian word, formerly used in English writing about art, meaning 'tinted' or 'a tint'.

4.29 wrote himself designated himself.

4.30 the ancient family of Tinto, of that ilk, in Lanarkshire Tinto is a prominent hill 11.5 km SE of Lanark: Tinto is hence a common local surname.

4.36 tailor in ordinary regular tailor: the phrase 'in ordinary' is normally used of court officials (such as chaplains-in-ordinary) regularly engaged by the monarchy.

4.36 Langdirdum fictitious, made up of the Scots words *lang* ('long') and *dirdum* (a word of various significances, notably 'uproar', 'scolding', and 'punishment').

5.12 sub Jove frigido *Latin* under the cold open sky. Horace, *Odes*, 1 (23 BC), 1.25.

5.27 as yet still.

6.2–3 a limb supernumerary the unusual positioning of the adjective after the noun introduces a facetiously formal or archaic note.

6.12 point d'appui *French* point of support, prop.

6.27–28 the Scottish Teniers, as Wilkie has been deservedly styled David Wilkie (1785–1841) was noted, as the Flemish David Teniers the Younger (1610–90) had been, for his paintings of peasant life. The comparison with Teniers was made, for example, at the Royal Academy Dinner in 1806 by the connoisseur John Julius Angerstein.

6.32 the nursery rhymes of Pope see Alexander Pope (1688–1744), 'Epistle to Dr Arbuthnot' (1735), lines 127–28: 'As yet a Child, nor yet a Fool to Fame,/ I lisp'd in Numbers, for the Numbers came'.

7.1 human face divine Milton, *Paradise Lost*, 3.44.

7.4 Wallace Sir William Wallace (1272?–1305), Scottish patriot, hanged and quartered in London.

7.16 had Christian faith with kept faith with.

7.19 Rubens Flemish painter Peter Paul Rubens (1577–1640), noted for his large-scale portrait groups of wealthy and noble clients.

7.23–24 the whetstone of mine host's wit compare *As You Like It*, 1.2.50: 'always the dullness of the fool is the whetstone of the wits' (Celia, of Touchstone).

7.28–31 the sloth . . . dying of inanition the sloth's habit of stripping a tree of its leaves and bark, dropping heavily from it (not being formed to descend), and painfully finding a new tree to feed upon is described in Oliver Goldsmith, *An History of the Earth, and Animated Nature*, 8 vols (London, 1774), 4.345–6.

7.40 Sir Joshua Sir Joshua Reynolds (1723–92), artist, portrait-painter, and first president of the Royal Academy.

8.1–2 muse of painting in classical literature there is no muse of painting; but the nine Muses were goddesses of the arts and intellectual pursuits in general.

8.29 long stitches *either* 'tedious', *or* (proverbially) 'carelessly economical' (Alexander Nicolson, *Gaelic Proverbs*, rev. Malcolm Mac Innes (Glasgow, 1951), 206: 'The lazy tailor's long stitch').

8.32–34 the majestic head of Sir William Wallace ... the felon Edward for Wallace see note to 7.4; Edward I, King of England, ordered his execution including half-hanging and decapitation.

8.43–9.1 the stag in the fable in Aesop's fable 'A Stag Drinking', the stag considers his branching antlers rather than his pitiful legs as effective against all his enemies, but his antlers catch in bushes, and he is killed by hounds.

9.11–13 Hogarth ... Domenichino, or some body else ... Moreland William Hogarth has a ragged artist painting an inn-sign in his engraving *Beer Street* (1751), perhaps to allude to the fact that artists were reduced to such straits. The Bolognese painter Domenico Zampieri (1581–1641) painted three outdoor frescoes at S. Onofrio, Rome in 1604–5, but Fiona Robertson is probably right in suggesting that the reference is deliberately vague. The artist George Morland (1763–1804), forced to hide on the Isle of Wight in 1799, was reduced to painting signs for inn-keepers in settlement of bills.

9.21 to boot into the bargain.

9.42–43 the prize at the Institution ... the hanging committee the British Institution, founded in 1806, awarded prizes in various categories (including historical compositions) from 1810 to 1817 for works submitted to the annual exhibition in competition. The Royal Academy of Arts held its annual exhibition at Somerset House in the Strand from 1780: the hanging committee would have hung Tinto's work in obscure or unflattering positions.

10.12 Swallow-street along with Little Swallow Street (the present Swallow Street) this was the principal thoroughfare between Oxford Street and Piccadilly. It was mostly replaced by Regent Street in 1817–20.

10.14–15 the Morning Post daily newspaper first published in 1772, noted for its coverage of the arts.

10.17 Mr Varnish alluding to the practice of finishing paintings with a thin layer of varnish.

10.18 on hand in his possession.

10.29 culs de lampe *printing* ornaments used to fill up blank pages.

10.30 serjeant of invalids sergeant in a reserve force of disabled soldiers.

10.31–32 Bothwell ... David Deans characters in *The Tale of Old Mortality* and *The Heart of Mid-Lothian*.

10.41–42 The ancient philosopher ... know thee the Greek philosopher Socrates (died 399 BC) is credited by Cicero with the adage: 'As a man's life is, so is his speech' (*Tusculan Disputations*, 5.47). Scott's formulation is probably influenced by Ben Jonson (1572–1637): 'speake that I may see thee' (*Timber; or, Discoveries* (1640), in *The Works of Ben Jonson*, ed. C. H. Herford, and Percy and Evelyn Simpson, 11 vols (Oxford, 1925–52), 8.625: *ODEP*, 760).

10.43 personæ dramatis *Latin* dramatic characters.

11.3–4 It is a false conclusion ... unfilled cann see *Twelfth Night*, 2.3.6–7 (Sir Toby).

11.6–7 that Pythagorean toper ... spoiled conversation the advice 'Don't speak a lot while you are drinking, for you will get things wrong' is attributed to Chilon of Sparta, a Greek philosopher of the 6th century BC. In fact, unlike his daughter Chilonis, he was not a disciple of the contemporary philosopher and mathematician Pythagoras.

11.7–8 a professor of a person professing themselves an expert in.

11.8 has occasion to needs to.

11.19–20 the serene and silent art . . . one of our first living poets the reference is to Thomas Campbell's phrase 'serenely silent art' in his 'Stanzas to Painting' (1803), line 33: *first* means 'most eminent', 'finest'.

12.23 Vandyke dress richly brocaded clothes with broad lace or linen collars usually worn by the men in the portraits by Sir Anthony Van Dyck, appointed Court Painter to Charles I in 1632.

12.39 the darkened tube of an amateur cultivators of the arts were wont to use such tubes to view landscapes as though they were paintings. An *amateur* is one who has a taste for the subject.

13.9–10 the name of Tinto . . . mists alluding to the nursery rhyme 'On Tintock tap there is a mist,/ And in the mist there is a kist,/ And in the kist there is a cap,/ And in the cap there is a drap,/ Tak up the cap, drink out the drap,/ And set it down on Tintock tap'. For Tintock Tap (Tinto) see note to 4.30.

13.24–25 the Ape of the renowned Gines de Passamonte Cervantes, *Don Quixote*, Part 2 (1615), Ch. 25: the (fraudulent) puppeteer's ape is reputed to be able to reveal events in the past and present, but not in the future.

13.43–14.2 the dramatic art of Mr Puff . . . Lord Burleigh's head see Richard Brinsley Sheridan, *The Critic* (1779), 3.1.119–30.

14.8 East Lothian and Berwickshire adjoining counties on the SE coast of Scotland: the Lammermuir hills straddle their common border.

14 motto *2 Henry VI*, 5.3.20–22 (Salisbury after the battle of St Albans).

15.5 Berwickshire or the Merse Scott uses 'the Merse' in the popular sense: strictly it is the plain occupying the south of Berwickshire and the eastern part of Roxburghshire.

15.6 the Lothians the counties of East Lothian, Midlothian, and West Lothian.

15.12 the Revolution involving the deposition of James VII of Scots and II of England and the acceptance by William and Mary of the English crown in 1688 and the Scottish in 1689.

15.15 Saint Abb's Head . . . Eyemouth Eyemouth is a fishing village 12 km N of Berwick-upon-Tweed, and St Abb's Head is a further 6 km N.

15.16 the . . . German Ocean the North Sea.

15.20 bending his mind to condescending to accept.

15.20 civil war of 1689 see Historical Note, 284.

15.21–23 although he had escaped . . . his title abolished for taking part in the rising in support of James VII and II in 1689 (see Historical Note, 284), Ravenswood was prosecuted for treason in a process before Parliament. Conviction could lead to execution, forfeiture of real and moveable property, and 'attainder of blood', which involved the loss of the right to inherit or to transmit a hereditary title. Ravenswood escaped all but the last penalty, enabling his son to inherit his remaining property, but no title, after his death.

15.32 great civil wars i.e. the civil wars of 1642–51.

15.34 skilful fisher in the troubled waters proverbial: see *ODEP*, 265; John Dryden and Nahum Tate, *Absalom and Achitophel*, Part 2 (1682), lines 314–15.

15.35 governed by delegated authority the Crown's power was exercised (often corruptly) by the Scottish Privy Council, and its members, the Scottish officers of state; although dominated by the Earl of Lauderdale from 1662 to 1680, the Council was an unstable body, wracked by the intrigues of councillors who were often motivated by their own shortage of money. 'Those best equipped for this elaborate game of financial charades were those who held office or influence' (Michael Lynch, *Scotland: A New History* (London, 1991), 291).

16.6 the Lord Keeper the Lord Keeper of the Great Seal of Scotland, and a member of the Scottish Privy Council.

16.8–9 extensive pecuniary transactions see Michael Lynch, *Scotland: A New History* (London, 1991), 291, for an analysis of the nature of the indebtedness of post-Restoration society in Scotland.

16.16–17 In those days there was no king in Israel Judges 17.6, 18.1, 19.1, and 21.25.

16.17–18 the departure of James VI. . . . England at the Union of the Crowns in 1603 James VI and I moved his court from Edinburgh to London.

16.20 court of St James's St James's Palace, built by Henry VIII, was one of the royal residences in London, and from 1698 to 1837 *the* London residence of the sovereign; foreign ambassadors are still accredited to the Court of St James's.

16.23 an Irish estate owned by an absentee the neglect of Irish estates by landowners who preferred to spend their time in England had long been a cause for concern: compare, e.g., Swift's *A Short View of the State of Ireland* (1728), and Maria Edgeworth, 'The Absentee', in *Tales of Fashionable Life* (1812).

16.32–33 the establishment of the throne in righteousness see Proverbs 16.12.

16.42–17.1 Abon Hassan . . . his own household in 'The Story of the Sleeper Awakened', from the *Arabian Nights*, the merchant Abon Hassan is transferred while asleep to the palace of the Caliph and treated as Caliph for one day (*Tales of the East*, ed. Henry Weber, 3 vols (Edinburgh, 1812), 1.315–40: *CLA*, 43). Scott follows Weber's form of 'Abou'.

17.8 Show me the man . . . law proverbial: Kelly, 289; Ray, 304; *ODEP*, 729.

17.18 the king's counsel the Law Officers of the Crown, especially the Lord Advocate, the King's Advocate or counsel, who looked after the royal interest in litigation, but also his junior colleague the Solicitor-General.

17.18–20 poured forth . . . concealment not identified.

17.26–29 it was believed . . . Macbeth in the days of yore see *Macbeth*, 1.5, 1.7, and 2.2.

18.6 airy wheel Milton, *Paradise Lost*, 3.741: Satan 'Throws his steep flight in many an Aery wheel'.

18.39–40 during the sessions of the Scottish Parliament and Privy-council the Privy Council, which had responsibility for public order, met fairly frequently throughout the year when Parliament was not in session, but at the time of the novel's action its business tended to be concentrated in the summer. It was at once the Scottish executive, a centre of legislative power, and a supreme court, but its members were chosen by the sovereign. Parliament met on specific dates, summoned by the sovereign.

19.8–9 founded, perhaps, rather in equity than in law Scott seems to mean simply that Lord Ravenswood's case was naturally just, or had justice on its side, but that the Lord Keeper's case had the strict letter of the law on its side. This might apply if the terms of the 'extensive pecuniary transactions' (16.8–9) between the men were oppressive, or if the elder Ravenswood had been fined, and the fine paid to the Lord Keeper (compare 47.27–31, and 220.43–221.5).

19.34–37 Contrary to the custom . . . service of the church prelacy, i.e. Episcopalian church government, was abolished in an Act of 22 July 1689, and Presbyterian church government established in a further Act of 7 June 1690. Anglican burial services were not expressly prohibited, but it was illegal for a minister to wear a surplice, and it was illegal for a minister who had refused to pray for William and Mary in 1689, and had been ejected from his parish as a result, to conduct religious ceremonies in public.

19.38–39 the tory gentlemen, or cavaliers these Tories are Jacobites, or supporters of the exiled James VII and II; they style themselves 'cavaliers' to recall the royalist faction during the Civil War.

19.40–41 The presbyterian church-judicatory of the bounds the local presbytery, the ecclesiastical court immediately superior to the parish kirk session.

20.5 Master Edgar's father having forfeited the title of lord, Edgar is not formally entitled to be called 'Master' (the title given to the eldest son of a viscount or lord): compare note to 15.21–23.

20.13 You'll rue the day ... answer see *Macbeth*, 3.6.42–43, with 'day' for 'time'.

20.17 dust to dust, and ashes to ashes see the (Episcopalian) Prayer Book's Office for the Burial of the Dead: 'ashes to ashes, dust to dust'.

20.19 countenances more in anger than in sorrow see Horatio's description of the ghost of Hamlet's father: 'A countenance more in sorrow than in anger' (*Hamlet*, 1.2.231).

21.3 Heaven do as much to me and more recalling Ruth to her mother-in-law Naomi: 'the Lord do so to me, and more also, if ought but death part thee and me' (Ruth 1.17).

22 motto see Child 116, stanza 162. The ballad was included in Percy, 1.159. 'Over Gods forbode' means 'God forbid'.

23.6 In fine in short.

23.9 made good substantiated.

23.25 an aggravated riot in law, 'aggravation' increases the seriousness of any crime. In this case a potentially violent assembly is arguably aggravated by stopping an officer of the Privy Council going about his lawful business.

23.26 stand committed are bound to act.

23.28 Blackness Castle a state prison 6 km NE of Linlithgow, West Lothian.

23.28–29 a charge of treason by the old Scots Law of Treason aggravated riot could be construed as sedition, and perhaps treason in certain circumstances. The old law was replaced by the Treason Act (1709).

23.33–36 Athole ... our administration for Athole (Atholl) and his son (who leant towards the Jacobite party), and the threat to the Whig administration in 1703–04, see Historical Note, 282–3.

24.4–5 in terrorem *Latin* as a warning.

24.6 a point of delicacy a matter requiring skilful handling.

24.16 I bide my time this motto was and is shared by several Scottish families.

24.19 Malisius latinised version of the English 'Malise'.

24.28–29 a bull's head ... was placed upon the table for the 'Black Dinner' of 1440 on which this incident is modelled, see *Minstrelsy*, 4.275–76.

25.5–12 Look not thou ... quiet die the lines are Scott's own.

25.23–24 Something there was of a Madonna cast she bore a certain resemblance to pictures or statues of the Virgin Mary.

25.36–40 distributing the prizes ... enchantment the description combines three allusions. In Milton's 'L'Allegro' (written *c.* 1631) tournaments are graced by 'ladies, whose bright eyes/ Rain influence, and judge the prize' (lines 121–22); in the first book of Spenser's *The Faerie Queene* the virgin Una, representing true religion, undergoes persecution at the hands of the hypocritical enchanter Archimago and the false Duessa; Miranda is Prospero's innocent daughter in *The Tempest*.

26.33 named after the head of her house according to David Hume of Godscroft, the house of Douglas was founded by royal decree in the 8th century, the first bearer of the name being a noble warrior called Sholto. See *The History* *of the House and Race of Douglas and Angus* (Edinburgh, 1644), [1]–4: *CLA*, 3.

27.15 the gourd of the prophet see Jonah 4.6.

28.4 Saul *interjection* upon my soul, upon my word.

28.17 man and mother's son proverbial: compare *ODEP*, 546.

28.21 Tristrem see Scott's edition of the 13th-century romance *Sir Tristrem* (1804), 1.27: 'More he couthe of veneri,/ Than couthe Manerious' (*Poetical Works*, 5.151, and note, 5.377–79).

28.22 hauds out presents his gun.

28.36–37 the bad paymaster ... before it is due proverbial: see *ODEP*, 614 ('Pay beforehand was never well served').

28.40 condictio indebiti *Scots law* an action to recover payment made in mistake or ignorance.

28.41–42 sue a beggar, and ... what follows 'Sue a beggar and get a louse' (Ray, 77; *ODEP*, 784).

29.6 Tyninghame estate, house and village between Dunbar and North Berwick.

29.8 stout old Trojan of the first-head, ten-tyned branches courageous fellow of great stamina, superlative, with ten-pointed horns.

29.11 whipt roundly in moved in smartly.

29.23–30 The monk must arise ... worth them a' these stanzas are based on an old quatrain referring to Liddesdale quoted in a note to Canto 4 of *The Lay of the Last Minstrel* (1805): 'Billhope braes for bucks and raes,/ And Carit haugh for swine,/ And Tarras for the good bull-trout,/ If he be ta'en in time' (*Poetical Works*, 6.126).

29.38 Ledington probably Lethington, then the home of the earls of Lauderdale. The house and estate, 2 km S of Haddington, were sold in the early 18th century and renamed Lennoxlove.

30.29 put them upon encourage them to tell.

30.35 Former in Scott's time a *former* was a carpenter's cutting tool.

31 motto *The Faerie Queene*, 3.7.5: Florimell sees the witch's cottage.

31.15 And every bosky bourne ... side Milton, *Comus* (written 1634), line 312.

31.24–25 scenes of deeper seclusion see Wordsworth, 'Lines Written a Few Miles Above Tintern Abbey ...' (1798), lines 6–7: 'Which on a wild secluded scene impress/ Thoughts of more deep seclusion'.

32.1 woman old Scott may be alluding to *The Faerie Queene* as in the chapter motto, but on all eleven pertinent occasions Spenser has 'old woman'.

32.8–9 as Judah is represented ... palm-tree Judaea is so represented in coins struck at Rome to commemorate the capture of Jerusalem (AD 72), in the years following that event.

33.29–30 I have drank the cup ... destined for me the utterance is rich in Old and New Testament overtones. The 'cup' is taken figuratively as those sufferings which God sends on a person or people at Psalms 23.5, 75.8, Isaiah 51.17, Matthew 20.23, and 26.39; it denotes joy and thanksgiving at Psalm 116.13 and 1 Corinthians 10.16.

34.28 an article in the sale one of the conditions of the sale.

35.1 driven matters hard on prosecuted matters in a harsh, uncompromising, insensitive way.

35.22 the judgment-seat i.e. at the Last Judgment.

35.28–36.1 harped aright the fear see *Macbeth*, 4.1.74 (Macbeth to the Apparition of an Armed Head).

35 note the Court of Session the supreme civil court in Scotland, of which Lockhart, as President, was head.

35 note Dalry Dalry House, Edinburgh; now in Orwell Place, formerly the junction of Fountainbridge and Canal Street.

35 note the Lawnmarket the western extension of the High Street, leading towards the Castle.

35 note as Jack Cade says ... occasion see the speech, actually by Cade's follower Smith the weaver, in *2 Henry VI*, 4.6.9–10: 'If this fellow be wise, he'll never call ye Jack Cade more; I think he hath a very fair warning'.

35 note special Act of the Estates of Parliament after June 1640 the Scottish Parliament consisted of three estates: nobles, representatives of the barons, and representatives of the royal burghs, but between 1662 and 1689 the old clerical estate was restored, and nine bishops were present at the March 1689 Parliament. The Act (1 April 1689) was special in that it dealt with a particular situation only: it declared that the use of torture in this case, to discover possible accomplices, was not to be regarded as establishing a precedent, or endorsing its earlier use.

35 note perfervidum ingenium Scotorum *Latin* very fiery temper of the Scots. The phrase is quoted by George Buchanan (1506–82), *Rerum Scoticarum Historia* (1582): see his *Opera Omnia*, ed. Thomas Ruddiman, 2 vols (Edinburgh, 1715), 1.321: 'Scotorum præfervida ingenia'. (Robertson)

36 motto *Romeo and Juliet*, 1.5.115–16.

36.38 point of state matter of dignified status.

36.39–37.14 Specimens continued ... Tankerville it is thought likely that the British white cattle are descendants of domestic cattle introduced by the Romans which became feral on their departure. The Hamilton, or Cadyow, herd can still be seen at Chatelherault Country Park, Hamilton, Lanarkshire, formerly owned by the Duke of Hamilton. Scott's belief, expressed in the Introduction to 'Cadyow Castle' (*Poetical Works*, 4.201), that they had been extirpated in the mid-18th century is almost certainly incorrect, and by 1835 there were some 80 animals. The herd at Drumlanrig Castle, Dumfriesshire, seat of the Duke of Buccleuch and Queensberry, was driven away to an unknown destination *c.* 1780. The estate and castle of Cumbernauld, Dumbartonshire, was owned by the Fleming family until 1875: a herd of white cattle roamed wild in a remnant of the ancient Caledonian Forest in the area until at least 1570 and may have survived in the park as late as 1730. The purest herd is that still surviving at Chillingham Castle, Northumberland, seat of the Earls of Tankerville. This was probably enclosed on the creation of the park in the 13th century: around 1810 there were 120 animals. Both the Chillingham and Hamilton herds have black tips on their horns and black hoofs, though it is probable that in Scott's time the Hamilton herd was hornless. The Chillingham herd is the less docile of the two and has pronounced remnants of a mane. Full details can be found in G. Kenneth Whitehead, *The Ancient White Cattle of Britain and their Descendants* (London, 1953). An engraving by Neele of the Strand after a drawing by Bailey showing a marksman aiming at three white cattle at Chillingham was published in 1794.

37.1 the accounts of old chronicles notably in Hector Boece, trans. John Bellenden, *The Hystory and Chroniklis of Scotland* (1527; reprinted as Vols 1 and 2 of *The Works of John Bellenden*, 3 vols, Edinburgh, 1821–22), 1.xxxix–xl; and in John Lesley, *De Origine, Moribus, et Rebus Gestis Scotorum* [Concerning the origin, customs, and military affairs of the Scots] (Rome, 1578), 19.

37.3–4 the shaggy honours of his mane compare Homer, *Odyssey*, trans. Alexander Pope, assisted by William Broome and Elijah Fenton (1725–26), 18.182: 'the graceful honours of his head'.

37.41 love strong as death see Song of Solomon 8.6.

38.6 walking sword small sword, or large knife carried for use as a weapon.

39.12–13 like a second Egeria ... Numa Numa Pompilius, legendary king of Rome, was said to have been advised by the water-nymph Egeria. The passage is probably designed to recall Byron's description of Egeria's fountain in *Childe Harold's Pilgrimage*, 4 (1818), 115–19. Scott reviewed the fourth canto for the *Quarterly Review* while writing the *Bride* (*Letters*, 5.223).

39.38   Malleus Maleficarum, Sprengerus, Remigius   only two works are involved here. The important collection of signs of witchcraft and the black arts, *Malleus Maleficarum* [The Witch Hammer] (Speyer, *c.* 1486), was the work of two Dominicans, Jakob Sprenger, and Heinrich Kramer (Henricus Institoris). 'Remigius' is the French demonologist Nicholas Remy, whose *Dæmonolatreiæ* (Lyons, 1595) to some extent replaced the *Malleus Maleficarum* as the leading authority on witch-hunting (Robertson). Neither work contains anything relating to the superstition referred to in this passage.

40.14   battle of Flodden   on 9 September 1513 the Scots under James IV were defeated by the English on the Northumbrian side of the border, the King and many of the Scottish nobility being killed in this national catastrophe.

40.29–30   a Grahame to wear green . . . Monday   it was believed that 'in battle a Grahame is generally shot through the green check of his plaid' (Scott's *Letters on Demonology and Witchcraft, addressed to J. G. Lockhart, Esq.* (London, 1830), 167). According to tradition, Robert the Bruce (Robert I, King of Scots, 1274–1329) resolved at a low point in his fortunes to determine his future policy by the success or failure of a spider struggling to build a web near him. On his way S to Flodden in 1513, William Sinclair, second Earl of Caithness from 1476, led forty of his men on a Monday over the Ord of Caithness, where all except one were killed.

41.27   Montero cap   Spanish hunter's cap with spherical crown and flap to draw over the ears.

43.7   her eloquent blood   see John Donne, *The Second Anniversary*, 'Of the Progress of the Soul' (1612), line 244: 'her pure and eloquent blood'. (Robertson)

45.29   incident to   liable to occur to.

46.24   in some sort   to some extent.

47.6–7   as soon comes . . . the auld tup's   proverbial: see Ray, 172, 280, and *ODEP*, 752. The lamb is Edgar Ravenswood, the auld tup (male sheep) his father.

47.10   A wilful man maun hae his way   proverbial: *ODEP*, 890.

47.11   year and day   legal term for a full year.

47.12   wind him a pirn   create difficulties for him.

47.15   he has not a cross to bless himself with   he has no money (old coins having been stamped with crosses, and *bless* meaning 'make the sign of the cross').

47.16   Turntippet   a *tippet* is a hood; to 'turn tippet' is to be a turncoat.

47.17–18   If he hasna gear . . . to pine   proverbial: see Kelly, 149 and Ramsay, 85. The second line refers to the torture of the boot, described in *The Tale of Old Mortality*, EEWN 4b, 280–82.

47.19   the Revolution   of 1688–89.

47.19–20   Luitur cum persona . . . law Latin   he is paid with the person [of him] who cannot pay with his purse. In spite of Turntippet's 'law Latin' this does not seem to be a standard legal maxim.

47.25   Hirplehooly   *literally* limp or hobble slowly or cautiously.

47.28   disponed upon   dealt with, transferred.

47.28   Lord Treasurer   the Lord High Treasurer was the Chancellor of the Scottish Exchequer before the Union.

47.29–30   Shame be in my meal-poke . . . nook of it   alluding to the deprecatory proverb 'Sairie [in a poor state, i.e. near-empty] be your meil poke, and ay your fist in the nook [corner] of it' (Ray, 304).

47.30   set that down for a bye bit   had it in mind for a snack.

47.33 you are like the miller's dog ... untied proverbial: see Ray, 308 and *ODEP*, 84.

47.36–39 I, wha hae complied wi' a' compliances ... thirty years by-past to 'comply' was in the late 17th century to accept the prevailing political and ecclesiastical authority. Those in public office had, from 1661, to take the oath of allegiance recognising Charles II as 'supreme governor of this kingdom', and, from 1681, the Test oath recognising Charles as supreme governor 'in all causes, as well ecclesiastical as civil'. Both oaths also involved a commitment to maintain the protestant religion and a renunciation of popery, but a new oath of loyalty promulgated in James's first indulgence of 1687 dropped the require-ment to maintain the protestant religion, and promised 'never to resist his power and authority'. After 1689 the oath of allegiance involved only a promise to be 'faithfull and bear true allegiance to their Majesties King WILLIAM & Queen MARY', and the Claim of Right, passed by Parliament with only five dissenting on 11 April 1689, declared that 'prelacy ... is and hath been, a great and insupportable grievance and trouble to this nation ... and therefore ought to be abolished'.

48 motto see Henry Mackenzie, 'Duncan: A Fragment from an Old Scots Manuscript' (1762), in *The Works of Henry Mackenzie*, 8 vols (Edinburgh, 1808), 8.7: *CLA*, 202.

48.30 One man is enough to right his own wrong Cheviot (271) recognises this as proverbial, citing this use.

48.36–37 but that I hold a hasty man no better than a fool see Proverbs 29.20.

49.3 a deeper stake *gambling* a more substantial or hazardous stake.

49.7 laid on imposed.

49.8 to boot moreover, in addition.

49.9–10 the Irish brigade a body of troops who entered the pay of the French King under the control of the exiled King James VII of Scots and II of England, according to the terms of the Treaty of Limerick in 1691.

49.16 on his own i.e. on his own resources.

49.19 the far end of a fair estate the very end of a fair amount of capital.

49.20 shift about change lodgings.

49.21 Saint Germains Saint-Germain-en-Laye, near Paris, where the exiled Stewart family held court after the flight of James VII and II in 1688.

49.23–24 the Chevalier 'Chevalier de St George' was the title conferred by Louis XIV of France on James Francis Stewart (1688–1766), who styled himself James VIII of Scots and III of England on his father's death in 1701.

49.24–25 the field the place assigned for a duel; actual combat.

49.26 perish from the way Psalm 2.12.

49.39 Versailles Louis XIV's great palace near Paris.

50.3 take and reclaim an eyess *falconry* capture a young hawk (eyas) and call it back as part of its training.

50.13 puts him to his defence obliges him to defend himself.

50.19 L'Espoir *French* the Hope.

50.20 Eyemouth see note to 15.15.

50.30–31 no time for grass to grow beneath their heels proverbial: see Ramsay, 82 and *ODEP*, 331.

50.38–39 art and part *Scots law* phrase denoting participation in a crime.

50.40–41 The dial spoke not ... murder John Dryden, *The Spanish Fryar* (1681), 4.2.81–82.

51.6 the Fatal Conspiracy i.e the Jacobite plot into which Craigengelt is trying to inveigle Bucklaw. Although Scott's own invention it is also a plausible title for a Jacobean or Restoration tragedy.

51.10–17 Alexander ... poor Lee Bucklaw gives a free version of

Alexander's speech concluding Act 4 of *The Rival Queens; or, The Death of Alexander the Great* (1677) by Nathaniel Lee (?1649–92): Lee suffered declining literary abilities, insanity, and an ignominious death as an alcoholic. *Come out* means 'make a début on the stage'.

51.19 **led horse** spare horse, led by an attendant or groom.

51.20–21 **set up** put in the stable, i.e. exhausted.

51.23–24 **this bout** on this occasion.

51.30 **neither art nor part** see note to 50.38–39

51.33 **my commission** i.e. his appointment as an army officer.

51.43 **Black Moor** blackamoor; blackskinned.

52.1–5 **Take a fat sucking mastiff whelp ... working it in** similar fantastic remedies can be found in 17th-century farriery manuals, e.g. Gervase Markham, *Markhams Maister-Peece; or, What Doth a Horse-Man Lacke* (London, 1610), which went through 21 editions (with varying titles) up to 1734 when more sober manuals finally rendered it obsolete. *Oil of spikenard* is aromatic oil derived from an Indian plant.

53.8–9 **he had gallows written ... his birth** Moslems believe that the decreed events of every man's life are impressed in divine characters on the forehead, but are invisible to mortal eyes. Variants of the idea came to have proverbial status in English: see Ray, 7, 109; Tilley, F590; and *Saint Ronan's Well*, EEWN 16, 262.13 (text and note).

54.9 **the salmon is off with hook and all** ironic allusion to the proverb 'A hook well lost to catch a salmon' (Ray, 120; *ODEP*, 383).

54.14 **Its good sleeping in a hale skin** proverbial: Ray, 296; Kelly, 220; Ramsay, 92; *ODEP*, 742.

54.15–16 **Little kens the auld wife ... hurle-burle-swire** proverbial: Ray, 299; Ramsay, 97; *ODEP*, 471. Kelly (229–30) suggests that Hurle-Burle-Swire is a particularly windy passage through a ridge of mountains separating Nithsdale from Tweeddale and Clydesdale.

54 **motto** see 'Graeme and Bewick', stanza 27, in *Minstrelsy*, 3.83 (Child 211).

55.13 **have more reason in your wrath to-morrow** compare Ephesians 4.26: 'let not the sun go down upon your wrath', and the proverbial 'Take Wit with your Anger' (Ramsay, 109).

55.15 **carry it off** dispose of the matter.

56.27–28 **sending, like one of Ossian's heroes, his voice before him** recalling such phrases as 'the terrible voice of Fingal' from James Macpherson's Ossianic poem *Fingal: An Ancient Epic Poem ... translated from the Galic Language* (London, 1762), 53 (Bk 4): *CLA*, 14.

57.13 **drawn bridle** pulled the reins so as to slacken our pace.

57.18 **Sathan** this spelling of Satan is not recorded in English usage after the 17th century, but survives in Scots.

57.19 **drawing up with** taking up with, entering into a relationship with.

57.23 **at the nearest** when we were very close to achieving our object.

57.34–35 **the devil is always at one's elbow** a proverbial sentiment: compare *ODEP*, 182: 'The Devil is never far off'.

57.37–38 **put my thumb under his belt** put myself in his power. Proverbial (see Ray, 307 and *ODEP*, 820).

57.41–58.2 **you have indeed nourished in your bosom the snakes ... one great goodly snake** proverbial: see Ray, 214; *ODEP*, 747.

57.43 **That's home as well as true** Cheviot (313) recognises this as proverbial: home means 'to the point'.

58.10 **et cæteras** *Latin* additional things.

58.11 **breaking a park-pale** making a hole in the fence of an estate, or trespass within the limits of an estate.

58.42–43   the expression of the English divine . . . Hell is paved with good intentions   proverbial: *ODEP*, 367. This form of the proverb is quoted by the Methodist leader John Wesley: *An Extract of the Rev. Mr. John Wesley's Journal from his Embarking for Georgia to his Return to London* (Bristol, [1739]), 26 (10 July 1736).

59.10–11   you should not drink up the last flask . . . ill luck in that   Scott is the only known authority for this belief.

59.20–29   cliff that beetled over the German Ocean . . . sheeted spectre   compare Elsinore in *Hamlet*, 1.4.70–71; 1.1.115.

60.14   the seven sleepers   seven noble Christian youths of Ephesus who, after taking refuge in a cave to escape persecution, were believed to have slept for 187 years.

60.18   in very blood and body   in true flesh and blood; having real human existence.

60.19   aroint ye   the approved command in Shakespeare for bidding supernatural beings begone: see *Macbeth*, 1.3.6, and *King Lear*, 3.4.122.

60.20–21   lith and limb   joint and limb (a standard Scots phrase).

60.31   men of mould   mortal men. The standard expression appears in *Sir Tristrem*, stanza 59, line 1 (*Poetical Works*, 5.165) and in *Henry V*, 3.2.22.

61.8   with a'   withal, besides.

61.13   this some months   for several months.

61.14   conform till   in accordance with.

61.14–15   as gude right is   as is very right.

61.24   let them care that come ahint   proverbial: let those who come after do the worrying (see Ramsay, 97).

61.27   ill convenient   inconvenient.

61.33   without doors   outside the castle.

62.5   out bye   away from home.

62.22   the Bass and North-Berwick Law   the Bass Rock rises from the sea some 5 km NE of North Berwick; North Berwick Law is a hill 1 km S of the town.

62.23   marshal ye up   conduct you ceremoniously upstairs.

63.1   neither hearth nor harbour   no place of shelter or entertainment.

63.3   Westminster-Hall   the Hall, in the Palace of Westminster, London, has an oak hammer-beam roof which was installed in 1397.

63.6   black jacks   leather beer jugs.

64.4   it is easy to put a fair face on ony thing   proverbial: see *ODEP*, 319 ('To put a good face on a thing').

64.5–6   as teugh as bow-strings and bend-leather   proverbial in origin: see Ray, 226 ('As tough as whitleather') and *ODEP*, 834 ('as tough as leather').

64.11   some gate   somewhere.

64.15   she's to pu'   she has to be plucked.

64.17   bide ye there a wee   stay there a short while.

64.37   under hiding   in hiding.

64.41   under distress   under pressure of adversity.

65.4–5   the nearer the bane the sweeter   proverbial: see Ray, 81 and *ODEP*, 557.

65.6–7   that's a' that's to trust to   that's all that's to be depended upon.

65.19   awfu' thunner   thundery conditions would be bad for storing beer. Compare note to 97.28–29.

65.21   engage fur   guarantee, warrant.

66.7–8   the Gowrie Conspiracy   on 5 August 1600 James VI was lured to Gowrie House in Perth by Alexander, Master of Ruthven, and claimed to have been threatened with death there, possibly in an ultra-Protestant conspiracy. James's followers killed the Master and his brother, the Earl of Ruthven. There were various fugitives from royal justice, including the younger Ruthven brothers, and other parties, such as Sir Robert Logan who then owned Fast Castle, and his law agent, George Sprott of Eyemouth, were implicated. See *Letters*, 8.456–59, and 'Fast Castle', in *Prose Works*, 7.446–57.

66 motto Scott's arrangement of two stanzas (2 and 4) from Part 2 of 'The Heir of Linne', a ballad included (in a version part traditional, part modern) in Percy, 2.313–14. See Child 267.

66.19 the lonely lodge the phrase in Percy is 'the lonesome lodge' (last stanza of Part 1 and stanza 1 of Part 2).

66.30 Favourable to calm reflection, as well as to the Muses, the morning for the morning as favourable to calm reflection compare Nicholas Rowe, *The Fair Penitent* (1703), 1.1.162; see also *The Antiquary*, EEWN 3, 39.20; and *Saint Ronan's Well*, EEWN 16, 214.10. Morning as favourable to the Muses alludes to the Latin proverb 'Aurora Musis amica [est]' ('Dawn [is] a friend to the Muses'): see *The Journal of Sir Walter Scott*, ed. W. E. K. Anderson (Oxford, 1972), 151 (28 May 1826), and *The Antiquary*, 176.22–23.

67.7–8 the exiled Earl of Angus ... a king's resentment Archibald Douglas, 6th Earl of Angus (?1489–1557), married Margaret Tudor, widow of James IV, in 1514, and from 1525 controlled the person of her son, James V. James escaped in 1528, raised support, and had Angus summoned before parliament to be tried for treason. Angus did not appear, and was outlawed; the royal army besieged his stronghold, Tantallon Castle, 4.5 km E of North Berwick, for 20 days, but failed to take it.

67.9 the sleeper awakened see note to 16.42–17.1.

67.24–25 your bosom-snake ... my vipers see note to 57.41–58.2.

67.34 as the ballad has it see 'Adam Bell, Clim of the Clough, and William of Cloudesly', Child 116, stanza 104. The ballad is in Percy, 1.129–60, these lines being at 149.

68.10 as the old song says 'I Have a green Purse and a wee pickle Gowd' is the opening line of a song in Allan Ramsay, *The Tea-Table Miscellany* (1724–29), in *The Works of Allan Ramsay*, Vol. 3, ed. Alexander M. Kinghorn and Alexander Law (Edinburgh and London, 1961), 58–59. It is also in David Herd, *Ancient and Modern Scottish Songs*, 2nd edn, 2 vols (Edinburgh, 1776), 2.94 (for both collections see *CLA*, 171). In Herd, the speaker woos his love Christy thus: 'I have a green purse and a wee pickle gowd,/ A bonny piece land, and planting on't,/ It fattens my flocks, and my barns it has stow'd;/ But the best thing of a's yet wanting on't.'

68.12–13 an end of an auld sang proverbial: Ramsay, 114; *ODEP*, 220–21. The phrase was used most memorably as a 'despising and contemning remark' by the Earl of Seafield on signing the Act of Union of 1707 (*The Lockhart Papers*, 2 vols (London, 1817), 1.223).

68.13 to boot into the bargain.

68.14 that gate in that manner.

68.17 putting it up again putting it back in your pocket.

68.22 gude right very right.

68.23 ta'en on bought on credit.

68.33 Eppie Sma'trash the surname suggests 'small trash', small or poor-quality business.

68.38 Luckie Chirnside the surname derives from a village 15 km W of Berwick-upon-Tweed.

68.39 mak shift manage.

68.41 to the fore alive, still in existence.

70.37–38 the Marquis of A—— Athole: for the Marquis, and from 1703 Duke of Atholl and the situation outlined in the following paragraph see Historical Note, 282–3.

71.8–9 probable change ... administration see Historical Note, 282.

71.29–31 **sloth . . . necks** see note to 7.28–31.

71.32 **watches for** awaits.

71.36 **one revolution too much already** i.e. that of 1688–89.

71.38 **my dream's out** my dream's out in the open, over, explained, revealed not to be a dream.

72.5–6 **our friend Ballantyne's types** James Ballantyne (1772–1833),
Scott's friend from boyhood, was manager of the firm of Ballantyne and Co.
which printed the Waverley novels.

72.15 **good liking** friendly or kindly feeling.

72.25 **forth of** out of.

72.29 **verbum sapienti** *Latin proverb* verbum sat sapienti: a word [is]
enough for a wise man.

72.29–30 **a word . . . fool** proverbial: compare Ray, 102, 171 and *ODEP*,
914–15.

72.32–33 **sliddery ways crave wary walking** *sliddery* means 'slippery',
'inconstant', 'untrustworthy': compare 'Fortune's slidd'ry ball' (Robert Burns,
'The Farewell. To the Brethren of St James's Lodge, Tarbolton' (1786), line
6). The next phrase echoes *Julius Caesar*, 2.1.15: 'It is the bright day that brings
forth the adder,/ And that craves wary walking.'

73.6–7 **our poor house of B——** Blair Castle, near Blair Atholl, Perthshire.

73.9–10 **These—With haste . . . delivered** a similar formula appears as a
motto in *The Antiquary*, with the comment 'Ancient Indorsation of Letters of
Importance', but is probably by Scott (EEWN 3, 109).

73.15–16 **Wit's Interpreter, or the Complete Letter-Writer** I. C.
[John Cotgrave], *Wits Interpreter: The English Parnassus; or, A Sure Guide to those
Admirable Accomplishments that Compleat our English Gentry, in the Most Acceptable
Qualifications of Discourse, or Writing, &c.* (London, 1655): see *CLA*, 111. *The
Complete Letter-Writer . . . With directions for Writing Letters, and the Proper Forms
of Address* (Edinburgh, 1768) is a Scottish version of the often-reprinted *The
Complete Letter-Writer; or, New and Polite English Secretary* (2nd edn, London,
1756).

73.26 **Saint Germains** see note to 49.21.

73.32–33 **crop-eared dogs, whom honest Claverse treated as they deserved** Covenanters whom John Graham of Claverhouse (1648–89), first
Viscount Dundee, persecuted during the 'killing-time' of 1681–85: *crop-eared*
means primarily 'short-haired', with ears exposed, but it also alludes to the
cropping of ears as a punishment.

73.34 **They gave the dog . . . hanged him** proverbial: see Ray, 98 and
ODEP, 302.

73.39–40 **the iron has entered . . . souls** see Psalm 105.18 as in *The Book
of Common Prayer*.

74.6–9 **To see good corn . . . wanton me** Burns records lines very like
these in the second of two 'old stanzas' to the tune 'To daunton me' in his copy of
The Scots Musical Museum: 'To see gude corn upon the rigs,/ And banishment
amang the Whigs,/ And right restor'd where right sud be,/ I think it wad do
meikle for to wanton me'. The lines refer to the Revolution of 1688–89. See
*Notes on Scottish Song by Robert Burns, Written in an Interleaved Copy of the Scots
Musical Museum with Additions by Robert Riddell and Others*, ed. James C. Dick
(London, 1908), 35–36. (Robertson)

74.10 **cantabit vacuus** Juvenal, *Satires*, 10.22: 'Cantabit vacuus coram
latrone viator' (The empty-handed traveller will whistle in the robber's face).

74.17 **treasurer or lord commissioner** for 'treasurer' see note to 47.28;
for 'lord commissioner' see note to 210.25.

75.3–4 **not a pair of clean spurs . . . old times** 'We are told, that when
the last bullock which Auld Wat [Scott's ancestor] had provided from the

English pastures was consumed, the Flower of Yarrow [his wife] placed on her table a dish containing a pair of clean spurs; a hint to the company that they must bestir themselves for their next dinner' (Lockhart, 1.67).

75.9   Saint Magdalen's Eve . . . her day   Caleb means to refer to Queen Margaret (1046–93) who married Malcolm III, King of Scots, in 1069. She was canonised in 1250, and her feast day is 16 November. Fasting on vigils (which would have involved eating fish rather than red meat) in preparation for a feast day was practised in the Church of England in the 16th and 17th centuries, and St Margaret's Eve might have been so distinguished by Episcopalians in Scotland.

75.11   reflection   Caleb means *refection* ('meal').

75.17   Out upon   *interjection* fie upon.

75   motto   see Joanna Baillie, *Ethwald: A Tragedy* (1802), 1.1.31–35, in *A Series of Plays in Which it is Attempted to Delineate the Stronger Passions of the Mind*, 3 vols (London, 1798–1812), 2.112: *CLA*, 212.

75.29   Light meals procure light slumbers   compare 'Who goes to bed supperless all night tumbles and tosses': Ray, 29; *ODEP*, 315.

75.34   view hollo   shout given by a huntsman on seeing a fox break cover.

76.10   Bittlebrain   'beat-brain'.

76.13–14   the freedoms and immunities . . . free-forestry   rights granted by Crown charter, encroachments on which could be severely punished under Acts of 1534, 1592, 1594, and 1617. The *freedoms* were the rights to hunt as the king could have done in a royal forest; the *immunities* were immunities from the king's normal right to hunt.

76.19   such a like right   a right of such a kind.

76.38   come at   obtain.

77.4–5   their bridles ringing . . . Elfland   the ringing bridles and court of Elfland recall the opening stanzas of the ballad 'Thomas the Rhymer': *Minstrelsy*, 4.86–87 (Child 37C).

77.10   serve the turn of   do instead of.

77.10   out o' the gate   absent, away from the castle.

77.27   fast on the feast day   i.e. while it is appropriate to fast in preparation for a feast day (see note to 75.9), one cannot properly do so on the feast day itself.

77.28   cast yoursell in the way of dining   put yourself in a position to dine.

77.29   cast about brawly for the morn   manage very well for the next morning (or day).

77.29–30   stead o' instead of.

77.31   mak some shift for the lawing   manage in some way to deal with the bill.

78.39–40   Take the goods . . . the great John Dryden says   see 'Alexander's Feast' (1697), line 106.

79.8   flesh and fell   flesh and skin; entirely (*King Lear*, 5.3.24).

79.12–13   blowing him at bay   blowing the horn to announce that the stag has turned to face its pursuers.

79.20   Hyke a Talbot! Hyke a Teviot!   'Hyke a Talbot' is given in Turbervile (112), *hyke* being a call to urge on hounds, and *Talbot* the generic name for a hunting-dog. The name *Teviot* derives from a tributary of the River Tweed.

80.17–19   the huntsman's knife . . . venison   the procedure follows that prescribed (with an illustrative print) in Turbervile, 132–34.

80.25   Taking unto himself heart of grace   plucking up courage.

80.32   Uds daggers and scabbard   meaningless oath (God's daggers and scabbard). See John Webster and Thomas Dekker, *Westward Ho* (1607), 5.3.23.

80.34   so that   providing that.

80.35   hunted at force   *hunting* run the game down with dogs; hunted in the open with hounds in full cry.

80.37   I durst have gone roundly in on him   I dared to attack him vigorously without delay.

80.37   use and wont   accustomed practice or procedure.

81.5–6   the Cabrach   mountainous area in W Aberdeenshire noted for hunting.

81.8–9   If thou be hurt ... lesser fear   see Turbervile, 124. Such doggerel couplets are the preferred vehicle for hunting lore in several 16th and 17th-century works.

81.14   break up   cut up.

81.15–16   if he breaks him up without drinking ... not keep well   the superstition derives from Turbervile, 128.

81.29   man or woman either   see *Hamlet*, 2.2.307–08.

81.32   with the precision of Sir Tristrem himself   see Scott's edition of the 13th-century romance *Sir Tristrem*, 1.41–48, in *Poetical Works*, 5.157–61.

82.20   unlooped and slouched   with the broad brim hanging down over the face, not looped up.

83.12   short mile   i.e. an English mile rather than a Scots mile which was longer.

83.28–29   ad re-ædificandam antiquam domum   *Latin* to rebuild the ancient house.

84.1–4   the words of the Bard of Hope ... encircle the sea   see 'Lines Written on Visiting a Scene in Argyleshire' (1800), lines 7–9, by Thomas Campbell, author of *The Pleasures of Hope* (Edinburgh and London, 1799).

85.16   but what he remarked   as to prevent him from noticing.

85.29   came and saw   alluding to the remark ascribed to Julius Caesar (102?–44 BC): 'Veni, vidi, vici' ('I came, I saw, I conquered').

85.39   mirk night   the dead of night.

86.12   the nakedness of the land   Genesis 42.9, 12.

86.14–15   red wud, and awa' wi't   stark staring mad, and out of his senses.

86.17   as mad as the seven wise masters   in *The Proces of the Seuyn Sages* seven wise men save their pupil Florentine from his imperial father's anger by telling a series of significant stories. The romance is included in the third volume of *Metrical Romances of the Thirteenth, Fourteenth, and Fifteenth Centuries*, ed. Henry Weber, 3 vols (Edinburgh, 1810): *CLA*, 105. In the third volume of his *Specimens of Early English Metrical Romances* (3 vols (London, 1805): *CLA*, 105), George Ellis gives a précis with extracts under the title 'The Seven Wise Masters'. In neither version are the masters at all insane.

86.21   Truce to   enough of; have done with.

86.32   Philistines   warlike people who constantly harassed the Israelites.

86.36   won into   obtained entry.

86.36   at the back of   following, behind.

87   motto   see lines 154–58 of Coleridge's poem (1798).

87.9–10   never hesitate between their friend and their jest   compare 'Better lose a jest than a friend': Ray, 125; *ODEP*, 54; *The Antiquary*, EEWN 3, 339.38–39.

87.21   Praise be blessed   God be blessed.

88.8–10   like Louis XIV. ... without directly lying   Louis XIV, King of France from 1643 till 1715, advocated keeping one's word inviolably, but he was a skilled economiser with the truth (e.g. 'treaties are not always to be observed literally').

88.21 the king on the throne to be taken as a proverbial phrase rather than literally.

88.30 the de'il of ony absolutely no.

88.31 the morn's morn tomorrow morning.

88.31–32 It sets the like of him *ironical* it is fitting for somebody in his situation.

89.5 post of audience listening post.

89.42 as free as the wind at Martinmas compare the proverb 'Where the wind is on Martinmas Eve, there it will be the rest of winter' (*ODEP*, 893). Martinmas is 11 November, one of the Scottish quarter-days, when various taxes and interest payments were due.

89.43–90.1 the honest old drivellers yonder of Auld Reekie i.e. the lawyers of 'Old Smoky' (Edinburgh).

90.2 a week of days a whole week.

90.13 cock of the pit plucky, spirited fellow.

90.13–14 thy very Achates your faithful companion, as Achates is to Aeneas in Virgil's *Aeneid*.

90.14–15 hand and glove—bark and tree proverbial expressions: Ray, 271; *ODEP*, 346, 556.

90.28 L'un n'empêche pas l'autre *French* the one does not prevent the other.

91.6 fooling him up to the top of his bent see *Hamlet*, 3.2.374–75.

93.40 Genius of the House tutelary and controlling spirit of the house.

94.22 designed for intending to travel to.

94 motto see John Fletcher and perhaps Francis Beaumont, *Love's Pilgrimage* (printed 1647), 2.4.1–4: 'put them off' means 'pass them off'.

94.37–38 this comes to hand … pint-stoup proverbial: *Guy Mannering*, Magnum, 4.207n.

94.41 de'il may care an expression of irritation.

95.4 the Bass the Bass Rock. See note to 62.22.

95.10 bits o' pigs handful of crockery.

95.11–12 hatted kitt preparation of milk with a creamy top, made of buttermilk, milk, sugar, and spices.

95.18 ever come hame to himsell by some chance (*or* in some degree) recover his wits.

95.37 Wull a wins! alas!

95.42–43 here awa', there awa' hereabout, thereabout.

95.43 like the Laird o' Hotchpotch's lands in English (but not in Scots) law *hotchpotch* is 'the blending or gathering together of properties for the purpose of securing equality of division, especially as practised in certain cases in the distribution of the property of an intestate parent' (*OED*).

96.6–7 was nae grit matter of preparation didn't take much preparing.

96.8 ordinary course of fare normal eating habits or diet.

96.8 petty cover, as they say at the Louver the French *petit couvert* ('small place-setting') means an unceremonious meal taken by a king or nobleman. At the period of the novel the Louvre was the royal palace in Paris.

96.19–20 gang on continue.

96.21 de'il but I dress ye I'll certainly prepare for you.

96.25 with reverence with its garnishings.

97.7 George Buchanan referring not to the renaissance humanist, but to the popular chapbook *The Witty and Entertaining Exploits of George Buchanan, who was Commonly Called, the King's Fool* (Glasgow, 1777). On pages 37–40 there is a set of 'Witty and Entertaining Jests, Epigrams and Epitaphs, &c.'.

97.23 white broth a rich soup, involving preparation over several days, whose ingredients include white chicken and ground almond.

97.26 as was weel her part which was proper for her to do.

97.28–29 the effect of thunner it is still a widely-held belief that thunder turns milk sour, the same atmospheric condition producing the two effects.

97.30 our haill dishes all our dishes.

97.32 command his countenance control his facial expressions.

97.42–98.1 the high-spirited elephant . . . a brother in commission see Oliver Goldsmith, *An History of the Earth, and Animated Nature*, 8 vols (London, 1774), 4.279. A 'brother in commission' is someone sharing a particular responsibility.

99.9 Henrietta Maria (1609–69), daughter of Henri IV of France and Queen of Charles I.

99.19 on any pinch in any extremity.

99.33–34 weary for his dinner Cheviot (378) explains: 'It was an old custom in Scotland, for a host to take his guest to the top of the tower of his house . . . in order that he might admire the view, and by means of the keen air gain a sharp appetite, and so, "Weary [yearn] for his dinner."'

100 motto see *The Canterbury Tales*, III (D) 1838–43: in all texts available to Scott the second line begins 'Have I' and the last word (as here emended) is 'suffisa(u)nce'. The French 'Je vous dis sans doute' means 'I tell you for sure', and 'I ne wolde' means 'I wouldn't wish'.

100.18 bold as any lion proverbial: see Proverbs 28.1 and *ODEP*, 72.

101.1–6 feu-rights . . . rights of commonty . . . feudal dependence . . . tenants at will 'feu-rights' were rights of property granted in perpetuity in return for payments of cash, kind, or service to the feudal superior. 'Commonty' was a form of shared ownership of land for the purpose of grazing animals or cutting peats. Tenants at will held land on a type of perpetual lease governed by ancient local custom; they had to pay rent and provide other services and their tenure was very precarious. Since tenancy at will is not strictly 'feudal' tenure, Scott is using 'feudal' here in a pejorative rather than a legal sense.

101.10–14 and footnote the royal purveyors . . . an hundred caverns Edmund Burke's speech of 11 February 1780 is quoted from the third volume of *The Works of the Right Honourable Edmund Burke*, published in various combinations of dates and with variations in the text by Rivington in London. Scott's version is close to that given in the 14-volume version (1801–22) at Abbotsford (*CLA*, 193): the third volume in this set was published in 1801. The emended page no. (280) is correct for all the versions of the Rivington collection examined.

101.17–18 awful rule and right supremacy *The Taming of the Shrew*, 5.2.109.

101.39 matter of understanding something understood.

102.8 kindly aid *Scots Law* contribution exacted by a feudal lord from a 'kindly tenant', one who occupied land on favourable terms under a special lease which gave a sort of hereditary right.

102.15 Conscript Fathers originally members of the Roman senate, now senators or legislators.

102.20 Dunse . . . Dingwall the writer Duns, 20 km W of Berwick-upon-Tweed, was the county town of Berwickshire. Dingwall is 'Dingwell' on his first appearance in the manuscript, and his Aberdeen accent suggests that 'Dingwall' is intended to suggest 'hit well' rather than to recall the town in Easter Ross. A 'writer' is a solicitor.

102.23 palaver 'as the natives of Madagascar call their national convention': *Saint Ronan's Well*, EEWN 16, 51.14–15.

102.35–36 compound or compensate compromise, or set off against a sum due by the creditor, in this case the feudal superior (Normand).

102.36 in fine, to agé as accords *Scots law* in short, to act as agent as may be necessary and legal.

103.18–19 he could not see it—'twas not in the bond see *The Merchant of Venice*, 4.1.257 (Shylock).

103.26–27 stouthrief, or oppression . . . termed it in Scots law 'stouthrief, or oppression by strength of hand' is theft aggravated by violence; 'via facti' is a Latin legal phrase meaning 'by means of an act', an extrajudicial but non-violent deed.

103.34 by the strong hand by physical force: see *Hamlet*, 1.1.102. When violence opposes the proper execution of a decree, the civil magistrate can ask the military to help to execute it 'manu militari'.

103.42 Maggy Lauder popular Scottish air first printed in Adam Craig, *A Collection of the Choicest Scots Tunes* [1730], 38. The words were published by David Herd in *Ancient and Modern Scottish Songs, Heroic Ballads, Etc.*, 2nd edn, 2 vols (Edinburgh, 1776), 2.72–73: *CLA*, 171.

104.2 El Dorado the golden land (or city); at first the name of an imaginary country of fabulous riches which Spanish travellers professed to have found in America; later a general term for Central and South America.

104.5 within its causeway within the paved area of the village.

104.16 gall and wormwood Lamentations, 3.19.

104.20–21 necessity was equally imperious and lawless alluding to the proverb 'Necessity has no law': see Ray, 139, Ramsay, 102, and *ODEP*, 557–58.

104.32 Cauld Kail in Aberdeen popular song published by David Herd: see *Ancient and Modern Scottish Songs, Heroic Ballads, Etc.*, 2nd edn, 2 vols (Edinburgh, 1776), 2.205: *CLA*, 171. Another version appeared in the third edition of Herd (1791), 2.160. The more literary version in *The Scots Musical Museum*, ed. James Johnson, 6 vols (Edinburgh, 1787–1803), no. 162, is attributed to Alexander Gordon (1743–1827), 4th Duke of Gordon. The tune appears in Domenico Corri, *A New and Complete Collection of the Most Favourite Scots Songs*, 2 bks (Edinburgh, [*c.* 1783]), 24–25 ('Cauld be the rebels cast'), as well as in *The Scots Musical Museum*.

104.38–39 in case the thunner should hae soured ours see notes to 65.19 and 97.28–29.

105.7–8 his presentation from the late lord in the Church of Scotland until 1690, and again from 1712 to 1874, the parish minister was nominated by a patron (usually the chief landowner) to Presbytery for admission to a parish. Between 1690 and 1712, and since 1874 a minister is elected by the parish congregation.

105.8–9 brewster wife woman who brews and sells malt liquors.

105.9 scored up added up and entered as an account.

105.12 stand his friend act the part of a friend to him.

105.15 a' comes o' taking folk on the right side everything depends on getting on the right side of people.

105.20 Loupthedyke *literally* 'leap the wall', a term used to indicate a wild, wayward, undisciplined person.

105.21 was about my lady i.e. was her personal maid.

105.26 he is e'en cheap o't he deserves it; he gets off lightly.

105.39 a canty carline see Robert Burns, 'The Author's Earnest Cry and Prayer' (1786), line 62.

106.15 cutty spoons short-handled spoons, usually of horn.

106.29–30 setting up their throats raising their voices.

106.31–32 A sight of you is gude for sair een proverbial: *ODEP*, 732.

106.34 the night tonight.

106.38 wad been would have been.

106.40 The ne'er a fit ye's gang you're not going a foot.

107.15 at e'en in the evening.

107.17–18 Ne'er a bit but she Good heavens! she.

107.20 gawsie cow, goodly calf proverbial: compare 'Like cow, like calf' (*ODEP*, 151).

107.34 Hout tout! nonsense!

107.37 Bidethebent endure the danger.

107.38–39 lying in the hills . . . a mountain-man between 1662 and 1690 the Covenanters, or mountain-men, sought refuge in the hills to worship in secret conventicles.

107.41 the Service-book either the Scottish Prayer Book, introduced by Charles I in 1637, or the Anglican Book of Common Prayer (as revised in 1662). However, the use of a liturgy was not required in the Restoration period: see Gordon Donaldson, *Scotland: James V–James VII* (Edinburgh, 1965), 364, and *The Tale of Old Mortality*, EEWN 4b, note to 94.18.

108.4 guide the gear manage the money economically.

108.10–11 ilka land has it's ain lauch proverbial: see Ray, 285 and *ODEP*, 441. *Lauch* is a variant of 'laich', an area of low-lying ground.

108.12 up bye yonder up there (some distance away, and suggesting an accompanying gesture).

108.13–14 Puncheon . . . Leith Puncheon, whose name means 'large cask', was (fictionally) cooper by appointment to Queen Anne at the exchange of the timber merchants at Leith, the port of Edinburgh. (Robertson)

108.15–16 frae hame away from home.

108.18 taks the tout takes huff.

108.22–23 sae she should, to set up for so she should be to have as her object.

108.26 what like what sort of person.

108.31 Hout awa nonsense!

108.39 Cauld be my cast may my fate be unpleasant.

108.41–42 a penny . . . twal pennies one penny stirling (0.4p), worth twelve pennies Scots.

108 footnote Monetæ Scoticæ scilicet *Latin* in Scottish money, that is to say.

109.16 toss him in a blanket Fiona Robertson suggests an allusion to the treatment of Sancho Panza for his master's non-payment of an inn bill (Cervantes, *Don Quixote*, Part 1 (1605), Ch. 17).

109 motto see John Fletcher, *Wit Without Money* (published 1639), 1.1.168–70.

110.4 council the linking with the parish kirk session suggests that burgh council rather than Privy Council is intended.

110.4 that I suld say sae alas that I should say it.

110.13 weary on him a plague on him.

110.16 Hout tout nonsense!

110.16–17 it's come to muckle . . . neither proverbial: 'Spoken when we reject the Proffer of a mean Service, Match, or Business, we are not come so low as that yet' (Kelly, 207). See also Ramsay, 92 and *ODEP*, 135.

110.18–19 hands aff is fair play proverbial: a fight is all right provided it does not become physical (see *ODEP*, 348).

111.2–3 in some sort to some extent.

111.7 what for why.

111.30 turn short off upon change direction abruptly to attack.

111.33–34 my substance disponed upon my goods handed over.

111.36 every twa words every other word.

111.36 gar you as gude pay you back in your own coin.

112.12–13 hills and hags, and caves of the earth see Hebrews 11.38.

112.18 Argyle Archibald Campbell (1629–85), ninth Earl of Argyll, took arms to oppose the accession of the Roman Catholic James VII and II in 1685.

112.22–23 The seed of the righteous ... bread see Psalm 37.25.

112.24 your fullness your abundance. There is probably an allusion to the marginal (i.e. alternative) translation of Exodus 22.29: 'Thou shalt not delay to offer thy fulness'.

112.30 hand and glove wi' proverbial: Ray, 271; *ODEP*, 346.

112.32–33 wad gar ye trow ... cheese proverbial: see Ray, 203; *ODEP*, 542.

112.34 cat and dog, hare and hound proverbial: see Ray, 174 and *ODEP*, 7 ('To agree like cats and dogs').

113.1 driving ower passing the time.

113.2 ower by yonder over yonder.

113.4 troth is he he is indeed.

113.6 putting up wi' staying with.

113.13 far aff far away from.

113.23 affordeth matter provides a cause.

113.24 Never fash your beard pay no heed.

113.25–26 I ken best how to turn my ain cake Cheviot (138) recognises this as proverbial.

113.43 bide a wee stay a little.

114.2–3 faced his companions down maintained to his companions' faces.

114.5–6 bent up his whole soul as a bow is 'bent up', strung ready for use.

114.7–8 might seem both spear and shield see Milton, *Paradise Lost*, 4.990 (describing Satan).

114.17–23 I have heard ... shuffle a saraband the source of this anecdote has not been discovered.

114.30–31 mak it better to make it more worthwhile to.

114.35–36 that of all great men ... about it Louis XIV (for whom see note to 88.8–10) is said to have responded to all requests by saying 'Je verrai' ('I will see about it').

114.41–42 make day and night of it *probably* make a day and night of it, behave riotously.

115 motto not identified: probably by Scott.

115.25–26 the sway of its Barons ... neighbourhood in Scots law, a *baron* is the owner of an estate created by direct grant from the crown. A grant of barony carried with it both criminal and civil jurisdiction: the baron court was competent to try all crimes except the most serious (murder, robbery, rape and fire-raising), and had power to settle disputes between feudal superior and vassal, landowner and tenant, etc. As feudal superior, the baron could grant exclusive possession and use of a heritable property to a vassal in return for payment of a feu duty which could be monetary or in kind or in service, or in any combination of the three; as landlord the baron could specify rents in money, kind or service, or in any combination.

116.7 put them mad ance once made them mad.

116.11 up bye there up there.

116.13 sic a lang head as he has since he has so much shrewd intelligence.

117.39–40 torches of wax ... tallow-candles i.e. candelabra of wax candles as distinct from single candles made of animal fat.

118.5 as strong as Sampson Samson, whose story is told in Judges Chs 14–16, is proverbial for strength. The formulation here also seems to draw on Samson's riddle about the swarm of bees and honey in the carcase of a lion (Judges 14.8–14).

118.8 in some sort to a certain extent; in an uncertain or undefined way.

118.27 excuse your waiting excuse you from waiting.

118.33–34   the Christian law . . . upon your anger   see Ephesians 4.26:
'let not the sun go down upon your wrath'.

119.39   your spirit goes before your wit   compare the proverb 'your
tongue runs before your wit' (Ray, 213; *ODEP*, 830).

121   motto   Philip Massinger, *A New Way to Pay Old Debts* (published 1633),
3.3.50–56: to be 'in a way to' is to be likely to do, to have a good chance of doing.

121.21–24   the versatile old Earl of Wiltshire . . . not of the oak   Sir
William Paulet (1485?–1572), first Earl of Wiltshire, is credited with this
remark in Robert Naunton's *Fragmenta Regalia*, which Scott edited: *Memoirs of
Robert Cary, Earl of Monmouth . . . and Fragmenta Regalia . . . by Sir Robert Naunton* (Edinburgh, 1808), 195–96: *CLA*, 231.

122.1   the Scottish cabinet   the Scottish Privy Council.

122.22   out of court   concluded, without the possibility of being re-opened.

**122.27–31   liable to be reviewed . . . remeid in law . . . regularity of
such a procedure**   in the Claim of Right (11 April 1689) the Scottish Convention of Estates laid down the constitutional and legal principles by which it
wished William and Mary to govern, including the right of every subject 'to
protest for remeed of law to the King and Parliament against Sentences pronounced by the lords of Sessione'. However, while in the period before the
Union of 1707 it was not disputed that a 'protestation for remeid of law' was a
competent method of appealing to Parliament, there was disagreement about
the extent of the right of appeal from the Court of Session. See also note to
19.8–9, and the text at 125.16–25.

**122.43–123.1   Scott of Scotstarvet's 'Staggering State of Scots States-
men'**   the exposure of the wiles and misfortunes of statecraft, *The Staggering
State of the Scots Statesmen for One Hundred Years, viz. from 1550 to 1650*, by Sir
John Scot of Scotstarvet (1585–1670), was circulated in manuscript until it was
eventually published in Edinburgh in 1754 (*CLA*, 17). (Robertson)

123.6–7   Fordun had quoted . . . in terra   *Latin* neither a rich man nor a
strong one, nay not even a wise Scot, shall last long on earth when envy prevails.
The source of this quotation has not been found. It does not appear in the
Scotichronicon by John of Fordun (d. 1384?) and Walter Bower (d. 1449), but
proverbial sayings were often thus attributed.

123.10   comes in   is elected.

123.12–13   fifth in descent from the Knight of Tillibardine   i.e.
Lady Ravenswood and the Marquis of A—— share a great-great grandfather.
The great-great grandfather of the historical Marquis of Atholl, and from 1703
first Duke, was Sir John Murray of Tullibardine, Earl of Tullibardine from
1606, d. 1613.

123.17–18   those unarmed and unable Mephebosheths   in 2 Samuel
Mephebosheth is conspicuous for his extreme lameness (4.4 and 19.26). Scott
is probably recalling Dryden's reference to 'lame Mephibosheth the Wisard's
Son' in his contribution to Nahum Tate's *The Second Part of Absalom and
Achitophel* (1682), line 405. (Robertson)

123.19   called over the coals   proverbial phrase, meaning called to account
(*ODEP*, 358).

123.20–21   have a crow to pluck with you   proverbial phrase, meaning
have fault to find with you (Ray, 184; *ODEP*, 157).

124.16   Sarah, Duchess of Marlborough   Sarah Churchill (1660–1744),
wife of the first Duke of Marlborough, and the formidable favourite of Queen
Anne, had Whig sympathies.

124.30   he had it in direction   he had instructions.

124.42   fill him drunk   make him drunk.

125.16–25   Since the Claim of Right . . . strict law   see notes to
122.27–31 and 19.8–9.

126.5 the Master might be reponed against the attainder i.e. his title, lost when his father was attainted of treason (see note to 15.21–23), might be restored, normally by Act of Parliament, though until 1707 a royal pardon would have sufficed.

126.38–39 driven on matters too hardly prosecuted matters too rigorously: Alice said 'You have driven matters hard on with the house of Ravenswood' (35.1).

127 motto Francis Beaumont and John Fletcher, *A King and No King* (acted 1611, published 1619), 3.2.43–6.

128.8–11 actions of compt and reckoning . . . expiry of the legal *Scots law* by an 'action of compt and reckoning' a creditor can force the debtor to give an account of transactions between them and pay any balance due. A *multiple-poinding* is an action initiated by a debtor to settle the competing claims of several creditors to his money and property. An *adjudication* is an action by which the heritable estate of a debtor is transferred to the creditor as security for and satisfaction of the debt, the debtor being able to redeem it by paying the debt within a certain time. A *wadset* corresponds roughly to an English mortgage, by which land is transferred as security for a loan, to be redeemed on repayment. Wadsets may be either *proper*, in which case the creditor holds the land as a proprietor, entitled to the rents and profits from the land until the loan is repaid; or *improper*, in which case the creditor may take the rents but must account to the borrower for an excess of rents over agreed interest. By 'poinding of the ground' moveables belonging to tenants occupying the land can be taken by the creditor, but only to the extent of their rent. A *declarator* is an action brought by an interested party to have some legal right or status declared, but without claim on any person called as defender to do anything. The *legal* is the period (5 or 10 years) within which the debtor has a right to redeem lands taken by the creditor, by paying off the debt. If the debt is not paid, the creditor can claim an absolute right over the property by obtaining a decree declaring the expiry of the legal. (from Robertson)

128.25 debitum fundi *Scots law* a debt that attaches to land. The bond in question was presumably a heritable one, creating a right over land that, as a *debitum fundi*, could be made effectual by poinding of the ground (see note above).

129.2–3 annual-rent . . . principal interest accumulated with the principal debt, ever increasing the sum due.

129.3–4 no nook or coign of legal advantage see *Macbeth*, 1.6.6–7: 'no . . . coign of vantage', i.e. no projecting turret as lookout position.

129.23 belted lords 'belted' refers to a distinctive accoutrement of nobility, although properly only earls are belted.

129.29 as moths into raiment recalling the Sermon on the Mount: Matthew 6.19–20, 25, and 28; Luke 12.23 and 33.

130.23–24 the reliques of the supper . . . morning meal echoing *Hamlet*, 1.2.180–81: 'The funeral bak'd-meats/ Did coldly furnish forth the marriage tables'.

130.28 standing cup cup with a base.

130.40–41 a messenger come to arrest me for debt a messenger-at-arms executed summonses for the Court of Session. Arrest for debt was only possible once the debtor had failed to respond to a summons from the Court requiring the repayment of the debt; failure to do so resulted in outlawry and imprisonment. For a more extended treatment, see *The Antiquary*, EEWN 3, 306.37–308.18 and notes.

131.10–11 the very moral . . . Stand, to a true man i.e. like a highwayman. See *I Henry IV*, 1.2.105–6 (Falstaff referring to Poins).

132.12 is in dependence *Scots law* awaits settlement.

133.10−11 woodie written on his very visonomy gallows written on his face: see note to 53.8−9.

133.11 twa and a plack a considerable sum of money, twice my worldy wealth.

133 motto not identified; probably by Scott. Jonah, a minor prophet, was held by fellow sailors to be responsible for a storm, was thrown overboard, and was swallowed by a 'great fish': see Jonah 1.1−17.

134.23 Coolie Condiddle *coolie* is a contemptuous name for a man; *condiddle* means 'filch' or 'destroy by wastage'.

134.24−25 theft under trust . . . honester folks *Scots law* theft in breach of a trust reposed in the thief was an aggravation of the crime, constituting a capital offence. Presumably Condiddle would have been a baron and would thus have been able to act as judge in his baron's court: see note to 115.25−26.

135.33−34 'Suum cuique tribuito' . . . Justinian *Roman law* give to each his own. This is one of the three fundamental legal precepts enunciated by the Roman jurist Ulpian (d. 228 AD) and codified on the instructions of the Emperor Justinian in 529-533 AD. The other two precepts were 'to live honourably' and 'not to harm another person'.

136.31 "over-crowed," to use a phrase of Spencer *The Faerie Queene*, 1.9.50; *The Shepheardes Calender*, 'February', line 142.

137.21 the Pretender James Francis Edward Stewart (1688−1766), who after the death of his father James VII and II in 1701 was the *pretender* (claimant) to the British throne.

137.28 Inimicus amicissimus *Latin* a very friendly enemy.

137.34 fidus Achates *Latin* faithful Achates. See note to 90.13−14.

138.1−2 Six heirs portioners . . . rich in Scots law, the heritable property left by a person who dies without male heirs was divided equally either between the individual's daughters, or between other female relatives of the same degree of relationship to the deceased. Lady Girnington's wealth has increased as the number of co-heirs sharing it has diminished. (Robertson)

138.2−3 march with adjoin.

138 motto not identified; probably by Scott.

138.25 furnish forth the Master's table see *Hamlet*, 1.2.180−81: 'the funeral bak'd-meats/ Did coldly furnish forth the marriage tables'.

138.26−27 could have eaten a horse behind the saddle proverbial: Ray, 197.

138.41 mind to hae seen remember seeing.

139.7 come to terms come to an agreement.

139.10 keep your ain state behave in a dignified manner.

139.17 Thomas the Rhymer Thomas Learmont of Erceldoune, a 13th-century poet from the Scottish Borders, was credited with rhyming prophecies of a gloomy turn, frequently published as chapbooks. Caleb's utterance is in Thomas's style, but it does not allude to any particular prophecy.

139.17 whose tongue couldna lie see the ballad 'Thomas the Rhymer' (Child 37C), stanza 17: *Minstrelsy*, 4.89. The 'Thomas' of the ballad, and the romance, was identified with Thomas of Erceldoune in the 15th century.

139.26 coming round coming to pass with the revolution of events.

139.27 Truce with enough of; have done with.

139.33 Kelpie water-demon, usually in the form of a horse, which is said to haunt rivers, fords, etc., and lure the unwary to their deaths.

140.8−10 what had they ado . . . a drap brandy see Historical Note, 282.

140.33−35 the language of the Duke . . . another father see *As You Like It*, 1.2.206−09.

141.5−6 up-bye yonder up there (indicating a place some way off).

141.19 broad piece name applied after the introduction of the guinea

(£1.05) in 1663 to the much broader and thinner twenty shilling piece (£1.00) of previous reigns.

141.21 put up put away, put in your pocket.

141.27–28 a wilful man ... maun to Cupar two synonymous proverbs which were often linked (Ramsay, 86; *ODEP*, 890, 161). Compare 47.10.

141.28–29 pity of your life your life may be at risk.

141.36–37 Wisely saith the holy man ... all men 1 Esdras 4.22 in the Apocrypha.

142.41–42 not feeling quite easy ... feelings see *Macbeth*, 1.3.144-46: 'New honours come upon him,/ Like our strange garments, cleave not to their mould/ But with the aid of use' (Banquo of Macbeth).

143.8 knows ... on which side his bread is buttered proverbial: *ODEP*, 438.

143.17 dochan dorroch *Gaelic* 'deoch an doruis', stirrup cup, parting glass.

143.31–32 as black as mourning weed [Lady Elizabeth Wardlaw], *Hardyknute: A Fragment* (1719), line 231: 'His tow'r that us'd with torches light/ To shine sae far at night,/ Seem'd now as black as mourning weed,/ Nae marvel sair he sigh'd'. (Corson)

144.5–6 with-drawing room drawing room.

144.17 Sir Thomas Hope and Lord Stair Sir Thomas Hope of Craighall (?1580–1646), Lord Advocate from 1626; for Lord Stair see Historical Note, 271.

144.21 a black silk Geneva cowl the form of skull-cap adopted from ministers of the reformed Church in Geneva by Scottish Presbyterians.

144.31 Ostade and Teniers Adriaen van Ostade (1610–85) and David Teniers the Younger (1610–90) specialised in genre pictures of low life.

144.38–39 awful rule and right supremacy *The Taming of the Shrew*, 5.2.109.

144.42–43 double chimnies wide fireplaces.

145.35 cedant arma togæ *Latin* let arms yield to the gown; let military power yield to the civil authority: Cicero, *De Officiis* (44 BC), 1.22.77.

146.1 Think of just imagine.

146.3 the Mull of Galloway the southernmost point of the western peninsula of Galloway, and thus of all Scotland, noted for its small, tough Galloway horses.

146.6 claw up both your mittens trounce you both.

146.11–14 "There was a haggis ... Fal de ral," &c see [Charles Kirkpatrick Sharpe,] *A Ballad Book* [Edinburgh, 1818], 69, no. 26: *CLA*, 161. The book was dedicated to Scott.

146.15 Mr Cordery the schoolmaster's name derives from Mathurin Cordier or Corderius (1478 or 1484–1564), whose *Colloquia Scholastica*, first published in 1564 and frequently reprinted, was widely used as a school textbook: Scott's publisher Archibald Constable was involved in the publication of an edition in 1807.

146.26 west away in the west.

147.5–6 as cautiously as if he had been treading upon eggs proverbial: *ODEP*, 218.

148 motto see Robert Tailor, *The Hogge hath Lost his Pearle* (London, 1613), 1.1. The speaker, Carracus, is about to abduct the daughter of old Lord Wealthy, not knowing that his treacherous friend Albert has just seduced her at night pretending to be Carracus. Scott included the play in his revision of Robert Dodsley's collection *Ancient British Drama*, 3 vols (London, 1810), 3.47-70: *CLA*, 43.

148.37 in course in due course.

150.33–34 the ways of Heaven ... beyond our fathoming compare

Isaiah 55.8: 'For my thoughts are not your thoughts, neither are your ways my ways, saith the Lord'.

151.13–14 a witch . . . them that suffered at Haddington between 1649 and 1677 several alleged witches were tried at Haddington, a town 27 km E of Edinburgh, and some were executed.

151.21–22 the usurer . . . ancient land-marks allusions to Old Testament transgressions: see particularly Isaiah 3.15 ('What mean ye that ye beat my people to pieces, and grind the faces of the poor?'), and Proverbs 22.28, 23.10 ('Remove not the ancient landmark, which thy fathers have set . . . Remove not the old landmark; and enter not into the fields of the fatherless').

151.30–33 if you know of any hare . . . a silver bullet ready for her Scottish witches were often alleged to have turned themselves into hares; a silver bullet was believed necessary to shoot anyone protected by the Devil.

152.3 the eyes of old Alice's understanding see Ephesians 1.18.

154 motto see Wordsworth, 'Poems on the Naming of Places', 4.37–40 (1800).

158.35–38 an emblematic ceremony . . . refused to receive from Ravenswood the division of a piece of gold or silver between lovers was accepted as a token of a contract of marriage.

159.29 the stab death by stabbing.

160.9 beside the mark close to the mark; close to the bone.

160.10–11 ne'er put fingers in your eye about it don't weep about it.

161.26–27 the ancient French adage . . . va se rendre a castle which parleys and a woman who listens are both ready to surrender.

162 motto see Philip Massinger, *A New Way to Pay Old Debts* (published 1633), 3.2.154–58. Scott omits the words 'or thou art lost. *Exit* MARGARET.' after 'command'. Margaret is the exploited daughter of the extortioner Sir Giles Overreach; Marrall is his protégé.

163.16–17 Religion . . . discord compare 1 Corinthians 14.33: 'For God is not the author of confusion, but of peace, as in all churches of the saints'.

164.6–15 His feelings . . . such sweet gentleness see Joanna Baillie, *Constantine Paleologus; or, The Last of the Caesars: A Tragedy*, 2.2.54–60, in *Miscellaneous Plays* (London, 1804), 322.

165.33–34 Law's scheme in 1717, the year after founding the Banque Générale in Paris, John Law (1671–1729) of Lauriston had set up the Compagnie d'Occident (Western Company) to develop the resources of French Louisiana. After feverish speculation the company collapsed in 1720. As Law was a known Jacobite the scheme was doubly risky for a British investor.

165.43 making a good hand of making a profit out of.

166.5 who would take . . . "the bit and the buffet" *literally* take 'food and blows': proverbial. Kelly (311) glosses it 'Bear some ill Usage of them by whom you get Advantage'; see also Ramsay, 109 and *ODEP*, 61.

166.15–17 this evil communication . . . in the patron see 1 Corinthians 15.33: 'evil communications corrupt good manners'.

166.42–167.1 Monsieur Sagoon . . . Seignor Poco . . . Meinherr Durchstossen imaginary fencing-masters (maîtres d'armes), whose names mean Messrs Filthy Pig, Little, and Thrust-through.

167.9–10 single rapier . . . case of faulchions a *rapier* is a sword with a long slender blade designed for thrusting as well as cutting; *single* means 'without dagger'. A *back-sword* has only one cutting edge. A *broad-sword* is a cutting sword with a broad blade. A *falchion* is a broad sword more or less curved with the edge on the convex side; a *case* is a pair.

167.13–14 small sword light sword with a triangular blade and a simple hilt, designed for thrusting rather than cutting.

167.15–16   the Chevalier de Chapon   the name means 'capon', 'castrated cock'.

167.16   bits of   an expression indicating depreciation.

167.26   Skioch doch na skiaill   Gaelic proverb, 'Sgìthichidh deoch an sgeul' ('The drink will weary the tale').

167.27–28   Sir Evan Dhu ... 1689   Sir Ewen or Evan Cameron of Lochiel (1629–1719), chief of the Camerons and nicknamed 'the Black' ('Dhu'), led his clan in support of Dundee's rising.

167.36–37   touching the hilt ... over the water   the traditional toast to the exiled James, accompanied by a gesture implying a pledge to military action.

167.40–41   lands and tenements   *Scots law* 'tenements' is almost synonymous with 'lands': it means rights in heritable property, typically land.

167 footnote   boon companions, don't preach over your liquor   Tilley (L332) gives several variants of this proverb.

168.4   the statutory penalties, 'in that case, made and provided' the penalties for treason could include death, the forfeiture of property, and attainder. As Bucklaw is not a peer only death and forfeiture apply. No specific source for the legal phrase has been located.

168.9   I'll pledge you ... bottom   see *2 Henry IV*, 5.3.54 (Silence sings).

168.24   Lammerlaw and Traprain   hills *c.* 12.5 km S and 6.5 km E of Haddington, East Lothian.

168.28   son of a Spaniard   Ravenswood has a dark complexion: see 171.13 (and note) where he is described as being 'black as the crook'.

169.3–4   wherefore droops thy mighty spirit ... so pale   compare e.g. John Milton, *Samson Agonistes* (published 1671), line 594 ('So much I feel my genial spirits droop'), and *A Midsummer Night's Dream*, 1.1.128–29 ('Why is your cheek so pale?/ How chance the roses there do fade so fast?'). (Robertson)

169.9   leading strings   reins to assist and restrain children learning to walk.

169.17   Castle-Cuddy   *cuddy* means 'ass'.

169.17   we were hand and glove   proverbial: see note to 90.14–15.

169.24   Katie Glegg   the surname means 'sharp-witted' and recalls 'cleg', a name for the horse or gad-fly.

169.37–38   the light of whose countenance   Old Testament phrase indicating God's favour: Psalms 4.6, 44.3, 89.15, 90.8.

170.3   the Pretender   see note to 137.21.

170.5   the dead palsy   palsy producing complete insensibility or immobility of the part affected.

170.9–14   Duchess Sarah ... the Duchess of Marlborough   for Sarah Churchill, *née* Jennings, see note to 124.16.

170.18   the Wansbeck   river in Northumberland.

170.21   put on the tapis   place on the tablecloth, i.e. bring under discussion or consideration.

171.7   Distance me   blow me! The expression derives from horse-racing: any horse which had not arrived at a certain point when the winner crossed the finishing line was 'distanced', or eliminated in that heat.

171.10   cut in   *card playing* join in a game of whist by taking the place of a player 'cutting out' (cutting an unfavourable card).

171.13   as black as the crook   proverbial: *OED*. A *crook* is a hook in a fireplace for hanging pots on.

171.18   kept no terms   had no dealings.

171.20–21   point ... capot him   the terms refer to piquet, a card game played by two persons, in which points are scored on various groups or combinations of cards and on tricks: *point* is the number of cards of the most numerous suit in one's hand after discarding; *quint* is a sequence of five cards of the same suit, which count as 15 points; *quatorze* is a set of four similar cards held by one player, which count as 14 points; to *pique* is to win 30 points; to *repique* is to win 30 points on cards alone before beginning play; to *capot* is to win all the tricks.

171.24   terms of jointure   in Scots law *jointure* is a contractual provision for a widow of an annual payment of money during her life, or a liferent assignment of the rents of lands.

171.26   comes down   i.e. from England.

171.26   takes ... in her own hand   herself takes charge of.

171.29–30   the very gates of Jericho   proverbial for a distant place (compare 2 Samuel 10.5): *ODEP*, 410.

171.30   the judgment-seat of Prester John   in fable, a powerful priest-king of early medieval times. He appears as Senapo, King of Ethiopia, in Lodovico Ariosto's *Orlando furioso* (1516–32), 33.106.

171.34   drop out   let fall.

171.38   make up   arrange.

171.40   starting for the plate   *horse racing* beginning to run a race with a silver or gold cup as the prize.

172.3   I would make his guts garter his stockings   proverbial: see *ODEP*, 297.

172.16–17   your boots and doublet ... as the man says in the play   see Sir Toby Belch in *Twelfth Night*, 1.3.10–11.

172.23   horse and away   see note to 197.10–11.

172.25   to boot   into the bargain.

172.30   wind ... finger   proverbial: see *ODEP*, 847.

172.32   old Sall of Marlborough   see note to 124.16.

172.34–35   John Churchill ... Dundee or the Duke of Berwick   John Churchill (1650–1722), first Duke of Marlborough, was the celebrated soldier and Whig statesman who served Charles II, James VII and II, William and Mary, and Anne in turn; he is best known for his victories over the French from 1702 in the War of the Spanish Succession. John Graham of Claverhouse (1648–89), Viscount Dundee, was killed at Killiecrankie fighting to restore James VII and II. James Fitz-James (1670–1734), Duke of Berwick, illegitimate son of James VII and II and Marlborough's nephew, fought for the French forces against Britain in Flanders and Spain.

173   motto   see the ballad 'Duke upon Duke' (1720), largely by Alexander Pope, lines 115–16.

173.35–40   It so chanced ... the British Parliament   Lady Ashton, as a Whig, is not just anticipating but preparing for the implementation of the Union in 1707 when Scotland elected 30 county and 15 burgh members of the British Parliament. Bucklaw has acquired control over 'a little separate interest', i.e. a number of votes which he can by custom control as laird.

174.6   setting up for the county   putting himself forward (for election as Member of Parliament) for the county.

174.6–7   carry the heat ... walk the course   *horse racing* win the heat ... win the race easily.

174.8   hollow votes   votes that could be easily won. The term *hollow* is used in horse racing to indicate victory against feeble opposition.

174.33   misprision ... of treason   *English law* the offence of concealing knowledge of a treasonable plot from constituted authorities, here applied metaphorically to marriage.

175.7–8   like Don Gayferos ... fair and true   see Cervantes, *Don Quixote*, Part 2 (1615), Ch. 26; trans. Motteux, revised Ozell, 4 vols (Edinburgh, 1766), 3.281. A figure from Spanish romance, Don Gayferos, is represented in the first scene of a puppet-show as playing at draughts instead of rescuing his wife Melisandra from Moorish captivity. A ballad is quoted by the puppeteer's boy: 'Now Gayferos the live-long day, / Oh arrant shame at draughts does play;/ And, as at court most husbands do,/ Forgets his lady fair and true.'

175.25   a middle resemblance   a resemblance partly to one thing and partly to another.

176.4–5 and footnote   Middleton's Mad World my Masters   Scott included Thomas Middleton's *A Mad World, My Masters* (1608) in the second volume of his revision of Robert Dodsley's collection *Ancient British Drama*, 3 vols (London, 1810): *CLA*, 43. The greeting is from 2.1.7–8 (2.264).

176.8   the Avenger of Blood   in the Old Testament, the man who had the right to avenge the murder of a kinsman: see Joshua 20.3, 5 and Deuteronomy 19.6, 12.

176.19–20   change a leg   the inside passengers in a coach sitting opposite each other were so close together that they could not change the position of their legs without the consent of the person facing them.

176 footnote   the umquhile John . . . that now is   in 1819 the 'present' earl was John (not Charles) Hope (1765–1823), 4th Earl of Hopetoun, who had succeeded to the title on the death without male issue of an older half-brother James in 1816. He was the son of John (1704–81), 2nd Earl of Hopetoun from 1742, by his second wife. The error may be deliberate, for the 4th Earl was a distinguished general in the Peninsular War, and, as Sir John Hope, well-known; but a mistake is more likely, for the Lord President of the Court of Session, under whom Scott must often have sat, was Charles Hope. Also, the 4th Earl had a younger half-brother called Charles (1768–1828).

176   footnote   Mars standing by . . . laurel   Matthew Prior, 'The Ladle' (1704), lines 35–36.

177.3–4   He turned his eyes . . . vision   see Alexander Pope's translation of *The Odyssey* (1725–26, with William Broome and Elijah Fenton), 11.733–34: 'I turn'd my eye, and as I turn'd survey'd/ A mournful vision'. (Corson)

177.9–10   the green and blue chariots . . . Constantinople   in the circuses of Rome and Constantinople four factions were represented by chariots distinguished by red, white, blue, and green colours. The rivalry of the blue and the green teams grew particularly virulent in Rome in the 1st century AD, and in Constantinople during the reign of Justinian (527–65) 'the sportive distinction of two colours produced strong and irreconcileable factions, which shook the foundations of a feeble government' (Edward Gibbon, *The Decline and Fall of the Roman Empire* (1776–88), Ch. 40).

177.16–18   Mon Dieu! . . . Il y en est deux! *French* My God! there are two of them! This story exists in more than one version. It appears as one of the *Ingoldsby Legends* by Thomas Ingoldsby, 'The Black Mousquetaire: A Legend of France', first published in *Bentley's Miscellany*, 8 (1840), 262–68, 365–76. Another version, by G. Lenotre (Louis Léon Théodore Gosselin, 1857–1935), entitled 'La Vision du capitaine' may be found in his *Suivant l'Empereur: croquis de l'épopée* (Paris, 1947), 173. Scott's source for the story has not been traced.

177.25   in the manner   in the act.

178.39   mending his pace   travelling faster.

179.3–4   put on to a hand gallop   urge their horses to an easy gallop.

179.19   pas d'avance *French* lead, precedence.

180.23   cavaliere servente *Italian* a man who devotes himself wholly to attendance on a lady.

182.32   to the boot   into the bargain.

182.39–40   scared by a dun cow . . . Guy of Warwick   after many heroic adventures Sir Guy of Warwick 'slewe/ A monstrous wyld and cruell beast,/ Calld the Dun-cow of Dunsmore heath;/ Which manye people had opprest' ('The Legend of Sir Guy', lines 97–100, in Percy, 3.103–11).

184.42 full dress elaborate dress appropriate for a public ceremony or formal meal.

185.40–42 younger branch of the house of Angus ... thrice inter-married see note to 67.7–8 and the text at 14.41.

186 motto the lines are not by Edmund Waller (1606–87); they are probably a Scott pastiche.

187.7 Scottish miles the Scottish mile was 1.8 km, or nearly one-eighth longer than the English mile.

190.13 as in Thessaly of old as explained at 192.12–13, a corpse had to be guarded 'least witches or fiends might play their sport with it'. Thessaly, in N Greece, was from early times regarded as the especial home of witches.

191.22–23 the meeting betwixt Macbeth and the witches ... Forres *Macbeth*, 1.3, especially line 77.

191.33 find out discover by searching.

191.33 Mortsheugh the name is generated from either *mort* ('death') and *sheugh* ('bury'); or *morts* and *heugh* ('cliff, ravine').

191.43 as light as a lark proverbial. Compare *ODEP*, 527: 'As merry (gay, happy) as a lark.'

192.18 light doun in the King of France's cellar to *light doun* is to 'land'. The allusion is to a story 'concerning one of the Lord *Duffus* (in the Shire of *Murray*), his Predecessors, of whom it is reported, That upon a time, when he was walking abroad in the Fields near to his own House, he was suddenly carried away, and found the next day at *Paris* in the *French* King's Cellar with a Silver Cup in his Hand' (John Aubrey, *Miscellanies*, 2nd edn (London, 1721), 158: *CLA*, 149).

192.21–26 They prick us ... amends o' them ... burn me until 1736, when witchcraft was abolished as a criminal offence in Scotland, those accused of witchcraft were investigated by Church courts as well as by the Court of Justicary or special commissions. Those suspected of witchcraft were pricked with needles to test for devil's marks, believed to be immune to pain, and were tortured to extract confessions by means of 'pinnywinkles' or 'pilliewinkis', vices which squeezed the fingers. To say a prayer, especially the Lord's Prayer, backwards was to invoke the Devil. In Scotland, those found guilty of witchcraft were strangled at the stake and then burnt (the last death sentence for witchcraft was in 1722). The phrase *pit us on* means 'subject us to', and *gi'e me amends o' them* means 'give me the upper hand over them'.

192.24 the foul thief the Devil.

192.28–29 a drap brandy to burn ... sugar a glassful of brandy would be burned in a saucer with half a tablespoonful of white sugar to remove part of the spirit and make a delicate tipple.

192.34 Annie Winnie see Historical Note, 285, note 5.

192.37 written on his brow see note to 53.8–9.

192.39–40 make you your market of that *probably* you can bet on it.

192.40 a sure hand a reliable source.

192.43 mony ane many a one.

193.5 Fashna your thumb don't bother yourself.

193.10 before the sark gaed ower his head i.e. at or before his birth.

193.25–26 confessions ... seventeenth century see Scott's *Letters on Demonology and Witchcraft* (1830), Letter 9.

193.41 The rich Abbey of Coldinghame Coldingham in NE Berwickshire was the seat of a Benedictine priory founded in 1098 by Edgar, King of Scots.

194.10 house leeks herb with pink flowers formerly often found growing on houses.

194.15–16   the house of mourning and the house of feasting see *Ecclesiastes* 7.2.

194.21   to give the meeting to to meet.

194   motto see *Hamlet*, 5.1.65–70.

194.35   when "the mind is free ... delicate" see Lear's speech to Kent before the hovel on the heath: *King Lear*, 3.4.11–12.

195.13   ken ... by head-mark recognising [people] by their individual facial characteristics; the term *head-mark* was originally used of sheep. See also note to 53.8–9.

195.42–43   saxteen pund Scots £1.33. By the end of the 17th century the value of the Scots pound had declined to a twelfth of that of the pound sterling. It was officially abolished by the Act of Union.

196.5   bite on the bridle experience frustrating restraint; endure hardship: proverbial (Ray, 178; *ODEP*, 62). There is also probably an allusion to the practice of punishing scolds by fitting them with bridles to restrain their tongues.

196.17–18   plenishing the earth see Genesis 1.28 and 9.1: 'Be fruitful, and multiply, and replenish the earth'.

196.19–20   harp, sackbut, and psaltery three of the instruments employed as a signal to worship Nebuchadnezzar's golden calf (Daniel 3.7). 'Sackbut' is the old name for a trombone; the 'psaltery', a zither-like instrument, was popular in biblical and medieval times.

196.29–30   de'il lift them may the devil be off with them.

197.2   de'il ane to mend other all equally bad.

197.8–9   this trumpeter Marine ... Lords of the Circuit in 1710 Francis Marine, Sen., is recorded as one of Queen Anne's Trumpeters for Scotland, whose duty it was to announce royal proclamations and attend the Circuit Courts; in 1716 he was joined as fifth trumpeter by Francis Marine, Jun. 'Lords of the Circuit' are the judges of Scotland's highest criminal court, the High Court of Justiciary which sits in Edinburgh. At specified times they go on circuit to hear trials elsewhere.

197.10–11   'Boot and Saddle,' or 'Horse and away,' or 'Gallants, come trot' versions of three of the five principal military calls, 'Boute-selle', 'À cheval' and 'Le marche'. Signals were given by trumpet and drum in the Scottish army from 1641.

197.13   what is all this to what has all this to do with.

197.19   other whiles at other times.

197.21   Bothwell Brigg the bridge over the Clyde where the Covenanters were routed by Royalist forces on 22 June 1679. See *The Tale of Old Mortality*, EEWN 4b, 249–59.

197.22   I behuved ... to I must needs.

197.29   de'il a not a.

197.31–33   twenty-fourth of June ... of a' days of the month and year the sexton is probably recalling the Scottish victory over the English at Bannockburn on 24 June 1314, leading him to re-date Bothwell Bridge, which actually took place on 22 June.

197.33–34   Hackstoun of Rathillet David Hackston of Rathillet in Fife (d. 1680), a prominent Covenanter, and one of the leaders of the party who assassinated Archbishop Sharp, near St Andrews, in 1679.

197.36   let abe let alone.

197.38   Andrea Ferrara high-quality Scottish broad-sword. 'Andrew Ferrara was a North Italian swordsmith of the late 16th century. His name became a mark of quality for Scotsmen in the 17th and 18th centuries, and many Scots swords bear his name, but it is doubted whether any of them are in fact his work' (*Waverley*, ed. Claire Lamont (Oxford, 1981), 452).

197.41 Gog and Magog leaders of the heathen nations: Revelation 20.8.
198.4 points of war military instrumental signals.
198.7–8 cut short ... as scripture says compare 1 Samuel 2.33 and Psalm 103.15.
198.9 we behoved a' to we all must needs.
198.12–13 taen the grund reached dry land.
198.23 my sartie certainly.
198.23–24 would I nould I whether I wanted to or not.
198.28–29 I couldna plaid whew upon a dry humlock I couldn't have played anything on a dried hemlock stalk.
198.39 bite and soup a little to eat and drink.
199.3 guiding us the gate treating us in the way.
199.4 life-rent tacks of our bits o' houses and yards written leases for life of our little houses and gardens.
199.6–7 my dainty bit mailing my handsome piece of arable ground held on lease.
199.17 Sarra a bit never a bit.
199.17–18 Let her alane ... draws near her trust her to make things unpleasant for everything that comes near her.
199.19 gate o't path in respect of it.
199.22–23 Cervantes acutely remarks ... madman see *Don Quixote*, Part 2 (1615), Ch. 18.
199.27 the great, as well as the small vulgar see Horace, *Odes*, 3.1.1–2, translated by Abraham Cowley in his essay 'Of Greatness' (no. 6 of 'Several Discourses by way of Essays, in Verse and Prose', printed in the final section of *The Works of Mr Abraham Cowley* (London, 1668), 125: 'Hence ye profane; I hate ye all;/Both the Great, Vulgar, and the small'). The second line is quoted by Belinda in William Congreve's play *The Old Batchelour* (1693), 4.3.144–45.
200.12 short cheer inadequate entertainment.
200.15–17 I can play ... Pattie Birnie Patrick, 'Patie' or Peter Birnie (b. *c.* 1635, and d. *c.* 1721) was a famous fiddler from Kinghorn, Fife. 'O wiltu, wiltu do't again!' was a tune he played on all occasions. The words and tune of 'The Auld Man's Mare's Dead' are attributed to him, although the words may have been by another; the words were re-worked by Burns (for words, tune and commentary see *The Poems and Songs of Robert Burns*, ed. James Kinsley, 3 vols (Oxford, 1968), no. 585 and note).
200.22 'Liggeram Cosh,' and 'Mullin Dhu,' and 'the Cummers of Athole' 'Liggeram Cosh' (Gaelic *gliogram-chois*, 'long-limbed person'), also known as 'Merrily Dance the Quaker' or 'The Quaker's Wife', was printed in Robert Bremner, *A Collection of Scots Reels or Country Dances* (London, [1766]), 53: the tune later appeared, with words by Burns ('Blythe hae I been on yon hill'), in *A Select Collection of Original Scotish Airs for the Voice*, [ed. George Thomson], 5 vols (London, 1793–1818), 3 (1799), No. 58. 'Mullin Dhu' is Scott's spelling of the reel 'Muileann Dubh' (*Gaelic* 'The Black Mill'): it can be found in James Stewart-Robertson, *The Athole Collection of the Dance Music of Scotland* (Edinburgh and London, 1961), 44. The same volume includes (252) 'Athole Cummers', which had been printed in Alexander M'Glashan, *A Collection of Strathspey Reels* [1780], 10.
200.25 a thought honest something of a Jacobite: see 89.37–39 (text).
200.26 'Killiecrankie,' and 'the King shall hae his ain,' and 'the Auld Stuarts back again,' three popular Jacobite songs included in *The Jacobite Relics of Scotland*, ed. James Hogg, 2 vols (Edinburgh, 1819–21), 1.32–33, 1–3, and 122–23. The tune 'Killiekrankie' was mentioned in 1692 and was printed in Neil Gow, *A Collection of Strathspey Reels* [1784], 26; that of 'The King Shall Hae His Ain' appeared in James Oswald, *The Caledonian Pocket*

Companion, Book 2 [c. 1746], 20; and that of 'The Auld Stuart's Back Again' appeared as a reel in *A Complete Repository of Old and New Scotch Strathspeys, Reels & Jigs Adapted for the German Flute* [c. 1810], 36.

200.37 my bread-winner see Allan Ramsay's 'The Life and Acts of, or An Elegy on Patie Birnie' (1721), line 17, where Birnie's fiddle is referred to as 'his Bread-winner' (Robertson).

201 motto the source has not been identified.

201.41 or so or something of that sort.

202.7–8 in the present view of a change in the event, which now seems likely, of a change in administration.

202.10 tongue of the trump the leading person (*literally* the vibrating fork in the Jew's harp).

202.28 indifferent good nooning quite a good midday meal.

202.32 spread . . . a table in the wilderness see Psalm 78.19.

203.14 went on continued further.

203.17–18 the Darien matter lent him a lift the Darien Scheme was initiated in 1695 to establish a Scottish trading colony on the Isthmus of Panama; its disastrous failure in 1699 was taken as a sign of Scotland's commercial weakness and helped to secure the Act of Union in 1707. This scheme lent Sir William *a lift*, i.e. gave him a helping hand: he had good information ('good intelligence') and sensible judgment ('sound views'), and thus sold his shares before the failure.

203.22 outsit his market delay making terms until the opportunity is lost.

203.27 to bell the cat with him in the Scots Parliament proverbial: see Kelly, 180; *ODEP*, 44. As well as the general allusion to the familiar fable of the mice proposing to put a bell round the cat's neck to apprise them of her approach, there is probably a recollection of Archibald Douglas, fifth Earl of Angus (c. 1449–1514), nicknamed 'Bell the Cat' for leading the conspiracy as a result of which James III's favourites were hanged in 1482: see *Tales of a Grandfather*, 1st Series (1827), in *Prose Works*, 22.320–23.

205.1 the fatal battle of Flodden see note to 40.14.

205.25 should been should be.

205.30–36 the principle of the Spanish generals . . . in the day of battle the reference has not been traced.

206.21 pease strae stalks and foliage of pea plant used as cheap fodder and bedding for animals.

206.40 loss of warld's gear loss of worldly goods and property: Robert Burns, 'Poor Mailie's Elegy' (1786), line 7. (Corson)

207.14–15 in the year that him they ca'd King Willie died 1702.

207.20 Aye did they, mony ane of them certainly they did, many of them.

207.26 made fast on us gained rapidly on us.

207.32 look about attend to.

207.38 as I live by bread compare Luke 4.4.

208.35–37 the Gut of Gibraltar . . . Algerine the Straits of Gibraltar . . . Algerian.

209.27–28 look a wee strange upon it behave in a slightly distant or aloof manner.

209.29 ring true i.e. show you are of the proper stuff, like a coin 'rung' on the counter to test that it is really gold.

209.40–41 the Council with the Queen see Historical Note, 282, 285, n.9.

209.42–210.1 ascending to the top-gallant . . . ropes as Corson points out, Scott is alluding to Tom Bowling's ladder of preferment in Ch. 41 of Tobias Smollett's novel *Roderick Random* (1748). He blends this with the image of the top-gallant, or highest pitch of aspiration, in *Romeo and Juliet*, 2.4.184.

210.9 fat the North-east Scots pronunciation of 'what'.

210.10–11 **the day ... the morn** today ... tomorrow.

210.15 **Ravensweed** not a misnomer but the NE pronunciation of a double 'o'.

210.23–24 **out by yonder** out there.

210.24 **the Bass** see note to 62.22.

210.24–25 **the Lord High Commissioner to the Estates o' Parliament** the sovereign's representative at the Scottish Parliament with its three Estates.

210.33–34 **whilk it is muckle to be doubted that he never will** which it's much to be doubted he ever will.

211 **motto** Thomas Campbell, 'Lochiel's Warning' (1802), lines 31–34. The Wizard predicts the effect of the 1745–46 Jacobite rising.

211.17 **Selkirk bannocks** rich fruit loaves from the county town of Selkirkshire.

211.33 **no ways** by no means.

212.8 **vassals ... men bound ... by law** in the feudal system the baron, having received a direct grant of lands from the monarch, would be bound to produce a specified number of armed men to serve in time of war; the baron in turn would require those to whom he feued the land to produce so many men for military service.

212.14–18 **What do ye want, ye dog? ... a new master** compare the exchange between Oliver and Adam in *As You Like It*, 1.1.73–76: 'Get you with him, you old dog./ Is "old dog" my reward? Most true, I have lost my teeth in your service. God be with my old master! He would not have spoke such a word'.

212.17–18 **ower auld a dog to learn new tricks** proverbial: see Ray, 99, 142 and *ODEP*, 805.

212.43 **down bye** down there.

213.3–4 **hail and fear** in perfect condition.

213.10 **Hout awa!** get away with you!

213.11–12 **Little's the light ... a mirk night** proverbial, though this instance is the only one recorded in *ODEP*, 470.

213.22 **in the sort** in that way.

213.30 **my certie!** exclamation of surprise.

214.5 **a grain's damage** the slightest harm.

214.20 **closing in to** drawing near to.

214.21 **train up weans ... in the way they should go** see Proverbs 22.6.

214.27–28 **Some gaed east ... craw's nest** see *The Oxford Dictionary of Nursery Rhymes*, ed. Iona and Peter Opie (Oxford, 1951), no. 150, 157–58, where the earliest Scottish version is: 'Hickery, pickery, pease scon,/ Where will this young man gang?/ He'll go east, he'll go west,/ He'll go to the crow's nest'.

214.33 **what cheereth the soul of man** see Psalm 104.15: 'wine that maketh glad the heart of man'.

214.39–40 **up bye yonder** up there.

215.23 **in some sort** to some extent.

216.9 **said it was Latin for a tass o' brandy** a traditional expression used as an apology for drinking a dram after the food in question: see *Swift's Polite Conversation*, ed. Eric Partridge (London, 1963), 144.

216.15 **that gate** in that way.

216.27 **chamber of dais** best bedroom.

216.37 **Low Dutch** Low German, spoken in N Germany and Holland.

217.3–5 **that which Teniers ... country village** for Teniers see note to 6.27–28. For possible self-portraiture in peasant surroundings, and for the form of glass referred to, see Jane P. Davidson, *David Teniers the Younger* (London, 1980), 12, and Plates 14 and 15.

217.7 **double ale** beer of twice the ordinary strength.

217.8 **a Scotch pint** four imperial pints (3.4 litres).

217.40 in fine in short.

219.1 a whiles a while's, a short space of.

219 motto probably by Scott, alluding to the proverb 'take Occasion (Time) by the forelock, for she is bald behind' (*ODEP*, 822-23). See also *Saint Ronan's Well*, EEWN 16, 245.27, and note.

219.38–39 the Tory party obtained . . . a short-lived ascendency see Historical Note, 282.

220.19 what Cromwell called waiters upon providence Oliver Cromwell is not known to have used this phrase in an ironic sense.

220.25 restoring him in blood . . . attainder when a person was attainted, they and their heirs suffered 'corruption of blood'; 'restoration in blood' involved readmission to the forfeited privileges of birth and rank.

220.38 the Canongate the former burgh adjoining Holyrood Palace in Edinburgh.

221.19 pize upon it! damn it!

222.27 in behalf of for the benefit of.

222.29–30 their hand has been . . . the immunities of God's kirk they have consistently supported the crown's oppression of the individual and the Presbyterian church in the covenanting troubles, and opposed the Revolution settlement giving powers to Parliament, and the Church of Scotland's freedom from external political control.

222.32–35 it has been my lot . . . knew them no more see Psalm 37.36 (Prayer Book version): 'I myself have seen the ungodly [Authorised Version: "wicked"] in great power, and flourishing [Authorised Version: "spreading himself"] like a green bay-tree'; and Psalm 103.16: 'For the wind passeth over it, and it is gone; and the place thereof shall know it no more'.

223.13 in foro contentioso *Latin* in an action contested in the law courts, where the parties have been fully heard and a decree (final judgment) made.

223.35 inter minores *Latin* between minors. The Keeper fuses two issues. Under Scots law, any contract concerning property (a betrothal between persons of this rank would normally have involved a contract as regards property) made by a person under 21 without the consent of parents ('natural curators') or guardians could be declared null; but a minor could marry without parental consent.

223.42–43 Time, the great physician, he hoped would mend all combining two proverbial sayings: 'Nature, time, and patience are the three great physicians'; 'Time cures all things' (*ODEP*, 556, 823).

224.22–23 which side of the hedge the sun had got to proverbial: see *ODEP*, 732, 'To be on the right (better, safe) or wrong side of the hedge', and 786, 'The sun does not shine on both sides of the hedge at once'.

224.30 keep her threep maintain her strongly-held position, stick to her guns.

225 motto *Richard III*, 1.2.227–29.

225.22 to boot to the good.

225.26 devil's tattoo idle drumming or tapping, as a sign of impatience.

225.28 double distanced see note to 171.7.

225.30 Cut me out of feather take my brilliance away.

226.7–8 as sulky as a bear that's lost its whelps proverbial: see Tilley, S292.

226.12 playing the back-game with a witness playing backgammon and no mistake. In backgammon the pieces are obliged under certain circumstances to go backwards.

226.16 Lothian see note to 15.6.

226.28–29 lies with . . . policy is in accordance with . . . political cunning *or* political objective.

227.23 a 'famous witness' *Scots law* an admissible witness of respectable character, who had not been declared 'infamous' by a sentence of the Court of Session or High Court of Justiciary.

227.38 Capote me imprecation derived from card game of picquet: see note to 171.20–22.

228.2 to boot into the bargain.

228.6–7 night-cowl ... considering caps nightcap (the article of dress and a drink) ... thinking caps.

228 motto see *The Comedy of Errors*, 5.1.62–66.

228.15 his faithful Achates see note to 90.13–14.

228.24 wait upon come respectfully to talk to.

229.41 in broad Scotch i.e. expressed in a plain-speaking manner befitting a Scot.

230.2 the three Lothians see note to 15.6.

230.3 the Canongate see note to 220.38.

230.8 except against object to.

230.10 out upon you expression of reproach.

230.14 upon a par *either* equal to each other *or* average.

230.30 Ratisbon Regensburg, in Bavaria.

230.35–37 the old song ... the new 'It's gude to be merry and wise,/ It's gude to be honest and true ;/ It's best to be off wi' the auld love/ Before ye are on wi' the new.' See 'It's gude to be merry and wise', lines 3–4, in *The Songs of Scotland, Ancient and Modern*, ed. Allan Cunningham, 4 vols (London, 1825), 2.352: *CLA*, 165.

231.24–26 your Pacolet ... this matter in the early French romance *Valentine and Orson* Pacolet is a dwarf servant with a magic flying wooden horse.

232.6 the casting of a fore-shoe the loss of a front horseshoe.

232.7 the 20th day from this is St Jude's St Jude's Day is 28 October.

232.8 Caverton Edge in the parish of Eckford, Roxburghshire, 6 km S of Kelso. Annual horse races took place here, from the period of the novel's action until Scott's time, at dates between late July and late October.

232.9 Kittlegirth *kittle* is used of a horse that is difficult to control, and *girth* suggests 'saddlegirth'.

232.25 to sign and seal since 1584 sealing had generally been unnecessary in Scotland, but the words imply finality and solemnity. (Normand)

232.27 to do and die variant of the proverbial 'to do or die' (*ODEP*, 192).

232.40–41 Posso, in Mannor Water Posso Craigs is a hill overlooking Manor Water 8 km SW of Peebles, Peeblesshire.

233 motto *The Comedy of Errors*, 5.1.78–82.

233.32 the revolution the French Revolution of 1789.

233.34–35 both in law and fact ... their parents actually, in fact rather than in law: see note to 223.35.

233.40–41 he made his choice ... the casket in *The Merchant of Venice*, 3.2 Portia's suitors choose between gold, silver, and lead caskets to decide who will marry her.

234.20–23 As this measure ... tyrannical the right of appeal to the Scottish Parliament was established in 1689, but extent of the right of appeal had not been determined (see note to 122.27–31). The politics of this particular appeal might well make it seem 'arbitrary' and 'tyrannical' in the circumstances.

235.2–3 the worst measures ... the worst Stuarts i.e the measures of Charles I and James VII and II, substituting government by decrees which were, in the words of the Claim of Right, 'utterly and directly contrary to the known laws' of the kingdom.

235.13–14 the civil, the municipal, and the canon law Roman law as received in modern times; the law of a particular state; and ecclesiastical law. These three laws had differing approaches to the validity of contracts.

235.14–15 **patria potestas** *Latin* in civil law, the power which a father could exercise over the members of his family. Although this power was never as extensive in Scots law as in Roman law, fathers had considerable rights over the custody, education, and property of their children. (Normand)

235.37 **the last consequence** the greatest importance.

236.33 **laying out of view** ignoring.

237.4–5 **a willow branch** willow was worn to lament a lost lover: there is probably an allusion to Desdemona in *Othello*, 4.3.26–58.

237.24–25 **pair of colours** commission of an ensign, formerly the lowest commissioned officer grade in the infantry.

238.13 **firm of purpose** Lady Macbeth rebukes her husband for being 'infirm of purpose': *Macbeth*, 2.2.52.

238 **motto** *The Faerie Queene*, 3.7.6.

238.34–35 **the Wise Woman of Bowden** a 'wise woman' is a witch, usually benevolent; Bowden is a village 4 km S of Melrose, Roxburghshire.

238.40–41 **herbs selected in planetary hours** planetary hours were one-twelfth of the natural day or night, and thus varied in length according to the season. Each hour was believed to be ruled by a planet, and each herb had particular virtue when plucked during the planetary hour appropriate to it.

239.15 **the stake and tar-barrel** barrels of tar were used in burning witches at the stake, usually after garotting.

239.15 **like Caliban's** see *The Tempest*, 4.1.196–98.

239.18 **matches** i.e. love-matches.

239.19 **Beelzebub** the Devil.

239.35 **"and mediciner"** probably rather a 'quotation' from popular speech than literature.

239.37–38 **the great enemy of mankind** the Devil.

240.13 **"lend an attentive ear"** probably rather a 'quotation' from popular speech than literature.

240.15–18 **Of fays . . . captive thralls** not identified. Scott also uses it as a quotation in *Minstrelsy*, 2.349.

240.22–23 **blue-eyed hag** *The Tempest*, 1.2.269 (Caliban's mother, the witch Sycorax).

241.9–12 **articles of dittay . . . Privy Council** the Privy Council would appoint a commission of local gentlemen, who authorised the sheriff to arrange for the selection of a jury. The 'articles of dittay' were the specific foundations of a criminal prosecution set out in an indictment.

241.11 **North-Berwick-Law** see note to 62.22.

241.13–17 **she had . . . another lady** see Historical Note, 281.

241.29 **rankling . . . wounded deer** compare *As You Like It*, 2.1.33–63.

242.23–25 **I'll have a priest . . . broken** William Congreve, *The Mourning Bride* (1697), 1.1.354–56: Manuel, King of Grenada, is frustrated by his secretly-married daughter's reluctance to marry the son of his favourite.

242.33 **the union . . . Zion** see Ezra 9.1–2, where intermarriage between Jews and neighbouring races is condemned.

243.8 **no inheritance in Jesse** see 2 Samuel 20.1, 1 Kings 12.16, and 2 Chronicles 10.16, where to have no 'inheritance in the son of Jesse' (David) is to be a dissentient among the Israelites.

243.9–11 **we are commanded . . . brotherhood with us** the language and sentiments are biblical, but there is no specific source.

243.25 **Moonshine** smuggled spirits.

243.27 **a sliding bowsprit** a running bowsprit, which was slid in to furl the jib.

243.28 Campvere (now Veere), on the island of Walcheron, Holland, where the Scots had a privileged trading post from 1444 until 1795.

244 motto see George Crabbe, *The Parish Register* (London, 1807), 2.284–9.

244.20 the articles the terms of the ante-nuptial contract regulating the property provisions on a marriage.

244.33–34 the deeds must be signed . . . happy on this belief there appears to be no other documented evidence, but it may be related to the old requirement that marriages be celebrated within canonical hours.

245.16 point d'espagne Spanish lace made with gold and silver thread.

245.19–20 sumpter mules mules used for carrying baggage.

245.30 the Copper Captain a sham captain: Michael Perez is so called in the dramatis personae of John Fletcher, *Rule a Wife and Have a Wife* (performed 1624).

246.1–3 as she had proved herself . . . land here see Exodus 20.12 (the fourth commandment) and Proverbs 3.1–2.

246.4 a better country Heaven (Hebrews 11.16).

246.6–9 the path of knowledge . . . causeth to err Proverbs 19.27: 'Cease, my son, to hear the instruction that causeth to err from the words of knowledge'.

247 motto see *Romeo and Juliet*, 1.5.52–53, 56–57 (Tybalt, of Romeo).

247.25 Spanish mantle cloak with a hood attached.

247.27 slouched hat see note to 82.20.

248.22–23 Him who brought peace on earth . . . mankind Jesus. See Luke 2.14.

248.24–25 God hateth the blood-thirsty man see Psalm 5.6: 'the Lord will abhor the bloody and deceitful man'. But the phraseology owes something to Proverbs 29.10: 'The blood-thirsty hate the upright'.

248.25 he who striketh . . . perish with the sword see Matthew 26.52 and Revelation 13.10.

249.21–22 the decisive interview . . . to demand whatever the moral position, Ravenswood had no legal right to such an interview.

249.32 depart in peace Luke 2.29.

249.33 the ancient Adam unregenerate humanity, as opposed to Jesus the new Adam. See 1 Corinthians 15.22, 45.

249.35 in the gall of bitterness and bond of iniquity see Acts 8.23.

250.5–6 add not fuel to firebrands proverbial or quasi-proverbial: compare the variants of 'Put not fire to flax' (*ODEP*, 260).

250.8–9 peradventure my grey hairs may turn away wrath varying 'A soft answer turneth away wrath' (Proverbs 15.1) and 'wise men turn away wrath' (Proverbs 29.8).

250.28 To-morrow, sir—to-morrow—to-morrow see *Macbeth*, 5.5.19 (Macbeth on his wife's death).

251.20–29 If a woman . . . disallowed her see Numbers 30.3–5.

252.13 under her own hand in her own handwriting; it is thus a holograph document, making it legally binding in Scotland.

253.7 a world's wonder an object of astonishment to the whole world.

254 motto Robert Southey, *Thalaba the Destroyer* (London, 1801), 7.430–31.

254.16 the disease was on the spirits i.e. her sickness was mental rather than physical.

255.40–41 Sir William Wallace see note to 7.4. The size of Wallace's sword and the strength of his blows have quasi-proverbial status: compare note to *The Antiquary*, EEWN 3, 204.40–41.

256.22 auld lang syne old times, old friendship.

256.22 for as braw as however splendid.

256.26 tenony hough stringy cut from a hind leg of beef.

256.26 mair by token the more so (i.e. all the more stringy by contrast with yours).

256.35 as if they served us for true love and likeing as if they gave us a dole because they truly liked us.

257.1 dead dole dole distributed on the occasion of a funeral.

257.3–4 My loaf . . . ne'er the worse see Reginald Scot, *The Discoverie of Witchcraft* (London, 1584), 245: compare *CLA*, 123.

257.5–6 God send us a green Yule and a fat kirk-yard alluding to the proverb 'A green Yule makes a fat Kirk-yard', i.e. a mild winter leads to many deaths (Ray, 36; *ODEP*, 337).

257.17–18 her winding sheet . . . is up as high as her throat already the superstition, which in general terms dates back to Homeric times (*Odyssey*, 20. 351–2), is located in the Hebrides, with details similar to those in the text, by Martin Martin in his *A Description of the Western Isles of Scotland* (London, 1703), 302. (Robertson)

257.18–19 Her sand . . . weel shaken the image is of an hour-glass, in which the sifting of sand from one compartment to the other marks the passage of time.

257.21 the fairy rings circles of dark green grass believed to be produced by fairies dancing, but actually due to the growth of fungi below the surface.

257.25–26 a bonnie red gown . . . a stake, a chain, and a tar-barrel see note to 239.15. Witches were strangled, then burned, sometimes in a tar barrel. *To the boot o' that* means 'besides that'. The red gown is probably metaphorical.

257.27 up early and doun late see *The Merry Wives of Windsor*, 1.4.93 (Mistress Quickly).

257.31 nae canny body unnatural, dealing in the supernatural.

257.34–36 a' the Scotch witches . . . North-Berwick Law for North Berwick Law see note to 62.22. The district was associated with witches because of the 1590–92 trials for alleged satanic rituals in North Berwick kirkyard (including flying through the air), and the trials at Haddington 1649–77. For a description of Scottish practices, see Letters 5 and 9 of Scott's *Letters on Demonology and Witchcraft* (London, 1830).

257.43 screwing up tuning.

258.1 the night tonight.

258.2 if the pins haud if the tuning pegs remain in place.

258.6 Presbytery and Synod presbyteries are the Church of Scotland courts superior to kirk sessions. Until they were discontinued at the end of 1992 synods were regional courts ranking between presbyteries and the supreme court, the General Assembly.

258.23 l'Amphitrion où l'on dîne see Molière's comedy *Amphitryon* (1668), lines 1703–04: 'Le véritable Amphitryon/ Est l'Amphitryon, où l'on disne'; i.e. the person providing the feast is the true host.

259.41–43 the key of the bridal-chamber . . . entrusted boisterous guests were thus excluded from the bedroom, and a reluctant bride or groom could not leave it.

261.4 at all rates at any cost, by any means.

261.24 The provincial judge of the district the local sheriff, or his depute or substitute, who were responsible for investigating crimes as well as conducting trials.

262.6 the Duke's Walk Scott explains in a Magnum note (14.356): 'A walk in the vicinity of Holyrood-house, so called, because often frequented by the Duke of York, afterwards James II., during his residence in Scotland. It was for a

long time the usual place of rendezvous for settling affairs of honour.' The walk
was situated below St Anthony's Chapel.

262.9–10   a sadder and a wiser man   at the end of Coleridge's 'The Rime
of the Ancient Mariner' (1798), it is said of the wedding guest that after hearing
the mariner's story 'A sadder and a wiser man/ He rose the morrow morn'.

262.21–22   an ower true tale   proverbial expression (Cheviot, 39), meaning something 'only too true'.

262   motto   from a poem composed by Alexander Garden on the death of Sir
James Lawson of Humbie in 1612, in Alexander Nisbet, *A System of Heraldry
Speculative and Practical*, 2 vols (London, 1722), Vol. 2, Appendix: compare
CLA, 11.

263.17   the day   today.

263.18   as black as the crook   see note to 171.13.

263.28   uphaud it for   warrant that it was.

263.32   led out the brawl   opened the dancing.

263.34–35   pride would get a fa'   proverbial: see Ray, 148 and *ODEP*, 647.

263.38   What should ail us to see them?   what should stop us seeing them?

263.43–264.2   there's a thirteenth . . . no be lang for this world   a
widespread superstition (derived from the Last Supper) that when there are
thirteen in a company one of them will shortly die.

264.42–43   Do not . . . urge . . . desperate   echoes Romeo to Paris at
Juliet's tomb: 'tempt not a desp'rate man' (*Romeo and Juliet*, 5.3.59).

268.27   life had lost to him its salt and its savour   compare Matthew
5.13 and Luke 14.34: 'if the salt have lost his savour, wherewith shall it be
salted?'

GLOSSARY

This selective glossary defines single words; phrases are treated in the Explanatory Notes. It covers Scottish words, archaic and technical terms, and occurrences of familiar words in senses that are likely to be strange to the modern reader. For each word (or clearly distinguishable sense) glossed, up to four occurrences are noted; when a word occurs more than four times in the text, only the first instance is given, followed by 'etc.'. Orthographical variants of single words are listed together, usually with the most common use first; in these cases separate references, divided by a semicolon, are normally given for each form. Often the most economical and effective way of defining a word is to refer the reader to the appropriate explanatory note.

a in 50.23, 75.3

a', a all, every title-page etc.; 96.29; for 61.8 see note

aback back 110.18

abe see note to 197.36

a-bleeze, ableeze ablaze 88.29; 198.12

about in attendance on 105.21

abroach a-foot 165.34

abroad out in the open air 24.36, 76.3, 145.19, 178.29

abune, aboon above, in good cheer 110.3, 196.28, 198.20; 68.40, 86.24, 214.22

acceptation favourable reception 81.18

accession assent, adherence 50.35, 50.37

accommodations accommodation 94.24, 99.4, 117.18

accompt account 166.34

accord see note to 102.36

acres landed estates 165.30, 168.31

address bearing in conversation, skill, adroitness, courteous behaviour 17.39 etc.

adjudication for 128.9 and 129.1 see note to 128.8−11

ado to do 140.9

advance distance in front 175.43

adverse holding an opposite position 16.39

advices communication from a distance 46.42

advised judged 128.38

ae one, a single 68.24 etc.

æther air 115.12

aff off 65.2 etc.; for 113.13 see note

affianced engaged 249.21, 250.1

afore before, in front of 68.16, 108.29, 141.3, 197.9

again against 64.42

against by the time of 232.24

agé act for another as a law agent or solicitor 102.36

agitated set in motion 158.35

ahint behind 61.24, 263.26

aid see note to 102.8

aiding helpful 243.11

ail see note to 263.38

aill ale 192.28, 195.41

ain own 61.7 etc.

airt direct 114.30, 210.12

aits oats 62.16

aiver carthorse, old horse 198.26

alane alone 199.17

alimentary providing maintenance 35.32

allenarly only, exclusively 213.16

allow deduct from the amount due 77.32

ally confederates 245.14

amang among title-page etc.

amateur person with a taste for a particular subject 12.39

ambi-dexter practising on both sides 46.2

amends see note to 192.21−26

an, an'¹ if 68.39 etc.; 105.23, 201.2, 210.24

328

an, an'² and 113.5; 192.34, 210.13

ance once 90.38 etc.

anchoret hermit 39.33

anciently formerly 36.37, 82.4

ane¹ one 61.22 etc.; for 192.43 and 207.21 see notes

ane² a 75.11, 114.14, 201.3, 220.33

aneath beneath 64.11

anent concerning, about 72.37, 219.21

aneugh enough 77.9 etc.

anglice *Latin* in English 111.28, 209.43

anither another 77.27 etc.

anker measure 114.14

annual *Scots law* annual payment from land or property 89.43

antique venerable 103.14

apple-woman woman who keeps a stall for sale of apples 73.37

appropriated appropriate 12.17

arena aren't 208.28, 214.38

aroint see note to 60.19

ass ashes 97.21

a'thegither altogether 85.35

attainder forfeiture of rights on conviction of treason 126.5, 220.25

atween between 206.43

auld old 47.6 etc.

auld-warld old-world 196.20

ava at all 112.16

avant-courier messenger sent on in advance 143.36, 205.5

aw all 64.33

awa' away 86.15 etc.

awe owe 77.32

aweel well 108.9 etc.

awful, awfu' awful, dreadful, terrible, sublimely majestic, commanding respect or fear 66.39 etc.; 65.19, 213.40

awsome dreadful 208.1

aye always 47.30 etc.

back-game see note to 226.12

back-sey (sir)loin 256.27

back-sword see note to 167.9–10

back-wynd back lane 6.35

baillie magistrate 90.8

bairn child 106.42 etc.

baith both 105.23 etc.

ball bullet, cannon-ball 50.24, 192.42, 198.17

band-string string for fastening collar or ruff 147.24

bandy band together 23.34

bane bone 65.5, 216.7, 256.28

bannock round flat cake made of meal and cooked on a griddle 64.32, 112.11; for 211.17 see note

barn-door reared at the barn-door 211.15

bartizan battlemented parapet 69.24, 140.12, 175.23

batoon (strike with) a stick 132.36

bawbee copper coin originally worth 6 pence Scots, one halfpenny sterling (0.2p) 197.10

be by 108.18

beaver hat of beaver fur 92.4

beck silent signal 211.30

bedesman humble servant 197.30

bedizened dressed in a gaudy or vulgar fashion 245.29

bedral beadle 197.29, 258.7

beetle-browed having prominent eyebrows 143.10

befa' befall 95.37

beflum befool by cajoling language 210.26, 210.27

beguiled mistaken 257.23

behint behind 85.36

behoof behalf 131.36

behove, behoove, behuve be proper 130.28, 205.27; need 56.31; for 197.22 and 198.9 see notes

beldame hag, witch 239.39, 241.2

bell-siller fee for ringing bell 195.40

bell-man town-crier 10.32

belly-god glutton 138.26

ben inner room, best room 106.9

bend-leather leather for shoe soles 64.6

bended cocked 197.43

bent degree of endurance 91.6

beseem befit 215.3

bicker drinking-cup, beaker, bowl 48.23, 81.15, 122.42, 217.8

bickering flickering 105.33, 106.3

bidding entreaty 68.16

bide await 24.16 etc.; stay, wait 64.17 etc.; dwell 105.22; endure, bear 209.7

biggonets linen cap 110.24

billet¹ letter 184.1 etc.

billet² piece of firewood 17.19

bink wallrack or shelf for dishes 105.37

binna be not 193.15

birkie¹ smart young fellow 145.24, 167.17

birkie² the card game beggar-my-neighbour 174.12

birling carousing 191.36

bit *goes with following word* indicating smallness, familiarity, or contempt 106.34 etc.; for 47.30, 95.10, 107.18, 166.5, 167.16, and 199.4 see notes

blackavised dark-complexioned 198.13

black-cock male of the black grouse 96.27

black jack leather beer-jug 63.6

blade-bone shoulder-blade joint 74.32

blaw blow 54.16 etc.

bleeze blaze 206.20, 214.18

blink brief bright gleam 222.31

blown out of breath 78.31

bluid blood 192.1, 220.29

bluidy bloody 197.28

blyth, blythe glad 64.41; 43.41 etc.

board table laid for meal 66.13 etc.

body person 107.43 etc.

bogle goblin, terrifying supernatural creature 64.12

bonnie pretty, lovely, fine, dear 105.18 etc.

bonnie-like *ironical* fine sort of 113.18

boon convivial 167.42

boot see notes to 9.21, 49.8, 68.13, 172.25, 182.32, 225.21, 228.2, and 257.25–26

bosky bushy 31.15

bottle-holder second to a boxer, supporter 165.26

bottom establish, base 6.4

bouk, bowk bulk 192.2; 198.20

boul handle 94.38

bourne stream 31.15

bourock mound 196.27

bowel disembowel 52.2

bower shady recess, arbour 24.42, 25.35; chamber 66.13, 206.18

brach hound hunting by scent 28.43

brae hillside, slope 29.27, 197.28

brake fern, bracken 233.7

branch antler 29.8, 146.24

brander *noun* gridiron 64.27

brander *verb* grill 138.29, 138.30

brattle make a confused and harsh sound 203.16

bravading defiant 19.41

brave worthy, excellent 82.28, 95.43,

107.26, 220.28; finely-dressed, handsome 257.34

bravery splendour 263.10

braw, bra' fine 197.31 etc.; 257.41

brawl (French) dance 263.32

brawly very well 77.29, 105.26, 108.27

breathing influence, inspiration 66.29

brent unwrinkled 195.17

brewis broth, stock made from meat and vegetables 106.4

brewster for 105.8 see note

bridal-shot discharge of firearms in celebration of a wedding 258.16

bride's-man bestman 245.13, 259.42

brig two-masted vessel 50.19, 216.11, 243.26

brigg bridge 197.21, 197.34

brimmer brimming cup 167.24, 168.12

brisket (joint of meat from) breast 29.1, 81.34

brither brother title-page

broad piece, broad-piece large, thin one-pound sterling gold coin 141.19, 218.15–16; 158.37

broadsword, broad-sword cutting sword with broad blade 198.18, 213.39; 167.9

broche roasting spit 108.40, 109.2, 110.4, 113.11

broidered embroidered 77.17, 215.21, 220.35

brood-hen breeding-hen 61.23, 64.5, 64.10

brutal animal 38.3, 135.37

brutally in animal manner 248.27

bumper cup or glass filled to the brim, especially for a toast 172.27, 204.31, 228.5

bumper-deep with deep drinking 91.9

bund bound 197.30

burthen refrain, chorus 74.12

busk prepare, adorn 108.1

but kitchen or outer room 105.31

by-past that have passed 47.39

bye for 47.30 see note

bye-play action apart from the main action, as in dumb-show 64.20

ca' call 112.27, 195.42, 207.15, 256.35

cabage cut off head of a deer close behind horns 81.12

cadgy cheerful 106.33

cake oatcake 113.26, 138.28

call whistle 32.43

callant lad 214.17, 257.12

campaign-cloak cloak used on a military campaign 99.17

canary light sweet wine from the Canary Islands 116.21, 118.1, 118.2, 181.36

cankered venomous, ill-natured 133.32

cann drinking vessel 11.4

canna can't 62.20 etc.

cannon-bit smooth round bit 227.5

canny pleasant, useful 106.2, 210.14; for 257.31 see note

cant word or phrase used habitually and unthinkingly, jargon 73.38, 171.22

canting whining, using religious language affectedly, hypocritical 90.9

cantraip spell 257.38

canty lively, cheerful, pleasant 105.39

capon castrated cock 64.27 etc.

capot, capote for 170.29 and 171.21 see note to 171.20–21; for 227.38 see notes to 227.38 and 171.20–21

car chariot 160.19

carabine carbine, gun half-way between pistol and musket 197.34

carbonaded scored across and broiled or grilled 115.21

car-cake small cake 211.17

career gallop, charge 38.3 etc.

careful sorrowful, anxious 206.38

carena don't care 141.20

carle churlish fellow 105.17 etc.

carline (old) woman 77.32, 105.39

carry conduct, escort, take 50.22 etc.; win, come first in 174.6; win in an election 174.9, 226.24; for 3.8 and 55.15 see notes

cast appearance, cast of features 25.24, 32.20, 48.17; type, kind 195.13; for 77.29 and 108.39 see notes

castor hat of beaver's or rabbit's fur 208.32

cattle horses 62.6

cauk see note to 3.5

cauld cold 54.16 etc.

causeway street or pavement laid with cobble-stones 90.8, 104.5

causewayed paved with cobbles or pebbles 208.34

cavesson restraining noseband fitted to horse's nostrils 227.6

certie see note to 213.30

challenge demand, call for 234.31

champion one who fights on behalf of another 55.12, 103.8

change-house inn 6.34 etc.

chap chop 141.32

chappin Scots half-pint (0.85 litres) 125.9

chappit struck 85.36

chase, chace unenclosed land reserved for breeding and hunting wild animals 27.32, 36.34; 37.19

chaumer chamber 66.6, 66.9

chaunce chance, happen 108.25

cheap see note to 105.26

cheek side 54.13

chicane, chicanery legal trickery 152.28; 236.32

chiel, chield fellow [1], 131.3

chimlay-nuik chimney-corner, hearth 95.1

chimlay chimney 95.23, 263.25

chimney-nook chimney-corner, hearth 54.13

church-judicatory ecclesiastical court 19.40

circumstance appendage, detail 6.9, 176.24

claiths clothes 76.43

clavering prating, talking foolishly 112.32

clavers gossip, nonsense 111.36

clerk scholar, one able to read and write 72.3

clockin-hen brood hen 198.4

clog impede 20.13

close *adjective* shut up indoors 28.13; concealed 49.15; close-fitting 144.20

close *noun* courtyard 35.35

clough narrow gorge 22.14

coat *heraldry* coat-of-arms 19.23

cockernony woman's cap with starched crown, gathering of hair in a band 105.42, 108.1

cogging wheedling 90.6

coign see note to 129.3–4

come came 95.22

comfit sweetmeat, sugar-plum 96.29

commodity occasion 72.37

commonty see note to 101.1–6

communication personal intercourse 166.15

compact *adjective* firm 238.13

compact *noun* agreement, contract 239.13

compass obtain 196.21

compassionate pity, commiserate 143.22

complacence pleasure, delight 44.13, 63.32

complacent pleasing, delightful 66.39

complaisance obligingness 78.31, 175.36, 175.37

compleen complain 198.8

composition compromise, agreement 120.12; settling of a claim by mutual agreement, compounding 203.29

compromise come to terms about 224.24

compromised exposed to risk 16.36

compt see note to 128.8–11

confidence trustworthiness 113.4, 205.15

conform see note to 61.14

confound confuse, mix up, fail to distinguish, overpower 11.18, 11.34, 94.31, 229.4

considerate thoughtful 74.20; careful 100.19

constant firm, persistent 24.19; unvarying 222.31

consummation end, death 133.14, 154.35

contemn(er) despise(r), scorn(er) 27.23, 103.36, 163.34

contrair contrary 88.22

convenient fitting, proper 75.6

cookie plain bun 211.17

copartment compartment 144.11

corbeille *architecture* carved representation of a basket 24.15

corse corpse 190.16, 196.10

couldna couldn't 77.10 etc.

council counsel 119.38

countenance patronage, favour, appearance of favour 53.39, 73.19, 142.43

coupe-gorge *French* cut-throat 132.32

course *verb* hunt 109.15, 148.34

course *noun* regular (postal) process 243.18

courser charger, stallion 6.14

cousin-german first cousin 174.7

couteau large knife worn as a weapon 29.13

cowl close-fitting cap, usually of wool 144.21

coxcomb simpleton 49.8

crack conversation 219.22

craft skill, dexterity 65.35; cunning 147.43

craig neck, throat 133.8

crave demand 72.33, 132.12

craven coward 48.33

craw crow 197.29, 214.28

crimp to decoy or trap men to act as soldiers or sailors 170.2

crook pothook 171.13, 263.18

crop-eared see note to 73.32–33

cross given to opposition 226.34; unfavourable, unpleasing 234.26; for 47.15 see note

crowdy oatmeal and water mixed and eaten raw 122.41

crown coin worth 5s. (25p) 7.12

cuckoo fool 49.8

cullion rascal 90.40

culverin a long cannon 140.11

cumber trouble 249.33

cummer, kimmer female friend 105.40 etc.; 219.22, 256.22

curator person legally responsible for managing the affairs of a minor 223.36

curiously elaborately, exquisitely, cunningly 48.41

cutty see note to 106.15

cutty-pipe short (clay) pipe 213.7

daffing fun 105.22; nonsense 108.31

dainty fine, handsome 199.7

damme *oath* damn me! 172.6

dandilly over-ornamented, fancy, pampered 257.10

dead-deal board on which corpse is laid 192.39

dead-foundered dead tired 61.40

decadent declining 5.30

declarant *Scots law* accused person making a statement before their committal 110.2

declarator see note to 128.8–11

declension decline, deterioration 4.34, 15.26

decored adorned 77.17, 106.12, 115.20, 117.29

decorement decoration, ornament 206.20, 215.20

decreet judgment, decree 223.13

decreet-arbitral decree given by

arbiters 35.31
deevil devil 95.2, 95.20
deevilry devilry 257.33
deformed rendered unsightly 5.6
de'il devil 86.15 etc.
deliberate studied 247.23
démêlée contention, quarrel 175.14
demisaker small cannon 140.11
demurrage payment for delay to vessel caused by the hirer 53.18, 53.25
denner dinner 77.26, 95.16
dentier more handsome (and large or plump) 112.8
depone testify 6.6
derange throw into confusion, disarrange 177.30, 247.26
derangement displacement 145.40
derogate fall away in character or conduct 4.31
design intend 35.33 etc.
designed bound for 94.22
desuetude disuse 99.31, 115.36
determination decision 249.15, 251.34
determined definite, fixed 237.40
develop disentangle, open out of enfolding covering 31.21
device emblematic figure or design 19.23
devious pursuing an erratic course 115.13, 115.14
devoir duty 115.34
devoted doomed 240.25
diet-loaf sponge-cake 217.11
digest endure, stomach 54.11, 88.34
dight prepared 66.13
dike wall 54.22
diligence speed, dispatch 173.6
ding drive 214.34
dingle deep wooded hollow 31.14, 31.21
dink neat, trim, dainty 108.6
dinna don't 62.10 etc.
dirgie, drigie funeral feast 59.11, 191.14; 195.41
disallow refuse permission to, forbid 251.26, 251.29
disconsolate dismal, cheerless, gloomy 59.30, 63.25, 86.5, 91.21
disgarnished stripped 91.21
disna doesn't 68.13, 77.13, 200.14, 256.24
displenished deprived of furniture 94.23

dispone for 47.28 and 111.34 see notes
distemperature ailment 233.23
dittay see note to 241.9–12
dogger two-masted fishing vessel 206.41, 217.30
doited foolish, silly 95.20, 112.32
dole distribution of charity 256.13, 256.20, 256.42, 257.1
dollar four-merk silver piece worth 4s. 5s. (22p) sterling, first issued in 1676 28.19 etc.
donative donation, gift 218.26
donjon-vault vault of great tower of a castle, inmost keep 87.38
donnart stupid 219.23
doo dove 68.37
doo-cot dove-cot 68.37
double duplicate 231.16; for 217.7 and 225.28 see notes
doublet(-buttons) (buttons of) close-fitting body garment 76.29, 81.30, 151.34, 172.16
doubt fear 50.23, 61.12, 68.12, 210.33
doubtingly fearfully, apprehensively 157.15
doun down 28.11 etc.
downcome fall, humiliation 195.26
downright direct, blunt 209.9
drap drop 68.36 etc.
drap-de-berry woollen cloth from Berry in France 76.36, 76.42
draw disembowel 64.15
driegh dreary 263.17
drink-money gratuity, in theory to be spent on drink 218.24
drollery comic picture, caricature 144.31
drought thirst 47.43, 88.33
drouthy thirsty 47.41
drucken drunken 111.34; drunk 200.28
ductile pliable, yielding readily to persuasion or instruction 164.24
dun *verb* press for money owed 10.13
dun *adjective* of a dull brown colour 182.39
dune done 192.42, 198.29
dung *past participle of ding* thrown, dashed 95.10; knocked 198.24; driven 219.23
dunshin nudging 216.15
durance imprisonment 90.2
duty expression of deference 205.25
duty-eggs eggs paid as part of rent to

feudal superior 98.11

dwining sickly, pining 257.28

easy moderate, not burdensome 4.1

eat ate 87.26

eat eaten 71.29, 165.38

eatche adze, carpenter's tool for slicing surface of wood 209.2

ebb shallow 195.34

ebullition boiling or bubbling over of sentiment 21.27

éclaircissement mutual explanation 162.11

ee, e'e, een, e'en eye, eyes 198.14; 108.28; 106.32, 214.19; 116.16

e'en *adverb* just, simply 105.26 etc.; even 139.8; really 195.27

e'en *noun* evening 107.15, 214.6

egad *interjection* a softened oath 29.9, 51.23, 169.21, 172.40

elder *noun* ruling elder, person elected to take part in the government of a Presbyterian Church along with ministers 243.26

elder *adjective* older 258.18, 259.26; ancient, earlier, former 152.20

Elizabeth-chamber room in Elizabethan style 13.27, 14.11

embattled furnished with battlements, crenellated 59.27

embrasure window opening with slanting sides 229.10

emergence emergency, pressing need 7.38

end part 111.17

eneugh enough 62.11 etc.

engine means 15.38

equipage outfit for a journey 173.5

equitable for 125.23 see note to 19.8–9

ever by any chance, in any degree 95.18

evermoe evermore 139.34

exciseman customs officer 140.15

exies hysterics 97.22

expede send 243.17

extenuated emaciated 232.28

eyess eyas, young hawk under training 50.3

fa' fall 198.10, 263.35

fa'an fallen 95.41

face appearance 8.12, 51.18, 64.4

factor estate manager 174.8

faculty ability, resources for doing something 206.6

failzie fail 210.11

fain obliged 82.9, 122.41

fallow-deer small yellow deer 27.38

far *adjective* long, a long 196.41, 263.12

far *adverb* greatly 257.23

fash trouble, bother 113.24, 209.7, 209.8

fashion mere form 47.25

fashna see note to 193.5

fat what 210.9

fay fairy 240.15

fear *verb* frighten 193.15

fear *adjective* see note to 213.3–4

feared frightened, afraid 64.11, 140.12

feckless weak, helpless 210.10

fell *noun* see note to 79.8

fell *adjective* fierce, strong, energetic 198.18

felon cruel, wicked 8.34

feu-charter document laying out the agreement between superior and vassal as to the ownership of real property 102.33, 103.18

feu-rights see note to 101.1–6

feuar somebody holding land on feu 7.10 etc.

fewmishes animal's droppings, tracks 159.24

first-head see note to 29.8

fit *noun* foot 106.40

fit *verb* fit up 145.35

flamb baste 111.28

flankards knots in the flank of deer 81.34

flee fly 192.17

flightering flickering, fitful, transient 222.30

fling move rapidly 98.17, 199.26

flisk whim 227.3

florentine pie 96.26, 97.23

flour flower 198.7

flourish swagger, talk big 197.40, 223.18

flow morass 139.33, 139.35, 267.38

flummery oatmeal jelly 218.9

flunkey livery servant, footman, mean cringer 86.36

flyting scolding 110.19

fog moss, lichen 194.10

foot-post messenger travelling on foot 161.18, 204.2

forbear refrain from (pressing) 231.30, 248.24

forbye besides 96.30 etc.

forebode prohibition 22.12

forespeak cast an evil spell over, especially by praising unduly 258.4

form¹ behaviour according to prescribed or customary rules 255.32

form² hare's lair 260.26

fortalice small fort 59.17

fou firlot, i.e. 1.25 bushels (53 litres) 62.16

found depend 111.43

foy farewell meal 8.5

frack bold, active, forward 77.15

frae from title-page etc.

frank generous, liberal 192.33

frankly generously 161.32

fraught ominously attended 84.21

freak whim 259.20

free-forestry see note to 76.13–14

free-handed liberal, generous 192.33

freets, freits (superstitious) beliefs 264.1; 116.17

frem, fremd strange 141.3; 213.16

friend *verb* befriend 125.40

frog ornamental toggle fastenings on a coat 144.40

fu' full 97.15

fudge turn out 201.40

fugitation *Scots law* sentence on a fugitive from justice, involving outlawry and confiscation of goods 134.7

fule fool 199.8

fullness see note to 112.24

fur for 65.21

furbeirs forbears 192.42

gab mouth 106.20

gaberlunzie beggar, tinker 3.8

gae go 29.29 etc.

gaed, gae't *past tense* went 191.42 etc.; 197.31

ga'en *past participle* gone 95.13

gallant (having the characteristics of, like) a fine gentleman or gentlemen 29.6 etc.

gallantly in a manner becoming a fine gentleman or gentlemen 255.17

gallantry polite behaviour towards ladies 142.5, 186.23, 228.31

galloway small strong horse originally from Galloway 79.11

gane *past participle of gae* gone 62.3 etc.

gang go 97.21 etc.

gang-bye go-by, action of passing without notice 210.28

gar make 95.3 etc.

garner-door granary door 115.12

garnish furnish, embellish 216.33, 216.35

gate manner, way, path 106.43 etc.; for 64.11 see note

gauger customs officer 7.9, 216.10

gaunch wound from a boar's tusk 81.6

gawsie handsome 107.20

gear money, property in general 47.17, 108.4, 199.8, 206.40

geizen'd cracked, leaky 209.12

genius guardian spirit 93.40

gentle *noun* person of gentle birth or rank 28.11, 95.4, 97.5, 213.16

gentle *adjective* noble, excellent 3.7, 4.31, 27.27

georgius gold coin with St George on the obverse worth 6s. 8d. (33.3p) sterling 105.23

gett brat 110.1

ghaist ghost 60.19

gie, gi'e give 111.14 etc.; 109.2 etc.

gif if 210.12

gill quarter of a pint, or one-eighth of a litre 48.40, 218.24

ginge-bread gingerbread 109.2

girn grin, grimace 193.15

girth barrel hoop 209.16

glazen glazed 199.7

gledge squint, cast a sidelong glance 213.17

glee squint, cast a sidelong glance 213.17

gleed glimmer 213.6

glent gleam, glint, sparkle 77.4

glower stare, gaze intently 108.24

gluve glove 210.13

goodsire, gude-sire grandfather 138.41; 197.5

gossip wise woman, female friend 30.5, 105.41, 117.31

gourd plant with a large fleshy fruit 27.15

gowd, goud gold 68.10, 141.5, 210.13, 263.18; 257.11

gowk fool 49.4, 86.36

graith furnishings, clothing 206.19

gramercy mercy on us! 87.4

grandee nobleman of the highest rank 245.4

gratefu' grateful 209.1, 256.35

gratification rewarding, (giving of a) gratuity 218.16, 218.20

gravaminous grievous, annoying, distressing 97.9

gree get on with each other 112.35

green-gaisling green gosling, simpleton 210.23

greet cry, weep 95.1, 108.32, 160.8

grey-beard jug, pitcher 211.19

grit great 192.20, 256.29

grogram coarse cloth of silk and mohair 105.41

ground-mail duty paid for the right of having a corpse interred in a churchyard 195.39

grounds dregs 65.32

grudge complain 263.19

grund estate 98.19; for 198.13 see note

gude good 28.14 etc.

gudeman, goodman, gude-man husband, head of household 106.32 etc.; 202.25, 208.27, 217.24; 107.35

gudewife, goodwife wife, mistress of a household 56.29 etc.; 14.13, 217.24

gude-will goodwill 209.10, 209.11

gudely goodly 213.39

gudemother mother-in-law 219.19

guerdon recompense, reward 140.29

guide *verb* manage, treat 108.10, 199.8, 215.16, 215.22; manage economically 108.4

guide *noun* manager 196.35

guinea 21*s*. (£1.05) 7.1

gunpouther gunpowder 207.28, 213.32

guse goose 112.7, 209.10, 216.9

gust fill the mouth with tasty food or drink 106.19

ha' hall 95.4 etc.

habit (riding-)costume 107.31, 265.26

hackney horse of middling size and quality used for ordinary riding 51.20, 51.43, 54.24

hadna hadn't 216.11

hae have 47.6 etc.

hag¹ witch, repulsive old woman 240.7 etc.

hag² soft marshy hollow in moor 112.12

hail, haill, hale *adjective and noun* whole, undamaged 54.14, 199.13; for 97.30 and 213.3 see notes

hair-cloth towel made of hair 69.13

half-crown coin worth 2*s*. 6*d*. (12.5p) 7.13

half-pay on reduced pay because temporarily laid off or permanently retired 202.17

hall-nook corner of a hall 116.19

hallan partition between door and fireplace 105.30

hame home 28.12 etc.

hand *verb* lead by the hand 91.27

hand *noun* source of information 192.40, 193.6, 193.9

handkerchief neckerchief 158.40

hanger loop or strap on sword-belt from which sword is hung 167.37, 168.6

hap fortune, luck 105.16

harbour *noun* entertainment 63.1

harbour *verb* entertain, provide a lodging for 204.30

harp give voice to 35.28

hasna hasn't 28.21, 47.17

hatch develop, produce 111.31

hatted see note to 95.11–12

haud hold 28.22 etc.

haven harbour 100.37, 215.7

head *noun* head-piece, decorative engraving at beginning of chapter in a book 10.28

head *verb* heed 110.19

head-mark particular characteristics of head and face 195.13

heather-cow tuft of heather 233.1

heaven-born *ironic* of celestial origin 5.32

hebdomadal week-old 86.13

heezy drubbing, something unsettling 208.3

hegh goodness! gracious! 47.20

hellicat good-for-nothing 86.32, 256.43

hersell herself 257.14

het hot 199.18

Hielandman Highlander 167.25

Hielands Highlands 103.29

High-Dutchman German 155.12

highly, high proudly, indignantly 6.41, 57.18

high-spirited high-minded 46.18

himsel, himsell himself 88.31 etc.; 95.18

hinder hind, rear 65.3

hold *noun* fortress 60.9

hold *verb* use (language) constantly 151.7

honest for 61.19, 89.35, 89.38, and 200.25 see 89.37–39 (text) honours distinctive feature, adornment 37.4

hoop-willow kind of willow used for making hoops 114.33

horse horses 77.42

hostler man who attends to horses at an inn 7.6, 54.31

hostler-wife woman who keeps inn or tavern 88.5

hough see note to 256.26

housewifeskap housekeeping 107.13

hout interjection dismissive of another person's opinion 107.8; for 107.34, 108.31, 110.16, and 213.10 see notes

how hollow 192.17

howbeit although 64.33

hum make an inarticulate murmur 20.12

humlock see note to 198.28–29

hurdle sledge 35.42

hurle-burle-swire see note to 54.15–16

huz, hus 198.37, 199.2; 197.38

hyke see note to 79.20

hypocritic hypocrite 144.25

ideot idiot 112.32, 147.18

ilka every 108.6, 108.10

ill see note to 61.27

ill-clackit misbegotten 109.40

ill-deedy mischievous, wicked 110.1

ill-willer enemy 72.18

impressed enlisted 117.33

improve turn to good account 96.14; use to one's advantage 255.7

impugn contest, call into question 23.20, 35.6, 128.37

in-dweller resident 87.32

inanition exhaustion resulting from lack of food 7.31

incumbent overhanging 31.39

indentured apprenticed 4.39

indite write 72.37

indulge *ironic* favour 87.39

inept *law* void, of no effect 223.36

infer imply 24.7

influence exercise of personal power (conceived of in an astrological image) 25.37

information *Scots law* a formal written accusation 134.40, 137.34

ingan onion 212.6

inlake shortage, reduction 29.10

inmate inhabitant, one of family

occupying a house 31.29 etc.; lodger, guest 131.39

insidious crafty 87.35

intelligence understanding, comprehension 64.40

interest personal influence 16.25 etc.; right or title to property 101.19, 129.4

inutility uselessness, unprofitableness 250.27

is as 104.36

I'se I shall, I'll 64.39 etc.

isna isn't 97.28, 139.6, 196.30

ither other 87.23, 108.2, 193.3, 198.11

Jacobite supporter of the exiled Stewarts 49.23 etc.

jacobus broad-piece, gold coin from reign of James VI and I, worth £1 sterling 51.42, 105.23, 155.9

jadd woman 111.33

jealous suspiciously watchful 18.29, 135.4

jeest jest 97.7

jess *falconry* hawk's leg-strap 232.38, 233.10

jib back out 226.35

joe sweetheart, dear 160.10, 209.25

jointure see note to 171.24

jow peal, stroke 195.24

jugglery trickery, deception 241.7, 241.21

just really, truly 65.18, 107.4

kail cabbage 104.32, 105.5, 105.6

kail-yard kitchen-garden 101.2, 199.21

kain payment in kind, especially of poultry, made by a tenant of land as part of their rent 68.39

kebbuck a whole cheese 65.6

keek peep 106.37

keel see note to 3.5

keepit kept 197.34, 198.30, 214.34; stayed inside 104.12

keiser emperor 216.19

kelpie for 139.33 etc. see note to 139.33

ken know 54.15 etc.

kenn'd *past participle (adjective)* known 201.6, 208.39, 214.36

kenna don't know 97.29

kenspeckle conspicuous 141.9

kimmer see cummer

kindly for 102.8 and 210.14 see note to 102.8

kippage state of excitement or anger 212.42

kirk-session the lowest presbyterian church court (at parish level) 110.4

kirk-yard churchyard 197.27, 257.6, 257.33, 257.38

kist coffin 195.40

kitchen-lumm kitchen chimney 95.42

kitt see note to 95.11–12

kittle *verb* tickle 111.35

kittle *adjective* tricky 201.3, 213.42

know-head hilltop 212.41

lacquey footman, valet 76.4, 88.12, 170.39

laird lord 7.8 etc.

lammer amber 105.41

landward from the country as opposed to the town 107.16, 107.17

lang long, for long 66.10 etc.

large lengthy 61.30

late-wake vigil kept over a corpse until burial 256.18

latest last 83.21

latitude freedom of action 114.27

latitudinarian liberal in religion 163.26

latter later, subsequent 193.41

lauch laugh 108.11

lawing reckoning, (tavern-)bill 77.31, 89.10

lead act as leading counsel 203.16

leaguered besieged 235.40

least lest 113.22, 192.13

leddy lady 77.1 etc.

leddyship ladyship 199.16

lee lie, falsehood 65.3, 213.20, 215.2, 215.9

leech doctor 81.9

leveret, leverit young hare 95.24; 96.26

life-rent see note to 199.4

lift *verb* take away 196.29

lift¹ *noun* see note to 203.17–18

lift² *noun* sky 212.6

like *adverb* likely 46.12 etc.

like *verb* please 68.39

limb agent 39.31

links sandy ground near sea-shore 264.40, 265, 18, 267,.39

lippening chance, accidental, unpremeditated 108.19

list please, care 257.18

lith joint 60.20

loon, loun fellow, rascal 62.30 etc.; 213.14

loot *past tense* let 198.36

lose *past tense* lost 198.28

loupen *past participle* leapt 147.20

love-knot intricate knot used as a love token 201.9

low-browed having a low entrance, gloomy 19.25, 60.11

lowe flame 61.12

Luckie, Lucky old Mrs, Goody 68.38 etc.

lug ear 108.12, 111.35, 198.16, 200.38

lugger small sailing vessel 214.31

lungies loins 192.35

lurdane ruffian 198.19

luve love 206.39

mail travelling bag, trunk 134.30

mail-box portable box for letters and other documents 134.38

mailing see note to 199.6–7

main a throw at dice 226.27

mair more 61.28 etc.

maist most 61.29 etc.

maister master 108.2, 112.42, 113.3, 113.12

major-domo head servant, butler 94.35

mak make 61.12 etc.

malignant disaffected, malcontent 18.3; applied by Covenanters to their religious opponents 243.8

managed controlled 256.2

manse minister's house 211.26

mantle suffuse cheeks with a blush 93.13

mark see **merk**

marks *hunting* footprints 159.24

marshal see note to 62.23

martingal strap arranged to keep horse's head down 227.5

Martinmas for 89.42 and 257.20 see note to 89.42

mattock tool for loosening hard ground 194.11

maun must 47.10 etc.

maut malt 65.19

meal-monger oatmeal dealer 232.9

meal-poke bag for holding oatmeal 47.29

mear mare 200.16

meat food 99.30, 263.11

mechanic handicraftsman 129.26

mediciner physician 239.35

melter male fish, especially in spawning time 75.14

merk, mark silver coin worth two-thirds of a pound Scots, by the late 17th century just over 1s. sterling (5p) 29.16; 128.22

Merse Berwickshire, or that part of it lying between the Lammermuirs and the Tweed 15.5, 142.28

messan cur, mongrel 143.9

metall'd spirited 167.28

mezzo-termine compromise measure 183.21

mickle much 64.42 etc.

mill snuff-box 109.1

mind remember 138.41 etc.

minister furnish 113.22

mirk dark, gloomy 213.12; for 85.39 see note

mirth joy 72.39

mischieve injure 257.39

misgi'e fail, go wrong 209.6

misgive suggest doubt or fear to someone 177.20

misprision see note to 174.33

mistak mistake 64.7

mither mother 105.22, 108.29

mony many 86.37 etc.

moral counterpart, likeness 131.10

mort note sounded on horn at death of deer 80.3

mortbleu *French oath* confound it! 54.8

moss marsh, moorland 106.36

mountain-man see note to 107.38–39

muckle much, a lot, great(ly) 87.21 etc.

multiplepoinding see note to 128.8–11

munt mount 197.22

murgeon grimace, contortion 256.43

musquetoon, muskettoon short, large-bored musket 38.29; 258.15

mysell, mysel, mysel' myself 62.6, 139.25, 198.7, 207.39; 47.31, 212.37; 258.7

na no 95.41 etc.

na not 196.34, 197.12, 198.1

nae no 43.37 etc.

naebody nobody 68.17, 216.16

naething nothing 96.2 etc.

naiad river nymph 39.30, 40.14, 40.33, 154.18

nane none 197.22, 264.4

napery household linen, esp. table linen 106.12, 215.21

nar never 106.33

natheless nevertheless 61.15 etc.

natural half-wit 147.17

naughty wicked 243.21

nearhand near at hand 87.27

needfu' needful 104.35, 193.14

needle-wark needle-work 206.19

needna needn't 216.15, 263.27

neest nearest 107.19

nice fastidious, difficult to please 64.39, 91.1; discriminating 229.1

night-cowl nightcap 228.6

no not 61.13 etc.

noble gold coin worth half a mark (6s. 8d. Scots, or by the late 17th century a little over 6d. (2.5p) sterling 210.13

nombles innards of deer used as food 81.33

nonsense nonsensical 96.28, 219.21

nook corner 47.30

nooning mid-day meal 202.28

north-country from the Highlands 200.20

nould see note to 198.23–24

nourice-ship post as a nurse 30.18

nowt cattle 155.10

o' of title-page etc.

obeisance curtsy 181.3

obscurity dimness, darkness 67.19, 91.25

observance deference, dutiful service 7.5

occasion ceremony 59.8

Od God 112.38

o'erseen mistaken, acting imprudently 148.11

offcome excuse 215.25

offices buildings for household work 59.25

on of 49.33 etc.

on-come sharp attack of illness 238.39

ony any 61.12 etc.

opinionative opinionated 217.31

or before 213.22

ordinance sacrament 106.35

ordinar ordinary 195.32

o't of it 62.12 etc.

otherways otherwise 89.41

ou, ow *exclamation* oh! 64.10 etc.; 62.15

oursells ourselves 257.43, 263.17

out *interjection* expression of indignant reproach 263.14

out-rider, outrider mounted attendant riding in front of or behind carriage 76.33; 194.17

over excessive 249.29

over-crowed triumphed over 136.31

ower too 67.41 etc.

owerlook take no notice of, neglect 106.42

owertake overtake 113.15

oxter armpit, under part of the upper arm 199.16

palfrey saddle-horse for ordinary riding 69.12 etc.

pands bed-curtains 215.21

parcel collection 104.28

parish-clerk see note to title-page

park-pale see note to 58.11

parochine parish 107.19

partial favouring one side 36.8

parts abilities, talents 49.42, 143.5

pass passage 87.38, 179.18

pat *past tense of pit* put 97.6, 97.27

patten clog 52.16

patter chatter, prattle 10.37

pearlings clothes trimmed with lace 105.35

pease see note to 206.21

pease-bannocks round flat cake made of meal produced by grinding peas, cooked on a griddle 165.38

peats *term of opprobrium* men 227.36

peculiar private interest, special concern 220.32

pedling feckless 106.18

pegh pant 198.26

pen-feather quill feather of a bird's wing 221.19

peril risk 72.33

person bodily figure 60.39 etc.

personage figure 192.34

petticoat-tails triangular shortbread biscuits 211.17

pettishness petulance 254.13

petty-fogging *contemptuous* concerned with minor legal issues, with suggestions of quibbling or chicanery 203.15

philtre magic potion 239.17

pick-maw black-headed gull 210.23

pickle small amount (of) 68.10, 192.29, 216.19

piece gold coin 170.4 etc.

pigs crockery 95.10

pinch difficulty, hardship 64.42; for 99.19 see note

pinched hard up 64.43; put into difficulties, puzzled 191.33

pine hurt, torture 47.18, 192.21

pinnace boat usually with eight oars 65.27

pinners (cap with) long flaps on either side 144.20

pinny-winkles instrument of torture for squeezing the fingers 192.21

pint-stoup tankard containing a Scots pint (4 imperial pints, or 2.25 litres) 94.38

piquet for 168.32 see note to 171.20

pirn bobbin, reel see note to 47.12

pit put 102.21 etc.

pit-mirk pitch-dark 64.13

pize see note to 221.19

placable capable of being placated, forgiving 158.33

plack see note to 133.11

plague trouble 232.39

plaiden made of twilled woollen cloth, usually tartan 155.30

plaister plaster 5.19, 216.29

plantain herb with broad flat leaves 33.14

planter colonist 202.19

pledge toast 63.9 etc.

plenishing furniture, equipment 206.18

plenty abundant 86.34

pliskie trick 110.12

ploy trick, piece of fun 263.35

plumdamas prune 96.28

pock-pudding *jocular* steamed pudding, Englishman 107.6, 107.8

poinding see note to 128.8–11

point see note to 198.4

policy diplomacy, political cunning 22.38 etc.

politician somebody keenly interested in politics 71.14, 73.37

polity civil order 129.16

poltroon coward 198.2

polygraphic precisely duplicate 177.17

poniard dagger 261.30

poor-man-of-mutton dish made from remains of a shoulder-bone of mutton 148.26

portioner see note to 138.1–2

post make haste 95.27

pot mug 5.25

pouther, powther powder 213.27 etc.; 206.40

pouthered salted, cured 216.8

prate chatter 160.2

preceese special, particular, noteworthy 107.1

precious used by Puritans of someone of high spiritual worth or standing 107.36

prelatical episcopalian 163.27

prelatist episcopalian 242.30

prelection lecture 235.14

premier chief officer 68.30

premised taken as stated 72.10

premium fee 7.2

premonition notification in advance 128.36

prent print title-page

presentation see note to 105.7–8

press affect, weigh down 82.11

press-money money paid to a soldier or sailor on enlistment 90.33

pretender claimant 239.20

pretty, prettier fine 57.39, 167.29, 203.15; brave(r), (more) gallant 55.27, 171.12

prick ride 113.30

primo *Latin* firstly 176.28

principal *adjective* excellent, prominent 61.28

principal *noun* combatant in a duel 253.22

professing making open profession of religious beliefs 242.29

professor see note to 11.7–8

proficience proficiency 6.17

proficient expert 173.25

propine a present, a tip 257.26

psaltery ancient stringed instrument 196.20

pu' pluck 64.15

pudding-sleeves large bulging sleeves drawn in at the wrist or above 105.35

puir, puirly poor(ly) 61.13 etc.

pund pounds 195.43

put¹ make 116.7

put² impose 206.2

pyking picking 216.6

quaigh, quegh shallow bowl-shaped drinking-cup 48.23, 48.39; 217.8

quality (people of) high rank or birth, good social position 55.20 etc.; skill 9.1

quarter quarter of a yard (9 inches, 23 cm) 198.16; quarter of a year 257.22

quean young woman 105.18, 110.16, 112.16, 215.9

quick living 199.6

quo' quoth 107.25, 209.19, 256.28

quotha indeed! forsooth! 215.14

racy excellent in taste 181.36

rade *past tense* rode 112.17

rae roe-deer 29.27

railly woman's short-sleeved front or over-bodice, worn on dress occasions 107.32

rat drat 171.40

raven-bones gristle on the brisket-bones 81.34

realize show or embody the truth of 71.28

reaving plundering 112.17

receipt prescription 54.31

receive accept 134.22

reckon give an account of one's conduct 35. 21, 35.23

reckoning bill 88.6; for 128.9 see note

recover pull back (a horse) on to its feet 132.40

red *adverb* see note to 86.14–15

red *adjective* old 257.23

red-coat soldier 103.32

redd tidied 219.18

rede advise title-page

reek rise 31.4; smoke 202.30

reested cured by smoking 211.16

refection meal 86.19

refer postpone 120.4

remeid redress, remedy 72.23, 122.29, 125.22

remember call to remembrance 40.39

repone restore to rights previously held, reinstate 126.5

resent show that one is displeased by something 20.4, 69.41

respect regard 256.33

reverence¹ for 96.25 and 97.23 see note to 96.25

reverence² bow 118.23, 118.28, 140.24, 144.2

review see again 153.22

revisal revision 244.15

rhematise, rheumatics rheumatism 199.6; 107.37

rifler *falconry* hawk which fails to take proper hold of its prey 232.41, 233.5

rigs land 74.6

rin run 257.1

ring-walk round walk made by

hunters 155.8, 159.22

ripely with mature judgment and consideration 128.38

romantic fantastic 262.16

rosemary fragrant evergreen shrub 192.9

round *noun* a dance in a ring 115.11

round *verb* whisper 96.16, 108.11

roundelay short simple song with refrain 29.20

roundly smartly 29.11, 80.37

roup sale by public auction 220.38

rudas hag 111.18

rue strong-scented evergreen shrub 192.10

rummer large drinking glass 225.21

runlet, rundlet cask 68.36, 204.18, 209.11; 114.14

sack general name for a class of white wines from Spain and the Canaries 49.23 etc.

sackbut early form of trombone 196.19

sacrifeese sacrifice 76.26, 76.28

sad-coloured dark or sober-coloured 76.41

sae so 28.13 etc.

saft soft 192.29

saint true believer 242.32

sair sore 106.32

sall shall 61.19 etc.

salute greet with a kiss 93.8 etc.

samyn same 176.30

sang song 68.13

sant saint, true believer 112.16

saraband slow and stately dance 114.22

sark shirt 193.10

sarra see note to 199.17

sartie see note to 198.23

saul soul 28.4 (see note) etc.

saumon salmon 125.11

saut salt 75.14, 125.11

saw proverbial saying 47.32, 55.15, 153.27, 187.30

sawn sown 208.43

sax six 196.28, 200.16, 256.23

saxpennys sixpence, a Scottish silver coin equivalent to a halfpenny (0.2p) sterling 256.24

saxteen sixteen 195.42, 197.32

say try 76.42

'sblood *oath, short for* God's blood 171.20

scape escape 219.30

scape-grace incorrigible scamp 57.20, 146.22, 147.18

scattergood spendthrift 47.27

scauded scalded 207.28

sclated slated 197.1

sclater slater 62.30

sconce 'wall-bracket' candlestick 144.43 145.22, 259.16, 259.41

score see note to 105.9

scour go in haste 108.34

scrambling unmethodical 69.4

scraugh screech 198.4

screech-owl barn-owl 192.32

screen head-scarf 37.25

screigh scream, screech 214.6

scrutoire (portable) writing desk 134.38

scurvy-grass plant believed to have medicinal properties against scurvy 130.27

scutcheon shield-shaped surface, or funeral hatchment, with armorial bearings 93.19

sea-mew seagull 22.5, 69.26

seat manner of sitting 108.23

se'enty-nine seventy-nine 197.32

sell self 215.3

seneschal steward 60.36 etc.

senior seignior, designation of Italian or Frenchman 114.23

sensible acutely felt, painful 123.41

sentence judgment, decision 221.24

separate belonging to oneself 173.37

sere withered 159.6

servitor manservant 138.22, 197.26

set *past tense* sat 88.4; *present tense* befits 88.31

sewer officer superintending service at table 24.27

shaloon closely-woven woollen material 217.27

shamefu' shameful 107.5

shaughled shuffled out of shape 227.32

shaw small wood, thicket 29.28

sheriff(-)clerk clerk to the sheriff court, presided over by the chief officer of a county 210.8, 210.29

shift *verb* employ evasion or subterfuge 47.4

shift *noun* for 68.39 and 77.31 see notes

shiver fragment 100.4

shool shovel 195.19, 198.15

shopboard a table or raised platform

on which tailors sit when sewing 5.4

shot-hole small hole in fortified wall through which to shoot 87.40

shouldna shouldn't 47.40, 195.34

shouther shoulder 192.34

shovel-board game which involves driving a coin along a polished surface 69.11

sic such 47.41 etc.

siccan such 65.19, 99.27

signify avail 65.3

siller silver 62.25, 141.5, 200.30

simmer summer 197.31

simplicity plainness, straightforwardness 245.40

sin since 263.30

single *falconry* middle or outer claw 232.42

sixpence coin worth 2.5 pence 56.33

skart pen-mark, scribble 47.35

skelder beg, especially posing as a disabled soldier 49.20

skirl shriek, screech 95.2 etc.

skirt coat-tail 146.35, 156.26

skreigh make people move by uttering a shrill sound on an instrument 197.28

sliddery slippery 72.32; uncertain 123.27

sloken quench 88.33

slouched worn with the brim overhanging the face 82.20, 247.27

sma' small 114.14 etc.

snap gingerbread biscuit 109.3

sneck-drawer crafty, deceitful person 112.32

sneck-drawing crafty, deceitful 168.13

snishing, sneeshing, sneeshin snuff 109.1; 212.17; 216.19

snood hair-ribbon 155.31

soi-disant self-styled 53.28

solan-goose gannet 210.23

soldan sultan 5.22

solicit petition 134.3

sombrous sombre, melancholy 59.31

soothfast reliable 175.9

sopite settle, adjust 126.3, 142.21

sort *noun* considerable number 29.6; for 46.24, 111.3, and 118.8 see notes

sort *verb* feed and litter 62.23; provide for 214.39

sough *verb* sing softly 139.25

sough *noun* rumour 257.30

soup *noun* small amount 95.11; for 198.39 see note

souple stout stick 257.40

souse heavily, with a thud 159.16

southern-wood aromatic deciduous shrub or plant 192.10

Southron English 107.8, 140.8

sowens oat and meal dish eaten like porridge 148.25

sowp sip, swig 68.34

spae predict 193.9, 239.16

speer invite 77.26; inquire 139.38, 196.27

spikenard see note to 52.1–5

spule-bane shoulder-bone 138.29

spunk spark, poor miserable fire 213.7, 214.16

stab death by stabbing 159.29

station position 158.25

staunchelled with stanchions or upright bars 59.38

stay await 108.17

steer disturb, pester 115.1

stick stab 191.41

sticket imperfect, bungled 263.28

stir be active 122.33, 258.6

stirring active 71.23, 123.15

stirrup-cup parting glass 143.17

stoup tankard, decanter 48.21, 63.6, 225.21

stouthrief see note to 103.26–27

strae see note to 206.21

strangely strongly, greatly 46.41, 70.28, 177.20

straught lay out 192.39, 193.15

streaking laying out 192.36

streekit laid out 257.8

streight straighten 191.16

strength stronghold 61.25

stude *past participle of stand* stood 61.7

suborner procurer, subverter of loyalty 239.26

subsidy contribution exacted by a feudal lord 102.8, 105.15

substance goods 111.33

suburb suburban 109.12

suddenly without delay 9.19

suld should 61.7 etc.

sum some 195.41

sumbody somebody 210.11

sumph sullen fellow 105.25

sumpter carrying baggage 245.19

sumpter-cloath cloth covering a pack-horse 77.17

sune soon 61.8, 116.12, 207.28

supply compensate for 140.21, 259.25

surbated foot-sore 81.12

sute soot 95.41, 96.27, 97.20

swanking smart 197.6

swarve swerve 198.16

swauk sudden heavy blow 198.18

sweepit swept 97.26

sybil prophetess, fortune-teller, witch 122.12 etc.

sybo spring onion 141.32

synde rinse 47.40

syne ago, afterwards 65.26 etc.

tablet wooden panel for painting 11.31

tack lease 57.32

tack see note to 199.4

tae one (of two) 198.17

taed toad 263.20

ta'en, taen *past participle* taken 56.30 etc.; 198.12

tait bundle, wisp 62.16

tak take 64.8 etc.

tap tuft 88.29; top 198.24

tapis see note to 170.21

tarpaulin sailor's 208.36

tarry stay for 114.13, 186.10

tass small draught or goblet for spirits 81.15, 216.9

tauld told 139.16

tauridor toreador, bull-fighter 136.1

telled, tell'd told 108.18; 193.3

temper habitual disposition 26.3 etc.; calmness 128.30

ten-tyned see note to 29.8

tenement building 31.35, 108.35; for 167.41 see note

tenony see note to 256.26

tenor course 27.19; *Scots law* exact wording, purport 72.7, 137.37

tent attend to title-page

term limit 243.41, 244.9

terrific terrifying 5.22, 44.4, 188.28

testor bed-canopy 215.21

teugh tough 64.5

thae those 116.6, 139.25, 197.21, 263.35

than then 47.40, 138.28, 192.41, 200.14

thank give thanks for 135.31

thegither together 97.30, 105.26

themsells themselves 196.8

thicksets trousers of stout cotton 8.25

thought see note to 200.25

thowless dissolute 111.33

thrall slave, prisoner 240.18

thraw turn, twist, distort 193.15, 199.17

threep see note to 224.30

through-stane horizontal gravestone on, at, or above ground level 196.27, 256.19, 263.6

thunner thunder 65.19 etc.

tide-serving obsequiousness 210.31

tiends parish land tax paid as part of the minister's stipend 105.8

tight vigorous, severe, lively, stout 50.16, 171.14

till¹ while 99.30

till² to 107.19

till't to it 196.41, 197.31

timmer timber 108.13, 207.27

tint colour, especially slightly or with delicate shades 11.28

tippence twopence Scots (0.14p) 263.11

tither other (of two) 198.17

tocher dowry 226.15, 226.18

tocher-good property given by way of dowry 203.26

tod fox 48.12 etc.

toilette dressing table 216.43

toils net(s), trap(s) 16.15, 24.14, 39.27

tokay sweet Hungarian wine 86.20, 86.25

tolbooth town hall, containing the jail 68.25

told reckoned 230.39

tone tune 197.12

tongue see note to 202.10

took struck 198.18

top-gallant highest point (literally, of a mast) 209.42

toun town 103.24

tout see notes to 107.34, 108.18, and 110.16

tow unworked flax fibre 88.29

town-end end of main street, edge of town 105.17

traducer betrayer 250.42

traffic business, intercourse 241.23

train line of combustible material to fire a charge 174.42

tredille card game for three players 173.24

trencher plate 106.15 etc.

trepanned inveigled 228.26, 252.13

trim adapt, adjust 47.4

Trojan see note to 29.8

troth truth, truly 108.22, 116.9,
195.16, 198.36; for 113.4 see note
trouble distress 244.39
troublous disturbed, unsettled 61.27
trow believe 86.35 etc.
truce for 86.21 and 139.27 see notes
truck barter away 133.31
trump see note to 202.10
trust supply goods on credit (for)
68.33, 105.9
tup ram 47.7
turn piece or spell of work 116.4
twa two 47.35 etc.
twa-lofted three-storied 197.1
twal, twal' twelve 85.36, 108.42;
263.36
twilight imperfect 72.42
twilt quilt 215.21
tyne each of the pointed branches of a
deer's horn 146.25, 146.27
typical symbolical, emblematic
168.41
umquhile former, sometime 176.40
uncase flay 203.28
unce ounce 256.25
unceremonious informal 161.33
unco terrible 208.3
under-hand secretly 161.20
unequal uneven 104.42; variable
241.24
unharbour dislodge from shelter 50.3
unprovided unfurnished 117.13
uphaud see note to 263.28
upper superior in authority 144.4
urge press (upon the attention), im-
portune, push 24.7 etc.
use habit 183.18
vacant free of activity 25.11
vague vagrant, shifting 115.11, 115.14
vaik fall vacant 202.8
van front part of a procession 19.32
vapour boast, swagger 168.5
various going in different directions
115.11
vassal (feudal) subordinate 18.20 etc.
vaticination prophecy 193.18
vau't vault 206.41
velveteens velveteen trousers 8.24
vera very 62.29
vestments clothing 5.6
vicegerent ruler exercising deputed
power 17.1
view plan 18.28 etc.
viewless invisible 235.43
vignette printed embellishment or

illustration unenclosed in a border
10.28
virginals a sort of spinet 143.11
visie look, survey 130.37
visionary unreal, fantastic 241.23
visnomy physiognomy, face 133.11
vivers food, victuals 97.22, 104.34
vizard mask 81.1
vulgar common people 40.21, 158.36,
199.27
wad would 43.37 etc.
wadna wouldn't 43.31 etc.
wadset(ter) for 49.15 and 128.9 see
note to 128.8–11
wae adjective sad 61.6
wae noun woe 65.26, 206.23
wage wager 133.11
wait await 154.41
wake party 186.25
walk ride slowly (round) 174.7,
253.40
walth plenty 64.26
wame belly 97.8
wand stick or switch for urging on a
horse 111.25
want lack, go without 77.11 etc.; be
lacking 239.7
wanton overjoy 74.9
wap blow 206.43
wardrope wardrobe 76.35
wared expended 226.21
wark work 47.41 etc.
warrand warrant 77.29, 196.3
warst worst 98.9, 197.27, 199.18,
213.3
wassail riotous festivity 58.10
wastland from the west of Scotland
197.22
wat wet 112.8
water-purpie brooklime, species of
speedwell found on the edge of
ditches 138.27
waur worse 65.2 etc.
wean child 106.34, 212.42, 214.21
weary yearn 99.33; for 110.13 see
note
wee little (bit) 68.9 etc.
weed, weeds garment(s), apparel
143.32; 238.25
weel well 43.40 etc.
weel-favoured good-looking 107.30,
108.22
weel-pouthered well-powdered
257.42
weid fever 108.33

well-a-day alas! 139.25

werena weren't 77.9

we'se we'll 192.30

westland from the west of Scotland 198.13

wether castrated ram 106.35

wha who 3.6 etc.

whample stroke, blow 209.2

whan when 116.6

whare where 107.35

wheen few 140.9 etc.

whew see note to 198.28–29

whiff smoke 105.42

whig 17th-century Scottish Presbyterian; supporter of the 1688–89 Revolution settlement 61.21 etc.

whigamore 17th-century Scottish Presbyterian 168.13

whigmaleerie decorative or fanciful object, knick-knack 3.6

whiles sometimes, from time to time 68.16, 214.36; for 197.19 and 219.1 see notes

whilk which 3.7 etc.

whim-wham fanciful objects 97.24

whin-bush gorse-bush 233.1, 233.7

whin-stane, whinstane whinstone, hard rock 192.20; 256.33

whinger whinyard, short-sword 53.32, 191.41

whisht quiet! sh! 62.9 etc.

white-hass oatmeal pudding cooked in sheep's gullet 107.10

whomling knocking down 198.24

whow interjection expressing astonishment and resignation 257.15

wi' with 28.13 etc.

wife woman 54.15, 200.27, 214.16, 216.19

wight person 31.6

wild-deucks, wild-deukes wild-ducks 112.8; 209.10

wile obtain 64.18

winding shrouding 192.36

winna won't 67.41 etc.

withie gallows rope 57.2

without outside 166.6

wold would 77.32

wonne dwell 31.6

wood-craft forest skills 28.23

wood-fee payment to a huntsman 28.38

woodie gallows rope 133.10

wot know 90.3

wraith a spectral appearance of a living person 60.19

wrang *adjective* wrong 62.5, 191.42, 213.18

wrang *past tense* wrung 199.20

wrang-headed wrong-headed 197.21

write sign 73.2; for 4.29 see note

writer lawyer, solicitor 102.20 etc.

wrought decorated with needlework 74.15

wud mad 86.15, 95.13

wull *noun and verb* will, wish 28.4, 102.19, 112.38; for 95.37 see note

wyte blame 68.23, 264.3

yard garden 199.4, 218.38

yate gate 61.7, 87.22, 88.21

yearth earth 220.31

ye're your 257.38

yestreen last night 87.22

yill ale 104.38

yoursell, yoursel yourself 77.28 etc.; 64.9, 212.42

yoursells yourselves 56.29, 219.22

Yule Christmas 257.6